FURY

Netanel stared back at her across the table and winked.

This is impossible, Marie thought. I am falling in love with this boy. But it is quite impossible. I'm Catholic and he's a Jew. All this is so alien to me he might as well be from the moon. His mother despises me, the rest of the family treat me as if I were some exotic animal from Africa. And there is what happened to Chaim; the same that happened to Nethanel a few months ago. Madness ever to contemplate loving him . . .

The Passover ceremony ended. "Next year in Jerusalem," the whole table said in unison.

Netanel looked across the table and smiled at her, a broad, delicious smile and she felt her stomach squirm like a puppy. Oh, *mein Gott*, she thought. This has already gone too far. I cannot stop this now. I cannot . . .

Also by the same author
and available from Coronet:

Venom
Deathwatch
Harem
Opium
Triad
Dangerous

About the Author

Colin Falconer was born in London in 1953. He is a journalist and has written for many national magazines and newspapers. He has travelled widely in Europe and South-East Asia and now lives in Western Australia. He is the author of seven acclaimed thrillers, all available in Coronet paperback.

Fury

Colin Falconer

CORONET BOOKS
Hodder and Stoughton

Copyright © 1993 by Colin Falconer

The right of Colin Falconer to be identified as the Author of
the Work has been asserted by him in accordance with the
Copyright, Designs and Patents Act 1988.

First published in Great Britain in 1993
by Hodder and Stoughton
A division of Hodder Headline PLC
A Coronet paperback original
This Coronet paperback edition 1996

10 9 8 7 6

A CIP catalogue record is available from the British Library

ISBN 0 340 59040 8

Printed and bound in Great Britain by
Clays Ltd, St Ives plc

Hodder and Stoughton
A division of Hodder Headline PLC
338 Euston Road
London NW1 3BH

For Helen, who believes in me

Foreword

No book is ever written through the endeavour of just one person, and I would like to thank those who gave me their time in the preparation and research of my story.

In Tel Aviv, Ruth Sobol and historians Dr Yaakov Sachs and Dr Yaakov Goren; in Jerusalem, Ruven Koffler at the Zion Archives, Dafna Rix of the Jerusalem Museum, Mulli Azrieli at Fink's, and Rivca Weingarten, who shared with me her memories of the siege of the Old City; in El-Bireh, Mrs Sameeha Khalil, of the Inash El-Usra Society. Closer to home, my thanks again to Anne Mullarkey for helping me find so many of the sources I needed.

I'd like also to thank my agents, Tim Curnow in Sydney and Anthea Morton-Saner in London, who helped me through many rough spots; and my editor, Bill Massey, who has such wonderful judgment in all but his choice of football team.

Although the background to this novel is a matter of public record, this is a work of fiction. To this end, certain errors are deliberate and a device of fiction; for example, there were two Haganah commanders during the siege of Jerusalem, David Halperin and Moshe Russnak, not one; and there were no kibbutzim in the area I have chosen for Kfar Herzl until the forties.

I have occasionally used someone's real name, in which case they appear as an historical character, peripheral to the story. Otherwise it has not been my intention to portray any real person or actual happening, and no such intention should be inferred.

Jerusalem
September 1992

I am here by Fury, and the Heart.

Moses in Christopher Fry's *The Firstborn*

PROLOGUE

West Bank, September 1992

The black and angry streets of Bethlehem.

Mulli Rosenberg sits, legs splayed, in the back of the patrol jeep, listening to the crackle of voices on the hand-held radio. A quiet night. The *intefadeh* had fallen into a lull; Rabin was talking to Assad, and the newspapers, at least, were talking about peace.

A siren wails somewhere in the night, and in the darkness he feels eyes watching him with silent venom. A jumble of graffiti is caught in the wash of the headlights, the letters "PLO" daubed with red aerosol paint in Arabic script on the rusted shutters of a shop. Underneath, had been scrawled in English, for the benefit of the tourists: "FUCK ISRAEL".

Mulli Rosenberg isn't a hero like his grandfather. He wants to be a lawyer. But first he must complete his three years' service in the army. In his khakis he looks lean and brown and young and scared.

He has never shot anyone.

He strokes the grease-warm barrel of the Uzi sub-machine-gun in his lap. There really was no choice, he has decided. Unless he wanted to grow up in a world like his grandfather's, there never was a choice.

Amman, Jordan

Wafa strokes her kohl-black hair, and lights another cigarette with trembling fingers. She finds it difficult to talk about Palestine without becoming upset.

She has huge brown eyes that glitter with passion as she talks. "My grandfather's name was Majid. His father was Sheikh Zayyad Hass'an al-Shouri, from the village of Rab'allah, near Jerusalem. My family are all Palestinians. I was born here in Jordan, but I am a Palestinian. A Palestinian. I cannot think of myself any other way."

There are tiny beads of perspiration on her forehead. Amman is a city of concrete and glass, of heat and dust and clamouring car horns. Outside, the heat hammers off the asphalt highway, drying the body like a raisin.

A late hamsiin is blowing, the hot wind that sweeps in from the eastern desert, yellow and foul, like the breath of a jackal. They say the hamsiin was blowing the day Christ was crucified.

The fan in the tiny office hums ineffectually in the corner. Wafa pauses to sip the gritty black coffee. "This is not my country. I have never belonged here. Until our case is settled I will never be happy. All my life I feel frustrated, always I feel this way. Why does the world not listen to our case? We can never rest, don't they understand? We will tell our children of our case, and our children's children. It can never be over for us."

Now it is difficult for her to swallow. She stares at the floor. "I try not to hate the Israelis but I know what they did to my father, and my father's father, and there is a stone in my heart. You understand? A stone.

"Take some more coffee. You have a moment, yes? I will tell you our story. All of it."

Speak unto the children of Israel and say unto them, when ye are passed over Jordan into the Land of Canaan:

Then ye shall drive out all the inhabitants of the land from before you, and destroy all their pictures, and destroy all their molten images, and quite pluck down all their high places:

And ye shall dispossess the inhabitants of the land, and dwell therein: for I have given you the land to possess it.

Numbers 33: 51–53

Part One

GERMANY, 1933

1

Ravenswald, Bavaria

It was Spritzer who brought them together.

He was an unlikely Cupid. He was a giant, seventeen hands at the shoulder, with pink, malevolent eyes. His iron-soled shoes rang on the icy cobbles as he walked, head bowed, sneezing at the chill air of the late afternoon. Behind him the wheelshoes of the Schultheiss wagon creaked under the load of heavy oak beer barrels.

He stopped outside the Hotel Alte Post; Emmerich the carter and his son started rolling barrels off the back of the cart down into the cellar. Spritzer stamped his right foot repeatedly on the cobbles, sparks flying. Netanel saw at once what was wrong: Emmerich had allowed the reins to become tangled around the horse's shoulder and hoof. Netanel slipped into the greengrocer and handed over a handful of pfennigs for two carrots.

He ran across the street, put his schoolbooks on the pavement and produced his bribe. "What's the matter, old boy?" Netanel said. "Here, you want a carrot?"

Spritzer eyed him suspiciously but took the carrot, sneezing into Netanel's hand by way of thanks. He saw the other carrot protruding from Netanel's jacket pocket. He nudged his benefactor aside, almost sending Netanel sprawling, and extracted it with the finesse of an old seamstress threading a needle.

While Spritzer was occupied, Netanel bent down and grabbed the horse's foot, and with one movement pulled it free of the traces. "There you go, old boy. How does that feel?"

Spritzer shook his great head and knocked Netanel into the wall. Netanel shrugged, picked up his schoolbooks and headed for home. He had gone nearly fifty yards when he heard someone yelling curses down the street and he turned to see what was wrong.

Spritzer was right behind him.

As soon as Netanel stopped, the horse began to inspect the contents of Netanel's jacket pockets with his teeth.

Emmerich waddled down the street in his knee-length leather apron and blue peaked cap. "Hey, what do you think you're doing? You trying to steal my horse?"

"He followed me, *mein Herr*," Netanel said, trying to prise the corner of his jacket from Spritzer's jaws.

Emmerich swore at the horse, and jerked at the reins. Spritzer shied away, and the rage returned to his pink eyes. "Why did he follow you, hein? What have you been doing?"

"He was caught in his reins. I helped him loose."

Emmerich looked at him as if he was crazy. "You helped him loose? You're lucky he didn't kick your brains out! *Verrückt!*"

Netanel recovered from his embarrassment, bridling at his interrogation by this *lumpen*. "I gave him some carrots first. He was hungry."

"You gave him something to eat?" Emmerich shouted. "He doesn't need anything to eat. He eats enough as it is. He eats like a horse!" Then he laughed suddenly, delighted with his own unexpected and unintended outpouring of wit. He looked back up the street to where his son, Rolf, was watching, hands on hips, outside the *Gasthaus*. "Do you hear that, Rolf? I said Spritzer eats like a horse!"

Netanel turned to go. He would not waste his time on this idiot any longer. But then he heard another voice behind him: "It's not his fault your horse followed him. Why didn't you have the brake on?"

It was a girl. She was the same age as Netanel; he knew her, her name was Marie, she was the new girl in his class at the *Realschule*, the high school. She was by far the prettiest girl in the class. She had hair the colour of chestnut, and her eyes were a radiant emerald. For two weeks he had been trying to summon the courage to speak to her; twice he had even approached her in the schoolyard, but then could think of nothing to say. He had just stood there and grinned at her and waited for his mouth to work. Until now he had been convinced that she thought him an utter idiot.

Now he felt the trance settle on him again and he could only stare at her as she berated the old carter.

"The brake was on," Emmerich was grumbling.

"If it was on, how did Spritzer drag his cart all the way down the street? And why don't you take better care of him, rather than have complete strangers fend for him?"

A crowd had gathered. "That's right, he never takes care of his horse," someone said, "he's always letting it wander."

"The way he treats it," someone else said, "it's not surprising."

"Someone ought to use his horsewhip on him one day."

Emmerich judged that the tide had turned. He led Spritzer through the muttering crowd, back up the Grossenstrasse. The old horse continued to toss his head against the traces, pulling Emmerich backwards and forwards like a marionette.

Marie turned to Netanel. "It's terrible, isn't it? Most people round here just turn their backs and look away. It's only when someone finally does something that they find their voice."

Netanel knew she was waiting for him to speak. Nothing occurred to him. He grinned and shrugged.

"You're Netanel Rosenberg, aren't you?" she said.

He nodded.

A long silence. "Well, goodbye, Netanel," she said, and turned to walk away.

Netanel felt the sudden blooming of panic. "Wait!" he shouted, alarmed at the tremolo in his voice. "Can I carry your books?"

Marie appeared startled by the request. "I do not have any books today," she said, spreading her hands.

"Well, do you want to carry mine?" Netanel heard himself say.

Marie actually laughed. The sort of laugh you save for those occasions when you find yourself in conversation with a certifiable lunatic, Netanel thought. Marie turned and walked away. Oh, brilliant, brilliant! Netanel thought. *Well, do you want to carry mine?*

Netanel looked back at Emmerich; the cart was back outside the Alte Post, and he was climbing on to the running board to put on the handbrake. His son was watching Netanel. On his face was an expression of the most pure hatred Netanel had ever seen.

He picked up his books and walked home.

Josef Rosenberg was one of the town's *bessere Leute*, one of the upper middle class of Ravenswald. Rosenberg Fabriken had been founded almost seventy years before by Josef's grandmother Esther. After her husband had died of consumption in 1864, she had started knitting stockings and selling them in the street in an attempt to keep her family of seven children, which included Josef's father, Mandel. She was good at her work, and after a while she was getting regular orders. Ten years later she had bought a manual knitting machine, and a few years later she had her own shop.

By the time Josef took over the business on Mandel's death in 1924, Rosenberg Fabriken was the largest single business in Ravenswald, employing six hundred people and exporting hosiery to Switzerland, France, Britain and even the United States.

The old lady who once sold her hand-knitted stockings on street corners would not recognise the kind of life I have now, Josef thought. I drive a modern motor car, live in a six-bedroom house with my own servants, and my wife hosts her own *Kaffeeklatsch* every Wednesday afternoon in the parlour, gossiping with a dozen of the leading socialites of the town. But that evening as he walked down the hill towards the town, his silver-headed cane tapping on the ice, it was an

6

effort to shrug off the black depression that had settled over him.

The world had turned so quickly. It was less than a year ago that the little Austrian Hitler had been appointed Chancellor. Fifteen million of his fellow Germans had voted for him! Soon after the "communists" had burned the Reichstag and the Nazi Party had suspended civil liberties and given the SA and the SS police powers. Now there was a new abomination: boycott!

Abraham Horowitz, who had a shoe shop in Theresienstrasse, had told him that SA men had begun to appear every morning outside his shop, trying to frighten his customers away. "Don't shop there, lady, they're Jews. Shop in a German store, *Gnädige Frau*!"

Jew-baiting was nothing new, of course. Hitler wasn't the first. He wouldn't be the last. Aryans, non-Aryans! What nonsense! They were all Germans, weren't they? His family had lived in Ravenswald for six generations. He had an Iron Cross second class for his services in the First World War!

He found he was walking faster, his cane tapping out an urgent tattoo in his agitation. He forced himself to slow his pace. Calm yourself, he thought. It means nothing. It will all blow over. The German people will not stand for too much of this nonsense.

Ravenswald nestled in a deep southern valley, surrounded by the enfolding arms of the Bavarian Alpen. The heart of the town dated from the thirteenth century, and was surrounded by crenellated walls and towers. A honeycomb of cobblestones and gabled stone and timber houses, stone fountains and arched gateways crouched inside. The town studied its reflection in the still waters of the Ravensee, overlooked by the brooding ruins of an old *Schloss* that stood on an isthmus of rock below the Ravensberg.

Every evening after work it was Josef Rosenberg's habit to walk the two miles from his home to the Hotel Alte Post to play skat with Landisberger, the doctor, and Schenke,

7

the solicitor. He had known the two men for years, they had been in school together. They had their own *Stammtisch*, their regular table, in the tavern, and they would play cards and drink beer until nine or ten in the evening.

This evening Rosenberg was surprised to find he was first to arrive; he took off his hat and his jacket and settled down to wait. At seven o'clock there was still no sign of Landisberger or Schenke. At eight o'clock Josef went home. The next night he waited again; the night after that he did not bother to come at all.

He saw Herr Doktor Landisberger the next day, in the Grossenstrasse. Josef stopped to talk to his old friend and was astonished when the Doktor walked straight past him, as if he were not even there. That same evening he saw him again, as he passed the *Bierstuben*; he was there with Schenke and another man, Dehlmer, the apothecary. They were at their Stammtisch and they were playing skat.

That was when the depression had settled on him; the reason for his sudden exile was quite clear to him. Neither Landisberger or Schenke were Jewish. Nor was the interloper, Dehlmer.

Suddenly Herr Josef Rosenberg, foremost businessman of Ravenswald, bessere Leute and employer of six hundred of the town's citizens, knew what it was like to be a pariah.

2

There were unsettling developments at the Realschule. One Monday, Lachter, their form teacher, did not appear for class. His place was taken by a teacher who introduced himself as Herr Professor Muller. He told them all that he was their new form teacher and Lachter would not be coming back. No explanation was given.

Muller was short and bald and owned a pair of astonishingly hairy, black eyebrows that appeared to inhabit his forehead like two large bristling caterpillars. But it was not this feature that occupied Netanel's attention on that first morning; it was the badge that he wore in his lapel. It was the size of a button, a black circle around a red circle around a white circle, with a tiny black swastika at its centre. It was like a small but deadly insect clinging to his lapel. The man, Netanel realised, was a fully paid-up member of the National Socialist Party.

Muller began his first class with a short history lesson; he explained how the German people had been committed to a century of poverty and degradation by the Treaty of Versailles and how it was time for the yoke that France had thrown around the nation's neck to be shrugged aside. He showed them a new kind of map of Germany; on it the Rhineland and Sudetenland, once part of "the Fatherland" as Muller called it, were coloured in black. It made them look like angry wolves, their jaws gaping open, about to strike.

"We must gobble up the wolves before they gobble us, or we will never be able to live in peace," he told them.

Netanel felt sick in his stomach. It was as if he were

9

in a courtroom, listening to a trial, knowing that at any moment the prosecutor would turn to the gallery and single him out from his peers to denounce him. Any moment he himself would be in the dock.

The suspicion grew to a certainty when Herr Professor Muller turned from history to the subject of racial purity.

"The German people are descended from the Aryans, the master race of mankind. The Aryans are physically and mentally superior to all other races and are characterised by certain physical features." He looked around the room. Netanel lowered his eyes, trying to avert the coming disaster. "You, boy!" Netanel looked up. The scene from the nightmare vision was being acted out. Muller's finger was pointing directly at him. "Yes, you! Come up here!"

Netanel got up slowly and walked to the front of the class. He could feel every eye on him. The room had suddenly turned to ice.

"Turn and face the class, boy," Muller said and he span Netanel around. Out of the corner of his eye Netanel could see Marie watching.

"Now here we have a true Aryan," Netanel heard Muller saying. "See the fair hair and the blue eyes. These are classic features."

Someone at the back started to giggle. Netanel dared a glance at Muller. The little man looked up sharply, disconcerted. But he could not spot the offender, and so he continued.

"Notice the head shape," Muller was saying. "It is not at all round like a Negro or a Jew. It is high at the back, denoting great intelligence."

A sound from the back of the room like a dog vomiting. Someone else had choked off their laughter by trying to disguise it as a cough. Netanel dared another glance at Marie. Her cheeks were red, and she was biting her lower lip so hard it was white.

"Notice too the physique. Tall and straight and lean."

Netanel was grinning now and a boy in the front row grabbed at his crotch, thinking he would wet his shorts.

"A classic Aryan," Muller repeated, and he heard

another laugh and looked around, frowning. "What's your name, boy?" he said to Netanel.

"Rosenberg, sir."

Muller's jaw went slack, and the caterpillar eyebrows began to work independently of each other. "Not the son of Josef Rosenberg, the factory owner?" *Josef Rosenberg, the Jew* hung in the air, unspoken.

"Yes, sir," Netanel said and the epidemic of snorting and coughing grew alarmingly.

Muller's face suffused to the colour of claret. "Sit down!"

Netanel returned to his seat. Muller turned his back on the class and stood facing the blackboard, groping for some inspiration that would dismantle the cast-iron image of utter foolishness which he had just created for himself. There was nothing. "Take out your history books," he hissed, "and answer the questions on page forty-five!"

Everyone did as they were told, thankful for the diversion and the opportunity to let out a little of their laughter as they bent over their books. Muller pretended to study his own notes, waiting for the blessed mercy of the lunchtime bell. But the little black swastika winked at Netanel through the rest of the lesson and its black malevolence promised Aryan revenge.

"I thought I was going to burst!" Marie said, as they turned off the Grossenstrasse. Netanel was carrying her books, strapped together with a leather thong, slung over his right shoulder.

"Notice the blond hair and the blue eyes. Typically Aryan!" she laughed, imitating Herr Professor Muller's solemn, deep voice.

"In a way he was right," Netanel said. "My great-great-grandmother married a Prussian cavalry officer. They say he even sported a duelling scar on his cheek."

"You'll have to grow your hair in long sidecurls so poor Muller knows who you are!"

Netanel looked at her. He was not sure whether to laugh

11

with her. He was not accustomed to a non-Jew treating his race and religion so lightly. But no, he decided, she was not mocking him. She really did think this whole thing was a joke.

"Not all Jews are the same," Netanel said, more seriously. "As not all Christians are the same. It is only the Oriental Jews, the Hassidim, who have the sidecurls."

"I think you would look very handsome with them," Marie said, and he felt his cheeks grow hot. She is teasing me now, he thought.

"I would rather have a duelling scar," he said. Strange, he decided, that what he had thought would be his greatest humiliation had instead been transformed into such a triumph. Marie had approached him after school and with the smile that made his knees turn to water told him that she too thought he was a fine example of Aryan physical and mental development.

"Thank you. I am going to be the first member of Hitler Youth who can recite from the Talmud!"

She had laughed at that, and he felt his shyness with her slough away.

They crossed the *platz* in the centre of the town. The Schöner Brunnen, the stone fountain outside the Rathaus, was frozen. The three cardinal virtues, represented by the pale angels, Faith, Hope and Charity, were cloaked in chill skins of ice. Fresh fallen snow balanced precariously on the wrought-iron signs that overhung the cobbled Grossenstrasse like banners at a parade.

"I live this way," Marie said.

"I know where you live. Your father took over the butcher's shop in Theresienstrasse."

She looked at him frankly. "How did you know that?"

"I asked around."

She was still staring at him. "Why did you do that?"

"Because I think you're the prettiest girl in class," he said, and he looked away, embarrassed.

But she did not laugh at him. "I'm not, but thank you anyway."

He turned and she looked up and smiled back at him. He

<hr />

12

felt a sharp pain in his chest. She is wonderful, he thought. And she likes me. *She likes me!*

The moment was broken suddenly, obscenely.

The paper bag landed with a moist plop at his feet, breaking open on impact, the contents splashing over the snow and over his socks and his legs. It had been filled with excrement; a human's, a dog's, it was hard to tell.

"*Jud, Jud, scheiss in die Tüt!*" someone yelled. "Jew, Jew, shit in the bag!"

There were three of them, lounging at the street corner, in their black Hitler Jugend *lederhosen* and brown shirts. Netanel recognised one of them: Emmerich, the carter's son.

Marie grabbed Netanel's arm and began to pull him away. "No, Netanel. Leave it. They are idiots. Forget it."

"I can't leave it."

Netanel pulled free, his eyes never once leaving his tormentors. As he crossed the street, he saw Emmerich was grinning.

"What are you doing with a nice German girl, Jew?"

"Who threw the bag?"

"It was good German shit," Emmerich said. "We should make you eat it."

Netanel measured the distance between himself and Emmerich. Two paces. The other two boys stood on either side, watching. The lightning rune on their armbands flashed a warning. If he went after Emmerich would they stand back and allow a fair fight? Of course not. One of them put his hand on his hip, the index finger pointing towards the dagger in its black scabbard.

"I don't want to see you with one of our nice girls any more," Emmerich was saying. "Go and fuck your mother, Jew."

Netanel moved even before the last word had left Emmerich's mouth. He took two quick steps and smashed his fist into Emmerich's face. Emmerich went down. Immediately the other two boys crowded in and grabbed him, pinning his arms. Idiot, Netanel cursed himself.

This was what they wanted. This is just the way they planned it.

The boys were older and stronger and they held him fast. Emmerich sat on the ground at his feet, cupping the blood that ran from his nose. He looked up at Netanel and grinned.

"We'll have to teach you respect, Jew pig," he said, and leaped up, arms flailing. The first two blows hit Netanel in the stomach and the chest, winding him. Netanel felt his body sag. He kicked out and his boot connected with Emmerich's knee and he heard him scream. The satisfaction of the blow lasted only a moment.

Something struck him sickeningly hard in the groin and the next scream he heard was his own. Then Emmerich's fist hit him hard on the side of the head and he blacked out.

Marie saw them drag Netanel around the corner. There was no one to help. Would anyone intervene against three Hitler Jugend anyway? She ran across the street. Netanel was on the ground now, and Emmerich and his two friends were kicking him.

"Stop it!" Marie screamed. "Stop it!"

Emmerich grinned at her. "It's only a Jew!" But he stopped.

One of them caught her wrist. "What does a nice German girl like you want with him?"

She tried to shake herself free. Netanel was lying prone, and there was blood in his hair and on the snow. "You've killed him!"

"No, we haven't killed him. Not that the Fatherland would miss one dirty Jew."

"Let me go!"

Emmerich nodded to the other boy. "Let her go."

She knelt down and tried to turn Netanel on his side. He groaned and his eyes flickered open. There was blood running from his nose, his mouth, everywhere.

"You pigs!" Marie screamed, but Emmerich did not hear

14

her. He and his two colleagues were already sauntering away, laughing and pushing each other, like it was all a game.

Marie cradled his head on her knees and tried to clean his face with her handkerchief. Suddenly there were people in the street again, she noticed. A few moments ago the Grossenstrasse had been deserted. Now everything was normal once more except the butcher's daughter had blood on her dress.

The Rosenberg house was known as the House in the Woods. It was set back from the road behind a high wall and an imposing wrought-iron gate, almost invisible behind stands of pines and willows that were wreathed at this time of year with snow and ice, giving the house the appearance of an ice palace. Marie helped Netanel up the snow-covered drive to the portico.

Netanel slumped down on the step. "No teeth missing," he mumbled, his index finger tentatively feeling inside his jaw.

"You'd better go inside and wash up," Marie said. Netanel's face and clothes were smeared with blood. One eye had already closed and there was a huge, purplish lump on his cheek and one of his nostrils was ripped.

"I'm all right," Netanel said. He looked up at her. "I'm sorry."

"I hate them," she whispered.

He shrugged. "You were right. They are just idiots."

Marie felt sick. She had never witnessed violence like that before. She was trembling.

"Netanel!"

They both turned. Netanel's mother stood in the doorway, her face white with shock. Her hands were bunched into fists in the folds of her long dress. She looked quickly at Marie, then at her son.

"Netanel, what has happened?"

"I'm all right, Mutti. It's nothing."

"Your face . . . what has happened?"

"You should have seen the other fellows," Netanel said.

Frau Rosenberg did not laugh. She called into the house for one of the servants. Then she took Netanel's arm and led him inside. Just before the door closed she turned and looked back at Marie.

"*Verdammt Deutschländer!*" she spat, and Marie was left alone on the portico, feeling something she had never really experienced in all her life as the daughter of a poor butcher.

Shame.

3

Marie Helder lived with her family in the apartment above her father's butcher's shop on Theresienstrasse. A wrought-iron sign overhanging the street announced "*Metzgerei*", in gold-painted Gothic script. Like many houses in Bavaria, the façade had been decorated with colourful murals. Green shutters had been painted around the windows on the second floor, and a fresco in red and ochre and gold portrayed the crucifixion of Christ. An unfortunate choice for a butcher's shop, Netanel thought. Typical of someone like Herr Helder not to be aware of the excruciating irony.

Netanel stared for a moment at the gutted pigs hanging from their shiny steel hooks in the window. Then he knocked on the heavy door that led to the stairs and the second-storey apartment.

A spy mirror was mounted diagonally outside the living-room window. Netanel saw Marie's face appear briefly in the glass, and then heard her running down the stairs. She threw open the door, breathless.

16

"Netanel!"

"Hello, Marie."

"What are you doing here? On a Sunday?"

Netanel looked beyond her, to the apartment. He saw a boy's face, at the top of the stairs, peering around the banisters. Marie turned. "Dieter! Go away!" Marie shouted. The face disappeared.

Netanel grinned. "Your brother?"

"Boys are such a nuisance, aren't they? Well, I mean brothers."

"I don't have any brothers. I'll take your word for it."

"What are you doing here?" She glanced up the stairs again. She felt a thrill of fear when she thought of what her father would say if he found her talking to Josef Rosenberg's son.

"Would you come to our house for tea on Friday evening?" Netanel said.

"Yes! I mean . . . I will have to ask my father."

"Of course."

"I am sure it will be all right." She would lie.

"Good."

They stared at each other. "Why didn't you ask me tomorrow at school?" she said.

"It took me all weekend to get my parents to agree. I wanted to come straight round before they had a chance to change their minds."

It was as if a cloud had passed over her face. "The butcher's daughter?"

"The Catholic butcher's daughter is the problem," he said. Then he grinned. "It's not really tea on Friday night."

"It's not?"

"It's the Passover."

"You're inviting me to your Passover?" Marie said, astonished. It was a Jewish celebration, she knew. The Nazis said it was when the Jews drank the blood of German babies.

"Please try and come." He looked up at the spy

17

mirror, saw a man's face appear there. The face quickly withdrew.

"I'll talk to my parents tonight," Marie said.

"Good." Dieter had appeared at the top of the stairs again. Netanel saw him making faces through the banisters. "Good."

"Netanel," she called after him. "What should I wear?"

"Just sidecurls," he shouted back at her, grinning. "Sidecurls and a black hat!"

The winter garden had been built on to the back of the house to accommodate the potted plants and palms that were Frau Rosenberg's passion. The room had huge windows all around, so that it stayed warm during the day even in the middle of winter. Frau Rosenberg would spend much of each day there, digging among the greenery with a small chrome spade; on weekends her husband would join her, reading the newspapers in the large wing-backed chair in the corner.

"I don't know why we have a *goyim* at our Passover Seder," Frau Rosenberg said.

"The boy likes her," Josef said. "He seems keen to invite her. Let it be."

"You can't trust a German. Have you forgotten what happened to him, what he looked like when he came home from Realschule that day?"

"We are Germans too."

"It did not stop those Hitler Jugend lumpen jumping on him in the street."

"How many of the ladies who attend your Kaffeeklatsch on a Wednesday afternoon are Jewish?"

"I am not talking race discrimination, Josef. I am talking about bringing a stranger to our Seder."

"Well, when we have met her she will no longer be a stranger."

Frau Rosenberg did not answer. She bent to another pot, turning the earth so viciously that it spilled out over the marble tiles. She dropped the spade with a clatter to the floor and went outside, slamming the door to indicate her displeasure. She stood on the verandah, her arms wrapped around her against the frigid March air. *Verdammt Deutschländer!* she swore under her breath. First they beat up her boy; then one of them invites herself to the Passover Seder.

She thought of her son's face the day he came home from school. It was a miracle nothing was broken; his ribs were a mass of bruises. Josef said it would all be all right in the end but how could everything be all right when these Germans could do things like that and no one did anything to stop them?

She was afraid. Josef did not know what he was talking about, did not know what it could be like. Her parents had come from Poland, she knew about pogroms. She could sense another one in the air, even here in Bavaria, no matter what Josef said.

Verdammt Deutschländer!

It was familiar and at the same time, totally alien. Netanel was the same, and yet, wearing his yarmulke, utterly changed. He saw the direction of her gaze and grinned sheepishly. "It's for the older men to hide their bald spots. Us young fellows wear one so as not to draw attention to them."

But the joke did not remove her feeling of alienation. She was an intruder. Josef tried to make her feel welcome, of course; everyone in the town spoke kindly of "*der Chef*". She had seen him many times around the town – usually in the back seat of his chauffeured car – but even he was utterly changed by the yarmulke and the prayer shawl he wore over the jacket of his suit. It was as if she had inadvertently stumbled on the wizard's den, found the real source of his power. A ridiculous notion, she thought, but there it was. She realised this fear the Nazis preyed upon was in her too.

Frau Rosenberg was more reserved than her husband; Marie felt the reproach in her eyes. In her eyes she was tainted by the misery of that afternoon when Netanel had been beaten.

Netanel introduced her to the rest of his family. There was his Uncle Mulu, a tall, stooped man with nicotine-stained fingers; Mulu's wife, Rachel, was a thin, nervous woman, a handkerchief twisting continually between her fingers. They had a daughter, about her own age, Bertha; an unfortunate name, Marie thought, for the poor girl weighed at least twice as much as she, and was only half as tall. And there was Eli, eleven, perched on the edge of his chair, sitting on his hands, blinking owlishly through tortoiseshell-rimmed glasses.

"This is Marie's first Passover," Frau Rosenberg was saying. "Netanel wanted her to see what a Seder was really like."

Marie saw the shadows in their faces. What was it? Suspicion? Contempt? Fear? Uncle Mulu lit a cigarette and Aunt Rachel twisted the handkerchief another turn, like a garotte. "It is a very special day for us," Rachel said. "It is nice to have a non-Jew with us to see how important it is." Twist-twist.

"But I suppose Netanel has explained it all to you," Mulu said.

"Marie's father is a butcher," Frau Rosenberg said, relentless.

"Nothing wrong with being a butcher," Mulu said.

It had never occurred to Marie before she met Netanel that there might be anything wrong with being a butcher. She looked at Netanel.

He was still smiling but his face was pale and his eyes glittered with fury. "I'll show you the Seder table," he said to her and guided her out of the room.

"I'm sorry," he whispered when they were out of earshot. "That was unforgivable."

"It does not matter."

"Mutti's side of the family has never left the ghetto."

She reached for his hand and squeezed it. "It's all right." It was the first time she had ever made such a gesture and the sudden intimacy between them scared her a little. "This is an adventure for me. I'll be the only girl in my confirmation class who's been to Passover."

"I'm ashamed of all of them. I shall refuse to talk to my mother again."

"Nonsense. If you want to see rudeness I'll invite you to come and celebrate Christmas with my father."

He opened the door to the dining-room. "Well, here it is anyway. This is the Seder table."

"It's beautiful," Marie murmured, in sudden wonder. Silver and porcelain shimmered in the candlelight of the menorah; the dishes and bowls appeared to be floating in the flickering yellow light. The table was dominated by a huge golden salver.

"Everything is a symbol for something tonight," Netanel whispered. "The little flat wafers are matzohs, unleavened bread. It reminds us how the Israelites had to leave Egypt so quickly they did not have time to wait for the bread to rise. There is a mixture of diced nuts and apple to symbolise the building materials of the forced labour. There is maror, the bitter herbs that recall the bitterness of bondage, and salt water for the tears of suffering. There is cress for the coming of spring, eggs to symbolise the offerings in the Great Temple, and the roasted lamb bone represents the sacrificial lambs that were slaughtered on the eve of the exodus."

"It is like stepping into the pages of the Bible."

"We Jews forget nothing. Wound a Jew, and in a hundred years you have a religious holiday."

She was not sure if he was mocking. "Is it important to you, all this?" she asked him.

He shrugged. "It's important to Mutti."

"But not you?"

"It's fun, but the Pharaoh was a long time ago. Do you believe in Santa Klaus?"

She smiled. "At Christmastime."

"There you are. I believe in the Seder at Passover. I'm sorry there are no German babies ready to be slaughtered. After everything Goebbels and Streicher have been saying, it must be disappointing."

"Well, you never claimed to be Orthodox."

He smiled at that.

21

They were interrupted by shouts from the hallway. "It's Aunt Esther," Netanel said. "You had better come and meet her too."

Aunt Esther had come from München, and she had with her her two sons, Michal and Chaim. Chaim was surrounded by the other members of the family, and everyone was shouting and crying at once.

Netanel and Marie hovered by the stairs. "What's happening?" Marie whispered.

"It's Chaim," Netanel said. "He looks like he's been in a fight."

Chaim was perhaps the same age as Netanel but shorter, dark-haired, not as broad in the shoulders. Both his eyes were almost swollen shut and a front tooth was missing. There was a purple bruise on one side of his face that made him look as if he had a whole orange in his mouth. The women, Frau Rosenberg and Aunt Rachel, were shrieking and patting him and embracing him at once, and Chaim winced and tried to pull away each time they touched his face.

"What happened?" Aunt Rachel repeated over and over, without taking breath to wait for an answer. "What happened?"

"It was the Nazis," Chaim's younger brother Michal shouted, hoping to draw some of the attention for himself.

"The Nazis did this? The Nazis did this?" Frau Rosenberg shouted.

"What happened?" Aunt Rachel repeated.

"I was just standing in the street – " Chaim said.

"It was a Nazi parade, SA men – " Michal shouted.

Esther waved them both quiet. "These SS men were watching. My Chaim did not salute the Nazi flag as it went past. Of course he does not salute the Nazi flag. He's Jewish, he's not allowed. But they take him into an alley and start to beat on him."

"Just because he did not salute the Nazi flag?" Josef shouted.

"He told them he did not have to salute the flag – " Michal said.

"– because I was Jewish," Chaim finished.

"So then they beat on him again," Esther said.

"Stupid to tell them he was Jewish!" Marie said to Netanel, and in that moment everyone fell quiet and stared at her. For a long time no one spoke.

Then Josef Rosenberg said; "Well. I am sure it will pass. Let us go inside now and celebrate the Passover."

Netanel cleared his throat. "Why is this night different from all other nights?" he said.

Josef Rosenberg, at the head of the table, read from the illuminated Hebrew text of the Haggadah, lying open on the table in front of him. He raised his hands, palm up. "This night is different because we celebrate the most important moment in the history of our people. On this night we celebrate their going forth in triumph from slavery into freedom."

So began the Passover feast, each course regulated by custom and the prayers and songs of the Haggadah of which each participant at the meal had their own copy. By the yellow light of the candles, they read the songs and prayers of the Seder, while Josef recounted the story of the exodus, the atmosphere in the room heavy with the aroma of herbs, chicken soup, roasted lamb bone, and the musk of the ruby wine that came all the way from Mount Carmel in Palestine.

They sipped the wine to symbolise joy while Josef recounted the story of the ten plagues against the Pharaoh, and then they sang the Song of Miriam, to celebrate the closing of the Red Sea on the Pharaoh's army. Chaim was given the honour of carrying a heavy silver goblet of wine from the room and placing it on the portico outside the front door so that the Prophet Elijah could take it as refreshment should he arrive during the feast.

Marie looked round the room. At Josef, reading from the Haggadah in the tone a kindly uncle might use to read his nephews a bedtime story; at Chaim, his battered face made all the more grotesque by the candlelight; at Aunt Rachel, the handkerchief still clutched between her fingers, corkscrewed tighter and tighter; finally at Netanel, his face a blank mask. What was he thinking?

He stared back at her across the table and winked.

This is impossible, Marie thought. I am falling in love with this boy. But it is quite impossible. I'm Catholic and he's a Jew. All this is so alien to me he might as well be from the moon. His mother despises me, the rest of the family treat me as if I were some exotic animal from Africa. And there is what happened to Chaim; the same that happened to Netanel a few months ago. Madness ever to contemplate loving him . . .

The Passover ceremony ended. "Next year in Jerusalem," the whole table said in unison.

Netanel looked across the table and smiled at her, a broad, delicious smile and she felt her stomach squirm like a puppy. Oh, *mein Gott*, she thought. This has already gone too far. I cannot stop this now. I cannot . . .

Part Two

PALESTINE, 1934

4

Kfar Herzl Kibbutz

Rishou Hass'an decided it was next to impossible to pick apples all day with a permanent erection.

It was unholy, it was torment, it was wonderful. These Jewish girls never covered their hair or their faces or their brown arms and legs. They worked all day in *shorts*, for the sweet love of Allah! He had never seen a woman's thighs uncovered before. He was hypnotised by the way the muscles rippled beneath the taut brown skin, how hairless they were, like a boy's. And then, whenever they picked up a basket of the apples . . .

Allah, help me in my sorrow! All the blood in his body drained into his virile member and he felt faint. These Jews were a curse sent to torment him. This Sarah was the worst. She worked right next to him, here in the orchard. What eyes! Dark brown eyes, that spoke to a man of all the pleasures of the couch and beyond!

Why does Allah try me this way?

One of the other Jewish boys was watching him. Asher, they called him. He knows! He knows what I am thinking and he would like to stick a knife in my ribs. Even for three Palestine shillings a day I cannot stand this any more! My seed is backed up in my belly like the Sea of Galilee!

Every day was a battlefield of glances. He watched her, she watched him, Asher watched both of them. Three pairs of eyes speculating with hunger, curiosity and murder, and not a word said.

If only she would not look at him that way. If only he

27

could feast his eyes on her brown legs and arms and that
shining charcoal hair and know she was forbidden and
impossible. But every day he would catch her looking at
him, and he speculated on what those looks might mean.
She was driving him out of his mind.

It was just too much. Even for three Palestine shillings
and fantasies to last a lifetime, it was just too much.

Rab'allah

"She is driving me crazy," Rishou said. "I can't sleep, I
can't eat. I don't know what to do."

"I've had more Jewish girls from that kibbutz than you
can count," Wagil said. "They're all whores. They're
begging for it."

"The next Jewish woman you fuck will be the first one.
You couldn't find your own stalk if it wasn't tied on."

Wagil flushed and slammed the flat of his hand on
the brass tray between them so the cups spilled and the
customers in Zayyad's coffee shop turned their heads and
grinned. Wagil hated to be mocked by his younger brother.
But Rishou was bigger, and there was little he could do
about it. "You don't know anything!"

"The sheep all bleat when you go in the barn," Rishou
said, still grinning, "but if I ever find a Jewish girl who
speaks your name with cow eyes I will give you a thousand
Palestine pounds."

Wagil tried to cuff his younger brother's face but Rishou
was too quick and caught his wrist.

"Wagil, Wagil! Don't be such a camel's ass!"

"You don't know what you're talking about!"

"Those Jewish girls might not cover their heads or
their long legs but their men protect them as jealously as we guard ours. If one of us sneaks over that
kibbutz fence they'll find us next morning with our
throats cut and our balls stuffed down our throats."

28

Wagil clapped his hands sulkily and the serving boy refilled their coffee cups from the *finjan*. The coffee house was owned by the Hass'an family. Zayyad Hass'an, their father, was *muktar*, headman, of Rab'allah. He owned much of the surrounding fields, and was the agent of the city effendis who rented out the remaining allotments.

He was muktar because he was the wealthiest man in the village, and his wealth in turn commanded respect. He had the finest house, the best horse, even owned the only raised bedstead in the village. His wealth was the source of his power, and here in the coffee house he smoked his water pipe and mediated in disputes, lent money, acted as intermediary for the villagers with the authorities in Jerusalem. One day perhaps the title of muktar would pass to Wagil – if he could prove himself capable.

"Let those Jews harm just one of us and we will raze their kibbutz to the ground!" Wagil said.

"Of course, that goes without saying. We will fire our guns at them from a safe distance, at least."

"They survive here only because of our much fêted patience and tolerance."

"And their much fêted searchlights and Enfield rifles."

Wagil scowled. His brother always had a clever answer for everything. Zayyad favoured him best. With Majid away in Jerusalem he was Wagil's only real threat. "Perhaps you should slip into the kibbutz one night and see what happens," Wagil said.

Rishou grinned. "Not even for you, brother. Not even for you!"

Kfar Herzl Kibbutz

"I don't like the way he looks at you," Yaakov said.

"How does he look at me?" Sarah asked him sweetly.

Yaakov knew that look of practised innocence in his daughter. "You know what I'm talking about. And I don't like the way you look at him!"

29

"How do I look at him?"

"Don't play games with me!"

They were in the communal dining-room of the kibbutz. The dining hall was the centre of their community, the hub of Kfar Herzl. The walls were bare stone and the narrow tables and benches were lit by just a few kerosene lanterns; but it was here that the fifty families of the kibbutz ate together, where they came to write to families left behind in Poland and Germany and Russia; where they came to talk and to dance. Most of all to dance. Even at the end of the hardest day of physical labour, there was always someone ready to pick up a guitar and bodies that had seemed too sore from work would rouse themselves into another celebration of freedom and life.

They were dancing now, just half a dozen of the younger men and women, but soon others would be dragged into the circle.

There would be more but so many were weak from the malaria, which was why he had hired the Arab labour for the harvest.

"If I see you talking to him, I'll smack your arse!"

"I'm not a little girl any more!"

"But I'm still your father. Remember that!"

They glared at each other across the table until one of the dancers noticed the fight and grabbed Sarah's wrist and tried to pull her to her feet. It was Asher.

Sarah snatched her arm away petulantly, but Asher was not denied easily. He grabbed her again, this time with both hands, and pulled her to her feet. Someone was strumming out the rhythm of the hora on a guitar, others sat on the tables and clapped their hands to the beat. The ring of dancers paced out the steps, two steps clockwise, one back, slowly at first then faster and faster, all of them laughing and singing at once.

Sarah joined in, but her mind continued to brood on what her father had said. He was right, of course. She was flirting with disgrace and danger here. Yes, their apple picker was a beautiful man, but to the rest

30

of the kibbutz he was just another dirty Arab. And yet.

She had never seen any man like him. Those eyes! They were like pools of dark water. She knew it was all illusion, a mirage of the desert. Behind that beautiful face there was probably just another cut-throat Bedouin. And yet such seductive, black eyes, such power and hunger . . . if for just one time she could . . .

Of course, her father was right. It was madness.

. . . And yet.

Rab'allah

The mournful cough of a hyena.

Rishou could not sleep. Whenever he closed his eyes he saw her: bare-headed, brown-legged, wide-eyed. Allah, I am only a man! How can I work and sleep with such temptation haunting me?

Wagil lay on his back on the mattress beside him, snoring. In the next room he could hear his father rutting like a bull with his second wife. Another temptation! Ramiza was barely a few months older than he, with the face of a ministering angel. May his father's stalk wither into a fig and drop off into the creek! He had arranged a marriage for Wagil already. When would it be his turn to take a wife?

He crept out of the house and stood in the alley outside, looking up at the scattering of stars. He groaned aloud. His balls felt the size of watermelons.

Far below, in the valley, he could hear the sound of voices drifting up from the kibbutz. The Jews were singing again. Wasn't a day's back-breaking work in the orchards enough for them?

The moon threw a ghostly luminescence over the stone and mud streets and the flat-roofed houses. He hugged himself against the chill of the night and wandered down the slope towards the orchards that were scattered over the slopes below.

Kfar Herzl Kibbutz

The kibbutz was surrounded by a barbed-wire fence, watchtowers dotted along its perimeter. There were flood-lights too, powered by generators, but these were only used to illuminate the cottages of the settlement. The wire fence was all that separated the olive orchards of Rab'allah from the stone terraced vineyards and apple trees of Kfar Herzl.

Rishou sat for a long time under the gently rustling branches of the olive trees staring at the brightly lit cottages and bungalows. She was so close. Dancing and laughing with those Jewish boys, her brother's friends. He groaned again.

Why was he moping and whining like this? He was no better than . . . than . . . Wagil! Where was his fire, where were his balls? Climb through the fence, he said to himself. You've been through enough times when you were a boy, with Majid, to raid the Jews' orchards.

He clambered through, ripping his robe on the wire, and made his way through the vineyards, in a low crouching run.

He lay face down at the first line of trees. It was nearly midnight and the kibbutzniks were filing out of the dining hall in ones and twos. The square outside the dining hall was floodlit; he could see everything clearly.

It was her voice he recognised first, husky, petulant. She was with a man. They came out of the dining hall side by side, Asher with his fists thrust deep into his pockets, sulky, Sarah trying to step ahead of him. He could see their faces as if it were daylight.

He felt a thrill of excitement and fear and longing in his gut.

They made their way to one of the cottages about fifty yards from the dining hall. Rishou scampered through the trees after them, clinging to the shadows. Suddenly he tripped on a root and stumbled, falling face down in the dry earth.

"What was that?" he heard Asher say.

"I didn't hear anything."

"I thought I heard something moving in the orchard."

Rishou willed himself into the earth, not moving. He saw Sarah run up the steps of the cottage and go inside. Asher hesitated, peering into the darkness. Then he seemed to shrug and walk away.

Rishou waited until he was gone and then moved on his belly through the orchard, closer to the cottage. Now what? he asked himself. Perhaps if I can find out which room she is in I can try and talk to her. But how, without waking her whole family?

One of the lights snapped on at one of the windows, and the silhouette of a woman was framed suddenly in the yellow light. It was her! It was Sarah!

She began to undress. He lay on his belly, not moving, not even breathing. She unbuttoned her blue denim workshirt. Then she leaned forward, staring into the orchard, almost as if she were looking for him, pressing the soft swell of her breasts against the window. He could almost feel the puff of her breath on the glass.

Rishou's fingernails clawed into the hard dirt. He held his breath, in agony. A part of him thought: She is doing this deliberately. But she could not know he was here. Could she?

She turned around and achingly slowly drew her arms back and let the shirt slide from her shoulders to the floor. "Turn around!" he hissed into the dirt. Sarah eased off her shorts, and they fell to the floor, out of sight below the level of the windowsill.

I can't see! Perhaps I could climb the tree, he thought, almost insane now. Or scale the watchtower and shine the searchlight into her room. Or I could jump head first through the window. Or . . .

The light went out.

He lay on his back, gasping for breath. His hand went to his groin. He was like iron. He could punch holes in a stone wall with his sacred member!

He rolled back on to his belly and examined the fifty yards of open space between the edge of the orchard and the cottage. Perhaps a small stone, flicked against the window. She would look out. He would not have to say anything. Just let her see him.

What then? She would scream and every gun in the kibbutz would be pointed at him!

I don't care! My father will come and claim my body and my corpse will have its virile member raised to Allah as thick and long as the trunk of a palm tree and Zayyad will be sorry he did not listen to my pleas for marriage sooner and he will build a shrine for me above Rab'allah and girls will pray at my tomb just to be fertile!

He got to his feet and started to run, in a crouch, towards the cottage. Almost immediately he heard a voice shout a warning in Hebrew. There was the crash of rifle fire and something zipped past his face. Allah help me in my sorrow! They are shooting at me!

He turned and weaved back into the orchard, cursing. More gunshots and a bullet slapped into the trunk of an apple tree a foot from his head. He continued to weave and run, his head bowed; he did not stop running till he was back in Rab'allah.

5

Rab'allah

A cluster of whitewashed cubes clinging to the Judean hills, Rab'allah was home for four hundred souls, descendants of one of the great Bedouin tribes who had turned their backs on the Negev two centuries before. The *fellaheen* of the village barely scratched a living from the barren hillside plots that they rented from the effendis in Jerusalem and Damascus. From these they coaxed just enough grain to eat or to use for barter or to feed a few head of sheep or goats. There was a communal orchard growing olives and figs.

The streets of Rab'allah were dusty in summer and clogged with mud in winter. Night and day the musts of the village clung to the air: there was the scent of woodsmoke from the outdoor fires; the sweetness of bread baking in the communal ovens; the steamy smell of fresh dung.

Dung was everywhere; the droppings of donkeys, sheep, cows, and goats and chickens, the dung that was their principal source of heat for cooking and for warmth, and for the fertiliser for the fields.

Time passed slowly from one harvest to another, marked only by the rites of marriage and birth and death. It was a way of life that had not changed in the lifetime of their fathers, or their fathers' fathers. The ritual of their daily lives was as certain as the passage of the seasons.

The social life of the village revolved around the tiny square at the centre of the town. On one side was the mosque; on the other the store, the khan, and the coffee shop, all owned by Zayyad Hass'an. Except for harvest time, the men spent their days in the coffee shop, drinking coffee, playing dominoes, boasting, arguing. It was here that Zayyad Hass'an, resplendent in his tunic of fine damascene silk and waxed handlebar moustache, held court. Wagil Hass'an, basking in his reflected glory, would read from *Falastine*, the Arabic-language newspaper printed in Jerusalem. As the only literate member of the community – apart from Rishou – he could hold his audience spellbound for hours. Often, as today, the temptation to embellish the accounts with his own prejudice proved too great.

"Jaffa: It was reported here today that an Arab girl, found raped and murdered this morning outside the main synagogue, was the victim of an attack by a Jewish gang."

There was a sharp hiss as the men sucked in their breath through gritted teeth and muttered into their beards.

Delighted with the effect of his improvised translation, Wagil continued: "Eyewitnesses said the gang pinned the girl to the ground and raped her repeatedly, before despatching her with their knives."

One of the men drew his dagger from his belt and plunged the blade into the dirt floor. "If I had been there I would have cut off their balls and stuffed them down their throats!"

There was a general murmur of agreement around the room that this was indeed the only honourable course of action.

"The Jews have been terrorising the city for months. This is believed to be the seventh attack of its kind in the last two weeks and the British police have refused to take action against the Jewish gang, even though they are all well known as rapists and murderers and unbelievers."

"We should kill all the Jews!" someone shouted.

"The Grand Mufti of Jerusalem, may God bless him and grant him increase, says that no Arab girl is safe any longer from violation even in her own home – "

"What are you reading, Wagil?" Wagil had not heard his

brother enter the coffee house. Rishou tore the newspaper out of his hand and scanned the page quickly. "Where is it? What were you reading?"

"I had finished," Wagil said.

"Here it is. It says one Arab girl was raped in Jaffa. It does not even say who was responsible!"

Wagil leaped to his feet and tried to snatch the newspaper back. "That is a different story!"

"Show me the real story then!" Rishou threw the tattered remnants of *Falastine* at him. "Show me the real story!"

Wagil's cheeks were burning with shame. "How can I? Look what you have done! No one can read this now, you've ripped it to shreds!"

"You read a little bit of Arabic and you make up the rest!"

"I did not make it up! An Arab girl was raped by Jews!"

"An Arab girl was raped. That is all it says!"

"It must have been Jews!" someone shouted from the back of the room. It was Izzat. Of course, Rishou thought. His uncle is on the Arab Higher Committee with the Grand Mufti.

Rishou looked around the room. "I do not have any great love for the Jews but we cannot blame them for everything."

"You're right," someone else said. "It's the British who are to blame!"

Rishou looked appealingly at his father. "Don't let him read if he's just going to make up lies about everything."

Wagil leaped to his feet again. "I can read as well as you!"

Everyone looked at Zayyad, awaiting his judgment. The muktar put down his water pipe and rose to his feet, the folds of his *abbayah* billowing around him like the wings of a great bird.

He crossed the room to stand in front of his eldest son. Wagil could not meet his eyes. Zayyad picked up the scattered sheets of the newspaper and crumpled them in

37

his fist. He cuffed Wagil around the ear with the loose sheets of newsprint.

"If you were as tall as you were stupid," he said, "Allah would have made you into a palm tree."

And he stalked from the coffee house.

The black Ford wound its way up the road from Jerusalem. It was the first time anyone had seen a motor car in Rab'allah, and the men swarmed out of the coffee house to watch. A crowd of urchins ran down to meet it, running alongside as it bounced over the rutted track. They slapped on the windows with their hands and tried to jump on the running board. A miracle if one of them is not crushed under the wheels, Zayyad thought.

When the motor car reached the outskirts of the village, there were at least fifty children swarming around it. Women scuttled squealing into doorways and a donkey hawed and stamped out of the way. Zayyad waited at the doorway, his arms folded.

The Ford braked to a stop, dust billowing around it. A short, balding European climbed out. He was wearing a western-style brown suit with white shirt and woollen tie. Everyone pressed forward to shake his hand and paw at his jacket, rubbing the material between grimy fingers. The man seemed wearily accustomed to this kind of welcome. He saw Zayyad and made his way towards him.

"You are the muktar?" he said, in heavily accented Arabic.

"I am Sheikh Zayyad Hass'an al-Shouri. Welcome to Rab'allah."

The man held out his hand. "David Schanenberg. I am secretary to the Land Fund at the Jewish Agency in Jerusalem."

"*Ahlan*," Zayyad said. "Welcome to my humble home."

Compared to the rest of Rab'allah, there was nothing humble about Zayyad Hass'an's house. It was built on the highest point of the village, with commanding views over the valley. While the other houses were built of mud, Zayyad's six-bedroom home was constructed of Judean limestone. There was glass in the windows, replacing the traditional wooden shutters, and instead of sitting on the floor on goatskin rugs, guests and visitors sat on benches upholstered with pillows embroidered by the seamstresses of Bethlehem. There was even, to the envy of everyone, an outside toilet.

Zayyad settled himself in the ancient stuffed armchair that was equivalent in prestige in Rab'allah to the Peacock Throne, and clapped his hands for his daughters to fetch coffee.

Schanenberg removed his jacket and sat on one of the benches that lined the walls. Faces crowded the doorway and the windows, eager for a glimpse of these important proceedings.

"I'll come straight to the point," Schanenberg said. "The Jewish Agency wants to buy some of your land. From the records in Jerusalem we've ascertained that you own a thousand dunams of land on the far side of the ridge. We want to establish a new kibbutz there."

Zayyad blinked at him. Among fellow Arabs Zayyad would spend at least half an hour drinking coffee and exchanging the usual pleasantries before discussing business. That, at least, was what civilised people would do. But the man had been invited into his home and it would be unholy to match insult with insult. "First we must drink some coffee while I consider this," he said.

"It is after all a useless tract of land as it stands now," Schanenberg went on, as if he had not heard. "The fellaheen to whom it is presently rented barely scratch a living from it."

Rashedah, Zayyad's youngest daughter, brought the copper finjan and two small handleless cups on a brass tray and placed it on the mat between them. She poured the coffee – Turkish style, thick and sweet and very strong, flavoured with cardamom seed – and withdrew.

"We are willing to pay a very good price," Schanenberg said.

Rashedah next brought a brass bowl filled with plums. Zayyad took one and wiped it on the back of his robe.

"Have a plum," Zayyad said, "and tell me about the drive from Jerusalem. Was it pleasant?"

Kfar Herzl Kibbutz

They rested for lunch in the shade of the apple trees. Cheese and olives, bread and figs were brought from the dining hall to the orchard and shared among all the workers. Rishou and two other Arab boys from Rab'allah sat separately from the kibbutzniks.

Occasionally Rishou dared a glance in Sarah's direction. She was sitting with her knees tucked into her chest, eating a fig. When she sat that way he could see the silky expanse of her thighs almost to her sacred place. Rishou dropped the hunk of bread he had been chewing back into the basket. He had quite lost his appetite.

Asher was watching him. "Someone broke into our kibbutz the other night," he said in Arabic, loud enough for Rishou to hear.

Rishou met his stare. "Bedouin?" he shouted back.

"The guard thought it was one of your people from Rab'allah."

"Then why didn't he shoot?"

"He did. But he aimed high."

Rishou grinned. "You mean he missed?"

"He thinks they were trying to steal from our orchard."

"Are any apples missing?"

"How would I know?"

Rishou's eyes widened in mock horror. "You mean you don't count them every morning?"

Sarah stifled a giggle and he felt a sudden glow of pleasure.

"You think it's funny that someone is stealing our apples?" Asher snapped.

"Perhaps he just wanted to see what they were like without their skins," Sarah said.

"What the hell do you mean by that?" Asher said.

40

Sarah shrugged and did not answer.

Rishou did not dare look back in her direction. *She knew!* Why else would she say such a thing? He thought back on that night. Had she known he was in the orchard before she went to the window?

Asher got to his feet. "Let's get back to work," he said.

Far above the orchard where they sat, Zayyad Hass'an squatted on his haunches under the gnarled and skeletal branches of a dead tree. The villagers called this The Place Where The Fig Tree Died. On one side of the ridge was the Kibbutz, on the other the thousand dunams of land that the Jewish Agency wanted to buy. And at what a price! Schanenberg had offered him thirty times what it was worth.

His commercial sense told him to take the offer. Another part of him wanted to tell the Jew to go piss up a camel's leg.

He could see their reasoning of course. With this other thousand dunams the two kibbutzim would form a strong bloc in the event of an attack. It made sense.

And Schanenberg was right, it was useless land, stony and hard and infertile. The fellaheen who sharecropped it barely made enough to pay their rents. The lower half was useless, bitter swamp, infested with malarial mosquitoes. A wasteland.

Yet he remembered when the effendis in Jerusalem had sold the Jews the three thousand dunams where Kfar Herzl now stood. He had negotiated an outrageous price, and everyone had laughed and slapped their thighs at how the Jews had been duped. Everyone agreed that when the Jews saw the land that had been bought for them they would turn around and head right back where they came from. It was wilderness and swamp; none of it had been farmed for generations.

That was ten years ago. It was Rishou, nine years old then, who had come running in from the fields shouting over and over: "The Jews are coming!" Everyone rushed out to watch.

41

There had been perhaps a dozen families, all dressed in the navy blue denim of kibbutzniks, men, women, small children, riding in the back of flatbed trucks, surrounded by rolls of barbed wire and farming implements and wheelbarrows. They were accompanied by another dozen Hashomer, the Jews' famous watchmen, on horseback, wearing the *keffiyeh* and flowing robes of Bedouin, carrying rifles and crossed bandoliers, trains of mules trailing behind them.

But when they arrived at their three thousand dunams of burned grass and swamp they had not turned back.

Instead, on that first day, they had set up their tents, dug defensive trenches and built fences of barbed wire. Within two weeks Kfar Herzl had its first stone building, with high watchtowers around the perimeter. The villagers watched, amazed, as the Jews turned night into day with floodlights powered by the hum of generators.

They planted strange-looking trees in the swamps, working through the heat of each day to dig ditches, while their mules dragged ploughs over the wretched fields. They built water-towers and dairies. A stone sleeping barracks was added to the central stone building, and others followed.

"When the rains come, they will give it up," the villagers told each other confidently. "When they start to die with the fever, they will see that Allah did not wish this land to be cultivated."

When the rains came, the Jews' fields flooded and their ditches collapsed and the kibbutz turned into a quagmire of mud that sucked the shoes off their feet and brought clouds of mosquitoes that killed many of them with the fever.

But still they did not leave.

And over the next year, as the villagers watched, a miracle took place. The strange trees – eucalyptus, the Jews called them – slowly sucked up the black, acid waters of the swamp and drained it. The Jews who had not succumbed to the fever rebuilt the ditches and the rest of the fetid waters drained away. They sprayed the swamp with strange white clouds of vapour and the next winter fewer of them died from the fever and the winter after that the swamp had become rich dark loam and the Jews began to plant their orchards there. They rebuilt the crumbling stone terraces on the valley walls, and planted new orchards of apple and plum trees.

The stony fields now had rivers in them that the Jews could turn on and off and they were green in winter and yellow with corn and barley in summer.

The villagers' exuberance subsided into sullen disbelief as they realised that the Jews were not as stupid as they had believed. The wilderness was now a paradise of orchards and fields. It was Allah's will that they should stay. *Insh'allah.*

A grudging commerce began between the two communities. Zayyad conceded that the Jews had become good neighbours. But another kibbutz, right here? Zayyad imagined the wasteland below covered with orchards and corn. Soon the whole of Judea would be swarming with these Jews!

He got up, and shook his head slowly, making his decision. It was Allah's will that some of His earth should remain as wilderness. It was unholy to think of this place any other way.

When David Schanenberg returned to Rab'allah, Zayyad Hass'an was again waiting for him outside his house. This time he did not extend his hospitality.

"I shall come straight to the point," Zayyad said, "you can go piss up a camel's leg."

Schanenberg threw his jacket over his right shoulder and squinted into the sun. "You want more money?"

"I shall not sell at any price."

"Well, that's a shame," Schanenberg said. "But it doesn't matter. Soon we'll own it all anyway. It's just a question of time."

"The earth belongs to Allah. You cannot own it all."

"We don't want it all," Schanenberg said. "Just Palestine."

And he got in his car and drove away.

43

6

Sarah.

Sarah with her arms wrapped around her knees, sitting against the trunk of an apple tree. Sarah pulling the fruit from the trees, her long brown arms and bare brown legs. Sarah smiling at him as she bent to throw another basket of fruit on to the donkey pannier.

Sarah, Sarah, Sarah.

He could not get her out of his mind. He tossed restlessly on his mattress but sleep would not come. This was impossible. He must tell his father he was not going back to the kibbutz to work. Make up some excuse. He could not stand it any more.

But if he gave up the work, he would not see her any more. And for all its pain and hopelessness, he did not want to give up the sweet torture.

He remembered again – did he ever stop remembering? – the night he had crawled through the wire. He closed his eyes and the image sprang perfect in his mind, with the supervivid clarity of repetition; the way she unbuttoned the shirt, then leaned against the window, her breasts swollen in the fold of her arms, then turning away and the bare shape of her shoulders and her back . . .

He sat up in bed, sweating.

The only girls he had ever seen without clothes had been his sisters. When they had been little they had played together barefoot in the streets, but as soon as they had reached puberty they had been made to wear long abbayahs. He could speak to them, boss them – that was his right, after all – but he had not played with them

44

or been alone with them since they were children. He had not seen them with their heads uncovered or their arms or legs bare since.

The Jewish girls drove him crazy. They laughed and teased the other Jewish boys, even held hands and danced with them. It was unholy, it was shameful. And he burned with envy.

Sarah, Sarah.

He dressed quickly and went outside. Without thinking, he ran down the hill towards the orchard. The wind had freshened and a cool breeze stirred the leaves of the olive trees. They whispered in the darkness as he ran, couriers of his desire.

He reached the wire and scrambled underneath.

There was no moon and the night was black, but Rishou had rehearsed this many times in his mind. He could have found his way to the cottage blindfolded. Was it only a week since he had last been here? He reached the apple orchard and kept up a low, loping run through the trees. He could make out the lights of the kibbutz in the distance. He had no idea what he was going to do when he got there.

He did not see the shadow waiting for him behind the trees.

Something hit him hard in the shin and he went down. A knife flashed in the darkness. Rishou rolled on his back and threw up an arm to protect himself. But he was too slow. A knee slammed into his stomach and the air rushed out of him. A hand went to his throat choking him and he felt the point of a knife against his neck. Another inch and it would sever the vein and he was dead.

He lay still, frozen, choking for breath, trying to glimpse his assailant's face, waiting for the death stroke.

"So it's you," a voice said. The knife stayed at his throat. "What do you want?"

He could not answer. Allah, help me in my sorrow, these Jews were worse than the Bedouin!

"I asked you a question! What are you doing here?"

45

"I came . . . to . . . see you."

"You were spying on me!" Sarah's voice hissed at him.

"No!"

"You have been spying on me through the window!"

She is going to murder me, he thought. All these secret looks that have passed between us were really just glares of contempt. She thinks I am just a dirty Arab. She is going to kill me!

"You're just so beautiful," he heard himself whisper to her. Oh Allah, what have I said? Now she will use the knife, for sure. I have heard about these Jewish women. They say they are every bit as tough as the boys. What humiliation to be killed by a woman! The gates of Paradise will be slammed in my face, Mohammed himself will curse me for shaming all of Islam!

"You think I'm beautiful?" Sarah said. There was a hint of softness in her voice.

"I can't stop thinking about you," Rishou said.

"Then what took you so long? Six nights I have been waiting here in the orchard!"

She withdrew the knife. He raised himself on his elbows. "You have been waiting for me?" he mumbled.

"What do you want? That I should write you a message in the sand with white stones? Should I ask Mohammed to fly a legion of angels from heaven to shake you awake and carry you here?"

"You knew it was me the other night?"

"I knew the next day. You are not a very good liar. I can read you better than an illuminated page from the Torah." She held the knife in front of his eyes. "Take off your clothes!"

I am dreaming this, Rishou thought. He scrambled to pull off his robe. He was ashamed to find he was trembling. He heard the rustle of fabric in the darkness and he reached out and felt her bare skin under his fingers. He gasped aloud and she squeezed her hand over his mouth. "Be quiet!" she hissed. "You'll bring the guard!"

She was kneeling over him. He felt her hair brush against his cheek and suddenly she was kissing him, her hot, sweet,

46

wet mouth against his. The warm softness of her breast
brushed his chest and he felt her fingers wrap themselves
around the swelling of his manhood.

This is too much, he thought. Allah, please do not let
me shame myself. If I release myself now I shall run away
and I shall not stop till I reach the furthest corners of the
earth. I shall run until I see a Red Indian and only then
shall I stop. Oh Allah, please do not let me be a boy when
tonight I need to be a man!

He felt himself throbbing involuntarily between the cool
grip of her fingers and he gasped and shuddered and
silently begged Allah to ride from heaven on El-Buraq
and kill him stone dead.

Instead he heard Sarah whisper, "Well, now we have
that out of the way, perhaps we can begin – yes?"

7

Rab'allah

Majid was coming back for the wedding. *In a car.*

Majid was the youngest brother, the favoured one.
Because he was the youngest, life had favoured him with
circumstance. Wagil had had his schooling from the imam
in the town mosque, squatting barefoot on a straw mat
and writing out his lessons in chalk on a piece of slate.
But by the time Majid was ready for school the British
had instituted a Department of Education school in nearby
Bethlehem, and when Majid had finished there, Zayyad
had so prospered that he was able to send him to the St
George's Anglican College in Jerusalem with Rishou.

It was already too late for Wagil.

Insh'allah. As Allah wills.

By the time he was of an age to get a job Majid could speak English and Hebrew as well as Arabic and Zayyad was able to use his influence to get him a job with the British as a storekeeper. It had earned the whole family enormous prestige.

Majid was too enterprising to remain a store clerk for long. He quickly proved himself invaluable as a translator and was recruited by a functionary in the office of the High Commissioner – Mandoob es Sami, the High One Who Has Been Sent – and was made his chauffeur and aide. Already he earned in a month what one of the poor fellaheen could not hope to make in a whole year.

And now he was returning to Rab'allah. *In a car.*

It makes the old Ford driven by Schanenberg look like a horse and cart, Zayyad thought, delighted. It was a stately Buick limousine with an engine that purred like a kitten with a bowl of cream.

And Majid! He looked wonderful! He wore a tarbush and a suit of woollen check, a silk shirt with stripes, and a tie of such magnificence that it dazzled the eye. It was of fine red silk and it featured a bare-headed western English girl *in her underwear*! Never in all his life had he seen such a treasure!

Zayyad awaited his son, settled into the great stuffed armchair that was the symbol of his authority in Rab'allah. Majid entered and knelt down to kiss his father's hand in the traditional manner.

"Yaba," Majid murmured, "Father."

"My son," Zayyad said. It had been six months since he had seen him. He has changed! Zayyad thought. He has a moustache and now he uses some sort of oil on his hair like a proper city effendi. Should I be angry or should I be pleased? He looks like an arse waiting to be pinched. But the car and these magnificent clothes! Everyone in Rab'allah was crowded in the doorway, gawking.

"Is that your motor car?" Zayyad said.

"In a manner of speaking," Majid said.

"Explain what you mean. I am just an old man now."

"Well, the car belongs to the secretary of the Mandoob

48

es Sami. But I drive it for him. So in some respects it is mine."

"He lets you keep it?"

"I must go back to Jerusalem after the wedding feast tomorrow. The British effendi and I have important business to attend to."

Zayyad nodded, satisfied. Such reflected glory would do his reputation no harm at all. By tomorrow it would be all over Judea that Zayyad Hass'an's son had driven his own motor car to Rab'allah for Wagil's wedding.

Zayyad leaned forward and fingered the soft silk of the golden-haired western girl in her underwear. Allah forgive me, he thought, but I am only flesh and blood. What would a man give to possess such a wonder! "How did you come by this treasure?"

Majid understood his father's meaning. The tie had cost him a small fortune in the bazaar in the Old City, but for the honour it would win him in his father's eyes, the price was small. He put his hands to his collar, loosened the knot and pulled it over his head. "It's yours, Father. I brought it as a gift."

"Aaahhhh, Majid, my son! What can I say? When you die may you go straight to Paradise and sit at Mohammed's right hand! Now show me this motor car!"

The urchins and old men clustered by the doorway parted respectfully to allow them to pass. Small children were swarming over the motor car like ants over a honey bowl. He clapped his hands sharply to send them scurrying away.

"Do you want to sit inside?" Majid said. He opened the door so that Zayyad could climb into the driving seat. Zayyad settled himself and looked around the interior, amazed. The seats were upholstered in leather the colour of red wine!

"It's a sixty series Buick with an overhead valve straight eight and clash-proof three-speed synchromesh transmission," Majid repeated, like a litany.

Zayyad turned the steering wheel and punched the horn, grinning as the noise sent the urchins who had ventured

49

closer scurrying away again. What a wonder. And it was his son's!

"Majid!"

Rishou ran up the street, laughing, Wagil scowling behind him. "Majid! Is this my little brother? It's really you?"

Majid turned and embraced him. "Rishou! You haven't changed!"

"You have! You look like a British major!"

"He looks like a pimp," Wagil said behind him. "Who owns the motor car?"

"Wagil, my brother! Do you like it?"

"There was a man from the Jewish Agency up here the other day," Wagil said. "His was better." And he walked on, pushing his way through the crowd, feigning disinterest.

Rishou and Majid watched him go. There was an embarrassed silence between them.

"How is Jerusalem?" Rishou said finally.

"Ah, Rishou, it is wild beyond imaginings! The women!"

Rishou waited for him to elaborate. "Well?"

"I have fucked so many times my virile member has a groove worn down the middle like the Damascus Steps!"

The expression on Rishou's face mirrored his disbelief.

"May Allah burn me on the Day of Fire if I lie!" Majid swore.

"Allah will burn you anyway!"

"You should come back with me! I can talk to the Mandoob es Sami for you. He listens to me! I will get you a job!"

"No, Majid, I want to stay here."

Majid lowered his voice. "You're crazy. Have you never noticed the stink here?"

Rishou stared at his younger brother. "What stink?"

They were interrupted by screams from the children and the hawing of a donkey as it scrambled away across the stones. Zayyad had released the handbrake and the Buick was rolling down the hill towards them. Zayyad's red silk tie flapped at his neck as he jerked frantically at the steering wheel.

"Bloody hell," Majid shouted in English.

The Buick swerved away to the left and slammed into the wall of a house. One of the headlamps shattered.

Silence.

Majid stumbled over. The damage was considerable. The left side mudguard had been stove in also.

Zayyad leaned out of the window and grinned, punching the horn. "This is wonderful," he shouted. "This is better than sex!"

Majid felt faint. He leaned against the wall. "How the bloody hell am I going to explain this to Mr Talbot?" he said in English and Zayyad punched the horn again and everyone laughed.

That night the sons slept together on goatskin rugs in a room leading off the dining-room of Zayyad's house. A jackal coughed in the darkness as it patrolled the dark borders of the village. Cows lowed in the barn, uneasy.

Rishou started to dress.

Majid stirred beside him. "Where are you going?" he whispered.

"I thought you were asleep."

"How can I sleep? I cannot stop thinking about Talbot effendi's Buick. What am I going to tell him?"

"Tell him the truth."

"If I tell him the truth I will lose my job."

"Lie then. You're good at that."

"May Allah forgive you. Where are you going?"

"Nowhere. Go back to sleep." Rishou slipped out of the house.

Rishou never tired of looking at her.

They lay side by side on the rough straw, their fingers intertwined. She was naked except for her shirt, which was unbuttoned. The moon was full and huge, framed by the gable of the barn, shimmering against a summer sky of purple and black. It threw shadows over the curves and valleys of her body. He leaned on one elbow and watched the rise and fall of her breathing.

No, he could never get enough of this. He could never stop touching or looking, never tire of this miracle that had happened to him. He untwined his fingers from hers and traced the contours of her thigh and belly. He was still damp from their lovemaking but already he felt himself stirring again.

He rolled towards her, nuzzling her cheek and shoulder, cupping her breast in his palm.

"Don't you ever get enough?" she whispered.

"Not of you."

She smiled. "*Hapzibah*."

"What does that mean?"

"It's just a Jewish word. I don't know. I can't translate it."

He kissed her eyelids, the lobes of her ears, the V of her neck, as she had shown him. She had shown him so much.

"Oh Rishou, I've never known any boy like you."

She meant it as praise but he felt the familiar stirrings of jealousy and rage and he pulled away. "Did you ever . . . do this . . . with other boys?"

She realised she had hurt him. "Didn't you ever do this with other girls?" she said.

"Of course." *No, never.*

She pulled his face towards her. "What's wrong?"

"Nothing."

"You think I'm a whore, don't you?"

"Of course not."

"Of course you do. No good Arab girl would do this."

52

She was right, he thought. If one of his sisters did this he would kill her.

"I'm the girl of your dreams and you despise what you dream about. Don't you?"

He rolled away from her. "Why do you talk to me this way? If you hate me so much why do you still meet me here? Or is it, you know, you want to see if us dirty Arabs are as exotic as they say. You're amusing yourself."

"What about you? Isn't that why you come? To be amused?"

"It's more than that for me."

"Of course it is. It's your pride."

"Why are we talking about this?"

"I'm sorry. I'm sorry." She ran her fingers through his hair. "Oh Rishou, if you were Jewish you'd be perfect."

"Well I'm not." He sat up and reached for his clothes.

Sarah lay back in the straw, her arms behind her head. "Will you come tomorrow?"

"I cannot. My brother Wagil is getting married." He slipped his robe over his head and started to brush off the straw.

"Did you know my father is coming to the wedding?" she said. "He is representing the kibbutz."

"My father told me."

"And when will they marry you off, my darling Rishou?"

"I don't know."

"Poor Rishou," she whispered. "You will hate it. You try hard to be a good Arab but the girl they will choose for you will never make you happy, and you will never know why."

"Stop taunting me!"

With one swift movement she wrapped her thighs around his chest and pulled him towards her. She grinned in the darkness. "Got you."

In spite of himself, he grinned back at her. "I pray to Allah I never have to fight you. You are as quick and devious as a scorpion."

"Come into my nest and let me sting you one more time, my fine Arab. In case you never come back."

"I'll always come back," he heard himself say and he wondered if it was true.

8

Rab'allah

The feasting and dancing for the wedding of the eldest son of the celebrated Sheikh Zayyad Hass'an al-Shouri would continue without interruption for four days. Relatives and close friends were expected to be present each evening, less important guests were assigned specific times. Those who travelled from distant villages slept overnight on mattresses in the orchards.

The men celebrated the occasion separately from the women, in a ceremonial four-poled Bedouin tent away from the main house. On the first evening the banquet consisted of several sheep's carcasses cooked whole, surrounded with heaps of steaming rice and raisins, stuffed with whole turkeys. The turkeys themselves were stuffed with chickens, and the chickens were stuffed with larks.

The ritual feasting was conducted with earnest gusto. The men ate with their right hand, their left behind their backs, in accordance with Arab custom. While quick practised fingers tore the juicy meats from the bones, voices were raised in laughter, or florid praise, in idle, ritual boasting, or in sudden, vicious quarrels that died as quickly as they began. The serving boys hurried in and out of the tent with heaped platters of meats and rice, hour after hour, until finally the men sat back on their haunches, patting their bellies and belching contentedly, while the gravy on the brass trays congealed among the ruin of bones.

Zayyad licked his fingers clean of the sticky juices and clapped his hands to signal that the sweetmeats and herb-scented coffee should be brought. The dancing began.

There were tambours and lutes and reed pipes made of steel. They danced the dabkah, a dozen of them in a semicircle, their arms on each other's shoulders, uttering the wild whoops of their desert Bedouin ancestors. They danced the sahja, fifty or sixty men in a long line snaking around the room, the rhythm created by the clapping of hands and the drumming of feet. Or they danced alone with their swords, the blades flashing around their heads in the firelight.

Zayyad sat in the place of honour, resplendent in a robe of green damascene silk, the red tie with the motif of the white girl in her underwear proudly displayed round his neck. Wagil sat at his father's right hand, Majid and Rishou on the left.

Zayyad considered them, these his sons. Allah had seen fit to burden him with five daughters and just three boys. *Insh'allah*. One day, one of them will be muktar of Rab'allah. And yet; the world is turning. Now these Jews crowd in from the outside, with their machines and their water ditches and their green lawns and their strange-looking cows. One of my boys will have to be far wiser than my ancestors, perhaps wiser than me.

"What is happening in Jerusalem these days?" he asked Majid.

"The Mufti is still stirring up trouble. He says that – "

Wagil snapped at the bait. "The Mufti is our only hope!"

"Enough, Wagil!" Zayyad said. "Let him finish speaking."

"The Mufti preaches sermons against the British and the Jews," Majid went on. "He says the British want to give all the land this side of the Jordan to the Jews."

"He's right!" Wagil said. "Look at how the Jews have taken over the valley here at Rab'allah."

"*Balderdash!*" Majid shouted, using the English word to intimidate his elder brother. "It was the effendi Jamal al-Husseini in Jerusalem who sold them the land. The Mufti's own cousin!"

"It's true," Zayyad said. "Even the Mufti himself has profited from selling land to the Jews. And perhaps he forgets also what it was like under Turkish rule, the taxes they imposed on us, and they gave us nothing. But the British build us hospitals and schools."

A poor point to raise in Wagil's presence, Majid thought. It was the British schools that made me smarter than him.

"The British give us jobs too," Zayyad went on. "Look how Majid has prospered! Why, he even has a wonderful new motor car!"

"They are just preparing the way for the Jews," Wagil said. "The Mufti says that they have told Jews all over the world that they can come here to live, and make it their own country!"

"How do you know what the Mufti says?"

"I can read the newspapers."

Zayyad snorted with derision. "Rishou says you make it all up."

Wagil stared at the carpet, his face a sullen mask.

"The British will protect us," Majid said. "When a Britisher gives his word, it is his bond."

Zayyad thought of the Jew, Schanenberg. "I trust the British, but I am not sure I trust the Jews."

"What do you think, Rishou?" Majid said.

Rishou's attention was focused on the other side of the room. Asher was there with the Jewish muktar, Yaakov, invited by custom as representatives of the kibbutz. It was hard for him to see them as enemies, even though he knew Asher hated him. And with good reason. It was obvious that Asher wanted Sarah for himself.

Rishou turned back to his father and his brothers. "I have nothing against Jews," he said. "And I, too, trust the British. Providing they have their hands in the air where I can see them and I am holding a loaded gun."

Zayyad laughed aloud. Majid looked disappointed. Perhaps he had been looking to Rishou as his ally.

56

Wagil raised his voice. "We must drive the Jews into the sea! Give me guns and ten good men and I would drive them out of Kfar Herzl myself!"

Zayyad frowned. "The trouble with you, my son, is you talk like a hurricane and fight like a flea's fart."

Wagil flushed. "The Jews – "

"Perhaps now is not the time to talk of this. Go and dance, enjoy yourselves. We will talk more about this later."

Wagil got up, sulking, and left the tent. Majid and Rishou exchanged glances and rose to their feet and joined the dabkah.

Zayyad sighed. It was obvious to him which of his three sons would one day be muktar, which one was best capable of dealing with the threat they now faced. What was it the Jew Schanenberg had said?

"One day we'll have it all anyway."

On the final night of feasting a delegation from the village was sent to El'Azar to fetch Wagil's bride, Hamdah. Rishou waited outside the house with Wagil, watching the procession make its way up the valley. They could hear the singing from a mile away, saw Hamdah in the midst of the crowds, mounted on a white horse. The young men milled around, whooping and firing their rifles into the air.

"There is something I have to say to you," Rishou said.

Wagil kept his eyes on the bridal party and said nothing.

"That day in the coffee house . . . I did not mean to give offence."

"You humiliated me."

Rishou felt his blood rise. "You were lying."

"You should have kept your mouth shut."

"Well, you know, it is your wedding day. I wanted to make my peace with you. I have said what I wanted to say."

"Make your peace with me!"

"I am your brother."

"You are a curse. All brothers are a curse. Haven't you realised that yet?"

Well, there, it was said, Rishou thought. They had been disguising their envy and mistrust of each other all their lives. They had been set against each other from the moment of their birth; for their father's affections, for his blessing, for the day when he would finally nod in their direction and bequeath one of them the mantle of muktar on his death. How could it be any other way?

"Yet I wish you well on your wedding day," Rishou said.

"May a thousand scorpions crawl up your arse and nest there!"

The bridal procession had arrived at the crest of the hill. Hamdah's father strode ahead beside Zayyad, the young men behind them, the women following the horse. Hamdah sat side-saddle in a long white satin dress that reached to her ankles, her feet covered with white stockings and white shoes. Her head-dress was a fortune in silver Ottoman coins and crude Bedouin jewellery. All that was visible of her face was her eyes, accentuated by kohl-darkened lashes and eyebrows. Her hands had been dyed crimson with henna.

Hamdah's brother helped her down from the saddle. She came forward, holding the ceremonial sword that she would hand to Wagil as a symbol of her submission to him. He took it and walked in front of her into the house.

Hamdah was thirteen years old and terrified. Her knowledge of what would happen on her wedding night was restricted to what her older married sister had told her one day at the well in her village.

"He has this big thing like an eggplant between his legs," she had said. "He sticks it into you and when the season returns you will have a baby."

"Does it hurt?" Hamdah asked.

Her sister had not been able to meet her eyes. "You must be brave," she said. "It is all over very quickly."

58

But Hamdah was not brave. Men terrified her. They were loud and they were hairy and they were stronger than she, and the thought of having an eggplant stuck into her made her shudder. Where exactly did the eggplant go? Like all the girls of her village she had not spoken to any boy besides her brother since she was eight years old, and all her life she had been told to cover up, cover up, cover up. If she sat with her legs apart her mother would slap her hard behind the ear. Shame! If she was ever caught touching her sacred place, her mother would suddenly appear and cuff her hard on the cheek. Shame! If she ever caught her looking hard at a boy, even one of her brothers, she would cuff her again. Shame!

Sometimes at night she heard the strange rutting noises from the room where her father slept with her mother and now she realised what she had been hearing. He was attacking her with his eggplant! She was frightened and she was ashamed and she wanted no part of it.

The hut had been set aside especially for the newly married couple to consummate their wedding in privacy. Outside, the rest of the wedding guests danced and sang, the men riding around the hut ululating and firing their rifles into the air. Hamdah felt like the victim of a public execution.

She faced Wagil in the darkness of the bedroom and watched horrified as he tore his robe over his head and came towards her, naked. His chest, arms, belly and thighs were matted with black hair. And from the midst of this disgusting forest rose the eggplant her sister had warned her about. She realised at a glance it could never fit inside any part of her without rupturing her fatally.

She screamed and threw herself on the floor in the corner.

Wagil stared at her, bewildered. "Hamdah?" he said. This was not supposed to happen, he realised, but he had no idea what to do next. His own sexual experiences had been limited to sodomising shepherd boys in the caves below The Place Where The Fig Tree Died.

He reached down to pick her up.

59

"*No!*" Hamdah screamed, turning her face away from the eggplant that bobbed a few inches from her face. She slashed with her nails like a cat, and Wagil jumped back in surprise.

What was he supposed to do now? "Hamdah?"

"Go away!" she sobbed and turned her face to the wall.

Wagil reached out again, tentatively. Hamdah squirmed away from him, as if he were a leper. The silver coins of her head-dress jangled. "Don't touch me!" she screamed. "I won't do it! I won't! If you try and touch me, I'll bite it off!"

Wagil put his robe back on and squatted miserably on the bed. Hamdah cowered in the corner, her arms around her knees, sobbing quietly, her face hidden in her hands.

The candle gutted and died.

The next morning at ten o'clock Zayyad Hass'an proudly strode the twenty paces that separated his house from the hut where his eldest son had spent his first night of marriage with his new bride. In the broad sash at his belt he had the ancient Parabellum that he would use to announce to the rest of the village and his other wedding guests the successful climax of the celebrations. It was customary to fire one shot for each of the couplings. There were five bullets in the pistol. He hoped it would be enough.

The villagers watched from a respectful distance as Zayyad hammered on the door. Wagil peered out. His face, Zayyad noted with alarm, looked drawn and there were dark shadows under his eyes.

"Well?" Zayyad said.

"Well?" Wagil said.

"Is it done?"

Wagil had the look of a cornered animal. He hesitated. If he said yes, Zayyad would demand to see the bedsheet as proof. "Something is wrong," Wagil whispered.

"You did not break her membrane of honour?"

"She will not let me come near her," Wagil hissed. "I think perhaps there is something wrong in her mind."

Zayyad swallowed hard. Unbelievable. "Perhaps there is something wrong in your pants!"

"I am not joking! I think she has gone mad!"

"All women are mad! Allah meant them only for making babies and baking bread, so what does it matter!"

"Please, yaba," Wagil whispered. "Can you not fire the pistol anyway? Do not shame me!"

"It is you who shame me!" Zayyad hissed, and he turned on his heel and stalked away. He could feel every eye in the village watching him, and the whispers cut him like a lash.

He saw Rishou waiting at the doorway of the house. "Father?"

"That boy couldn't fuck his way out of a brothel!" he snarled and stormed inside.

9

Kfar Herzl Kibbutz

If Paradise is like this, Rishou thought, I shall die tomorrow.

Angel-white clouds scudded across the night sky as leaves murmured in the warm breeze. He lay on his back, the hard earth against his naked skin, Sarah on top of him. *On top of him!* How did she persuade me of this? he wondered.

She sat astride him, motionless, her fingers entwined with his. She would wait until his breathing was almost normal again then she would squirm her hips against him to hear him gasp with pleasure, moving in long, circular rhythm and then as suddenly she would be still again, ignoring his desperate pleas for her to continue.

61

"I like having you like this," she murmured. "What does it feel like to have a woman control you for a change?"

"You're a she-cat," he said, his voice hoarse.

"You want me just to lie there like one of your Arab girls?"

He wet his lips with the tip of his tongue. His mouth felt as dry as if it were midday. He could not wait any more, he knew it. Every slight movement made his body jerk like a puppet on a wire.

Her fingers untwined from his and she slipped off her workshirt. She took his hands and held them against her breasts. "No, that's too hard," she whispered. "Just gently. Like this. And this."

He let her move his hands across her body, letting her show him. A miracle, Rishou thought. This Jewish woman is my religion to me. I submit to her totally. What is happening?

"Rishou . . ." she murmured.

"You are driving me mad . . ."

She moistened the palms of his hands with her mouth and drew them down across her nipples. "What are we going to do, Rishou?"

"I don't know."

"I never stop thinking about you."

He felt every muscle in his body stretch taut. "Seeing you every day in the orchard I think I am going to go out of my mind . . ."

She moved again and Rishou heard her sob. He put his hand to her lips to stop her crying out and he felt her bite hard into the soft flesh of his palm.

"Please, Sarah . . ."

She moved again, urgently, and carried them both over the edge of the precipice.

Sarah leaned forward and kissed him. "*Hapzibah*," she whispered.

"What does that mean?"

"I told you, you do not have the words in your language."

He ran his fingers through the silk black hair against his cheek and closed his eyes. Something was happening to him and it frightened him. Every time he came here, he felt that he left a little of Rab'allah behind.

He was frightened now. He had seen a few of the poor fellaheen who had become drunk with too much hashish. They no longer smoked it for rest and ease as other men; it had become a craving and they could not live without it. They were useless for anything else, and their families starved. Now it was happening to him with this girl.

But what was the cure? He could not marry her, and she could not marry him. Every minute they spent together was stolen.

He felt her breast brush against his chest as she kissed him, her mouth wet and hot and sweet. Oh Allah, what can I do?

"What are you thinking?"

"That I have dreamed you. That you are some *djinn* that has bewitched me."

"Perhaps I am."

"Then don't let me ever wake – "

"Is it so hard to imagine? That a girl can be more than just a piece of property? Does it frighten you so much?"

Yes, it does, he thought. "Are all these Jewish girls like you?"

"You want to try them all?" she teased him. "You want to make the kibbutz your harem? I think my father might not like that."

"You are too much temptation for men. All of you."

"No, it's just that you Arabs are obsessed with sex. At the kibbutz a woman is the equal of any man."

Rishou had never heard such an absurd notion in his whole life. "How can that be?" he said.

"I am a Sabra, I can use a gun and a knife, drive a tractor, work in the fields at harvest time. What does a man do that I can't?"

"But who looks after the children and cooks the food?"

63

"During the day they are cared for by women volunteers. As for the food, we all take turns in the kitchen, even the men."

"It is unnatural."

She shook her head. "So unnatural you creep here in the darkness to taste a little of the spirit you have quite squeezed out of your own women. Is that not true, Rishou?"

Well, yes, he thought. Possibly. But he could not admit that to her, and because he had no answer, he was angry. He sat up, and searched for his clothes. "You need a good beating," he hissed.

"I'd break your arm if you tried."

"I shall not come here again!"

"Yes, you will," she laughed. But her laughter was cut short.

A single gunshot shattered the night.

Rishou heard the zip! of the bullet a moment before it slammed into the tree trunk by his head, showering them with splinters of bark. Sarah threw herself to the ground, instinctively rolling for cover behind one of the trees. A true sabra, Rishou found himself thinking, even as he scrambled in the dust for his clothes.

A guard must have spotted them. Sarah shouted something in Hebrew. He turned and saw her standing upright, naked, shielding his body with her own, preventing the rifleman from taking aim.

"Sarah!" he shouted.

"Run! Go!"

He stumbled into the darkness. By the time he reached the fence the siren was wailing the alarm. He knew it would be the last time he ever came secretly to Kfar Herzl. He threw on his abbayah and scrambled through the wire, tearing his cheek and wrist in his haste.

Rab'allah

Wagil sat on the edge of the bed and wrestled with his pride. For three days now this hideous nightmare had continued. Hamdah still crouched in the same corner in which she had thrown herself that very first night. She would not even speak to him.

Last night, in a rage, he had thrown her on the bed, intending to achieve by force what he had so far failed to do by charm, entreaties and threats. Hamdah had shocked him not only with her strength, but also by her ruthlessness. He had not realised any woman could be so spiteful. She had bulk and muscle far beyond her years and a talent for fighting that included eye gouging and liberal use of the knees and feet. After ten minutes of bitter combat it was he who had retreated first, his face torn, his groin tender agony.

But he had to do something. He knew at any moment his father would rap once again on the door, and demand the proof of his manhood. He dared not disappoint him again.

Trembling, he went outside and fetched a sharp knife.

The villagers stood in hushed and dreadful silence as Zayyad Hass'an stepped from his front door and strode for the third time to the hut from which Wagil and his new bride were yet to emerge. Strange weepings and cries had been heard from there during the night and many interpretations had been placed on their meaning.

Rishou waited to one side, holding Zayyad's horse by the halter, in forlorn expectation.

Zayyad rapped on the door. Almost immediately it was thrown open. Wagil stood in the doorway, grinning in triumph.

"You have done it?" Zayyad's voice was hoarse with strain.

Wagil thrust a bedsheet into Zayyad's arms. Zayyad shook it out, and examined the copious, fresh bloodstains with evident relief.

"Six times," Wagil said.

Zayyad looked suspicious. "I have only five bullets."

"Then you will have to get another one from somewhere."

"It is the morning of the third day. In the circumstances, five bullets will have to suffice." He took the pistol from his waistband and fired five times into the air. Then he climbed on to Al-Tareq and galloped through the village, waving the bloodied sheet above his head to signal to the rest of the village that Hamdah's membrane of honour had finally been broken in marriage by his son.

Wagil sagged against the door, relieved. He examined the deep wound in his thumb, where he had cut it with his knife. The wound was deep and would probably fester but the humiliation was finally over.

As Zayyad rode back up the hill on Al-Tareq he suddenly reined in the horse and the rest of the villagers stopped in their tracks also, their cheers dying in their throats. They were staring at the lone figure trudging up the hill through the olive trees.

As he came closer Wagil recognised him. It was the muktar of Kfar Herzl, Yaakov Landauer. What could be wrong, for him to come up here alone and unannounced at this time of the day?

In another time and place Yaakov Landauer might have looked scholarly; the sparse fluff of hair was prematurely white thanks to five years as a political prisoner in a Russian jail. But now the white European skin had been burned the colour of polished mahogany by constant exposure to the sun, and the ice blue eyes that glittered in his face revealed the steel that the prison wardens in the Pale and the grit of the Palestinian desert had forged in him.

In the coffee house he leaned towards Zayyad and those eyes were quite unafraid, even though he was surrounded by hostile Arab faces. "Someone broke into our kibbutz last night and raped my daughter."

Zayyad felt even the hairs on his belly stand on end. Rape. This was how men died with their throats cut, how wars started.

He forced himself to portray calm. "Are you certain of this?"

"We have known each other a long time, Abu Wagil," Yaakov said, calling Zayyad by the honorific, "Father of Wagil". "You know I would not come here just to blow smoke. One of your people broke the wire. I want to know who it was."

"I shall tell you the truth," Zayyad said. "I don't know." And he thought, Well, I know who it isn't. It isn't Wagil. He can't even fuck his own wife, never mind your daughter.

Rishou was sitting on Zayyad's right. "She told you she was raped?" he said suddenly, and Zayyad was aware of a lethal silence in the room. Yaakov stared back at Rishou with icy hatred. Allah, help me, Zayyad thought. He thinks it is Rishou!

"We want the offender brought to justice," Yaakov said.

"She said she was raped?" Rishou repeated.

Yaakov did not answer.

Zayyad addressed himself to Yaakov. "Did your daughter recognise her assailant?" he said, gently.

"It was dark."

"As so often happens at night," Rishou said.

Allah, make him be quiet! Zayyad thought. Let him not be such a young fool! "You are sure in your mind it was someone from this village?" Zayyad said, trying to sound as ingenuous as possible.

"Who else could it be?"

"A Bedouin perhaps?"

"It was no Bedouin."

"Was the girl hurt in this . . . attack?" Rishou said.

Yaakov still did not answer. It occurred to Zayyad that if the girl had been hurt, Yaakov would have said so. That could only mean two things: that she was not hurt, and her attacker had fled before he could succeed with his intentions; or that it was not rape.

He looked at Rishou and wondered.

"What happened to your face?" Yaakov said to Rishou.

"I fell from a horse."

Zayyad had not noticed the cuts on his son's face; his attention had been otherwise occupied that morning. But there were indeed fresh wounds on his cheek and wrists.

"They look like the sort of cuts you get from barbed wire," Yaakov said. He turned back to Zayyad. "I ask you once again, Abu Wagil, will you assist us in finding out who was responsible for this cowardly act so that we can bring the offender to justice?"

Zayyad considered. If he said no, it would be tantamount to a declaration of hostilities between the kibbutz and the village. If he said yes, it would seem that he had submitted to these Jews in front of the whole village and he would lose the people's respect.

It was good to have friends. But it was better in the eyes of Allah to wave a gun in someone's face. He was sympathetic to the situation Yaakov found himself in; he did not personally dislike the man. But there really was nothing else to do.

But before he could answer Rishou leaned forward and said, "I am curious about something. What does 'Hapzibah' mean?"

The Hebrew word had a startling effect. Yaakov's cheeks flushed the colour of dark grapes and he leaped to his feet. "From now on armed guards will patrol the perimeters of the kibbutz day and night. Anyone found trespassing on our property will be shot on sight!"

He stamped out of the coffee house, the sullen crowd of villagers parting grudgingly for him.

Zayyad stroked his beard. "What was that word you used?"

Rishou shrugged. "Hapzibah. It's Hebrew. Do you know it?"

"Every old Arab knows what it means," Zayyad muttered, "I didn't spend my youth screwing donkeys."

Rishou stared at his father. "Then tell me."

"It means 'I love you.' Where in Allah's name did you hear it?"

10

al-Naqb

Sheikh Daoud al-Khatab al-Husseini was waiting to greet them at the doorway of the sprawling sixteen-room house that looked over the village of al-Naqb. He was dressed simply but judiciously, in black robes and a tarbush with a white sash that denoted his position as a *qadi*, an Islamic judge. His beard was carefully combed, flecked with iron and grey.

Zayyad had come here only after very careful consideration. He knew he was forming a potentially dangerous alliance. Sheikh Daoud was a distant cousin of the Grand Mufti of Jerusalem, and also a member of the Arab Higher Committee, a group of effendis and clerics who were agitating for an end to British rule, fostering some absurd notion of uniting all the Arab communities west of the Jordan into one nation.

From Zayyad's point of view, any brains that Sheikh Daoud may once have possessed had filtered out through his ears like sand under a door, but he remained a man to be reckoned with. As muktar of al-Naqb, a respected imam, and confidant of the Grand Mufti, he was a formidable friend. From another point of view any alliance would be like inviting a jackal into your barn, and in normal times Zayyad would not have considered taking such a drastic step. But these were not normal times. Perhaps the times would never be normal again.

It was essential to find a suitable wife for Rishou. If the young man continued to use the kibbutz as his personal harem there would undoubtedly be reprisals, and he did not want his favourite son brought home to him one day wrapped in a sheet.

It was also apparent that there would soon be trouble over the Jews and he had already decided that he did not want Rab'allah to become involved. What he feared was not so much the Jews, but the Mufti. An alliance with Sheikh Daoud was, in the light of recent events, a prudent tactic.

Zayyad and Rishou dismounted and Daoud came to greet them.

"*Ahlan wa-sahlan*," he said. *May your way to my tent be through a smooth valley.*

"A blessing on you also," Zayyad answered.

"Sheikh Zayyad, it is indeed good to have you honour my house with your presence. Please come inside."

"Thank you, Sheikh Daoud," Zayyad answered. "It is I who am honoured."

Daoud led them inside. The house was square-built, two storeys of hand-cut limestone. They were ushered into the *majlis*. The room was spartanly furnished. There was a Koran stand, with illuminated Koran in one corner, a crystal flower vase and religious reference books lining one wall. There was no art, for the Koran forbade the representation of life in images.

The *diwan* was a line of chintz cushions, stuffed with cotton. Daoud's own seat of honour was a small silk cushion placed in one corner, opposite the window, where it was favoured by the prevailing breeze. There were thick rugs on the floor, and in the middle of the room a brass tray piled high with honey cakes and other sweetmeats.

Zayyad and Daoud sat and for half an hour exchanged pleasantries, enquiring of the health and welfare of each other's families, from wives and children to distant cousins. They sipped sweet mint tea and nibbled on the *halwa* and sugar-encrusted almonds and sesame cakes. The conversation was punctuated with the continual click-click of their *tespi*, prayer beads.

Rishou remained solemn and silent, as was the custom.

Finally Zayyad said, "Sheikh Daoud, you are one of the leaders of our community, a pillar of wisdom, and celebrated by the whole of Palestine as a man of great piety and learning."

"It is very kind of you to say so. Allah alone knows that you yourself are considered one of the pillars upon which the whole fabric of Islam is founded here in Judea. Your courage and virtue are celebrated in every town where there is a mosque."

"I thank you for your words. My son Rishou is also a fine boy, blessed by Allah with great wisdom. He does not drink or seek amorous entanglements with shepherd boys, and his reputation from here to Jerusalem is as perfumed as gum arabic. One day he may even be muktar of Rab'allah. All he needs to make his life truly blessed is a bride. I have long considered this matter and we have now come to ask, with the utmost respect, for the hand of your daughter Khadija in marriage. Naturally we thank Allah that he has shown such great wisdom in wishing the honour of being related to you."

"The honour, of course, is totally ours."

"It is kind of you to say so."

Daoud clutched at his heart and for a moment Rishou thought the old man was about to have a fatal seizure. "Ah, my Khadija!"

"Her virtue is of renown all over Palestine."

"She is indeed the jewel of my heart. Her purity is a comfort to Allah himself. It will tear at my heart to have to give her up."

The jackal means to extract a small fortune from me! Zayyad realised. "All Islam rejoices in her goodness," he said.

"I must be completely honest with you," Daoud said, lowering his voice. "There have been many enquiries after her. One poor wretch after another has insulted me with his offer. Should a man offer a trinket in exchange for a gemstone?"

Zayyad allowed the question to hang unanswered in the air.

71

"She is a priceless treasure, a wonder of God, a gift from Allah himself. She can also make baskets."

"Thanks be to Allah. Mohammed himself rejoices in such a one."

"Naturally we have heard also of Rishou and his many admirable qualities," Daoud said. "In that regard I could perhaps let her go for as little as the paltry sum of one hundred and fifty pounds."

Zayyad thanked Allah he was sitting down or he knew he would almost certainly have fainted. Instead, he ran his fingers through his beard in silent contemplation and smiled.

Two hours later, a price had been agreed. It had not been easy. The two men had torn at their beards, made supplications to Allah for divine intervention, even wept a little. At one point Rishou was convinced that they would produce their daggers. But at last a bride price was arrived at without the spilling of blood; one hundred Palestine pounds, a local record, plus ten pounds for each of the girl's uncles.

"There is one additional problem," Daoud said.

Zayyad braced himself. "And that is?"

"My Khadija has a maternal cousin, Izzat Ib'n Mousa, who has previously asked for her hand in marriage. I turned him down, but of course, he could cause trouble."

Zayyad sighed. By tradition a boy always had first claim to his cousin, and if he wished, this Izzat could indeed cause trouble. He could disrupt the wedding, force the bride to dismount from her horse, commit suicide in front of the bridal party, or, worse, challenge his rival to a fight.

"I shall arrange that he will be compensated for his great loss," Zayyad said.

Daoud bowed his head in recognition of Zayyad's concession. "Then I shall speak to the boy," he said. "And let us thank Allah for blessing us with such a happy union."

And ask Him where I will get the money to pay for all this, Zayyad thought.

*　　*　　*

After Zayyad and Rishou had left, Daoud sent a messenger to the home of Izzat's father, summoning the boy to his presence.

"I have just received some good news," he told Izzat. "Sheikh Zayyad has honoured me by asking for the hand of my daughter, Khadija, for his son, Rishou."

Izzat stared insolently back at him.

"Sheikh Zayyad is not a generous man, as all Palestine is aware. I had to argue with him long and hard to extract some measure of compensation for you. I hope that you will be duly grateful."

Izzat mumbled something unintelligible.

"Well?"

"You promised her to me."

Sheikh Daoud controlled himself with some difficulty. He was an unappetising creature, this Izzat. The two halves of his face seemed never to match, as if brought from two separate moulds by Allah and joined together incorrectly in a moment of inattention. His eyes were never focused correctly and the sparse tufts of his beard only added to his sour demeanour.

"Sheikh Zayyad is muktar of Rab'allah. Apart from being a man of some influence, the village he controls will have great strategic significance in any armed struggle against the British overlords. An alliance between our families is much to be desired. Your own pain is insignificant in comparison."

Tears of self-pity welled in Izzat's eyes. "But you promised!"

"I promised to consider it. That was all. Now listen to me. I have extracted the monumental figure of fifteen pounds from Zayyad as compensation for you. You will accept the money with good grace and you will make no trouble at the wedding. Is that clear?"

Izzat did not raise his eyes from the carpets. He kissed Sheikh Daoud's hand perfunctorily, and shuffled from the room. Like a diseased dog, Daoud thought with contempt. How could he possibly be related to me? Allah is mysterious in many ways!

73

11

Kfar Herzl Kibbutz

The apple harvest was almost over. Because of the malaria
it had taken them longer this year. When Yaakov returned
from Rab'allah he had ordered that the kibbutz no longer
employ Arab labour.

The kibbutzniks sat under the shade of the trees to eat
their lunches. Sarah returned her share of bread and olives
and cheese to the basket, untouched.

"Not hungry?" Asher asked her.

Sarah shrugged.

"You have to eat."

"I've no appetite."

Asher crumbled the earth in his fist. She was so beautiful. He loved her and he wanted to protect her. The
thought of that dirty Arab with his hands on her . . .
Hapzibah!

"You've been like this for weeks. Won't you tell me
what happened?"

"I don't want to."

Asher picked up a stone and threw it into the dirt. "You
have heard the news, I suppose?"

"News?"

"The muktar's son is getting married. The boy who was
working here in the orchards with us. The one who was
always staring at you."

Sarah did not react. "So?"

Asher's voice dropped to a whisper. "It was him,
wasn't it?"

"For God's sake, leave me be!" Sarah jumped up and walked away from him. She didn't want him to see the bright, hot tears in her eyes. Of course she had heard about Rishou's marriage! Despite her father's ban on trade and labour exchange between the kibbutz and Rab'allah, people loved to gossip, and news still filtered through by a mysterious process as old as mankind itself.

So Rishou finally had his good little Arab girl!

Why did she let it hurt so much? He had been an adventure, that was all. She had known that from the very beginning. It had been a stupid, irresistible, insane, exotic adventure and she had known that it would end as suddenly as it had begun.

So why did she feel like this? Why could she not look at the orchard without thinking about him, why had she lost nearly half a stone in weight, why could she not close her eyes at night without seeing those intense dark eyes and grinning, arrogant smile?

She leaned against the trunk of an apple tree, suddenly crushed with grief. She had tried to conquer him like a man. And she had ended up loving him like a woman. Weak, weak.

Give it time, Sarah. This pain will go away in time.

al-Naqb

There were three stages to the wedding. It began with the engagement ceremony, and afterwards the news of the betrothal was spread to the surrounding communities by word of mouth. Two months later, an Islamic judge would declare the couple man and wife in a formal religious service, the *katb al-kitab*. The wedding itself, however, did not take place until three or four months after that. Three days of singing and dancing and feasting traditionally climaxed in the consummation of the union.

*   *   *

On the day of his engagement to Khadija al-Khatab, Rishou arrived at his bride's house on horseback, accompanied by his father and mother. He was understandably nervous. Today, when he gave her the ring, he would meet his promised wife for the first time.

Once again Daoud met them at his front door and led them inside. The living-room was filled with members of the sheikh's family, his wife, his brothers and his wife's brothers. The usual greetings and lavish compliments were exchanged. Mint tea was sipped, and the men fingered their prayer beads.

Finally Zayyad took the sheikh's right hand, bowed from the waist, and kissed it three times, raising it each time from his lips to his forehead in the traditional gesture of respect.

Afterwards Daoud raised his hands, palms upturned, towards heaven and recited a sura from the holy Koran. Everyone in the room repeated the words after him. Daoud's brother, Moussa, then crossed the room and embraced Zayyad and Rishou. He led Rishou into the adjoining room.

Khadija was there with her sisters. She was wearing a long dress of white silk, and her head was covered with a scarf. Rishou stared at her. She was young, no more than sixteen, with huge brown eyes and a face that could have been sculpted by an artist.

Praise be to God! Rishou thought. At least she is not some moon-faced child like Hamdah. In fact, she is quite beautiful. She will help me forget about Sarah soon enough. With her I will rediscover the same pinnacles of pleasure that I discovered with the Jewish girl. Everything will be all right. This ache I feel is just the seed backed up in my belly. Everything will be all right again.

She dissolved under his scrutiny and burst into a fit of giggling, hiding her face in her hands. Moussa barked a sharp command and she subsided. She obediently held out her right hand and Rishou placed the plain gold band on her finger.

*   *   *

Izzat watched Zayyad and Rishou ride away from al-Naqb and his envy and rage tasted sour in his mouth. He spat into the dirt. He had known Khadija since he was a child. It had been an unspoken understanding that one day he would have her. Now his uncle had betrayed him for politics and they wanted to pay him off and have him surrender like a woman.

Well, he would show the Hass'ans that not everyone would grovel at their feet. If he could not have her, neither would Rishou. He would see to that.

12

Rab'allah

Everything was in readiness for Rishou's wedding. Tents had been erected in Zayyad's orchard for the men and women, the feast had been prepared, the house that Wagil had occupied on his wedding night – "all three of them!" Zayyad had shouted, still unable to let go of that bitter memory – was ready.

Zayyad and Daoud walked slowly in front of the procession, as it wound its way up the valley from al-Naqb. They had prayer beads entwined in their fingers, and their steps were measured and dignified. Behind them Khadija was mounted on a white horse, the male members of her family crowded around her, singing and chanting. Occasionally one of them would fire his rifle into the air and the women would shriek a piercing "ool-ool-ool-ool-ool!" in admiration.

Izzat watched from his eyrie on the ridge above the valley. The ancient First World War Mauser was cumbersome and it took him long minutes before he finally settled it comfortably into the hollow of his shoulder. He flicked up the sight, and took a practice sighting into the gully directly below where he lay.

The procession was a hundred yards away.

If only he could stop this trembling in his hands. I have to do this, he told himself. I have to defend my honour. I must kill Khadija and show her how much I love her.

The sweat was stinging his eyes.

He would show them, especially that festering ulcer on the arse of a camel, his uncle! Wouldn't he be delighted when his daughter landed in the dirt at his feet.

Fifty yards, forty, thirty.

He was shaking so hard the muzzle of the rifle bounced on the ground and loosened a small avalanche of stones. He wiped his right hand on his robe to dry off the sweat.

Fire and run. They will never know it was you.

They were almost below him.

Now! *Now!*

The sound of the rifle shot alarmed no one. The men in the wedding party had been randomly firing their rifles all the way from al-Naqb. But suddenly Sheikh Daoud fell in front of Khadija's horse, screaming and clutching at his foot.

Zayyad pointed up at the ridge. A man holding a rifle appeared for a moment silhouetted against the afternoon sky before he fled.

"Haaaaiiiiy!" Daoud was screaming. There were gouts of blood spattered on the hem of his robe. The horse bucked in alarm and Khadija screamed. Two of her brothers leaped at the reins.

Zayyad was first to react. Unarmed, he scrambled up the steep slope. Two other men followed, clutching rifles. Loose scree slowed their progress and Zayyad was panting hard when he reached the crest. Their would-be assassin must have escaped by now.

But they found Izzat lying on his back in a gully a few yards away. He had tried to leap across the dry creek and had landed short, breaking his ankle. He was crying.

"Izzat!" Zayyad growled.

"It wasn't me!"

"What were you trying to do?"

"The gun went off by accident!"

One of the men raised the butt of his rifle menacingly.

"You shot your uncle in the foot!"

"It was an accident!"

Two of Khadija's brothers helped Sheikh Daoud up the slope. He was cursing with pain, and his injured foot trailed blood in the dust behind him. When he saw his nephew his expression changed utterly. His distress was replaced with fury. "You!"

Izzat scrambled for the Mauser he had dropped in the gully.

Daoud aimed a kick at Izzat's ribs and his nephew screamed and curled into a ball. Daoud howled with pain as his weight fell on his injured foot.

"You tried to kill me!" Daoud screamed.

"No!"

"*You tried to kill me!*"

"No, I was aiming at Khadija!"

This last utterance made Daoud speechless with rage.

He kicked his nephew again and Izzat scrambled away down the slope on his hands and knees, babbling with fear.

Daoud gasped and fell again. "Diseased son of a whore!" he shouted and then realised what he had said. Allah forgive him. Izzat's mother was, after all, his own sister-in-law.

Khadija's brothers were about to go down the slope after Izzat but Zayyad pulled them away. "Leave him," he said. "It is my son's wedding day. There has been enough bloodshed."

They picked up Daoud and carried him back to the procession, and the wedding continued. When they reached Zayyad's house they dressed the sheikh's foot and propped him with cushions next to Zayyad in the great tent. Zayyad slipped the qadi some Black Label whisky from his secret cache to help ease the pain. After several glasses, Daoud

79

was numb to all sensation and the alliance between the houses of Hass'an and al-Khatab was cemented.

Burning incense mingled with the heavy perfume on Khadija's body, arousing Rishou's senses. A single candle burned in the darkened room. His new wife stood by the bed in her bridal dress, her eyes pinpoints of fear and apprehension behind the fringe of Ottoman coins that framed her face.

"Don't be afraid," Rishou whispered. He reached up and removed the heavy head-dress. "I won't hurt you."

Khadija covered her face with her hands and giggled.

Her giggles annoyed him. "Take off your dress," he growled.

She was trembling. He reached down and lifted the long robe over her head. She was naked underneath. She took a step away from him, crossing her arms protectively over her breasts.

Rishou's breathing was tight in his chest. She was indeed beautiful, he thought. Her skin was like bronze, her long hair glossy and almost blonde. Crusader blood in her history perhaps. She was not as skinny as Sarah, heavier in the hips, her belly more rounded.

It was hard to swallow. "I won't hurt you," he repeated, and he put his arms around her. "It will be all right."

It had to be all right. If he was ever to have a peace with himself again, it had to be all right.

But it was not all right.

He lay on his back and listened to the late night revellers dancing and singing and he wished he was with them, anywhere but in this room. Poor Khadija. It was not her fault. She did not know there was more. How could she know?

What had gone wrong? Khadija was beautiful, her body was soft, her membrane of honour was intact. What more could he want?

He wanted Sarah. That was what he wanted. He wanted Sarah.

Khadija was awake also. She lay curled under the sheet, staring at him in the flickering candlelight. "Rishou," she whispered.

Ah, she speaks, he thought. She can do more than giggle. "Yes?"

"Do you like me?"

"Yes, I like you," he said. But I do not love you, he shouted into the cavernous loneliness of his own mind. Sarah was right. No docile little Arab girl will be enough for me. Not now.

But what can I do? What can I do?

Kfar Herzl Kibbutz

In Kfar Herzl they were dancing the hora. Yaakov Landauer had just announced his daughter's engagement to Asher Ben-Zion.

As one of the boys strummed out a rhythm on a cheap guitar, Sarah clapped her hands and sang and laughed, as they expected her to do. There really was no choice. Besides, Asher was a good man, he was strong, and kind, and he loved her, she was sure of that.

She must have been crazy to do what she did. Her father said the trouble between themselves and the Arabs would only get worse. The rioting in Jaffa and Jerusalem had come to an end for now, but the fighting could flare again any day. What had she been thinking of? These were her people. What she had done was tantamount to a betrayal.

Tonight she had rejoined her brothers and sisters.

Asher left the hora ring, his chest heaving from laughter and the dancing. He held out his hands to her. "Come and dance!" he said to her.

Sarah danced, but after a while she felt faint, and Asher took her outside for air. The night was cold, and the sweat on their skins dried quickly.

"I love you," Asher whispered.

"I love you too," Sarah answered, and returned his kiss. But over the shouts of the hora she could hear the sound of the flutes and drums at Rab'allah, and it was all she could do to forget that Rishou was gone.

Part Three

GERMANY, 1935

13

Ravenswald

Josef Rosenberg sat alone in his study, smoking a cigarette. He was wearing the old black velvet smoking jacket
that he had put on every night for the last twenty years
on returning home from work. The velvet was paper thin
at the elbows, and crushed almost to grey by the years of
wear, but Josef had resisted all his wife's efforts to throw
it out. It was a private tradition, and such traditions of
comfort and familiarity were important to him.

On his desk, in a gilt frame, was a photograph, yellowed
with age. A young man, dressed in the braided uniform
of a cavalry officer, a cigarette dangling rakishly from the
corner of his mouth, posed in front of a painted backdrop
of the Alps. He had one foot on a chair, and his right elbow
rested on his knee. He looked as all young soldiers do,
Josef thought, before they discover that wars are charnel
houses and not parade grounds.

Over twenty years had passed since the photograph
had been taken. It was difficult to imagine himself as he
was then, eager and unafraid. So much had changed,
in himself, and in the world. The young pretender had
become der Chef; he had grown wealthy, while his country
had been impoverished by war.

And now the wheel had turned again. Der Chef had
become a pariah while a starving, defeated people had
become the master race.

He unlocked the second drawer of his desk and took
out a small metal box. Inside were two medals, a strip

of ribbon, and a lead bullet, the only souvenirs that the young man in the photograph had brought back with him from the war. He took them out one at a time, caressing each one with his fingers, invoking their memories; the Iron Cross, second class, attached to a metal strip covered with ribbon-like material, a memento of his service in the German army over four years; a ruby-studded half moon, awarded to all the survivors of his regiment by the Ottoman government, in recognition of their service at Salonica; and the flattened lead bullet that had dropped out of the periscope he had used to peer over the top of a trench one day in 1916.

There were other souvenirs, less tangible, that he carried with him always: the cold, numbing dread of violence that still sometimes woke him in the night; and the memory of a friend dying by inches beside him in a trench, as he tried to stuff his belly back into its cavity. His friend had not screamed, just grunted horribly like a dog vomiting. He had finally died, after what seemed like an eternity, convulsing in Josef's arms.

He had learned to live with his nightmares, but what had happened to his country in the intervening years had been less easy to bear, for himself, for all Germans. The Treaty of Versailles had put a boot on their neck for the last fifteen years. He could understand the Nazis' rage at the French and the British; what he did not understand was their hatred of their own people.

The National Socialists had labelled him a Jew, as if he were some filthy ghetto dweller in a gaberdine coat. What was a Jew? His own family practised only the most liberal form of Judaism, attending the synagogue only on the Sabbath and high holidays. They dressed like Germans, not Hassidim, and they spoke and acted and thought like Germans. They even ate ham – kosher ham, of course, as the family joke went.

The government said all Jews were parasites, bleeding the poor. He could not comprehend how his fellow Germans could be taken in by such blatant lies. Yes, he was wealthy, but it was because of Rosenberg Fabriken that six hundred and eighteen men and women in the town had jobs, with generous wages and conditions. Before the Nazis he had been a popular and well-respected man.

His sister Esther was a widow; her husband had lived and died in a little shop in Augsburg, mending watches. His brother Mulu was a teacher – until the Nazis had thrown him out of the school in München where he had been employed. Neither of them were the hook-nosed capitalist of Streicher's caricatures.

Jews? They were Germans. Good Germans! *Anständige Leute*, good decent Germans!

He heard the back door click shut. Netanel, he thought, coming on tiptoe up the stairs. There was the telltale creak of the top step. He smiled, grimly. He was trying to creep back to his room without alerting his mother that he had been out. That meant he had been seeing the Helder girl again. The boy was so transparent.

"Netanel!"

The study door was ajar. Netanel peered in.

"Father . . . I thought you were downstairs, in the parlour."

"Obviously."

"Did you want to see me?"

"Come in and sit down."

Netanel crossed to the armchair next to the fire. There were tiny droplets of rain on the shoulders and lapels of his overcoat.

"Where have you been?" Josef asked him.

"Frederic and I went to the Odeum. There was a Tom Mix western showing."

It sounded too pat, Josef thought, a rehearsed reply. Josef drummed on the surface of his desk with his fingertips. "Did you listen to the radio tonight?" he said, finally.

Netanel shook his head.

"The Nazis have passed new laws. You and I are no longer German citizens."

Netanel snorted with disgust. "That's ridiculous!"

"I agree. But that is now the . . . ridiculous . . . law. It seems we will also have to let Hilde go."

87

"We are not allowed to hire cooks now, in Hitler's utopia?"

"From today it is forbidden for Jews to hire female domestics under the age of forty-five years."

"Idiots!"

"They are rescuing the flower of the nation's womanhood from ravishment at our hands."

"I couldn't fit my arms round her waist, let alone ravish her."

"There is more, Netanel. That is just the good news."

Netanel could not meet his eyes. He is an intelligent boy, Josef thought. He must have seen this coming. "They have invented a new word. *Rassenschande*. Racial disgrace. It is the word they have coined for any intimate relationships between their master race and the rest of us."

Netanel leaped to his feet. He went to the window, his hands bunched into fists at his side. He thrust them deep into the pockets of his overcoat.

"I know you are still seeing the Helder girl," Josef said.

"I want to marry her."

"Marry?" What could the boy be thinking of? Even in normal times . . . "I think after today that is quite impossible."

"Nothing is impossible."

"They have passed these laws to prohibit such a thing. There is nothing anyone can do."

Netanel turned away from the window and threw himself back into the armchair. "This suits you, doesn't it?"

"What does or does not suit me is no longer the – "

"You claim to be a liberal, but the thought of me marrying a *goy* –"

"Mind your tongue!"

"– just turns your stomach, doesn't it?"

Josef stared at him, unsure how to proceed. This is unfair, he thought. If only you knew how often your mother and I have argued about this. It is she who is against this girl, she is the one who cares what the rabbi will say. Now I find myself arguing her case in her place.

"All that is irrelevant now," he said.

"Is it?"

Josef felt himself losing patience. A boy wanting to defy his parents was one thing. Defying his country's laws was quite different. "There is nothing either of you can do about this."

"Forgive me, Father, but I do not agree."

Oh, Netanel, Josef thought. I am sorry. This was not how it should have been for you. There should not have been this misery in your life. I intended for you to have everything. The family business, your own house, security. Who could have foreseen this?

"Listen. It is bad for us now, but it will get better. This sort of thing has happened before, it will no doubt happen again. We must remain inconspicuous, and the storm will pass. Perhaps in Berlin and München things will be the worst, but if we get on with our lives, and stay within the laws, it will not be too bad here. No one in France or Britain will allow these maniacs to go too far."

"They have already gone too far. How can you stand this? Every day there are new signs. We could not get into the cinema tonight. There was a sign outside: 'Jews not welcome here'. Not welcome! The wages you pay them are welcome enough! For years, right through the Depression, their jobs were welcome! How can they do this to us?"

"It will pass."

"I cannot live this way!"

"Son, listen. You are young, you must learn patience. There have been Rosenbergs in this town for six generations. There have been these kinds of troubles many times. They never last. This is our country. I fought in the Great War, so did your Uncle Mulu. It's not the German people doing this, it's Hitler and his gang. Very soon people will have had enough of these Nazis and kick them out."

"I wish I could believe that, Father."

"It is true. You will see."

Netanel's eyes were suddenly fierce. "I want to marry Marie."

"She's not of our faith, Netanel . . ."

"I love her!"

"When all this is over . . ."

"No! Perhaps this will never be over! If we cannot marry in Germany then perhaps we will have to go somewhere else."

Josef felt a chill in the pit of his stomach. He could endure these Nazis, but he would not lose his son because of them. Everything had been for Netanel. There was no point to Rosenberg Fabriken if there was no Netanel. The young man who now sat so erect and determined in front of him was his life's work.

"I will not let you do that," Josef said.

Netanel rose to his feet. When he spoke his voice sounded hoarse and strained. "I'm sorry. I love her. Nothing will make me give her up."

He strode out of the room.

Josef sat for a long time, staring into space, numb to all feeling. He had no idea Netanel felt so strongly about this girl. He knew, of course, that he still saw her from time to time; it was obvious that all those nights he had said he had been seeing Frederic or Marx he had, in fact, been seeing Marie. Their son was far more resourceful than Frau Rosenberg imagined.

He lit another cigarette.

It just could not be allowed to go any further. He loved his son too much to let him throw everything away on a gentile. In good times, he would not have stood in his way. After all, his own great-great-grandmother had married a Prussian. But times were not good. If Netanel would not be sensible, he would have to be sensible for him.

14

Hermann Helder was appalled. The sign outside his shop was quite plain:

> *Juden sind hier nicht erwünscht.*
>
> Jews not welcome here.

And now here was the town's best-known Jew, der Chef, Josef Rosenberg, walking straight in off the street. The little bell on the front door announced his arrival. Hermann panicked. What was he supposed to do? He could not serve him, of course. But he could not throw him out either. Not der Chef.

Why was he doing this to him?

Josef stood in the sawdust, his hands thrust into the pockets of his jacket. "Herr Helder? *Guten Tag.* My name is Rosenberg, Josef Rosenberg. I have to talk to you."

Hermann gaped at him.

Josef made a slight movement of his head in the direction of the sign that had been pasted in the window. "I did not mean to embarrass you, Herr Helder. But this is important."

"Come in the back," Hermann said, with sudden inspiration. He ushered Josef into the back room. He looked over his shoulder to make sure no one saw him. *Mein Gott!* If the SA found out . . .

The storeroom reeked of offal. The carcasses of several pigs hung from shiny hooks on the ceiling and half a

91

cow lay partially dismembered on a wooden bench in the middle of the room. Hermann pulled up two wooden chairs and indicated that Josef should sit. Then he went to the back door and shouted for his wife to bring coffee.

Hermann sat, wiping his hands on his apron. "This is an unexpected surprise, Herr Rosenberg."

"I realise I am not welcome here, Herr Helder. I would not have come if this was not of the utmost importance."

Hermann gave him an oily smile. "Take no notice of that stupid sign. That Emmerich boy made me put it up. I had no choice."

"Of course."

Hermann licked his lips and waited. He was conscious of the fine cloth of Josef's suit, and the expensive homburg that der Chef held on his lap. He was also painfully aware of the proximity of the butchered calf. Without thinking, he found himself wiping at the bloodstains on his apron. "So what can I do for you, Herr Rosenberg?"

"It is about your daughter, Marie."

The smile vanished. "My daughter?"

"What I have to say may distress you."

Hermann was confused. "It is Marie's day off today. She has gone to München, to the zoo."

"I know. She is meeting my son there."

Hermann put out a hand to steady himself against the bench.

"You did not know?"

Hermann shook his head, unable to answer. The little bitch had been deceiving him! She had lied to his face! Oh, he had known she had been seeing the Rosenberg boy for a while. But he thought he had put a stop to that months ago. If the Nazis found out . . .

"We must stop this," Hermann said. "I'll not have her running around with a Jew." It was out of his mouth before he could stop himself.

"Quite," Josef said.

Frau Helder appeared carrying two white porcelain mugs. The blood drained from her face when she saw Josef. She looked questioningly at her husband, but he

92

ignored her. She put the two mugs of steaming coffee on the bench, next to the carcass.

"Thank you, Inge," Hermann said. "Look after the shop for me. I have important matters to discuss with Herr Rosenberg."

Frau Helder hesitated. She glared at Josef, in order to make it quite clear to him that he was unwelcome, and left.

Hermann rubbed the shiny patina of his scalp. "What are we going to do?" he said.

"I think we're agreed that this cannot be allowed to continue."

For a moment Hermann felt an involuntary surge of resentment. Why? he asked himself. Because I am only a butcher? Is that what you are concerned about? He was comforted by reminding himself that in this situation, he was superior. Now it was his offspring who had chosen beneath herself – thanks to Hitler.

"No, of course. I appreciate you coming to tell me."

"What else could I do?" Josef answered, genuinely surprised.

"What do you propose?"

"I have spoken to my son about this, but he openly defies me. In the event of his intransigence in this affair – and hers – I think the best course would be to arrange for them to be separated."

"I am not sure I follow you, Herr Rosenberg."

"Let me be frank. I feel badly about what I am doing, Herr Helder. My son obviously cares for your Marie very much. Separating them is obviously going to hurt him – hurt both of them. However, it must be done. So what I propose may be some measure of compensation to her."

Hermann had not the slightest idea what Josef was talking about. "I understand," he said. "Please continue." He sipped his coffee.

"I propose that Marie goes away to the university in Berlin."

Hermann almost choked, and the scalding coffee was

redirected up his nose. He spluttered, wiping his mouth and nose on his apron. "I can't afford that!"

Josef leaned forward, his homburg balanced on the forefingers of each hand. "Perhaps not, but I can, Herr Helder."

Hermann stared at him. Hope and hatred were born together. Having a daughter at university! He would be the envy of everyone! And Marie was a pretty girl; in Berlin she would have a much better chance of meeting a man of wealth and reputation. Perhaps even someone with connections to the National Socialists!

At the same time Hermann felt an overpowering urge to smash the Jew in the face. Rosenberg was flaunting his wealth at him, reminding him that he could do for Marie what he could never hope to do.

"Go on," Hermann said.

"I will pay for your Marie to go to the university. It is a long way, so she will have to board there. She will be away for most of three years."

"You are very generous."

"Three years is a long time. Perhaps the National Socialists will no longer be in power when she returns. Who can tell? One day she and Netanel may be able to see each other again, if they still wish it. Or perhaps they will forget each other."

"For myself, I have never been against the Jews, Herr Rosenberg. I think it is terrible what is happening." Best to leave my choices open, Hermann thought.

"Of course. All good Germans think that way," Josef said.

They discussed the details of their arrangement while Josef's coffee grew cold on the stained and fat-smeared bench beside him. Finally he stood up to leave.

Hermann held out his hand. Josef took it, reluctantly, as if he were being offered a handful of raw kidneys.

"You are a great man, Herr Rosenberg," Hermann said.

"I am afraid not all of Ravenswald thinks so."

"One more thing . . . you will not mention to anyone . . ."

". . . that I am paying for the fees for Marie's tuition? That would be rather defeating the purpose, would it not?"

Hermann was delighted. "Of course."

Josef left.

Hermann watched him through the window of his shop. Der Chef was very generous, but perhaps he ought not to feel too grateful. After all, it was true what the National Socialists said. These Jews had sucked them all dry for years. It was only fair that they should get some of their own money back.

The Helders always dressed for dinner on Friday; it was a family tradition. Hermann wore his best suit and the shirt with the press stud collar, his black tie worn in such a way as to disguise where the shirt had frayed. Inge wore her floral print dress, and young Dieter had chosen his new Hitler Jugend uniform. Marie noticed that the khaki brown shirt had been carefully pressed, and the knot in the black neckerchief must have been tied by her mother. And he was wearing his dagger! It had a black hilt with "Blood and Honour" engraved on the blade. Ridiculous! A boy of fifteen with a dagger!

Frau Helder had made omelette, stuffed with chopped kidneys, mushroom and asparagus, and an enormous bowl of salad. Marie could feel her father's eyes on her through dinner. Finally, as he forked the last of the omelette into his mouth, he asked her, "How was München?"

Marie's cheeks flushed hot. "Busy as always," she said. "There are posters everywhere." There was a silence and she felt compelled to talk through it. "'The Jews this, the Jews that. The Jews are destroying Germany, the Jews are trying to take over the world.' I don't know why people read such nonsense."

Dieter looked at her as if she had spoken a blasphemy, but said nothing. Her father shrugged. "Yes, Hitler certainly has a thing about the Jews. But he has done a lot of good, you must admit."

"Like what?" She looked at Dieter. "Like dressing schoolboys up as stormtroopers?"

"You apologise to your brother," Frau Helder said.

"Now, now," Hermann said, uncharacteristically composed, "everyone is entitled to their opinion."

Her father's equanimity unsettled her. Yes, she thought. There is something in the air. *He knows*.

"Germany has been on her knees too long," he said. "He is making us a proud nation again. And look at unemployment! He's certainly doing something about that."

"Yes, military conscription and forced labour in armaments factories."

"Ah, but you are just prejudiced because of the Rosenberg boy."

"Perhaps that is what made me unprejudiced."

"Dirty Jew!" Dieter sneered.

Marie stunned all of them with the speed of her reaction. In one movement she reached across the table and slapped her younger brother hard across the face. They all stared at her. The outline of her fingers showed livid against the fair skin of his cheek.

"Dinner is over," Hermann snapped. "Inge, Dieter, leave the room."

Frau Helder recognised the menace in her husband's voice from other occasions. She got up and guided Dieter out of the room. The door closed with terrible softness behind her.

Hermann wiped the grease from his chin with a napkin and leaned back in his chair. "A fine performance," he said.

"He asked for it."

"Perhaps. Well, how is Netanel Rosenberg these days?"

Marie tried to prepare herself for what was coming. "How should I know? You ordered me not to see him any more."

"But you saw him today, didn't you?"

All right, she thought, he does know. Well, I am not going to grovel. She looked him in the eye. "Yes," she said.

96

He drew back his hand and hit her. The force of the blow snapped her head back. "That's for Dieter," he growled. "Perhaps that will teach you some respect."

Marie put her hand to her mouth. Blood on her fingers. The blow hurt her terribly and she wanted to cry but she would not give him the satisfaction.

Hermann stood up, and leaned across the table. His cheeks were mottled with fury, the tiny capillaries delineated against the skin, like a spider's web of fine crimson thread. "Are you out of your mind? I told you to stay away from him for your own good!" He slammed his fist on the table and the crockery rattled. "You defied me!"

"I love him."

"Don't you read the newspapers? It is Rassenschande! You can be arrested just for talking to these people now!"

"I don't care."

"It has nothing to do with whether you care or not!" Again he slammed his fist on the table and a glass of water spilled over the tablecloth. "You will destroy all of us if you continue this way and I will not allow it!"

Marie tasted the metallic taint of her own blood in her mouth. "I don't care," she repeated.

Hermann rubbed his face with his hands. "You don't know how this hurts me," he said softly. "I had such high hopes for you."

"Working in the shop weighing your sausages for you?" she said, and was surprised how much she hated him at that moment.

He sighed and sat down once more. "I was not going to tell you just yet, but I have . . . well, been putting money aside for your education for many years. Now I finally have enough."

"Enough for what?"

"I have enrolled you in the university in Berlin." He spread his hands. "Did you really think I intended my beautiful daughter should work in a butcher's shop for ever?"

Marie was too stunned to speak.

"It means you will be away for three years. A long time, I know, although of course you will be with us on the holidays. But it will be for the best. Things can change. Perhaps one day Hitler will be gone and you and Netanel can see each other again. If not, then you can find yourself a good job somewhere. You don't want to spend your whole life in one little town."

His voice was soothing, hypnotic. He spoke as if everything was already decided. She was moved, of course; she had not realised the sacrifices he must have made but . . .

. . . But she knew what she wanted. She would not betray Netanel and she would not betray herself. "I am going to marry him."

Hermann accepted this news with apparent calm. "Even if your mother and I said yes, Hitler says no."

"It doesn't matter what Hitler says."

Hermann was silent for a long time. He studied her, as if by staring at her long enough and hard enough he could somehow see inside her mind and divine her thoughts. "Ah," he said finally. "Now I see."

"It's not that I don't appreciate – "

"You think you can get out of the country. You are planning to run away with him, aren't you?"

"I love him, and he loves me."

"Love! Tell that to the border guards! You would never get permission to leave, even if you had papers! And you cannot get papers without my permission, at your age! So what are you going to do, hein?"

He was laughing at her now. One moment he offers me his sacrifice, the next he mocks me, she thought. What did he really want? She got to her feet, still dizzy from the blow to her mouth.

"Sit down!"

She ignored him. "I don't know how we will do it, but we will find a way. Thank you for your offer, Father, and I really appreciate what you must have done to try and help me, but I don't want to go to university. I only want Netanel. Somehow we will find a way to be together."

She left the room.

"You silly bitch!" Hermann screamed and picked up his plate and threw his dinner in the fire in rage.

15

The rhythmic tramp of boots on cobbles, a fluttering red, white and black Nazi banner, neatly pressed brown uniforms, gleaming leather belts and boots. It was a stirring display, a Wagnerian dream of pageantry and precision; Gothic spirits rising from a chivalric past to herald new dawns. The crowding of the medieval houses and the mist that clung to the streets exaggerated the impression.

The Brownshirts sang as they marched.

> *Wenn vom Messer spritz das Juden Blut,*
> *dann geht's noch mal so gut.*
>
> When Jewish blood spurts from the knife
> then everything goes well in our life.

People stopped and stared. Marie looked at their faces. Many of them were smiling, or looked sternly proud. Mothers urged small children to cheer.

Everyone was going mad, she decided. The emperor had new clothes and they were khaki brown, with lightning runes on the shoulder patches. Hitler's crazed dreams had become a national vision. Der Führer had hypnotised them all. Now all Germany believed that getting rid of the Jews was going to solve everything.

"They are a stirring sight, aren't they?" a voice said.

It was Rolf Emmerich. The shabby son of the beer carter

99

had undergone a transformation in the last two years. His appearance both frightened and impressed her: white hair, white eyelashes, white, humourless smile; black leather boots, black leather overcoat, black shirt and tie. It was as if the whole uniform had been designed to contrast the beauty and bleakness of his Aryan features.

He was Untersturmführer Emmerich now, the local Nazi boss of Ravenswald. It was remarkable really. The Nazis seemed deliberately to promote these lumpen to positions of power. It seemed that the humbler the circumstances of your birth, the more likely you were to rise quickly in the hierarchy. Not so surprising perhaps, she decided, when the organisation was fuelled by the rage born of poverty and humiliation. With the Nazis, the natural order of things was reversed. The least educated were best qualified; they were less likely to question the party's philosophies, were more in need of scapegoats for their life's failures and pain.

As the local SS organiser, Rolf's principal duties involved the harassment of the town's Jews. He had finally found a position, she thought, which harnessed all his talents to the full.

He was watching her with eyes as cold and blue as a winter sky. "It is good to see so many of the townspeople have come to applaud our local SA volunteers," he said.

"I have to be going," Marie said and tried to push past him.

He caught her arm and held her, grinning. "What could be more important than talking to your town's Untersturmführer?"

"I can think of a number of things. Throwing a stick for my dog, for example. Let me go."

His smile vanished. "You should be more careful."

"Don't threaten me. I'm not scared of you."

"Then perhaps you do not know me well enough."

"I already know you better than I could have ever wished."

He pulled her closer to him, his fingers locked on her wrist. She cried out with pain. People looked

100

around, but turned away again when they saw Rolf's uniform.

"Listen to me," he said, softly. "I know you're still seeing that dirty Jew. You could get yourself in a lot of trouble. I cannot protect you for ever."

"What do you mean, protect me?"

"How do you think you've got away with this for so long?"

"Got away with what?"

He grinned. "Don't play games."

"My friends are my affair."

"You're very snotty for a butcher's daughter, you know."

"And you behave exactly like the son of a peasant!"

He squeezed her wrist tighter, smiling at the bright tears in her eyes. "You're being very foolish."

"I want to know how you think you're protecting me."

"Everyone knows you're going out with a Jewboy. You're not just going against your own people, you're going against the law."

"Get away from me!"

"As Untersturmführer, I can keep people from acting against you. But I can only do so much."

"I don't need your help."

"I only do it because I like you." He tried to kiss her.

"No!" She lashed out with her shoe, kicking his shin, and squirmed away from him. "Pig!"

He let her go but his face was chalk white with fury.

Marie looked around. The Nazi parade had turned the corner into the next street. A few people were still standing around, but they kept their eyes averted. The watchmaker was sweeping outside his shop, his back towards them. There was a jeweller's precision to the way he ignored her. Another man crossed the street to pass them on the other side.

"You saw what he tried to do!" she screamed at them. "Don't you care any more? Don't you have any decency?"

Rolf thrust his hands in the pockets of his greatcoat.

101

"You'd rather kiss a dirty Jew than a good German?" he asked her.

"I'd rather kiss a pig than a Nazi!" she screamed and ran home.

Josef Rosenberg's office was panelled in mahogany and oak, the room dominated by a portrait of Josef's father, Mandel, sombre in winged collar and morning coat and pince-nez. The heavy oak desk was positioned in front of the window, the surface reflective as glass. In one corner was a burgundy leather banquette and a carved oak table where each morning Josef and Netanel drank coffee from Dresden porcelain and discussed the day's business before the siren sounded to announce another day's production.

Frau Hochstetter had been with the company for as long as Netanel could remember, had been hired by Mandel Rosenberg himself. She was a tall, thin woman with spectacles and grey, neatly kept hair. At exactly twenty past eight she brought a coffee pot and two cups and saucers on a silver tray, as she had done every working morning for the last twenty-five years.

When she had left, Josef poured the coffee and they sat and discussed the latest order they had received from the United States, but Netanel seemed vague and inattentive. "What's the matter, Netya?" he said, finally.

"Father, this is no good. We have to get out."

"What are you talking about?"

"We must get out, while we still can. Like Mulu."

He saw his father flinch. Josef had still not recovered from that shock. Mulu had left Germany without telling anyone, not even his brother. The Nazis had forced him from his teaching job the previous year and Josef had been supporting him and his family ever since. Then one day he took a phone call from Esther. Mulu had emigrated to Palestine, taking his whole family with him. Josef had received one letter, six months ago. Mulu had thanked him for all his help, and promised to repay all his debts; after that, he had heard nothing more. Josef still regarded it as a personal betrayal.

102

"We should give up all this to wade round in the Huleh swamps?"

"If we sell now we can get our money out of the country through Switzerland. We can start again somewhere else."

"Start again? This business took seventy years to build. You can't just start again like that!"

"We have no choice."

Josef stared at him, awed by his audacity. "You think you can lecture me now, is this it? You are out of school two years and already you can teach your own father how to run his business!"

"The *Risches* – the anti-Semitism – is getting out of hand – "

"Ever since there have been Jews in Germany there has been persecution! You think this is something new?"

"There were never Hitler and Streicher before – "

"There have been plenty of Hitlers and plenty of Streichers!" Josef slapped his fists on his thighs in exasperation. "We're going to throw away seventy years' work for two madmen? It will pass!"

"They do not want us here any more, Father! They are boycotting every business except ours – "

"Yes, of course! Of course every business except ours! Even Hitler cannot survive for long without foreign currency. For all their rhetoric they need people like us, with export industries! Maybe they will harass the little watchmaker, the doctor, the shoe mender, but they won't touch us!"

"I wish I could believe that . . ."

"A year from now no one will even remember this Hitler's name."

"You're blind!"

Josef curbed his temper. "You're young," he said.

Netanel put down his cup, stirred more cream into his coffee with his spoon. He watched the swirling bands dissolve as he braced himself for what was difficult to say. "If you won't go, then I must."

Josef controlled himself only with difficulty. "Go? Where will you go, Netya?"

103

"Does it matter? Just away from this country."

"Not just 'this country'. Your country. You're German, you were born here."

"I'll never be a German. Not if you listen to Streicher."

"What else could you be?"

"Right now, I no longer care. I just want to be with Marie."

"Ah! So that is what has brought about this urge to run away!"

"I'm not running away!"

"I need you here to – "

"You cannot make me stay!"

"Perhaps not. It's true the Nazis are letting a lot of Jews leave Germany. But there are not many countries who will give them visas. Especially when they have no money and no skills."

Netanel lowered his eyes, too proud to beg.

"Ah, I see! You want money, don't you?" Josef said. His voice was not cruel, just sad. "But you must see I cannot help you buy your own ruin. Be sensible. Even if you could get out, what about this Helder girl? The government is not allowing any so-called Aryans to leave the country. Well, all right, supposing you pretended just to go away for a holiday and then married outside the country, in France, perhaps, or in Holland. No one will give you a resident's visa. Eventually you would have to come back to Germany and you would both be arrested. Besides, where will you marry, have you thought of that? She is a Catholic, you are a Jew. Everything about this relationship is impossible."

The siren sounded for the start of work.

"Please, Netanel," Josef begged, "it stands in the face of all common sense. Just let it be. It can never happen. I am sorry."

"I won't let it be. Somehow I'll find a way," Netanel said, and he walked out.

16

Netanel sat in the conservatory, the newspaper spread on his lap, his eyes closed. Outside, the sun was weakening, but it was still warm and yellow through the glass. His mother was busy with her plants, re-potting a willow sapling. She hummed as she worked.

Netanel glanced back at his paper. In München, a Jewish banker had had his house burned to the ground by a gang of fascists. Every day now there was some new outrage: a Jewish businessman beaten; a car belonging to a Jew had its tyres slashed; some other poor wretch was sent to prison for listening to foreign news broadcasts. Today there was a photograph of a woman walking out of a greengrocer's. The caption read: "Do you know this woman? Yesterday afternoon she was seen entering Weinstein's Grocery Store. She is a traitor to the German people!"

Netanel threw the paper on the floor in disgust.

His father was wrong. It was not going to pass; it was going to get a lot worse. Yesterday Esther had rung. Chaim had been beaten again. He had been walking near the Marienplatz when a parade of SA had marched past carrying the swastika banner. Everyone in the street stopped and gave the Nazi salute. Chaim did not know what to do. It was illegal for Jews to salute the Nazi flag but remembering his previous experience Chaim raised his right arm and shouted "*Heil Hitler!*" with everyone else. Unfortunately two local Hitler Jugend toughs had recognised him.

"Dirty Jew!" one of them shouted and they dragged him into an alley and beat him up.

Esther was talking about emigrating to Austria. She had a cousin in Linz.

"What's the matter?" Frau Rosenberg asked him. Her hands were black with rich earth. It always fascinated Netanel to see her with dirt on her hands. Away from the conservatory or the garden she would not think of touching anything that was not immaculate.

"The news depresses me," he said.

"Then don't read the newspaper, *liebling*. I never do."

He smiled. Such an elegant solution seemed perfectly logical to his mother. Ignore something and it will dissipate, like vapour. "Not reading the newspaper did not help Chaim."

"There is always trouble in the city," she said, and returned her attention to her potting.

So much a mother, and so much a child, he thought. Lately he had found himself thinking of her not as his parent, but as his responsibility. He supposed that it was a sign of his passage into manhood. He guessed that soon she would need him as much as he had once needed her. One bond was as strong as the other.

"It is much more than a little trouble," he said. "I wish you would talk to Father."

"About what, liebling?"

"About what is happening in Germany. We need to take this seriously. We must make plans." When she did not comment he went on, more forcefully. "The National Socialists will not be content just to boycott our businesses and harass us in the street. It could get worse. We must be ready to get out, if necessary."

"What does your father say?"

"He says that Hitler will not last."

"I am sure he knows best."

Netanel could have strangled her. How typical of her to reply to his concerns with platitudes. As he watched her with her plants he was reminded of a little girl playing with her dolls. She always left Josef to take care of her, abdicating all responsibility for herself.

But the image of her was shattered just as swiftly by her

106

next question. "Have you seen that Helder girl recently?" she asked.

"Father has forbidden it," Netanel said, carefully.

"It cannot work, you know."

"That's what he said, also."

"I was thinking about you and this Marie. She seems like a very nice girl, very sweet. I was wondering how such a sweet, nice girl would cope with being Jewish."

"You seem to have managed very well."

"Yes, but I was born to it. You know, Netanel, it is all a matter of degree. Oh, the wives of our anständige Leute come to my Kaffeeklatsch, but they have never invited me to join their tennis club. A small prejudice, hardly significant, but when you think about it, it is just a small step from that to beating my family in the street. But it has always been that way, so we busy ourselves with our daily lives, and when things get a little worse, we are prepared. But if your father says everything will be all right, then I believe him."

Netanel felt a sudden admiration for her. It was plain to him then that what he had mistaken for artlessness was actually a stoic acceptance of life. If she trusted Josef's judgment too much, it was to her credit, not her fault.

For himself, he felt only despair. "They are going to turn on us like a rabid dog, Mutti."

"And so you want your little goy to get bitten too?" she asked him.

He did not answer her. She went back to her task, kneading the soft earth with her fingers, singing tunelessly to herself, once again completely absorbed with her own green, moist world.

The Rosenberg house had been built on ten acres of land on the edge of town. It had been built with an eye to the views; Josef's study overlooked the Ravensee, a narrow blue neck of water snaking between the green pine forests that clung to the feet of the Alps; Netanel's bedroom afforded glimpses of Ravenswald's Catholic church with its clock and bell tower and the sombre grey stone of the Rathaus.

There was a far better view of the town from the end of the garden. It was here that Mandel Rosenberg had built a rotunda, nestled among the pines and willow, out of sight of the main house. Netanel remembered spending long summer afternoons here with his parents when he was a boy; sometimes Mulu and his family would be invited, and they would sip cool drinks and picnic on *liverwurst*.

Lately the rotunda had assumed a more important place in his life. It provided an ideal place for him and Marie to meet in secret.

The day had been warm, but the clear Alpine night had a crisp edge. Netanel shivered as he made his way through the garden. He saw a shadow move in the rotunda and his heart beat a little faster. What was he going to say to her? What could he possibly say?

When she saw him she threw herself into his arms and they clung to each other for a long time without speaking. A breeze rustled the trees, the lights of the town winking between the leaves.

"What are we going to do?" Marie whispered.

He did not answer her. He had worried the problem in his mind all day, and had found no solution. They could not go on as they had, meeting in darkened doorways; cuddling in the cinema, leaving ten minutes early to avoid prying eyes; stealing kisses in the Jewish cemetery. They were trapped. Germany did not want them, but Germany would not let them go.

She stood on tiptoe and rested her forehead against his. "I won't give you up," she said.

He kissed her gently, wondering how he would muster the courage to push her away.

"Say you won't let them break us apart, Netya."

"Marie . . . things are going to get very difficult."

"It doesn't matter."

"My father says Hitler cannot last. But what if he does last? Even another five years? What is going to happen to

108

us Jews? They are going to impoverish us. They are going to drive us back into ghettoes like they did in Poland and Russia."

"I don't care. I just want to be with you."

"You have no idea what you're saying."

She took his face in her hands and made him look at her. "Don't talk like this. You frighten me. We must not give up. You said it yourself. There must be some way."

"Marie, without your father's help, we cannot get you out of the country. And even if we could, what sort of life can I promise you? I'll have no money, nothing. You want to risk so much so you can help me pick potatoes in Palestine . . .?"

Marie covered her ears. "Stop it! I won't listen!"

Netanel pulled her hands away. "I'm telling you the truth!"

She started to hum.

"Don't be so childish!"

"I can't hear you." She continued humming.

In spite of himself, Netanel laughed. "You idiot!"

"See? That's more like it. You get so serious sometimes. You paint everything so black."

"It is black! There is no way we can – "

She started humming to herself again.

"Marie!"

"Mmmmmmm – I'm not listening – mmmmmmmm . . ."

"*Whether you're listening or not there's nothing we can do!*"

She punched his chest with both her fists. "Stop saying that! You want to get rid of me, is that it? You've got another girl?"

"Yes, there are hundreds of them. Good German girls just can't get enough of us Jewish boys. Pariahs are the fad at the moment."

"Is it a Jewish girl?"

"Why would I want another girl? You're the only girl I have ever wanted!"

She smiled and then said more gently, "Then that is

all that matters. If we love each other, we can survive anything."

"Don't be naïve."

She turned his face towards her and kissed him on the lips. He kissed her back, harder. Her arms went around his neck and the kiss went on and on. She had never kissed him this way before, so passionately. She moved her body against his, slowly and rhythmically, simulating the act of love. He was shocked, and excited, and confused. Finally he pushed her away.

"What are you doing?" His voice did not sound like his own.

"Make me pregnant. Make me pregnant and they will have to let us marry."

"No . . ."

She lifted up her skirts. "Do it," she whispered. "I've wanted you to for so long. Make me pregnant and then no one can stop us!"

Netanel wanted her so badly. But another voice inside his head screamed at him: *This is not going to solve anything! You are just going to drag her down with you! Is that what you want? Do you love her so much that you would let her sacrifice herself to the same nightmare you want so desperately to escape?*

"Please, Netanel, do it."

"No, Marie . . ."

He felt her hand move to his groin. The touch of her was like an electric shock coursing through him. He shuddered and pushed her hand away.

"*No!*"

Anger and hurt played across her face. She turned away and smoothed down her skirts. He thought she might cry, but when she finally spoke her voice was tight and hard. "I did not think you would give up so easily."

"All I can think of – "

"If you love someone, you don't stop to think! That calm, analytical brain of yours – "

"I won't let you do this! I love you too much – "

"You don't love me at all!"

110

"This is not the way!"

"It's the only way! You're just frightened of the risk! Well, damn you then! Give in to them! Perhaps it's right what they say about the Jews!"

She ran off into the darkness. Netanel started to follow her, then stopped. There was nothing left to say. They had said too much already. He listened to her footfall fade into the distance and then turned and went back towards the house.

17

The body of Christ, the blood of Christ.

The line of men and women and children waited patiently for their communion with God, on this the day of days on the Christian calendar. Marie watched Rolf Emmerich fall to his knees before the priest to accept the bread and wine into his mouth. As Rolf returned to the pews he smiled at her.

The sky was grey and heavy and the gloom of the church was lit with candles. A manger had been carefully prepared, with painted alabaster figures of Joseph and Mary and the child arranged on straw. The only sounds the shuffling of feet, the murmuring of the priest and the occasional muffled fall of snow dislodging from the eaves.

There were perhaps half a dozen brown SA uniforms among the congregation. Goodwill to all mankind, Marie thought. The priest stooped to offer the host to a Brownshirt. A tortured Christ watched from the cross on the stone wall above their heads: INRI – KING OF THE JEWS.

Hermann, Inge and Dieter knelt, and were blessed with man's communion with God. She knelt also, took the morsel of bread between her lips, and sipped the heavy, ruby red wine from the chalice, aware of the heavy must of the priest's robe. Today of all days the act of communion gave her no pleasure.

I hate these people, she thought. I hate them all. I hate them for their hypocrisy and their crippling prejudices and I hate this priest who does not have the moral force or the simple courage to rebuke them for what they are doing.

She went back to her place among the pews and fell on her knees and prayed.

The priest stood at the porch to bid farewell to his congregation.

"Merry Christmas, Father," Hermann said.

"Merry Christmas," Father Zoller answered. "I hear young Marie will be leaving us soon."

Hermann looked as if he were going to burst. "That's right, Father," he said, his voice booming in the porchway, "I am sending her to the university in Berlin."

Oh, he is enjoying this, Marie thought. He tells everyone who comes into the shop, rings the whole family to remind them each week, practically accosts strangers in the street. He is playing the part of a rich man for once in his life.

Still, I should not be ungrateful. What else do I have to cling to at the moment? It is for the best.

"We must thank God for his goodness," Father Zoller said.

"Of course," Hermann said, not entirely pleased with this perception.

The snow underfoot was thick and soft and new. Snow decorated the gravestones and vaults, made them appear almost festive. The air was frigid and echoed like a mausoleum.

Marie walked quickly ahead, her breath freezing on the air in thick clouds. Frau Helder hurried after her. "Marie, are you all right?"

112

"I'm sick of the lot of you," Marie said but her mother could not hear her. Frau Helder walked faster to catch up, almost slipped on the ice.

"What's wrong?"

"I want to be alone! Merry Christmas!" Marie shouted at her and stamped off.

Frau Helder looked for her husband. Hermann had buttonholed Herr Doktor Landisberger, whom he had forced into a discussion about the relative merits of educational institutions in Berlin. "Hermann!" Frau Helder called.

Landisberger, striking at his chance, excused himself from Hermann's company. Hermann looked irritated. "What is it?"

Frau Helder merely nodded in Marie's direction. Hermann caught only a glimpse of her before she turned the corner and disappeared over the bridge towards the town. "Where is she going?"

"Perhaps she's going to wish her Jewboy Merry Christmas," Dieter said.

Hermann cuffed him smartly around the ear for his blasphemy. But he had an uncomfortable feeling that perhaps his son was right.

The sky was a watery blue, and the air bit like a razor. The light was so clean and bright that every surface shone like polished glass. A pale yellow sun reflected off the new snow so fiercely it hurt the eyes; it bounced from the glacial calm of the Ravensee in sheets, and shimmered and dazzled on the soaring walls of the valley.

The House in the Woods looked desolate. The trees were draped with wreaths of frost, and the icy skeleton of the ivy vine clung to the façade like the bones of a long-dead parasite to its host. Marie hesitated outside the great iron gates. Perhaps the family had gone away to Switzerland for the holiday. She heard that der Chef liked Geneva.

She reached into her pocket and took out the little box in its festive wrapping. Well, if Netanel was not there she would leave it for him. He would know who brought it.

The brass knocker boomed like a cannon. She waited. Finally there were footsteps in the marble hallway beyond and the door opened. One of the Rosenberg servants opened the door.

"*Guten Morgen*," Marie said. "Is Netanel Rosenberg at – "

"Wait a moment," the woman said, and the door closed again.

She had not seen Netanel for nearly three months. At first it had been her choice. She had been sure he would come looking for her, and when he did not, her pride was stung. Every day she had silently damned him to all the demons in hell, but every night she had prayed that he would have a change of heart. After he had humiliated her with his rejection that night in the rotunda, she had promised herself that she would not be the one to break their estrangement. But this morning, of all mornings, she could not stay away.

The door opened behind her. "Netanel! I – "

"Fräulein Helder. How can I help you?"

"Frau Rosenberg!"

"I am afraid Netanel is not home at the moment." Frau Rosenberg noticed the gaily papered box in Marie's hands. "Is there something I can do for you, perhaps?"

"I was hoping to see Netanel," Marie said, lamely. She felt stupid. She thrust the gift-wrapped box into Frau Rosenberg's hands. "This is for Netanel."

"How very kind," Frau Rosenberg said, not without grace. "I will make sure he gets it."

"Thank you," Marie said. She was surprised. Frau Rosenberg's expression betrayed none of the hostility of their last encounter. Instead, she seemed concerned, even compassionate.

"I had better go," Marie said.

"Wait a moment," Frau Rosenberg said. "I . . . I don't know how to . . . well, I didn't realise that you and Netanel . . ."

114

"We don't see each other any more. This is just a Christmas present and – a going away gift too, I suppose."

"I heard you are going away to Berlin to study. I wish you every success. I mean it. You seem like a very nice girl. I am very sorry for what has happened."

Marie had not expected this. Suddenly, she felt angry. If the Rosenbergs had shown this much understanding a few months ago, perhaps it would not have come to this. "I am sorry too," Marie said. "Goodbye, Frau Rosenberg."

She turned to go.

"Marie!"

Netanel stood in the doorway, his face creased in a frown. He was staring at his mother, and the package in her hands. "What's going on?"

Frau Rosenberg's demeanour changed completely. "Why can't you just leave well enough alone?" she snapped at him.

"What are you doing?"

"Just trying to save you from yourself!" she shouted. All pretence slipped away and she gave Marie a look of cold anger. She threw Marie's gift at Netanel and went inside, slamming the door.

Netanel was in his shirtsleeves. He shivered against the cold. "I was in my room. I heard your voice. No one told me that – "

"I brought you a Christmas present," she said. She stared at Netanel, her eyes hungry for him. He looked beautiful, fair and tall and lean. She just wanted to throw her arms around him and hold him and she despised herself for her weakness.

He stared at the gift, embarrassed. "I don't know what to say . . . thank you."

"Well, open it."

He fumbled with the wrapping. Inside was a small red velvet box. He opened it and removed the cotton wool wrapping. It was a Star of David, sterling silver on a silver chain. He held it up to admire it. "You shouldn't have done this," he said.

115

"The jeweller is boycotted, of course," she said. "You don't know how difficult it was to arrange this." Yes, she did want him to know, wanted him to know the risk she had taken on his behalf.

"It's beautiful. What can I say?"

They stared at each other in awkward silence.

Finally: "I hear you are going to Berlin."

"As soon as the holidays are over."

"Well . . . good luck."

"Good luck? Is that it? Is that all you can say?" She had promised herself she would not cry, but now the tears welled in her eyes, angry and scalding hot.

He spread his hands. A helpless gesture.

"Don't you love me?" she said.

"You know I do."

"Then why won't you fight for me?"

"Because I love you," he said.

"That doesn't make sense."

"You think you understand the danger, Marie. But you don't."

"Damn you, Rosenberg," she said.

She turned and ran down the white driveway.

They were all there, her cousins from Oberammergau, her spinster aunt from Augsburg, her crippled uncle from München. Dieter was strutting around the platform in his Hitler Jugend uniform; her mother had donned her best hat and frock; Hermann had on a brown three-piece suit he wore only for church and for funerals, a silver fob watch he could not afford to have repaired in the waistcoat pocket. Her mother was crying and Hermann was shouting to anyone on the platform who would listen that his daughter was going to the university in Berlin.

They were early and the ten minutes until departure time dragged. The bonhomie and excitement became strained.

Her little cousins ran too close to the edge of the platform and her aunt screamed, ushering them away.

116

Meanwhile Dieter marched the length of the platform, in a vain search for communists or Jews in disguise.

Finally the train arrived, trailing a huge banner of steam. A porter helped load Marie's luggage while she said her goodbyes. Frau Helder's tears approached hysteria.

A station-master in a bright red cap signalled with his baton that the train was ready to depart. Marie clambered aboard, leaning out of the window of her compartment to finish her goodbyes.

As the train steamed out of the station, Frau Helder waved her handkerchief, her face screwed tight with despair. Hermann had one thumb tucked into his waistcoat, playing out the role of gentle and haughty provider. Dieter ran alongside the carriage the length of the platform, demonstrating his physical prowess to Marie's fellow passengers.

But Marie was no longer watching her family.

She was looking for Netanel. Even now she thought he might appear just for a moment, beside the railway tracks, to wave and to give her the comfort of a last farewell. But her only companions as she left Ravenswald were the gentle rhythm of the train wheels and the endless soaring white of the Bavarian winter.

Part Four

PALESTINE AND GERMANY, 1937

18

Jerusalem

Like a well-sucked lemon, Majid thought. Dry and sour
and her juice all used up.

Majid Hass'an did not like Mrs Elizabeth Talbot. She
was tall and thin and pale, like a stick insect that never
saw the light of day, he thought, something you might
find under a rock. And no meat on her at all, nothing
for a man to get a good grip of. All bones. Poor Talbot
effendi, he thought. It must be like fucking a lamppost.

Talbot effendi had gone home to Britannia last year on
a holiday, and when he returned he had announced to his
household that he had brought back with him the new
Mrs Henry Talbot. It had been a shock, since Talbot
effendi had given no hint before his departure that he
had been considering taking a wife. Majid assumed it had
all been arranged for him, by his father.

Maijid had long considered that what Talbot effendi
needed was a woman. But oh, not a woman like this
one.

Elizabeth Talbot was a scourge sent by Allah. Within a
week she had assumed complete control of the household,
and Talbot effendi had retired to the salon with his books.
The formerly relaxed pace of life had been swept away.
Mrs Henry Talbot called it a new broom.

There were three servants; an ancient cook, Hasna; old
Abdollah who fed the chickens and cleaned the toilets
and tended the garden; and Majid himself. As chauffeur, houseboy, and servant, he had been accustomed

121

to exercising his authority over Hasna and Abdollah, and even, sometimes, Talbot effendi himself. Mrs Elizabeth Talbot – The Rod That Allah Sent To Test Us, as he had named her – had changed all that. Now, he was treated with almost the same curt indifference as Abdollah, old shit-on-his-hands himself.

Allah help me in my sorrow.

It was intolerable. She was, after all, only a woman, not much older than himself; yet she treated him like a donkey on the end of a rope, for the love of Allah. His father would die of shame if he knew. In consolation he reminded himself that she was a Britisher and so perhaps her spirit was loftier than, say, an Arab woman's.

He found further solace in the fact that Mrs Henry Talbot treated her own husband little better than she treated him. In fact, Talbot effendi disappointed him greatly. The great man had the deportment of a lion and the liver of a sheep.

It proved something his father had told him from the day he took his first tottering steps: Let a woman once rise above you and she will shit on your head for the rest of your life.

This morning, thanks be to Mohammed and all his caliphs, she was in a good mood; unusually cheerful, in fact. He brought the car to the front door and when she emerged she was dressed in a long white dress of fine white muslin, the inevitable broad-rimmed hat, and even, may Satan turn his back in shame, perfume. His nostrils twitched as she climbed into the back seat of the Buick. Perfume!

"Where to, Lady Talbot?" he asked. The "Lady Talbot" honorific had been his own invention.

"The Husseini Quarter. Try not to hit any camels this time."

"Yes, Lady Talbot." Unforgiving bitch!

The Husseini Quarter was on a plateau between the Nablus and Jericho Roads. Majid drove slowly along the Bethlehem Road under the walls of the Old City, trapped in the crawl of the afternoon traffic, buses belching black smoke, the Arab donkey carts indifferent to the honking of horns around them.

They passed the Damascus Gate. The markets around the gate were teeming with people: Arabs in white keffiyehs; Hassidim in the black of European *shtetl*, sidecurls flapping under their broad-rimmed black hats; Orthodox Jews wearing white yarmulkes and business suits. Arab women with baskets piled with vegetables scrambled for a place on the already crowded buses that would take them back to their villages in the surrounding hills, and small children moved among the crowds selling prayer beads to Muslims and crucifixes to Christian pilgrims.

Two snot-nosed urchins ran up to the Buick waving photographs. "You want bicture of Tomb of Hully Vuggin?" they sang. "Only two biastre!"

The Rod That Allah Sent To Test Us wound up her window and ignored them.

They turned on to the Nablus Road. When they reached the streets of the Husseini Quarter, they left the squalor and noise of the Old City behind. The Arab villas were hidden behind high walls, their gardens neatly tended, calla lilies in bloom. The streets were green-shaded and cool.

"The next street on your right," Mrs Henry Talbot said.

Majid did as he was told.

"Stop here."

A spreading fig tree uncurled its long branches over a saffron-painted stucco wall. Majid glimpsed a white-painted villa hidden behind the olive trees. He thought he saw someone appear briefly at a second-storey window, and move away again.

He jumped out and opened the door for Mrs Henry Talbot. "Wait here," she said and hurried through the gates. The door to the villa opened and she disappeared inside.

Very mysterious.

Majid got back behind the wheel. He turned the car

123

radio to an Arab station and settled down to wait. The cacophonous melody of lutes and drums was interrupted to broadcast a report of a bomb blast in a Jewish commercial district in Tel Aviv and a British patrol being ambushed near Nablus. The Mufti has been busy, Majid thought. Then the music returned.

It was late spring, and the afternoon droned with insects. Majid took off his jacket and loosened his tie. The tie was pale green and without decoration, another innovation of The Rod That Allah Sent To Test Us. She had forbidden him from wearing any tie of more than one colour. She had even dared to say – to his face – that his taste in clothes upset her digestive system.

Blooming bitch, he muttered to himself in English.

After a while, he started to doze.

An Arab effendi in a tarbush and grey business suit left one of the villas further along the street. Two men in traditional Arab dress, abbayahs fluttering around their ankles, got out of a black Vauxhall parked on the other side of the street and walked towards him. Majid closed his eyes, the yellow sun streaming in through the windscreen, warming the soft leather upholstery. His head lolled on his chest.

Two loud bangs, like a motor car engine backfiring.

He opened his eyes, saw the effendi lying on his back on the footpath. There was a pool of dark blood around his head, and some of it had sprayed up the wall beside him. The two Arabs ran back to their car and jumped in. It would not start. One of them leaped out again, holding a cranking handle.

A fat woman waddled into view. She knelt beside the stricken man, screaming hysterically at the two men on the other side of the street. Suddenly she noticed Majid sitting in his car and ran towards him. Majid waved her away with his hands and locked all the doors.

She beat on the windscreen with her fists. "My husband has been shot! Help me! Please help me!"

The two Arabs – the man's assassins, no doubt, Majid

124

realised – had given up on the old Vauxhall. They fled on foot along the street.

"I am not a doctor!" Majid yelled at the woman. "Go away!"

The woman hawked deep in her throat and spat on the windscreen. She ran back inside her house.

Why does Allah do this to me? Majid thought.

The woman would get the police. The police would want to interview him, perhaps interview Lady Talbot as well. The Rod That Allah Sent To Test Us would be furious. Whatever she was doing – and several alternatives had suggested themselves, each as unlikely as the other – he was sure she would not be pleased with this turn of events.

He leaned his fist on the horn and kept it there. Faces appeared at the upstairs window of the villa. He waved frantically to get their attention. Moments later a young Englishman, tall and very fair, stepped out of the front door. He was wearing a white open-necked shirt and white slacks but Majid noticed that the trousers were not buttoned properly and the shirt was badly creased.

However, he seemed perfectly composed. A real Britisher, Majid thought. He wound down the passenger window and the man leaned in.

"I say, you little Arab shit, what are you doing?"

"A man has been shot, effendi! Look! Just there!"

The Englishman frowned and looked in the direction Majid was pointing. The man lay in the dirt, like an abandoned suit of clothes. His wife reappeared, keening and wringing her hands.

"What rotten luck," the Englishman said. "We were just starting to have a good time."

"We must leave here, effendi," Majid said.

The Englishman considered a moment. "Dirty little Arabs," he muttered. "Why can't they go and shoot each other somewhere else?"

He wandered back inside.

Majid fidgeted in the front seat. He turned up the radio so he would not have to listen to the fat woman's grief.

Several children gathered around and stood and watched, fascinated. In the distance Majid could hear the klaxon of an approaching police car.

Minutes later it turned the corner, brakes squealing as it came to a halt in the middle of the road. Two khaki-clad policemen jumped out. They spoke hurriedly to the weeping woman who pointed up the street in Majid's direction. One of them walked towards the car.

At that moment the door of the villa opened and Elizabeth Talbot appeared. She was running, her hat held in one hand, while she tried to pin back her hair with the other. The fair-haired Englishman stood framed in the doorway, watching her. She hurried through the gate and almost collided with the policeman on the footpath.

"My apologies," the policeman said, and touched his cap. The chevrons on his arm denoted him as a sergeant. He spoke faultless English but one glance at his complexion and his colouring told Majid he was probably Jewish.

This should be interesting, he thought.

The Rod That Allah Sent To Test Us gave him a withering glance. Majid jumped out to open the door for her.

"Just a moment," the sergeant said. "I'd like to speak to your chauffeur."

"I am in a hurry," Elizabeth Talbot said, and her tone made it clear that she was not accustomed to being addressed by policemen.

"A man has just been murdered, ma'am."

"Oh? And why is this of interest to me?"

"The man's wife says your chauffeur saw the whole thing."

Elizabeth looked over the policeman's shoulder, saw the fat woman, her hands raised to heaven, shrieking prayers for vengeance to Allah. "For goodness sake, Sergeant. It was only a fucking Arab."

The man blinked. The word was delivered with such perfect elocution it might not have been an oath at all. For a moment he could not find his voice.

"Anyway, my chauffeur was not out here. He was

inside, in the kitchen with the other servants. Weren't you?" she said to Majid.

"I was inside, in the kitchen with the other servants," Majid repeated.

"Well, we'll need a statement."

Elizabeth threw her hat into the car and took a step towards the policeman. "Do you know who you're talking to?"

Beads of sweat appeared on the policeman's forehead.

"He saw nothing. I saw nothing. Neither of us wants to make a statement. Is that clear? And if you bother me again I'll have you shipped back to Germany. All right?"

The police sergeant's face was mottled with fury. For a moment Majid thought he might risk a confrontation, but then he turned on his heel and walked away. Why throw away his career for one Arab?

As they drove away, Majid glanced at The Rod That Allah Sent To Test Us in the rear-vision mirror. She had succeeded in pinning her hair but long strands had worked loose and now hung wild around her face. Her cheeks were suffused with a soft pink. So, he thought, the lemon still has some juice!

She caught him staring at her. "Do you know who that Englishman was, Majid?"

"No, Lady Talbot."

"He is a captain in the Royal Suffolks. He won a bronze medal at the last Olympic Games for fencing. If you breathe a word of this to anyone I shall have him insert an epee up you. Is that clear?"

Majid's grin fell away. Blooming bitch. One day he would have to remind her she was only a woman.

al-Naqb

Sheikh Daoud's breath smelled of cardamom and tobacco. He leaned closer to Zayyad, the fingers of his left hand worrying his tespi, the other holding a slowly burning cigarette.

"The Mufti has asked that all of Palestine rise in a *jihad*."

"So I have heard," Zayyad answered.

"He often asks me what his great friend Sheikh Zayyad is contributing to the cause."

Great friend? Zayyad thought. I have never even met the man. "And what do you tell him?" he said, fencing gently.

"I change the subject."

Zayyad sipped his coffee, strong and bitter and herb-scented, while he composed his thoughts. Had the Mufti really called him his great friend? Allah forbid he should ever be a friend of the Mufti. It was a guarantee of a bullet in the neck.

Years ago the Mufti had started preaching his jihad, shouting out sermons in the Grand Mosque in Jerusalem about a united Arab Palestine, addling everyone's brains. Palestine! What was Palestine? Palestine was strangers he had never met, effendis from Jaffa and Jerusalem he despised! His country was Rab'allah, his king was Allah. The Mufti was a poison the people drank when they were so parched of hope they would swallow anything.

Even so, a lot of what he said was true. The Jews were taking over, flooding into the country from some town called Germany. The British said they would not let the Jews take over, but it was clear now that the British would do whatever they considered expedient.

The troubles had begun a year ago, when the Mufti had managed to persuade the faithful in Jaffa that the Jews had defiled Jerusalem's Grand Mosque. A mob had streamed through the streets towards Tel Aviv and massacred a number of Jews in the bazaars. Since then, the killings and bombings and rioting had become a daily event.

If it was just Jews being slaughtered he might have applauded. But it was clear to Zayyad that the Mufti's main targets were other Arabs. He was using the troubles to rid himself of his political enemies, which included almost every teacher and doctor and moderate man in Palestine. Just last week Majid had seen a Christian Arab effendi gunned down in the street in the Husseini Quarter.

If it were not for Rishou's marriage to Khadija, which had made him a blood relation of both Daoud and the Mufti, he was convinced his own assassination would have taken place long ago.

Sheikh Daoud had formed a band of "Holy Strugglers" in al-Naqb, gangs of unemployed youths looking for an outlet for their rage. They were armed with a motley selection of antique hunting rifles from the time of Lawrence, and rambled around the hills at night, sniping at British forts, burning orchards at the kibbutz or cutting power lines. By day they slipped back into their villages to sleep off their adventures.

Zayyad thought they were a joke.

"The Mufti looks forward to the day when you raise your own army at Rab'allah," Daoud said.

"We all look forward to that day. But Rab'allah has just four hundred people. If you take away the old men, the women and the children, we could not raise an ambush, even if you included the sheep and goats."

"Where is that much-celebrated Bedouin fighting spirit?"

"It is tempered by that much-celebrated Bedouin wisdom."

Daoud drew on his cigarette and his face was tight with disdain. "No good Arab can stand by while his country is at war."

"What country? You have been to my country. It sits on a hill two miles away. It is called Rab'allah."

Daoud's lips pursed into a frown. "The Mufti would be displeased if he heard you say such things. It could be dangerous."

"Ah, then your meaning was that I should raise an army to protect myself from the Mufti, not the Jews?"

"A man should cultivate friendships if he is wise."

"He should also keep his back against the wall. If he is wise."

Daoud digested this response. He threw the stub of his Four Square out the window where his grandsons scrabbled for it in the dust. He took his time in lighting another. "It is fortunate you have a friend on the Higher Committee. You should not try the Mufti's patience too far, Zayyad."

"I shall remember your words, brother."

"I hope you will," Daoud sighed. "But I doubt it very much."

19

Rab'allah

When Zayyad returned from al-Naqb he threw himself into his armchair and his second wife Ramiza hurried in from the kitchen to wash his feet in an enamel bowl that was set aside expressly for this purpose. He sat in morose contemplation while she ministered to him.

Later, Wagil and Rishou returned from the coffee house. They kissed his hand and sat at his feet while they reported their day's labours; Rishou had collected the rents from Beit Shabus and Deir Jebrin; Wagil had read the newspaper. The women brought them their food and left them. The three men sat cross-legged on the rug and ate with their fingers from a common plate. Wagil spoke about the latest reports of the uprising from Jerusalem and

Jaffa; Rishou concentrated on his food; Zayyad brooded on his conversation with Sheikh Daoud.

When they were finished, the leftovers were sent to the kitchen for the wives and children. Zayyad's daughters scrambled for the honour of washing his fingers and drying them.

Zayyad resumed his position in the armchair and sat for a long time, moodily picking the straw padding from a rent in one of the arms. Finally he announced, "Fetch the women. There is something we should all discuss together."

Zayyad Hass'an was, in his way, a liberal man, perhaps even a radical by Sheikh Daoud's standards, in that he sometimes allowed the women to voice their opinions on matters that concerned them all. Naturally they could only speak when invited to do so, but even this concession was regarded by some in the community as a dangerous precedent.

Zayyad's first wife, Soraya, entered first. Her wrists and ankles jingled, heavy with silver and gold bands. It was Zayyad's way of displaying his wealth without personal ostentation. Zayyad's second wife, Ramiza, entered next followed by Hamdah and Khadija. They sat beside their men on the rug at Zayyad's feet.

Zayyad cleared his throat. "I have spoken this afternoon with Sheikh Daoud. He conveyed to me felicities and other warm words from the Mufti of Jerusalem himself."

He heard Wagil draw in a breath in awe.

"He also conveyed to me the Mufti's desire that the people of our village should join him in his rebellion."

Wagil nodded vigorously. "We will drive the British into the sea and take back all the lands that the Jews have stol – "

"Shut up," Zayyad said softly, and without rancour. "I told Sheikh Daoud that I would consider the Mufti's request, but in my own heart I am troubled. I have seen many seasons. I remember the way things were when the Turk was in Jerusalem and I have seen the way the British

131

have ruled us. For my own part I prefer the British. Now the Mufti says we should rule ourselves. By that I assume he means that he wants to take over himself. This prospect does not lift my heart with exultation. For the last year I have seen the way the Mufti rules – may God protect him and grant him increase, of course – and that is by putting a bullet in the head of those whom he personally dislikes. However, I have no love for the Jews and I have begun to suspect that the British are not going to protect us from them, as they promised they would. So what should we do? I am undecided. I will listen to counsel."

"If we do not fight the Jews will swallow up all our land!" Wagil shouted. "We must fight to the last drop of Arab blood!"

Zayyad turned to Rishou. "Do you agree with your brother?"

"I would perhaps agree with him more if the Arab blood was not being spilled by the Mufti's mercenaries. Besides, the Jews at Kfar Herzl have been our neighbours for the last fifteen years, and they have lived peacefully enough. The Mufti is a troublemaker."

"He is the saviour of Palestine!" Wagil shouted.

"What is Palestine? Ten thousand villages like this one! We don't care about them and they don't care about us!"

"Enough," Zayyad said. He turned to Soraya. "What is your opinion?"

Soraya, aware of the honour being accorded to her, spoke softly. "Abu Wagil, when the Turks were here they made us pay a lot of tax money and they gave us nothing in return. The British do not ask for so much and they give us schools and even a hospital at Bethlehem for when the children are sick. They have brought us jobs too. Majid has a fine motor car and a house in Jerusalem with a toilet inside. Why shoot the British for giving us all these things when we did not shoot the Turks for robbing us like jackals?"

Zayyad turned to the other women. "Have any of you anything to say on this matter?"

Ramiza and Hamdah stared at the floor. Hamdah

secretly wished that Wagil would go out at nights and shoot at the British instead of trying to force his eggplant into her. Khadija giggled and covered her face with her hands. She thought they should do whatever her father, Sheikh Daoud, said they should do, but she did not have the courage to say so.

Zayyad sighed. "I am not happy," he said. "If we fight, we cannot win. The British army is too strong. They have tanks and planes and as many cigarettes as they can smoke before a battle to calm their nerves. But if we do not fight, I fear they will give the Jews more land and soon there will be barbed-wire fences in the places where our grandfathers grazed their sheep." He pulled another handful of straw from the armchair and crumpled it in his fist. "But I will not have my sons, or any of the young men of Rab'allah carried home in sheets for the Mufti of Jerusalem. The British have been our friends for twenty years. We must trust them not to betray us."

"We betray the Arab cause and all Islam!" Wagil hissed.

Zayyad stood up smartly and boxed him round both ears. "Talk back to me and I will cut off your toes and throw them in the stew!"

Wagil lowered his head, shamed, but his eyes burned with his anger. One day . . .

"Leave me, all of you," Zayyad said. He turned to Soraya. "Fetch me my water pipe. And the whisky bottle," he added in a whisper. "I wish to make my heart glow again."

One by one they trooped from the room. Zayyad slumped into his armchair. Allah, help me in my sorrow! Anything I do now will be wrong. May the Mufti's beard turn into fire ants and chew off his face! May his balls turn into coconuts and drop on his foot!

Why did Allah send such men to us?

Captain Terrence Mannion looked around in disgust. An open sewer ran the length of the village and his nostrils twitched in protest. Children swarmed around him, pawing his uniform, smearing snot on his khaki shorts.

The muktar who came to meet him scattered the urchins with a clap of his hands and extended his palm in greeting. He had a grey beard and a face as wrinkled and brown as a walnut. He wore a camel-hair abbayah, and a sash of red damascene silk at his waist, but the green and red tie at his neck detracted from his air of dignity.

Mannion exchanged a glance with the corporal who sat, stony faced, behind the wheel of the jeep. "My name is Captain Mannion," he said. "I am here on official business." He spoke in English, assuming Zayyad would understand.

"Welcome to Rab'allah," Zayyad replied in Arabic. "Would you like to come into my home and drink coffee? I have sent for my son, Rishou. He speaks English like the King of Britannia himself and he will help us converse."

"Is there anyone here who speaks English?" Mannion asked him.

"I don't understand," Zayyad said, in Arabic.

"I'm terribly sorry. I don't understand," Mannion said.

They blinked at each other and fell silent. Zayyad was greatly relieved to see Rishou marching up the hill from the coffee house.

Rishou pushed his way through the crowd. "I am Rishou Hass'an," he said to Mannion and seized his hand. "This is my father Zayyad Hass'an al-Shouri, muktar of Rab'allah. How can we help you?"

"Ah, you speak English," Mannion said with evident relief. "My name is Mannion, Captain Terrence Mannion. I need to talk to your father. It is a matter of great importance."

"Please come inside. We shall take coffee. Then we shall talk."

Zayyad had his daughters fetch coffee and offered Mannion some of his stock of Black Label whisky, which Mannion politely refused. Through Rishou, Zayyad informed the British captain that his eldest son drove a Buick, and expressed his sympathy to the captain that his own vehicle did not have a roof and windows. Mannion, in turn, explained to Zayyad that he was a member of the Suffolk Regiment and that his own village was a place called Ipswich. At present his home was the Allenby Barracks in Jerusalem.

"There has been a lot of trouble with certain Arabs recently," Mannion said.

"It has not escaped my father's attention," Rishou translated.

"The British have always tried to be a friend to the Arabs."

"He says your greatness is legend."

"But the situation is becoming intolerable."

"My father offers you his sympathy and hopes you will not blame him personally when you return to Ipswich."

"That is why we have been forced to instigate stricter controls over the villages. From now on each muktar will be officially appointed and approved by the High Command in Jerusalem and will be answerable to us for all local activities."

"My father says he has always been a friend to the British but Rab'allah conducts its own affairs without interference."

Mannion shifted, uncomfortable with the duty he had been assigned. "In future all muktars will be expected to report any suspicious activity in their area to the British authorities. If they do not, they will be held directly accountable."

Rishou translated this for his father. Zayyad stared at him. "What does he mean?"

"I think they are threatening us," Rishou said, in Arabic. "They want us to become their spies."

"I cannot do that!"

"What do you want me to tell him?"

"Tell him to go piss up a camel's leg!"

"My father," Rishou translated, "thanks you for the honour that you do him, but says he must refuse. He is already muktar of Rab'allah, appointed by his own people. He maintains his own authority here, he cannot countenance interference."

Mannion's cheeks turned pink. "I am afraid he has no choice. This is a civil emergency."

"My father assures you of his friendship and his respect and prays that God grants you increase and still says no."

"I am sorry he feels that way," Mannion said. He was unaccustomed to sitting cross-legged on the floor and he was eager to end the interview. It was quite clear that he was making no progress here. "Is it true that he is related by marriage to Sheikh Daoud, a member of the so-called Arab Higher Committee?"

"The sheikh's daughter is my wife," Rishou said.

"I see," Mannion said. That settled the matter. He stood up.

"Is he angry?" Zayyad asked Rishou.

"I don't know," Rishou said. "He asked whether you were related to Sheikh Daoud."

"Let us give him a gift to console him perhaps for our refusal," Zayyad said, and he loosened the red and green tie that Majid had given him. He gave one last, baleful look at the girl with the blonde hair and wonderful breasts who had been embroidered on to the front, and looped the tie over Mannion's head.

"It is a gift," Rishou explained to Mannion.

Mannion stared at it. Jesus Christ Almighty. "Please thank your father for his generosity."

They shook hands. Mannion jumped into his jeep and nodded to his subaltern. The children scattered as the jeep roared away, scattering dust and small stones.

"Do you think that will be the end of it?" Zayyad asked Rishou.

"I hope so," Rishou answered.

But in his heart, he doubted it.

20

Everyone in the coffee house was shouting at once. They screamed their oaths and shook their fists and surrendered themselves to the small consolation of rant. It would take a little while for the full import of the news to be absorbed, Zayyad thought, and then defeat and impotence would settle on them again like dust.

The British had appointed Sheikh Jamil, the clan chief from Beit Shabus, as muktar of Rab'allah and the surrounding district.

It was unforgivable.

By this one action the British had displayed their ignorance of Rab'allah, of Palestine, of Arabs everywhere. At a stroke, they had undermined an institution that had been in place for thousands of years. Zayyad was humiliated, the entire village had been insulted, and the British had underlined their utter contempt for Arab honour.

Who was this Sheikh Jamil? the villagers shouted. A minor clan chief, living in a stone hovel. He even paid rents for his fields to Zayyad himself!

"He is a shit-eating son of a diseased dog," Wagil shouted, "and I will personally take my knife and cut his throat!"

"We will blow up the fort at Latrun!"

"We will avenge ourselves on any British soldier who dares step into our valley again!"

"We will throw the British out of Palestine and a thousand tanks won't save their spotty arses!"

"Sheikh Jamil will mourn this day!" Wagil shouted again. "I will cut out his liver and feed it to my dog!"

Zayyad got up and went outside. The shouting did not abate. He knew from experience that they could keep this up for hours. As a young man he had done it himself.

A hot wind rushing in from the Jordanian desert seared his lungs like the blast from an oven. It came each year at the end of spring, blowing day and night without relief. The spring flowers wilted and died and the hills turned tinder brown, behind a dirty and choking sepia haze. The wind would blow for weeks without respite. It was known as the hamsiin, from the Arabic word for fifty; the fifty-day wind. It drove everyone to the edge of madness. It was a dangerous time of year, the season of hot tempers and clan killing.

Zayyad found Rishou sitting alone by the well, his back turned against the wind. A dust devil swirled between the mud-brick houses.

"What is happening?" Rishou said.

"Wagil has laid plans to defeat the British and has devised a thousand ways to torment Sheikh Jamil to death," Zayyad said. "All that remains now is for him to do it."

The baking wind moaned across the empty square. The sun beat down on the white dome of the mosque and hurt the eyes.

"I want you to go to Jerusalem for me," Zayyad said. "I want you to talk to Majid. He must tell this Talbot effendi what has happened and ask him to intercede for us with Captain Mannion."

"I will leave straight away."

"Thank you. And Rishou . . ."

"Yes, Father?"

"Tell him I want my tie back also."

Off Salah ed-Din Road

Majid lived in a two-bedroom flat with his wife and two small children, a son and a daughter. It was oppressively hot inside, and the noises of the traffic and the cries of children playing in the street below came from the open windows.

Majid wore a charcoal grey suit with a wide white stripe, and a dark blue MCC tie he had bought in the bazaar. He was effusively welcoming. They embraced at the doorway, and then the children were paraded before him, and his wife, Mirham, was ushered forward.

"Welcome. Jolly splendid," she said in English, giggling, and fled to the kitchen.

"Sit down, sit down," Majid said, and they squatted on the rug by the window, but it was no cooler there. The hamsiin's hot breath was tainted with petrol fumes and the debris of the city. Majid went to the RCA Victrola record-player that occupied a place of honour against the far wall under the *Bismillah*. He had so far been able to afford to purchase just one recording of Arabian music and he put it on the turntable, placing the needle reverently on to the edge of the grooves, as the salesman in the shop had shown him.

"It was very expensive," Majid said, with evident pride.

"You have done very well."

Majid grinned with pleasure and squatted down opposite his brother. "This is a wonderful surprise," Majid said, and Rishou saw that he meant it. "How is our father?"

"He is well in health," Rishou said, carefully, and Majid's face clouded with concern. He had known that only a crisis of some weight would have brought Rishou to Jerusalem so unexpectedly. But he put his concern aside. There was the ritual of asking after brothers and sisters and cousins first.

Mirham brought coffee and placed a brass tray of honey cakes on the rug between them. Majid leaned towards his brother and whispered, "There is whisky if you would prefer."

139

Rishou shook his head. He still maintained the pretence of being a good Muslim.

Majid asked after each member of the family in turn, and enquired after the pleasantness of Rishou's journey. Finally, he said: "So what has brought you here, brother?"

"It is our father."

"What has happened?"

"The British have betrayed us, Majid. They have appointed a new muktar in place of our father."

Majid laughed. "They can't do that!"

"They have done it. They wanted Father to spy for them. When he refused they appointed Sheikh Jamil as the new muktar of Rab'allah."

"Jamil does not know one end of a donkey from the other."

"The British said they would protect us from the Jews. They lied to us, Majid. Now they spit on our village."

"The British don't lie."

Rishou was surprised that his brother might try to defend the British actions. "We are humiliated. Something must be done."

Majid sipped his coffee. "I will talk to Talbot effendi."

"Our father believes you are his best chance." He paused, awkward with his next words. "It may be difficult to rule Rab'allah without British approval."

"Not difficult, impossible."

"Sheikh Daoud has spoken to our father," Rishou said. "He wants him to, you know, recruit villagers for the Mufti of Jerusalem."

"The Mufti! That dirty little Arab!"

Dirty little Arab, Rishou thought. Did he really say that?

"Father has tried to delay on this as long as possible."

"Stay out of it! The British will crush the Mufti. Anyone who sides with him will be thrown into prison. Stay out of it!"

"It will not be easy, now the British have done this." He felt a bead of perspiration drop from the point of his chin into his lap. "Do you think you can persuade this Talbot to help us?"

"We sit down together every day to discuss the situation here in Palestine. I will arrange things, do not worry. Now then, on to more pleasant things. First you must have something to eat. Then I will show you Jerusalem, little brother! Things that will make your eyes stand out from your head on their stalks!" He laughed and clapped his hands. "Don't look so gloomy! Mirham – more coffee!"

It was like no Arab gathering Rishou had ever seen. The room was in darkness, crowded with effendis in tarbushes and western clothes, sitting at tables and chairs drinking whisky. There was an Arab orchestra with flutes and tymbals, like at a wedding, but no one was dancing. Instead they stared at a raised platform that was illuminated with electric lights. The men had sweat on their lips and glassy, distant expressions in their eyes.

There was a woman dancing on the stage, a Syrian, and she was almost naked. She wore just a flimsy piece of sparkling cloth to cover her breasts and her loins, the rest of her body and face veiled with a gauze that was transparent in the strong light. There were cheap gems in her nostrils and her ears and braided into her long black hair; a large blue stone glinted in her navel.

Rishou was hard as a palm tree with desire for her. He wondered what would happen when she finished her dance. Would they all rape her, all these strangers, one after another?

She writhed in time with the lutes and drums, the muscles of her thighs rippling under her skin, her breasts keeping a rhythm of their own. Rishou wiped the palms of his hands on his abbayah.

"What is going to happen?" he whispered to Majid, who was grinning with the same, unfocused expression as the others.

"Just watch," Majid said.

The woman came down the steps of the stage, her arms held out from her body, her hips thrusting in time with

141

the urgent beat of the tymbals. She came towards their table. Rishou swallowed hard. He could see everything now, each bead of sweat on her face, the tautness of her breasts where they were squeezed between the sequins, the quivering flesh of her belly.

What now? he wondered. Is she going to launch herself over the table and thrust her sacred part straight into our faces?

She danced in front of Majid who laughed and withdrew one Palestinian pound from his wallet. She arched her back, moving in rhythm with the music, so that her hair trailed on the ground behind her and her jewelled fingers clutched at her own ankles.

I am going to spill myself all over the floor if this goes on much longer, Rishou thought.

Majid leaned forward and placed the pound note inside the sequinned covering of the woman's right breast. He ran his hand lasciviously along her flanks, but almost at once she shivered away from him and wriggled across the floor as another group of men summoned her, waving their money in the air in supplication.

"Look at her," Majid said, his voice hoarse. "She has a bottom like two steaming puddings wobbling on a tray!"

Yes, it was wonderful, Rishou thought, a Paradise on earth. Perhaps that was what was wrong. This was not Paradise. If Allah had meant women to push their sacred places into a man's face he would have put them higher up.

Majid would soon be lost to them. He wore a suit, he taught his wife English words, he called the Mufti a dirty Arab. He was becoming an effendi, like the effendis who had sold their valley to the Jews, and brought this war down on them. He was forgetting his village, and he was forgetting the old ways.

Rishou glimpsed the future, and in that vision there was no place in it for Rab'allah and good Arabs like his father and no place for the simple fellaheen who had been his neighbours all his life. He realised that no matter what he or Wagil or his father did now, they would be drawn into the vortex of the vast, modern world outside.

21

Ravenswald

Colonel Weber of the Schutzstaffeln arrived at Rosenberg Fabriken in a Mercedes limousine, a red and black swastika fluttering on the bonnet. Netanel watched the chauffeur run around the car to open the door. He glimpsed a small, round-faced man in a black peaked cap before he disappeared from view through the front doors and into the reception area directly below.

"He's here," Netanel said.

Josef barely glanced up from his papers. "He's five minutes late. Hitler would not be pleased."

"I wonder what it is this time?"

"We shall know soon enough."

Father looks perfectly calm, Netanel thought. As if this is a routine visit from our bankers rather than the SS. Sometimes Josef's poise struck him with awe; at other times he was merely frustrated with it. He wondered if he really understood how bad things were.

Frau Hochstetter knocked lightly and stepped into the room. "There is a Colonel Weber outside to see you," she said.

"Tell him I'll be with him in a moment," Josef said.

A moment later the door flew open and Colonel Weber appeared, Frau Hochstetter fussing behind him like a ward sister with an unruly patient.

"I'm sorry, Herr Rosenberg, he pushed past me – "

Poor Frau Hochstetter, Netanel thought. She is not used

143

to dealing with bullies. Until Hitler, all their clients and colleagues had been gentlemen.

"It's all right," Netanel said, and he crossed the room to greet their visitor. The SS had visited them many times in the last four years. Always a new face, each time an officer even more arrogant and more stupid than the one before.

"*Heil Hitler!*" Colonel Weber shouted.

They take themselves so seriously, Netanel thought. Have they any idea how ridiculous they look? "*Heil Rosenberg!*" Netanel said, and he returned the salute.

Colonel Weber did not appreciate the joke. He was shorter than Netanel and he had the blunted features of a pit bull. He removed his cap; completely bald. Whatever blond Aryan hairs had once grown there had disappeared long ago. He unbuttoned his overcoat and sat down, uninvited.

He ignored Netanel. "You are Herr Rosenberg," he said to Josef.

Josef indicated his son. "We are both Herr Rosenberg. Why not take a seat, Major?"

"Colonel," Weber corrected him.

Josef smiled at Netanel, sharing the joke with him. "Yes, Colonel. Of course. Shall I ask Frau Hochstetter to bring us coffee? Frau Hochstetter is the lady you trampled on as you barged in here."

"I do not have time for coffee. I am here on business."

Netanel sat down. "What is it this time? Two of your people audited all our books last month. We are paying all our taxes, including all the new ones."

"Nice office," Weber said, looking round the room. But his expression was of a man who had just bitten down on something bitter and unpleasant.

"Thank you," Josef said.

"How long have you been bleeding the people of Ravenswald?"

"We have been providing employment and bringing wealth to this town for nearly seventy-five years, Colonel Weber."

144

"You Jews like to twist words. We know what you're really up to."

"You said you had business here," Netanel interrupted. "Or do you want just to sit here and abuse us?"

Weber pulled a wad of documents from the inside pocket of his overcoat. He threw them on the desk. Josef picked them up and glanced through them quickly. They all bore the official eagle and swastika emblem of the National Socialist government.

"This is absurd," Josef said.

"What is it now?" Netanel asked him.

"They are reducing our import quota by forty per cent."

"Why?"

"Be thankful we let you stay in business at all," Weber said.

"All right," Netanel told him. "We'll cut our workforce by forty per cent."

"We will not allow you to do that. If even one job is lost, we will fine you the exact amount of that person's salary."

Netanel glanced at his father. Josef shrugged his shoulders and returned his attention to Weber. "Very clever, Major – "

"Colonel."

"– you force us to cut our profits by forty per cent while still maintaining our overheads. You are forcing us to sell."

Weber did not react.

Netanel threw the papers on the desk. "Instead of smashing our windows, you smash our profits."

"The orders are effective immediately. That is all." Weber got up to go.

"Colonel Weber," Josef said. "Do you want us to starve?"

"If you starve, you starve. *Heil Hitler!*" He clicked his heels and gave the salute. "You forgot '*Heil Rosenberg!*' this time!" he said in a mock whisper to Netanel, and walked out.

Josef and Netanel sat for a long time in silence.

"What are we going to do?" Netanel said finally.

Josef's face was the colour of ash. His head seemed suddenly too heavy for his shoulders. "There's nothing we can do. I should have listened to you a long time ago, Netya." Josef Rosenberg threw his fountain pen on the desk, a gesture of surrender. "We cannot continue here any longer. It's over."

Netanel said nothing. What was there to say?

"We must sell up. The Nazis leave us no choice." He managed a weak smile. "Perhaps they have saved us a little patch of mud in the Huleh swamps."

Netanel's attention was focused on his shoes.

Josef Rosenberg put one hand to his face to hide the sudden hot welling of tears. A man can forgive himself for many things, but being a fool is not one of them.

22

Rab'allah

Izzat had spent a lot of time around Rab'allah lately, Wagil noticed, sitting in the coffee house, arguing and gambling. Wagil welcomed his presence for Izzat was a ready ally in the many debates about the Mufti's rebellion, although Zayyad was afraid he wanted to make trouble for Rishou. Another mark in his favour, Wagil thought.

Izzat was waiting as Wagil made his way back up the hill from the coffee house. It was dusk and the Judean hills were bordered with a purple haze. The dropping of the sun should have meant a welcome relief from the torments of the day, but the hamsiin was still hot and fetid, like the breath of a jackal.

"I want to talk to you," Izzat said.

"What about?"

"What you said the other day about cutting out Sheikh Jamil's liver. Did you mean it?"

Wagil felt a shiver of alarm. Was Izzat crazy? Of course he had not meant it! If a man made good on every threat he made, there would scarcely be a dozen Arabs left in all Judea. "Sheikh Jamil can count the days he has left on this earth on the fingers of one hand." He kept walking. He had to get away from this lunatic.

"I will help you," Izzat said.

Wagil felt his panic rising. "This is a matter of honour for the Hass'an family. It has nothing to do with you."

"Sheikh Jamil has sided with the British, so he is not just your enemy, he is the enemy of all Palestine. Did you know I have joined the Holy Strugglers?"

No, Wagil thought, I did not know that. It is a miracle that your uncle would even contemplate letting you loose with a rifle after you left him with three toes missing on his left foot and a permanent limp. "I am forming my own band in Rab'allah," Wagil lied.

"Your father has spoken against it."

"I am my own man now."

"If only all Arabs were like you," Izzat said. "We should run these Jews out of Palestine in a week!"

Wagil accepted the compliment with a solemn "*Insh'allah*," and walked faster.

But Izzat kept pace with him. "So we are agreed then? Sheikh Jamil must face the consequences of his betrayal."

"Let him know I am sharpening my blade!"

"We will do it together. Tomorrow night!"

Wagil almost stumbled and fell. Kill Sheikh Jamil? Bring the British soldiers and a clan feud down on all their heads? Was he mad? If he was so eager to see blood spilled, why did he not do the deed himself? "I shall do it alone. It will be no more difficult than snapping the neck of a chicken."

"You underestimate him, my friend. He has bodyguards

147

with him night and day. He knows the dangers of what he has done. You will not get close enough to use your knife, celebrated though it is."

"I shall find a way," Wagil said, delighted that Izzat had furnished him with his excuse for failure.

"If you had a gun you could do it," Izzat went on, relentlessly. "I can get you one."

"I want to see the dog's eyes when he dies."

They were almost to the top of the hill, at the house. In a few moments I can get away from this madman, Wagil thought.

"I think you are afraid," Izzat said.

Wagil span around. "Wagil Hass'an is not afraid of anything!"

"Your father's right. You talk a big wind and fart like a beetle!"

"I will cut out your liver!"

"Your father is ashamed of you. Everyone knows it."

Wagil swayed on his feet. He should reach for his knife, he knew, but his arms hung useless at his sides. Izzat grinned, enjoying himself. His eyes bored into him, as if he could see into his head, see every frightened shadow that dwelt there.

"I can get you an Enfield," Izzat said. "It will cost you ten pounds, but it will be worth it. It can shoot for twenty miles. We can kill Sheikh Jamil and be back in our villages before he hits the ground. We'll be heroes. Even the Mufti will hear of our great feat."

"Ten pounds is a lot of money," Wagil said.

"Then sell some of Hamdah's jewellery. It will be worth it. Do you want your father making fun of you in the coffee house for the rest of your life?"

Is that how the rest of the people see me? Wagil wondered, and he suddenly wanted to move his bowels. Has my father really made me so ridiculous? "I will shoot out Sheikh Jamil's heart," he said, "and then I will kill you."

"I am not your enemy, Wagil. You will see."

Wagil heard the trap close. "I fart in your face!"

Izzat ignored the insult. "Bring the money to the coffee

148

house tomorrow. If you do not have the money, bring jewels. I will arrange the trade through my uncle. He buys guns all the time for our *mujahideen*. He will get you a fine rifle, you will be the envy of all Rab'allah!"

Wagil turned and walked away. He wanted to weep. Izzat had led him up a high mountain and the way back had crumbled away behind him. Now he would have to jump or he might as well put on the veil and be a woman. He wanted to be angry but he was only very, very afraid.

"We will be heroes!" Izzat called after him, in the darkness.

Heroes, Wagil muttered. He wanted desperately to be a hero. But all he could see in his future was death.

Talbieh

Henry Talbot sat at the table in the courtyard while Majid fetched his breakfast. It was the time of the day that he liked the best. It was cool out here on the flagged stones, and his neighbour's fig tree had spread its long branches over the wall and offered shade from the early morning sun. He relished this hour of peace and solitude; Elizabeth never rose before midday, and he was able to enjoy his breakfast alone.

The courtyard formed a long rectangle, the top half enclosed by the wings of the house. At one end double glass doors opened on to the main sitting-room; on the right, a wooden door led to old Hasna's quarters; on the other was the kitchen and dining-room. The rest of the court was surrounded by a high, whitewashed wall, with niches of blue and white ceramic cut into it, holding terracotta flowerpots of geraniums. At the far end of the yard two tall Aleppo pines snuggled next to each other, whispering in the breeze like adolescent lovers.

Majid brought Talbot's breakfast on a silver tray; Rose's marmalade, butter, toast, crisp-fried bacon, an omelette, and a pot of Ceylon tea. He set the tray down, carefully arranging the heavy silver knife and fork on each side of the plate. He placed the toast rack in the centre of the table next to the butter and marmalade, and poured tea from the silver teapot into a china cup.

He set the napkin on Talbot's lap, as he had been shown, and picked up the silver tray, about to return to the kitchen. Instead he hesitated, waiting by Talbot's shoulder.

Talbot put a piece of the omelette into his mouth, and then looked questioningly at Majid. "Something wrong, Majid?"

"Forgive me, effendi. I have woes which afflict me greatly."

Talbot suppressed a smile. He had lent Majid some old schoolboy grammar texts to help him with his English, but some of the results had been bizarre. "Can I be of any help?"

"If you will excuse me, effendi, that is my wish."

Talbot put down his knife and fork and wiped his lips with his napkin. "Well, you'd better tell me then."

"It is a matter of some delicacy, effendi. My father, as you know, is a great man in his village. He has been muktar at Rab'allah for many years. Now he has been terribly humiliated. A British army soldier has come and appointed another as muktar, someone no better than the droppings of a diseased camel, if you will pardon me, effendi. It is a calamity of terrible proportion. My whole village is full of woe. My father is the King of Britannia's most loyal friend, as everyone in Palestine knows, and it is impossible to describe in mere words the injustice of this act."

Talbot sipped his tea. He knew all about this new policy of the government's. The directive had come straight from London, where they thought they knew all about Arab affairs in Palestine, having recently, no doubt, bought themselves a map of Jerusalem. It was galling, but as Mandate officials he and every other British civil servant in Palestine were sworn to see that such directives were properly administered, even if they violently disagreed with them.

"What was this British soldier's name?" he asked.

"His name was Captain Terrence Mannion," Majid said, repeating what Rishou had told him the night before. "He is the muktar of Ipswich."

"All right. Leave it with me, Majid. I will make enquiries and see what I can do." It was unlikely that he could do anything, of course. The army was merely carrying out official government policy. But if this Mannion had made a personal judgment in the field, perhaps he might be able to use his influence to persuade him to reconsider. On the other hand, the British army resented interference from any civil servant, especially one from their own country, so it might well be a forlorn hope. But he could try.

"Thank you, effendi," Majid said. "My family will be utterly grateful. Splendid. Jolly splendid."

"I cannot guarantee anything."

"Yes, effendi. Yes, of course," he said, but it was obvious from Majid's manner that he already considered it as good as done.

Majid disappeared into the kitchen, and Talbot returned his attention to his breakfast. Damned shame what we're doing to these people with our dithering, he thought. We won't make a stand against the Mufti and we won't make a stand against the Zionists. We're the jam in the sandwich and one day we're going to find ourselves being squeezed out.

Beit Shabus

Izzat and Wagil hid among the fig trees above the village until dusk, and then picked their way carefully down the slope, rifles clutched in their right hands. A full moon rose above the hills, huge and blood red.

Their noses knew they were close to the village before

151

their eyes; the scent was a familiar amalgam of cardamom and incense and sewage. When they reached the edge of the orchard they threw themselves down on their bellies and waited. The village was in darkness except for the muted orange glow of cooking fires. They heard dogs quarrelling in the dirt over scraps and a man relieving himself in a nearby ditch.

The moon climbed the night sky, illuminating the village like one of the Jews' searchlights. It was easy to pick out Sheikh Jamil's house. Clan heads all had stone houses, and they were the only ones who could afford outside toilets. The sheikh had also purchased a kerosene lantern, at great expense, and it glowed from the windows of his house, high up the hill, with a fierce white light.

Wagil lay quite still, heard the sound of his own blood roaring in his ears. He had no idea what to do next. The plans they had made did not extend further than buying an extra rifle.

"What now?" Wagil hissed.

"We'll hide near the house and wait for him to come out."

"What if he doesn't?"

"Then we will come back again tomorrow," Izzat said, and Wagil detected a tremor in his voice. This camel's arse is more frightened than I am, he thought. He is praying that Sheikh Jamil will not appear so he can say that circumstance conspired against him.

"That sounds like a good plan," Wagil said, and the blackness of his panic was lightened by the first stirrings of hope. They would lie here for a while in the dirt, until everyone was asleep, and then go home. He would have a gun to show everyone and he could go on making up as many lies as he wanted. Perhaps tonight would not turn out so badly after all.

Izzat rested his forehead on the stock of the Mauser. Now that the waiting had taken the edge from his fear, fatigue had overtaken him. He closed his eyes and thought about his uncle. For three years he had lived with the humiliation

152

of the events at Rishou's wedding. When Sheikh Daoud had formed a band of Holy Strugglers at his village, he had bestowed on Izzat the rank of lieutenant, the lowest rank then on offer. Everyone else was either a major or captain. They might just as well have made him regimental mascot.

Well, now he would show them how great he was. And if he missed with his shot and the bodyguards fired back at them, he would drill Wagil through the back and leave him there as sacrifice while he made his escape. There would be no falling down gullies this time.

Wagil stroked the barrel of his new rifle, enjoying the cool feel of the metal, the sense of masculine power it gave him. Izzat had been as good as his word. It was a bolt-action Lee Enfield, and Izzat said that Lawrence himself had fired it at the Turks. Wagil doubted that it could truly fire twenty miles but it was a fine weapon just the same. From now on, he decided, he would carry it with him everywhere.

It was late. Soon, he decided, they could make their way back through the fig orchards and the ordeal would be over. He would have proved his bravery to Izzat.

He could hear the murmur of men's voices carried on the night wind from Sheikh Jamil's house. Izzat said that he had at least five bodyguards with him at all times, and they were all armed with rifles. It was madness to have even contemplated this, he thought.

But what a story it would make tomorrow at the coffee house! With a few embellishments, of course.

The moon had moved far across the sky. The night was still, given up to the rhythmic rustlings of the cicadas. Wagil shook Izzat's shoulder. "Wake up."

Izzat started awake. "What is it?"

"Nothing. They are all asleep. Let's go home."

Izzat rubbed his face. "All right. But you suggested it first."

"Nothing is going to happen tonight," Wagil said, and as he looked up he saw movement in front of the house. A tall

153

man, holding a kerosene lantern in his right hand, stepped out of the door and began to make his way towards the outhouse. The lantern illuminated his face clearly; it was Sheikh Jamil.

Before they could react he disappeared inside the toilet.

"It's him," Wagil said.

He could hear Izzat's breathing.

"It's him," he repeated.

"I know."

"What are we going to do?"

Izzat wiped his hands on his abbayah and sighted his rifle. Wagil copied his movement. *Allah help me!* From the toilet came the sound of Sheikh Jamil breaking wind. It was followed by a loud groan as he voided his bowels.

Izzat giggled, a high-pitched, nervous sound.

Wagil felt as if there were an iron band around his chest. It was going to happen. They were going to do it!

The door opened and Sheikh Jamil stepped out, holding the lantern above his head, making himself the perfect target.

I'll let Izzat fire first, Wagil thought. Perhaps he won't do it. Perhaps he will leave it too late.

Sheikh Jamil was almost back at the house.

Wagil watched him through the sight, his vision blurred with sweat, praying, praying.

The sound of the shot was so close it made him cry out. He saw Sheikh Jamil stagger and slump down the wall. The kerosene lantern fell out of his hand, the glass splintering on the ground.

Darkness.

Wagil lay quite still, listening to the sound of Izzat running. He couldn't move. We did it, he thought. *We did it!* Fear, panic, awe pounded through his veins. Men rushed out of the house, their cries of alarm echoing through the village.

I have to get away from here!

He leaped to his feet and started to run. He suddenly realised he did not have his gun. Too late to go back for

154

it. He ran faster, gulping in lungfuls of air, tripping and scrambling on the rocks underfoot.

A shadow loomed ahead of him. Something hit him hard in the chest and he slammed backwards on to the ground.

He sat up, gasping for breath. The man he had collided with sat up too, gaping at him in surprise. This close, his face was plainly visible in the light of the full moon. It was Naji, Sheikh Jamil's nephew. He knew him, they sometimes drank coffee together in the coffee house!

Wagil leaped to his feet and stumbled away, through the trees.

Allah help me. What shall I do now?

23

Rab'allah

When Captain Terrence Mannion returned to Rab'allah he was expecting trouble. He brought with him a British CID inspector and two Jewish members of the Palestine police. In the armoured car behind him was a squad of infantrymen from the Royal Suffolks.

The murder of Sheikh Jamil was a direct challenge to British authority in the area. Fortunately, the perpetrator had been recognised at the scene and the witness, the dead man's nephew, was willing to testify in court. Mannion was convinced the assassination had been inspired by the Mufti and it vindicated his decision to remove the existing muktar from his position of influence.

This time, as the convoy wound its way through the narrow streets, there were no children, no curious faces; they were greeted with hostile stares and sullen silence. Everyone knew why they had come.

When they reached the muktar's house, Zayyad and Rishou Hass'an were waiting for them.

"I have a warrant for the arrest of Wagil Hass'an," the CID inspector, Cooper, told Rishou.

Rishou translated this to Zayyad, then turned back to Cooper. "My father wants to know why you want to take his son."

Cooper glanced at the crowd of villagers pressing in around them. Mannion's men looked nervous. They were grouped in a semicircle behind them, their eyes watchful. Their rifles were still at slope, but the knuckles on the stocks of their guns were white.

Cooper was a big man, over six feet three inches, and he had twelve years' experience of this work in the Holy Land. He had faced down hostile crowds before; he knew how to bluff.

"Last night Sheikh Jamil was murdered at Beit Shabus. There are several witnesses who saw your son fire the shot that killed him." Well, only one witness perhaps, and he only saw him after the fact. But such subtleties could wait for the courtroom. At the moment he needed to make a good impression.

Rishou translated what Cooper had said.

Zayyad looked incredulous. "My son does not own a rifle and he does not have the brains to kill anyone with one if he had. The boy couldn't find his own member in the dark if it wasn't tied on."

"My father says his son does not own a rifle," Rishou translated, "so he could not possibly have done this."

"We have witnesses," Cooper insisted. "You must tell us where he is."

"I have authority to use force if necessary," Mannion added, and Cooper winced. Bluff was one thing. Stupidity was something else.

"My father says to tell you he has made a pilgrimage to Mecca," Rishou said, "and to go piss up a camel's leg!"

*　　*　　*

Wagil stood behind the door of the house and listened to the argument between the British policemen and his father. On the other side of the room the women watched him, their faces white with terror. Wagil was ashamed to be hiding here with the women, listening to his father make jokes about him.

"The big policeman says he has a sworn statement from a witness," he heard Rishou telling his father.

Naji! Wagil thought. I should have cut his throat!

"Then my son must have a double," Zayyad was saying. "And if they find him, tell him I will happily swap him for Wagil."

Wagil gritted his teeth and willed back the angry tears. The injustice of it seared him like a hot iron. He had had Sheikh Jamil in his sights, hadn't he? So it was Izzat who fired the shot. Did it matter? It was luck that Izzat had been the one to kill him first. Did he then deserve to be humiliated in front of everyone like this?

"They say they have a warrant to search our house," Rishou told Zayyad.

"Then you had better call out to your brother to get out from under the bed and jump out the window quick," Zayyad said.

"No!" Wagil screamed and he stepped out into the sunlight.

Cooper smiled. This was an unexpected development. He had not expected the muktar's son to still be here. This was going to look good on his record.

Zayyad threw up his hands in despair. "What are you doing?"

"I did it!" he shouted at his father. "I did it. Not Rishou, not Majid, me! Your first son, the one who cannot find his cock in the dark! I took your revenge for you." A thread of saliva spilled from his chin. He turned to the rest of the villagers. "I did it! I killed Sheikh Jamil! With one shot! Boom!"

"Shut up," Zayyad said.

"No, not any more! I won't shut up for you any more!

157

You always make fun of me to everyone! I did it! I killed him!"

With a nod of his head Cooper signalled for the two policemen to grab Wagil. One of them forced his arms behind his back while the other efficiently locked on the handcuffs. There was an angry murmur from the villagers.

"Don't be stupid, Wagil," Rishou was saying. "If you confess to the police they will hang you!"

Wagil ignored him. "Are you still ashamed?" he shouted at Zayyad. "Do you want to find the other Wagil and trade me for him?"

The two policemen pulled Wagil towards the jeep. Rishou tried to stop them but Cooper insinuated his bulk in the way. "Don't sign anything, Wagil!" Rishou shouted. "They'll hang you!"

"What's going on?" Mannion asked Cooper as they backed towards the jeep. "What are they shouting about?"

Cooper's knowledge of Arabic was limited. "I think the muktar's son is telling them he did the murder. I don't think his brother's very happy about it." He kept his big frame between Wagil and the other Arabs until his prisoner was seated in the back of the jeep between the police.

The soldiers made an orderly retreat to their armoured car. The crowd pressed in after them. "Let's get out of here," Mannion said.

Rishou had jumped on the running board of the jeep. "Don't sign anything, Wagil. I will go and see Majid, and Talbot effendi will get you out of prison. Just don't confess to them!"

Mannion started the engine and crunched the jeep into gear. The impetus jerked Rishou from the running board. The jeep sped out of the village, Rishou and a number of the villagers running after it. Several of them stopped to pick up small stones and hurl them in the jeep's direction. Then the armoured car rumbled out of the square, sending them scattering into the alleys and doorways on either side.

Rishou watched the trail of dust as the convoy made its way back down the valley. When he turned around the square was empty. Everyone had trudged away, the women to gossip and weep at the well, the men to sit in morose silence in the coffee house.

Zayyad spread his hands in a gesture of despair. His father, who had been a giant for all of Rishou's life, suddenly looked very small and very old.

Jerusalem

Wagil felt light-headed, as if he had smoked too much hashish. He could tell the Britishers were impressed with him. He had not displayed to them even the slightest sign of fear. Cooper seemed to admire the calm with which he had described the assassination of Sheikh Jamil; how he had waited, with infinite patience and courage outside the sheikh's house and then drilled the sheikh through the forehead with his first shot, even though the night was black; how he deliberately left his rifle behind because he would not sully his hands further with any weapon required to dispatch such a diseased dog as Sheikh Jamil.

An Arab policeman sitting beside Cooper translated everything into English, and a British policeman sitting at a card table in the corner of the room banged away on an ancient typewriter, transcribing it all on to clean white sheets of paper. When he had finished they asked him to sign his name at the bottom of the typewritten page and he hesitated for only a moment.

They would all be talking about him in Rab'allah. His father would be tearing at his robe and crying to Allah to forgive him for all the insults he had hurled at his eldest and bravest son; Rishou would be skulking, ashamed, in his shadow now and for ever; Hamdah would be weeping, doomed to spend the rest of her days in torment now she realised how she had spurned such a hero.

159

And Izzat! What must Izzat be going through? Wagil wondered. He must be convinced by now that I have named him to the British. When he discovers I have saved his yellow jackal's hide, what will he think? Will he offer up his prayers to Allah for my sake? Or will he spit up his bile in useless anger, knowing he did not have the courage to join me in Paradise as a true martyr for Palestine?

Martyr!

He knew he should be afraid, but instead he just wanted to laugh in these policemen's faces because in the end it was all so easy and he only wished he could be there at his own funeral to see all their faces, and drink in their sorrow and regret.

Cooper looked at the piece of paper in his hand with the expression of a man who has received a small but unexpected gift. This would look good on his record. So many of these internecine assassinations had gone unsolved and unpunished in recent months. This one made him look like Sherlock Holmes.

He studied his prisoner. The man was obviously a few shillings short of a pound. Look at that stupid grin on his face and the unnatural glaze of his eyes. He suspected there was more to this, but you should never look a gift horse in the mouth, as his mother used to say. He had a signed confession, and that was that as far as he was concerned.

He had told the stenographer to omit the part about Wagil drilling the deceased through the forehead. In fact, the bullet had entered the victim's right lung, and the old sheikh had taken several painful, gurgling hours to die. Still, in his experience every murderer liked to elaborate a little.

There was a rifle standing in the corner of the room. Cooper got up and brought it over to the table, holding it carefully at the rim of the stock and the point of the barrel. He laid it on the table in front of Wagil.

"Tell him this gun was found at the murder scene," he said to the interpreter. "Ask him if it belongs to him."

The interpreter translated. "Yes, he says that is the rifle he used to kill Sheikh Jamil. He asks that it be returned to his family."

"We'll have to see about that," Cooper said. It was all so neat. A signed confession, even a rifle left at the spot from which the bullet was fired. The only problem was the ballistics report. The bullet which killed the sheikh was a .257 and the rifle on the table was .313. Also, there were no powder burns in the barrel, so it was certainly not the murder weapon, contrary to what Wagil Hass'an would have them believe.

Cooper decided he would not waste his precious time trying to fit the facts to the solution. Not for one dead Arab. The ballistics report could easily get lost in a file somewhere. It had happened before. And the problem about the powder marks could be solved just as simply. As soon as the interview was over he would go outside and fire the rifle into a tree.

Why this fool would want to confess to a murder he obviously had not committed was beyond him. But he was not employed to understand people's motives, just to solve crimes. The bastard had said he did it. What did it matter whether he did or not?

"All right, take him to his cell," he said to a constable. "But no rough stuff. Make sure he gets plenty to eat. Bastard's done me a favour, least I can do is show some gratitude."

Henry Talbot stood on the balcony and stared at the panorama of the city with the same reverence he had experienced on his very first day in Jerusalem, almost three years before. He could never overcome the sensation of having been transported through time and dimension into the musty pages of a Bible. The name Jerusalem had assumed a mythical quality, like Babylon and Jericho. At school in Guildford it was not until he was in third year that he had realised that the city still existed. Every time he looked at the city he could hear boys' voices echoing along draughty cloisters:

161

I shall not cease from mental fight,
Nor shall my sword sleep in my hand
Till we have built JER-U-SALEM!
In England's green and pleasant land . . .

England had instead built its own monuments on
Jerusalem. On the crest of a rise in Julian's Way the
King David Hotel dominated the Jerusalem skyline, an
ugly six-storey slab of concrete, one wing home to a
thousand minor government departments, part of the
vast bureaucracy that the British had brought with them
to Palestine; and in the distance were the tree-clad slopes
of Mount Scopus, scarred with the neat white lines of the
British War Cemetery, a permanent reminder of the price
they had paid for the Holy City, the crosses even more
significant of sacrifice here, the white graves as stark as
bone against the dark background of pines.

To the south, beyond a grove of olive trees, stood the
wooded rise where the High Commissioner of Palestine
had his residence. The place's name was the Hill of
Evil Counsel, a joke that was not lost among the local
population. There, remote among the tranquillity of the
rose bushes and Aleppo pines, Sir Alec McIntosh faced a
Pandora's box. Balfour had released the demons in 1917
when he had promised Palestine to the Jews. The British
government of the time had allowed the Jews to flood into
the country, and although they had now put restrictions on
Jewish immigration, it was too little, too late. Along with
the monster of Zionism, Balfour had unwittingly released
another devil: Palestinian nationalism.

These two beasts would shake the very earth of Palestine,
Talbot decided, shake it with forces it had not experienced
for two thousand years. He feared they would shake the
High Commissioner off his hill, and send the walls of the
King David tumbling to the ground, and add more white
crosses to the cemetery on Mount Scopus.

But there was nothing he could do to stop it, as there
was nothing he could do about the next grave now being
dug in the baked earth of the Judean hills above Rab'allah.

162

The report he had received from the police sergeant at Jerusalem CID headquarters was conclusive. Wagil Hass'an had made a full signed confession. There was absolutely nothing he could do to save him. Poor Majid. He had begged him for help, pathetically convinced that Talbot had the power of Pilate over his brother. What was he going to tell him?

The government would hold Wagil Hass'an accountable for the murder of Sheikh Jamil; yet if we were truly to apportion blame, Talbot thought, what about Mannion? He was the one who had incited these passions by arbitrarily replacing Zayyad Hass'an with his own spy. He had some fault in this.

And if we are to follow the tributaries of blame to their source, he decided, then we should also hang the fool in Whitehall who first dreamed up this stupidity; the man who, without knowledge or experience of Arab affairs, thought it appropriate to issue the directive Mannion sought to carry out. Blind ignorance had killed Sheikh Jamil, and blind ignorance had written Wagil Hass'an's death warrant.

And blind ignorance would kill many more before the Mandate in Palestine was finally declared at an end.

24

Sir Alec McIntosh looked up from his desk as Talbot entered. His First Secretary stood behind him, holding a file, indicating where Sir Alec should sign his name on the papers in front of him.

"Ah, Talbot," he said. "Won't keep you a moment."

"Yes, sir." Talbot waited until Sir Alec laid down his pen.

Sir Alec leaned back in his chair. "Got a strong stomach?"

Talbot wondered where this line of enquiry might lead. "Same as the next man, I suppose, sir."

"There's an execution tomorrow morning at the prison. I need someone to attend on behalf of His Majesty's Government. I would have sent Simpson but he's in Acre at the moment."

Talbot felt the blood drain from his cheeks. "I see."

"Ten o'clock. Be there in good time, won't you?" The First Secretary laid another document on the desk in front of him and the High Commissioner picked up his pen.

"Yes, sir," Talbot said, and he left the room.

Wagil was handcuffed, unshaven and dirty. He sat cross-legged on the floor of his cell, his head bowed. He did not look up when the warden unlocked the door, even when he heard his father's voice.

"Wagil," Zayyad moaned. "What have they done to you?"

Zayyad squatted down and shook him by the shoulders. Wagil raised his head. He was pale, and there were dark bruises under his eyes from lack of sleep.

"My son," Zayyad murmured.

"So you are proud of me at last!"

"Please forgive me."

Wagil did not answer him. He looked up at Rishou. "Ah, little brother."

Rishou heard the tremor in his voice. He does not want to die now, Rishou thought. Whatever madness made him sign that confession, he does not want to die now.

"What are they saying about me in the village?" Wagil asked.

"That you are a lion and a hero of Palestine," Rishou said. Well, some of them were saying that. Others were saying he should have run away and hid with the Bedouin, that he was crazy to have surrendered so easily. But Sheikh Daoud was delighted of course. Any enemy of the British was a friend of the Mufti, and he was gratified that Zayyad

164

had finally proved his loyalty to the cause with the sacrifice of his eldest son.

"There is still a chance," Zayyad said. "Majid has spoken to Talbot effendi. He has written to the King of Britannia himself!"

"I had to do it," Wagil told Zayyad. "I knew Rishou did not have the stomach for it."

A snake to the end, Rishou thought.

"Forgive me," Zayyad was saying. "Say you forgive me for the wrong I have done to you."

"At last you see what a lion I am! This son of yours who cannot find his member in the dark!"

"Please, Wagil. I have humbled myself, in the sight of Allah. Give me your forgiveness so I can live the rest of my life in peace!"

Wagil shook his head. "I will never forgive you," he said.

In the morning, with the sun rising from behind the Mount of Olives, there is a mist haze over the Jordan valley; but at dusk the light is clear and luminous, and the grey ramparts of the mountains are suffused with violet, the shadows of the gullies stark and sable.

Henry and Elizabeth Talbot watched the light show taking place before them with detached interest. They drank their limes and bitters in silence, alone with their own private disappointments. They dressed formally for dinner, as was their custom, Talbot in a tuxedo, Elizabeth in a white muslin gown, and went downstairs.

The bells of the Church of the Holy Sepulchre tolled the angelus, and the muezzins called the faithful to prayer.

The city still shimmered with heat, but here, in the black-and-white-tiled dining-room, it was cool. The rose-wood table was set with Irish linen napkins and Wedgwood china. A piece of Waterford crystal, smeared with pink lipstick, rang as Elizabeth circled the wet rim with a forefinger.

"Please don't do that," Talbot said.

"Bothering you, dearest?"

"It weakens the crystal."

"Stupid of me. I should hate to vandalise our best dinnerware."

"I don't mean to be sharp. I have a lot on my mind."

Elizabeth lowered her voice. "I hear Majid's brother is going to swing tomorrow." She put a hand to her pretty throat and squeezed, lolling her tongue from the side of her mouth.

"That's not funny."

"Well not if one is the one about to swing, I suppose. But you only have to stand and watch, don't you, dearest?"

"That is quite bad enough."

"I have never seen a hanging. I shall rely on you for a detailed description."

Majid crossed the courtyard from the kitchen carrying two plates. Lamb chops and baby potatoes. They sat in silence as he set down the plates and refilled their glasses with French burgundy.

Elizabeth watched Majid return to the kitchen. "He is bearing up rather well, don't you think?"

"Can we drop this subject, please?"

"I'm sorry, dearest. Is it upsetting you?"

"Perhaps you would like to witness the execution in my place."

"I shouldn't mind."

"You should have been born a man."

"So should you, dearest."

Talbot ignored the remark. He cut the lamb, bloody juice running from the pink centre. He imagined it was her heart.

"Does he know you're going to be there tomorrow? When they hang his brother?"

"No."

"How droll," Elizabeth said, and she sipped her wine, and dabbed at the vermilion stain on her lips, "how terribly droll."

25

It was hot inside the execution chamber. There were no windows: the only light came from an electric bulb in the ceiling, covered with an iron grille. The room was empty except for the scaffolding.

Sweat ran into his eyes, stinging like salt, and beads of it trickled down the length of his back. His shirt was soaked.

Yet he felt cold.

The governor was a Yorkshireman, Weatherby, a short man with a thick egg-yellow moustache that reminded Talbot of a straw broom. There were heavy pouches under his eyes and his cheeks were a patchwork of tiny veins. Drink, Talbot guessed. He was dressed for a funeral, in shabby black suit and tie, but his demeanour was of a man waiting for the delayed start of a third division football match.

Weatherby looked at his watch. "Dreary affairs, hangings."

"I wouldn't know," Talbot said.

Weatherby grunted. "I've dropped more than I can count these last twelve months." He dabbed at the sweat on his face with a handkerchief. "I've spoken to your Simpson about this. Ten o'clock is too late for this sort of business. You should have a word with that Alec Whatsisname. Tell him we should get under way much earlier int' morning. Too damned hot by ten o'clock in summer."

Talbot realised Weatherby was talking about the High Commissioner. "I shall bring it to Sir Alec's attention," he said.

Weatherby looked at his watch again. "I do hope this one don't make a fuss. Some of them do, you know," he said, as if Talbot should find it surprising that men were sometimes reluctant to die.

"Perhaps he will find comfort in his faith. I take it an imam will be present?"

"A what? No, no, we have none of that here. If they wants a priest, they can have one. If you ask me, that's mumbo jumbo enough. When you die, you die, the rest is between you and the worms."

"You refuse a condemned man the succour of his religion?"

Weatherby looked at Talbot with an expression of utter disdain. "If you have complaints about the way I do things, Mr Talbot, you'd better tell old Whatsisname. But I run a tight ship here, and I don't have any time to have vicars in bedsheets boogerising around."

Heavy footsteps in the corridor outside. The chief warden led in the execution party. Wagil followed, dressed in the traditional scarlet uniform of the condemned. He was chained hand and foot, supported by a warden on either side. When he saw the gibbet, he screamed and started to struggle.

Weatherby blew through his moustache. "Oh, bloody 'ell, a screamer. Too hot for screamers today. Isn't it, Mr Talbot?"

The bedroom was still in darkness. The Rod That Allah Sent To Test Us did not rise before noon as a rule, but this morning she had specifically requested that her breakfast be brought to her at ten o'clock. Majid instinctively understood the perverse nature of the request. Ten o'clock was the time set for his brother's execution.

"Good morning, Majid."

"Good morning, Lady Talbot."

She was wearing a heavy lace nightgown and eyeshades made of black felt. She lay on her back, her arms folded across her chest. Like a corpse laid out for wailing, Majid

168

thought. Does she lie this way when her English captain covers her?

"Put it on the table."

Majid placed the covered silver breakfast tray on the table by the bed. Egg all mixed up and bits of pig and blackened bread. He did not understand how people could eat such disgusting things.

"Draw the curtains, will you?"

The windows were set deep in the thick stone walls, keeping the house cool. Majid drew the heavy gold brocade curtains and yellow sunlight flooded into the room.

The Rod That Allah Sent To Test Us blinked as she removed her eyeshades. She sat up. "A glorious morning."

"Yes, Lady Talbot."

"It's going to be a wonderful day."

Was she taunting him? "Yes, a wonderful day, Lady Talbot."

"Run my bath, will you?"

Majid went into the next room and ran hot water into the clawfoot bath. Such luxury still awed him. His own father would bathe once a week, the women heating pots of water in the kitchen and pouring it into a tin bath in the living-room. In Rab'allah it was considered a great extravagance. But here was this Britisher woman taking a hot bath every morning, the water running freely out of a tap. She had sweetly perfumed soap and bottles of lotions lining the shelves and even something called a sponge to wash the dirt from her body. Not that she ever did anything to make herself dirty. The most labour she ever performed was pulling out her piano stool.

He returned to the bedroom. "Your bath is ready, Lady Talbot."

Elizabeth got out of bed, and with one motion lifted the nightgown over her head. She held out her hand. "Fetch me my towel, will you?"

Majid did not hear her. He could only stare. The Rod That Allah Sent To Test Us was indeed skinny, as he suspected, her breasts were small, but her nipples were

169

pink – *pink! like roses!* – and her flesh was as white as milk. She had freed her hair from whatever arcane devices she used to restrain it and he was astonished to find that it was not straight but hung around her shoulders in black coils.

This is not happening, he thought. I have caught a fever of the brain and this is some sort of mirage.

"Did you hear me? I said, fetch my towel."

He took a step towards her.

"What are you doing?" There was alarm in her voice.

"You are beautiful," he said.

"I hope you are not going to take advantage of this situation. I am quite helpless. There is nothing I can do to stop you."

He took another step towards her. Allah, help me! If I touch her, they will hang me too!

"I tried to fight you. You were too strong," Elizabeth said.

"You're begging for it, aren't you?"

"There was just nothing I could do."

Majid undid the buttons of his trousers. "What you need is a good Arab cock."

"Possibly," Elizabeth said.

What was he thinking of? At this very moment his own brother was meeting a martyr's death. How could he even contemplate this? Had not Majid sacrificed everything for Palestine? Was it not this woman's husband who was at this very moment watching own brother jerk at the end of a rope?

Her skin was cool and soft and white. White! Fuck Palestine, fuck the British. And fuck Wagil too.

Wagil's hands were cuffed behind his back, his ankles chained together. A warder pinioned his elbows on either side. But still he somehow managed to delay the moment of his dying by several minutes. He resisted with his bare heels on the concrete, leaving bloody smears on the floor. He fought them with all the strength he had, while the men struggled and sweated and swore.

"FATHER!" Wagil screamed, "FATHER, HELP ME! PLEASE HELP ME!!"

Weatherby had had enough. He nodded to the chief warden who took out his baton and with great precision hammered it into Wagil's stomach, then slammed it down over his shoulders. Wagil sagged, his spirit broken.

"Get on with it," Weatherby said.

Talbot felt faint, and steadied himself against the wall.

They dragged Wagil to the scaffold. He gasped out something in Arabic.

"What did he say?" Weatherby asked.

"He said, 'See the way a Hass'an can die,'" Talbot translated.

Weatherby snorted with derision and nodded again to his chief warden, who took a black hood from his pocket and placed it over Wagil's head. He put the noose in place and drew it tight. Talbot was suddenly aware of a foul odour in the room. Wagil had soiled himself.

Weatherby held a handkerchief to his nose. "Jesus Christ." His hand went to the lever at the foot of the scaffold. "Get clear!"

The wardens stepped back. He slammed the lever over.

Wagil fell through the wooden trapdoor that was set in the concrete floor under the gibbet, only to be brought up short as the rope ran out. The shock shook the scaffolding, and Talbot thought he could hear Wagil's neck break. The hangman's knot, Talbot was relieved to see, had been a good one. Wagil hung limp, the neck twisted at an obscene angle from the body, already dead. Silence now except for the panting of the wardens, still recovering from the struggle with their victim.

"Well, we all saw the way a Hass'an can die," Weatherby said. "Like every other bloody wretch who comes in here. Well, that's it, Mr Talbot. Hope to see you again some day. Don't forget to tell old Whatsisname about those earlier starting times."

Talbot hurried out, desperate to get out of these dark

171

cellars, away from the terrible, creaking sound of the swinging rope.

Majid stared at the vaulted ceiling, his hands behind his head. In his mind he was composing the story he would tell the next time he returned to Rab'allah. He toyed with the small black moustache on his upper lip. It was a fine moustache. It made him even more handsome, he decided. Perhaps it was the moustache that had finally driven The Rod That Allah Sent To Test Us crazy with desire for him.

Elizabeth sat up and reached for Majid's shirt, and wiped herself with it. She tossed it at him and got up from the bed. "Thank you, Majid, that will be all."

He stared at her in astonishment. His shirt! What had she done with his *shirt*? It was the most disgusting thing he could possibly imagine. And she was a Britisher *lady*!

"I said, that will be all, Majid."

"But Elizabeth . . ."

"Majid, in the circles in which I move, a single act of intercourse does not constitute a formal introduction. If you ever call me that again, I shall have to ask my husband to dismiss you." She put on her robe and stared at his body with the expression of a woman examining used goods at a market. "I believe you are married?"

He reached for his clothes. He did not like her looking at him like that. "Yes," he said.

"I beg your pardon, Majid?"

"Yes, Lady Talbot."

"Well, a word of advice. If I were you I should go home and practise my technique before performing in public again. Now I shall go and take my bath. Take the breakfast things as you go."

The bathroom door closed. Majid dressed and hurried out of the room. Blooming bitch! Blooming, blooming bitch!

Part Five

GERMANY AND PALESTINE, 1938

26

Ravenswald

The vine leaves on the front of the house had turned a
rich red-brown with the coming of autumn. They were
facing another winter and for the first time in Netanel's
life he feared it. As a child it had meant ice-skating and
snow-heavy pine branches brushing the window panes and
Hanukkah, the Feast of Lights, and his mother's warm
broths and bird tracks on the lawn like tiny arrows. But
this winter there would be only large, cold rooms and
watery *Knochensuppe* and dread.

Familiar sounds he had grown up with were suddenly
silent; like the maids opening the shutters in the mornings
or Mr Taborski shovelling the coke into the boilers in the
basement under the house. But now the servants were
all gone.

Mutti now prepared and served all the meals herself.
"It is no hardship to me," she said. "When I was a girl
I had to do everything at home. I had five brothers and
they were no help *at all*."

Netanel soon learned to stoke the boiler himself, but
then the coal man refused to deliver any more coke: "I'm
sorry, Herr Rosenberg, I really am, but the SA have been
to see me, and they have warned me not to sell any more
coal to Jews." So with each shovelful the black mountain
shrank a little more. Soon it would all be gone.

The factory was gone too, sold. They had been paid
one-third of the true value of the business, and their buyer
had counted himself a generous man to give even that to a
family of desperate Jews.

175

They had been cheated again. But a few weeks after the sale, the Nazis found a way to compound even that humiliation. The government informed them that they were confiscating their personal bankbooks and they were unable to withdraw the proceeds of the sale from the bank. Almost overnight Josef Rosenberg's wealth evaporated.

But by then the question of personal wealth had become academic. The Deutschmark had lost ninety per cent of its value on overseas markets since 1935, so their money would be virtually worthless outside Germany anyway. They had simply waited too long to get out. For a time the Haavara Agreement had made it possible for Jews to emigrate to Palestine and transfer their money with them, but once the Arab rebellion was under way, the British attempted to pacify the Arabs by closing off Jewish immigration.

Another escape route was closed.

The concern for material possessions quickly became subordinated to the more pressing problems of mere survival. Fortunately Josef Rosenberg had been a prudent man and had not kept all his money in the bank; he had cash hidden in a safe, inside the house. "It was put aside for a rainy day," he told his wife. "And believe me, it's raining hard right now."

Some of that money was used to buy food; most of it went in bribes to Nazi officials. Every day Josef Rosenberg trudged the streets of München, trying to obtain a precious visa out of the country for himself and his family; each day his efforts became more urgent. The news from abroad was all bad. The French and British allowed Hitler to reoccupy the Rhineland, in breach of the Treaty of Versailles. They looked the other way when Hitler sent his tanks and planes to crush the Spaniards. Then, just five weeks ago, they had persuaded the Czechs to allow Hitler to annexe the Sudetenland.

They were sorry, but there was nothing they could do.

Just like the Rosenbergs' coal man.

*   *   *

176

They sat down to a pauper's meal consisting of watery, unpeeled boiled potatoes and *Matjes* herring, salt herrings. The room was frigid and they wore their overcoats to the table. They needed to conserve their fuel now, and Netanel would only light the boilers after sunset, when the temperatures dropped below freezing.

Netanel chewed a little fish, without appetite. "I was listening to the radio tonight," he said.

Josef nodded. "I heard."

Frau Rosenberg looked up. "What is it?"

Josef cleared his throat. "A Jewish boy broke into the German embassy in Paris today. He shot one of the officials, the Third Secretary. Ernst vom Rath."

"Is he dead?"

Josef shook his head. "No, but he is very seriously wounded. He may not survive."

Frau Rosenberg forked a morsel of herring into her mouth, as if it were lobster. "Good," she said. "One less Nazi."

"You don't understand," Josef said. "If he dies there will be serious trouble here. Very serious trouble."

Frau Rosenberg took some moments to digest this perspective. "How can things get any more serious than they are?"

"I admit, it's hard to imagine," Josef said. He allowed himself the luxury of a small, tight smile. And he added, "Perhaps it's as well we will not be here to find out if it is possible."

Netanel looked up. "What was that?"

"I have our visas here in my pocket. We are leaving Germany!"

They stared at him. Frau Rosenberg was first to break the silence. "Where?"

"Chile."

"Chile? South America?"

Netanel stared at his father. South America! A cold, oily cocktail of relief and fear settled in his stomach. He suddenly saw himself an impoverished alien in a strange and distant country.

But at least this nightmare would be over.

He realised also, in that moment, that he would never see Marie again. A part of him had clung to the frail hope of some fairy-tale ending for them. Now he brought that hope to the light and let it die.

"Chile!" he whispered. "It's the end of the world."

"No, Netanel," Frau Rosenberg said softly, and she looked around the room, at the cold radiators, at the salt herrings on the plate, and at the three of them in their overcoats, "no, this is the end of the world."

"We leave in a month," Josef Rosenberg said. They nodded and continued to eat in silence, each alone with their thoughts.

27

Hermann was listening to Wagner on the radio, Inge was darning socks. The *Herrenvolk*! Marie thought. *Der Führer*'s master race. She felt a little guilty about her contempt for them. They have sacrificed so much for me, she thought. Or had they? she wondered. Hermann had suddenly announced that his savings had run out, and Marie would not be able to complete her degree. He now seemed content to have her work behind the counter in his butcher's shop again. It was as if the last three years had meant nothing.

But they had meant something to her. In Berlin she had experienced the full hysteria of National Socialism and it had terrified her. Everyone she had met was infected with it. Where had it come from, this Jew-hating, this preoccupation with national destiny? It was like living in an insane asylum.

"We are going to get a new motor car," Hermann announced.

"A motor car?" Marie said. "How can you afford such a thing?"

"Der Führer has announced that every German should own a motor car. Not just the damned Jews." Something else she had noticed on the last few occasions she had come home. It was not Hitler any more; it was der Führer. It was all he ever talked about.

"Is he going to send us one?"

Hermann looked up sharply from his edition of *Der Stürmer*, annoyed at the implied sarcasm. "It is part of a plan. We are paying five marks a week."

"As soon as the factory is finished," Inge said, "we will have our new motor car."

"When will that be?"

"Next year," Hermann said. "Der Führer has promised."

"I shall not sell my bicycle just yet then – "

The radio announcer interrupted *Der Ring des Nibelungen* and they felt silent. Third Secretary Ernst vom Rath had died in a Paris hospital. The announcer read a statement from the Berchtesgaden: the Third Reich would not tolerate any more provocation from the Jews. The cowardly assassination of vom Rath would not go unpunished.

Hermann nodded. "The Jews have gone too far this time."

"Der Führer has been good to them until now," Inge said. "I think this time they have tried even his patience a little too much."

Marie stood up and left the room. She could no longer even endure being with them. Five-mark motor cars and Hitler being good to the Jews! Had they ever stopped to listen to themselves?

Netanel, what is going to happen to you?

Netanel woke to the sound of tyres crunching on the gravel driveway. Torchlight swung across the windows. There were muffled shouts as someone started hammering on the front door.

Netanel stared at the clock. Two in the morning. What

179

was happening? His bedroom door opened, and Josef switched on the light.

"Netanel, it's the SS!" Josef's sparse, grey hair was comically awry from sleep. Fear made him look suddenly very old.

Netanel jumped out of bed and reached for his dressing-gown. It was freezing cold. Netanel went to the window. There was an army truck parked in the forecourt. The crashing continued downstairs. It sounded as if there were at least half a dozen of them.

"What are we going to do?" Josef said.

"I'll go," Netanel said. "Stay here with Mutti."

He ran down the stairs and across the hall. He was too late to save the lock. The wood splintered and the door flew open. Men in black uniforms rushed through. They were all armed; one of them had used the butt of his rifle to break open the door.

One of the men ran straight towards him and hit him in the face with his fist. Netanel fell backwards and his head smacked on the tiled floor. For a moment he lay on his back, stunned.

"Stay where you are, Jew, and perhaps you won't get hurt." He knew that voice; it was Rolf Emmerich.

Netanel struggled to sit up, his head still dizzy from the unexpected blow. Rolf's knee-length shiny black leather boots swam in and out of his vision. He heard the sound of china smashing, drawers crashing to the floor, and from somewhere, his mother screaming.

"I said, stay where you are."

Rolf's boot slammed into his ribs and Netanel collapsed, choking. Another kick and he felt a searing pain in his kidneys.

"Leave him!" he heard his father shout.

Josef ran down the stairs, but stopped suddenly, his face grey. Rolf had drawn his pistol and was pointing it at his head.

"*Heil Hitler!*" It was Weber. He was standing in the doorway, flanked by two SS stormtroopers.

"Colonel Weber!" Josef shouted. "I suppose you have

come to see for yourself how your representatives in Ravenswald behave!"

"Yes, Herr Rosenberg. I must admit, I am impressed."

Netanel tried again to get to his feet, but the room span around him and he slumped to his knees, cold greasy sweat erupting on his body. His fingers clawed at the balustrade on the stairs, and he retched on the floor.

Weber looked on with an expression of disgust. "*Heil Rosenberg*," he said.

Rolf laughed.

Netanel could see the SS at work in the dining-room. They had found the Spode china tea-set. It was hand-painted with tiny roses; it had belonged to Netanel's great-grandmother. They took it from the glass cabinet and threw each piece separately on to the floor.

"Look at what these Jews have got," one of them shouted. "They have everything and we have nothing!"

His colleague drew his dagger across the portrait of Mandel Rosenberg that hung above the old fireplace, then carved a star of David on to the polished oak surface of the dining-room table.

"Why are you doing this?" Josef shouted.

"We are searching for arms," Rolf said. "If you try to resist us, we will shoot you."

"We have no arms! I am a respectable businessman!"

"You are a Jew, aren't you? Like the filthy Jew who shot Herr vom Rath."

"Pigs!" Netanel gasped. "Nazi pigs – "

Rolf's boot smacked into the side of his head and Netanel went over on to his back, groaned once, and passed out.

Josef tried to go to his son but two stormtroopers pinned his arms. "Herr Rosenberg," Weber said, "I've a warrant for your arrest."

This was not happening! Josef swallowed hard, tried to keep the fear out of his voice. "Arrest? On what charges? For what crime? For having my son beaten in front of my eyes. For seeing my house smashed to pieces by young thugs . . ."

"It is *Schutzhaft*, Herr Rosenberg, protective custody."

"Protective custody? The only people I need protecting from is you!"

"The German population is demanding revenge on you Jews for what you did to Herr vom Rath. We cannot guarantee the safety of certain Jews any longer. You will be taken to the KZ at Dachau for your own safety. If you resist, my men have orders to use force."

I am dreaming, Josef thought. In a moment I will wake up and go downstairs and have breakfast with Rachel and Netanel and drive to the factory and it will all be a bad dream.

"Herr Rosenberg. Are you ready?"

Rachel was at the top of the steps, screaming. He wanted to comfort her, wanted to go to his son, who was bleeding all over the cold tiles, but he was too numb to move. What will happen to Rachel? he thought. She cannot fend for herself. And look at my son! He needs a doctor! What is going to happen to them?

The stormtroopers dragged Josef outside into the waiting car. The last sounds he heard as he left the House in the Woods were his wife's screams as she collapsed in the snow.

Marie woke to the sound of breaking glass.

She slipped on her dressing-gown and went to the window. There was a truck parked under a streetlight outside Horowitz's shoe store at the end of Theresienstrasse. Half a dozen stormtroopers were clustered outside, and one of them was breaking in the door with the stock of his rifle. The shop window was smashed and a Star of David had been painted on the remains of the glass with thick black brushstrokes. The paint seeped down the glass like blood.

The SS ran inside and moments later Marie heard screams and laughter. Feathers fell like snow into the street as one of the stormtroopers leaned out of Horowitz's second-storey window and emptied the feather comforters one by one.

Meanwhile two figures in dressing-gowns waddled across the street, stepping carefully in their slippers over the shards of glass strewn on the cobbles. They bent down and began to fill two bags with shoes from the smashed display window.

When they were finished, there were feathers in their hair and on their clothes. They looked almost comic, Marie thought. And she perhaps might have laughed at them but it was her own mother and father and instead she wanted to weep with shame and disgust.

28

Near Rab'allah

Majid steered the Buick up the winding road from Jerusalem, his fist punching the horn. The truck in front of him crawled along the centre of the road, belching black smoke from its exhaust. Majid leaned out of the window.

"Move over, you flaming bastard!" he shouted, in English, using an expression he had learned from the British officers in their jeeps along the Jaffa Road.

It was the first days of autumn. In Rab'allah the women would be busy at the grape harvest, the men would be slaughtering sheep, boiling the meat for fat, getting ready for winter. He could see the first sheep fires on the horizon, the smoke smudging the watery blue sky, drifting lazily upwards. Not a breath of wind.

Majid swerved to the right and raced the truck for the

next corner. A British army lorry rolled around the bend. He swerved violently in front of the truck, heard the truck driver yell a curse at him – "Son of a whore!" – and the army lorry blared its horn. He grinned and waved. *Insh'allah*. Thanks be to Allah, it was ordained that this was not his day to die.

The road snaked through the Judean hills. He steered one-handed while he shifted through the wavebands on the Buick's radio. He found Radio Damascus. The oriental music was interrupted every few minutes for hotly delivered news items on the war in Europe. The Mufti's great friend and ally, Hitler, had invaded Poland. Majid had heard of Poland. It was where a lot of the Jews came from.

Majid was not sure what to think about this. Perhaps it was a good thing. The Mufti said Hitler was going to get rid of all the Jews for good, and if there were no Jews, Palestine would not have any problems. But what if he did not get rid of them, as the Mufti said? What if he only chased them out of Poland and they started coming here again? Talbot did not like Hitler, he said he was a troublemaker like the Mufti, and Majid had never known the British to be wrong about things like that.

He turned off the Jerusalem–Tel Aviv road and headed up a stony track towards Rab'allah. The Buick bumped over potholes and rocks. Majid kept his foot on the accelerator. He wanted to raise the largest possible dust cloud so that everyone in the village would know he was coming long before he arrived, and a suitable welcoming party could be arranged.

He heard a sharp ping! and looked down. There was a bullet hole in the coachwork no more than six inches from his right knee and an exit hole on the floor between his legs. Someone was shooting at him! He slammed on the brakes and jumped out of the motor car before it had even stopped rolling, throwing himself face down in the dust.

When he looked up he saw half a dozen men scrambling down the slope towards him, each of them armed with a rifle. He was about to run, then realised he knew one of them. It was Izzat.

Son of a whore! He jumped to his feet. "You dirty little Arab!" he shouted at him as soon as he was within earshot. "May Allah roast your cock slowly on the Day of the Fire!"

"Majid!" Izzat laughed. "So it's you! Did we scare you?"

Now Majid recognised two of Izzat's companions. They were fellaheen from Rab'allah: one of them paid rents to his father, the other was an idiot from birth and half blind. He spent his days squatting outside his mother's hut, dribbling. They said when he wiped his arse he licked his fingers dry. And some maniac had let him loose with a gun!

It was an odd assortment of weapons for all that. Izzat had a Mauser, another one had a First World War clip-loaded Springfield; the rest of them were mostly armed with single-shot antique hunting rifles. The Holy Strugglers! He thought they had been disbanded.

Majid recovered his composure. He pointed at the Mauser. "Is Daoud giving away another of his daughters?" he said to Izzat. "Are you out here practising for the wedding?"

The jibe struck home. Izzat stopped grinning. "You were lucky," he said. "We are on a training exercise out here. You should have asked permission before coming through our territory. You could have been killed."

"Not if you were doing the shooting."

"We were not aiming at you. If we were, you would have stayed on your face on the road."

Majid was suddenly conscious of his clothes. His silk suit and Miami Beach tie were covered in dirt. He began to dust himself off, furious.

"Look what you've done!"

"You look like a real city effendi, Majid. I bet the little bend-over boys in Jerusalem love you in that suit."

The Holy Strugglers laughed.

"Go piss up a camel's leg! Anyway, what are you and

185

these women doing roaming around the hills without an escort? You could get hurt."

"We are training to kill Britishers, not bend over for them."

"The Mufti has declared the rebellion at an end. The British gave us what we wanted. As they said they would!"

"It was men like us that forced them to give in." A murmur of agreement from the others, even the idiot, who did not have any idea what Izzat was talking about. "The war is not over yet. Not until we've run every last Britisher out of Palestine!"

"If you're doing the shooting, they'll have to limp out," Majid said and he spat on the ground and went back to the Buick. As soon as he turned his back, he experienced a shiver of fear and doubt. Surely Izzat would never shoot a brother Arab in the back? No, not even Izzat would do that. But he walked quickly.

Look at the hole in the Buick. How would he explain that to Talbot effendi?

He got in and drove on to Rab'allah.

Rishou Hass'an watched his brother, unsure whether to envy him or despise him. What Izzat was saying about him was true. He *had* become a real city effendi. He ate pork, he smoked cork-tipped Craven As, he wore silk suits and brightly coloured ties from America, he went to Jerusalem nightclubs. Yet even though the villagers hated the effendis, they recognised that for one of their own to be accepted in Jerusalem was a real achievement.

But what was the cost? Rishou wondered.

So much was changing. The Mufti was no longer in Palestine, but his influence was as strong as ever. Earlier that year the British had tried to arrest him, but he fled to Lebanon, where he still continued to incite his jihad against the British from Beirut. He knew he could not defeat the British with weapons, so he did the next best thing: he made the Mandate ungovernable.

In the end the Mufti's gangs and the disparate bands of

Holy Strugglers had not chased the British into the sea as they had promised they would; yet they had forced the British to relent. The government had announced that there would be no more Jewish immigration, and no more land sales. They even committed themselves to an Arab Palestine within ten years, the Mufti's ultimate goal.

The Mufti's gangs had killed more Arabs than Jews, and more Jews than Britishers, and in doing so he had established a new authority, even above that of the muktars, an authority that had not been challenged for two thousand years. Everyone in Palestine was in fear of him.

Rab'allah was different too. Since Wagil's death, Zayyad had changed. He hardly ever spoke, and spent hours every day sitting in his armchair staring at the framed photograph of Wagil on the wall. He lit incense underneath the picture each morning and evening in memory of the family's great hero and martyr. Zayyad went often to the mosque to ask Allah to honour his son in Paradise and to ask forgiveness for his part in his death.

It was Rishou now who visited the outlying villages to pronounce *sulhas*, and collect the rents; it was he who dealt with the new British district commander, and bargained with the Bedouin nomads for the skins which he sent to the market in Jerusalem; it was left to him to supervise the harvests in the orchards and vineyards and fields.

Rishou had three children now, two sons and, by Allah's will, the burden of a daughter. Ali was four years old, Rahman was three. The last wet season he and Khadija had made another, a girl, and they had called her Wagiha in memory of his brother, the martyr.

His brother, the idiot! Rishou thought. The one who did not have the sense to run when he was told and had thought it was worth being strung up on a rope to pay back his father. His brother, may Allah turn him over hot coals for eternity!

Perhaps Wagil should have been more like Majid, he thought. A real Britisher.

*   *   *

Majid toyed with the knobs on the Buick's radio while the rest of the men clustered around, jostling for a better position. Rishou watched from the window of the coffee house, Zayyad beside him, the water bubbling in the silver *narghiliye* beside him.

"I have covered women in this car," they heard Majid say.

"How many?"

"Too many to count! Do you count how many figs on your trees? A lot!"

"What's this hole here?"

Majid rolled his eyes. "One night I took a Britisher lady out in this car. Her husband found me lying with her and fired his gun at me. That is the hole the bullet made!"

Heads craned forward for a closer look and Majid looked up at Rishou and winked. Then he saw Izzat's face in the crowd and immediately regretted this embellishment to his story. He turned up the volume of the music until some of the men covered their ears and told him to stop.

"Do you have to pay them?"

"Pay them?" Majid shouted. "They pay me!"

The crowd roared at that one.

Rishou shook his head. "My brother is a natural show-off."

Zayyad sucked on his pipe. "He always was," he said.

The clash of the music was suddenly stilled and everyone fell silent. The announcer on Radio Damascus was almost sobbing with excitement. The British and French had declared war on Germany.

The music returned and everyone spoke at once.

"What does this mean for us?" someone shouted at Majid.

"Nothing!" Majid shouted. "Talbot effendi says the British army will beat the Germans as they beat them in the time of Lawrence."

"The Mufti says Hitler is our friend," Izzat shouted and everyone turned and stared at him.

"How do you know what the Mufti thinks?" Majid asked him.

"My uncle travelled to Damascus last spring to speak with him. He says the Germans have promised him that they will run every last Britisher out of Palestine."

"The Britisher army is invincible," Majid said. "They even have cars with guns on them. I have seen them myself in Jerusalem."

"Anyway, why should we trust the Germans?" someone else shouted. "If you invite someone into your house you have to be sure he does not want to live in it himself. The Britishers got rid of the Turks, but then they wouldn't go. Who is to say these Germans won't do the same thing?"

Izzat jumped on the Buick's running board. "Because they are not like the Turks and the Britishers! They hate the Jews just like us! They won't let any Jews in their country! Besides, the Mufti has spoken to them and he has given his word. Do any of you think he is cleverer than the Mufti?"

The excitement aroused by the news on the radio had been transformed to tension. Rishou watched Izzat working the crowd and for the first time he sensed real danger.

For a long time he had considered him a fool. When Sheikh Daoud's Holy Strugglers had disbanded, Izzat had formed a new band with half a dozen others, even more stupid and idle and crazy than himself. He had even recruited Tareq, the son of a poor widow, born half blind and simple. He called himself Field-Marshal Ib'n Mousa and roamed round the hills with his recruits, where they fired their guns randomly at rocks and small animals. Everyone in the district thought Izzat was a joke, even his own uncle.

No, especially his uncle.

But perhaps not, Rishou thought. If he was a joke, he was a very bad one.

"This is our chance," Izzat was saying. "Why do you think the Britishers gave in? Because they knew they would have to fight the Germans and they needed all their men for that, because they are afraid they will lose!"

"The British have too many soldiers," Majid argued.

189

"They will win easily. If we do not help them, they might change their mind about the White Paper."

"What is this White Paper?" Izzat sneered.

"It is the agreement the Britishers have made, to stop the Jews coming here and buying land. They have promised us our own Arab Palestine!"

"You talk like a woman! Who cares about pieces of paper? Who cares about promises? This is our land! We must take it back from the invaders! Anyway, Majid Hass'an, how do you know so much about what the Britishers will do?"

Be careful, Majid! Rishou thought. He fought back an impulse to get up and slap his hand over his brother's big, idiot mouth.

"Talbot effendi discusses everything with me," Majid said. "I am like a personal adviser. He does nothing without consulting me first!"

"You're just his handmaiden," Izzat said, and Rishou thought, Get out your knife now, Majid, or you will have to live with that slur for the rest of your life. He looked at Zayyad, but his father continued to smoke the narghiliye, apparently unconcerned.

Majid hesitated, and Rishou saw the fear in his eyes. *And if I saw it, everyone here saw it too.*

Majid decided against attempting retribution for the insult. He tried one last, elaborate boast. "I go everywhere with Talbot effendi," Majid said. "Next week I am going to Acre with him. All the way to Acre! I am taking him in my car!"

This news had the effect Majid had anticipated. None of the villagers had ever been to Acre. They murmured among themselves, impressed. Majid grinned in triumph at Izzat; the gambit was all the more satisfying because it was true.

"Which route are you taking?" Izzat asked him.

"We will go along the Bab el-Wad to Latrun, and then right up the coast through Jaffa and Haifa. If you come to the Bab el-Wad I will wave to you as I go past."

190

"Will there be an escort?" Suddenly there was silence, except for the shuffling of feet.

"Why would we need an escort?"

"A man like that, the man who hanged our great martyr, Wagil Hass'an, your brother! It could be dangerous for him to ride through the Judean hills without an escort."

"He did not hang my brother."

"He was there, wasn't he?"

"Talbot effendi did not kill my brother!"

"He's a Britisher. Britishers killed your brother! Wagil was a hero for Islam and Palestine and he has yet to be avenged. If you are afraid to do it, then tell me when you will be on the road, and the Holy Strugglers of al-Naqb will avenge him for you!"

"Talbot effendi is innocent of any crime!"

"What sort of a woman are you? Your brother was hanged from a rope and you try to defend the Britishers!"

"Talbot effendi did everything he could to help us," Majid protested, but every face in the crowd was hostile to him now.

"What are you, Majid?" Izzat said, pressing his advantage. "Are you an Arab or a Britisher?"

Rishou could see what was happening, but he was powerless to stop it. His brother and his big mouth! Majid looked desperately at his father, and everyone imitated him; without a word being spoken, the final judgment in the matter was handed to Zayyad.

He smoked in silence for a long time. Finally he laid the water pipe aside. "I have tried to keep us from this conflict," he said. "For many years I too thought the Britishers were our friends, that they did not lie. I was also afraid that this fight would bring only misfortune on all our heads, so I did not join the struggle against the Britishers. As my reward they tried to disgrace me, and then they murdered my eldest son. I see no good coming from this, but I cannot rest until Wagil is avenged. In this then, I agree with Izzat lb'n Mousa. Talbot effendi will pay for the death of my son."

191

"Father, I beg you to reconsider," Rishou whispered.

Zayyad turned towards him. "Rishou, I want you to go too. You can take Izzat and his troupe of donkeys with you if you want. But you will kill him. Do you understand? You. You will restore the honour of the Hass'ans. That is all I have to say."

Izzat grinned at Rishou in triumph. Majid slumped behind the driver's seat of the Buick and put his head in his hands. What had he done? What had he done?

29

Talbieh, Jerusalem

"You indulge him far too much," Elizabeth said. "He's only a servant, you know."

"It doesn't hurt to treat one's help with a little decency."

"You let him drive our car away for the weekend! That's a little more than just decent, Henry. That's positively saintly."

Talbot slipped on his dinner jacket and adjusted his bow tie in the mirror. "We didn't need it, we weren't going anywhere. Besides, it's not our car, it's the government's."

Elizabeth emerged from the bathroom. She was wearing just stockings, suspenders and pants. She went to the bedside table, put a cigarette in an ivory holder and lit it. The cigarette-holder was a recent affectation, and Talbot loathed it. He suspected she knew this, and it encouraged her.

He turned away – why couldn't she dress properly before she started smoking anyway? – and went to the window. Majid was polishing the Buick. It was parked in the forecourt under a gnarled and ancient olive tree. The branches reflected in the maroon coachwork like a mirror. Majid did an excellent job; he tended and pampered the car as if it were a thoroughbred pony.

"It's got a hole in it," Elizabeth said.

"What has?"

"The Buick. It's got a hole in it." Elizabeth leaned against the wall, crossed her arms over her bare breasts and drew on her cigarette. "You're not much good at noticing things with holes in, are you?"

He looked up at her. He wished she'd dress. He reflected on this last cryptic remark and decided the barb must be aimed at him. "I suppose not," he said.

"You really didn't know, did you?"

"What sort of hole?"

"A little one."

"How did it get there?"

"Why don't you ask him?"

Majid saw Talbot at the window, looked up and waved. Talbot raised a limp hand in acknowledgement. The Buick looked in excellent condition from where he was standing. If there was a hole in it, he was sure he would have noticed.

"Perhaps you're more interested in looking at Majid," she said.

"Would you like to explain that remark?"

"Sometimes I just wonder what really interests you, Henry."

He felt panic rising in him. He hated being alone with her like this. She was not an unattractive woman. But in a moment she might expect him to perform for her, and he couldn't, and then there would be the silent looks of rebuke and the lingering sense of failure.

"We'll be late for dinner," he said.

He opened the door.

"Why did you marry me, Henry?"

Well, it seemed like a good idea at the time. What could he tell her? That she had seemed like an indispensable accessory for an ambitious young diplomat? A decorous and socially acceptable wife was a prerequisite, like having

193

been to the right school, and good passes in English and French. He had not meant to hurt her, of course, and she seemed just as keen as he was. He was even thought of as a good catch in some circles.

Anyway, it was all his mother's idea.

"I am very fond of you," he lied.

"Do I disappoint you?"

She was going to press him. She liked to argue when she was almost naked. Perhaps she thought it gave her an advantage. "No, of course not."

"Are my breasts not big enough for you?"

He felt himself blush. "For God's sake, Elizabeth!"

"You never want to touch me."

"There is a time and a place for everything."

"Well, I have the time." She smiled, and her fingers slipped down the front of her pants. "And I have just the place."

"We'll be late for dinner," he said, and went out, closing the door.

They followed the ancient walls of the Old City past the Zion Gate. The sprawling, ugly tower of the old German convent on the Mount of Olives came into view, below it the army of white tombstones that marched up the hill from the Jewish cemetery.

Talbot sat in the back of the Buick, his briefcase resting on the seat beside him. Every weekday morning at this time Majid would take him to the High Commissioner's residence for the start of his day's work; he would pick him up again just before sunset. Talbot enjoyed the leisurely drive, staring at the fabled hills of the ancient city, trying to imagine them as they were a thousand or two thousand or three thousand years ago. But lately his muse had been distracted by other portentous events taking place a long way away. His country was now at war.

In Palestine, Sir Alec McIntosh had been replaced by Sir Harold Macmillan. The new High Commissioner had assured his staff that their job was to maintain the status quo: "The White Paper was intended to placate the Arab

Higher Committee while the attentions of our government are focused elsewhere. Some time in the not too distant future Palestine may be strategically important. From now on we must go out of our way to maintain good relations with the Arabs."

It was the reason for his trip to Acre next week. Macmillan had ordered himself and Simpson to brief all the regional administrators personally.

"You have not forgotten we are going to Acre," Talbot said to Majid.

Majid gave a nervous laugh. "No, effendi, I have not forgotten. I have thought of nothing else."

Majid has been behaving strangely, Talbot thought. Ever since his recent visit to Rab'allah. I wonder what's wrong? "Have you ever been to Acre, Majid?"

"No, Talbot effendi, never. The prospect is very enthralling." Another nervous laugh.

Talbot leaned forward. He remembered what Elizabeth had said about a hole in the coachwork. She was right. There it was, by Majid's right knee. He was suddenly angry. There was a limit to his tolerance.

"Majid, would you mind telling me what happened to the car?"

"Effendi?"

"There's a hole there, by your knee. You must have noticed."

"I am so sorry, Talbot effendi. A thousand times a thousand apologies! I throw myself in the dust at your feet and beg your forgiveness!" Majid turned around in his seat so that Talbot might obtain a better view of his contrition. Talbot saw the rear of a donkey cart approaching rapidly and forced Majid to return his attentions to the road.

"Just tell me what happened!"

"Bandits," Majid said.

"Bandits?"

"It is a bullet hole, effendi. They fired at me because they thought I was a Britisher. It is only Allah's will I was not killed!"

"Or wounded in the knee, at any rate."

"The hills are crawling with dirty Arabs!"

"The army commander seems to think the roads are quite safe."

An elderly Arab wobbled to the centre of the road on his bicycle. Majid slammed his fist on his horn and passed him so close that the old man lost his balance and fell. Majid seemed not to notice. "Judea is still very dangerous, effendi. You must tell the Mandoob es Sami you will be in great danger when you go to Acre."

"Nonsense."

"I am very afraid for you. Please believe me, we should not go through the Bab el-Wad."

"What other way is there?"

"We can go north to Ramalla, Talbot effendi. Then across to Lydda."

"The roads to Ramalla are awful. It will add hours to the journey."

Majid licked his lips. He was sweating, Talbot noticed, yet the morning was still cool. "The Bab el-Wad is not safe. Please do not make me drive that way."

Talbot's irritation was replaced by alarm. "You know something, Majid?"

"I am the brass monkeys, Talbot effendi. Hear no evil, see no evil, smell no evil. Do not ask me how I know, I beg you, but I know. Let us not go that way. I will make up the time, I will drive faster around the bends."

Talbot considered. Why would anyone want to shoot him? The rebellion was supposed to be over. But Majid seemed genuinely frightened. "Perhaps I could arrange a military escort," he said.

Majid went pale. "No, no, please, Talbot effendi, if we take soldiers there will only be more shooting and more men will be killed. It is better if we go another way, and there is no trouble. No more holes in the car."

Talbot sat back and admired the tall Aleppo pines that stood sentry around the High Commissioner's house. He was not a stupid man; Majid obviously knew more than he was saying.

He would have to think about this.

30

Dachau

The wind moaned through the barbed wire. The man removed his cap and ran his hand across the stubble on his skull. They had shaved his hair. Bad enough that they had dressed him in these ridiculous striped pyjamas but to shave his hair like this. Josef Rosenberg. A good German citizen!

Thank God it would all be over soon. Hitler had pushed the people too far this time. They would not tolerate this. Any day they would kick them out of office and things would get back to normal. If they resisted, Chamberlain and the French would force him out. Yes, it would all be over soon.

And the insurance money should be through any day. He just hoped Rachel had remembered to send in the claim.

München

Netanel looked at his watch. Three o'clock. Six hours they had made him wait! There was a cold draught in the tiled corridor and he was hungry, but he had not dared to go out to buy lunch – even if he could find a shopkeeper who would serve him – because he knew the Nazi clerks would use that as an excuse to pass him over altogether.

It had been over a month now since they had taken Josef. That night almost everything in the house had been destroyed; all the windows had been smashed or kicked in, the glass ankle deep on the floor of the conservatory. It glittered in the winter sun like frost.

Netanel had decided they would live in just two rooms to conserve fuel. He converted the drawing-room into a bedroom for his mother, while he slept on the sofa in the living-room. They used the kitchen and downstairs bathroom for washing and cooking. He closed the doors on all the other rooms, leaving the broken glass and china and splintered furniture where it was. He sealed under the doors with blankets as best he could to keep out the draughts.

It took him a day to haul the rest of the coke from the boiler-room. He built a fire in the living-room and boarded up the smashed windows with pieces of broken furniture.

He left the rest of the debris in a pile on the driveway, along with the slashed and vandalised paintings. The empty square patches of wallpaper in the living-room depressed him but it was better than staring at "JUD" smeared over the face of his grandfather.

They were left with a sofa, its upholstery torn apart with a knife, and his father's favourite green brocade armchair, miraculously untouched. He scrubbed with turpentine to remove the red Star of David on the dining-room wall.

The following morning he dressed in his best suit and walked into town to catch the train into München.

That morning's stroll through the streets of his home afforded him a broader perspective of Kristallnacht. The synagogue was a smouldering shell, and the Jewish cemetery beside it had been desecrated, the stones overturned and defaced with swastikas. The glass from the shopfronts that had littered the streets had been cleared away – evidently Emmerich's men made the shopkeepers get down on their hands and knees and pick up every fragment themselves – but the Jewish shops were deserted, their windows boarded up, many of their owners having joined his father on the train to Dachau.

He passed Horowitz's shoe store and recognised the

Helders in there, bartering with the old cobbler. He stopped and listened. It seemed Hermann and his wife had stolen all the shoes from the display window on Kristallnacht but they were angry because they had discovered that none of the shoes made a matching pair. Now they were bargaining with old Horowitz, without apology. Ten right-foot shoes for one new pair.

Netanel had with him the rest of their Deutschmarks – despite their best efforts, Rolf's lumpen had not found the safe. The money was bundled in the briefcase on his lap. Ten thousand marks. That was the amount the SS clerk had told him, on his last visit, that would be needed to expedite his father's release from the KZ at Dachau.

What would they do when Josef was released? he thought. Their exit visas for Chile had expired at the end of November. New ones would cost more money. Well, they still had possessions they could hock. Once his father was free, he would find some way to get them all out. Palestine perhaps. The responsibility was his now.

If only Josef had listened to him three years ago, they could have got out with everything!

He looked at his watch again. Ten past three. Perhaps they would leave him sitting here all day. They had done that to him countless times. Usually the clerks did not even inform him they were going home. They just left. At half past five two SS soldiers simply picked him up and threw him on the street.

He looked at his newspaper. On the front page was a photograph of a great column of people marching under guard through the streets of Linz. They were carrying cardboard suitcases and rucksacks and they had Stars of David pinned to their coats, even the children. Netanel scanned the faces and wondered if Esther and his cousins were among the faces. They had run away once and now the Nazi tentacles had just reached out for them again.

A dark-haired young man in a black Schutzstaffeln uniform and horn-rimmed spectacles stepped into the corridor. "Rosenberg," he said, and went back into his

199

office. Netanel left his newspaper behind and jumped up to follow.

The office was small and cramped, dominated by a huge, grey filing cabinet in one corner. The clerk himself looked like any harassed bureaucrat. He held out his hand for Netanel's papers. Netanel fumbled in his jacket pocket and brought out his identity card. It was one of the new ones, stamped with a large Gothic letter "J" for Jew. It identified him as Netanel Israel Rosenberg. The "Israel" was an innovation too; after Kristallnacht every Jewish male was required to add "Israel" to his name so there could be no possible confusion about his true identity.

The man looked at the papers then flicked the card back across the table. "What is it you want?" he said without looking up.

"My father is being detained at Dachau – "

"Yes?"

"I was told I might be able to arrange his release." Be polite, Netanel, he told himself. This little *scheiss* has your father's destiny in his pale hands.

"What is he there for?"

"He has done nothing wrong. When he was arrested – "

"What is he there for?"

"Protective custody."

The clerk's spectacles flashed as they caught the light. He toyed with his pen and stared. "What is his name?"

"Rosenberg. Josef Rosenberg."

"Josef *Israel* Rosenberg," the man corrected him. He wrote the name on a form. "Address?"

Netanel gave him his father's details, his date of birth, his occupation – the clerk snorted with contempt – and date of arrest.

"It costs a great deal of money to transport a prisoner of the Reich from one place to another. And it makes a lot of paperwork."

"I have brought ten thousand marks with me."

"Good. Leave it on the desk. You can go now."

Netanel sat there. Was that all there was to it?

"When will he be released?" he said.

"You can go now," the clerk repeated, and Netanel wanted to press him further but dared not. But just to leave the money there?

What else could he do?

He stood up and left the office, leaving behind the briefcase and the precious ten thousand marks.

Ravenswald

The House in the Woods looked deserted from the outside. The heaps of broken furniture, the discarded paintings, the boxes of broken glass and broken china piled up on the driveway, the boarded windows, all gave the impression the house had been long abandoned. Only the skein of smoke from one of the chimneys hinted that there might be life inside.

Netanel let himself into the house with his key. His mother was sitting in the armchair in the darkened living-room, staring into the fire.

"You should have the lights on," Netanel said. He flicked the switch but nothing happened. He tried another in the drawing-room, and the kitchen.

They had turned the power off.

Mein Gott! But Emmerich and his friends knew the small, intricate ways of torment! Netanel had been prepared for this, but not quite so soon. He went to the pantry cupboard and took out one of the boxes of candles, lit one, and carried it into the living-room.

"Here. We have some light," he said.

"You should let the servants do that," Frau Rosenberg said. "That's what they are here for."

Poor Mutti, he thought. Ever since they had taken Josef, she had not been herself. Sometimes she was lucid, but at other times her mind was anchored in the past. She is trying to escape, like every Jew in Germany is trying to escape, he thought. Only she has sought her refuge inside her own mind.

If I can only get Josef back, she will be all right.

"Do you want something to eat?"

"Yes, ring for Hilde. I think it's fish tonight."

"I'll make some soup."

"Josef should be home soon. Tell Hilde supper had better be ready or Herr Rosenberg will be furious. He does not want to be late for his card game."

Something caught Netanel's eye. There was a brown paper parcel on the floor by the armchair. It was addressed to his mother.

"Who brought this?" he asked her. The postman had long ago stopped delivering letters to their door.

She stared at the parcel as if she had never seen it before. "Perhaps Hilde put it there," she said.

Netanel picked it up. There was no postage stamp, but the National Socialist eagle and swastika insignia were imprinted above the name and address. Netanel tore off the buff paper. Inside was a cardboard box. He opened it. It contained a small metal pot and a typewritten letter bearing the official seal of the Schutzstaffeln.

It read:

Frau Rosenberg,

We enclose the ashes of your husband, Josef Rosenberg, who was shot while trying to escape from protective custody at Dachau. He was cremated in line with official government policy. There is an outstanding charge for transport which will be sent to you separately.

Ernst Hasler,
Commandant,
Dachau K.Z.

31

The man did not introduce himself. "There was an advertisement in the paper," he said. "You have books for sale." He waved the newspaper in Netanel's face as if it were a search warrant. The advertisement was ringed in black ink. "Can I come inside? I don't like being seen going into a Jewish house."

He was a thin, neat man, with short blond hair. The breast and side pockets of his overcoat were piped with green, and he wore a jaunty Tyrolean hat with a badger brush set at the back, in the traditional manner. He wore thick horn-rimmed spectacles that made his eyes appear twice their normal size.

Like a stick insect, Netanel thought.

He opened the door. "Come in," he said.

The cold black-and-white-tiled hall was empty and the broken windows had all been boarded up. Netanel wore a scarf over his suit to keep out the chill of the empty rooms. He felt like a house agent trying to sell a house that had been abandoned for years because of a ghost story.

"Where are the books?" the buyer said.

"This way."

Netanel led the buyer up the stairs to his father's study. He opened the door and for a moment he almost expected to see Josef sitting at his desk in his worn velvet smoking jacket, poring over family accounts. But the room was empty. Josef's splintered desk was rotting away on the portico with the other furniture smashed by the SS on Kristallnacht. Now only the bookshelves remained – one of them had been hurled to the floor but the heavy walnut had withstood the impact – and their feet echoed on the parquet floors and left imprints in the thin rind of dust.

The buyer frowned, like a pearl dealer confronted with a handful of misshapen baroque. "What do you have here?"

"It depends what you're looking for," Netanel said.

The buyer ran his finger along the bindings. He raised his eyebrows. "Heine?"

"You like Heine?"

"Heine is hard to find. Most of these have ended up on bonfires." He took out *The Harz Journey*, flicked through the pages. "It's in good condition," he said grudgingly.

"My father always said that a book was the sum of a man's thoughts, and as such it was to be revered, not burned."

"Depends on the man. Depends on the thoughts." He took another volume, Josef's favourite, the *Buch der Lieder*, the Book of Songs, from the shelves. Netanel curbed an impulse to snatch it away. It was his father's favourite and it seemed almost a sacrilege. Like a barbarian crushing a flower in his fist in a vain effort to discern the scent.

I'm sorry, Father, he thought. But it's no good to you now.

"I can perhaps take some of these off your hands."

"How kind. If you will excuse me saying, you do not look like the sort of man who reads Heine."

"They are collector's pieces."

"So you want them because Hitler has made them rare? You are very astute."

The buyer surveyed the rows of books. "Erich Maria Remarque," he murmured, impressed. "I'll give you ten marks for the lot."

And I'll throw you out of the window, you little shit. "No less than fifty."

The buyer reached into his jacket and produced his wallet. He took out four ten mark notes. "Forty."

Netanel took the money. "You have just got the biggest bargain of your life."

"I get bargains like this every week," the buyer said. "Not that I have anything against the Jews personally."

"Hardly anyone does. Only Hitler."

"Quite so. Do you have a box I can put these in?"

Hermann closed the shop every day at five o'clock. Winter was drawing in, and it was dark by the time Marie flipped over the sign on the front door: CLOSED. She heard Hermann grunting as he lifted a lamb carcass off his workbench and carried it out to the cool room in the back yard. Marie went to the trays, took two veal steaks and some lamb chops and wrapped them in paper. She tucked the package into the cardigan she wore underneath her apron.

By the time Hermann returned to the shop Marie had finished packing away the rest of the meat trays. Her petty larceny was not noticed.

The wind rattled the boarding at the windows and tiny flurries of snow found their way through the cracks. Netanel and his mother huddled around the small coal fire for warmth, blankets wrapped around their shoulders.

Netanel had prepared them bowls of thin Knochen-suppe, vegetable soup flavoured with a little carefully preserved chicken stock and a few marrow bones.

There was just one small candle, fluttering in the draught. Soon the last of the coal would be gone, and they would have to burn the furniture.

Despite the loss of the ten thousand marks, they still had a little money left, but no one would take it. It had now become apparent to Netanel that the National Socialist government and the majority of people of Ravenswald were quite happy to let them starve.

But not everyone. One night he had heard footsteps on the portico. When he went outside he found a parcel lying by the doorstep, and saw the grocer, Muller, riding away on his bicycle. The parcel contained tins of food and condensed milk.

Other packages appeared: bread, a few vegetables,

perhaps a liverwurst. They were always left during the night, as no one would dare be seen near the House in the Woods during the day. Once Netanel thought he saw Frau Hochstetter hurrying away. When he looked on the portico step he found a small basket containing eggs, bread, milk, even a little meat. That night he and his mother had enjoyed a feast.

But how much longer could they live off the charity of the few people of Ravenswald who still remembered der Chef kindly? How long before Ubersturmführer Emmerich frightened them off too?

"Josef is late from his cards," Frau Rosenberg said.

"He's dead, Mother. He's not coming home."

"He is getting later and later. He works hard, I know he needs his pleasures. But I shall have to talk to him about it."

"He's dead. You can't talk to him."

"He does like his cards."

There was a gentle rapping, from the back door.

"That will be him now," she said.

Netanel put down his soup. What now? He forced himself to remain calm. It could not be SA, they would come straight through the front door with axes, no timid tapping at the washroom door. So it must be a friend. Perhaps another delivery of food!

He took off the blanket, lit another candle from the one at his feet, and went into the hallway. God in heaven. It was like a tomb out here. There was a sheen of ice on the tiles and his breath crystallised on the freezing air. He crossed the hall, carefully picking his way over the wreckage that still remained from Kristallnacht, and made his way to the washroom at the back.

Whoever it was, they must have come through the garden, from the path through the wood.

He opened the door, shielding the candle from the draught. A figure stood huddled in the darkness, coat and woollen hat dusted with snow, a thick scarf obscuring the face.

He held up the candle. Those eyes. He would have recognised them anywhere; in a sea of faces he would have known those eyes.

"Marie," he whispered.

He pulled her inside and shut the door. "It's so dark out there," she whispered. "I almost fell down the basement steps."

He could not speak.

She pulled the scarf away from her face and grinned at him. "You thought I'd forgotten about you, didn't you?"

"Did anyone see you?"

"I could hardly see myself on a night like this." She reached into her pocket and brought out a little package, wrapped in stained white paper. "The butcher does home deliveries now. It's an extra service for his good customers."

He took the proffered gift. "You should not have done this! Sometimes the Nazis watch the house. It is a terrible risk."

"No one saw me." She shivered. "It's freezing in here. Is the whole house like this?"

"We're trying to save our fuel. We're living in two rooms now."

"Do you have a fire? I'm so cold!"

He hesitated. This is dangerous for her, he thought. I should send her away. But he couldn't do it. In a world of darkness, there was at last a little light.

"This way," he said.

They cooked the steaks in their own juices on the kitchen range. The smell of the frying veal pinched the glands in his tongue, and his belly growled with hunger. "Fresh meat," he whispered. "I'd forgotten what it was like."

The candle flickered as another gust of wind whistled through the boarded windowpane. "I should send you away. If you're seen here, you'll be arrested."

"I can't stand by and watch you starve. I know the danger."

He put an arm around her, drank in the warm smell of

her hair, the scent of her cologne. He felt a surge of joy, the first time he had felt anything but the emptiness of dread and despair in long months. He tried to forget the nightmare world outside. Right here, right now, he had a miracle and he would not think about anything else.

"How did you get this food? Won't your father find out?"

"He never checks on me. Why should he? Besides, some of the customers I don't like, the ones I know are National Socialists, I charge them a little more deliberately when I weigh their purchases. Enough to pay for what I brought to you tonight. So it's not really stealing and I make the Nazis contribute to a good cause – even if they don't know it!" She looked up at him, and suddenly the smile was gone. "I can't believe what they did. Not just to you, to all the Jewish people in the town. They are not human."

"But they are human, Marie. Humans have been doing this to us for two thousand years. You just need someone like Hitler who lets people be what they really are."

"Not all people."

"No," he said, "not all people." He looked into her face. What could he do? For her own sake she should have stayed in Berlin. For himself he thanked God for bringing her back to him.

He kissed her gently on the lips. "The steaks are nearly ready," she said. "Let's surprise your mother with them."

"Thank you for coming here," he said. "But I can't let you put yourself in this danger for me any more. You mustn't come again."

"All right," she said. "If that is what you think."

But they both knew she would come again. They both knew that it was a lie.

Part Six

PALESTINE, 1939

32

Bab el-Wad, Jerusalem–Latrun Fort

The shadows were thin and pale, and the scrub danced in the heat. Trucks rumbled up the gully, engines roaring in protest, the crunch of the gears echoing around the narrow walls. Then silence again.

The Holy Strugglers of Judea squatted under a stand of pines. Black eyes stared watchful from the folds of their keffiyehs. They cradled their rifles against their shoulders and waited in stoic silence.

"He's not coming," one of them said.

"He said he would be on the road an hour after dawn. It is almost midday."

"We will wait," Izzat said. What else was there to do? Izzat did not want to return to Rab'allah, even though he was hungry and thirsty and cold. If they went back without having fired their rifles, they would be the butt of whispered jokes in the coffee house. He would delay that particular humiliation as long as possible. Damn Majid! May a thousand bees swarm on his testicles!

Near Lydda

The trip had taken eleven hours; if they had come through the Bab el-Wad the journey would have taken them less than half that time. I wonder if the detour was really necessary? Talbot thought, as Lydda appeared below them on the plains, squat and white in the yellow light of late afternoon.

"You think we are safe from bandits now?" Talbot said.

Majid laughed, as if Talbot had made a joke that he did not quite understand. "Quite safe now, Talbot effendi. Perhaps we should come back this way also. Just to be on the side of the safe."

"Whatever you think is best, Majid," Talbot said, and he laid a hand on his driver's shoulder. A good chap. He did everything that was expected of him without complaint. And he seemed to be truly concerned about his welfare. In many ways he felt more comfortable with him than with Elizabeth. "Whatever you think is best."

Bab el-Wad, Jerusalem–Latrun Fort

The twilight was pure and soft, accentuating the contrasts between shadows and light, every rock and bush and gully perfect in line and shade. The horizon faded to violet as the sun dipped below the Judean hills. The temperature fell with it.

The day was over, wasted.

Izzat kicked at a stone, watched it pick up speed and roll down the slope almost to the edge of the road. "He has told the Britishers about our plan. He is a coward and a traitor!"

He heard the sound of a motor engine around a bend in the road. They all craned their heads, the triumph of habit over reason. It was another truck, a British supply vehicle, its headlights already blazing. It rumbled on down the road towards Latrun.

Suddenly Izzat found himself staring down the black, malevolent eye of a rifle. He uttered a sob of terror and jerked backwards.

"I'm going to blow a hole in your head," Rishou said.

"No," Izzat whimpered. He looked for his loyal band of Holy Strugglers. No help there. "No, please."

"You wish to insult one of my family, you son of a whore?"

"As Allah is my judge, I did not mean it!"

"There could be a thousand reasons why the Britisher did not come this way today."

Izzat could think of only one, but expressing it was the reason he now had Rishou's rifle shoved in his face. "Your brother's courage and honour is famous in these parts. Everyone knows it."

Rishou considered.

"Let Allah burn me on the Day of Fire!" Izzat shouted desperately. "I meant no harm!"

"You called him a traitor and a coward!"

"A figure of speech, Rishou. I abase myself before your brother's legend!"

Rishou lowered his rifle, honour satisfied. He stalked away.

For a moment Izzat considered shooting him in the back, but rejected the thought almost as soon as it occurred to him. It would destroy his image with the Holy Strugglers and, anyway, Zayyad would kill him. There would be another day to settle with the Hass'ans.

33

The Place Where The Fool Shot His Uncle

There were two riders, wearing the blue denims of
kibbutzniks. They were leading a line of four ponies;
they had been buying stock from the traders in Jerusalem,
Izzat decided. They appeared to be unarmed. Easy targets. Compensation, perhaps, for a wasted day. And the
unbranded horses would be a satisfactory bonus.

Izzat signalled his intentions to the rest of his band and
they squatted down to wait below the crest of the ridge. It
was the same spot he had chosen five years ago to ambush
Khadija's wedding party.

He knew what the people of Rab'allah called this place
now. Well, a couple of dead Jews would stop them
laughing. Tomorrow, the exploits of the Holy Strugglers
of Judea would be sung through the hills.

A full moon rose over the hills, throwing phosphorus
light over the gully. Where was Rishou? Izzat wondered.
Perhaps back in Rab'allah by now. He hoped so. He did
not want to share the glory.

He put his finger to his lips. The others nodded their
heads, the whites of their eyes pronounced in the darkness.
There was the sound of trickling liquid; in his terror, Tareq
had lost control of his water.

Izzat peered over the lip of the ridge. They were close,
no more than fifty paces away. "Kill them!" Izzat screamed
and he aimed his Mauser and fired.

"*Allah y Akbar!*" roared from half a dozen throats.
There were orange flashes all along the ridge as the

214

Strugglers fired into the gully. A horse bellowed in protest, then, in the silence following the first volley, Izzat heard a high-pitched shriek, like a woman screaming. The line of ponies galloped away down the trail towards the kibbutz. One of the riders escaped with them.

"Follow me!" Izzat shouted and scrambled down the gully. They had done it! Allah, the Merciful, the Compassionate, please let there be at least one dead Jew down here. Even better let him still be living so they can make him eat his own testicles!

A horse whimpered in pain somewhere close by. Then they all heard it; another cry, unmistakably human. "The other one is still alive!" one of them said.

"We'll have some fun," Izzat said. He could make out the silhouette of the horse ten paces away. The rider was struggling to crawl away. Izzat ran over.

The horse had fallen on its side and the Jew's leg was trapped underneath it, "Please," the Jew sobbed, "please . . ."

"A woman!" Izzat shouted in triumph.

"Allah is indeed great!" someone else said.

They stood in respectful silence, awed by the extent of Allah's bounty. None of them had ever raped a Jewish woman before and they waited for Izzat to tell them what to do.

"Please . . ." the woman said.

"Get her out from under the horse," Izzat said.

Two of them grabbed her arms and pulled. She shrieked in agony as the task was accomplished, then passed out.

"Sons of whores!" Izzat said. "Now look what you have done. She is no good to us like that. Wake her up!"

"How?"

Izzat went to the dying horse and found a water bottle on the saddle. He bent over the wounded woman and tipped the contents on her face. She moaned softly.

"Hold her down," Izzat said.

"Please . . ." Sarah said. The horse snorted and kicked. "My horse . . . help my horse . . ." Sarah raised her head

215

and tried to sit up. She gasped with pain. Two Strugglers grabbed her and pushed her back on to the ground.

Izzat stood over her and lifted his robe. "Look at this, Jew. See! Our weapons are better than yours!"

"Please . . ."

"Our barrels are longer!" The Holy Strugglers cheered. "And we shoot for twenty miles!"

". . . please . . ."

The horse grunted and died.

"Now I shall show you how good my aim is!" Izzat knelt between Sarah's legs.

She gasped with pain, ". . . please . . ."

The crack of a gunshot in the darkness. A bullet slammed into the hillside just feet away.

Izzat jumped to his feet, scrambling for his rifle. "What's happening?"

More shots.

The Strugglers groped for their weapons; some of them started clawing their way back up the ridge, trying to get away.

"Jews!" It was Rishou's voice, somewhere above them. "The Jews are coming! Quick, let's get out of here!"

Three more shots.

The moon had disappeared behind a dark bank of cloud. Izzat saw the orange flash of rifle fire above him. They had no chance against the kibbutzniks. They were better trained for night fighting and they had better rifles.

He ran.

"Izzat!" someone screamed.

It was Rishou. "Where are they?" Izzat shouted back at him.

Something hit him in the buttock and he turned round to see who it was. But his leg was numb and would not take his weight. He fell.

He was hit! By the Prophet's beard, he was shot!

"Help me!" he screamed.

He had to get away. Allah, help me in my sorrow! He tried to get up but his leg collapsed underneath him. The

Jews were coming! The Jews were butchers and animals! He had heard stories of what they did to their prisoners. "I am wounded! Help me! *Rishou!*"

The sons of dogs were going to leave him!

But then someone grabbed his arm and began to haul him over the hard ground, back up the ridge. He scrambled for purchase with his good leg. Another shot zinged into the rocks a few yards away and a splinter of stone hit him in the face. "Hurry!"

They reached the crest of the ridge and the other man fell on his belly, panting with the effort. It was Tareq, Izzat realised. Of course, only an idiot would stay behind to help the wounded. Izzat tried to crawl, dragging his wounded leg behind him.

They had to get right away from here. "Carry me," he hissed at Tareq. "Without me, you have no leader!" He wondered what had happened to Rishou. He hoped the Jews had got him.

Sarah lay on her back, unable to move, conserving her strength to ride the waves of nauseating pain. She braced her shoulders against the ground, and her fingers clawed at the dirt as she tried to fight it. The pain was savage, undreamt of. Let me die, let me die!

"Sarah?" A man's voice, rich and masculine, came to her from a bittersweet past. My mind playing tricks, she thought. She opened her eyes but she could not see a face in the darkness.

"It's all right. They are gone," the voice said. "Is the pain very bad?"

Couldn't be real, couldn't be him. She closed her eyes again.

"Sarah, talk to me! Open your eyes!"

She felt his hands lift her head, and warm breath on her cheek.

"Rishou?"

"Sarah, please open your eyes!"

"Can't be you . . ."

"What did they do to you?"

217

". . . mustn't stay here . . . my people are . . . coming."

"It's all right."

"They will . . . shoot you."

"There are no kibbutznik. Only me."

She didn't understand. She had heard the gunshots, and the Arabs shouting in alarm as they ran. Nothing made sense. Why was he here? The pain made it impossible to think properly.

Her mouth was dry, she couldn't swallow.

"It was me, Sarah, I fired the shots! It's all right now."

She clutched his hands in hers. "It hurts so much!"

"Shhh. You'll be all right."

"You . . . have to splint . . ."

"I don't know how to mend legs, Sarah."

Another jolt of pain and she squirmed against him. Rishou, Rishou. So long since she had seen him. Yet having him with her now seemed the most natural thing in the world. He would hold her and help her through this. He had guided her through the limits of pleasure, he would get her through this pain.

"Did those sons of whores hurt you?"

She shook her head. She had only dimly been aware of the Arabs who had tried to rape her. "Only when they pulled me . . . from under Meshaq . . . my horse . . . Rishou . . . where is Meshaq?"

"The horse is dead, Sarah."

She groaned as another spasm of pain hit her. "Oh, Rishou, help me . . . it hurts . . ."

"I can carry you to the kibbutz."

"Splint . . . you must . . . splint first."

He felt for the injury. She was wearing shorts, and Rishou ran his fingertips along her bare right leg. He had reached a point midway along her right shin when he heard her gasp, and her body went rigid. The leg was deformed, twisted outwards; bone shards had pierced the skin, and the leg was damp with blood.

"Straighten it," Sarah gasped. "Splint to . . . the other leg."

218

Rishou took out his knife and ripped three strips of cloth from the hem of his abbayah. Then, as an afterthought, he cut another. She would need something to bite down on. The pain would be worse than any torture.

He squatted beside her. "Sarah?"

"Hold me."

He stroked back her hair from her forehead and gave her a little water from the goatskin bottle at his belt. Five years since I have seen her, he thought. Five years! Those nights in the apple orchard could have been yesterday. He picked up her hand. It was cold and greasy damp. He felt the metal band on the finger of her left hand. So! She was married now.

What is wrong with me? he thought. I have betrayed my own people for her, helped a Jew against a brother Arab! All I know is that I have never loved anyone or anything as I love this woman. She might have a Jew husband now, but in her soul she is mine. She always will be.

"I am going to set the leg," he said.

"You're a dream, aren't you? . . . The pain is making me . . . imagine, Rishou, I dream you . . . so many times."

And I have dreamed you, he thought. How many times have I been with Khadija and brought myself to the sublime moment by thinking of you? "I am going to set the leg," he repeated.

He took a strip of cloth and pushed it into her mouth. He braced her knee with his left hand and gripped her ankle. He had seen Zayyad do this once, a long time ago, when one of his brothers had fallen from a horse. You had to pull slightly as you moved the limb or the bones would grind together like a gourd and pestle.

Sarah took the cloth from her mouth. "I think about you all – "

Rishou straightened the leg.

Sarah's body jerked like a string pulled taut and she screamed; the scream echoed through the dark hills as if it would never end.

*　　　*　　　*

219

Yaakov heard it, from just a hundred yards away; he almost retched with despair, Sarah! *Sarah!*

So close!

"Down there!" one of the men shouted.

Yaakov spurred his horse down the steep gully. The Arab's robe was the only white in the darkened valley. A dark and lifeless shape lay at his feet. Sarah! *He has been using his knife on my daughter.*

He reined in his horse, raised the rifle to his shoulder and fired. The white abbayah was an excellent target. The Arab fell.

Yaakov spurred his horse on, and jumped from the saddle, scrambling across the rocks to his daughter's motionless body.

"Sarah . . ." His hands searched her body, and he almost wept with relief when he found her clothes untouched. No blood!

"Sarah!" he shouted. Her face perhaps? What had the bastard done to her face? No, no, she was all right, there was no blood. He shook her by the shoulders. "Sarah, wake up!"

Horses' hooves drummed the ground. Asher and the others were around him now. "Is she all right?" Asher was suddenly beside him. "What have they done to her? Is she all right?"

Yaakov found a pulse. She was alive! "I think so," he said.

Asher cradled her head in his arms.

"What shall we do with this one?" one of the others said.

Yaakov stood up. The Arab was lying spreadeagled on his back. There was a dark stain across the front of his robe. "Bastard!" Yaakov screamed. "*Bastard!*" He kicked him. The Arab groaned and tried to roll over. Yaakov kicked him again. "He was torturing her!"

Yaakov knelt down and grabbed a fistful of Rishou's hair. He jerked his head back. "Can you hear me, Abdul?" he said in Arabic.

"Name's . . . not . . . Abdul," Rishou grunted.

Yaakov took out his knife. "We're not like you," he hissed. "We don't do this for pleasure. But unless you tell me what happened, I can carve you up as well as any Arab."

"You Jews . . . learn fast."

Yaakov slammed the handle of the knife against the bullet's exit wound in Rishou's shoulder. Rishou screamed.

"No . . ." Sarah opened her eyes, tried to sit up. "No!"

Yaakov twisted around. "Sarah!" He hugged her, sobbing with relief. "Oh my Sarah! Thank God in heaven! What did he do to you?"

"Leave him . . . was helping me . . ." Sarah said. She tried to push Yaakov away. The pain made her cry out.

"It's all right now," Asher said.

". . . he saved my . . . life." She reached for Rishou's hand. "Help him," she whispered, "help him . . ."

Rab'allah

Yaakov and Asher reined in their horses a hundred paces from the village. Rishou was slumped across the back of Asher's stallion. His blood had seeped along the animal's flank, leaving a sleek, dark stain that glistened in the feeble light of the setting moon.

Rishou groaned.

"You'll have to help him," Yaakov said to Asher. "He's lost a lot of blood. Leave him as close to the village as you dare."

Asher hesitated, remembering Levi's lifeless body. It was Levi who had alerted them. Minutes after they had helped him from his horse, he had died, an Arab bullet through his chest.

Yaakov read his thoughts. "He didn't kill Levi," he said. "You heard Sarah. This one showed mercy. Help him."

Asher dismounted. He grabbed Rishou's robe and pulled him down from the horse. Rishou groaned and

221

sank to his knees. Asher put Rishou's good arm around his shoulder and hauled him to his feet.

Rishou gasped.

"What's the matter, Abdul? A little pain never hurt anyone."

"It's just being so close to a Jew. The smell is overpowering."

Asher dragged Rishou up the horse trail towards Rab'allah. Rishou held on to him, his left arm hanging useless at his side, his legs barely holding him upright. "One day we're going to settle with all you sons of whores," Asher said. "Levi was a good man, a good Jew. He was worth twenty of your filthy fellaheen."

"I do not know who killed him. That is the truth."

"You would not know the difference between the truth and a pile of camel shit!"

"I know what camel shit looks like. I have my arm around some right now."

Asher pulled away and Rishou pitched forward on to his face. "You're the one who worked in our orchard, aren't you?"

"You have a good memory."

"You're the one Sarah had moon eyes for."

"She's the most beautiful woman I've ever seen."

"She's also my wife. You have another fifty yards to crawl, Abdul. With any luck you won't make it."

Rishou lay quite still, summoning the remains of his strength. After a while he heard the Jews' horses set off back down the trail. When he was satisfied the Jews were gone, he started to crawl up the path to Rab'allah. Sarah is a beautiful woman, he thought, but I don't think I will ever get on with her friends.

34

It seemed as if everyone in Rab'allah was crowded into Zayyad's house. There was a mood of celebration. Wagil had been avenged; even Zayyad seemed pleased with the night's events. The sobering consequences could wait till later.

Rishou's mattress had been brought into the main room, so that everyone could gaze upon the bullet hole in his shoulder. The bullet had passed straight through, but he was weak from blood loss and the women had packed the wound with a poultice of herbs to draw out the poisons.

But he was allowed little rest.

"Tell us the story again," someone urged him.

Rishou sighed. They had all heard the story a dozen times. "We made an ambush in the Bab el-Wad," he told them. "Just after dawn we saw Majid's car. But the Britishers had tricked us. Talbot effendi was escorted by a force of at least fifty British soldiers and three armoured cars. But we decided to attack anyway, even though we were hopelessly outnumbered."

It sounded absurd, even to him, but the legend had been forced on him. When Rishou had staggered into the village the night before, Izzat and his Holy Strugglers had already recounted their story, and Rishou had been careful not to contradict it; he did not want to be questioned too closely on his own role in the shooting of Izzat. So he had merely added his own heroic elaboration.

Three of the Holy Strugglers were now among his audience. They behave towards me as if we were comrades from a thousand battles, Rishou noticed. I would love to

223

see their faces if they found out who was really shooting at them last night.

"I shot a Britisher through the heart at a hundred paces!" Tareq shouted.

"I cut out a liver with this knife!" another said, and held up a rather ordinary bone-handled knife for them all to admire.

"What happened after the ambush?" Zayyad said, on cue.

"We scattered them with our first volley," Rishou recited, "but by then Majid's car had disappeared towards Latrun." Was this really the best story that Izzat had been able to invent? Rishou wondered. Perhaps it was the pain of his wound that had made him delirious.

"On the way back to Rab'allah the Jews were waiting for us," Tareq said, unable to hold back any longer. "They had machine-guns."

"Izzat was wounded as we charged them," another of the Strugglers shouted, and Rishou wondered if anyone had thought to ask how he took a bullet wound in his pimply arse while he was running forwards. He cursed himself for the poor shot that he was. He had been barely twenty paces from Izzat when he heard him call out, identifying himself among the running men. A good marksman would have drilled him through the middle, even in the dark.

"Tell us what you did then, Rishou!" someone shouted.

Rishou told them how he saw the Holy Strugglers carry the heroic Izzat off in their arms, while he decided to hold back the attackers with just his rifle.

"There were at least two hundred of them," Zayyad said proudly, elaborating on Rishou's own story, in which he had modestly claimed only a force of two dozen.

"We gave them a lesson they'll never forget!" Tareq added.

One Izzat will not easily forget either, Rishou thought. Now he has two holes in his arse. He would have liked to have been there when Sheikh Daoud's doctor pulled out the bullet with his forceps.

The effort of talking had tired him. He closed his eyes

and slept. After a while the villagers drifted away to the coffee house, to relive the battle with the other Strugglers and to describe in detail to each other what they would have done if only they had had the good fortune to have been there.

Zayyad sat beside his son, saw the first flush of the fever bloom in his cheeks. He needed rest, and good herbs. But he could not have either, not yet. He would have to get him out of Rab'allah, send him to hide among the Bedouin in the Negev. The British would come about the dead Jew. There would be questions, and anyone nursing a bullet wound was inviting a noose around his neck. Unless, of course, their uncle was on the Arab Higher Committee. Like Izzat.

He wondered what had really happened last night. Perhaps he would never know. One thing he was sure of: whatever put the hole in Izzat's buttock, it wasn't a Jewish machine-gun.

The Place Where The Fig Tree Died

Rishou swayed in the saddle. It was as much as he could do to stay on his horse, but his father had impressed on him the need to get out of Rab'allah without delay. From the crest of the ridge he could see a small tail of dust moving up the horse trail from Jerusalem towards the village. Probably Captain Mannion, he thought, or Inspector Cooper.

The two men with Rishou looked uncomfortable. If Rishou died, there would be no point in returning to the village. Zayyad would publicly absolve them of all blame and then come in the night and cut out their hearts. The previous night's incident had restored to the old muktar all his former vigour.

"We must hurry," one of them said.

Rishou's shoulder ached unmercifully and the fever

made him light-headed. He blinked away the sudden nausea that threatened to overwhelm him. "Yes, yes," he said, but still he lingered. Down there, beyond the vineyards and the orchards was the kibbutz. He wondered about Sarah. The Jews had good doctors. He was sure they would mend her leg.

He looked back at Rab'allah. At least two years, his father had said. Of course, he would miss Zayyad, as he would miss his two sons, Ali and Rahman. And Khadija – well, she was a good cook.

But he guessed he would not miss any of them as much as he had missed the Jewish girl who had taught him so much in those apple orchards. He would pay anything for one more night with her under the moon. But that was impossible now. One day he would be muktar of Rab'allah, and he would have to face the realities of the new Palestine. He must never again put himself in the position of raising a rifle at his own brothers, even if one of them was Izzat Ib'n Mousa.

He would remember her often, when the moon was full, or when the apple harvest was near. But he was a man now, an Arab, and Sarah Landauer must be consigned to the secret places of the past, for ever.

Part Seven

GERMANY, 1941–2

35

Ravenswald

Herr Nöldner made a point of informing all his customers that he had nothing personally against the Jews. Yes, he supported Hitler. After all the man had got Germany back on its feet again. But he, personally, was not anti-Semitic. He thought what was being done to them was a terrible shame.

A terrible shame, Netanel thought, but also a wonderful windfall for Herr Nöldner, because Herr Nöldner owned the pawnbroker's shop. Once he barely scratched a living in Ravenswald – most of the town had at least one member of their family in employment at Rosenberg Fabriken and making a living wage – but now he was one of the bessere Leute. In fact, he had recently bought Herr Doktor Köhn's house from his widow for the bargain price of thirteen thousand marks. Köhn had caught pneumonia at Dachau.

Herr Nöldner's personal fortunes had risen with Hitler's; when the first Jews had started leaving Ravenswald in 1934, they had been forced to sell whatever they could not afford to take with them. When they could not sell privately they came to him. Later, when emigration restrictions became more strict, and Jews were allowed to take virtually nothing of value, Westphalian ham replaced *bratwurst* on Herr Nöldner's table.

Even those Jews still remaining in Ravenswald were forced to use his services. They had no choice but to barter personal items just to pay for basic food like bread and milk, and even these had to be purchased through an intermediary.

But it was Kristallnacht that paid for Herr Köhn's six-bedroom house on the hill overlooking the town. Legislation was passed in the Reichstag prohibiting Jews from owning valuable metals, such as gold or silver, and even small luxury items such as wirelesses.

The queues outside Herr Nöldner's shop grew longer and longer.

Netanel's memories of these events were bitter. He had wandered through the ruins of his house collecting the silverware; the baroque cutlery, the silver coffee pot, the menorah and ornamental salver they used for the Passover, the candlesticks they used for the Feast of the Lights. He had packed it all in two leather suitcases and taken it to Herr Nöldner who offered to pay him by weight of the metal.

"But most of this silver is antique!" Netanel shouted at him. "The menorah itself is over two hundred years old!"

Herr Nöldner shrugged his shoulders. "I am sorry. Times are difficult. What can I say? Personally, I have nothing against the Jews, but . . . well, you know how it is these days. Next!"

Netanel had taken Herr Nöldner's offer. He had no choice. The law said he had to sell, and no one else would pay more.

But the halcyon days had passed for Herr Nöldner. There were just a handful of customers in his shop this morning. They were all Jews, and like Netanel they wore an armband on their overcoats, a black Star of David stencilled on yellow cloth. It was law now. They could not go out in public without this mark of the pariah.

They sat in miserable silence, waiting. One had a piece of old carpet, tied with string; another man – it was the shoeseller, Horowitz – had a phonogram with a broken handle. Such a cornucopia of riches! Netanel thought.

A cold drizzle of rain misted the window.

"What have you come to sell?"

Netanel looked around. The speaker was a small man,

230

with shiny black hair, thinning on the crown, that looked like a monk's tonsure. He had eager and watery brown eyes, like a dog, and the creases on his face looked as if they were lined with dust.

"I have a piece of Meissen china," Netanel said.

The man nodded, to indicate his sympathy with Netanel's situation and held up a brown paper bag. "Look in here. Good leather shoes. But I never wear them any more. So why not sell? I told my wife, what's the good of shoes you never wear? Still, it's not so bad for us, harder for you. You're der Chef's son, aren't you?"

"That's right," Netanel said, warily.

"I'm Amos Mandelbaum." He put out his hand. "I used to work at the factory. You probably don't remember."

Netanel shook his head. "No, I'm sorry."

They shook hands. "He was a good man, your father. A great man. It was a tragedy what happened to him. I said to my wife, 'What they did to that man is a tragedy.' When all this is over, they'll build a statue to him right in the middle of the square. You'll see."

"They already have a statue. Of King Ludwig."

Mandelbaum seemed not to hear. "Twelve years I worked at the factory. Every Passover, all the Jewish workers got a bonus. He was a good man, a great man. Still, we mustn't be gloomy."

I'm not gloomy, Netanel thought. I have a visa for Cuba for myself and my mother. It was not the United States, but it was close. We catch the boat-train from München to Hamburg on December 23rd. So indeed – why should I be gloomy?

But what about this Mandelbaum, and all these others who had to stay behind? Perhaps that was why he was reluctant to talk. Guilt. He had the money to pay the bribes and the fares; they did not.

"I heard a joke the other day," Mandelbaum said.

"A joke?"

"Hitler and Goering are arguing. Goering says to Hitler, 'You know, the Jews are really quite smart.'

"'Prove it!' Hitler says.

231

"So they go into the nearest china shop they can find and Goering picks out a tea-set. 'Watch this,' he says to Hitler and he points all the handles to the right. When the German owner comes over, he says to him, 'I'm looking for a set of china just like this one, but I need a left-handed set.'

"The man says that it is the only one he has in the shop and he will have to contact the wholesaler to see if he can get another.

"So Hitler and Goering go to a Jewish shop. Goering does the same thing again. 'I need a set of china cups just like this one,' he says to the Jew, 'but I need a left-handed set.'

"'I'll see what I can do,' the Jew says, and he takes the tea-set out the back, turns all the handles round to the left, and comes back out again. *Meine Herren!* he says. 'You're in luck! I have just one left! Shall I wrap it for you?'

"So Goering buys the tea-set. When they get outside he turns to Hitler and says, 'See, I told you the Jews were smart.'

"And Hitler says, 'That's ridiculous. It proves nothing. The Jew was lucky. He had them in stock!'"

Mandelbaum rocked back in his chair, laughing. "Do you understand?" he said. "He had them *in stock*!" He laughed again.

Horowitz had turned away from the counter, his face blank with despair. He pocketed the meagre coins Nöldner had given him and went out. Netanel watched him trudge away through the rain, his eyes down, careful not to attract attention to himself. A Jew with his head held high was inviting trouble these days.

"Next," Herr Nöldner said.

Netanel went to the counter. Herr Nöldner studied him over the rims of his half-moon spectacles. The smile was benign, and a gold tooth flashed in his lower jaw. "How can I help you, Herr Rosenberg?"

Netanel took a package from his overcoat pocket. It was wrapped with newspaper, and tied with string. Netanel

232

opened it carefully. Inside was a porcelain figurine, a small boy in lederhosen sitting on a gate. It was one of a pair; its partner had been a blonde girl in a blue dress carrying a basket of flowers. She had been trampled underfoot by the stormtroopers on Kristallnacht, but the boy had somehow miraculously escaped their attentions.

Netanel was loath to part with it; the Meissen figurines had flirted with each other in the glass cabinet in the drawing-room for as long as he could remember. Another link with the past being bartered away.

"An ornament," Herr Nöldner said.

"It is Meissen," Netanel corrected him.

"Are there any others?" Herr Nöldner said, betraying that he knew more about Meissen than he pretended.

"The other was broken."

"A great shame. If you had the pair . . ."

"I told you, it's Meissen. Even alone it is worth something."

Herr Nöldner put the figurine on the counter and assumed the pained expression of a man whose hands are tied by circumstance. "I wish I could help you. I'll give you five marks, to take it off your hands. After all, you have been a good customer."

"Five marks!"

Herr Nöldner held up his hands. "It's a lot for a simple ornament, I know. But I want to help if I can."

"You little shit!"

Herr Nöldner took a step back from the counter. "I will not be insulted by the likes of you! Take it or leave it."

Netanel looked around the shop. The other men had their eyes on the floor, studying the faded patterns of the carpet. What a pathetic sight we are, Netanel thought. The flower of European Jewry clustered in a pawnbroker's shop, begging for coins.

He picked up the figurine and smashed it on the edge of the counter. He dropped the shattered halves on to the floor.

"Now it's a pair," he said.

As he walked back to the House in the Woods, the chill rain fell harder. He kept his head high and stared every one of the townspeople right in the eye.

Goering's Guns for Butter campaign had begun to bite. It was impossible to get real butter or cream now. Everything was *ersatz*, a substitute. There was ersatz butter, ersatz rubber, even ersatz fabrics. People joked about buying a new suit and having green leaves sprout from the lapels, or buying a dress that grew branches.

Tonight, at dinner, Hermann had thrown away his bread and margarine in disgust. "This is shit!" he had shouted, and practically spat it on to the plate. "I would rather eat my bread dry than eat this muck!"

There were only three of them at the table. Dieter was now with the Sixth Army in Russia. During the summer Hitler had opened a second front and invaded the Soviet Union. In August they received a letter from him saying that he was in Smolensk, and that he would be celebrating Christmas in Moscow. In the newspapers Russian names dominated everything. Bialystock, Minsk, Kiev, Leningrad. The radio announcers crowed victory after victory as von Bock and his generals converged on the Russian capital.

"We will show those communists a thing or two," Hermann had announced that night from his armchair as he read the letter. "Dieter says there are lines of prisoners as far as the eye can see! It's a good job we have Poland or we would have nowhere to put them!" He laughed at that. It was a good joke.

Apart from the ersatz butter, the only other problem for Hermann and Inge was the motor car. They were still paying their five marks every week, but as yet there was no sign of their promised Kraft dürch Freude Wagen. The factory had been finished in 1939, as Hitler had promised, but by then the war was under way and the factory was fully occupied producing vehicles for the German army.

Now it was the third winter of war, and in Ravenswald

everything was covered in ice. The freezing rain was turning to snow and it was already dark by four o'clock in the afternoon. Children were ice-skating on the Ravensee.

After dinner Marie sat down with Hermann and Inge to listen to the radio. For once, the news was not dominated by events on the Russian front. Germany's friends and allies, the Japanese – tall, blond and Aryan to the core! Marie thought with disgust – had attacked the American fleet at Pearl Harbor.

The whole world was going mad.

Much later in the broadcast, while Hermann was dozing off in his chair, the newsreader announced another piece of legislation from Berlin concerning the Jews, and Marie started in her chair with such violence that Hermann woke.

"What's wrong?" he said.

"Nothing," she said, but her mind was racing. As from today, Goering had told the Reichstag, no Jew under the age of sixty was allowed to leave the country.

Netanel's last avenue of escape was gone.

36

It was Hanukkah, the Feast of Lights. Netanel lit every candle in their dwindling store, two dozen bright white flames chasing away the shadows from the corners of the tiny room that had defined the perimeters of their sanctuary ever since Kristallnacht. It was extravagant, but Netanel justified the waste by assuring himself that in another two weeks they would no longer need the candles. They would be on their way out of Germany.

Everything except the day-to-day essentials was packed. Netanel had stuffed two suitcases with clothes; household goods, sheets, crockery and linen had been packed into the wooden chests that now lined one wall of the room. Everything had been ready for their journey for almost a month, ever since Netanel had returned from Berlin with the precious visas. Now there was just the waiting; listening to the snow falling from the roof, the lonely whine of the wind, the crackle of logs in the grate.

"Your father should be home soon," Frau Rosenberg said.

Poor Mutti, Netanel thought. Every day she retreats further into her own fantasies. How will she cope with the journey? How will she cope with living in a new and alien country?

All Netanel knew about Cuba was a listing he had found in one of his father's encyclopaedias: that it was an island in the West Indies, the capital was Havana, and the economy was based on sugar and tobacco. What would happen to them when they got there? Would Mutti still want to know when Josef was coming back from his card game? Would she still expect Hilde to fetch her her afternoon *kaffee*?

It seemed unreal, a child's daydream. Yet the visas were stamped, and their tickets for the passage between Hamburg and Havana were on the mantelpiece above the fire. He knew what his last act on German soil would be: as he stepped off the dock on to the gangplank he would save one mouthful of good Jewish spit for "the Fatherland".

He heard tapping on the kitchen door. Marie! He got up and went through the drawing-room and into the kitchen. He threw open the door and Marie hurried inside. A draught of bitterly cold air followed her. Netanel slammed the door shut again quickly.

"Your cheeks are red," he said, grinning, and hugged her. It had been almost a week since he had seen her.

She pulled away from him. He knew straight away that something was wrong.

"What is it?"

"Nothing," she said, too quickly, and held out the package that was concealed under her coat. "Veal and

236

liverwurst and bratwurst. I'm sorry I could not come before. You must be starving."

"Thank you."

She took off her coat. Netanel hated himself for his weakness; he should never have allowed her to continue with this. Each time he told her that this must be the last time, but they both knew it was merely a charade. Neither Netanel nor his mother could survive without her now. She bought groceries with the money he gave her, stole meat from her father's shop, brought him the rumours of who was offering visas, which country was accepting refugees. But most of all she brought companionship and solace, and that one commodity that had become priceless and rare: kindness.

She would have given him much more, if he had let her. But she was already taking terrible risks; to make her his lover was to drag her down with him to doom.

Yet it disturbed him too how effortlessly his reason controlled his passion. He saw too much of his father in himself, a man whose first instinct was to think. Even though Netanel felt he was doing the right thing, the just thing, he despised himself for it.

Marie went into the living-room. "You've lit the candles."

"It's Hanukkah. The Feast of Lights. When I was a child we had them blazing all over the house."

"You should be saving them," she said, and Netanel had his first clue as to what was wrong.

Frau Rosenberg looked up from the fire. "Who's there?"

"*Guten Abend*, Frau Rosenberg."

"Netanel! We can't have gentiles in the house!"

"But, Mutti, look what Marie has brought us!" He held up the parcel of meats.

"Herr Rosenberg will be back from his cards very soon. We can't have gentiles here when he gets home!" She returned her attention to the logs in the grate.

Marie went back into the drawing-room. This was where

Frau Rosenberg slept; Netanel had dragged one of the beds down from upstairs for her.

Marie sat on the edge of the bed. She folded her arms across her knees, hugging herself. She could not meet his eyes.

It's bad, Netanel thought.

"Thank you for coming," he said.

"Father thinks I am at the cinema."

"One day he will catch you out."

"He has caught me out before. So I make up another story. If I told him the truth he would never believe me." She laughed, a high-pitched tremolo. She was trying too hard.

He sat on the bed beside her. "Something's wrong."

She hesitated. "I don't know how to tell you."

"Just do it. Please."

Her voice was anguished. "Liebling, what are we going to do?"

"Tell me what's happened!"

"It was on the radio tonight. They have cancelled all emigration for any Jewish person under sixty years old."

Netanel hung his head.

He was surprised at his own reaction; it was almost as if he had been expecting this. Cuba had never seemed very real anyway. This was like waking up from a pleasant dream. Perhaps the real despair would come later.

"What are we going to do?" Marie said.

"You are going to go away from here tonight, and you are not going to come back."

"You have said that before. You don't mean it."

"I do mean it. You're just too stubborn to listen."

"There must be some way!"

"They have slammed the last door in our faces. Perhaps I should wait another thirty-five years. I will be old enough then."

"Don't give up hope, liebling. Go back to Berlin. Perhaps there is someone you can bribe."

"What with? I have sold everything. The car paid for the grease at the Cuban embassy for the visas."

"You still have the house. You can offer the deeds."

"Perhaps." He would try, of course. But he had lost his belief. He was convinced now that they would never get out of this hell.

Marie took his hand. "Don't give up hope."

"What hope is there?"

"Oh, Netya, I don't understand. They say they don't want any Jews, but now they won't let you go. I don't understand . . ."

"I think they just enjoy it. They would miss us if they did not have us around to kick any more. They would have to find someone else to blame for everything that goes wrong."

"You'll get out. You'll find some way, I know you will."

"The hell of it is, a part of me does not want to go. If I escape the Germans, I have to leave you behind."

She put her arms around him. Her hair was soft as silk against his cheek, and the scent of her cologne aroused the ache inside him. It was like a fist in the pit of his stomach. Take her, he thought. You might only have this moment. You don't know what will happen tomorrow. If you get away, if you don't, either way you lose. Just take this moment.

But then you will make her a Jew too. Your kiss is the kiss of death. You are the Jew Midas, your touch is the mark of the pariah.

"I love you, Netanel."

He pushed her away. "Go now."

She grabbed his hand. "Please . . ."

"No! We won't starve. Frau Hochstetter still leaves parcels now and then and sometimes one of the townspeople comes by and throws bread on the driveway. It's very uncomplicated. They don't say they're sorry, we don't say thank you. Perhaps it's better that way."

"I mean it. I do love you. I never stopped."

"In the end it doesn't make one little bit of difference. I'm a leper. You can't touch a leper."

239

"But I want to touch you," she whispered.

He stood up. "Just go!"

She went into the kitchen, put on her coat, and wound the scarf round her cheeks. She went to the door, hesitated. When she turned back to him, her eyes flashed with anger. "I don't need you to make my decisions for me! You can't stop me coming here. I love you, and I'll love you till the end. I'll never betray you. Never!"

When she had gone, Netanel stood for a long time staring at nothing, his fists opening and closing in silent torment. Then he went back into the living-room and started to snuff the candles, one by one, until just a single candle was left burning, their only light on this winter's night.

37

Marie saw a thin man in a grey cloak overcoat and a Tyrolean hat walking past the shop. A massive chestnut draught-horse, standing stock still on the cobbles outside, suddenly turned its great head to one side and pushed the man into the window. The man yelped and lost his balance. He scrambled to his feet and hurried away.

"Spritzer," Marie said.

Emmerich, the carter, was halfway through the front door. He saw the passer-by fall and swore under his breath. He saw Marie and removed his denim cap. "That horse has the foulest temperament of any animal I ever saw."

Perhaps because you beat him all the time. "What can I do for you today, Herr Emmerich?"

"I came to see your father, Fräulein."

"He's out the back. I'll tell him you're here."

Hermann was butchering a pig carcass. He came out and waved Emmerich into the back room. Marie went outside. Spritzer stood in the street, tossing his head against the traces of the heavy cart, the breath from his nostrils crystallising on the chill March air.

"Spritzer, it's me, Marie. Do you remember?" She produced two sugar cubes from her apron. She kept them as treats for any small children who came in the shop. "I've brought you something."

The old horse studied her with malevolent pink eyes. If he did remember her, it seemed the recollection did not conjure pleasant associations for him. But a sugar cube was a sugar cube. He accepted them, without grace, sneezing wetly into her hand.

Then, satisfied that she had nothing else to offer, he showed his gratitude by ignoring her, instead of pushing her through the window with his nose.

She tried to stroke his mane but he jerked his head away. Spritzer was tough. He could be tamed but he could not be bought.

A customer went into the shop and she had no time to seduce him further. "Be good, Spritzer," she said and he snorted in disgust.

"What did he want?" Marie asked after Emmerich had left.

"Just business," Hermann said.

"We shouldn't do business with people like that. He's a pig."

"Now you watch your tongue. His son is an important man now. He's a Stürmbahnführer in the SS."

"Doing what exactly?"

"Secret work," Hermann said, and nodded profoundly as if he were Albert Speer and privy to such secrets.

"Is he fighting the Russians like Dieter?"

"The SS is one of the elite units."

"Should I be impressed?"

Hermann clucked his tongue, impatient with her intransigence. "Young Rolf Emmerich kept a torch burning for you for many years. You missed your chance there."

"You know how it is. I was distracted by nausea."

"Such a clever tongue you have now you have been to university! Look where it has got you. You are nearly an old maid. A girl your age should be married by now."

"It's not my fault, Father, it's Hitler. He wants all the nice young boys for his army."

"So what do you do with your life? You go to the cinema every week. Inge wants to know when you're going to make us grandparents."

"Does she have any suggestions?"

"What about Rudi Hoettges?"

"He is half blind and congenitally stupid. The army refused him, even as a clerk. Even the Gestapo didn't want him."

"Don't make jokes about the Gestapo!"

"Any young man left in Ravenswald is either a cripple, a mental defective or Jewish. Perhaps you'd like me to go back to Netanel Rosenberg and ask him if he'd still like to marry me?"

Hermann went white. "Be still! If you even so much as mention his name again in my house I will beat you black and blue!"

Hermann looked up and saw Herr Netzer, the postman, on the other side of the street. He went around the counter and threw open the door. "*Guten Morgen*, Herr Netzer!"

Netzer waved. His job had become harder since Hitler had opened the Russian front. Everyone wanted letters. Handwritten ones. It was the ones with the official stamp of the Reichstag everyone dreaded.

"Anything for me this morning?"

"Nothing, I'm sorry."

Hermann closed the door. Over a month since they had heard from Dieter. On the radio there were reports of glorious victories at Kharkov and in the Crimea. But the last they had heard from Dieter was a long and desperate letter about truck radiators freezing and men losing toes and fingers to frostbite.

Hermann disappeared into the back room. Marie heard the angry chop-chop of the cleaver as he continued with his work.

There was just one candle to light the Seder. This Passover there was no matzoh, no bitter herbs, no wine for Elijah. Instead they ate black bread with ersatz butter, sweetened with a thick treacle made from beets.

As Netanel recited the story of the exodus, he stared at the Jewish Star that a stormtrooper's knife had carved into the surface of the table. Let my people go: the words echoed in his head. Five thousand years and nothing had changed, except this time there was no Moses to lead them, and no God to avenge them with his ten plagues.

He recited the stories and the prayers, and they ate in silence. When he had finished they all whispered, "Next year in Jerusalem." But Netanel wondered if there would be a next year, in Jerusalem, or anywhere else.

"I have to go home now," Marie said.

Netanel kissed her lightly on the cheek. "Thank you for coming."

"You should not allow gentiles in the house," Frau Rosenberg said. "Your father will be home soon."

38

"Where did you go last night?" Hermann said.

I was at a Passover. Oh, you know, just with some Jews. "I went to the cinema," she said.

"Is that all you ever think about?"

Marie put on her apron. "Shall I open the shop?"

"What did you see?"

"It was a western. Tom Mix."

"America! They are our enemies, our bitter enemies! And the cinema shows Tom Mix westerns!" He snorted with disgust and went into the back room. There was a large carcass laid out on the bench. That's the biggest cow I've ever seen, she thought.

"Who did you go with?"

"Ilse." Ilse had been told to cover for her. Ilse thought Marie was seeing Rudi Hoettges. Ilse was even more stupid than Rudi.

"Ilse! That girl could frighten away a gorilla! How do you hope to meet young men if you keep company with girls like that!"

"Ilse is very sweet. You shouldn't talk about her like that."

"You're not getting any younger," Hermann grumbled.

"Who is?"

"You always have an answer. I should never have sent you to university. All you learned was to talk back to your father."

She folded her arms and stared at him. "Why did you send me?"

He did not answer. He took a large knife from the wall and began to sharpen it.

"What sort of animal is that?" Marie asked him.

"It's a horse. What does it look like?"

"Horse? You're selling horsemeat?"

"Keep your voice down!" He looked around the corner of the door to make sure there were no customers in the shop. "Who's going to tell the difference?"

"Why do we need to sell horsemeat?"

"It's cheap! There's a war on, if you didn't notice! Times are hard. A clever man needs to find ways to make a little extra profit for himself if his family is not to suffer. If I had a pawnbroker's shop I would be rich by now. But as I am only a poor butcher, I have to do the best I can."

"Where did you get this poor beast from?"

"From old Emmerich. I did him a favour. I paid him more than the knacker would. Once he's in the bratwurst, who's going to know?"

Spritzer. Father, you pig!

She heard the bell ring in the shop. The postman, Netzer, stood at the counter, and he could not meet her eyes. "Just one for you today," he said. He handed her the letter and walked out quickly.

The typewritten envelope bore the eagle and swastika emblem of the Reichstag. It was addressed to her father, but she immediately tore it open, her fingers trembling. Perhaps he was only wounded.

She read it and walked into the back room.

Hermann saw the letter crumpled in her fist and put down the cleaver. "Dieter?" he said.

She nodded.

He looked desperately around the room like a drowning man searching for driftwood to cling to. He put a hand to his mouth and made a sound like a sneeze as he tried to choke back tears. Marie stared at him. She had never, ever, seen her father cry. "What are we going to do?" he said.

Marie wanted to comfort him but she was too numb to move. Hermann gulped down his grief and took off his apron. "I will tell Inge," he said. "You had better close up the shop."

She stared at the carcass on the bench and thought about her brother. She tried to remember him as he used to be, before the Hitler Jugend, when he still wore lederhosen and played with his tin soldiers on the stairs; not frozen to death in a field in Russia, his flesh frozen and bleeding and raw, like Spritzer over there.

Like horsemeat.

A skein of smoke drifted lazily upwards, into an ice blue March evening sky. The House in the Woods was more like a battered farmhouse in a battlefield, Marie thought. The rondavel had gone a long time ago to help board the windows; now most of the trees were

245

gone too. Netanel had chopped the small ones down for firewood, and only the big willow and two old firs remained.

Marie ran quickly up the path and sprinted across the back garden to the kitchen door. Netanel answered her knock, peering out from the gloomy interior, surprised. She had never come while it was still light. "What's wrong?" he whispered, as he ushered her inside.

Marie stood shivering by the kitchen table.

"What is it?" he repeated.

"Hold me," she said.

He put his arms around her and she leaned against him, needing his strength, his comfort. "Tell me what's wrong," he said.

"It's Dieter." It was stupid, she knew. She and Dieter hadn't even liked each other, not for years anyway. When he joined the Hitler Jugend she had despised him, and the last time she had seen him he had been wearing his new Wehrmacht uniform with two chevrons on the shoulder, and they had barely spoken a civil word. But he was her brother. Once she had played with him in his cradle and when he had taken his first steps she had been there to cheer him on.

She wasn't angry at the Russians. It was Hitler she hated. He had taken away her little brother and turned him into a swaggering monster and death was just the final postscript to the transformation.

"I'm sorry," Netanel whispered. "I'm so sorry."

"Who is there?" Frau Rosenberg called. "Is that Josef? Is he back from his cards?"

"It's no one, Mutti," Netanel answered. He led Marie into the drawing-room, lit the candle by the bed and shut the door.

Marie sat on the bed. "We don't even know how he died."

Netanel put his arms around her. There was nothing he could think of to say.

"He never grew up," Marie said. "He never had the chance. I always thought one day we would be brother

246

and sister again. That we would look back and laugh at all this. He was just a little boy playing soldiers."

"Shhh," Netanel said, stroking her hair, "it's all right."

"It will never be all right again. You don't believe it, and neither do I. They have made all our lives hell." She was angry now. Grief would come later. It was clear to her now that none of them had a lifetime, that for her, for Netanel, for everyone she knew, there might only be a few months, a few days, perhaps just a few hours. Dieter's death had given birth to a cold fury and a determination to count off every minute that remained to her as an inviolate treasure.

She took off her coat, unbuttoned her cardigan and reached behind to unfasten the buttons on her dress.

"What are you doing?"

She took his face in her hands, her eyes fierce. "When is it going to be you?"

"What are you talking about?"

"They want to take everything away from us, Netya, and we've let them! We have been so afraid of what will happen we have let them take everything we wanted. Soon they'll take you too!" She stood up and pulled the dress over her head.

"No," Netanel said. It wasn't meant to be like this. He picked up her dress and pushed it back into her arms. "You don't know what you're doing."

She twisted away from him. "They're going to take you away from me somehow. But they can't take now. Every moment I have with you is one moment I will not regret when you're gone." She wrapped her arms around his neck. "I'm cold. Are you going to let me into your bed or do you want me to stand here and freeze?"

It had been urgent and awkward. When he was twenty years old Netanel had lost his virginity to a prostitute in München. He had learned only a little from the experience, and only a little more on his return visit. But since that time eligible Jewish men had not been greatly prized in Hitler's Germany and further opportunities had been limited. What else he knew, he had learned from books.

It was over too quickly. He was barely inside her when he felt himself close to the edge. He pulled out of her, heard her murmur "No," and then a shuddering climax enveloped him and he lay panting on top of her, feeling guilty and spent and ashamed.

She stroked his hair. "You did not have to do that."

"You might be good at . . . deceiving your father. But I think even Hermann might suspect . . . if you brought home . . . a baby."

"Was it all right for you?" She had heard from her cousin that the first time was never good. It hurt more than she had expected.

"It was wonderful." *Mein Gott*, what about his mother's sheets?

They lay quietly for a long time. Marie had thought that lovemaking would bring them a feeling of intimacy. Instead she felt only embarrassed and awkward.

The door to the living-room opened. "Is that you, Josef?" Frau Rosenberg said. Marie gasped and pulled the sheet over her head.

"Shut the door please, Mutti," Netanel said.

"Are you in my bed?"

"Yes, Mutti."

"Are you tired?" She squinted into the shadows. "Oh, Netanel. Who is that?"

"It's Marie Helder, Mutti. She came to visit us."

"Oh, Netanel. You've brought a gentile into the house!"

Unexpectedly, Netanel laughed. "Yes, Mutti, I am afraid so. Now go back inside and sit down. Father will be home soon."

The door closed.

They lay in the darkness, listening to the sound of their own breathing. "Once that would have been my worst nightmare," he whispered. He pulled the sheet away from her face. "Adolf Hitler seems to have put things in perspective for me."

She opened her eyes. He was laughing. Suddenly the awkwardness between them was gone. She started to laugh too.

"I should have locked the door," he said.

"It doesn't matter. Rather your mother than the Gestapo."

He kissed her and stroked a lock of hair from her face.

"I'm sorry. It wasn't very good, was it?"

"That was just practice. Do you want to try again?"

Marie closed her eyes and let him love her. She tried not to think about Dieter, or her father, or any of it. There would be time for all of that later. She knew that finally she was doing what she should have done years ago. She was with the man she had chosen, and she had wasted so much time.

39

As summer wore on, other names crept into the radio broadcasts in the evenings: the German army took Sebastopol on the Black Sea and converged on Stalingrad; their Japanese allies landed on an island called Guadalcanal somewhere in the Pacific; Erwin Rommel's Afrika Korps were sweeping towards the Suez Canal. The announcer claimed that soon British Palestine would be in German hands, together with the whole of North Africa.

Hermann no longer took much interest in the conduct of the war. He had become sullen and morose since the news of Dieter's death; meanwhile Inge had taken to her bed, and had stayed there. The doctor visited her regularly, investigating every new complaint and imagined suffering, and prescribed endless medicines. But Marie knew what was wrong with her mother; she had lost the will to go on.

Visiting the House in the Woods was much more

difficult for Marie during the long, hot days when the sun did not set until after nine o'clock in the evening. Lovers came to the woods behind the house, and this increased the danger of her being seen. She found herself longing for the cold winter nights when few people ventured beyond the town streets and she had the protection of darkness.

Because of the risk, she rarely visited the house more than twice a month. On those occasions they fell on the bed in each other's arms almost at once, for their years of self-imposed restraint had dammed a flood of urgent need. Marie did not know how she had lived so long without a man in her life. She had sinned against her Church and outlawed herself in the eyes of her country, and she had never been so happy in her life.

Her cousin Heidi, who was married, had once told her that sex was difficult and painful at first. But then one day, she said, her cheeks red, it becomes wonderful.

Heidi was right. She and Netanel had quickly lost their awkwardness and embarrassment with each other and one day this other magical and unexpected thing happened to her body. The first few times she had felt nothing, but then, as their lovemaking became gentler, a shuddering tension built inside her and one night it had broken in a shattering explosion that left her weak and exhausted and ecstatically happy.

When she opened her eyes Netanel had been smiling at her.

"Does this mean I am going to hell?" she whispered.

"Because you enjoyed it?"

"I'm a good Catholic girl . . . I'm not meant to enjoy it."

"Of course you are. Didn't your mother ever tell you anything?"

"I can't imagine her ever enjoying anything . . ."

At that one moment she had never felt so close to another human being in her life. They were joined physically and emotionally and it no longer mattered to her what the priest or the government or her father said. When

250

tomorrow came with its darkness and bitter hatreds, there would still be this to hold on to.

"What is it like for you?" he asked her. "At the last moment?"

"It's like . . . I can't describe it. It's like a warm glow. And it just grows and grows. All over my body. What about you?"

"For me? . . . I don't know . . . it's a little like a sneeze . . ."

She feigned outrage. "A sneeze?"

She had succeeded in embarrassing him. "It's just the feeling," he stammered, ". . . like the sensation . . . only not in my nose . . ."

She pretended to cuff him. "Should I say 'Bless you' every time?"

"If you like. Better make it 'Gezuntheit'. That's Jewish."

"My whole body feels as if it turns into a rainbow of colours and you sneeze!" He grinned, and she ran her fingers through his hair. "I never thought I'd laugh when I was in bed with a man. I thought it was supposed to be a serious business."

"With my mother in the next room shouting at me not to bring gentiles into the house? How can we be serious?"

She put her arms around him. He was losing weight, she had noticed. Netanel and his mother had used up their stock of food during the last winter and now they barely survived day to day. Lately Marie had taken to buying groceries and leaving them in the woods to reduce the risk of being seen. But her secret errands were already an open secret with her girlfriend Ilse and with the grocer. It was only a matter of time before she was betrayed.

She touched the silver Star of David that he wore at his neck, her Christmas present to him all those years ago. "Don't ever give up," she whispered. "No matter what happens. Promise me."

"I promise."

One day there would be a time, she thought. This could

251

not be all there was. One day there must be a time
when they could lie here for as long as they wanted
without fear.

Another time she whispered to him, "If you could get away
from here, where would you go?"

He thought about it for a long time. "Palestine," he said
finally. "The Zionists say one day Jews will have their
own country there. Can you imagine it? Somewhere we
wouldn't be foreigners any more. Where being called a Jew
wasn't an insult? Somewhere they couldn't take anything
away from us ever again?"

It was late evening, nearly ten o'clock, but the sun had not
long set behind the distant Alps, and the air was warm and
smelled of hay. Marie climbed the stairs to the apartment,
aware of the delicious dampness between her legs. She
experienced a thrill of fear, as she always did when she
returned from one of her clandestine visits to the House
in the Woods.

She assumed an air of casual boredom as she opened
the door. She froze. There was a stranger sitting drinking
schnapps with her father in the living-room.

He got up and gave a slight bow of his head, the heels of
his polished black leather boots clicking smartly together.
"Good evening, Fräulein Helder," Rolf said.

Marie looked at her father. "What is he doing here?"

Hermann looked frightened, and did not answer.

"I came to see you," Rolf said, smiling at her.

He has changed, she thought. The swagger of the
bully had been replaced by a more sinister brand of
self-assurance. He wore the chevrons of an SS Stürmbahnführer on his uniform, and his death's head cap grinned at
her from the table by the window. He looked sleek and
beautiful, like a wolf. The face of a god and eyes like
winter.

"Where have you been?" he asked her.

"That is no business of yours."

"Your father says you were at the cinema."

252

Marie concentrated her attention on her father. "Why did you let him in?" she said to Hermann.

He did not answer her, but his eyes pleaded with her for silence. He looked utterly miserable. So! Even he is intimidated by the carter's son now!

"Come and sit down," Rolf said.

Hermann yawned and stretched and rubbed his eyes. When the elaborate pantomime was finished, he said, "I'm tired. I think I must excuse myself. I have to be up early in the morning."

Thank you, Father, Marie thought. Thank you for your protection. Are you frightened of him or have you already worked out some way this brutal little upstart can be of use to you?

"Goodnight, Herr Helder," Rolf said.

"Goodnight, Stürmbahnführer Emmerich. Goodnight, Marie."

"I should go to bed too," Marie said.

Hermann looked at Rolf then back to her. "But your guest . . ."

"He's not my guest."

Rolf smiled with his mouth, but his eyes glittered with rage. "Let her go to bed if she wishes, Herr Helder. I thought I might have something to say to her that might help her. But if she is tired, perhaps it can wait until another day." He picked up his cap.

Marie could not refuse the bait. "How do you think you are going to help me?"

He merely smiled, the corners of his mouth creasing upwards. The enigma of his expression taunted her. Does he know? she thought.

She had to find out.

She put down her coat and seated herself in the armchair by the fire. She heard Hermann's bedroom door click shut. Rolf sat down opposite her, and took his time lighting a cigarette.

"How was the film?" he said. His head was wreathed in blue smoke.

"What film?"

253

"The film you saw tonight. At the cinema."

"Is that why you came here tonight? To discuss the cinema?"

"I came here to see you. I have always admired you, Marie. It is only a pity that my duty to my country has kept me away from Ravenswald for so long."

"I had not realised you had been away."

The smile disappeared. It was like a cold draught through the room. Without the smile, the viciousness in his eyes was all she could see, and Marie felt naked. He hates me, she realised. He wants me desperately but because he has no power over me, he hates me.

"Do you still prefer your little Jewboys to good Germans?"

Has he seen me? She made her voice hard and confident. "What do you want, Rolf?"

He leaned back in the chair, affected once more an air of casual superiority. "I was sorry to hear about your brother."

"He died for the Fatherland. Who could hope for anything more?"

If he perceived the irony in her voice, he did not remark on it. "You could have saved him, you know."

"Saved him? How could anyone have saved him? He died in Russia. We don't even know what hap – "

"He need not have been there. A transfer could have been arranged. He could have served the Reich in other ways."

An intriguing idea, Marie thought. "In what ways do you mean?"

"It doesn't matter. What is important is having friends." He leaned forward. "Friends who have a little influence."

"Like you?"

"You have misjudged me, you know. I can be a very good friend."

"What exactly do you do, Rolf? You are in the army, I can see that. But where have you been fighting?"

"I told you. There are more important ways to serve the Reich."

"You're a cook, is that it? You make sandwiches for the Wehrmacht."

He leaped to his feet. "Shut up, you little slut!"

Marie jumped up too. He was a head taller than she, and Marie was frightened of his anger and his strength. But she would not let him intimidate her in her own house.

"Don't try and visit me again, Rolf."

She watched the rage melt from his face. He fought to control his temper, aware he had lost his advantage. The savage smile returned. He feigned a leave-taking and casually picked up his cap from the table. "By the way, whatever happened to that little Jewboy of yours?"

He's just baiting you, she told herself. "I don't know."

"I heard he's still here in Ravenswald. I thought they would have put him in a KZ by now. For his own protection."

Marie said nothing, aware that he was watching her intently.

"Still, he won't be around much longer. Goodnight, Marie. Thank you for your hospitality."

"What do you mean?" She ran over and blocked the doorway. "What do you mean, not for much longer? What is going to happen to him?"

He grinned. There was a strange look in his eyes. What was it? Triumph? No, more than that. She decided it was – relish.

"They are rounding up all the Jews tonight," he said. "Tomorrow morning Ravenswald will finally be *Judenrein* – Jew-free."

The blood drained from her face, and she felt the dread congeal in the pit of her stomach like cold fat. Rolf watched her, savouring her reaction.

Finally, he said, "Goodnight, Marie. Sleep well."

She waited for a while after he had gone, then fetched her coat and put it back on. It was clear to her what she had to do now.

255

40

Netanel was asleep on the banquette in the living-room. Frau Rosenberg shook him awake. She was in her white nightgown, and the light of the candle threw dark shadows on her face.

"There's someone banging on the kitchen door," she said.

Netanel sat up and listened. Yes, he could hear it. The tapping was soft, but urgent. If it was the Germans they would have simply kicked the door in. There was only one person it could be.

He dressed quickly, pulling on trousers and a shirt.

"Do you think it's your father?" Frau Rosenberg said.

Netanel took the candle from her, went through the kitchen and unlocked the door. A shadow slipped past him. "Marie?"

He shut the door and held the candle closer so he could see her face. Her expression told him everything he needed to know.

"Who is it?" Frau Rosenberg called. Long grey strands of hair hung in front of her eyes as she peered into the kitchen.

"It's all right, Mutti. You go back to bed."

"I don't know where your father is. He should have finished playing cards by now."

"Go to bed," Netanel repeated. When they were alone he put down the candle and took Marie in his arms. "When?" he whispered.

"Tonight."

"You should not have come!"

"I had to warn you. You have to get away."

"Get away where? Where is there to run to?"

She was trembling. "You can't let them take you!"

He took her face in his hands and kissed her gently on the lips. "There's nothing to be done. Goodbye, Marie."

"You have to hide!"

Calmly: "I told you. There is nowhere to hide."

She stared at him. He was right. There was nowhere to run. No one would give them shelter. No one. "Then get out of the house! Just for tonight. Until all the arrests are finished!"

"If we hide tonight they will come back tomorrow. I've been ready for this for a long time now. It's all right."

"It's not all right!"

Panic, grief, despair surfaced together. If there was such a thing as God how could he allow this? Why can't they all just leave us alone? She threw her arms around him and clung to him.

"I'm ready," he whispered, "it's all right."

But it's not all right! she wanted to scream at him. It would never be all right! When they took him, they would take away her faith in a compassionate God and her belief that there was anything decent worth living for.

"You have to go," he said. "They mustn't find you here."

"No!" I don't care if they shoot me, she thought. You are all I want and without this love to sustain me I am just a butcher's daughter in a dirty apron.

"You have to go!"

But suddenly it was too late. They both heard the tyres turn on to the gravel driveway and the shouts as the soldiers spilled out in their heavy boots. Netanel grabbed her by the shoulders and propelled her towards the kitchen door.

"NO!"

"They're here! GET OUT!"

Voices at the front door: "*Aufmachen, Polizei!*"

Netanel threw open the door and pushed her out. "Run!"

She heard boots stamping around the side of the house.

A door splintered open inside the house. There were shadows moving among the trees, and the sound of men's voices, very close, and long fingers of torchlight groping for them.

"Run, Marie, for God's sake, please run!"

No, I won't! Let them take me! I will spit in their faces!

Netanel was silhouetted in the doorway. A shadow loomed behind him and she heard a dull thud. He groaned and fell. She wanted to run to him but suddenly there were hands all over her, pulling her to the ground. Someone shone a bright white light in her face, blinding her.

"Who is it?"

"It's a woman – "

"That's Helder's daughter. What's she doing here?"

"– dirty Jew lover – "

"What do we do with her?"

"Bring her inside, let the colonel decide – "

Then she heard another voice calling from the kitchen, soft and dreamlike. A voice from another time, when the world was ordered and sane. It was Frau Rosenberg.

"Josef," she called to the darkness, "Josef, is that you?"

Part Eight

41

The platform was jammed with people, most of them women and children and old people, clutching cardboard suitcases and tiny bundles of possessions tied with string. With so many people, Netanel thought, you would expect a hubbub of voices; but no one here spoke above a whisper. The fear was tangible. It hung in the air like a chill mist. The soldiers with their machine-pistols looked on and in the dull light of the station lamps their faces were blank and grey as the walls.

"Where are we going?" Frau Rosenberg said.

Netanel kept his arm around her and guided her through the mass of bodies. People instinctively drew away from him. He guessed the encrusted blood on his face must mark him as a potential source of trouble. "I don't know, Mutti. I'm here. It will be all right."

"I don't understand. Who were those people? I want to go home."

They had not even allowed them to dress. His mother was still in her long white nightgown, he had on only the thin shirt and trousers he had thrown on to answer Marie's knock.

Marie!

Where was she? They would not bring her here, not with the Jews. But what would they do to her? If only I knew she was safe. She should not have come, if only . . .

All he remembered was waking up on the ground surrounded by soldiers, and hearing his mother's screams. Then he was dragged to his feet and a Gestapo officer had shone a torch in his face.

"Are you Rosenberg?"

He could not see his inquisitor but he recognised Weber's voice. He did not answer but then Weber said, "Yes, it's him."

Netanel and his mother were bundled into the back of a military lorry between three soldiers. He was afforded a brief last glimpse of the white portico of the House in the Woods glinting in the moonlight like dry bones; then the lorry roared away and his home was left behind and a part of him knew he would never see it again.

He tried to talk but his head was still numb from the blow and his tongue felt twice its normal size. "Where's Marie?" he whispered to his mother but then one of the soldiers hit him with the butt of his machine-pistol and he blacked out again.

A train pulled into the station, brakes squealing, steam curling from the boiler in dense white clouds. There were perhaps a dozen enclosed wagons behind. At once the German guards came alive; the wagon doors were thrown open and they began shouting commands, pushing people inside.

Netanel was carried forward by the press of people. He clutched his mother's hand. He was terrified they would become separated. He knew she could never cope on her own.

"What's happening?" she shouted to him.

"Just hold on to me."

"I want to go home now."

"We can't."

"I want to go home!"

A man in a broadcloth cap tried to shove his way between them. Was he so eager to go to his doom? Netanel wondered. He brought his elbow up sharply into the man's nose, snapping his head backwards. The man stared at him in dull surprise and cowered back.

Netanel pulled his mother towards him, put a protecting arm around her. They were shepherded into one of the boxcars. People were packed tight against each other on the floor, and there was no light. Somewhere a child was crying.

Netanel found a space for them against the front wall

of the wagon. As he squatted down he felt someone shove him. "Look out!" a man's voice said. "Watch where you're treading!"

Netanel's temper broke. "Do you think I want to sit on your lap like this, idiot?"

"I don't like this," Frau Rosenberg said. "Let's go home!"

"I told you, we can't!"

"Why are you angry at me? I haven't done anything."

"I'm sorry, Mutti. Just don't ask me if we can go home any more, all right?"

The doors slammed shut and they were left in darkness. A woman started to scream.

"Shut that cow up!" a voice yelled.

Someone struck a match close by to light a candle. The fragile flame illuminated a man's face. "See, it's not so bad," he said. "A little cramped, but not so bad."

The man's voice was familiar. Netanel realised he knew him; it was Mandelbaum, the man from the pawnbroker's, the joker, Mr Cheerful. He suppressed a groan. He would have preferred the Gestapo dungeons. Perhaps Mandelbaum would not recognise him in the gloom.

"I know you, don't I?" Mandelbaum said.

"I don't think so," Netanel answered.

"Yes, of course, don't you remember? In the pawnbroker's? Mandelbaum, Amos Mandelbaum! You're der Chef's son, aren't you? Hey, everyone, Rosenberg's Netanel is here!"

"So, we should have a celebration?" someone said.

Mandelbaum seemed not to hear. "What happened to you? That's a nasty cut on your head."

"Just an accident. I walked into a Gestapo colonel."

"You should have that fixed when we get to Czechoslovakia."

"Where?"

"That's where we're going. They're sending Jews there from all over Germany. You have to work but there's plenty of food at least."

"How do you know all this?"

"I heard some soldiers talking. Trust me. By the way,

263

have you met my family? This is Rula, my wife, and these are my children, Ruth and Sophie." He shone the candle on their faces; Netanel saw a tired-looking woman with lank, grey hair – it must be deflating living so long with such relentless cheerfulness, Netanel thought – and two teenage children, both girls, their eyes wide and frightened. "Do I have the honour of addressing Frau Rosenberg?" Mandelbaum held out his hand to Netanel's mother. "I was sorry to hear about your husband. He was a great man, a truly great man."

Frau Rosenberg drew back from the proffered hand as if it were a dirty rag. "Josef will be back from his cards soon," she whispered and hid her face in Netanel's shoulder.

The train trundled through the night, squealing and rattling, stopping for minutes or hours, then rumbling on again, jerking, slowing, stopping, rolling again, stopping, endless. Netanel studied the huddled mass of humanity by the light of Mandelbaum's candle, listened to the curses and the exchange of blows over the unavoidable encroachments on space. Already, it is like a madhouse, Netanel thought. Some cried, others argued and kicked, still others, like his mother, sat silent and withdrawn, already half mad from the shock of what had happened to them.

Pray God this journey is not a long one, Netanel thought. If they do not let us out of here soon, the children and the old people will not be able to endure it.

The train rumbled to a stop once more, Mandelbaum shook Netanel from his reverie. "What's the matter?" Netanel asked him.

"I can never sleep on trains."

I can never sleep on trains. Was this another joke, or was he serious? Was he mad or simple in the head? "Have you ever been on a train like this one?"

"It will be all right. We shall be there soon." He took a wallet out of his jacket pocket and opened it. Inside, there was a photograph of a young man. Netanel examined the snapshot in the flickering light of the candle. A smiling youth with dark, wavy hair.

"Your son?"

"Shimon. He went to Palestine when he was sixteen. He sends us letters. He is working on something he calls a kibbutz near Jerusalem. As soon as everything is normal again here, we will bring him back home. It's no life for a young man out there in the desert. We told him that, but he wouldn't listen. The Zionists had filled his head with nonsense."

"You would rather he was here with us, in this cattle truck?"

Mandelbaum stopped smiling, but only for a moment. "This will pass."

Someone fidgeted irritably in the darkness behind them. "*Ruhe! Ruhe!* Can't you be quiet! We're trying to get some sleep!"

"Sleep?" Netanel shouted back. "How can anyone sleep in here?"

Mandelbaum grinned sheepishly and took the photograph. "He's right," he whispered. "There are other people to consider."

He put the snapshot back in his wallet. He reached into the leather bag propped between himself and his wife, took out a Thermos and poured coffee into a tin cup and passed it to Netanel.

Netanel accepted it, feeling the stirring of guilt. So, he told himself, you don't like the man but you are still prepared to drink his coffee. You were pampered in the House in the Woods for too long. You forgot that a man's measure is not the sum of his character but his capacity for kindness.

"Thank you," he said. The coffee was black and strong and sweet. It warmed his insides and he felt a little better.

He was aware of his mother's head on his shoulder. It felt heavy, a good sign. She was asleep. He considered waking her and offering her some of the coffee, but decided they would surely be stopping soon and she could drink then. Better to let her sleep. He put his arm around her shoulders and pulled her towards him, making her as comfortable as he could.

Netanel saw a shadow rise from the huddle of sleeping bodies. Near the doors was a large tin can, the only means they had been given for relieving themselves. A small boy straddled the can, and Netanel heard the splash of his water. Suddenly the train jerked back into life and the boy stumbled forward and kicked the can, spilling it over the floor. Men and women howled in disgust and the boy started to cry, stumbling back over the sleeping bodies to his family on the other side of the wagon. Curses and insults followed him.

"It was an accident!" Netanel shouted. "Leave him alone!"

"It's all right for you," an anonymous voice called back. "You haven't got to sleep in piss the rest of the night!"

Netanel closed his eyes. Let this nightmare be over soon!

The lemon yellow tracings in the slats of the boxcar were Netanel's first clue that a night had passed. He could not remember sleeping. He crawled to the edge of the car and peered out.

They had stopped yet again, at a train station somewhere. The platform was deserted, except for two German soldiers with machine pistols. He could make out a sign further up the platform: Trebon. So, Mandelbaum was right. They were inside Czechoslovakia.

A troupe of railway labourers trudged past, carrying picks and shovels, bare feet limping on the gravel. They had yellow stars pinned to their clothing. They were mostly women, some very old, but there were children as young as five or six. Two Brownshirt guards walked behind them, rifles slung casually across their shoulders.

For a moment one of the women looked up at the railcar, her face etched with deep brown lines of misery. This is the future, her eyes seemed to say. Then she was gone, and the sound of the Brownshirts' boots on the gravel receded in the distance.

Netanel turned away. God help us all.

The day went on for ever, minutes dragging by in peaks of hope and troughs of despair. Once the train shunted to a stop and did not move for hours, while the sun turned the boxcar into a gloomy and desperate furnace. Netanel's body was soon slick with sweat; it trickled through his hair, down his chest, seeped into his clothes. Men and women groaned and cursed, stripping off to their underclothes. The air was soon fetid and thin. It was not yet one o'clock by Netanel's watch when panic set in.

At the back of the car a young woman started to wail: "My baby's dying!" Her screams went on and on: "My baby's dying, my baby's dying . . ." The infant that had been suckling at her breast lay in her arms with its toothless mouth slack.

A young man jumped to his feet and beat on the doors with his fists, screaming for water. Another man joined him, then another. Suddenly there was a stampede towards the doors. A woman and two young children screamed, caught up in the mêlée.

"Look at these people," Mandelbaum said. "It's shameful!"

The crowd around the door were fighting each other with their fists and their feet. A man screamed and fell, holding his face.

"We have to stop this," Netanel said.

Mandelbaum made a clucking noise with his tongue. "People should maintain a certain standard," he said. Despite the heat, he still wore his tie, and his jacket was draped neatly over his knees.

"Give us water!" someone was shouting, as his fists beat time on the door. "We are dying! Give us water!"

A rifle butt hammered against the side of the boxcar. "Shut up in there!" a soldier shouted. "What do dead men need water for?"

Silence.

267

The men crowded around the door went back to their places, and a terrible quiet fell over everyone in the wagon. Suddenly they were all faced with their own deceptions. There was no refugee camp in Czechoslovakia as Mandelbaum had said. They were being sent somewhere to die. Was that so surprising, after Kristallnacht?

Mandelbaum offered Netanel the last of his coffee. It was tepid and bitter, but Netanel accepted it gratefully. It would at least moisten his lips and mouth. He offered some of the coffee to his mother. She shook her head. "I want to go home now," she said.

"We can't," Netanel whispered.

"I don't like it here."

"There's nothing we can do."

He put his arm round her. Frau Rosenberg wept. Just let it soon be over, Netanel prayed to the darkness, to the God in whom he had not believed since he was a child. Let it soon be over.

And look after my Marie.

Another night.

The day had beaten them, had sucked them dry; now they lay in the dense and humid fug of their own vapours, sprawled across each other in imitation of death, too weak to protest against their treatment, too drained to beg. The infant had wailed its hunger all day, but now, thankfully, the baby too had fallen silent.

Netanel was propped against the wooden slats of the wagon, all his concentration focused on the effort to breathe. Frau Rosenberg's head rested on his lap.

Suddenly there was a piercing shriek in the darkness.

"My baby!" the young mother was screaming. "My baby is dead!"

She screamed again and again and again. In the darkness Netanel heard voices try to comfort her, but she would not be still. Then Netanel heard a soft, mellifluous man's voice, perhaps a rabbi, reciting the prayer of Kaddish, the mourner's prayer.

"*Baruch dayyan emeth*," he heard someone else say, in Hebrew.

Blessed be the infallible judge.

The mother sobbed out her grief through the night and her moans seemed to speak for all of them.

42

How long had it been since the journey began? Had there been two nights, three? It was impossible to remember. The nightmare montage had become formless and shapeless. Consciousness had blurred into dreams, a half world of tormenting illusion. Sometimes he would find himself stretching out a hand for a cold glass of water and then his body would jerk back to reality and there would be nothing there except the darkness and the stink and the moaning.

He sat up and looked around. Mandelbaum was awake, his daughter's head cradled in his lap. At first Netanel thought she was dead. Her lips were cracked and swollen and her eyes sunken in her head like a cadaver. But suddenly she called out in her sleep and Mandelbaum stroked her hair to soothe her. Mandelbaum's tongue was swollen with thirst. He said something but Netanel shook his head, unable to understand him.

"All . . . a mistake," he repeated.

A mistake! How could these people still cling to their stupid self-deceptions? How many Mandelbaums had there been? How many good little Jews like his father who thought things could never get worse? Even when the Germans took everything they owned and massacred their families and sent them to torturous deaths they thought that, well, tomorrow perhaps, things will be better; someone will say they are sorry, it is all a terrible mistake, and all the little Mandelbaums will nod their heads in understanding and start all over again. That was the way it had always been.

The Mandelbaums of this world! Netanel thought bitterly. That is why I am here; because my father was a Mandelbaum. My whole race is made up of Mandelbaums and they have doomed the rest of us!

The infant's death had been followed by others; mostly old people, some of the young children. Who knew how many? Even the most pious were now too exhausted and dehydrated to repeat the Kaddish, and the stench of death and excrement was unbearable. How long would this go on? Or did the Germans plan to shunt the train endlessly around Europe until the human cargo inside was all dead? Perhaps that was a fitting end for people who never had a homeland of their own.

A man crouched by the door, pulled out his penis and urinated into his cupped hand. He brought his hand to his mouth and gulped down the contents. Netanel envied him his drink.

He looked down at his mother. Her mouth was open as she slept, and the chevrons of light that slanted through the boxcar threw the bones of her face into sharp relief, and he could see the outline of her skull. Her nightgown was filthy and torn and he pulled the neck of the garment together to cover her more modestly.

All her life, he thought, she had been sheltered, but it was an illusion, a house of straw. There was no shelter for the weak.

None.

Oswiecim, Poland

The doors opened with a crash.

It was night, but the station platform was floodlit and people screamed with pain, covering their eyes against the sudden glare.

"*Raus, raus!*" SS soldiers were shouting up and down the platform. "*Schneller!*" One of them jumped into the boxcar and kicked at the sprawl of occupants with his boots. "*Raus!* OUT!"

Netanel stared at this apparition in confusion, shaken from black empty sleep, trying to remember where he was. The soldier grabbed his shirt and threw him towards the door. He stumbled on to the platform. There were shadows milling everywhere, clutching suitcases and bags. Men and women and children called to each other, stunned and disoriented by the bright lights and the blows of the guards and the sudden release from the terrible prison. Their voices were hoarse from thirst and hunger and fatigue.

"Mama, where are you?"

"Here!"

"Where's here?"

"Esther, Esther!"

"What's happening? Will someone please tell me what's happening?"

"My husband! *I've lost my husband!*"

Netanel stared at the outside of the boxcar that had been his jailor and tormentor for . . . how long? Someone had scribbled on the side, in chalk:

DANGER! CONSIGNMENT OF DIRTY JEWS

And underneath:

Jews will be destroyed by German Kultur.

Netanel looked around. The platform was strewn with luggage, suitcases yawning open, empty; here, a little tortoiseshell brush, there a tin saucepan, a child's doll. Where had they come from? Why did the rail track stop so abruptly at the far end of the platform?

There was classical music being piped through the station loudspeakers. "Die Valkyrie." Wagner.

The SS guards were grouped around them now, grinning at a mother who was adjusting the clothes of her small children, but the grins were without warmth. Something was obviously very funny but Netanel felt like a man who has arrived at a conversation too late; everyone is laughing and he has missed the point of the joke.

Where was Mutti?

He pushed his way back through the crowd to the boxcar. The floor of the wagon was littered with bodies. My God! So many?

"Mutti!"

A guard shoved his truncheon into Netanel's stomach, winding him. As he doubled over, he brought it down hard across his back and sent him sprawling across the platform. Netanel brought up his knees, prepared for a beating, but it did not come. There was no venom in the attack, Netanel realised. It was just standard procedure.

Someone pulled him to his feet. "It's all right!" Mandelbaum whispered. "Look!"

A row of military lorries were drawn up outside the station. Some of them had a white circle with a red cross painted on the side. The guards pushed them into lines, separating the older men, women and children. Mandelbaum tried to cling to his wife and his daughters but a guard shoved him away. For the first time, Mandelbaum showed signs of protest. "Rula!" he shouted. "Sophie, Ruth!"

"Not now," the guard said. "Together again afterwards."

"After what?" Netanel shouted.

The guard snatched the suitcase from Mandelbaum's hands and threw it to one side.

"My case!"

"You get your luggage back later," the guard said. He pushed Mandelbaum back into line with the other men.

"Are you going to gas us?" he heard a woman ask one of the guards.

"What do you take us for? Barbarians?" the guard grunted.

Suddenly, another vision. Skeletons in striped pyjamas, their skulls shaved smooth, appeared on the platform and moved silently through the crowds. They had a curious, shambling gait, their heads bowed, arms rigid, like ghosts rising from a graveyard. Some of them piled the discarded luggage on trolleys, others climbed into the boxcars and heaved the corpses on to the platform.

Netanel saw one of them roll his mother out of the door of the boxcar like a sack of potatoes. She landed on her head. Netanel thought he could hear the bones crack. She lay there for a few moments in her soiled nightgown, twisted and grotesque, and then more bodies dropped on top of her and she disappeared from view.

Netanel wanted to cry, to rage, to fight, to feel something, but thirst and exhaustion had left him numb. Like sacks of potatoes from the back of a cart, he thought over and over.

The women and children were marched towards the lorries with the red crosses, flanked by guards with Alsatian dogs on chain leashes. Sophie looked back and waved. Mandelbaum smiled and waved back as he watched his family climb into the back of a lorry.

When they were gone, the men were led to the lorries waiting on the other side of the station building, each one silent with his own thoughts, praying for death, praying for a glass of water.

43

The sign above the wrought-iron gate read:

ARBEIT MACHT FREI
YOUR LABOURS SHALL SET YOU FREE

They all stared at it from the back of the open lorry, each of them composing their own future from the random clues. "See . . ." Mandelbaum croaked. "Work camp . . . they won't . . . kill us."

A huge city, row upon row of identical brick buildings, passed them in the darkness. When the convoy came to a halt they were surrounded by SS, who roared at them to get out of the trucks. Only the SS can bellow like that, Netanel thought. He wondered if it was perhaps a qualification for induction. The men with the most raucous voices entered the SS; the rest went into the Wehrmacht.

They were herded into a large, empty room and the door was slammed shut behind them. Netanel looked around. There were perhaps fifty other men like himself, with stubble on their chins, lips cracked and bleeding, eyes blank with confusion and dread. The harsh glare of a single lightbulb leeched the colour from their faces.

In the corner of the room was a tap. Everyone in the room was staring at it. None of them had drunk anything for days. There was a sign on the wall:

IT IS FORBIDDEN TO DRINK THE WATER.

No one moved.
The joke was monstrous. Are we all Mandelbaums?

Netanel thought. Are we going to die of thirst because a sign tells us we cannot drink? He shoved the man in front of him out of the way and turned on the faucet. He knelt and opened his mouth under the stream. The water was warm and brown and tasted like a swamp.

He spat it out.

The others watched him, and the agony of his discovery was reflected on all their faces. Netanel pressed his head against the cold, damp wall in despair.

This was the end.

Soon the SS would come with their machine-pistols and finish them off. They waited, and the long, silent minutes dragged by.

Perhaps I died on the train after all, Netanel thought. This is hell, a place where you are tormented with thirst and brought to a room where the only water is rotten, where you wait for a death that will not come. Yes, he imagined that this was what hell must be like. Endless suffering, with no blessed escape from life into death.

Someone at the back of the room fainted and his skull cracked on the floor as he fell. The sound jarred Netanel back to the memory of his mother, how the shadowy figures in pyjamas had treated her like just so much discarded luggage. She was dead. He said the words aloud, trying to make it real to himself.

"She is dead."

Perhaps she was the fortunate one.

An SS guard threw open the door. This is it, Netanel thought.

He understood now what the tap was for. They have to wash away the blood afterwards. There must be a drain in the other corner. Perhaps, before the train, he would have tried to put up a fight. Now, he no longer cared. Let's just get it over with.

"Out," the guard said.

They were led across the compound to another building, into some sort of change-room. There were pegs all around the walls. "Take off your clothes," the guard said. "Put all your money and jewellery in the pockets so it won't be stolen."

Stolen? Netanel thought. By whom? He took off the Star of David that Marie had given him and hid the metal star in his fist.

"In there," the guard said.

Naked and filthy and exhausted, they did as they were told.

The door clanged shut behind them.

They were in a shower-room, ankle deep in cold, filthy water. They looked at each other. What was going on? Someone knelt down and started to lap the putrid water like a dog.

What exquisite refinement was in store for them now?

Nothing happened.

Suddenly bells clanged to life, and an icy torrent of water burst over their heads from the showers. Everyone shouted out in shock and surprise. Netanel opened his mouth and let some of the water run into his mouth but he spat it out again immediately. It was rank also. Some of it leaked down his throat and he retched.

He scrubbed at the dirt and filth from the train, and the encrusted blood in his hair. He cleansed himself automatically, and as he busied himself with the task, another thought struck him. If they were going to kill them, they would not shower them first!

A demon was born in him then, a demon called hope. It tore him from his grief and his anger and whispered to him that although his mother was murdered, and he was now a prisoner and a slave, there might still be some way for him to survive.

Their heads were shaved to the accompaniment of shouts and blows from the guards and, still naked, they were lined up in alphabetical order to have numbers tattooed on their arms.

Netanel became prisoner 81305.

They were given uniforms, caps, jackets and trousers of grey and blue stripes, with their number sewn on the front

276

of the jacket next to a red and yellow Star of David. Their only other possessions were a tin soup bowl the size of a basin and a pair of wooden clogs.

They dared not look at each other because they saw reflected in each other's appearance the same vision that had greeted them when they arrived at the station of Oswiecim: shambling, bowed figures in pyjamas, with shaved heads, creatures without dignity or power.

Survive? Netanel thought. I have joined the living dead.

That evening they squatted in the dirt outside the barracks, with their ration. The camp was a babel of voices, Polish, German, Yiddish, Russian, shouts and threats and entreaties in a dozen languages.

"A piece of advice," someone said. "Never rush to the front of the queue when they serve the soup." Dov was a camp veteran. He had been transported to Oswiecim from the Warsaw ghetto four months ago. He could speak good German; he said he had been educated in Berlin.

"But we haven't had food or water for days," Netanel said. He had drunk down half his "soup" in one gulp. Soup? A pint of salty water, flavoured with cabbage leaves and some pieces of turnip.

"You are a High Number. You don't know anything," Dov said, and he slurped the soup into his mouth with a metal spoon. "The quicker you learn, the better it will be for you."

"Learn what?"

There was pity and scorn in Dov's pale blue eyes. He was big-boned, although most of the flesh had wasted off him, but there was still a hint of strength in his size and in the intensity of his eyes. "Listen. Forget everything you ever knew before you came here. Try and imagine you just dropped here out of the sky. Now you have to start all over again, like a little baby. So. The first thing you must learn is never to stand at the front of the soup queue."

"Why?"

277

"Because only the liquid is at the top. It is always thicker at the bottom."

Netanel watched Dov eat, spooning in the scraps of vegetable from the bottom of the bowl first.

"Where did you get the spoon?"

"I can get one for you. It will cost you a ration of bread."

"All right."

"I'll have it for you tomorrow. Then you give me the bread."

Netanel tried to force some more of the foul stew down, but his stomach rebelled. He spat it out. Dov stared at him, open-mouthed.

One of the other prisoners shuffled towards him, his bowl held in front of him like a beggar. He kept bowing his head, like a dog that was accustomed to regular beatings. His eyes pleaded with Netanel for the rest of the soup.

Netanel pushed it towards him but before the man could grab it, Dov snatched it away. "Another rule. You don't waste good food on Müsselmen. You have to look after your friends in here."

Dov poured the rest of Netanel's soup into his own bowl.

"What's a Müsselman?"

"You'll find out soon enough."

The "Müsselman" shuffled back to his corner of the hut.

"Are all the meals as bad as this?"

"What other meals? The only other meal is breakfast. A slice of bread and a cup of coffee."

Netanel bit off a hunk of the bread. Some of the crumbs fell on his jacket. Dov started to pull them off with his fingers, transferring them quickly to his mouth, like a monkey picking fleas.

Netanel pushed him away. "What are you doing?"

"Hold your bowl under your chin," Dov said. "Like this. Then you won't spill anything."

Netanel looked across the yard at Mandelbaum; poor, empty-headed Mandelbaum, who still thought he would

278

get back his luggage and clothes, and be reunited with his family. He watched him draining his soup bowl to the last drop, holding his bowl under his chin to catch the breadcrumbs like a Low Number.

Poor empty-headed Mandelbaum? He will live longer than me.

There were endless streets of two-storey brick barracks. Netanel, Mandelbaum and the others were assigned a dormitory. The bunks were no more than wooden planks, covered with straw and rough sacking. They were tiered four high, divided by three corridors, stacked to the roof.

There were insufficient places for everyone, so Netanel was forced to share his bunk and his one filthy blanket with Mandelbaum. Netanel tried to sleep, but the straw made him itch and the maddening bites of the lice would not let him rest. His tongue felt like a piece of leather; his head throbbed with pain.

"This will be the last outrage for the people of Germany," Mandelbaum said.

I will do the Germans' job for them, Netanel thought, I will kill him before they do! "What are you talking about now?"

"What do you think the people of Ravenswald will do when they wake up and discover what Hitler has done now? You cannot just deport hundreds of good Germans from a town and get away with it."

"Yes, you can."

"No, this time he has gone too far! They will rise up!"

"No one cares what they do to us."

"Neither do I!" someone hissed. "Go to sleep!"

Sleep? Sleep?

The barrack lights were still on. "They never turn off the lights," Dov had said. "Not ever."

But then, quite suddenly, they were plunged into darkness for a few blessed seconds before the lights flickered on again.

"My God, do they never give up trying to find new ways to torment us?" Netanel said aloud.

"That's not the Germans," Dov said from the bunk below. "Some poor swine's thrown himself on the electric wire."

Netanel could not sleep; he lay awake, imagining the body frying on the wire; hearing his mother's skull hitting the platform, over and over; trying to form the words of a prayer for Marie.

When exhaustion finally overtook him he was jerked awake by the sound of water splashing into a tin bucket as one of the sleepers got up to urinate. The sounds continued without interruption through the night. The huge amounts of water in the soup had filled all their bladders. Once, out of habit, Netanel tried to check the time but the tattooed number on his wrist stared back at him, mocking him.

But they had not taken all of Netanel Rosenberg's possessions. He felt the sharp spines of the David Star still in his palm and he hid it away under the sacking of his bed.

The lights flickered on and off twice more during the night and men relieved themselves into the bucket while others ground their teeth and moaned and whimpered in their fitful sleep.

This way Netanel Rosenberg spent his first night in Auschwitz.

44

It was still night when they were shaken from their beds and herded into the main assembly square, the Appelplatz, for roll-call. Harassed and pummelled by shouting guards, they were lined up in columns of five, four deep, blocks of twenty, groups of one hundred.

Brutality and order, Netanel thought. The two rocks on which our new Germany has been founded.

The Orphan was waiting for them. He was not an appetising sight, this time of the morning. I wonder where they found this one? The Hamburg docks probably. He had the face of a boxer and the small, bright eyes of a predator. Like them, he wore a striped uniform and cap, but instead of the red and yellow star of a Jew sewn on his jacket, he had the green triangle of a criminal. Also, unlike them, he wore good leather boots and was holding a solid rubber truncheon.

He slapped the truncheon in his palm as he addressed them. "Well, *meine Herren*, welcome to Auschwitz. You *Häftlinge*, you dirty Jews, have had it good long enough while good *Reichsdeutscher* like me have been starving for a crust of bread. Well, *Herrgottsacrament*, the wheel has turned and now you will find out what it's like to do an honest day's work. Do any of you have a degree from university?"

A man in the front row half raised a hand in the air. Dov, standing beside Netanel in the second row, uttered a soft, low moan.

The Orphan stepped forward, brought his club up from the level of his knees and into the man's groin. The man

281

uttered a shrill scream and fell to his knees. The club came down on the back of his skull. He crumpled over on his side.

The Orphan rolled the man on to his back, put his boot on his throat and held it there. The man gurgled and died in front of them.

"This is what I think of intellectuals," the Orphan said. "So don't ever try and make a fool out of me."

When it was over, the man was dragged away and roll-call began. The body was accounted for. It did not matter that one had died, only that none had escaped.

The roll-call went on for hour after hour. The numbers were counted off in blocks by the *kapos*, and were checked and re-checked with the SS officers. They stood in their lines, dull from sleep and shivering with cold, and waited for the next torment.

Netanel was still stunned by what he had witnessed. It was not the violence – God knows, he had seen the SS and the Brownshirts in action first hand, and he knew what men like that were capable of – but the casual indifference with which the man had been killed. The act had been performed with the practised skill of a chef breaking open an egg. Three precise movements and it was over, without passion, without anger. The Orphan had killed a stranger in order to prove a point. No one among the thousands of prisoners or scores of other kapos and SS in the Appelplatz had even bothered to turn around and watch.

"Does he kill one of us every morning?" Netanel whispered to Dov.

"No, only when he has High Numbers to impress. You know how he got his name, the Orphan? He murdered his mother and father. With an axe."

How can anyone hope to survive in here? Netanel thought. The psychopaths are the guards and the sane are their prisoners.

Dawn was leeching shape into the world when the roll-call finished. The camp was like a small brick city, endless

282

streets of barrack buildings encircled by watchtowers and barbed wire. A dark shape resolved into the charred remains of one of the prisoners who had thrown themselves on the electrified fence during the night.

After roll-call they were formed into work squads, *Arbeitskommandos*, and they stumbled off to work in their heavy wooden clogs. Netanel thought he heard a band playing the sentimental marching tune "Rosamunda". Delirium. But he turned around and there they were, men in drab uniforms like himself, with violins and trumpets and a drum, formed up by the gate to farewell them, as if they were regiments marching off to some patriotic war.

As they passed under the gates the Orphan cried, "*Mützen ab!*" and they all removed their caps in deference to the grinning SS guards who were waiting with their dogs to escort them to work. Netanel looked back once, and glimpsed the legend inscribed in wrought iron on the front gates:

AND YOUR LABOURS SHALL SET YOU FREE

Netanel learned quickly.

He learned to save half his bread from the breakfast ration to eat mid-morning at the Farben factory when he was so faint from carrying the heavy clay tiles that black spots danced in front of his eyes and he wanted only to sink to his knees and die.

He learned to ignore the stench and the flies and eat it in secret in the latrine, so no one would try to steal some as he ate.

He learned to judge when the night bucket in the barracks was almost full, so he would not be the last one there and be required to go to the latrines in the middle of the night and empty it.

He learned always to remove his cap when an SS guard passed by so he would not collect a beating.

He learned always to roll up his sleeve and show the number tattooed on his wrist to receive his food ration.

He learned never to draw attention to himself.

He learned to say "*Jawohl!*" whenever any instruction was issued to him.

He learned to judge the best place to be in the soup line by the size of the vat.

He learned that if he left his spoon or his shirt or his bread ration unguarded, even for a moment, it would be stolen.

He learned to make a bundle of all his belongings, from his tin bowl to his wooden shoes, and sleep on it at night.

He learned that everything was valuable; any rag, no matter how inconsequential or how filthy, could be used as a towel or for extra padding inside clogs to protect the feet.

He learned never to think about tomorrow.

He learned to try not to think at all.

But there was still one more important lesson to learn, and he learned it from Amos Mandelbaum.

Every morning at reveille Netanel dressed quickly so as not to leave anything unguarded. Almost immediately the room sweepers drove them out, shouting and shoving them with their brooms, turning the air opaque with dust. Netanel stumbled to the latrines and washrooms. They had five minutes at most before the morning rations of coffee and bread were issued, and latecomers received nothing at all. Netanel saw one man urinate as he ran, to save time.

The washrooms were dank and draughty, the brick floors covered with a grim and slippery layer of mud. The walls were covered with frescoes. Netanel wondered whether they were a sort of bad joke, or mockery, or just some twisted and humourless separation of the mind, the work of some SS functionary unable to perceive absurdities.

One of the frescoes portrayed a good prisoner, stripped to the waist, soaping his face and body; the legend underneath said:

So bist du rein
(Like this you are clean)

Another frescoe showed a filthy Müsselman, with a large Semitic nose and grimy uniform dipping just one finger in the washbasin. Underneath it said:

So geht's du rein
(Like this you come to a bad end)

A bad end! Netanel thought. Not washing in this freezing water is a bad end; being beaten to death with a rubber truncheon is just camp discipline.

Mandelbaum was at the washbasin next to Netanel. He watched him strip off his cap, shirt and jacket and place them carefully between his knees so they would not be stolen. Mandelbaum went through the motions of making a lather from a tiny piece of dirty soap and the cold, brackish water – an almost impossible task – as he washed his face, arms, and body.

Then he dried himself diligently with his jacket.

Netanel splashed a little water over his face and watched him with pity. Poor, simple Mandelbaum. What was the point? Washing so diligently burned up the precious energy they would desperately need later at the Farben factory and, anyway, within half an hour at the work site they would both be as dirty as each other again.

"I saw you in the latrines," Mandelbaum said, as they crouched against the wall of the barracks with their bowl of coffee and their hunk of bread. "I noticed you have stopped washing properly." There was a note of injury in Mandelbaum's voice, as if Netanel had somehow let him down.

"What is the point of it? If you want to keep pretending we are still members of the human race, that's up to you."

"I am surprised that you should take that attitude, Herr Rosenberg. You, of all people."

285

"It's a waste of time and energy."

"No, Herr Rosenberg, it is not a waste. Not a waste at all."

"In another hour you will be as dirty as I am. The Orphan will see to that."

"That is not the point."

"What is?"

"Washing is an essential part of being a human being. It is not only a daily renewal of hygiene, it is a renewal of our dignity as human beings. If we let them take that away we have nothing left."

"How can we have dignity, Mandelbaum? They shave our heads and make us piss in buckets and dress in striped uniforms like clowns. We forfeited our dignity the day we walked through those gates!"

Mandelbaum shook his head. "You see, it is harder for you, Herr Rosenberg. You have always had respect. Dignity has come so easily for you. You have never had to remind yourself of it."

"What are you saying, Mandelbaum?"

"They can treat us like animals, but if we choose not to behave like beasts they cannot win. Perhaps you think I am simple, Herr Rosenberg. But every day the act of washing helps me survive."

Survive! The word was like a blasphemy. How could a man still harbour thoughts of tomorrow when every dawn brings hunger and torture and deprivation? Perhaps the only sane men were the ones draped over the electric wire.

Yet there was Marie. Remember Marie.

"I would still rather save my energy," Netanel said.

But the next morning at reveille he ran to the latrines, stripped off his jacket and shirt and washed.

45

It was quickly apparent to Netanel that some prisoners were in much better shape than others. In fact, there was a rigid hierarchy in the camp, and the ordinary Jewish inmates – the Häftlinge – were at the bottom of the pile.

The first distinction between prisoners was the colour of the triangle on their uniforms. There was pink for homosexuals, violet for Jehovah's Witnesses, red for politicals, green for criminals, and two triangles of red and orange, forming a David Star, for the Jews. The masters of the camp, for most purposes, were not the SS guards but the green triangles – the criminals.

The green triangles were the Prominenz, the aristocracy of the camp. For them were reserved the best jobs. Most of the kapos, the prisoner guards, were green triangles. Their position enabled them to get extra rations of food, they were provided with camp luxuries like tobacco and insect powder, and there was even a brothel filled with Polish Häftlinge girls, the Frauenblock, for their private use.

But not all the kapos were Reichsdeutsche criminals. Some were Jews, who through favours and bribes, and excessive demonstrations of brutality, had turned their back on their own to save themselves. The German kapos were like the guard dogs, Netanel thought, they were born brutal and knew no other way. For the Jewish kapos, he had nothing but contempt.

Together with the kapos, each block was administered by a Blockälteste, a block elder, and his assistants, the Stubenältester. Most of these, also, were German or Polish criminal or political prisoners; but among these also were

Jews who had bartered their souls for better conditions and a fragile hope of survival. The Blockälteste on Netanel's barracks was a man named Mendelssohn. They said he was a Hassidim from the Warsaw ghettoes.

He lived separately from the rest of them, in a large room in the corner of the barracks, with the Orphan, the Stubenältester and a handful of favoured friends. Netanel had seen inside the room only once, when the door had been inadvertently left half open. There were tables and chairs to sit on, and shelving for glasses and dishes. There were even ornaments, imitation flowers, and pictures cut from magazines, as well as proverbs praising order, discipline and hygiene.

But the sight that made Netanel ache the most was the beds; proper beds with pink silk quilts. It was hard to imagine the Orphan sleeping contentedly beneath a pink silk quilt.

Suddenly Mendelssohn appeared in the doorway, and slammed the door in his face.

"This is the whole world," Dov said, when Netanel told him about it later. "The whole world packed into a few acres. The few Prominenz, the privileged, looking after themselves and keeping their power with cheating and with strength. And there's the rest of us, working for a few crusts, starving and struggling."

They were sitting among the orange dust and broken bricks in the Farben factory, shaded by a low wall from the relentless afternoon sun. The watery soup had swelled their stomachs but could not revive the exhaustion in their limbs. Netanel rested, mouth open, his limbs at awkward angles, like an abandoned puppet.

"You're a communist, then," Netanel replied.

"A Zionist. I wanted to go to Palestine before the war. The only way we Jews will ever redeem ourselves is through the land and through labour. But then the Germans invaded and I was trapped."

"My father said Palestine was nothing but swamps and deserts."

"Spoken like a good German."

"Perhaps Palestine is just another dream. Jews are not a nation, we are a religion. Sometimes not even that."

"Then why don't you give up your country and your religion? Renounce it!" Dov smiled, knowingly. "You would have liked to, wouldn't you? But the Germans won't let you."

"I am a German."

Dov grinned again. "Then tell them to make you a kapo."

"I would rather die first."

"You probably will. How long do you think anyone survives in this place unless they can organise themselves into becoming one of the Prominenz?" Dov leaned closer. "You know what these bastards do, Mendelssohn and the Orphan? They get fifty loaves of bread for our ration. They are supposed to cut each loaf into ten pieces. Instead they cut them into eleven. Simple. So at every meal they make five loaves. What they don't eat themselves they trade for other things on the black market."

"If you know all this why haven't you tried to organise something for yourself?"

Dov shrugged, and his eyes were evasive. "I have."

"What?"

Dov hesitated, then pointed to a group of four kapos who were standing in conversation by the wooden hut that served as a site office. "See that one on the right, the big one with the long chin? That's Lubanski. He's in charge of the Kartoffelschalen Kommando, the Potato Peeling Command. I sold him my gold tooth and he has promised me a place with him. I start tomorrow. This is my last day working in this shitty heat, carrying all these bricks. It's easy work, in the kitchens, and if you take a few potatoes, who is going to know?"

"I don't believe you."

Dov opened his mouth and pointed to the dark and still bloody gap in his lower jaw where a tooth had been.

Netanel closed his eyes. Any minute the siren would sound again and they would have to face five more hours of relentless crushing labour in the hot sun. "I have nothing to give him," he murmured.

"He'll take anything. He's a mercenary bastard."

Netanel remembered the silver Star of David and he made his decision. There was no law that said he had to suffer with the rest of them. There was only one law here: survive one more day.

He lay on his bunk staring through the barracks room window. The Silver Star of David was hidden in his right fist; he could feel the points of the star in the flesh of his palm. He waited.

Lubanski emerged from the barracks opposite and make his way towards the Appelplatz with his familiar long-boned stride. Netanel sprang from the bed. The sudden movement did not attract much attention. Many of the inmates did the same thing when they were suddenly stricken with diarrhoea and had to hurry for the latrines.

He ran across the street: "Herr Lubanski!"

The kapo stopped and turned.

Netanel pulled off his cap. "May I speak with you?" he said.

Lubanski took two steps towards him and put his hands on his hips. "What do you want, Häftling?"

"I understand you are in charge of the Potato Peeling Command. I would like a place on your kommando. I am willing to pay." He held out his palm and revealed the silver Star of David.

Lubanski examined it, carefully. "The Potato Peeling Command," he said. He closed his fist so that two points of the Star protruded from between his knuckles. The blow was delivered with such speed that Netanel did not see it coming. He felt a numbing blow to the side of his face and fell backwards.

Then Lubanski's knees pinned his shoulders to the ground and the beating started.

He arched his back and tried to roll free but the kapo was too heavy. He heard a voice shrieking from far away and realised the screams were his own.

It went on for ever, then stopped as suddenly as it had begun. He heard men's voices shouting angrily, was aware of others standing over him. This is it, Netanel thought. They are deciding how best to finish me off.

"Netanel?" a voice said softly.

He recognised that voice. It was Chaim, his cousin, Chaim, who was arrested by the Germans in Austria before the war. He was dead by now. That meant he was dead too. "Chaim? Has it stopped? Is it over?"

"Netanel, is it really you?"

Netanel tried to open his eyes but he could not see.

"Thanks to God that it is over."

"Potato Peeling Command!" he heard someone hiss in disgust.

"He's a High Number, he didn't know!" Chaim said.

"Chaim?"

"I would not have recognised you. It was your voice. When I heard your voice . . ." He stood up and barked an order. Netanel felt himself being lifted by the arms and feet. He was finally set down on a straw bunk and he heard Mandelbaum's voice whispering in his ear, "He really messed you up. Do you have much pain?"

Netanel could not answer him.

He was alive, and there was no gratitude in him. Only disappointment.

The pain came the next morning.

Mandelbaum helped him to the washroom, risked his own place in the soup line to wash some of the dried blood from his face. One of Netanel's eyes was swollen shut and his mouth was split open in two places. The points of the Star of David had torn holes in his cheek and his eyelids and his lip.

As Mandelbaum helped him away from the washbasin Netanel saw Dov standing in the line, watching him.

"It was only meant to be a joke," he said.

Netanel did not answer him.

"Anyway, what were you doing all the time I've been here, eating this watery piss for food and hefting bricks? Sleeping in a good bed, eating good German food! You're a Jew, same as me. Why weren't you here as well?"

Netanel staggered away.

"Maybe this makes up for it," Dov said.

They assembled in their ranks in the Appelplatz. The Orphan summoned prisoner 81305 from his place and marched him away to the western side of the square, near the wire. Chaim was waiting for him.

"Herrgottsacrament! Look what that bastard did to your face!"

Netanel stared. It was his cousin, and yet it was not. The last time he had seen Chaim was just before he left for Austria with Aunt Esther and Michal. He was still in short trousers then. The thing he remembered most was the large purple and yellow spot on his chin.

Chaim. Well, that was who he said he was. In the shadow-and-light play of the searchlights from the towers, the man in front of him had the raw, seamed face of a boxer. There was absolutely nothing to connect him to the pimply face of the cousin he remembered. He looked more like one of the Brownshirts who had made a personal pastime out of beating him.

"Is it really . . . you?" Netanel mumbled through his torn mouth.

"It seems we have both lived a hundred times in the last seven years, Netanel." He stepped closer. "How long have you been here?"

"A week . . . maybe two . . . don't . . . remember."

"I can help you, Netanel! I know this place, how it works. I should do. Four years I have lived in Hitler's charnel houses."

"Aunt Esther?" Netanel said, and the familiar name sounded like a foreign tongue. "Michal?"

"Dead," Chaim said, and he did not attempt to explain.

"Potato Peeling Command! Did you really say that to Lubanski, of all people?"

Netanel said nothing. What was there to say? He was a High Number, a stupid Häftling, and he still had not learned.

"Lubanski used to be a professional boxer. If I hadn't come along he would have killed you."

Netanel said nothing. He was thinking now about his cousin, the kapo, the Jewish kapo.

"He thought you were making fun of him!"

Chaim looked beyond Netanel's shoulder to the rows and rows of filthy, shabby uniforms and their cropped and bowed owners. "Look at them. They come from everywhere. Hassidics, from Warsaw and Lublin, gypsies from Romania, ignorant little shoemakers and tailors from the ghettoes. How did we get mixed up with all this rabble? We may be Jews, but we're Germans too, good Reichsdeutscher."

"We're just . . . Jews."

"I'll help you," Chaim said. "I can get you a job as a Stubenälteste in my block. Maybe I can even persuade someone to make you a kapo."

Netanel shook his head. "Don't want . . . your help."

"Don't be an idiot!"

"Rather die . . ."

"What?" Chaim took a step towards him, his face twisted in disbelief. "Look at you! Covered in blood and vermin and filth, and you've only been here two weeks!" He tore open Netanel's jacket. "I can see the bones of your ribs already. You're like an anatomy lesson! You won't even last a month at this rate!"

"Got . . . dignity."

"Dignity?" Chaim laughed, incredulous.

"Won't . . . betray my . . . people."

Chaim's voice was suddenly hard and dangerous. "When you were der Chef's son you had dignity! Now you're just a piece of filth in a striped uniform! Don't you understand? This is a death camp. The only way out of here is through the chimneys at Birkenau! When your strength is all used up they kill you! Is that what you want?"

"Won't be . . . a kapo."

Chaim spat on him. "Damn you!" He hawked and spat again. "Damn you, you self-righteous bastard! Don't presume to judge me!"

Netanel returned his stare but said nothing.

"I can save your life!" he hissed.

"Maybe . . . get me . . . on the Potato Peeling . . . Command," Netanel said.

"Get back to your place, prisoner 81305," Chaim said.

46

In early November it started to rain. It rained for ten days, turning the camp into a swamp. The smell of damp and mould overlaid the sweet smell of the chimneys at Birkenau.

Their Arbeitskommando had been moved from the Farben factory to the shunting yards at Buna. Netanel found himself shivering at the bottom of a three-foot ditch, shovelling the clinging mud with stiff, repetitive motions, trying to allow as little of his skin as possible to come in contact with his clothes, which were icy and soaked.

There was no colour in anything, the railyards and huts and horizon blending into the amorphous grey of a bitter and waterlogged landscape. A goods train moved past them, and Netanel looked up, staring without seeing, his eyes as dumb and uncomprehending as those of a small animal caught in a trap.

The white-painted legend passed in front of his eyes.

Deutsche Reichsbahn . . . Deutsche Reichsbahn . . . Deutsche Reichsbahn . . .

"Winter's coming," Dov said, beside him. The rain dripped steadily from the end of his long nose and on to his jacket.

Winter, Netanel thought. I have been here nearly four months.

"Nothing like a good Polish winter. Kills seven out of every ten men. They say if there was no winter, Hitler would have invented it."

"I heard a good joke about Hitler," Mandelbaum said.

Netanel stared at him. He still could not make up his mind if Mandelbaum was simple or wise, victim or survivor. Countless times since he had arrived here, he had experienced this same sensation, that it was all some elaborate and bizarre joke. Now here was Mandelbaum telling his funny stories in a freezing ditch, as if he were in a *Bierkeller* in München.

"I don't want to hear it," Dov said.

But Mandelbaum ignored him. "Hitler gets up in the morning, and he looks out of the window and he sees the sun come up over Poland. 'Good morning, Mr Sun,' Hitler says.

"'Good morning, Mr Hitler,' the sun says.

"Then, after lunch, Hitler walks out in the garden and he looks up in the sky and he sees the sun high over Germany and he says, 'Good afternoon, Mr Sun.'

"And the sun says, 'Good afternoon, Mr Hitler.'

"Then, that evening, Hitler looks out of his window and he sees the sun setting in the west, and he says, 'Good night, Mr Sun.'

"And the sun says, 'Get fucked, I'm in England now.'"

Netanel threw back his head and laughed.

Suddenly he felt the Orphan's truncheon across his shoulder-blades. "What are you laughing at, Jew shit?"

Netanel returned to his digging. "I just enjoy my work, Herr Kapo."

The Orphan turned away, scowling. The Häftling was obviously going crazy. Why wouldn't he, knowing winter was so close?

* * *

295

Winter brought with it its blessing and its curse.

The Arbeitskommandos were allowed to work in the snow and the freezing rain, but they were not allowed to go out in the fog or the dark, for the simple reason that both these things afforded the prisoners a chance of escape. So working hours were shorter, eight o'clock till four o'clock through the darkest months.

But those hours were torment beyond Netanel's experience. They were forced to stand for hours in the bitter darkness of the Appelplatz at the beginning and end of every day, made to labour in the marshalling yards in icy rain wearing just a cloth jacket and trousers. Every waking minute, from reveille to the blessed moment when they returned to their barracks, Netanel would dance from foot to foot, slapping his arms against his sides, trying to keep warm.

He spent part of his precious bread ration in order to acquire gloves. He lost hours of sleep repairing them when the stitches broke.

As Dov had predicted, the winter soon began its grey harvest. Every morning the Stubenältester dragged the dead from their bunks, stripped them, and piled them outside the barracks door, to be collected by the men of the Leichenkommando.

One Sunday Netanel watched them at work. There were four of them. One stood by the pile of bodies, another by the truck, a third balanced on a small stool, the other positioned himself on the tray. They passed the dead from one to the other in their makeshift assembly line, hauling the frail and skeletal corpses by their hair, or by their arms or by their legs. They seemed dead to all horror. They did not once flinch at the way the bones cracked when they hit the frozen boards of the lorry.

After all, what does it matter to the dead now? Netanel thought. Broken bones cannot hurt them any more, or the truncheons of the kapos, or the yellow fangs of the dogs.

Soon Netanel became indifferent to the dead also. He no longer walked around the corpses he found outside the barracks, just stepped over them like everyone else.

After a while he paid them as much attention as he did the chimneys of the Krematoria or the reflectors mounted on the watchtowers or the yellow long-tailed rats that now ran freely through the barracks with as little fear as domestic cats.

Netanel learned how to survive.

Death, he learned, began with the shoes. If the shoes fitted badly, or the feet were not sufficiently well protected, then sores would form and in the sodden conditions they would soon become infected. The infected area would swell, the rubbing would get worse and the wound would become larger and deeper. Netanel had seen how the wet and frozen toes of fellow Häftlinge quickly developed gangrene and rotted. They would develop a strange shambling gait as they tried to continue. Finally they would shuffle to the infirmary for treatment, but the SS knew there was no cure. *Dicke Füsse* – bad feet – was a death warrant. The victims rarely came back. They escaped, like so many others, through the chimneys at Birkenau.

Netanel became obsessive about his feet. He washed and dried them every evening before sleeping, without fail. He collected even the smallest scrap of paper or cloth to wrap around them to protect them from the damp and the chafing of the wooden clogs. Any spare paper he would stuff under his shirt for extra protection against the cold, but his feet would always receive first attention.

With every passing day, the confidence grew in him that he was going to survive. He had to survive.

For Marie.

The day began invincible.

The camp bell rang in the cold black dark long before dawn, cutting across restless sleep. The terror of the coming day and the familiar hunger was like cold lead in the pit of the stomach.

The night guard turned up the lights and walked along the line of bunks. "*Wstvac*," he said, softly, in Polish: "Get up." He never had to speak above a whisper. They had all

297

been awake for a long time, bracing themselves for the coming, impossible confrontation.

Netanel dressed and ran across the frozen ground to the latrines, washed quickly, chest, arms, face, scalp, not just his hands as the Müsselmen did. Then he shoved his way to the best place in the queue for the coffee and the precious bread ration. He spent time making sure his feet were clean and well protected in his wooden clogs, then hurried to the main square for Appel.

He shivered for hours in the freezing rain while the kapos counted out the roll-call. His body shook uncontrollably. He was beaten. The fight had not even begun and he knew he could not win, not today. Already his fingers were so stiff with cold he could not feel them. Surrender now. Let them shoot you. The odds against you are too great.

A few more minutes. I will count to a hundred and if I am still standing then, I will decide again.

No sunrise, just a leaching of shadows from a grey, hostile world. They marched off through the gates, stumbling, bowed shadows, their morale gone. The camp band played "Rosamunda".

I cannot do this. Not a whole day. Today I am going to lose.

The railyards waited, a battlefield of frozen concrete, iron and mud. Everything grey and cold. The only colours were the rainbow veils of petroleum on the frozen black puddles. A mist of vapour rose from pipes and rails and boilers that had frozen overnight. In the distance, the steeple of Auschwitz pushed through the mist.

They marched to the siding office, and the Orphan made a second roll-call and entrusted them to the civilian Meister, Lentner, a taciturn Pole with a weeping egg-yellow moustache and grey eyes. He never looked at them directly. He averted his eyes, like a spectator at a fight where the loser stays on his feet too long.

The Orphan went off to sleep in the Meister's hut, next

298

to the hot stove, sheltered from the driving sleet and the freezing mud.

I cannot do this, Netanel thought. There is no strength in my arms. I cannot fight again today.

"*Bohlen holen*," Lentner said, and pointed to a frozen pile of sleepers standing at the side of the tracks. Near by was an enormous cast-iron cylinder on a goods wagon. Netanel saw the intent: they were to build a pathway from the sleepers so the cylinder could be rolled from the wagon to the sheds.

The sleepers were frozen to the ground and each one weighed as much as a healthy man. He and Mandelbaum bent to the first sleeper and hoisted it on their shoulders. Ice slid down Netanel's neck, and the iron plating bit into his shoulder bone. As he took the weight of it, he felt his knees start to buckle.

They staggered forward, the ice and mud sucking at their shoes. Count the steps, Netanel thought. Ten, eleven. I cannot do this all day! Give it up now! Twenty-one, twenty-two. Let them shoot you! Escape through the chimney. Thirty-five, thirty-six. Bite your lip. Harder. Can't feel anything. Fifty-three, fifty-four. Harder. Some blessed pain to override everything else. Seventy, seventy-one. Nearly there, just a few more steps. Eighty-three, eighty-four . . .

Eighty-eight steps.

You did it!

They dropped the sleeper.

Netanel stood, open-mouthed, his shoulder and arms throbbing in rhythm with his heart. For a few moments he could not see or hear. Rain beating cold on his face felt good.

I cannot do that again!

Mandelbaum swayed on his feet; his eyes were sunken and inflamed, like skinned plums. "That wasn't . . . so bad," he said.

The Orphan appeared at the hut door. "Get working, Jew shit!"

They staggered back to the pile of sleepers. Netanel

tried to calculate how many trips they would have to make. Fifty of us in the kommando. Two to a sleeper. Perhaps a hundred sleepers.

Four trips.

Perhaps I can survive this. Then I will decide again.

After the second journey he was deaf and blind to everything. He stood gasping, his arms limp at his sides. His legs were too heavy to move, his feet mortised to the ground.

I cannot do it again!

Netanel staggered slowly back to the pile. Too soon he had arrived. "I have to go to the latrine," he told Meister Lentner.

Lentner shrugged and pointed to Levin. Levin was old and weak, the kommando's "Scheissbegleiter" – toilet companion – charged with the task of accompanying prisoners to the latrine, and ensuring they did not try to escape. That there was anywhere to run to, that Levin could stop them if they did! Another bad German joke.

The visit to the latrine saved one trip. When he returned he saw a lorry splash through the mud, loaded with the day's ration. It must be close to mid-morning, Netanel decided. The noonday break was in sight. For the first time the day was vulnerable. Perhaps if he could just get through to noon . . .

There were only the heavy sleepers left; those at the bottom had inches of ice frozen to their surface, heavy iron plates still nailed to them.

"We'll wait until they scream at us," Netanel whispered to Mandelbaum. "Even if it costs a blow from the truncheon."

Finally the Vorarbeiter, the Orphan's assistant, was attracted by their dawdling. He bawled at them to get to work. They somehow hauled one of the sleepers on to their shoulders. The rain fell harder, stinging their faces . . .

. . . One, two . . .

Soaked through, knees buckling, shaking with exhaustion and cold, they picked their way through the cloying mud.

300

Twice they fell to their knees.

Not as far this time, perhaps just twenty paces . . .

Almost there.

. . . eighteen, nineteen . . .

They were there!

He detected the aroma of hot soup on the wind. It was almost time for the ration. The day was no longer so fearsome an opponent. They had seen the worst. Half an hour more to hold on. I can manage that, Netanel thought. Then food, then rest. Then I'll decide again.

The midday siren.

They trudged to the hut to receive their ration of soup from the Orphan. Despite their pleas, he would not stir the pot. He was saving the pieces of potatoes and parsnips at the bottom for himself.

But at least the liquid bloated their stomachs and warmed their insides and Netanel was grateful for that. He licked out his bowl and then crouched round the stove inside the hut with the others. The fragile warmth started to dry their clothes, and the vapour rose from them like a cloud, a dense, humid fug that smelled like mushrooms.

Netanel listened to the rustle of the sleet against the window, and closed his eyes. He dropped quickly into a black sleep.

He woke a few minutes before one o'clock. A dark instinct stirred him, whispered that this brief mercy was almost over.

He heard the Orphan's triumphant whisper: "*Alles heraus!*"

Netanel stepped back outside, gasped at the shock of the wet and the cold. Three more hours. Yes, he could do it. The day was looking weaker now. He could beat it, he could win.

The siren from the carbide factory cut across the deepening grey. The driving sleet and wind had begun to ease. Another joke, Netanel thought. Now the day's work was

301

over and they were returning to camp, this additional torment was no longer required.

The Orphan arranged them *zu dreine*, in threes, for the march back to camp. The Orphan called out the rhythm.

"*Links – links – links . . .*"

They still faced the long torture of the Appel, but after that there would be the bread ration and then they could rest. Netanel staggered, head down, but inside there was a growing sense of elation. He had won! This morning the odds had seemed too great, his opponent too strong. But he had beaten him. First by habit, then by endurance, finally by determination.

He had won again today, as he had yesterday, and the day before.

And tomorrow he would do it over again.

47

The iron wheels squealed as the train rolled to a stop. The guards moved quickly, slamming back the doors on the wagons. "*Heraus! Heraus! Mach schnell, SCHNELL!*"

The crumpled knots of humanity spilled on to the platform, blinking in the white phosphor of the lights. Marie hugged her woollen coat tighter about her shoulders. Hermann had given it to her the last time she had seen him – how long ago? – at the police headquarters in München.

The guards shoved their way through the crowds, pushing the women and children to one side, bullying the people into lines. Children cried out, women screamed for their husbands. A guard dog brought down one of the men and started to maul him.

A guard grabbed her by the arm and pushed her into

a line with the other women. She did not try to resist. This was one of the death camps she had heard about, she realised. They were going to kill her.

They had taken long enough about it.

The woman in front of her had an infant clutched to her right shoulder, a small boy and a girl clinging to the hem of her coat. "Daniel, Rachel, hold on to me, you hear? Just hold me tight." She turned to the old man on her right. "Don't push!"

Marie stumbled along with the crowd towards the waiting trucks. She wondered if this was where they had taken Netanel. Well, it did not matter now.

Someone stepped towards her.

"Come here," the SS man said. "The major wishes to speak to you. Lucky little bitch, aren't you?"

One Sunday in every two was designated a rest day. It was a time for scavenging, for everything was useful. Bits of wire could be used to tie shoes, paper could be padded under the jacket as insulation, any rag of cloth was useful as a towel or as extra protection for the feet. But today it was too cold even for that and so they lay on their bunks and watched the rain fall plop, plop on the windowsill and silently gave thanks to whatever gods they still cherished that at least they did not have to work.

Netanel felt Mandelbaum reach into the straw under their bunk. He furtively handed his treasure to Netanel in his cupped hand. It was a photograph, creased and folded so many times that its subject was almost beyond recognition. "My boy in Palestine."

Netanel glanced at it and passed it back. Mandelbaum clutched it to himself, like an icon. "You hid it all this time?" Netanel said.

"When we were in that changing-room, I knew those bastards were not going to give us our clothes back. When have you ever been able to trust a German?"

"That was clever, Mandelbaum."

Mandelbaum allowed himself another look at the photograph before returning it to its hiding place. "Perhaps he won't want to come back to Germany now. Not after what they've done to his mother and me."

Come back? What Jew, in his right mind, would ever want to set foot inside Germany again? Mandelbaum perhaps. "He is better off where he is."

"He was a fine boy, you should have seen him. Good at his studies, his rabbi had high hopes. But the last couple of years . . . I don't know what gets into children sometimes. When he said he wanted to go to Palestine I couldn't believe it. These Zionists had addled his brain. I begged him to change his mind, but he wouldn't listen."

"It's just as well, isn't it?"

"Perhaps, Herr Rosenberg, perhaps."

"Perhaps?"

"Things will get back to normal one day soon. You'll see."

He's mad, Netanel thought. Or perhaps his delusion is just a way of staying sane. And what about you, Rosenberg? he asked himself. What is your madness? That you will see Marie again one day?

At least it has stopped me from becoming a Müsselman, like Dov over there.

"I wonder what my wife is doing right now?" Mandelbaum said.

Dov was lying on his bunk watching them. Now he sat up, resting on one elbow. "Your wife and your children are just soot in the Birkenau chimney, idiot."

"Shut up, Dov," Netanel said.

"They put them in the ovens the same night they arrived, Mandelbaum. Your family vanished in a puff of smoke."

"Shut up!" Netanel said.

The big Pole shrugged and lay back on his bed. "Idiots!"

Dov had undergone a change with the onset of winter. He no longer tried to organise for himself, had crossed the boundary from the saved to the drowned. At some imperceptible moment he had lost the will to struggle. There was a feverish look in his eyes, and he walked in a curious shuffle, his eyes downcast. What meat there had been on his bones had wasted off him. He smelled of faeces, sores and sweat, and continually talked of death. Because he no longer tried to organise, there was no advantage gained in being with him, so everyone avoided him.

He had expended his use. He had become, in the camp argot, a Müsselman.

"When the people find out what is happening here, they will rise up," Mandelbaum said. "You will see. They will rise up and things will get back to normal again."

The freezing rain dropped plop, plop on the windowsill.

After the midday soup ration, they assembled in the drizzle for another roll call and then returned to their barracks. As soon as they were inside, the Blockältester unexpectedly shouted, "*Blocksperre!*" In the language of the camp, it meant the block was being closed. A deathly silence fell over the room. They all knew what it meant but only Dov dared say the word aloud for them.

"Selection!"

The doors were locked and Mendelssohn lined everyone up in pairs, while the Orphan ran up and down the corridors between the bunks with his rubber truncheon beating anyone who was too slow or too terrified to get to his feet.

"Who's ready for the chimney? How about you, Jew shit? Come and see the good doctor, he'll fix your complaint!"

The Orphan marched them across the Appelplatz to the bathhouse.

"All right, Jew shit, strip off!"

It was raining harder now. They took off their clothes and waited, shivering, in the rain, spidery arms wrapped around their chests.

"Inside! One at a time," the Orphan said.

Netanel was one of the first. Inside, the camp commandant and several SS officers sat at a table with one of the camp doctors. Netanel recognised him; it was Mengele. The doctor looked up at Netanel as he entered and gave him a beatific smile. He was a handsome man, elegantly dressed, exuding calm. One of the officers recorded Netanel's number.

"81305."

With a slight movement of his head, Mengele nodded casually to the door at the side of the bathhouse and Netanel went out.

Mendelssohn and the Orphan were waiting. "You're lucky, Jew shit," the Orphan whispered. "You get to come back with me to the railyards tomorrow."

Netanel looked back at the bathhouse door. Others came through and he nodded at them, to let them know they had passed the selection. Mandelbaum came out, but not Dov. In ten minutes the selection was finished and they were marched back to the yard in front of the bathhouse and told to put their clothes back on.

As the Orphan escorted them to the barracks, Netanel felt in his top pocket. While he was being assessed for the ovens, someone had stolen his spoon.

As soon as the Orphan had gone, there was an outbreak of whispers. "Poor Dov," Mandelbaum said.

"Where is Moshe? Did they select Moshe?"

"Has anyone seen Mendel?"

"What about Jan? He was no Müsselman! Surely they didn't pick Jan!"

An old rabbi from Lublin fell on his knees and began to thank God in a loud voice for saving him from death. Netanel pushed the old man to the floor.

"Shut up! There's no God listening to you! Do you think that was God sitting in judgment in there? It was the Germans!"

There was a shocked silence. Mandelbaum got up and pulled on the sleeve of Netanel's uniform.

"Come away, Herr Rosenberg. He's a rabbi. Leave him."

"He's shit!" Netanel screamed. "He wants to thank God because some other poor bastard has been selected to die in his place!"

"Come away, Herr Rosenberg, please come away."

The rabbi stared at him, uncomprehending. Netanel threw himself on his bunk. The sussuration of whispers began again.

Netanel expected that they would not see Dov again, but a few minutes later those who had been selected for death were marched back into the barracks. The room fell silent.

Some of the selected men were crying, others prayed, most, like Dov, were silent, almost taciturn. He lay down on his bunk.

His neighbour, also selected, tugged at his jacket. "Why did they pick me?" he shouted. "I'm no Müsselman! Why did they pick me?"

"Because you're a Jew!" a voice shouted, laughing. The Orphan, Mendelssohn and the Stubenältester stood at the doorway of the *Tagesraum* and watched the display. It was, after all, a free entertainment.

"They wrote my number down by mistake!" someone shouted. He appealed directly to Mendelssohn. "Look at me, I have months more work left in me, Herr Blockältester! Tell them they've made a mistake!"

"Certainly I shall tell them," Mendelssohn said. "The next time I see Dr Mengele I shall tell him. Next month some time!"

The Orphan liked that one. He and the rest of the Stubenältester roared. Then they all went back inside and the door to the Tagesraum slammed in their faces.

Silence.

Dov sat up. "Rosenberg, do you want to buy a spoon?"

"Why would I want a spoon?"

Dov shrugged. "Do you . . . or not?"

"How did you know mine was stolen?"

"Half a ration of bread. The usual price. Yes or no?"

"You're going to die. What do you need with bread?"

"I don't want to die hungry, Rosenberg." He held out the spoon.

Netanel took it. Half a ration of bread to a dead man. Waste.

"Don't feel sorry for me," Dov said. "You are dead too. All these poor little Häftlings are dead. It's just a question of time before it's your turn. So don't feel sorry for me."

And he started to laugh.

"Well, Marie, how delightful to see you, here of all places. Silesia does get a little grey and drab this time of year. Why don't you sit down here? Thank you, Sergeant, that will be all."

Major Rolf Emmerich walked around his desk and held out a chair for her. When she was seated, he took a packet of cigarettes from the desk and lit one. He offered her one.

She shook her head.

"It was most fortunate for you I happened to be there at the station this morning. It is not my regular duty. I have only recently been transferred here from Buna. If I had not seen you . . ."

Marie held her hands in her lap and concentrated on the floor.

He leaned forward and forced her chin up. "What are you doing here?"

"Where is here?"

"Oswiecim. In the south-west of Silesia, in Poland."

"It's a death camp, isn't it?"

A muscle in his jaw rippled. "Now what makes you think that?"

"Why don't you kill me and be finished with it?"

"Why would I want to do that? Hermann would never forgive me."

"What do you want?"

Rolf drew on his cigarette and weighed her in his gaze. "First, you answer my questions. How did you get to be on that train? The shipment was supposed to be entirely Jews from Theresienstadt."

Marie shrugged her shoulders. Why should she tell him anything?

When he spoke again, there was a harder edge to his voice. "I can find out soon enough. A few phone calls.

But I would rather hear it from you. It would be a gesture of friendship. You might need a friend now, Marie. You are a long way from home."

He is right, she thought. There is no reason to give up. "I was arrested in June by the Gestapo."

"What for? No, let me guess." He grinned again. "Did it have anything to do with your Jew lover?"

"They found me at his house. I was sleeping with him."

Rolf stood up suddenly, as if he'd been stung. He realised he had given himself away and tried to cover his gesture by walking slowly to the window. "Go on."

"I was interrogated and I spent God knows how long in the prison in München."

"Did they hurt you?"

"Would you have liked that?"

"Don't be stupid," he snapped.

"I don't think they could make up their minds what to do with me. They sent me to Theresienstadt. Then two days ago I was put on a train and sent here."

"Theresienstadt is a summer camp."

"I must have gone at a bad time. It was winter."

He turned from the window and leaned on the back of her chair. "You don't know how lucky you are."

"Yes, it's obvious, isn't it?"

He stroked her hair. She flinched, so he took a handful of hair in his fist and pulled her head towards him.

"This is not Germany. You have a lot to learn. The first thing to learn is that you must be nice to me. If you want to stay alive."

"You decided I want to live so badly. I didn't." She gasped as he twisted his fingers tighter in her hair.

"There are many ways of dying. Many ways. The worst kind is when you are still breathing long after you are dead."

He kissed her throat.

"I shall give you a choice." He let her go and walked round his desk and sat down. "What do you think happened to those women who were with you on the train?"

"I imagine they are all dead by now."

He nodded. "Yes, it is a pity, but those are our orders. You see, it creates problems. Women here are very scarce. This morning did you see the big building just beyond the main gates?"

Marie nodded.

"That is the Frauenblock. To be frank, it is the camp brothel. It is reserved for the use of the Aryan prisoners, as a reward for performing certain duties. These men, you understand, are not the best that Germany can produce. Most of them unreasonably violent, a few of them are psychopaths. The girls are mainly Polish, and they are kept very busy I'm afraid. We are always short of girls because for some reason many of them die after a few months." He paused to draw on his cigarette. "So here is your choice. I can arrange for you to be sent to the Frauenblock and you can have your pick of our country's most depraved criminals as your sexual partners. Or, I can arrange for you to take up a post of some comfort inside the camp, and in return you will be required to satisfy just one customer, a man of quality, position and some gentleness on occasion."

"You."

"It is a good bargain, I believe." He stubbed out the cigarette and leaned back in his chair, his hands behind his head. "I waited a long time for you, and you refused me. Well, I thought, so be it. But now fate has brought you here. Here it is not necessary for me to plead my case. The choice is yours."

Marie hid her face in her hands. It would have been easy to have chosen death, to have gone away screaming defiance. She had prepared herself for that ever since she was arrested. But to die slowly, by brutality and rape in a death camp brothel . . .

She removed her hands. Damn him. She would not let him see her break. "Am I really so desirable?"

"We shall have to find out . . . won't we?"

Netanel saw Chaim waiting outside the Meister's hut when their Arbeitskommando arrived at the marshalling yard.

The snow had vanished but the coal-stained slush seeped through Netanel's shoes.

Chaim called him out of line. "So you survived the selection?"

Netanel nodded.

"Herrgottsacrament, have you any idea what you look like?"

"They took my shaving mirror."

"You don't have to go on with this."

"Neither do you."

Chaim snorted in disgust. "I was at the barracks this morning when the Leichenauto came for your friends." He nodded towards the chimneys at Birkenau, visible this morning for the first time in weeks. A black-yellow smoke drifted lazily into the frigid blue sky. "There they go now."

"If you want to help me, get me an easier kommando."

"They don't let the Jews have the easy jobs."

"Thank you, Chaim. Your mother would have been proud of you."

Chaim shrugged. "It's a long winter, Netya. There are new Häftlinge arriving all the time. You survived this selection. You don't really think you'll survive the next one, do you?"

He walked away.

Netanel watched him go, the large black "K" stencilled on the back of his prison jacket. A Jew like me. But I cannot betray my own conscience, sell my soul as Chaim has done. They can beat me, but they cannot break me unless I agree to become one of them.

Yet I want to survive so much; to know Marie is all right.

The Orphan hit him between the shoulder-blades with his truncheon. "Back to work, Jew shit! The good doctor didn't save your skinny arse so you could stand around in the sun dreaming!"

Netanel shuffled towards the others, standing in line to receive their day's tools at the Meister's shed.

Marie . . .

Part Nine

PALESTINE, 1943

48

Talbieh

Henry Talbot took his breakfast on the patio. It was a bright, still morning. The best time of year, he thought. Swallows swooped and played in the branches of the spreading fig, and sparrows pecked around the flagging and fidgeted overhead in the vine trellis, feeding on the sweet black grapes, while old Abdollah sat on a wicker stool in a corner of the courtyard shelling peas.

Talbot felt a sudden, but familiar, pang of guilt. Whenever he caught himself out enjoying such moments, he felt like a truant schoolboy. He reminded himself that in England right now his sister was probably standing in a ration queue, and his younger brother was watching rain drip through an olive drab tent somewhere on Salisbury Plain. Their war seemed so far away.

Yet it had come so close.

It was this time last year that Rommel had converged on El Agheila, just ninety miles from Alexandria. The Mufti, who had fled to Berlin after the start of the war, made frequent appeals on Radio Damascus for the Egyptians to stage a revolt. For a few weeks it seemed almost inevitable that the German Panzers would roll through Cairo and Jerusalem, as they had Paris and Warsaw, and for weeks the lights had burned through the night on the Hill of Evil Counsel and in the David Building, as the British administration prepared for an ignominious exit. Instead the German rush had broken at Alamein and now Rommel's Afrika Korps was crushed, its remnants trapped on the Cape Bon peninsula.

No doubt it was all a great disappointment to the Arabs.

Majid appeared with a fresh pot of tea. He placed it carefully in the centre of the table, fussily brushed away some crumbs of toast, and waited.

Talbot glanced up at him apprehensively. Their relationship had become complicated recently, and now he wished he had not so recklessly fudged the distinction between master and servant.

"How are you this morning, Majid?"

"Splendid, thank you, Talbot effendi." He hesitated. "In fact, effendi, there was something I wished to ask you."

Knew it, Talbot thought. One of his little schemes has run foul of the Palestine police. "Are you in trouble?"

"Oh no, effendi. It is my youngest son, Yusuf. He is to be circumcised this Saturday."

"And you'd like the day off? By all means, we shall manage."

"That is very kind, effendi . . . I wondered also if you and the Rod – Lady Talbot, would do my family the honour of your presence?"

Talbot put down his newspaper. "It is very kind of you to ask us, Majid." The invitation was a great honour, Talbot realised. It might also be rewarding. What Elizabeth would think was another matter.

"It is to take place in my village, Rab'allah. You will come?"

"I shall have to discuss it first with Lady Talbot." But why not? he thought. It was all in the cause of good British–Arab relations; assuming, of course, that they did not still wish to assassinate him.

Rishou parked the black Plymouth taxi in the street outside Majid's apartment and punched the horn. Majid leaned out of the second-storey window and waved. A few minutes later he reappeared, resplendent in his best western-style suit of wide check. Mirham followed behind him in a *thaub* of white silk, a black scarf wrapped around her face. The same contrast of styles was reflected in their sons and daughters.

Majid jumped in next to Rishou, while Mirham and the children piled into the back. Mirham and the oldest boy were struggling with large sacks.

"Sugar," Majid beamed. "Good Britisher sugar. Tate and Lyle."

Rishou grinned back at him. "Father will be delighted."

"The Britishers have been good to us," Majid said, conveniently ignoring the fact that the British knew nothing at all about the transaction. "How are you, Rishou?"

"I am well, Majid."

"How is the taxi business? Do we prosper?"

"At this rate we shall be the most prosperous Arabs in Jerusalem. We shall be invited to tea with the Mandoob es Sami."

The taxi had been purchased with money largely provided by Majid. The war had been kind to him. Talbot had entrusted Majid with the purchase of all their household requirements, and Majid took a fifteen per cent commission from this weekly allowance.

"As easy as scooping cream from a bucket," he had boasted.

He used this money to buy items readily available from the British quartermaster stores – such as tinned food and kerosene – that fetched a handsome price in the souks on the black market. In this way he regularly doubled or even trebled his profits. He had reinvested the proceeds in the Plymouth and a taxi licence.

As he drove Rishou studied him from the corner of his eye. Majid was getting plump. There were extra rolls under his chin and his belly bulged over the waistband of his western-style trousers. Yes, Rishou thought, the Britishers have indeed been very good to us.

They had not meant to be, but they were.

Rab'allah

When Rishou was not working the taxi, it was left parked outside the coffee shop, radio blaring, so the customers could listen to the news bulletins from Damascus. Syria was under the control of the French Vichy government and the reports on the war's progress were quite different from the ones they heard on the British radio station in Jerusalem. One thing, however, had become quite clear. The Germans would not now be arriving to throw the British out of Palestine. The miracle the Mufti had promised would not take place.

"We were betrayed," Izzat shouted when the broadcast finished. It had become his personal litany.

"*Insh'allah*. It is God's will," Zayyad said.

"Is it God's will for us to sell our apples and our figs and our sheep to the Britishers, even sell our labour to their army? Is this the way to fight our enemies?" There was stillness inside the smoky room. Everyone knew it was Zayyad's decision to sell produce to the Mandate government and to allow some of the villagers to work as labourers at the RAF base in Jerusalem. Izzat's accusation was tantamount to a challenge to his authority. How would Zayyad react?

Oriental music blared from Rishou's taxi.

But it was Majid who spoke first. "The Britishers are not our enemies," he said.

"They are in conspiracy with the Jews!"

Majid leaped to his feet. "How? How are the Britishers against us? Look at you! Are you starving? All over Palestine there is a shortage of sugar, coffee, rice, wheat. But I get it for you. How? From the Britishers! Some of you have bicycles now, you can buy Player's instead

318

of rolling tiny cigarettes with bad tobacco. Jamil Sinnawi has his own outside toilet because the Britishers gave him work in their army stores. And look at how you are all dressed!" Self-consciously, a few of them peered through the haze of cigarette smoke at each other. Some of them had western-style jackets on under their abbayahs, many of them owned wristwatches, clutched packets of Player's cigarettes. Perhaps Majid was right. "Would you have all these things if it were not for the Britishers?"

"All gifts come from Allah," Izzat said.

"Perhaps the Jews were a gift as well," Rishou said.

A few men laughed and Izzat's face turned a mottled pink. "The Mufti says Adolf Hitler is the sworn enemy of the Jews. So he is a friend to us. The Britishers are the enemy of Hitler. So the Britishers are our enemy too!"

"The Britishers have promised to give us our independence. The Britishers don't lie," Majid said.

"Why should anyone have to give us what is ours by right? If we had risen up together and fought when the Mufti declared the jihad, the Germans would be here now!"

Majid tried to shout him down but Rishou held up his hand. "No, brother, our friend is probably right. Perhaps that is what would have happened. But tell me, Izzat, how did the Mufti, you know, plan to get rid of the Germans?"

"The Germans would have left us in peace to rule ourselves."

"But if they like us so much, they might have wanted to stay."

"They have given the Mufti their word."

Rishou shook his head. "You know, Izzat, your intelligence is not exactly something from which poets would draw great inspiration."

Izzat's mouth twisted in contempt. "I did not go to the Britisher school like you did, Rishou, but I know what I see. The Jews have come here and taken our land away from us. The Britishers let them do it. When you walk up to the Place Where The Fig Tree Died and look over the valley, what do you see? You see Jews. Jews on what was once our land."

"It was a swamp."

Izzat ignored him. "What about the Jews who built a farm near my village at al-Naqb? My grandfather grazed his sheep on that land."

They say he did a lot of other things to his sheep there, as well, Rishou thought. But Izzat had made his point. "What is done is done. The Britishers have promised no more Jews will come."

"There are already too many! We don't want Jews flaunting their women at us, with their naked legs and arms, we don't want their men staring at our women, we don't want them taking the wilderness Allah made in His wisdom, we don't want them taking our fields – "

"Enough," Zayyad said.

The room fell quiet. Every head in the room turned towards the muktar. Zayyad knew he should have silenced the argument sooner, but if he did not let the young men speak out here, they would whisper among themselves in secret. For nearly a decade this thing with the Jews had been tearing his village apart. Izzat was right. The Jews now resided on land that had been theirs for hundreds of years. But it was too late to do anything about that now.

"The Britishers have given us their word that Palestine will be entrusted to us. Meanwhile they bring us prosperity such as we have never had before. We must trust them."

Izzat pointed to the grainy photograph that was framed high on the wall, garlanded with fresh flowers. Wagil. "How can you still trust them after what they did to your son?"

Zayyad closed his right hand into a fist. "What would you have us do, Izzat? If I do not trade with the Britishers, some other muktar will." Your uncle Daoud, for one. He is a revolutionary only when it does not affect his dealings on the black market.

"We must do as the Mufti commands."

"And return to the old ways? Will you tell Jamil Sinnawi to go back to his stony fields and sweat all day in the sun for a few bushels of rotted barley?"

"It is time to claim Palestine as our own! The Britishers

320

are not invincible. Look how they turned white like women when they thought the Germans were coming!"

"If we have patience there will be no need to fight. I do not want other fathers to weep for their sons as I wept for mine."

"If we do not act soon we will all weep!" Izzat shouted and he jumped to his feet and ran out of the coffee house. No one spoke. The music from the Plymouth overlaid the fidgeting silence.

Zayyad shook his head. Curse the Mufti, curse Sheikh Daoud, and curse Izzat Ib'n Mousa! May Allah strike him with lighting and blow off his balls!

49

As Rishou made his way back from the coffee shop, he heard Rahman calling his name. Rahman was the younger of his two sons, the quiet one. Rahman ran to meet him and grabbed his hand.

"What is it?" Rishou said. "What's wrong?"

"Quickly!"

It was Ali, his elder boy, Ali, the boisterous one, the one with the same cocksure self-assurance he had possessed as a child. Ali, the one who always had to prove he wasn't afraid. He had picked a fight with Hamad, one of the boys from the village, three years older, a head taller. When Rishou arrived, Ali already had a bloodied nose. He was lying on his side in the dust at the back of the house, Hamad standing over him. Hamad's friends looked on.

When Ali saw Rishou, he jumped to his feet. Pride, Rishou thought. He has enough of it for all my children.

Hamad saw Rishou and took a step back, uncertain. Ali

took advantage, rushing in, his fists flying. A wild punch snapped Hamad's head back. Hamad reacted instinctively, and his fist hit Ali on the side of the head. Ali tottered and fell on his behind.

Khadija ran towards them from the side of the house. "Stop it!"

But Rishou grabbed her wrist and held her, shaking his head.

"But he's hurt!"

"Be silent!" Rishou told her.

Khadija searched his face, saw the stone in his eyes. It would be dangerous to argue with him further.

Ali picked himself up.

Hamad put his hands at his sides. He glanced fearfully at Rishou. "All right, Ali. That's enough. I don't want to hurt you."

Ali rushed him again and landed two more punches before Hamad could retaliate. Hamad was panicked into the punch, and he hit as hard as he could. Ali fell on his back.

Khadija gave a small cry, like a bird wounded in a trap.

Hamad looked again at Rishou. He wanted this to end. If he really hurt Ali, Rishou might thrash him. But he could not just walk away without looking like a fool.

"That's enough, all right, Ali? Friends." He reached down, offered the younger boy his hand. Ali grabbed him and pulled him on to the ground, and for a brief moment, he was on top. He pummelled the older boy with his fists, twice, three times. But Hamad was too big. He threw him off with a shrug of his shoulders and as Ali fell sideways he hit him on the side of the jaw and Ali fell on his face.

Hamad leaped to his feet. There was blood oozing out of his mouth. He was genuinely frightened now. Why didn't Rishou stop this? Ali was a little shit-eater, but he didn't want to hurt him.

Khadija wanted to go to her son but Rishou's grip on her wrist was unyielding. Ali rose slowly to his knees, spat the dirt out of his mouth. There was blood all over his face.

"Stay down," Rahman hissed at him.

322

No, he'll get up, Rishou thought.

Ali got up.

"The Englishman's coming!" one of Hamad's friends shouted; he had seen the dust from Talbot's car. Immediately the other boys lost interest in the fight, and ran off. Hamad, relieved, followed them.

Ali looked at Rishou and at Khadija.

"Go and wash your face at the well," Rishou said.

Ali stumbled away; Rahman went with him.

"You should have stopped it," Khadija said.

"He has to learn to fight."

"Hamad is bigger than he is."

"We cannot always pick our enemies."

"He is only a child."

Motherhood has changed her, Rishou thought. I used to think of her as an empty bucket in which her father had tipped all his opinions. Now she has her own priorities: her sons. "One day he is going to be a true Hass'an," Rishou said.

"No. One day he is going to take all your tears."

The Rover Ten trundled up the dirt road. It was spring, and the hills were ablaze with flowers; wild irises, poppies and anemones in yellow, pink and scarlet pushed up between the stones. It was furnace hot inside the car, and the Judean hills rippled in the heat haze. Soon the hamsiin would return.

"Tell me, Henry," Elizabeth said, fanning herself furiously with a scented handkerchief, "what is involved in this delightful little function this afternoon?"

"It's a circumcision ceremony. It's a very important occasion for an Arab child. Like an English child's confirmation, I suppose."

"Without the foreskin."

"Quite."

The Rover bounced over a rut and Elizabeth gave a small cry and steadied herself with a hand on the dashboard. "Am I invited to the torture session, or do I wait outside and count the screams?"

323

"For God's sake, Elizabeth!"

"Don't worry, Henry. It's a diplomatic occasion. I shan't embarrass you by vomiting or anything."

"We are only expected to attend the feast afterwards."

"You mean we have to eat it?"

Talbot took a deep breath. She was being deliberately obtuse, of course. She would enjoy this, in her own perverse way. It would be a good story to relay to her gin-soaked friends at the bridge club.

This afternoon's trip had been commended by the High Commissioner. It was now government policy to woo Arab sympathies where possible; recent broadcasts on Radio Jerusalem had featured items alleging that Hitler employed a Jewish physician and that the King of England drank Arab coffee. Rumours that the Nazis had been killing Jews in large numbers in death camps – Talbot believed such stories had been outrageously exaggerated in America – had been suppressed for fear of arousing Arab sympathies. British officials had even been reprimanded for publicly criticising the Mufti, who was living in Berlin and actively promoting support for Hitler.

They reached the crest of the hill and saw the flat-roofed huts of Rab'allah above them, surrounded by orchards of plum and olive and fig trees. Below the trees, stony fields fell away to a dry wadi.

"Rab'allah," Talbot said.

"Oh," Elizabeth said, "how quaint."

The smells were what one noticed first. The rich, pungent odours of charred wood, smoke, dung, urine and sun-warmed, wind-cooled bodies. It was the raw smell of life, of birthing and begetting and dying. It evoked the uninterrupted rhythm of centuries, a pungent aroma unbroken since the time of Abraham.

As he looked around the press of faces, at the curious veiled eyes and unshaven faces and brown, broken teeth Talbot appreciated for the first time the nature of the forces that were in conflict in this most ancient of all countries. These people represented the natural and ordered rhythm of life as it had been since the time of the Book; the Jews were the twentieth century. They brought irrigation, and shorts on women, and science, and European thought. In these ancient, Biblical faces, he saw the inescapable collision of modern man with his own heritage.

"Oh, my God, the stench," Elizabeth said. "I'm going to faint."

They were pressed against the side of their car. Everyone wanted to touch them. The women, it seemed, were especially fascinated with Elizabeth's dress. Another tried to pull off her hat.

"For God's sake, Henry, do something!"

"What do you suggest, Elizabeth?" Talbot snapped as another veiled harridan tried to grab her crocodile-skin handbag.

Talbot was relieved to see Majid pushing his way through the crowd, resplendent in a wide check suit and purple silk tie.

"Talbot effendi," he shouted. "Lady Talbot! How wonderful you could come!" The crowd parted in deference to him.

Talbot shook his hand, gratefully. "Good afternoon, Majid, I hope we're not too late."

"Of course not, splendid!"

Elizabeth pointed to one of the riders who had escorted them from the road. He was a handsome man, with a rich, black beard, dark eyes and a cruel, mocking smile. He was leaning on the pommel of his saddle, watching them. "Who is that?" she asked Majid.

"That's my brother, Rishou, You will meet him later."

"I hope so," Elizabeth said.

Talbot felt a stab of irritation. For a woman of such breeding, Elizabeth sometimes displayed no sense of decency whatever.

"I am sorry for all this crush," Majid said. "I am afraid everyone is very curious about you."

"It's not their curiosity I mind," Elizabeth said. "You can't blame people for curiosity. Now hygiene – that's another matter."

Talbot glared at her. Majid pretended not to understand.

"This way," he said, and he led the way towards Zayyad's house. "My father wishes very much to meet you."

Once they were inside, Rishou sought out Majid. "So that is the great Talbot effendi and his woman," he said.

"Yes, splendid people! Had them both!"

50

There were eleven of them in the room: Zayyad, Talbot, Majid, Zayyad's wives, Soraya and Ramiza, Khadija, Mirham, the two boys, Rahman and Yusuf, Naji Azzem the circumciser, and Rishou. It was a resonant moment in the boys' lives; from this moment, they would be branded for ever as either a lion or a goat. Ali had been circumcised the previous year and had barely flinched. As the knife flashed in the dimly lit room he had shouted: "I am a Hass'an and I am accustomed to pain!" just as Rishou had taught him to do. Rishou had reason to feel proud of Ali. Rahman was another matter. He had no idea what he would do.

The boys lay on the floor, naked from the waist down, staring at the ceiling. Rishou waited and listened to the whispers around him. Majid was explaining to Talbot, in English, that the man who would perform the operation was also the local barber and the lute player at weddings.

Khadija, meanwhile, was baiting Mirham. "Look at your Yusuf. He hasn't got much of a birdie, has he? What is Naji going to cut off?"

"He is younger than your Rahman," Mirham said. "It will grow."

"I've found bigger lice on my donkey," Khadija said and

Rishou suppressed a smile. What a wicked little mouth. "Look at my Rahman," she went on, remorseless. "Only six and he's built like a horse. His birdie will be the envy of all the girls when he is grown up."

But Khadija's bravura did not last beyond the moment when Naji produced his razor. It was the same one he used for shaving the men. As he bent to his work she rushed outside.

Talbot, Rishou noticed, had gone pale.

As Naji worked, Rahman continued to stare at the ceiling. Rishou watched him intently, but could not detect a change in his expression. His jaw was clenched shut, his eyes unblinking. Ah, my Rahman, he thought. I am proud. You have not shamed me.

It was over.

Soraya, Rahman's grandmother, bent to attend him. She smeared the wound with sheep fat to soothe the pain, and then she wrapped his penis in cloth and sesame seed oil as a dressing.

Now it was Yusuf's turn.

At the first spurt of blood the little boy shrieked and tried to get away. Majid and Rishou had to pin his arms and legs so Naji could finish the operation. Naji was forced to work much more slowly and carefully, and Yusuf's shrieks seemed to go on for ever. Mirham ran outside sobbing.

When it was over Soraya bent to minister to him also. The boy was sobbing like an infant.

Rishou looked at Majid. He was white with humiliation.

Nobody noticed that Talbot had fainted.

Zayyad uttered a brief sura of thanks from the Koran and the feast began.

There was pita bread, chick peas mashed with sesame seeds and garlic, steamed grape leaves filled with nuts and currants, deep-fried balls of crushed wheat and chick peas, lambs' livers, yogurt, tomatoes, onions, fish balls on skewers, squash, okra, and leeks.

Afterwards Zayyad clapped his hands and his daughters and granddaughters brought the main course: spit-roasted

327

chickens; couscous; whole lambs' heads; lamb testicles flavoured with herbs, cinnamon and garlic; spring lamb chops on a bed of rice, spiced with saffron and dill and sour cherries; bananas, melons and grapes for dessert.

They sat cross-legged, Arab style, on piled rugs on the floor. Elizabeth sat with her knees drawn to one side, as if she were riding a horse. She was the only woman present and Talbot was painfully aware that the other Arabs in the room were leering at her stockinged legs, imagining they were being discreet. Even Majid, damn him. Elizabeth, being Elizabeth, was enjoying herself. She did not even seem to mind that her white dress was being ruined on the carpets.

She leaned towards him. "Did you enjoy watching them mutilate their children?" she whispered.

"Try and make an effort, Elizabeth."

"I thought I was being perfectly charming. How much more friendly can I be? Would you like me to sleep with the chief over there?" She nodded in Zayyad's direction.

"No. But don't let me stop you."

"Very droll, Henry."

Zayyad knew they were talking about him. He smiled, and with his index finger he pulled an eye from the cooked sheep's head. It made a sucking noise as it came out. He offered it to Talbot.

"I think he prefers testicles," Elizabeth said.

Talbot took the proffered delicacy.

"Close your eyes and think of England," Elizabeth said, by way of encouragement.

Talbot swallowed. For king and country, he thought. Christ Almighty!

When the meal was finished, Zayyad's daughters fought with each other for the honour of washing Zayyad's fingers. Elizabeth raised an eyebrow and looked at her husband. "I imagine you find a lot to admire here," she said.

The girls returned to the kitchen to fetch the coffee, double boiled and laced with cardamom.

Zayyad leaned back, patted his belly, and belched.

"If he breaks wind I simply must ask you to take me home," Elizabeth said, smirking.

Talbot ignored her.

Zayyad produced a small jewelled box and, to Talbot's amazement, took out a stick of hashish. Majid passed him his water pipe – the narghiliye – and Zayyad crumbled some into the bowl. He lit it and offered it to Talbot.

Talbot turned to Majid. "Please tell your father thank you, but I don't smoke."

Zayyad considered this a moment. "Go and get the whisky," he said to Majid in Arabic. It was hidden in a special cache behind the barn along with the firearms.

After Majid had gone Elizabeth turned to her husband. "How much longer do we have to be pleasant to these beastly people?"

"We shall take our leave shortly. Are the men bothering you?"

"With the exception of Majid's brother, they all strike me as troglodytes." She took out her compact mirror and lipstick. A deathly silence fell in the room. Elizabeth looked up, innocently, and smiled at Rishou. "I really think this is taking diplomacy a little far, Henry. I'll have to lie in the bath and soak for a week when we get home. Where will they send us next? Borneo?"

"Please shut up, Elizabeth."

"You probably feel at home. Isn't buggery an Arab word?"

Talbot sipped his coffee and smiled at Zayyad, who mimed that he should eat more baklava. Talbot wished Majid would hurry back.

"These people live like niggers, Henry. Why the British government thinks it has to fawn to them is beyond my understanding."

"Many things are beyond your understanding, Elizabeth, but we don't have time to go through them now."

"Well, don't forget I haven't let you down, Henry. I would not have denied you your diplomatic coup. I went to a good school, remember. I can squat in the dirt with the best of th – "

Majid appeared with the whisky bottle.

Talbot held up his hand. "No thanks, Majid, I don't think I will."

"I'll have one," Elizabeth said.

Zayyad stood beside Rishou and watched Talbot drive back down the dirt road towards Jerusalem. He was angry. He knew when he was being patronised. He had offered this Britisher and his wife his best hospitality and they had treated him like he was a simple Bedouin, a savage. It had been apparent in their whole manner. These Britishers had no respect. It was why he had told Rishou not to reveal to them that he spoke English as well as his brother.

"What did they say when Majid went to fetch the whisky?"

"The woman talked about us as if we were, you know, people of the left hand."

"Never in my life have I witnessed such rudeness. She flaunted her legs at us as if we were eunuchs! And the Britisher effendi allowed it!"

"It seems they are pleasant to us only because their king in London wishes it. The woman complained endlessly about the offence we gave to her nose."

Zayyad's lips twisted with contempt. So this is the great Talbot effendi, of whom I have heard so much! he thought. These were their great friends from King George! May a leprous camel fart in his face! May Allah turn the woman's womb into a palm tree and may she give birth to hairy coconuts!

He turned to Rishou. "What happens when the war finishes and they do not have to be good to us any more?"

Part Ten

POLAND, 1943

51

Oswiecim

The sun rose cold and white from a horizon of grey mud. Today it seemed a little warmer than it had the day before. There was no east wind to penetrate their jackets on the Appelplatz.

It was spring. He had survived almost nine months at Auschwitz.

He had started the winter as a High Number, but he met the spring as a veteran, a survivor, a Low Number. The tattoo on his arm set him aside from the others. He was a living fossil, a dinosaur. Of the pathetic knot of humanity who had shared his misery in the boxcar from Ravenswald, only he and Mandelbaum remained.

There were new High Numbers now, first graders to be bullied or duped out of their precious and holy ration. Low Numbers could persuade High Numbers to pay three rations of bread for a spoon; Low Numbers could convince High Numbers that the infirmary was giving away real leather shoes and that they would look after the High Numbers' soup while they ran and got themselves a pair; Low Numbers could tell when the night bucket was almost full by the noise it made when it was used, High Numbers went at the wrong time and were sent out into the snow by the night guard to empty it.

There was a simple test to tell a High Number from a Low Number. High Numbers would save a portion of their morning bread ration for later; Low Numbers would eat it all at breakfast, because their hunger would not be stayed, and because they knew their stomach was the safest place to keep the grey, pasty treasure from thieves.

In the past, bitter season Netanel had learned to organise.

At the evening ration he would sell half his portion of bread for two pints of soup. From the watery broth he would extract the meagre pieces of vegetable and then sell the soup to another prisoner for half a ration of bread. He would then repeat the transaction again and again, sometimes half a dozen times in an evening.

Three times that winter he had sold his shirt for extra rations. Each time he approached the Orphan afterwards and asked him for a replacement.

"What happened to your shirt, 81305?"

"It was stolen," Netanel said. "In the washroom."

"You sold it."

"No, sir, it was stolen."

The Orphan took down the hollow rubber truncheon from its hook in the Tagesraum and beat him around the shoulders and the ribs until he lay screaming at his feet. Then he gave him a new shirt.

Netanel calculated the price was reasonable.

Pride stood in the way of survival and it had to be discarded. Shining shoes for the Orphan or for Mendelssohn was usually worth an extra half ration of bread.

He volunteered for the team that brought the coffee to the barracks in the morning and fetched the soup on Sundays. It meant losing half an hour of sleep to stagger across the frozen Appelplatz in the snow and wind, but it was worth it because it gave him the opportunity to steal a turnip or a carrot or perhaps even a potato from the kitchen. Vegetables could be eaten raw or traded on the black market for bread or extra rations of soup.

He sold the Orphan two gold molars for four rations of bread each. The Orphan removed these treasures himself with pliers. Netanel was amazed how easily the teeth came away from his gum; starvation, the Orphan observed, laughing, had some side benefits. By now he was inured to pain; all he could think of was the bread.

This transaction led to another lucrative piece of *Organisierung*. He would approach a High Number and offer him two rations of bread for a gold tooth; if the Häftling proved hesitant, he might offer two and a half, or even three. He would then take the seller to the Orphan who removed the tooth, paid the agreed price and gave Netanel the balance of the standard market rate – four rations.

It was a good trade, even though Netanel knew the Orphan was getting twenty rations per tooth from the Meister at the railyards.

But no matter how well he organised, there was no escape from the continual hunger. He could endure the cold, the work, and the beatings, but it was the hunger that broke the spirit.

Hunger was his shadow, dogging him, tormenting him, driving him, day after day after day.

Endless, endless hunger.

Sometimes at night he watched his fellow prisoners sleep, saw how they licked their lips and moved their jaws, anticipating some meal conjured in their mind. It was torture even to watch them for he knew these visions well; he had the same dreams every night. In the mornings when he woke the cold ache of their residue would not leave him. He was like an adolescent constantly dreaming of sex.

In his dreams he could smell herring frying in a pan; felt the crumbled texture of a rich *torte* on his tongue; saw juices dripping from a roasted cut of beef. But the promise was never consummated; in his dream someone would jog the fork from his hand, or call his name, or steal the plate. He could never sate his hunger, even in his mind.

Hunger made the belly swell, hollow like a drum.

Hunger stole the fat from his thighs and changed the shape of his body so that he no longer looked like a man.

Hunger left sores on the backs of his feet that would not heal.

Hunger made his head ache every morning, left him light-headed and faint at night.

Hunger made it impossible to think of anything but the next ration.

Hunger made it impossible to think.

Hunger.

Once he and Mandelbaum had been sitting outside the barracks, in the snow, eating their morning ration of bread and coffee. Mandelbaum had received a much larger ration of bread and Netanel found himself unable to avert his eyes from the sacred grey slab in the other man's fist. Envy and rage smouldered like cold fire.

"How did you get so much bread?" he hissed.

Mandelbaum was watching him too. "Do you want to trade?"

Netanel could not believe his ears. The idiot. "All right," he said, and held out his own meagre ration.

He accepted the prize in his other hand and Mandelbaum snatched Netanel's ration away. They stared at each other.

Netanel realised he had been tricked. Now he had the smaller ration. How had Mandelbaum managed that?

"You tricked me," Mandelbaum said.

"Do you want to trade again?" Netanel said.

Mandelbaum held out the ration. Netanel snatched it away and tossed the other piece of bread back to him.

It had happened again. Mandelbaum still had the larger ration.

They stared at each other, bewildered.

"Do you want to trade again?" Netanel said.

"What's the point? You always get the biggest piece."

They ate their ration in silence, confused and defeated by the illusion. The hallucination was a common one; just another torment to be lived with. Auschwitz had many more.

Once he had even imagined he had seen Marie.

It was only for a moment. It was a Sunday and he had been assigned to a special kommando to clean up the perimeter fence. The SS turned off the wire so they could pull a body off the spikes, and then, with the guard behind them, they walked between the rows of wire collecting the refuse blown through the fence by the wind.

The fence separated their part of the camp from the SS administration and barracks. Netanel looked up for a moment and saw a girl walk quickly out of one of the Gestapo offices.

"Marie," he whispered.

"*Schnell, mach schnell!*" the SS guard shouted and jammed the butt of his rifle into his back.

Netanel bent to continue his work. When he dared another glance she was gone, disappeared into the grey and frozen rains of Auschwitz, and he realised it was just another illusion, another torment invoked by the demons in his mind.

The evening ration had been distributed over an hour ago, but a few Müsselmen still squatted on the floor scraping their bowls with their spoons, frowning with concentration as they turned them in the dim light, searching for some morsel that had somehow been overlooked. An old Jew who had once been a doctor in a hospital in Warsaw moved around the bunks offering to tend wounded feet and corns for a half ration of bread; on another bunk a man who had been a tailor in Lublin squinted as he worked with his precious needle and thread, organising another extra ration for himself.

Mendelssohn appeared at the door of the Tagesraum. "Who has broken shoes?" he shouted.

Men fell over each other in the rush to be one of the first through the door. Only the first dozen or so would get new shoes; the rest would have to wait for another opportunity the next evening. What kind of incarnate evil could find ways to torture men over such a simple thing as shoes?

A few minutes later another bell rang, and the night guard planted himself on a chair by the door and the lights dimmed.

Mandelbaum curled into a ball on his bunk, so that no one could see him remove the photograph of his son from the straw.

"The rats have been eating my boy," he whispered.

"Better him than you," Netanel said.

"They have chewed half the face away. When he is gone, everything is gone. I shall be ready for the Krematorium."

"Don't talk like that," Netanel said. But he was right. It was a different Mandelbaum these last few months. He was a Müsselman now. When he took his shirt off you could count his ribs. It was like an anatomy lesson. Netanel reckoned you could even count the bones in his head. But what was worse was the smell of him; Mandelbaum had stopped washing. Netanel had decided that was how the SS chose who was next for the chimneys: by the smell.

"Sophie is dead, my little Ruth is dead. How can they do such things to children?"

"They're not dead," Netanel heard himself say. "They went to the women's camp at Birkenau, with your wife. You said so yourself."

"No, it's all over. I'm ready now."

Netanel stared at the bunk above his head and tried to think of some way to keep Mandelbaum alive. Why is it so important? he wondered. Because he is my last tenuous link with Ravenswald, and some other self I used to be? Because I knew him as a name before I knew men as numbers?

Or because without him to despise I will have no one to despise but myself?

"Look, I heard a rumour today. The guards do not like what is happening here. Even they are sick of all this killing. Some of them are planning to turn their guns on the commandant and free us."

"No, Herr Rosenberg, no one is going to help us. They are going to kill us all sooner or later. Why wait?"

So the madman has become sane, Netanel thought, and I have joined the battalion of fools who deal in daydreams. The bell rang and the last rites of another day in bedlam were played out.

52

Marie waited while the schreiber flicked through the sheaf of orders. He exuded an air of self-importance, as if the dispatch was a secret correspondence to him from the Führer himself. He looked up at her, leering at her body. The sports outfit that was the required uniform of a läuferka – a prison courier – did not flatter her, but in a place like this, the clerk thought . . .

"Wait here," he said, and took the papers into the next office, shutting the door behind him.

Marie went behind his desk and slid open the drawer of the filing cabinet. She knew what she was looking for. Twenty-three women from Block 41 at Birkenau had been selected for the Krematorium, among them three members of the camp underground. She quickly removed their identity cards from the file and replaced them with other cards concealed in her track-suit pocket; cards that belonged to women gassed five months ago.

She had performed this simple operation half a dozen times. As one of the läuferki she was allowed to move freely about the camp, carrying orders from the central administrative building to the outlying blocks, which extended for several kilometres through guardposts and checkpoints. Her duties had made her a prime recruit for the prison underground.

When the clerk returned she was standing at attention in front of his desk, as she had been when he left the room. He did not notice the patina of sweat that glistened like grease on her forehead.

"That will be all," he said.

She felt his eyes on her as she walked out. Pig, she thought. An SS clerk, and he behaves like Goering. One day, I would love to tell you how many times I have doctored your precious files while you've been strutting round your colonel's office. But I don't suppose there will ever be such an opportunity.

One day I will be discovered and shot. So why do I do it? I could have been gassed at Birkenau or suffering right now with all these other starving and shaven skeletons around me; instead I have a room to myself and enough food to eat. An aristocrat in hell.

Recently she had seen a German newspaper lying on a desk, and she had been startled by what she had read: "tactical withdrawals" all along the Russian front; "redeployments" in Northern Africa. They were losing. The war would have to end soon, Hitler would have to negotiate. The army might even try to get rid of him. The nightmare would have an end, after all.

So why do I still risk?

Because of what Rolf has done to me, she thought. And to make them pay for killing my Netanel.

SS Major Rolf Emmerich sat on the chair by his bed, the soft black leather of his boots gleaming in the dull glow of the bedside lamp. He was in his shirtsleeves. He smiled softly as the guard escorted Marie into the room.

"Thank you, Sergeant," he said to the man, "that will be all."

The door closed softly.

Rolf reached on to the bedside table and picked up a packet of cigarettes. He lit one, still smiling.

"My pretty Marie."

"Do you want to do it now or do I have to listen to you talk first? I can never decide what is worse."

Rolf shook his head, feigning shock. "You try so hard to hurt me, don't you? Why do you do it, liebling? Has it not occurred to you that I am the best friend you ever had?"

"I thank God for it every night."

"And so you should. Where would you be without me, hein?"

Marie forced a yawn. "Shall I open my legs for you now?"

His smile vanished. She did hurt him, because she knew he wanted more than sex. She exacted her price, measure for measure.

"First I have something to show you," he said.

"That will make a change."

"Oh, my Marie. You used to be such a prim little girl. Where did you get this dirty mouth?"

"I've been mixing with the wrong people, I suppose."

His uniform jacket was hanging over the back of his chair. He took a thin stack of file cards from the pocket, each one emblazoned with the official eagle emblem of the SS. He held them under her nose and casually flicked through them with his thumb.

"Do you know what these are?"

"They are identity cards."

"Which ones?"

Her eyes were dull. No fear, as he had hoped, or even surprise. "The ones I switched over in Colonel Schrantz's office today?"

"That was stupid, Marie."

"Forgive me, but it would seem to me the stupid one is the idiot of a clerk who let me do it right under his nose."

Rolf dropped the cards on the bed. Unexpectedly, he started to laugh. "You're quite right. I think perhaps it is time he moved his desk a little closer to the fighting." He threw himself on the bed, and put his hands behind his head. "But what should I do with you?"

"I don't care."

"I think you do. Oh, perhaps you might not care if I sent you to the Krematorium. The Frauenblock though – that is another matter."

He saw her swallow hard against her fear.

"Yes, that is your weakness, isn't it, little Marie?"

"So . . . is that my – punishment?"

He sighed. "I don't know. I have another 'housemaid' now. She is a läuferka too, like you. She is much nicer to me than you are, and she does not do stupid things like this." He indicated the identity cards at the foot of the bed.

"I shall throw myself on the wire before I go there."

"Yes, I believe you would. That would be a waste. And what should I tell your father?"

They stared at each other in silence.

"Take off your clothes."

Marie stripped and lay down on the bed. She put her hands behind her head and concentrated on the ceiling. He leaned across and put his hand on her breast, kissed her on the mouth. "Marie," he whispered. "I could help you so much more if you would let me. I could perhaps even get you out of this place."

"Could you get me away from you?"

He pulled off his belt angrily and jerked down his uniform trousers. He pulled her legs apart and rolled on top of her. "Why don't you close your eyes and pretend I'm your Jew lover?"

"How can I? Every time I breathe in, I smell you."

He squeezed her breast, hard. She flinched and instinctively pulled one hand from behind her head to protect herself. He grinned. "See? You do feel. You only pretend you don't feel anything."

"I feel disgusted."

"It doesn't matter to me, Marie. This is all I want."

He forced himself inside her. She uttered a small cry but her face remained expressionless. It's always like this, he thought. She lies there, she doesn't even try to fight me. It's like making love to a corpse.

"I don't care, Marie," he repeated. "This is enough for me. You don't have anything else to give me anyway."

"He was bigger than you, Rolf. Did I ever tell you that? He made yours look like a peanut."

Rolf grimaced. He was losing his erection. The bitch was castrating him. "He's dead now. I selected him out

342

myself. You should have seen him. His legs were like matchsticks."

"Are you enjoying this, Rolf? I can't feel a thing."

He moved more urgently. Damn her. He was losing it completely.

"Go on, Rolf," she whispered, "go on. Rock me to sleep."

He pulled out of her. "Turn over."

She stared at him. He slapped her once, very hard.

"Turn over!"

She shook her head. He hit her again, caught her wrist and pulled her on her side. She fought him. He hit her twice more and she screamed and clutched at her mouth. There was blood on the pillow. He forced her wrist behind her back and held it there.

Yes, this was better. He had his erection back now.

"I'll make you feel," he whispered in her ear. "I'll make you moan for me like you moaned for your Jewboy."

God help me! Marie thought. God help me when venom dresses as passion and the devil is free to do as he pleases.

She lay sobbing into the pillow. Rolf sat naked by the bedside, tendrils of smoke curling up to the ceiling from his cigarette. He casually stroked the smooth and pale round of her shoulder. She was cold with drying sweat. "I am sorry if I hurt you," he whispered.

"Dear God in heaven . . ."

"The first time is always the worst. It will get easier."

She dragged herself off the bed and pulled on her clothes, painfully.

"You see. You can lose your virginity more than once, Marie."

Was he insane? she thought. Perhaps madness was just the freedom to do as you pleased, without restraint, without controls. Rolf's madness was the madness all Germans were infected with.

"I love you, Marie," he whispered.

"One day I'm going to kill you," she whispered, and limped out.

53

In his mind Netanel named it the Dance of the Dead Men. Every evening they returned through the camp gates, moving with the spastic shuffle of men whose shoes always hurt, whose bodies were exhausted beyond pain and whose spirits were drained of any aspiration but to eat a hunk of grey bread and lie down on a lice-ridden straw mattress.

The kapos shrieked and slashed at them with their rubber truncheons but Netanel had long ago become indifferent to the shouts and the blows. His mind was focused totally on the ration. Another day over, another victory won.

But after Appel a bell rang and someone shouted, "Blocksperre!"

Mendelssohn and the Orphan were grinning at them when they filed in. Mendelssohn gave everyone a card with his name, age, number and nationality printed under the SS eagle, and the Orphan's unterkapos herded them on to their bunks. The word was whispered like a plague from mouth to mouth through the rows of huddled, frightened men: "Selecjwa!"

"Selection!"

"This is the end for me," Mandelbaum said.

"You'll be all right," Netanel said. "Spend a quarter of your ration for a shave. It will be worth it. You still have time."

Mandelbaum groped in the straw mattress for the

photograph. It was gone. "The rats have eaten my boy," he mumbled.

"You'll be all right," Netanel repeated, but it was hard even to look at Mandelbaum when he was naked. The varicose veins in his calves were bigger than the muscles in his arms. "You'll be all right." It was a small comfort he heard repeated endlessly around him as men tried to reassure each other.

"They won't choose you. You're no Müsselman."

"It won't be your turn. You're still healthy and strong."

"They're only picking out the sick ones. You'll be okay."

"I heard they're not sending people to Birkenau any more. They're going back to Theresienstadt."

"They're not choosing German Jews, just Poles."

"They won't choose a High Number . . ."

"They don't select Low Numbers . . ."

The door to the Tagesraum burst open and the Orphan rushed out. "All right, you bastards, strip! *Schnell, schnell!* Get in here with your cards, hurry up!"

Clutching their cards, they were herded into the Tagesraum. It was a cold night and the press of warm bodies was not unpleasant. Everyone held their cards above their heads so they would not get lost or crumpled.

Like schoolchildren on an outing, Netanel thought.

There was a cracked mirror on the wall. In it Netanel saw a huddle of staring skeletons with shaved skulls, their heads too large for their bodies, their faces distorted by starvation into grimaces of ugly fear. He saw a tall man with the cicatrice of a scar, jagged and pink, down one side of his face, his scalp and cheeks covered with greyish stubble, jostling for space. He looked familiar. Someone he had known in school perhaps, changed almost beyond recognition by time and injury.

. . . Me.

Oh my God. Great, sweet God, it's me.

But it can't be me! That man is a monster, ugly and misshapen, like all these other ghetto wretches. I don't look like them!

The outer door of the Tagesraum was thrown open. Outside, the reflectors on the watchtower had turned the night white as phosphor. There were just three of them, waiting: an SS major, Mendelssohn and the Orphan.

Netanel recognised the SS major instantly. It was Rolf Emmerich.

"I am dead," Netanel murmured.

Rolf looked beautiful, a fallen angel in black. The artificial light framed his face with shadows, like a Vermeer portrait, lent him a ghastly aura of ethereal perfection. His eyes glittered like sapphires, reflecting light without absorbing it, and his smile was beatific and kind.

Mendelssohn was on his right, the Orphan on his left. Smaller than Rolf, dressed in prison garb, they appeared as minions from the underworld, emphasising Rolf's dark splendour.

The moment was broken by the voices of the unterkapos. "*Heraus! Heraus! Mach schnell, schnell!*"

The first man ran towards Rolf – stiff-legged, buttocks so scrawny you could make out his thigh bones – and handed him his card. Rolf handed it to Mendelssohn. The man was herded away to the side, shoved back into the barracks through another door. All over in a few seconds. His fate, whatever it was, had been decided.

Netanel watched carefully. One at a time they were pushed out of the door; Rolf took the card, handed it either it to Mendelssohn or the Orphan, then the next man was running towards him.

Who was life? Mendelssohn or the Orphan?

It took just a few seconds for each man to be judged. After all, Netanel thought, it did not matter if Rolf made a mistake. If a fit man was written down for the gas, or a sick man spared, it was of no consequence. It was important only that a certain number should die in order to make room for new arrivals.

An old man shuffled forwards. He was limping, and Netanel could hear his breath sawing in his chest. Rolf grinned, and there was no mistaking what that smile meant. He handed the card to Mendelssohn.

346

So.

Mendelssohn was death.

The Orphan was life.

"Goodbye, Herr Rosenberg," Mandelbaum whispered.

Mandelbaum was shoved forward. Rolf took his identity card and slapped it against the palm of his black-gloved hand, deliberating. He glanced over Mandelbaum's shoulder, and seemed to hesitate. In that moment one of the unterkapos grabbed Netanel's arm and shoved him forwards.

Rolf looked up and their eyes met. This is it, Netanel thought, will he send me to the gas or will he put me aside for some other, more exquisite, torment?

54

Netanel ran forward and handed Rolf his card. Rolf glanced up at him, and for a moment their eyes met. And there was no sign of recognition in his face. None at all.

When he looks at the card he will know, Netanel thought. But Rolf did not look at the card, and in that moment Netanel knew what was going to happen. It was over in a moment.

There were two cards in his hands.

Two cards.

Of course, Mandelbaum! Rolf had been too slow to make his judgment on Mandelbaum, the unterkapo had been too quick ushering Netanel forward. There was nothing to be done. Rolf was already looking over Netanel's shoulder at the next man. He overcame the aberration in the process by handing one card to his right, to Mendelssohn, the other to his left, to the Orphan.

Netanel glanced down. The Orphan, life, was holding Mandelbaum's card.

For a moment he was about to protest. But what would he say? Wait, you have made a mistake? Would he scream for mercy, for justice, to Rolf Emmerich, son of a beer carter, major in the Schutzstaffeln? There were no mistakes in here. You lived or you died, and it did not matter to anyone else.

The unterkapos were already hustling him away towards the barrack doors. He did not feel the sting of the truncheons on his bare back and buttocks. His Organisierung, the desperate struggle for survival through the Polish winter, his Low Number, it all counted for nothing now. He might just as well have thrown himself on the wire that first night.

All because of Mandelbaum.

He wanted to weep with frustration. Why go through all that pain to have it end now?

And I just wanted to see Marie once more.

Netanel sat on his bunk and did not bother to dress.

"They're going to send you to a special camp," Mandelbaum said.

"What?"

"They're going to send you to a special camp. It's not the gas, not this time. I heard Mendelssohn tell one of the others."

Netanel looked up at Mandelbaum. He was smiling. He really believed it. He had had his reprieve and now he was crazy again.

"You still believe what Mendelssohn says?"

"Why would he lie?"

"It makes his job easier. And because he enjoys it."

"You'll be all right. You'll see. It's not the gas this time."

"Just fuck off and leave me alone, Mandelbaum."

The ugly little shit. He is trying not to be happy because he is going to live and I am going to die. Well, why not? I would be happy too, if I were him. But I'm not, I'm marked for the gas. And I would like to tear him apart with my hands because it's his fault.

"They are giving out the ration. You'll get a double share. That's something to look forward to, isn't it?"

A double share, Netanel thought. I am a dead man so now they give me a double share. Something to look forward to. Mandelbaum is serious. He really thinks I should be grateful.

"It will be all right, Herr Rosenberg."

He wanted to hit him to shut him up, but there was no strength left in him so instead he got dressed and took his bowl to the table at the end of the barrack and asked Mendelssohn for his extra ration.

When the bell rang the next morning, and the night guard passed along the bunks with his whispered "Wstvac", Netanel did not move. Mandelbaum jumped off the bunk, dressed quickly and ran for the shower block. The unterkapos ignored Netanel. After all, he did not exist any more.

He had the bunk to himself for the first time since he arrived at Auschwitz. He could stretch out on the scratchy straw without feeling the hard wooden edges of the cot biting into his bones. Now in his last moments in hell, he could find small luxuries in those things which all his life had barely attracted his attention.

His emotions see-sawed between elation and cold dread. In one moment he was light-headed with relief that the future was finally decided; the next the black terror of death made him want to run in blind panic.

The barrack was silent; empty now except for the other sleepers, the waiters for death like himself. He felt like a ghost. The world was turning around him but he no longer took part. He could observe but could not be seen.

Outside his former inmates shuffled off in the darkness for morning Appel. He stared in silence at the fading shadows as the grey dawn light crept across the cement floor. What was the hurry? Why was the day so eager to come?

*　　*　　*

They came mid-morning.

"*Achtung!*"

They leaped from their beds and the Orphan and his unterkapos harried them into lines. Mendelssohn sat at a folding table by the door. The men in the front of the line showed him the tattoos on their arms, and he made a small tick beside the appropriate number on the typewritten sheet in front of him.

"Is it the gas, Herr Blockältester?" he heard one man ask.

"No, no, you are going to another camp. You have my word on it. On the grave of my mother!"

Rot in hell, Mendelssohn! Netanel thought.

The Leichenauto was a large van, painted grey, with a metal chimney protruding from the roof. Because of fuel shortages most of the camp's transport had been converted to run on wood as well as on gasolene. The SS driver sat in the front, staring straight ahead.

"Get in! Hurry!" one of the unterkapos shouted, pushing them into the back.

I am going to my death, Netanel thought. Death. It did not seem real; I suppose it never seems real to anyone. No one ever thinks they are really going to die.

There was a bench running along each side of the van. Netanel sat down. Nobody spoke, no one looked up. The door slammed and left them in semi-darkness. Netanel realised it had all been done without the aid of a single SS man. One German criminal and a few yellow Jews and our whole nation bows its head and is led off to extinction.

The Leichenauto juddered into life and they drove away. He glanced into the corner. No fire in the grate. They were using gasolene today.

Someone started to pray.

"Aren't you all ashamed?" Netanel said aloud.

No one answered him.

"No one will ever know," Netanel said. "We are going to die and no one will ever know our sufferings. They lead us away by the nose, like cattle, and we did not fight back once. They are going to kill every Jew in the world and there is no one to resist them."

Still, no one spoke.

"Someone has to survive! There has to be a revenge! There has to be a redemption for us . . ."

Silence.

They are dead already, he thought. They died at the selection.

"I did not want to be a Jew, they made me one! How can you die this way? How can you ever rest in your graves, any of you?"

He stared at the chimney in the corner of the van. Perhaps I could fit in that, he thought. Well no. *I* couldn't, Netanel Rosenberg could never fit his big body into such a space. But the man I saw in the mirror in the Tagesraum, he could fit.

"I swear I will have revenge for all of you," he said.

He wondered later if any of them even saw what he did. He crouched down by the chimney and raised his arms above his head, and forced his head and shoulders into the flue.

He could not breathe. The choking soot was in his nose and mouth, but he fought down his panic. He kept pushing until he was standing in the grate. The tips of his fingers reached the edge of the chimney.

He would wait until they stopped, he decided. Then he would pull himself up.

Small breaths, he told himself. You won't choke if you control your breathing and don't gulp in too much soot. Not much room for your chest to expand, but enough.

Feeling strangely calm. Waiting.

The van lurched to a stop. A sudden stillness, then the crunch of boots. Netanel curled his fingers around the lip of the chimney and pulled himself up. Just enough room to bend his knees a little, so that his feet were out of sight . . .

No good, he couldn't hold himself, his arms were too

351

weak. Perhaps if he braced his knees and elbows against the sides . . .

He heard the SS guard shouting, "*Heraus! Heraus! Los! Los!*"

He waited for the hammering of boots on the metal floor of the van, the triumphant shouts as they pulled on his legs and dragged him out of his hiding place.

Instead he heard the doors slam shut.

Now what?

Stupid, he thought. Stupid! What have you gained, except a few hours? You cannot open the doors from inside so how are you going to escape? And where can you run to? The whole of Auschwitz is a prison!

He eased himself out of the grate, and crawled into the corner.

Outside the SS guards were still screaming instructions to their victims. There was the hollow thud of a rifle stock on bone.

The van's engine shuddered to life again.

What now?

The Leichenauto rolled to a stop. Netanel heard the driver climb out of the cab, slam the door and walk away. Another door slammed and then there was silence.

He's taken the Leichenauto back to the garage, Netanel thought. I'm inside the SS compound! Desperately, he tried the door. Locked.

There was nothing to do now but wait.

He had cheated death. But only for another day.

55

Yawning, SS Corporal Dieter Overath threw open the doors of the Leichenauto, a tied bundle of loose faggots under his left arm. There was another gasolene shortage and they had received instructions to use the wood again. He cursed. He hated using the wood. He got his uniform dirty from the chimney and besides, the engine never had enough power. You had to light the fire and keep it stoked the whole time. With gasolene you just turned the key and cranked the handle and you were away.

He climbed into the back of the Leichenauto and almost shit himself.

"Herrgottsacrament!" There was a Jew in there!

The man was naked and covered with soot. He was crouched down in the corner, black as a negro, the whites of his eyes staring from his head like two little moons. A ghost! A ghost from the chimneys come back to haunt him!

He dropped the bundle of wood.

Calm yourself, Dieter, he told himself. Anyone can see the Jew is alive; very much alive and very frightened. But what is he doing in the back of the Leichenauto?

"Who are you?" he hissed. "What are you doing in my van?"

The man just stared at him.

Soot. Herrgottsacrament, the chimney!

"You stupid little shit, what are you trying to do to me?"

The Jew said nothing.

What was he going to do? He could get his rifle from the

cabin and shoot him. Then what would he tell the major? If Emmerich found out about this he would get transferred to the Eastern front, like the colonel's clerk. The Jew had been marked off on the forms, he was supposed to be dead. He couldn't take him back to Birkenau now, not without the appropriate paperwork. He would be reported. Of course, it wasn't his fault, it was the idiot who designed these stupid vans, but Emmerich wouldn't care about that.

He slammed the doors and locked them. What in the name of Holy God was he going to do?

The Leichenauto shuddered to a halt in a street just off the Appelplatz. Overath jumped out. He looked around quickly to satisfy himself that no one was watching then threw open the rear doors.

"Get out!" he hissed. "Quick, you little shit, get out!"

He jumped in, grabbed Netanel by the arm and threw him out of the van. Netanel landed on his back in the mud. Let someone else find him and figure it out, Overath thought.

"You Jew shit, why did you do this to me?" he hissed. He slammed the doors shut and climbed back behind the wheel. He drove away through the mud, praying that Major Emmerich did not find out what had happened.

The barracks was empty.

Netanel went to the shower block and washed the soot off his body, then returned to the barracks and sat naked on the edge of the bunk, waiting for the others to return. They were a poor family, and Mendelssohn and the Orphan were cruel parents, but they were all he had.

No one moved, no one spoke. They would not even look at him.

"Hello, Mandelbaum," Netanel said.

Mandelbaum squatted on the far end of the bunk and ate his ration as if he were not there.

"Mandelbaum? It's me, Rosenberg."

"Go away," Mandelbaum whispered.

Netanel stood up and joined the queue for the ration. Immediately the customary pushing and jostling stopped. The line of men parted for him. As usual, Mendelssohn and the Orphan were distributing the soup and the bread. They saw him and whispered urgently to each other.

Netanel showed the Orphan his number.

"Next," the Orphan said.

"But Herr Kapo – "

"Next!"

I am a dead man, Netanel thought. You cannot see a dead man. You cannot talk to him, and you cannot give him his ration. They do not know how to deal with me any other way. If they acknowledge I am not dead, they might be blamed and they will be punished. So they have to pretend I am invisible.

There is only one thing I can do.

A dirty yellow dawn, flat grey fields beyond the wire. Chaim saw a naked and dirty figure stumble across the Appelplatz. He did not recognise him. He slapped the thong of his whip into his palm and strode across to intercept this interloper. Perhaps some Jew who had gone crazy. He would deal with him.

"Chaim."

"Herrgottsacrament!" Chaim whispered. He stared at the scar, the one that crazy Lubanski had given his cousin. "Netanel?"

"Help me . . ."

"But where are your clothes? What happened to you?"

"Just help me. I'll do anything. I'm going to get these bastards, all of them. Help me."

Chaim smiled. "You want to be a kapo, do you?"

"I'll join the SS if I have to. Don't let me die. I have to make all this mean something."

"It just means you survive, Netanel. That's all."

"That's enough. For now."

Chaim smiled. "Well, we'll see." He nodded towards

Birkenau. An ugly brown smudge hung on the horizon over the forests. "They've started early. Anyone you know?"

Netanel shook his head. "Not any more," he said.

Part Eleven

POLAND AND GERMANY, 1944–5

56

He would never, as long as he lived, forget the smell of the summer of 1944. Burning human flesh gives off a choking, clinging odour that is at once nauseous and sweet. The weather was hot and dry, the sky had turned smoke-red, and the sunsets were long and rose pink and beautiful. The trailing smoke of the chimneys became the feathery banners of the lost souls who arrived in ragged battalions at the train station.

The death factory was fuelled day and night by boxcars of Jews from Hungary and Italy, and trainloads of gypsies from Romania. Most of them never knew Auschwitz as he knew it; they were there only long enough to be counted, stripped, gassed and burned, and all that remained of their passing was a broken suitcase on the platform, a boy's football between the tracks, a child's doll discarded on the banks of the sidings.

But the sunsets they made for those left as witness were glorious.

Soon the Krematorium had reached capacity and was unable to burn all those who were gassed, and Netanel was put in charge of an Arbeitskommando sent to excavate deep trenches in the forests above Birkenau. When the work was done the SS arrived with truckloads of corpses. Even Netanel found it hard to breathe and after two years in Auschwitz he thought he was used to any stink.

Netanel's kommando were ordered to throw the bodies into the trench and douse them with benzene. Then an SS sergeant threw in a match.

A black plume of smoke rose hundreds of feet into the sky.

Still the trains kept arriving. All night, every night, he lay on his bunk and heard the wagons rattle into the sidings. It seemed the nightmare had no end.

He was in the forest with his kommando, watching the flames spit from another trench of the dead, when a grey SS lorry pulled up on the slope below him. Two SS sergeants jumped out. One of them hauled a wheelbarrow from the back of the truck.

There were a dozen children inside.

"Who'd like a ride?" one of the sergeants shouted. He was a big, cheerful, red-faced man with close-cropped blond hair. A good German father, Netanel thought.

The children fought with each other for the first ride.

The man laughed, picked up a little girl and sat her in the wheelbarrow. "Hold on!" he shouted. He ran up the slope and the girl – she was no more than five, Netanel guessed – screamed, delighted.

The man took her over the rise, out of sight of the others. He headed towards the flaming ravine.

"God in heaven," Netanel whispered.

He closed his eyes. But that night in his bunk he could still hear the child's screams, and the screams of all the other children who followed her. It stripped his soul like a flail and he made a silent vow to the dead child that he would survive and ensure such obscenities never happened again.

Netanel took the half loaf of bread from the table, and scooped up a handful of cigarettes. On the camp's black market if bread was coin, cigarettes were the highest denomination currency.

Chaim was playing chess at the table with Alexandr; Shlomo was asleep on his bunk. Netanel went out the back door of the hut and waited in the shadows. A few moments later he heard the soft, foot-dragging shuffle of a Häftling.

"Mandelbaum?"

"Herr Rosenberg . . ."

"Here." He gave him the bread. Mandelbaum immediately began tearing chunks off it with his teeth. Netanel waited; he understood this kind of hunger. Even now, when he could organise everything he wanted, he did not forget. It was like being poor; even if you one day became rich you still saw every small waste as a blasphemy.

"How are you doing, Mandelbaum?"

"There was another selecjwa yesterday."

"I know. You're all right?"

He tore off another hunk of the bread. "I worry they will make a mistake."

"One day at a time. It will soon be over. The British and the Americans are in France."

Mandelbaum continued to tear at the bread. "You heard what happened to the Orphan?"

"Yes, I heard." The Gestapo had caught him selling gold teeth to Meister Lentner at the railyards. The gold teeth, of course, were German property, redeemable at the ovens when their owner had no further use for them. Trading in them was illegal. The Orphan had escaped the noose however; they had shown great mercy and sent him to work in the mines on the Silesian coalfields.

"When all this is over I am going to find him and spit in his face," Mandelbaum said. The bread was nearly gone.

"You won't see him again," Netanel said. The average life expectancy for prisoners in the coal mines was three months.

Mandelbaum crammed the last of the bread into his mouth and leaned against the hut in a sort of ecstasy. When you suffer all the time, Netanel remembered, a little less pain can be the most exquisite form of pleasure.

"Bless you, Herr Rosenberg."

"Here," Netanel said. He gave him the cigarettes. "You can buy anything with these on the black market. But first see if you can trade them to Mendelssohn for an easier kommando."

Mandelbaum hid the cigarettes inside his jacket.

"Don't let anyone know where you got them."

Mandelbaum leaned closer. The stink of him! "Wher

all this is over," he said, "I am going to join my son in Palestine."

"What would you do in the desert? You'll come back to Ravenswald with me."

"You won't go back to Ravenswald, Herr Rosenberg. None of us can ever go back now."

No, you're wrong, Netanel thought. I have one reason to return. I have to find out what happened to Marie. "Come back tomorrow night. Perhaps I can organise a little more bread."

Mandelbaum shuffled away. He was a freak, a Low Number who had survived two years as a Häftling. Even Mendelssohn deferred to him now. Among some of the prisoners he inspired something like awe, and perhaps hope. He had survived because of Netanel. He was Netanel's living absolution for his betrayal of his fellow men.

Chaim looked up from the chess board. "You should be careful."

Netanel did not answer him.

"The SS should not find out you are soft on a Jew Häftling."

"After morning Appel I'll hit him just as hard as you. What I do with my bread at night is my business."

"Nothing is your business, Netanel. Not in here."

Netanel threw himself on his bunk.

He shared the *Stübe* with Chaim and two other kapos, German Jews like himself. These days he had a single bunk to himself with a real mattress, a warm blanket, even sheets. There was a tiny kitchen with a hotplate and a shelf for food. Food! They were given margarine and jam as part of their rations. They also received treasures like tobacco and insect powder and these could be traded on the black market or at the hospital for luxuries such as tinned food and fresh eggs. There was no bedtime curfew so they played chess after the last bell and long into the night.

The four of them had withdrawn from the common law,

were hated, and, in turn, became hateful. Companionship existed only among themselves.

"I overheard two SS officers talking today," Chaim said. "Someone tried to kill Hitler."

"There's always rumours," Alexandr said.

"It didn't sound like a rumour. They said someone planted a bomb under his desk. Rommel was one of the plotters."

"Rommel!"

"That was what they said."

"What happened?" Netanel asked him.

Chaim shrugged. "I don't know. Hitler is still alive anyway. But these two SS fellows were worried. The Americans and British are pushing east. They think they will be in Paris within weeks." He looked at Alexandr and then at Netanel. "You know, the end of the war is going to be a very dangerous time for all of us."

There was a long silence as each of them forced themselves to think of the unthinkable; a day when their conduct might be judged by the standards of an outside world they had all but forgotten.

But there was an even worse prospect: that they would be judged by their fellow prisoners. In the event of such a fate, the hangman's noose might seem a mercy. Who will speak for me? Netanel thought. Only Mandelbaum. The others hate me as I hated the Orphan and Mendelssohn and the rest. No one will ever believe it was not just the determination for revenge that forced this betrayal. I am not even sure I believe it myself.

"We must be away from here before then," Alexandr said.

"I agree," Chaim said. "But how are we going to do it?" He looked down at the chessboard and moved his bishop, taking Alexandr's queen. "Checkmate," he said.

57

The autumn went on and on, bright and warm, as if the approach of the Allies had banished winter, heralding an endless Narnian summer. Then one day the warm silence of the camp was shattered by the shock waves of an explosion. It rolled through the camp from the direction of Birkenau.

Soon afterwards Netanel heard distant voices sing the Internazionale, in Polish and German and Russian. Inevitably it was followed by the barking of commands in German, and the dull pop of Schmeissers. Screams followed by silence.

Within minutes the news was all around the camp. A group of Sonderkommando had blown up the Krematorium.

October, and the days were still bright and blue. The barrage balloons hovered over the Carpathian mountains like monstrous insects, and the steeple of Auschwitz – a nice touch, the church, Netanel thought, another of God's little jokes – was still visible above the forest. But now the evening air had begun to chill. Even the Allies' approach would not hold back one last Auschwitz winter.

Netanel's kommando was unloading bricks at the Carbide factory. The work was demanding but he had learned his new trade quickly. Shouting and cursing and pummelling men's backs with hollow rubber truncheons was not such a difficult task when you remembered the gas ovens at Birkenau and the children's wheelbarrow rides in the Buna forest. Someone had to settle the debts of the past and pay for the future, and these bastards were plainly not up to it.

It was easy to despise the Häftlinge, in fact. He understood now how it came so easily to the SS. A starving man
with his back bowed under a load of bricks invited either
scorn or pity, and pity was foreign to this place. These
Jews had let this happen to them: each of them had relied
on the compassion of their enemies or the intervention of
their friends, just like his father. In the end they had been
abandoned, and still they would not fight back, and they
had dragged him down with them. He began to think of
them as if they were as much his enemy as the SS.

A Häftling tripped and spilled his load of bricks. He lay
groaning on the ground. Netanel ran over and clubbed him
between the shoulders with his truncheon. "Get up, you
dirty Jew!"

The man looked up; a skeletal face with a stubble of grey
beard and yellow-streaked eyes. He grinned and bobbed
his head in deference. It was Mandelbaum. "Please, Herr
Rosenberg . . ."

"Get up, you bastard!" Netanel hit him again. It was a
kindness, in a way. He remembered how a greater pain
helped you forget the lesser ones, and kept you going.

Mandelbaum struggled to his feet.

"Pick them up!" Netanel screamed at him.

Mandelbaum tried, fell to his knees again. Netanel
looked around; two SS were watching. He hit him a
third time.

"Mandelbaum, for God's sake! Get up!" he hissed.

"I can't do it any more . . ."

"Get up, you bastard!"

The siren sounded. The end of the day. Relieved,
Netanel hit him twice more and turned away, apparently
disgusted that the siren had ended his game. The two SS
guards chuckled and walked away.

Netanel looked back. Mandelbaum was still on his
knees. He wouldn't make the winter. His absolution was
about to be withdrawn.

When they got back to the Appelplatz Netanel noticed
a gallows had been erected on the patch of lawn in

front of the square. So! This evening there was to be cabaret.

Netanel counted his kommando and shouted the number to the SS sergeant: "*Kommando 58, sieben und sechzig Häftling, Stärke stimmt!*"

"Squad 58, sixty-seven prisoners, number correct!"

The searchlights were on, and the gallows was illuminated like a stage. Now for the theatre, Netanel thought. A Häftling was dragged out of a nearby building by two SS guards and hauled up the wooden steps on to the platform. His face was swollen and there were scabs around his lips and eyes. He could not stand without support.

SS Major Rolf Emmerich ascended the platform.

"Häftling 183095 has been condemned to death by orders of Gestapo High Command in Berlin for crimes against the people of Germany. Last month communist factions within the camp conspired to sabotage German property. In his full confession Häftlinge 183095 has admitted that he smuggled explosives from the Union factory to the communist traitors at Birkenau. Do you all understand?"

"*Jawohl!*" thousands of voices echoed.

Emmerich nodded at the guards. They dragged the man to the trapdoor and looped the noose over his head and drew it tight.

"Comrades!" the man shouted. "I am the last one!"

Netanel clenched his hands into fists, felt the nails bite into the flesh of his palms, swallowed down the sudden bite of shame. Yes, some had fought back, he thought. They had not all gone meekly to their deaths in the ovens, like sheep. But my way is better. If I can only get out of this place, one day I will prove it.

A long, shuffling silence.

Then, unexpectedly, "Comrade, we salute you!"

Netanel looked round to see which idiot had just signed his own death warrant. The man had his hand raised to his forehead in salute. There were tears glistening in the blackened creases of his old face.

Mandelbaum.

Rolf leaped from the platform and reached him in one stride. One blow bent him double, another sent him sprawling on to his back. He put his boot on Mandelbaum's throat and looked around at the thousands of ghostly, staring faces.

"Anyone else?" he said.

With a barely perceptible nod of his head, Rolf gave the order. The trapdoor opened and prisoner 183095 jerked and twisted on the rope. The band broke into a Strauss waltz and the prisoners filed away while the man slowly strangled to death.

"You!" Rolf shouted.

God in heaven, Netanel thought. He means me.

Mandelbaum was writhing and gurgling at Rolf's feet. "Kill him," Rolf said.

For a moment Netanel could not move. Rolf was watching him, waiting. He turned to one of the SS guards who was standing at the foot of the gallows. "Give him your truncheon!"

The guard took the wooden club from his belt and shoved it into Netanel's arms.

"He's in your kommando," Rolf said. "Now kill him, or I'll kill you."

He took his foot off Mandelbaum's throat. Mandelbaum rolled on to his side, gasping breath into his lungs. Rolf stood back.

I can't do this, Netanel thought.

Out of the corner of his eye he saw Rolf unclip the holster on his belt and take out his Lüger pistol. "Hurry up, kapo!"

Mandelbaum is dead anyway. There is no choice. Everything I've done, I've done for a reason. For the children in the forest, for my dead companions in the Leichenauto. I cannot die until I have made amends.

He raised the club.

He looked down at his uniform. Like pulping a watermelon, he thought. The juice goes everywhere. Bits of Mandelbaum on his face, and glistening on Rolf's boots.

"Leave him there for the Leichenkommando," Rolf said, and walked away.

Netanel looked up. A woman was staring at him. There was a white armband on her sleeve: "LÄUFERKA". She was absorbing everything, and it seemed as if what she saw had soaked into her like a stain.

Marie.

In that moment Netanel Rosenberg died.

The SS guard snatched the club from his hand and wiped it on Netanel's striped uniform. He replaced it in his belt and followed SS Major Emmerich out of the square.

Netanel looked around. Marie was gone. Only his kommando remained in the square, their eyes averted.

Absolute silence.

"Ah, my pretty little Marie," Rolf said. He was standing by the window, smoking a cigarette.

The guard closed the door and Marie sat on the edge of the bed.

"You're grey. You're not sick?"

She shook her head.

"You saw the execution?"

She nodded.

"Did it upset you?"

She did not answer.

"Your father was a butcher. It's no different. It's just meat."

Marie took a deep breath. She started to tremble.

"What's the matter, for God's sake?"

Still she did not answer.

He slapped her face, hard. "You're becoming quite tiresome."

She seemed to be having trouble breathing.

"What is it? For God's sake, say something!"

She lowered her head and her hair fell around her face.

Herrgottsacrament! He turned away in disgust and stubbed out his cigarette in the ashtray by the bedside table.

"I think we shall have to do something about you, liebling. I think we shall have to teach you some gratitude."

He went to the window and lit another cigarette. The Fliegeralarm sounded. He cursed softly, then bent down and turned off the bedside lamp. *Scheiss!* The Russians.

He could hear them now. The drone of the unseen enemy, remorseless. Every night they sent over their bombers, every day their armies came closer. The Russians in the east, the Americans in the west. A vice, squeezing out their lifeblood.

He felt the ground shudder as the first of the bombs fell, saw an orange flame blossom for a moment in the night sky. Another, another. Getting closer. He turned away from the window and in that moment the glass blew in and he was knocked to the floor.

He heard Marie scream. When he picked himself up, she was lying face down on the bed sobbing. He rolled her over. Just shock.

Perhaps that was what she needed. Shock treatment.

He went back to the window. One of the bombs had hit an acetylene gasometer at the railyards. The Appelplatz was illuminated with a sunset of orange flame.

Time was running out. These were the last days. A time of desperation, a time to take what you could and run.

58

The Frauenblock was on the second floor of the administrative building, just inside the main gates. The SS guards had free access to its facilities whenever they pleased; it was also available to Aryan criminals serving their sentences as kapos or Blockältester. They could earn chits for good behaviour redeemable at the whorehouse once a month.

Herr Kapo Lubanski approached the desk at the top of the stairs and threw his chits on the desktop. He hooked his thumbs in the belt of his uniform trousers and waited. The Frauenblock supervisor, a green triangle like himself, looked up and grinned.

"Herr Lubanski, what can we do for you today?"

Lubanski said nothing. His features were hard and set like a marble statue. He always looked as if he was about to spit.

"We have a new one," the supervisor said.

"Another of your ghetto Jew bitches?"

The supervisor shrugged. It was fun baiting this one. Insane, of course. Completely verrükt.

"No, this one is a good Aryan."

"What's a German girl doing in here?"

"Who cares? You'll like her, Lubanski. She still has a lot of fight in her."

Lubanski tried not to show his excitement. He must control himself. He had killed whores before, in Hamburg. But he dared not do it here, not to a Reichsdeutscher. The SS might not like it.

*   *   *

The supervisor heard screams coming from the room at the end of the corridor. He was accustomed to it. Some of the girls got a little hysterical when they were told to do something unusual.

He checked his clipboard to see who was using the room. Lubanski! He should have known! Well, he hoped he did not mess the girl up too badly. She had become something of a favourite with some of the SS, and fresh meat was getting harder to find.

As the Russians advanced, trains continued to pour into the railway yards of Oswiecim, but now they came from the east, and only the sickest and weakest of their cargo were fed to Birkenau. Since the reverses of the summer, the Gestapo High Command had begun to look on the Jewish problem from a different perspective; they realised the Jews might be more useful to Germany alive, as labour for their crippled armaments factories.

As the numbers inside the camp swelled, conditions deteriorated even further, even for the Prominenz. Rations were reduced, and the scarlet fever, diphtheria and typhus that the refugees had brought with them did not honour the hierarchy of Auschwitz. Guards, Häflinge, Blockältester and officers, all were stricken.

And every night the bombers came.

Netanel was at the Buna railyard when the first daylight raid struck the camp. He heard the sirens and instinctively looked skywards; when he looked back his kommando were already running across the tracks for the shelter of the trees. There was nothing to do but follow them.

He had just reached the trees when the first bomb hit the quartermaster's hut and the ground jumped under his feet. Hissing wood and metal slammed into the grass around him.

He kept running.

A second explosion, a third.

He threw himself face down into the soft grass. A shipment of rolling stock filled with gasolene exploded into a fireball. A stick of bombs chased each other along the railyards, and the ground shook underneath him, crump-crump-crump-CRUMP!

As he watched, he wondered at the beauty of destruction, the poetry of it. Flame and smoke and tearing. The end-over-end grace of falling debris, a small boy's satisfaction of demolition.

Destroy it, Netanel thought. Destroy it all.

He heard someone, somewhere, cheering.

His kommando, his fellow prisoners, his enemies, they were all around him, in the grass, Netanel realised, lying on their swollen bellies, chewing the dandelions and chicory leaves for their hunger even as they sheltered from the bombs. They would like to kill me, Netanel thought. Soon they may have their chance.

But they are too late.

I am already dead.

The vision he had seen the night he murdered Mandelbaum had not been the work of his fevered and tormented imagination, after all. Chaim had told him Marie Helder had been a läuferka in the camp for twenty-two months. All this time, she had been so close. The bastards! They had made her suffer so much just for loving him. They had brought her here so that she could witness the moment he took arms with the devil and whatever private purpose he had for survival had gone.

Now it was all for the dead ones.

The searing flames of the burning railyards were reflected in his eyes. Let the rage sustain him, for rage was all he had left inside now every other human emotion had been cauterised from his soul.

Lubanski unfastened the buckle of the belt securing the girl's wrists to the bed. She groaned and rolled on to her side. There was blood on the mattress, he noticed. The sight of it excited him, and he would have liked to have stayed to continue the session with her but the supervisor was hammering on the door. His time was up.

The sirens were still wailing. It sounded as if the Russians were bombing the railyards again. It was the first time they had attacked in daylight. They must be very close.

He dressed quickly. The girl was crying, softly. When the war was over and he got back to Hamburg he must pay for one just like her and do the job properly.

59

SS Major Rolf Emmerich looked up from his desk. The sergeant saluted and led the prisoner into the office. Rolf dismissed the guard, put down his pen and picked up his cigarettes.

They had cut her hair. A pity. He preferred her with her hair long. The pallor of her skin accentuated the plum-coloured bruises around her eyes, and her lip was swollen and split in two places. But the starkest change was in her demeanour. Her shoulders sagged, the tilt of her head was gone. Her eyes were pink-rimmed and empty.

Rolf lit his cigarette and relaxed in his chair. "Have you nothing to say to me?"

"Please," she whispered.

"It's strange. So many people want to be popular. I hear you have been very popular. But it can be a curse, don't you think?"

"Please, Rolf . . ."

"You don't look well. Have they not been looking after you? I shall talk to them, see if we can improve your conditions there."

Her shoulders trembled. "Don't send me back . . ."

Rolf grinned. He had been too kind, too indulgent. He should have done this a long time ago. "I don't know, Marie. I have a new housemaid now. She is very good to me."

"Please."

He sighed, as if generosity was draining his own resources. "I offered you my friendship, my protection. You laughed at me."

Marie slowly raised her eyes. "Please don't send me back."

How wonderful to see her this way! "It is beyond my power now."

Marie dropped slowly to her knees. "I'll do anything."

"Do?" He sounded puzzled. "What is it you think I want you to do? I offered you my friendship and my trust and you betrayed me. All I wanted was your friendship in return."

"I . . . I am . . . s-sorry."

He grinned. "Are you, Marie?"

"I was wrong. Don't send me back. Please don't send me back."

He crossed the room, took a handful of her hair and forced her to look up at him. "Say you love me."

"I . . . love . . . I love you."

"Say it like you mean it."

"I love you, Rolf."

He released her. "I don't know. Perhaps it's too late now."

"I love you!"

What a change! A month in the Frauenblock had worked a miracle. A shame what it had done to her appearance. "My little Marie. I'll do what I can. It won't be easy. Would you like your old quarters back?"

Marie started to cry.

"You can come to my quarters tonight. We shall see if you have learned to be truly grateful. Then I shall decide."

He had the guard take her away just as the Fliegeralarm started up again. Bastard Russians. Well, they were too late. He had what he wanted. One simple act of contrition at his feet and all the humiliations of his past were cancelled out.

New Year's Eve.

The starless night smelled of snow. Netanel stood at the

374

window of his Stübe and stared at the wire. There was no one out there, no one at all. Last year the SS compound had been full of shouting, drunken Germans but tonight it was deathly quiet. The camp was starting to empty; the most able-bodied workers had already been sent west to Germany to work in the armaments factories.

Chaim walked in. He had organised some schnapps from one of the guards. He poured steaming coffee from the kettle on the stove into two tin cups and tipped in the schnapps. He handed one of the cups to Netanel as he joined him at the window.

"They are going to abandon the camp very soon," he said.

Netanel nodded and said nothing.

Chaim sipped his coffee. "Two and a half years I have been here. It is like a home to me now."

Netanel stared him. God in heaven, he was serious.

"We should make plans."

"Plans? How can we make plans? We will have to wait for the opportunity and when it comes, we must not be slow."

"I'll follow the SS before I stay behind with the prisoners."

"They will not give us that opportunity, Chaim. Believe it."

Somewhere in the camp a voice began to sing the Internazionale. Other voices joined in. Men's voices first then the women's; the voices were filled with hope, and triumph. The song drifted across the still, cold night. Something is stirring in the warm ashes of Birkenau, Netanel thought. From the charred soot of all the Amos Mandelbaums we are going to rise as an army of phantoms and of men, and that army's anthem shall be: Never Again.

Rolf Emmerich heard the singing too. Doom has a madness to it, he thought, a lawlessness that sates the desires like a drunk with a bottle. What such moments do for the passions! Three times tonight already.

So it is finally over, and I shall savour the end with all its acute and bittersweet flavour. At the very last moment I shall make arrangements for my own survival, but right now I shall behave as if I do not care. What I have is an absolute freedom and few men will know it as I do now. I have lived twelve glorious years of soaring patriot's dreams, and I shall never experience its like again. I shall live, but never like this. Like every warrior, I shall cherish this, my great campaign, for the rest of my life.

Marie was asleep. He turned on the bedside lamp and her eyes opened suddenly, wary and afraid. Until the last few days he still thought she might one day show him some genuine affection. It had been a vain hope. Perhaps it was better this way. If she had ever really loved him, he might have tired of his obsession long ago. And what was life without obsessions?

He studied her critically. He had had his barber cut her hair properly – they had just chopped it off in lumps in the Frauenblock – but there was nothing to be done about the bruises just yet. He drew back the sheet. She had lost weight in there. He would get her some of the Red Cross rations, perhaps.

A part of him wished for the Russian planes to come again. He enjoyed doing it during a bombing. Danger always added something to the experience.

"Say you love me," he said, and rolled on top of her.

"I love you," she whispered.

"Beg me to make love to you again."

"Do it to me, Rolf."

"Say it like you mean it."

"Please, Rolf. Make love to me . . ."

He moved his hips in slow luxury. "Wrap your arms and legs around me."

She groaned and writhed underneath him. She is a good actress, he thought, she submits well, and that is all that matters. Invasion and conquest. It was the only real pleasure to be had in life.

60

There was a revolver in the middle of the table.

Marie did not know the other girl. She had blonde hair and china blue eyes and she would have been beautiful if not for the ugly greyish stains under her eyes, the mark of her personal torment. She was watching Marie from beneath hooded lids with the air of a beaten dog.

Rolf lit a cigarette and leaned against the windowsill. "She is a Jewess," he said to Marie. "Can you believe it? They brought her here from the Poznan ghetto. A Jewess! Blonde hair and blue eyes and a Jew! I wonder what Julius Streicher would say?"

Marie looked at the girl, then at the gun.

"Her name is Rebecca," Rolf said. "She is seventeen years old. She is my other housemaid. I hope you're not jealous."

Marie cleared her throat. "Why have you brought me here?"

The rumbling of distant artillery rattled the window-pane. "Can you hear that, Marie?"

"The Russians."

"Yes, the Russians." He looked out of the window. "They will be here any day. The army has lost its balls. They don't want to fight any more. We should never have invaded Russia. It was der Führer's one mistake. There's too many of the bastards."

Marie could not take her eyes from the revolver.

"In an hour, I and a few brother officers shall be leaving here. Unfortunately, there is room for only one more passenger, and I am having much difficulty deciding who I shall take with me."

Well, that was not completely true. If they were going to rush ahead of the rest of the troops, they would require an "important prisoner" to escort "urgently" to Berlin. Two prisoners would be an unnecessary indulgence, when so many of his brother officers were so eager to leave. He returned his attention to the two girls. "Which one of you shall I take?"

"Why don't you choose?" Marie said. "I am sure either of us will be prepared to make the sacrifice and stay behind."

Rolf smiled. "I care for you both too much to leave you to the mercy of the Russians. Who knows what they will do to you?"

His fingers drummed on the windowsill.

"So this is my idea," he said.

Both girls looked at the revolver.

"We shall let fate decide. On the table in front of you is a revolver. There is one bullet in the chamber. You will simply hold the gun to your temple and pull the trigger and whoever finds the bullet first . . . well, she has to stay behind." Rolf picked up the gun. He snapped open the mechanism and spun the chamber with his index finger. He slapped it back in position and removed the safety.

He put the revolver in front of Rebecca. "You first," he said.

He returned to his position by the window.

Rebecca looked at Marie then at the gun. She picked it up; it was heavy for her, and she had difficulty coiling her index finger around the trigger. She lifted the gun to her temple.

"Don't do it," Marie said.

The click of the trigger echoed in the room like a thunderclap.

Rolf laughed. "Well, Marie, now it is your turn."

Rebecca slammed the gun down and pushed it towards Marie.

Marie did not move.

"If you decide not to play my little game, I will have to shoot you anyway," Rolf said. "There is only room for one

378

more in the car and if you forfeit your chance, well . . ."
He shrugged his shoulders.

Marie picked up the gun. It was unbelievably heavy.
Do it, she thought. Do it and get it over with. There's no
choice anyway.

It was difficult to support the weight and work the stiff
trigger mechanism as well. As she fired, it jerked in her
hand and if there had been a bullet in the chamber it would
have blown off her face.

She dropped the gun.

"The odds are getting shorter," Rolf said.

The two girls stared at each other. "Don't do it,"
Marie said. "If we both refuse to play his little game,
he will have to decide himself. This is one pleasure we
can refuse him."

Rebecca seemed not to hear. She picked up the gun and
held it to her head. She clenched her eyes shut, and her
hand began to shake.

"Don't!" Marie shouted.

Click!

Rebecca pushed the gun across the table to Marie with
both hands, as if she was heaving an iron-cooped barrel.

"One chance in three," Rolf said. "The game becomes
more interesting."

"I won't do it," Marie said.

Rolf unclipped the holster at his waist. "Would you like
me to do it for you?"

Marie hesitated, then picked up the revolver. She held
it to her temple with two hands to steady the weight. If
she had the bullet she wanted it to go where it should.
The lever resisted her.

Click!

Marie lowered the gun. A drumming noise on the table,
like a death rattle. Rebecca's fingers. The girl's entire body
was shaking.

No! Let it be me! Marie thought, and she raised the gun
again. But Rolf was already standing beside her and he
snatched the gun from her grasp. "You've already had
your turn," he said.

He walked to the other side of the table. Rebecca did not move. A trace of saliva had spilled on to her chin.

"I think she is quite caught up in the excitement of the game, aren't you, liebling? Would you like me to take your turn for you?" He put the barrel of the revolver against the blonde girl's head. The drumming got louder. "This to win the game," he said and fired.

Click.

Rebecca started to cry. She folded her arms across her chest and her head sank on to the table, her shoulders shaking. Rolf set the gun on the surface of the tabletop and slid it across to Marie.

He grinned wolfishly. "What a shame," he said.

Marie picked up the gun.

Wrapped her finger around the trigger.

Pointed it at Rolf's grinning face.

And fired.

Click.

Rolf threw back his head and laughed.

Marie pulled the trigger again and again.

Click, click, click.

Rolf took the gun from her fingers and snapped open the chamber. He showed it to her; it was empty. "I am sorry," he said. "Just my little joke. I was playing with a stacked deck." He placed both hands on the table and leaned towards Marie. "I wanted to see what you would do."

"I told you one day I'd kill you," Marie said. "I meant it."

"It seems all your gratitude has just been hollow. All this time you have been deceiving me." He took the Lüger from his holster and put the barrel between her eyes. "What should I do with you?"

"Kill me."

Rolf grinned. Perfect white teeth. "All right," he said. He turned his head and looked at Rebecca. She was sobbing, her lower lip quivering like a small child's. Rolf shot her in the head.

Marie stared at the wall. There was a fine spray of blood, like a spray of crimson ink drops. Rebecca's legs were splayed over her upturned chair.

Rolf holstered the pistol and lit another cigarette. "I was beginning to tire of her anyway. You are far more entertaining." He exhaled the smoke through his nostrils, in a long sigh of near regret. "We leave in half an hour."

61

It was evening when the word went through the camp: evacuation. There were rumours that most of the SS officers had already left in their staff cars. It was the end; but the last hours, Netanel knew, would be the most dangerous time of all. When they left Auschwitz, they left the protection of years of jealously guarded privilege.

The snow crunched underfoot, the wind was bitter and stung like a razor. The crump of artillery rumbled across the horizon and the sky was illuminated by the flash of rockets, a few of them landing very close, panicking the guards. The SS were jumpy and dangerous. Netanel heard the crack of gunfire as the SS punished those slow in joining the march; the guard dogs howled, infuriated by the noise and the movement.

They marched through the wrought-iron gates for the final time.

Corpses were dotted along the sides of the road, like litter, frozen into bizarre postures. Netanel trudged through the snowdrifts with his head down, keeping close to the man in front to shelter himself from the wind. Chaim had organised rucksacks for them and loaded them with extra

rations of bread and treacle and margarine he had stolen
from the kitchens. God alone knew where they were going
and how long it would take them to get there. It was worth
the extra weight on your shoulders to know at least you
would not starve on the way. Netanel and the rest of
the kapos were well fed and in better condition than the
Häftlinge; they had the strength for the march if only they
could fight off the effects of the cold.

"I heard we are going to Matthausen," Chaim said.

"I have heard rumours too. That there are machine-guns
set up along the sides of the road and they are going to cut
us all down and leave us for the Russians to bury."

"They won't do that," Chaim said.

"Why not?"

Chaim stared at him and did not have an answer.

An old Müsselman stumbled and slumped to his knees,
exhausted. An SS man rolled him out of the line of
marchers with his boot. He held his Schmeisser at the
man's head and fired. He walked on.

"Bastard," someone said.

"Ari was old and slow," someone else said. "He had it
coming."

Yes, Netanel thought, he did. It was the least cruel thing
he had seen in two and a half years inside the camp. The
guard shot him because he was slowing the pace of the
march. That was all. He did not do it out of spite, just
because he was a Jew.

They reached the siding at dawn.

Netanel slumped to the ground, and scooped a handful
of snow into his mouth to slake his thirst. A grey light was
seeping across the sky from the east.

Chaim fell to his knees beside him. "Herrgottsacrament,"
he murmured. "How much further?"

The silhouette of a train emerged from the darkness.
There were a dozen empty flatcars behind it.

"They're taking us back to Germany," Netanel said.

SS men worked their way along the line of slumped
figures, hitting indiscriminately with their rifles. "Get in!

382

Get in!" One of the guards fired his Schmeisser into the air. Shadows rose to their feet and staggered towards the flatcars.

Chaim was about to swing up on to one of the flatcars, but a guard caught him and pulled him back. "You! Come here!"

"I am a kapo!" Chaim protested.

The guard pulled the rucksack off his back. "I don't care if you're the Reichsführer himself!"

Chaim tried to reclaim the food. "It's mine! I stole it!"

The guard lifted the butt of his rifle in one swift movement and Chaim's head snapped back. He put his hand to his mouth and when he took it away two of his teeth were cupped in his palm.

"Now you," the guard said to Netanel. "Or you get the same treatment."

Netanel pulled the rucksack off his back and handed it over. The press of the crowds carried him into the flatcar. The men closest to him were leering at him. So much for you Prominenz, their looks seemed to say. Now you're just another piece of shit, like us.

There was hardly space enough to breathe, a mass of wrecked humanity in freezing, sodden cotton, tight-packed against each other. The stench was overpowering; a cocktail of sweat and sores, mould and fear. The metal floors of the flatcars were crusted with ice. Netanel started to shiver violently from the cold.

Chaim squatted next to him. He had his right hand cupped against his mouth, and blood was oozing between his fingers. He uncupped his other hand and stared at the two broken teeth.

He started to cry. "Bastard . . ."

"What did you expect?"

The swelling on his upper lip and the missing teeth made it hard to understand him. ". . . knew him," he said. ". . . kapo six years . . . knew that bastard . . ."

"You're still a Jew, Chaim. What did you expect?"

The train began to move. No one spoke. Men shivered

and stared unblinking like corpses, blind to everything but their own personal suffering. The only sounds were the rhythmic clatter of the wheels and the moan of the wind. The sky was the colour of lead.

It started to snow.

Near Lübben, Germany

The Gasthaus was full but Rolf commandeered three rooms in the name of the SS, one for Colonel Hauptmann, one for Major Schenke, and one for himself and Marie. Their driver, Sergeant Netzer, would have to sleep in the car. Someone would have to guard it, anyway.

They had driven right through the night. It was safer to sleep during the day. During daylight there was danger from enemy fighters.

Rolf led Marie up the stairs past the hostile eyes of the innkeeper and his wife. She was in handcuffs, as befitting an important SS prisoner. When they reached the room, Rolf sat her down on the bed and locked the door. He threw off his uniform jacket and lit a cigarette. His hands were shaking.

"How far are we from Berlin?" Marie said.

"We're not going to Berlin." He started to pace the room. "The war is going badly. The whole eastern front is collapsing."

"I'm so sorry, Rolf. Is there anything I can do?"

"Shut up!" He slapped her hard across the face, but was immediately contrite. "I'm sorry," he said. He took a key from his pocket and unlocked the handcuffs. "I didn't mean to hurt you." He massaged her wrists. "These are necessary. You are our prisoner."

"Four SS to guard one girl. Are you sure it's enough?"

He did not answer her. Sweat shone on his cheeks like a glaze. He got up and went to the fire, threw his cigarette into the coals. "Colonel Hauptmann wants to go west, and surrender to the British."

"And me?"

"You can be a great help to us. You can tell them how we looked after you, helped you escape. How I saved you from the gas chambers."

She stared at him. "You really mean it, don't you?"

"Don't make jokes, Marie. Try and be grateful, for once."

"Don't worry. I shall not forget a single thing you have done for me."

"If you are going to be difficult, perhaps it's better we don't take you with us."

"I don't give a damn what you do." After the Frauenblock, after seeing the caricature that was once her lover beating one of his fellow inmates to death with a wooden club, why would he think that life still remained so precious?

"I think we can do it," Rolf was saying. "We have all the right papers. It will be easy until we get near the front lines."

"What will you do after the war, Rolf? Cart beer?"

There was a soft knock on the door. Rolf opened it. It was Colonel Hauptmann. There was a swift and whispered conversation.

"I will see you later," Rolf said.

"What is happening?"

"The Colonel asked if he might be alone with you for a while. Be nice to him, hein?"

Major Schenke was waiting outside in the corridor. He leered past Rolf at the locked bedroom door. "I had her once when she was in the Frauenblock."

"Shut up."

Schenke's face reddened. Who did the bastard think he was? They were all in the shit together now. "Will she help us?"

Rolf shook his head. "We'll have to get rid of the little bitch. Tonight, after Hauptmann's had his fun."

Bielawa, Poland

Day turned to night turned to day. Snow settled on still, grey faces, on stark, grey stubble, on drab, grey uniforms. Everything the colour of lead, Netanel thought, like a pencil drawing, a frieze by Modigliani. The train had stopped, had been stopped for hours. They had travelled slowly ever since leaving Oswiecim, stopping often to let other trains past, supply trains perhaps, or troop transports. There was no toilet so they sat in each other's filth and no one spoke because it was too cold and it required too much effort. When dawn broke the SS guards were still staring at them over the muzzle of the machine-gun set up on the flatcar in front. Idiots, Netanel thought. Even if we had the strength to run, where could we go?

It was impossible to stand up, or even to move. Men slept or gazed in trance-like exhaustion at the sky.

How much longer?

He fought sleep. He knew that if he slept he would not have the strength to fight his way back to consciousness, and then it would be the end. He had come too far to surrender now.

He thought about Marie. In his mind he composed a hundred speeches of explanation that he could make to her should he ever see her again, but his soliloquies were for his own conscience, and in the end he scorned them all. He had joined the damned. So be it. It would make easier the task he had set himself.

He heard heavy boots crunching on the snow outside and the bolt on the flatcar door was thrown back. A guard barked at them to get out. A few men rose stiffly from their haunches, shrieking from the pain of stiff and frozen joints.

"We're here," Netanel whispered to Chaim.

He reached up and grabbed the edge of the car with numb fingers. The man in front of him started to crawl towards the open door, and it gave him just enough room to push himself upright. Herrgottsacrament! His knees would not unbend.

"Raus! Raus! Schnell!"

"Help me, Chaim," he whispered.

He forced his legs straight, gasping at the agony in his joints. "Chaim?"

He shoved him hard, with his left fist. Chaim fell on to his side, cold and hard as a statue, his gloved hands still clasped around his knees, striped cap pulled down over his ears. Frozen in his time, Netanel thought. Auschwitz was his home. Now he will wear its stripes for ever.

62

Near Lübben

They set off late in the afternoon.

Hauptmann sat in the front seat next to the driver, Netzer. Marie was in the back between Rolf and Schenke. She was handcuffed again. Schenke was leering at her.

The road was choked with army traffic. A long line of troop transports lumbered east towards the Russians.

"Poor bastards," Schenke said. "Look at them. Not one of them is over seventeen."

The youths in the back of the lorries cheered and waved at them as they passed. "Idiots," Rolf muttered.

They did not see the fighters. They came low out of the sun, rushing across the plain at less than a hundred feet, their wingtips almost brushing the tops of the chestnut and plane trees. Their first warning came when a grey Volkswagen jeep a hundred yards away from them burst into flame. The bullets skittered down the road towards them, devils of snow skidding into the air as they came.

"Get off the road!" Hauptmann screamed.

Netzer did not have time to react. Marie instinctively

threw herself forward, heard the windscreen shatter into fragments. Someone screamed. The Mercedes lurched off the road into a ditch and stopped.

She blacked out.

When she came to, the door was open and Schenke was gone. There was blood over the shattered windshield. Hauptmann was hunched forward in the front seat, gurgling. Marie felt something pressing down on her right shoulder.

Rolf.

His head was a pulpy mess. She rolled away from him and he slumped face down on the floor.

She saw a flash of silver metal as the fighter roared low over the road, saw the red star painted on the fuselage. She heard the cough of the fighter's machine-guns, felt a scalding rush of air as a truck exploded.

She had to get away.

She leaned across Rolf's body, groped in his right-hand pocket for the keys. Her hands were shaking. Which key, which key? The metal bracelets snapped open. She threw the keys away and started to run.

Rolf opened his eyes. He tried to reach for the Lüger in his holster but he could not move his arm. She was getting away, damn her. A brown field, specked with white, her silhouette getting smaller and smaller.

Near Bielawa

They followed winding country lanes, away from the main highways. Allied planes patrolled the skies overhead, but when one of them buzzed the column the guards would move closer to their charges. They were taking no chances.

Netanel's shoes lacerated his frozen feet. He could feel the blood squelching between his toes. What had Dov taught him? Death starts with the shoes. He took them off and tied them round his neck, walking barefoot through the snow.

388

They found a dead horse lying by the side of the road. Netanel ran across with several others and tore off chunks of meat with his teeth and fingers. He chewed it raw, sucking out the blood and juice. The guards pointed at him and laughed. To hell with them. It might be the difference between life and death. He had done worse.

They found a deserted farmhouse. The guards herded them into the barn. There were only a couple of hundred of them left and they fell exhausted into the straw, curling up beside each other for warmth. Sleep enveloped Netanel quickly, pulling him down into the merciful blackness of temporary oblivion.

They reached the main highway.

It was clogged with people and abandoned vehicles. The refugees struggled along on foot with bursting suitcases of clothes, pushed carts with precariously balanced and rope-tied bundles of furniture, hauled wagons piled with saucepans and books and chickens squawking in cages, dragged cows and pigs and sheep tethered with rope. The Poles were running once more, this time back into Germany, away from the ancient enemy Russia, towards the Allies coming from the west.

Before the guards had realised what had happened, the column of prisoners melted into the mêlée and in that moment the SS seemed to accept that the charade was over. Other prisoners drifted away from the column and ran into the fields. Netanel followed them. Stacks of hay had been left to rot in the fields the previous autumn. He threw himself into the first haystack and lay quite still.

He heard the murmur of life all around him and realised the hay was alive with people.

"It's all right," someone said, "the bastards are leaving!"

Netanel peered out. The guards had joined the column of refugees. They were leaving them behind.

He was free. He had done it. He had survived.

Part Twelve

PALESTINE, 1945

63

SS Eretz Israel

Anything would be better than this, Netanel found himself thinking. Anything at all. Even Auschwitz.

The ancient freighter groaned and rolled. Netanel threw out a hand and held tight to the metal pipe to which his bunk had been fixed, fought back another giddying wave of nausea. Sweat like cold oil soaked his clothes.

Please, let this end soon!

Canvas hammocks had been hung between the pipes, five rows high. The air in the hold was thin and stale, but the decks were awash under freezing, twelve-foot seas and so they were trapped. The stench alone is going to choke me, he thought. Vomit lapped the metal decking like bilge.

Endure! he reminded himself. As you learned to endure the hunger and the cold and the beatings. Survive each tormented minute as it arrives, and endure.

The ship rolled again, and Netanel gasped, thinking they were about to capsize. Men screamed and retched, others fell from their bunks, those who had been whispering their prayers now shouted them aloud, beseeching the God of their ancestors to intercede once more.

They were just a day's sailing from the coast, but Palestine was as far away as ever.

It had taken so long.

First there had been the long months spent inside the camp in Poland, waiting for the war to end. While he was inside the DP camp, the Brichach – the word meant

393

"escape" in Polish – contacted him and organised money and false identity papers. When he was released he became Daniel Herzog, an Austrian Jew from Graz.

The cities were in ruins, and every road, every train station, was choked with refugees. Borders were closed down as the occupying armies tried to restrict illegal emigration, and trap fleeing Nazi officials. Netanel could have returned to Germany but there was nothing for him there now. He knew in which direction his own salvation lay.

In mid August he crossed the frontier into Czechoslovakia. The border guards had been bribed by Brichach and he had no trouble.

At the beginning of September he crossed into Austria and the British Occupation Zone. For the first time in twelve years he saw a Star of David worn with pride. The badge was sewn on a British uniform, the wearer a Palestinian sabra from the Jewish Brigade, camped just across the border at Tarvizio.

Netanel had thought then that his journey was almost over. But it was just beginning.

The British, the local Brichach representative informed him, were trying to stem the flood of refugees pouring out of Europe and into Palestine. They had closed the border with Italy.

So Netanel hitch-hiked to Villach near the Italian frontier and walked across the border, illegally, just after dawn. The air was bright and frost-cold, the sun rising over a broad, cultivated valley, dotted with white. In the distance the Carnic Alps glistened like a rampart of ice. He thought for those few wild hours that he was leaving the darkness in him on the other side.

When he reached Tarvizio the Jewish Brigade had already moved on. He came to a farmhouse and his fractured German-accented Italian drew hostile stares from the men until he drew a Star of David on the ground. They smiled sympathetically then, invited him inside, fed him soup and one of the men took him into Tarvizio on a creaking cart. From there he caught the train to Trieste. The carriages were jammed with refugees, people hanging on to the doors and windows. The only space he could find for himself was on the roof. He clung on desperately, for the whole journey, pressed flat on the ice-encrusted metal to avoid the numbing December wind and the endless tunnels.

In Trieste he was one of hundreds of Jewish refugees rounded up by the Mossad Aliya Bet, an organisation set up by the Yishuv in Palestine to beat the British blockade. They fed and clothed him while he waited for a boat. One night, dressed as Jewish Brigade soldiers, he and a hundred and fifty others were driven out of the city to an isolated stretch of coast. The *Eretz Israel*, an ancient, rust-stained freighter, waited in the darkness at the end of an unlit jetty. Five hundred men and women crammed on board in slanting, freezing rain. Netanel Rosenberg, the good German citizen, accustomed all his life to wealth and respect and comfort, was homeless, alone, and embarking on his own crusade to the Holy Land.

Tel Aviv

SECRET

TO: DISCID HAIFA, rpt DISCID HAIFA
FROM: PLACID

162/17/8/1   17/12

SS *Genoa*, renamed SS *Eretz Israel*, left Trieste 8/12, sighted 300 nautical miles west of coast 1300 hours, 17/12, headed east at 10 knots. Imperative we intercept. Estimate arrival after sunset 18/12.

Decoded: RJ
1735 hrs 17/12

Mordechai Yarkoni was chief of staff of the Haganah, the Jewish Agency's military underground. He poured from the brass coffeepot on his desk and read the telex again. It had been relayed from one of their agents in Jerusalem just half an hour ago; PLACID was the British codeword for CID headquarters in Jerusalem.

They were in the Red House, the Haganah's own headquarters, an anonymous five-storey building in HaYarkon Street. The window looked out over the beach. The wind sifted sand across the boulevard below and the Mediterranean was cool and grey and flecked with white.

Yarkoni passed the telex towards the handsome young man on the other side of the desk. He was a sabra, you could tell that by looking at him, Yarkoni thought. The *saabra* was the desert pear that thrived in the Palestinian wilderness because it had evolved a prickly outer shell that protected it from the aridity and from desert scavangers. It was also the nickname the Palestinian-born settlers gave themselves. They all wore a black moustache, like a badge, and they all had this same air of quiet assurance that men only attained from a life spent in perpetual combat against the desert and against other men.

Yarkoni waited until Asher Ben-Zion had finished reading the message and said, "A British Sunderland spotted them yesterday, two hundred miles south-west of Famagusta. They've been held up in heavy seas but we anticipate they should arrive off Haifa about midnight."

"How many people on board?"

"Five hundred and forty-six."

Asher raised an eyebrow. "That's a lot of Jews."

"More than we've tried before. We have to show the British that they cannot stop us. More particularly, we have to show the Arabs."

Asher nodded. "What if the British make the intercept?"

"The captain has been told to run the ship aground. On no account must the British be allowed to stop her. We have to get everyone off, and disperse them in Haifa and Acre as quickly as possible. All our people have been put on alert."

This feat of communications alone, Asher thought, was remarkable. The radio in the adjacent office kept Yarkoni in touch with every Jewish settlement and Haganah command post throughout the whole of the Yishuv, from Acre to Eilat.

"Who will be in charge of the operation on the land?"

Yarkoni sipped his coffee. "You will," he said.

Asher tried to disguise his elation. There were no formal ranks in the Haganah; in an organisation of equals, men achieved authority through reputation and experience. He had thus been effectively handed his first command. "I won't let you down," he said.

"If you do, I'll break your head," Yarkoni said. He meant it.

64

Rab'allah

Reception on the Phillips radiogram had deteriorated during the day. A storm was moving in from the Mediterranean, and static was breaking up the signal. The Arab music, tinny flute and drum, came in waves like the rhythm of cicadas; fading away until it had almost vanished, then stronger again until the noise was almost deafening.

The Holy Strugglers of Judea sat in a circle by the coffee house window. Rain wept from the eaves and the carpets smelled of mould. Winter was a bad time. Babies died of the cough, and the cold rains drove the sheep and goats into the caves where they huddled side by side for sanctuary. Most years, there was nothing to do but sit here and argue or make babies to replace the ones that were lost.

But this year was different; this year the Jews were coming.

"We have to fight," Izzat was saying, his voice low, "as we fought in the time of the Mufti. Remember how the Britishers wanted to divide up our land and give it to the Jews? We fought then – we must fight again now!"

"If only the Mufti would return," someone said. The Mufti had disappeared after the war, and no one knew his whereabouts. There were unconfirmed reports that he was in a French prison.

"The Mufti is making new plans," Izzat said, his tone suggesting he knew far more than he was able to divulge.

There was a ripple of excitement. "You have heard something?"

"I meet regularly with Sheikh Daoud."

"The Mufti is still alive?"

Izzat had no idea. "The sheikh communicates with him regularly. Through him the Mufti has relayed a personal message for all of his brave Strugglers!" There was a sharp intake of breath. The Mufti himself! "He has commended us all to continue our jihad even if it demands from us the last drop of precious Arab blood!"

The announcement had the reaction Izzat had hoped for. The Strugglers grew fierce and leaned towards him, committed anew.

"I shall not lay down my rifle while there is one Jew still living in Palestine," one of them said.

"May Allah burn me on the Day of the Fire if I ever rest until we have driven the Jews into the sea!"

"We are with you, Izzat! What will the Mufti have us do?"

Izzat lowered his voice. "Now the Britisher war is over, the Jews are preparing to come here in thousands, tens of thousands!"

They all nodded. They were familiar with the stories in *Falastine* of immigrant ships running the British blockade, of hordes of refugees waiting on the European shores to flock into Palestine.

"The Britishers only pretend to send them away. The Britisher pasha Bevin wants them to come here, because he does not want them in Britannia. I would not trust the

398

British any more than I would trust a Bedouin in the dark with a sharp knife! We must fight!"

A low murmur of agreement.

"I have a plan, a plan for which Sheikh Daoud himself has given his blessing, may Allah grant him increase, a plan that will – "

They all fell silent as the music on the radiogram was interrupted by the voice of the announcer on Radio Damascus. He began to read a prepared news item on the death camps the Britishers had claimed to have discovered in Germany and Poland. The announcer said independent Arab observers now claimed these camps did not exist.

The announcer's voice faded under the whine of the static: ". . . been reported . . . an elaborate plan by the Zionist Satan . . . world sympathy for . . . Jewish invasion of Arab Palestine . . ."

The bulletin ended with a report that three thousand Jewish immigrants had been landed near Acre two nights before.

Izzat looked around the circle of grim faces, eyes glittering in the quickening gloom of the afternoon. No one present seemed to doubt that such a conspiracy was possible, or underestimated the magnitude of the threat they now faced.

"You see," Izzat said.

"But the pictures," one of them protested. Photographs of the German gas ovens had been spread across the pages of *Falastine* for weeks at the end of summer. Back then they had been cause for celebration.

"Anyone can fake a picture," Izzat said. "It is the easiest thing in the world. Besides, if these stories were really true, why is it that the Britishers and the Americaners will not harbour the Jews themselves in their own countries? No, it is just a trick."

The logic of the argument was inescapable.

"Tell us about your plan," someone said.

Izzat leaned forward, drawing invisible maps on the carpet with the sweep of his forefinger. "Every morning at eight o'clock a bus leaves the Jaffa Gate for Tel Aviv.

It is crammed with Jews, and it is never guarded. We can choose our own place for the ambush. It will be easier than picking figs from a tree. The harvest will be a rich one," he added, for the benefit of those of his followers whose valour was tempered with avarice.

"What about the British?"

Izzat grinned, hawkishly. "Let me take care of the British."

Silence. This sounded good. A great blow against the Jews, with little danger and the chance of some loot as well. They could hardly wait to get home and oil their guns.

"Show us your scar," someone said.

Izzat stood up and lifted his robe. He turned around. The purplish hole in the flesh of his buttock was livid against his skin.

"Tell us the story again!"

Izzat allowed himself to be persuaded. "It was the night we ambushed fifty horsemen from the kibbutz," he began. "I killed a dozen that night, and cut off their balls! One of them lay beside his horse, pretending to be dead. As the Jews broke and ran, I chased them, and he shot me from behind – "

"He was aiming for your brains, and he only just missed!"

Everyone turned. It was Zayyad.

Izzat dropped his robe and turned around, his face white with anger. "Do you come to lead us in our jihad, Abu Wagil?"

"What holy war? All that is holy to you is your ambition."

"Palestine is what is holy to me! I only carry on the fight that was started by the great martyr, Wagil Hass'san, your son." He indicated the little shrine in the corner of the coffee house, and the yellowing portrait that hung there.

Zayyad studied the faces grouped around Izzat. Several of the men were from al-Naqb, the rest from his own village. Most of them were fellaheen or idiots like Tareq. "What are you all doing here?"

No one answered him. My authority over them is ebbing

400

away, he thought. I can smell their desperation, it clings to them like stale sweat. "The coffee house is shut. Go home!"

No one moved.

"All of you! Get out!"

They filtered out. Finally only Izzat remained.

"Why do they listen to idiots like you?" Zayyad wondered aloud.

"They do not want to see their land stolen, their women raped and their children hoisted on bayonets."

"You talk like the Mufti."

"The Mufti talks for all of us."

"The Mufti opens his mouth and the wind blows his tongue about."

"What would you have us do, Abu Wagil? Stand by and let the Jews kick us into the desert?"

What will I have them do? Zayyad thought. Izzat was right, one day they would have to fight. But to fight well, a people needed good leaders, not murderers and opportunists in clerics' robes. They needed weapons that would not blow up in their hands.

"If you endanger this village I will cut off your toes one by one and ram them down your throat," he said. "Now get out."

After Izzat had gone, he slumped on to the divan by the window.

Rishou, Rishou . . . what am I going to do?

65

SS Eretz Israel

The storm eased enough for those with the strength to battle up the swaying gangways to the deck. The grey sea foamed and heaved. Netanel hung on to the rail, gulping in the freezing, salt air, tasting the bile in his mouth, closing his eyes against the giddying wretchedness that squeezed his guts like a fist.

When he opened his eyes once more he found himself staring at the gaunt, shrunken profile of Blockältester Mendelssohn.

He was hanging on to the rail a few feet away, thinner and paler than Netanel remembered when he was overlord of Block 51, but there was no mistake. It was him. They stared at each other for the moment of mutual recognition and then both looked away.

Netanel was too stunned to react. He continued to stare at the sea. Shame and hatred returned slowly, with memories so raw and painful and vivid that he groaned aloud.

I should denounce him! he thought. I can be the instrument of retribution. I will tell everyone on ship who he is and what he did at Auschwitz and they will take him and pitch him into the sea.

But almost at once he remembered: how can I denounce Mendelssohn when I am as guilty as he? You forfeited the right to accuse when you became a kapo. You have Mandelbaum's blood under your fingernails. Your silence guarantees his.

He stared at the grey, cold ocean for a long time and when he looked up again, the deck was empty and Mendelssohn was gone.

The storm rushed ahead; the sun set behind them in a clearing sky. The decks were milling with people now, straining for their first glimpse of Palestine. Many of Netanel's fellow travellers that evening were survivors of the German death camps like himself, and for all of them the first sighting of their promised land was endowed with mystical significance, like Noah's vision of the rainbow after the flood. It would be the sign that the ordeal was finally past.

There must be three or four hundred on deck now, Netanel decided. Only those too weakened by seasickness were still below. The faces around him were gaunt, almost translucent in the greenish aura of the storm's twilight. Despite the cold, some men were in their shirtsleeves, enjoying the bite of the air after the suffocating atmosphere of the holds. All of them had numbers tattooed on their wrists or forearms, stark against their marble-white skin.

There were several false sightings as they searched the horizon for the coast, praying for one glimpse before the light faded.

The man next to him turned and grinned. Netanel could not guess at his age – thirty, forty, fifty, it was hard to tell with veterans of the wire. He was missing two teeth on one side of his mouth. "We are finally home," he said in German.

"This year in Jerusalem," Netanel said, paraphrasing the Passover prayer.

"You are German?"

"Before the war I lived near München. What about you?"

"Frankfurt. But I lived in Belgium since 1936. My parents sent me there to get me away from the Nazis. Can you believe it? Three years this couple looked after me. Nice people. He was a postman."

"What happened?"

"His own brother betrayed him to the Gestapo. Can you believe it? I never found out what happened to them."

Netanel glanced down at the man's wrist. "Where did they send you?"

"Maidanek. Fifteen months I was there." He pointed to the gap in his mouth. "A kapo knocked them out. Rifle butt. A Jew like me, and he did that. Can you believe it?" He held out his hand. "My name's Chaim, everyone calls me Hymie. What's yours?"

Netanel thought of his own cousin Chaim, frozen like a board on a flatcar somewhere in Poland. "Rosenberg. Netanel Rosenberg."

"You know anyone in Palestine?"

Netanel shook his head.

"My cousin lives in Tel Aviv. He went there in '34. His whole family. I told him he was crazy. How are you going to live in a place like that? I said. Those were my actual words. 'How are you going to live in a place like that?' Can you believe it?"

"None of us could have seen what was coming."

"His name's Uri, Uri Aizenberg. He has a restaurant on Dizengoff Street. You should look him up. Maybe he can help you find a job."

There was a loud shout, taken up by others, and suddenly everyone was pointing. There was a dull yellow streak on the eastern skyline, like a pencil line drawn across the horizon of the sea.

"Palestine," Hymie said, reverently, like a prayer.

As they drew closer to the coast the golden sand-dunes of Akko Bay and the dark green-black of the pines on Mount Carmel at Haifa emerged in stark relief against the gathering slate grey of the thunderheads over the land.

The sun dropped, and golden fingers pointed them the way home.

Then it was night, and they sailed on through the bitter dark, towards the orange glow of the Haifa refineries. The veterans of the wire filtered back to their holds to be warm and wait out the last few long hours before they would finally be home.

Haifa

Three men and one woman were hunched over a table in a tiny room above a restaurant in HeHaluz Street. Rain slapped against the window, leaking under the pane to gather in a widening pool around their feet. The remains of a meal of omelette and salad lay scattered around the table among the glasses and an uncorked vodka bottle.

Asher looked around at the others. "We've just had a signal from the captain of the *Eretz Israel*. He will land our guests at ten o'clock tonight near the village of Qiryat HaGefen."

The man on Asher's left, David Shapira, was dressed in the khaki uniform of a sergeant in the Jewish Supernumerary Police. He tapped the table with his forefinger. "The earlier the better. We must have them all hidden here and in Acre before dawn."

The other man, Uri Ben-Carmel, spoke. Like Asher he did not wear a uniform but as the local manager of the Egged Bus Company he played a vital role in the Haganah's plans. "I will have four buses standing by, and I have managed to persuade some of the Solel Boneh drivers to bring their trucks to the rendezvous point."

"How many can you guarantee?" Asher asked him.

"At least six. There are three others, but . . ." He shrugged his shoulders. "They say they have families and they are worried."

"What else have you arranged?"

"We have at least two dozen taxis. All good Haganah men."

"What if something goes wrong?" the policeman asked.

Asher told them about the telex they had intercepted from CID headquarters in Jerusalem.

"They will be waiting, then," Shapira said.

Asher shrugged. "Yes, we have to assume that. But there is a Haganah team on board. They will ensure that the captain delivers his cargo to the beach, whatever happens. After that it's up to us."

Ben-Carmel took a swallow of his vodka. "Even so, it will be almost impossible to get them into Haifa and Acre tonight. There will be roadblocks everywhere."

"Yes. We may have to take most of them inland to the kibbutzim at Kfar Atta and Kfar Yassif."

The others fell silent.

"We will have to arrange something else to keep the British occupied," Asher said.

"What do you have in mind?" Shapira asked.

"Obviously, we need to stop the British getting to the rendezvous. But first we will have to ensure that they do not arrive in strength. That's where we need you, Rebecca."

Rebecca Orenstein nodded, slowly. She was a large-boned girl, with the faint shadow of a moustache on her upper lip. She wore khaki shorts and a denim blouse, and sat with her legs splayed and her arms folded on the table, like a man. But when she spoke, her voice was soft and mellifluous, in contrast to her appearance.

"I have two dozen Palmachniks ready. You only have to give us the word." The girls of the Haganah were treated as any man; many were members of the Palmach, the organisation's elite military wing.

"What sort of armoury do you have?"

"We have seven Sten guns, thirteen rifles, ten handguns of various calibres and a two-inch mortar."

"How many rounds for the mortar?"

"Only three I'm afraid, Ash."

"Hand-grenades?"

"Perhaps a dozen."

Asher gave her a rueful smile. "It's enough. It's better than throwing rocks."

"We've done that as well."

"All right. Uri, you're in charge of the transport. That's taken care of. Shapira, we'll need you to arrange a few

406

delays for the British between Haifa and the rendezvous. And you, Rebecca. I'm afraid I'll have to ask you and your Palmachniks to attack the British fort at En Josef."

66

SS Eretz Israel

The ship swayed and groaned as another wave rolled beneath it.

Netanel lay in his hammock listening to the drumming vibration of the engines and the excited chatter of the people around him. Now they were close to their destination, everyone had come alive again. Their fear and despair during the storm were forgotten.

He heard a voice shouting in German, an ugly voice barking a command. Would these nightmares never go away?

Then he heard it again.

It wasn't his imagination . . . everyone else was listening too.

Now he could make out the words: "This is Captain Sunderland of Her Majesty's Navy. You have illegally entered the waters of the Palestine Mandate. We are coming aboard. If you do not stop your engines immediately, we will be compelled to fire on you."

The vibrations of the hull increased. They were putting on speed!

Netanel leaped from his bunk and ran to the companion-way.

The deck was washed in the phosphorus glare of a searchlight. Netanel held up his hand to shield his eyes. He could make out the silhouette of the navy patrol boat less than a quarter of a mile away on the port side, heading across their bows.

"*Eretz Israel*, this is your last warning. If you do not heave to, I shall have to fire on you."

The *Eretz Israel* continued to pick up speed. The patrol boat was almost directly ahead of them now, positioning herself between them and the land.

People swarmed on to the decks from the holds. An officer ran to the railing alongside the bridge screaming at them to return below.

Netanel heard something ping! against the metal above his head, as if someone was throwing coins at the bridgework. Suddenly women were screaming and there were three bodies lying on the deck.

There was a panicked rush for the hatches.

It took several moments for Netanel to realise what was happening. The patrol boat was firing on them!

Belatedly, he threw himself on to the deck.

The whine of the engines had risen to a scream, the boat juddering underneath him as it reached full power. The patrol boat's Vickers gun fired again. Bullets bagatelled around the deck, ricocheting from the bridgework.

I have to get below, Netanel thought. But the hatchways were jammed with people. He saw a woman scream and crumple to the deck, clutching her leg. She was trampled under the surging mass.

Netanel peered over the bulwark. The captain of the *Eretz Israel* was steaming straight at the patrol boat, which was now perhaps less than fifty yards away.

Another volley of machine-gun fire punched huge holes in the upperworks of the ship, the trajectory now too high to endanger anyone on the deck. The windows on the bridge blew in.

He braced himself for the collision.

It never came.

Netanel looked back and saw the patrol boat wallowing in their wake on a black sea. The captain was still screaming at them through the loudhailer, but Netanel could no longer make out the words over the howling wind and the cough of the Vickers gun.

Two bodies lay prone in the darkness a few feet away. A black river trickled from one of the bodies into the scuppers. The patrol boat's searchlight swung around again, suddenly illuminating the deck and the dead men's faces. One of them was Mendelssohn.

The other was Hymie.

Can you believe it? he thought.

En Josef

The British Tegart fort dominated the coast road, perched on top of a hill just a mile north of the town. There would be only a skeleton watch, Rebecca knew. The last thing the British would expect was to be attacked inside one of their own forts.

Three rounds from a two-inch mortar was like throwing felafels at an armoured car, but if they could lob the shells inside the walls it might be enough to cause an hour's panic. The important thing was to make the garrison think it was a concerted attack.

She crouched in a shallow depression below the walls and signalled for two Palmachniks to bring up the mortar. It was raining heavily again, and as they ran their boots splashed in the mud.

Calculation of the trajectory was pure guesswork. At this range, it shouldn't be too difficult, she decided. I could toss an orange to the guard on the wall if I had a decent run up.

She set the mortar herself, and kissed the precious two-inch shell before she dropped it in. She had always hoped to fire it in anger, but she supposed it would not be wasted if it helped five hundred of her fellow Jews get into Palestine.

The WHOOSH! of the mortar erupted in the silence.

There was a white flash, followed by a heart-stopping explosion. A siren went off inside the walls and she heard

British soldiers shouting out in alarm, and an officer screaming orders.

A hundred yards to her right a Sten gun raked the walls. In the darkness she heard other guns bark into life. Her Palmachniks were ringed around the fort. If they were careful with their ammunition, and kept moving, they could almost be mistaken for an army.

Qiryat HaGefen

Asher stood on the beach searching the darkness for the SS *Eretz Israel*. The moon scudded in and out of the clouds making visibility difficult. Rain had plastered his hair across his face, and beads of water dripped from his chin.

As the moon came out again he raised his field glasses and picked out the silhouette of the freighter to the north of the bay. There was a light blinking urgently on the sea to her stern. That would be the British patrol signalling the shore.

He put down the glasses, and swore, softly, under his breath.

"What is it?" Ben-Carmel said.

"She's too far north. She's steaming too close to the reef."

Asher ran back up the beach to his car and fetched the Aldis lamp from the boot. He had to warn her before it was too late.

Haifa–Acre Road

Captain Tom Hughes of the 6th Airborne steered his jeep around the line of stalled cars, his hand pressed on the horn. Finally he stopped and climbed out, staring in the direction of his headlights in frustration and disbelief. He was a Yorkshireman, and not given to mincing words. "What the fookin' hell's amiss 'ere?"

The road was completely blocked. Both trucks lay on their sides, surrounded by police cars and ambulances. Onlookers were crawling over the wreckage and crowding around the medical personnel as they worked.

A policeman in a khaki uniform ran through the rain and saluted smartly. "Sergeant David Shapira of the Jewish Supernumerary Police. Sorry to hold you up, Captain. I'm afraid there's been an accident."

"Get this fookin' mess off the fookin' road!"

"We're trying to sort it out as fast as we can."

"Fook me!" Hughes roared. It would take hours to get this chaos sorted out. His patience was being sorely tried. First he had had to send half his force to En Josef when the colonel in charge of the fort there – he knew the man, a complete idiot, and a Londoner of course – had reported he was under siege from a superior force.

Now this.

Hughes shoved the smaller policeman out of the way and strode through the crowd. A man was lying on his back near one of the trucks, his face a mask of blood. The other driver was still trapped in his cab and two Supernumeraries were trying to extract him.

The rain beat down harder.

Wait a minute. There was something wrong.

"They must have collided head on," the Jewish sergeant was saying. "The loads are all over the road. I don't think we can get it properly sorted out until morning."

Yes, there was definitely something wrong! All this rain. Two hot engines. There should be *steam*.

He kicked at the truck's bonnet. Eaten through with rust. It had been painted over. "Corporal! Give me your fookin' torch!"

Hughes bent down and took a closer look inside the bonnet.

"What's the matter, Captain? Have you spotted something?"

"Yes, I have. This truck don't have no fookin' engine!"

411

Shapira shook his head. "Amazing."

"Fookin' miracle, I'd say." He grinned. "But then, this is the country for fookin' miracles, ain't it?"

Shapira grinned back. "I suppose so."

Trucks with no engines. Bricks and iron pipes all over the road. In other words, a roadblock, Hughes thought. A few police cars and ambulances, and some injured civilians to add to the confusion and the delay. These kikes were brilliant sometimes.

Hughes grabbed Shapira by the shirtfront and bent him backwards over the mangled cab of the truck. "I'm going to have your fookin' arse for this, lad," he growled and stalked back to his jeep.

SS Eretz Israel

Netanel was standing close to the bows, and he could see the breakers smashing white around the old Roman walls below the dunes. An Aldis lamp blinked through the rolling mist of sand and foam.

The crew were screaming orders, trying to get everyone back on deck.

The freighter juddered with the force of sudden impact and the grinding of the ship's metal hull on the reef was so agonising that Netanel put his hands to his ears and screamed. He was thrown forwards and struck his head on a bollard and blacked out.

When he opened his eyes the ship was listing on to its port side, the white maelstrom of the waves rushing to meet him. There was no time to think. He dived feet first into the sea and the cold water rushed over his head.

En Josef

Rebecca cursed at the pain in her hand. The blood was still seeping through the dressing. Three fingers gone. Besides herself, three other Palmachniks had taken wounds. That was enough for one night. The British reinforcements would be here soon.

Almost on cue she looked back towards Haifa and saw the flicker of a signal lamp from the road. The British convoy had been spotted.

A burst of automatic fire raked the ground five yards from where she lay. "Withdraw," she shouted to her second-in-command. "Send up the red flare! Let's get out of here!"

Qiryat HaGefen

There were heads bobbing everywhere, like scores of tiny corks. The *Eretz Israel* was skewered on the reef, stuck fast at an angle of forty-five degrees. She was impaled on the rocks, and the sea would slowly break her up and destroy her.

A breaker rolled over him and crashed on towards the beach. He heard someone screaming.

"Leah! Leah!"

The woman was flapping at the water, trying to reach the struggling body of a little girl. Netanel struck out for the child, and pulled her head above the surface. He swam with her towards the shore.

It was less than a hundred yards but the undertow made progress slow and exhausting. Netanel battled with the current until he reached the back of the surf and then rode in with it towards the shallows. There were lights on the beach now and he could hear people shouting.

Someone ran through the shallows towards him and dragged him up the beach. "Take the child!" Netanel shouted.

The little girl was snatched from his arms and Netanel collapsed on his knees in the rushing foam.

He looked up. Men and women were streaming from the village. They were dragging ropes out to the breakers or linking hands in human chains to reach those still struggling in the surf. Hurricane lamps dotted the sand and car headlights illuminated the beach.

Other Jews helping Jews, he thought. For the first time!

He staggered back into the water. It was easier swimming with the current. He found the child's mother, exhausted, past the backbreak. He grabbed her under the arms and swam across the current this time towards the northern end of the beach.

Haifa–Acre Road

Hughes cleared the road behind the "accident" by the simple expedient of giving the drivers of the other cars a choice: drive their vehicles into the ditches or he would have his trucks shunt them in nose first.

While his troops cleared the bricks and iron pipes by hand, ropes were attached to one of the wrecked trucks and two lorries pulled it off the road. It took almost two hours but finally he had cleared a way through for his convoy.

He was grinning when he got back to his jeep. Shapira sat in the back with Hughes's corporal. The corporal held a revolver pointed at his head. "Better fookin' late than fookin' never," Hughes said. "That's what I always fookin' say, anyway!"

Qiryat HaGefen

Four times Netanel had swum out to the wreck. Now he crouched on his knees in the soft, rushing sand and coughed the salt water from his lungs, preparing himself for one more journey.

This time he did not have the strength. But he would go anyway.

He stumbled back through the breakers. Someone grabbed his arm. "What are you doing? You're exhausted! Go back!"

Netanel knocked the man away with his fist. He dived through the next wave and was lost from sight in the dark, swirling sea.

Asher stared after him. Crazy. The man was plainly exhausted.

He dived after him.

There were still people in the water, too many. He dived through the next wave, came up on the far side of the break, felt the current sweeping him out towards the wreck. Netanel was already fifty yards further out. A woman was struggling to support a small boy. Netanel reached them, tried to help them back to the beach. The woman struggled, panicking.

When Asher reached them, he grabbed the boy, who was unconscious now, supporting him under his left arm. He followed Netanel, swimming across the undertow. After almost a quarter of an hour they had still not reached the back of the break, and Netanel had slipped behind.

Asher saw the trailing end of a rope snaking across the surface of the water. He grabbed it. They saw him from the beach and started to haul him in. As soon as he reached the shallows men ran splashing through the waves and took the child from his arms.

Asher coiled the rope over his shoulder and swam out again.

The undertow had carried Netanel and the woman back

towards the reef. It was as much as Netanel could do to keep their heads above the water now. Another few minutes and they would both drown.

"I'll take her!" Asher shouted. "Grab the rope!"

Netanel coiled the lifeline around his wrist, his eyes staring wide with exhaustion. "Hang on!" Asher shouted. He trod the dragging water, waiting for the men on the beach to see them and pull them in.

Haifa–Acre Road

Hughes stood up in his jeep and pointed a finger at the man in the woollen yarmulka. "Get your fookin' animals off the fookin' road, *fookin' now!*"

The man spread his hands and answered him in Hebrew.

"What did he say?"

"He said that God in His wisdom made sheep before he made motor cars," Shapira translated.

Hughes snarled and climbed out from behind the wheel. There must be at least two hundred sheep milling around his jeep. It was the middle of the night. "God in His Almighty fookin' wisdom also made fookin' machine-guns and that's what I'm goin' to use on his fookin' sheep if he don't get them out the fookin' road!"

Shapira translated, approximately, what Captain Hughes had said to the shepherd. The man blinked in the headlights of the jeep and the trucks. "Tell him he is most welcome," the man said to Shapira. "As you yourself know, for it was your suggestion, I stole them from an Arab. I shall not be upset if the British captain slaughters every last one of them and barbecues them over an open fire but their Arab owner will doubtless weep a river of tears."

"He says go ahead and shoot," Shapira said to Hughes.

Hughes turned to the driver of the truck behind him. "Drive straight through," he roared. "Straight fookin' *through!*"

* * *

Asher heard the approach of the convoy from the beach, saw the headlights arcing across the sky from beyond the hills. "Hurry!" he shouted to Ben-Carmel. "Here they come. Hurry!"

They carried the unconscious figure between them up the beach and rolled him over the tailboard of the nearest truck.

"Go!" Asher shouted. He ran up and down the line of trucks and taxis, kicking doors closed, screaming at their drivers. "The British are here! Get out of here! Go!"

When Hughes arrived he ordered his corporal to turn on the searchlight mounted on the back of his jeep and aim it at the beach.

"Fookin' hell," he muttered.

The sand had been churned by a thousand footprints. Men and women were still floundering in the water, dragging survivors of the wreck from the water, or clinging together in human chains to try and reach those who no longer had the strength to swim.

Heads appeared briefly in the beam of the light, bobbing on the grey sea. The great black silhouette of the *Eretz Israel* groaned and creaked out beyond the surf.

Hughes turned to his corporal. "Tell Sharpe to position his platoon along the road and stop anyone trying to leave this fookin' beach. Then get Alderson and Finch and tell them to get ready to get their boots wet."

"What are you going to do?"

"I'm not a fookin' animal, Shapira. There's people fookin' drowning out there!"

"It's your fault," Shapira said. "They survived the Nazis just to die a hundred yards from Palestine."

"No, Sergeant, it's not my fookin' fault," Hughes said. "Maybe it's fookin' Bevin's, or maybe it's fookin' Ben-Gurion's, but it's not fookin' mine. All right?"

Fook them all, he thought. What a horrible *fookin'* mess!

FOOK THEM ALL!

67

Jerusalem

Sarah shivered and tucked her fingers inside the sleeves of her woollen jersey. Outside, by Damascus Gate, a cold wind whipped the flowing robes of the Arabs milling around the buses. Little Jewish children hurried home from school in long skiing trousers and woolly hats, laughing and squealing, cheeks burnished bronze from the cold.

She looked at her watch. He was late. The serving boy poured her more coffee and she held the tiny handleless cup to her face and warmed her nose and cheeks with the steam.

"A thousand apologies," he said, in Arabic. "There were business matters I had to attend to."

Sarah shrugged and indicated a chair. He seemed to make a point of being late, as if he wanted to make it clear to her that he was in control. It must be hard for him to deal with a woman, she thought.

He had told her his name was Ishmael. He had short, curling hair, flecked with grey, and a Chaplinesque moustache that was often affected by Arabs with pretensions to the effendi class. His clothes were well cut, even if his taste was execrable, and his ties were all made of embroidered silk and painful on the eye.

Her other contacts attempted anonymity, but Ishmael was by far the most conspicuous single individual in the café, if not all of Damascus Gate. In all likelihood he wanted other Arabs to think she was his mistress. It would not readily occur to anyone that she was a member of Shai, the intelligence arm of the Haganah.

Outside, it was getting darker. All over the city the cries of the muezzins echoed from the minarets calling the faithful to the evening prayer. The words faded on the rush of the December wind.

After the serving boy had brought him coffee, Ishmael lit a cigarette and leaned across the table, smiling, revealing a golden eye tooth. He certainly behaves as if this is a lovers' tryst, she thought. "You have brought the money?" he said.

"I told you, Ishmael. There will be no money until you provide us with something worthwhile. We are not going to pay you just to sit here and drink the coffee I pay for."

"How do I know I can trust you?" he said.

It was an astounding proposition for a traitor to put forward, but she said, "Without trust, what is life?"

He grinned and allowed his gaze to drop insolently to her breasts. He switched to English. "You are a beautiful woman," he said. His dark eyes bored into her.

These Arabs, she thought, they penetrate you with their eyes. "We are here to do business," she said.

"Why don't we go somewhere and fuck?" he whispered in English.

Typical of a town Arab, she thought. They think using words like that is a sign of sophistication. She held his gaze with her eyes and did not answer.

"There is a hotel just round the corner," he said.

"All right. You go ahead. I'll meet you there." She sipped her coffee. "If I'm not there in half an hour, start without me."

He laughed, a cheerful sound that came from deep in his chest, like the bubbling of a narghiliye.

Now his masculinity has been established, Sarah thought, perhaps we can begin. "We have been meeting here every week now for a month. You have still to tell me anything really useful."

"I told you it might take time."

"This is a simple transaction, Ishmael. You are the

419

merchant, I am the buyer. I pay nothing until you offer me something I can use."

Ishmael leaned forward, holding his cigarette near his lips in a furtive posture that all but announced to the room that he was about to impart a secret. "One of your buses is to be attacked."

Sarah raised an eyebrow. "Which one?"

"The morning Egged service to Tel Aviv. They plan to kill all the passengers, loot their belongings and burn the bus."

"When?"

"Two days' time. It will be ambushed in the Bab el-Wad."

"How many men? What kind of weapons?"

Ishmael drew on his cigarette, and the tobacco crackled like firewood. "About a dozen," he said. "Don't worry about their weapons. They'll probably do themselves more harm than anyone on the bus."

"How did you come by this information, Ishmael?"

His face became sulky. "You wanted something you could use. I have given it to you. Now you pay me."

Sarah shook her head. "If the bus is attacked, we will pay you. I'm not giving you money for some story you perhaps just invented."

"You think I would do that?"

"I am sure of it."

He shrugged. "What are you going to do?"

"We will take precautions."

He stubbed out his cigarette and switched back to Arabic. His eyes speculated. "Perhaps I do not want to be paid in money . . ."

"That's all we are offering."

"A pity." He looked at his watch. It was expensive, she noted. An American Rolex. "I have to go."

"Evening prayers?"

He grinned, but his eyes were cold. He must hate this, she thought, having to barter with a woman and being taunted in return.

She watched him leave. Information, she had been

420

taught, was important, but knowing what motivated your contact was equally valuable. You could not control your flow of information unless you understood its source. So what had made Ishmael seek out the Haganah?

Some Arabs informed because they heard there was easy money to be made. The city effendis were an especially rich seam to mine. They were softened by city living and addicted to the city's pleasures; their loyalties were blurred by the dictates of self-interest.

Others treated it as a game, as if the outcome of the conflict between their own people and the Jews were separate from the results of their own perfidy. Greed blinded them to the onrushing future.

Others used them simply as a means of settling a grievance. Let the Haganah kill my enemy, and spare me and my family the consequences of a blood feud should I do it myself.

She wondered to which category her Ishmael belonged.

In the corner an Arab in a dirty white abbayah was fingering his tespi beads, quietly reciting his prayers. His name was Levi Bar-Ayal; he was a Shai agent, like herself. Sarah nodded to him. He got up and followed Ishmael through the crowds outside the Damascus Gate.

Haifa

The old Fiat wound its way up the slopes of Mount Carmel, past the Arab-style brownstones and apartment buildings, leaving the teeming streets of the waterfront and Hadar far behind. Asher parked the Fiat outside a pension house that was almost hidden from the road behind a tall stand of pines. He got out and went inside.

The owner, Levitski, took him up to a room on the second floor. Netanel was sitting in a chair by the window, staring down at the port through the mist of rain. The wind rattled the window in its frame, and moaned around the eaves.

"Shalom." Asher held out his hand. "My name's Asher Ben-Zion. I am with the Haganah."

Netanel looked up at his visitor, but if he recognised him from the previous night he gave no sign of it. "Shalom."

Asher slumped into a chair. There were dark shadows under his eyes. "Forgive my appearance. I have not been to bed for nearly forty-eight hours. There has been a lot to arrange."

Netanel nodded, but said nothing.

"What is your name?" Asher asked him.

"Rosenberg. Netanel Rosenberg."

"Do you remember what happened last night, Rosenberg?"

"I remember I got very wet."

"There are at least half a dozen who owe you their lives." He studied this Rosenberg more closely. A scar on the right side of his face had healed badly and pulled the lid half closed over the eye. His lip had once been badly torn in two places and pulled down the corners of his mouth in a permanent sneer. More like the face of a villain than a hero, Asher thought.

How old was he? he wondered. There was a lot of white in his close-cropped hair, and the skin was pulled taut over the bones of his face. Perhaps forty.

Levitski had provided him with fresh clothes, but the shirt was too small for him and the sleeve did not conceal the blue tattoo on his wrist. His hands were never still, Asher noticed. They moved constantly, the fingers working ferociously. But the most unsettling thing about this man was his eyes. They were dull and lifeless, like the fish heads down at the market at the waterfront.

"You have remarkable resources of courage," Asher said.

"Is that what you think?"

Asher shook his head. "Well, it's what I thought at first."

"And now?"

"Now I wonder if you weren't almost hoping you would drown."

Netanel untwined his fingers with what seemed like a great effort of will. Suddenly Asher was aware that at last

422

he had this man's attention. "How many did you save last night?"

"Of the five hundred and forty-six people on board we estimate that just over three hundred made it to the shore. The rest either drowned or were rescued from the ship this morning by the British."

"You managed to hide the rest of the survivors?"

Asher shook his head. "Unfortunately not. The British may have picked up perhaps as many as a hundred, either from the beach, the village or at roadblocks. The rest are scattered all over the northern coast, here in Haifa, in Acre, or on kibbutzim away from the coast. There are eight of your comrades in this pension alone."

"So. Only two hundred?"

Asher bristled at the implied criticism. "In the circumstances, it was more than we could have hoped for. It is two hundred more Jews in Palestine who otherwise would be rotting away in DP camps in Europe. Europe doesn't want any more Jewish refugees. We do."

"You really think the British will give us our own Jewish state here?"

"No, I don't think that's what they want to do. We will have to persuade them."

"You will use force against them?"

"We'll employ whatever means necessary. This land was promised to us by God in the time of the Pharaohs and by Balfour in 1917. Imagine that! We have the word of both Jehovah and the British! Palestine is our twice-promised land."

"Then why do they want to stop us coming now? They fired on us last night. I saw two men lying on the deck, dead, with British bullets in them. I thought the British were on our side. I thought it was just the Germans who wanted to kill us!"

"It is just politics."

"Everything is just politics. Hitler and Streicher were just politics. Gassing children is just politics."

Asher shrugged. "The British want Arab oil, they are frightened of Russian expansion, they want to keep their

423

airfields here. So even though they feel sorry for us, and cry their tears in buckets at the Nuremberg trials, they have decided to court the Arabs. The thing you have to learn about the British, Netanel, is they know only two political positions. They are either bending over forcing you to lick their arse, or they are on their knees licking yours."

"What have you people done about it so far?"

"When Ernest Bevin, their Foreign Minister, cut immigration to one thousand five hundred a month the Jewish National Council declared a one-day protest strike. It had the effect of a mosquito bite on a camel's rump."

"And so?"

"And so the council has decided it is time to fight. During the Arab riots in 1936, the Haganah was used only for defence. Look what happened. The British gave in to the Arabs. The lesson is clear."

"And you think you can beat the British?"

"Not in a proper war. But we do not intend to fight a proper war. Sooner or later the British will have to go. We want them out, and so do the Arabs. One of us will win Palestine. Personally, I would rather eat a mountain of camel turds than live under the rule of any Arab. So we have to win. We have nowhere else to go."

"We needed men like you in Germany, twelve years ago."

"It was what happened twelve years ago in Germany that made men like me." He fished in the pocket of his jacket and produced a manila envelope. "This is for you."

"What is in here?"

"New identity papers. You're a free man now, Netanel Rosenberg. What do you intend to do with your new freedom?"

Netanel sat forward and suddenly the dullness in his eyes was gone. "There is only one reason I came to Palestine. I want to help build a homeland, a place where a Jew can be safe. A place where he knows he will not lose his business, his home, his children, his woman, his parents, his family, and his life just because he is a Jew. What I have lived through must never happen again. I don't want freedom – I want to chain myself to your cause. Our cause."

Asher considered. "It isn't easy, Rosenberg. As an army we have no rank, officially we have no existence. We have few weapons, and if you are found in possession of one of the few guns we do have the British will throw you into Acre prison for the next five years. At the moment, all we have is our hopes and dreams."

"After three years in Auschwitz, it's an embarrassment of riches."

"How old are you?"

Netanel had to stop to think. "I was born in 1916."

Good God! Asher thought. Not yet thirty! Young enough to fight with the Palmach.

"No family?"

Netanel thought briefly about his mother and father. He had never really had time to grieve. For a moment an image of Marie flashed across his mind, and he discarded it. "Not any more."

Asher stood up. "Good. Be ready to leave here at ten minutes' notice. Consider yourself Haganah. We are your family now." He went to the door, hesitated. "In a way, you know, I am sorry. We need men like you, as many as we can find. But in a way it doesn't seem fair. You come from one war, and now you find yourself in a new one."

Netanel shook his head. "No, it's not a new war. It's the same one. It started a long time ago, and it's about time we finished it."

Jerusalem

Sarah's flat was in Rehavia, in the middle of the Zion quarter, a few hundred yards from the Jewish Agency. A stand of pine trees grew close to her window and as

425

she worked in the kitchen she could hear the branches creaking and rustling in the wind.

It was the seventh night of Hanukkah, marking the triumphant revolt of the Maccabees in 167 BC. An eight-tipped menorah stood on her dining-room table, seven of its eight candles alight. In the windows of the flats opposite she could see the lights of dozens of other menorahs like her own. From the flat along the corridor she could smell someone frying *latkes*, potato pancakes.

There was a knock on the door. She looked at the clock. Nine o'clock. "Who is it?" she shouted.

"Levi."

She opened the door. Levi Bar-Ayal had discarded his robes and keffiyeh – a wise precaution in Rehavia, Sarah thought – and now wore a knee-length coat and a scarf. He slipped past her and sat down at the table.

"It's cold," he said.

"It's winter. Any luck?" she asked him.

He nodded. "After he left you he took a taxi from Damascus Gate to a house in Katamon. He was there for a couple of hours. I made some enquiries. It's owned by a woman, an Austrian. Her neighbours say she's a prostitute. Could be they're just jealous, I don't know."

"So now we know how he spends his money."

Levi shrugged. "Could be. Afterwards he got another taxi back to the Old City. He went into a small olive oil factory. That was where it got really interesting."

"An olive oil factory?"

"I made some enquiries in the coffee house a few doors away. Don't worry, I was discreet. The owner only needed a little encouragement; he told me about everyone in the whole street."

"What did he say about Ishmael?"

"He thinks he's a . . ." Levi stopped himself. ". . . he implied he engages in unnatural sexual practices. It also seems the olive oil factory is a family concern. Owned by the Hass'an family from Rab'allah, a little village about twenty miles outside Jerusalem."

426

Sarah felt the blood rush from her face. "Yes, I know it."

"Our friend's name is Majid, Majid Hass'an. It seems he provides all the money, his brother does all the work."

"What's his brother's name?"

Levi looked puzzled by the question. He frowned, trying to remember. "Rishou, I think. Rishou Hass'an. Why? Is it important?"

Sarah lay in bed, her hands behind her head, and watched the stars blinking their cipher through the branches of the pines outside her window. The cold of the sheets and the aching loneliness of the bed depressed her. She wondered what Asher was doing tonight. After all these years she had almost persuaded herself that she loved him.

And now, suddenly, that name again.

Rishou!

She had not seen him since the night of the ambush. The next day he had disappeared and she had heard nothing more of him until tonight. He had remained an icon in her memory, a bright and shining secret she cherished in her private fantasies.

If she closed her eyes now she could still smell the apple trees and the soft desert wind; could smell his skin, a dusty scent like cardamom and good tobacco. She could still see the way he looked at her, the deep black eyes that seemed to see right into her soul. Lately she had longed for that time more than ever, pined for the way she had felt then. The devil had been in her when she was young, and she had been willing to take any risk. She had dared to cross borders, to touch the forbidden and the taboo. It had liberated her, as nothing she had ever done since.

Rishou!

His face, his memory, his name, were inextricably entangled with her youth, with feelings far more powerful than anything she had ever felt for any of her own kind. He was in her blood now. Yes, she supposed, that was exactly it. He was, in every way, in her blood.

She felt the sharp, poignant pain of a self that had

427

somehow been lost and she lay awake, into the night,
planning.

68

There were only eight tables in Fink's, but more rumours,
lies and betrayals had been whispered over each of them
than in all of Jerusalem's other restaurants combined.
Since its opening in the early thirties it had become almost
a private club for the British intelligence community.

Today Major Ian Chisholm sat by the window, smoking
cigarettes, nodding occasionally to colleagues entering
or leaving by the street door. David Rothschild, the
proprietor, welcomed him personally. He left a beer and
a plate of schnitzels on the table.

Despite his rank, Chisholm had the hard, raw-boned
appearance of an NCO, his nose flat, his face seamed
with scars. He looked like a streetfighter; in fact, his nose
had been broken playing grammar school rugby, and the
scars on his face had been caused by flying glass during
the Blitz.

The war had been good to Ian Chisholm. Without Hitler
he would probably have spent most of his army career as
a junior officer. His father had been a greengrocer; hardly
the sort of pedigree his regiment was looking for. But
breeding did not stop bullets or deflect shell fragments,
and by the time of Germany's surrender the greengrocer's
son was a major.

Chisholm looked at his watch. Late.

A few minutes later Majid strolled in. He was wearing a dark pinstripe suit and a red silk tie. Chisholm
almost groaned aloud. For God's sake. He looked like
a gangster.

"Hello, old boy," Majid said. "Sorry I'm late." He sat down and clicked his fingers in Rothschild's direction. "Beer over here."

Chisholm clenched his jaw and forced himself to smile. Who the hell did this little gyppo think he was? He hated wogs at the best of times, but a wog with an English accent affecting public school airs was, in his opinion, worse than a black or a chink or a bog Irish.

"How are you today, Mr Hass'an?" Chisholm said, forcing himself to be polite, if not pleasant.

"Splendid. Just splendid."

"I'm pleased to hear it."

Rothschild brought Majid his beer. Chisholm raised his own glass and said, "Cheers."

The things he did for king and country. He had heard a lot of funny rumours about this Majid. There were whispers that he was dealing quartermaster's stores on the black market; there were other stories too, nasty ones, about him and some toffee-nose on the High Commissioner's staff.

Still, orders from above were quite clear: fraternise with the Arabs, harass the Jews. Harass them! If the government let the army do their job properly they'd do more than just harass the bastards. It was a British Mandate, British territory, and if the kikes didn't tow the line they should be given a few lessons at the sharp end of colonial diplomacy. What was it they said? "You can do anything with a bayonet except sit on it." Still, orders were for a softly, softly approach. And fraternisation. We must remember to fraternise.

"What have you got for me?" he asked Majid.

"Trouble," Majid whispered.

"Where?"

"On the Bab el-Wad road. The morning Egged bus to Tel Aviv."

Chisholm nodded slowly. "When?"

"Tomorrow morning."

"What is it? Ambush, bomb, what?"

"Ambush."

"All right," Chisholm said. As far as he was concerned,

the Arabs could do what they liked as long as no British soldiers were hurt and the process of government was not disrupted. Majid was just one of a number of contacts among the Arabs who kept him informed about possible trouble. It worked to the benefit of both sides.

As it was, the army sent a patrol up the Bab el-Wad every morning and every evening to ensure the road stayed open for British traffic. The morning patrol would be back in Jerusalem by the time the Egged bus reached the wadi. The wogs and the kikes could blow each other to kingdom come.

"You will not send troops to intervene?" Majid asked him.

"Intervene in what?" Chisholm said and he drained his beer.

"Splendid," Majid said. And he thought: Allah, help me in my sorrow! All this deception is a strain on the health! But what could he do? He was a loyal Arab but good sex was so expensive these days.

Judean Desert

Netanel was less than fifty yards away when they saw him. The gazelle raised their heads, their ears twitching violently, and then darted away, skipping over the stones in the dry river-bed.

Yaakov Landauer appeared at Netanel's right shoulder. "Not bad. For a beginner."

"What did you expect? They're wild animals."

"A good Palmachnik would grab them by the tail and see what they had for lunch." Yaakov took off his khaki slouch hat and wiped the sweat from his forehead, exposing the mahogany brown skull and the fringe of white hair. He stood up.

How old is he? Netanel wondered. Fifty-five? Sixty? Older than my father was when he died, certainly. Yet

430

look at him. No softness on him anywhere. Hard and gnarled like the trunk of an olive tree.

The rest of the group was straggling over the rocks towards them. "Now we march!" Yaakov shouted. "When we reach the cliffs there, we'll see how much you kids have learned about rock climbing!"

Netanel had arrived at the kibbutz at Kfar Herzl over a week before. He had travelled with fourteen others, ten men and four women. Most of them were like him, veterans of the wire, smuggled in on the ships of the Aliyah Bet. Their new identity papers said they were farm labourers, and at the British roadblocks the driver had told the soldiers they were travelling to the kibbutz to help with the harvest. The soldiers let them through.

Most of them were Polish, two were Hungarian and there was one other German like himself. They conversed with each other in Yiddish but as soon as they reached the kibbutz they were encouraged to use Hebrew, a language which until then had been only a written language, like Latin, the language of their scriptures.

It was night when they arrived. Netanel was taken to a wine cellar under the communal dining hall and questioned in the semi-darkness by three men whose faces he could not see. He learned later that one of them was Yaakov Landauer, Haganah commander for the kibbutz.

Two candles, an ancient Bible and a Beretta pistol were then placed on the table in front of him. With one hand on the dusty scripture, the other on the cold metal of the gun, the three men invoked what they called the supreme conscience of Zionism and invited him to swear his allegiance to the Haganah.

Forty-three thousand Palestine Jews had served with the British forces during the Second World War, to help defeat the Germans. They also wanted to receive proper com training, and combat manuals were painstakingly pilfe from British army barracks all over the Middle East. The manuals found their way back to the Haganah.

Netanel and his fellow recruits were given a crash course in British soldiering. While the kibbutzniks were out in the fields Yaakov Landauer gathered the latest recruits in Kfar Herzl's communal dining hall and gave them their basic training.

Weapons were brought from the kibbutz's cache – the kibbutzniks called it their *slik* – which was hidden under a concrete floor in the henhouse. They were shown how to break down and reassemble revolvers, pistols, rifles, Sten guns, even a Hotchkiss machine-gun.

They were taught judo.

They were taught first aid.

They were taught intelligence-gathering.

They were taught interrogation techniques. Some of the methods, Netanel thought, would not have been out of place in Auschwitz.

They were taught the rudiments of signalling and map-reading.

They were taught survival techniques.

There was hardly any time to eat, let alone sleep.

Then they were taken into the desert.

"The first thing you have to learn," Yaakov announced, "is how to jump out of a moving truck."

Security was paramount. As part of their basic training Haganah recruits were driven into the desert late in the afternoon and told to leap off the backboard. The truck would not slow down. They were then required to find their way to a rendezvous point using the night navigation methods they had been taught in the classroom. Apart from preventing detection by British patrols, it was a quick – if dangerous – test of a new recruit's abilities.

But this was just their initiation.

They learned to march through the night.

They learned to patrol without compass or light.

They learned how to stalk prey – first animals, then humans.

They learned rock climbing.

432

They learned how to throw grenades, using oranges stuffed with potatoes as dummy grenades.

And when it was over, they marched again.

Exhaustion, hunger, thirst. It was not a new experience for any of the death camp survivors. But it was the young sabra recruits who held up to it best. Their bodies were lean and hard and accustomed to the hardships of the desert. A new breed of Jew, Netanel thought. Tough, arrogant, athletic. If they had fair skins and blond hair, they would be the kind of Aryans that Hitler dreamed about.

The moon rose above the desert, impossibly huge, its seas and craters clearly visible. He had never seen any moon like this before, not in Ravenswald. Then he had never paid any attention to it. But here in the wilderness, where his ancestors had perhaps once slept in goatskin tents and grazed sheep, he felt once more in harmony with the rhythm of the natural world, as if he had travelled back in time, to a barren and sun-baked Eden, to a moment in history when he was free of the sin of murder, when Amos Mandelbaum's blood was not sticky on his hands because it was still yet to happen.

Sleep, deep and black. Amos Mandelbaum stood behind the counter in the pawnbroker's shop. "What do you have for me today?" he said.

Netanel pushed a wheelbarrow up to the counter. In the wheelbarrow was a little girl, holding a truncheon. "I could give you more if you had a pair," Mandelbaum said.

The door swung open and Mendelssohn burst in. He pointed his finger at Netanel. "You lied to us! You're a Nazi!"

"No," Netanel said, "you don't understand."

"You're a Nazi killer!"

"No . . . !"

"Come on, on your feet!" Yaakov barked, shaking him awake. "You've had your rest. Now we march again. If you boys want to be Palmachniks, you have to prove to us you have the belly for it!"

Netanel staggered to his feet in the darkness.

There were only six of the original group left now, plus four sabras. The rest had been broken by the regimen of forced marches and lack of sleep. But they won't break me, Netanel thought. If I fail this test, I might as well be dead.

He followed the silhouette of Yaakov Landauer down the rocky incline, the backpack and the weight of the Sten gun cutting into the flesh of his shoulder through his black jersey. Amos Mandelbaum walked beside him, his silent companion.

Twelve days.

Twelve days with little sleep, little food, only just enough water. Every muscle in his body screamed for rest. His arms and legs had been torn on rocks and desert scrub. His feet were bleeding from the endless marches. He was dizzy from fatigue and thirst.

But he had done it. It had all been worth it. The training was over and he was a Palmachnik now.

Yaakov Landauer squatted down next to him and handed him a rifle. He nodded towards the tin can that had been set up on a boulder a hundred yards away. "One round," he said. "That is all the ammunition we can afford. It is your graduation present."

They were in a wadi; the high walls that surrounded them would cushion the noise of the shots. A jackal patrolled the clifftop like a sentry on a parapet, searching the rocks for easy pickings.

Netanel took the rifle, aimed.

Missed.

Yaakov grinned and slapped him on the shoulder. "Don't worry, we want soldiers, not snipers. Tonight we go back to the kibbutz, you can rest up for a couple of days. Then we start again."

Netanel looked up at the cliff. The jackal was gone. No easy pickings here, Netanel thought.

Not any more.

434

69

Bab el-Wad

Izzat sat on his haunches, the ancient Mauser cradled between his knees. He stared at the sinuous coils of the road winding through the hills from Jerusalem. The wadi could not have been more perfect if Allah Himself had created it specifically for the purpose of ambushing Jews. In fact, he decided, that was probably the very reason Allah had brought it into being. Even back then, before time began, He had foreseen that there would come a time when the Jews would try to trespass on their land.

Perfect. Perfect hiding places behind the rocks and boulders of the slopes, perfect sighting for a rifle down into the gully; a perfect trap between the high walls, no hope of escape.

He looked at the heavy wristwatch he wore beneath the flowing sleeve of his abbayah. Almost time.

Jerusalem

The blue and silver bus of the Jewish Egged Company was about to leave the station when a Jewish police sergeant climbed inside, spoke softly and urgently to the driver, and then ordered everyone off. Half the passengers were women, half a dozen were children. They filed out of the door without complaint.

Their places were quickly taken by two dozen members

of the Jewish Supernumerary Police, dressed in civilian clothes. Each of them was a member of the Haganah, and each of them was armed. As the police were the only individuals among the Jewish population who were allowed by law to carry weapons, they made no attempt to conceal their armoury, which included rifles, Sten guns, and Beretta 9mm pistols.

As soon as they were inside the bus, the driver started the engine and the morning service for Tel Aviv set off for the Bab el-Wad.

Bab el-Wad

Izzat grinned. This was going to be easy.

He waited. His men had orders not to shoot until he had fired the first shot.

But one of his Strugglers became impatient. He saw a puff of smoke and heard a CRACK! echo around the rock walls. Idiots! Izzat thought. They have opened fire too soon! The gleaming windscreen of the bus shattered. Bullets punched into the metal sides of the bus from both sides of the gully.

Izzat joined in, firing, reloading, firing again. The bus swerved off the road and stopped.

Easy.

"*Allahu Akbar!*" Izzat shouted and he raised his rifle in the air and led the charge down the wadi.

Something was wrong.

Izzat stopped in his tracks, his own well-developed instinct for survival alerting him to the danger. His Holy Strugglers streamed past him, robes flying, scrambling down through the pines, firing their rifles as they ran.

Every window on the bus was smashed. Every window. Of course, he thought, they would have been smashed by our bullets.

Or would they?

Even in his most sanguine moments, he did not pretend that there was one of them who could hit a camel with a large melon at a range of three yards.

Something was definitely wrong.

Some of the glass had been smashed from the inside.

Suddenly gun barrels appeared at the windows. A trap! he realised. And now it was too late to withdraw.

The air whined like a host of angry bees as someone began to fire a semi-automatic weapon. Rifles and revolvers joined in the fusillade and a rain of bullets sent the stones around his feet kicking into the air like dust-devils. All around him his Strugglers screamed and fell.

By the hundred holy names of Allah!

He turned and fled back up the wadi, followed by the bleeding and screaming survivors of the Mufti's army.

70

Jerusalem

It was the evening before Shabbat, and the square around the Damascus Gate was packed with crowds: black-hatted Hassidim shuffled off to prayer, sidecurls swinging; Arabs in black checked keffiyeh made their way to the mosque to answer the call of the muezzin; nuns with white wimples hurried to evening mass.

Today, Majid was early. He was sweating despite the cold drizzle that had stained the shoulders and broad lapels of his suit. He mopped at his face with the purple silk handkerchief that he extracted from the breast pocket of his suit.

"Hello, Ishmael," Sarah said. "Congratulations."

"Six dead, four of them from my own village," he whispered in English. "Another three wounded!"

"They were armed. Unlike the women and children who would have been on the bus if you had not warned us."

"This wasn't meant to happen!"

Sarah produced a small packet, wrapped with brown paper, from the pocket of her coat. "You'll find we have been most generous."

Majid snatched the package from the table as if it were a pornographic magazine. "This wasn't mean to happen!"

Sarah shrugged her shoulders. "What was meant to happen? The women were meant to be raped, the children mutilated?"

"I am a good Arab. Four of those men were from my own village." He wiped his forehead and glanced quickly around the café.

Sarah sipped her coffee. "You haven't counted your reward."

Majid held the package between his knees and tore it open. He put the contents in his pocket. He seemed calmer. "That's a lot of money."

"There's a lot more, provided you are prepared to earn it."

Majid leaned towards her. "I didn't know you were going to kill so many! May Allah burn me on the Day of the Fire if I lie!"

I have a feeling He will burn you anyway, Sarah thought. I wonder if Rishou knows about this? I doubt it. "What did you think we were going to do? We have a right to defend ourselves."

"You could have just cancelled the bus."

"Then your friends would have attacked another one. The men who died had weapons, they have gone to Allah as martyrs. Think of the ones you saved. Innocent women and children."

"They were only Jews," Majid said, and then he realised what he had said and found something of particular inter-est on the floor.

"Just give us the information we want," Sarah said, eventually. "We will make sure you are rewarded."

"I cannot help you any more. That's it. I'm a good Arab."

Her superiors in Shai had anticipated this. They had told her what to do. Even so, it was not a pleasant prospect. But what was there in Palestine right now that could be construed as pleasant?

"I cannot let you do that . . . Majid," she said.

The sweat erupted on his upper lip as thick as dewdrops. His eyes widened and she saw the play of his thoughts on his face, as the realisation hit him.

"You little whore," he said in Arabic.

"Your real name is Majid Hass'an, you come from a village called Rab'allah, you own an olive press in the Muslim quarter. You see, we know everything about you. You may think you are a good Arab but I wonder what your comrades in the Holy Strugglers will think if they find out what you have done?"

"You can't . . ."

Suddenly there was steel in her voice. "Don't be so naïve. What do you think is happening here in Palestine? We are fighting for our lives! They killed millions of us in Europe and no one lifted a finger. If we lose Palestine we have nowhere else to go. This is a war, Majid. We will do anything because we cannot afford to lose!"

Majid stared at her. A war? For as long as he could remember there had been trouble between Arabs and Jews. It was like a tribal feud. He had never considered that there might be a day when it would be actually resolved, one way or another. But this girl was serious! She really thought the Jews could win, take Palestine away from them. The very notion made him feel sick to his stomach.

He forced the thought from his mind in order to consider the more immediate threat to himself. The Haganah knew who he was, were obviously prepared to expose him. He could never allow that to happen.

And besides, he needed the money.

Old City

The Hass'an Olive Oil Company was situated in a rundown
two storey building with a coffee house on one side and a
brass merchant on the other. It was evening and the brass
merchant was pulling down the shutters on his shop. A
Sudanese hawker had set up a little brazier by the roadside
and had begun roasting peanuts.

A woman, covered head to foot by a black abbayah,
only her eyes visible behind her veil, stopped to stare
in the window. Three men were working at the press
in the gloomy backroom, their faces beaded with sweat.
The woman watched them, unnoticed, then moved on,
indistinguishable from the hundreds of other Arab women
who had walked the street that day.

But she was different in a very fundamental way.

She was Jewish.

Sarah Landauer watched Rishou work the press. He had
taken off his shirt and wore only a white vest, and sweat
glistened on his back and shoulders. He has changed, she
thought. The boy she remembered from the apple orchards
had gone. He was a man now, his shoulders broader,
his chest deeper, his beard darker. She felt something
squirm inside her. She thought seeing him would make
the memory of him easier, would exorcise his ghost from
his mind. But suddenly she realised nothing had changed.
She still wanted him.

It was dangerous standing here. She must go. She had
indulged a foolish whim. She made a silent promise to
herself that she must never return.

440

Part Thirteen

PALESTINE, 1946

71

Atlit

The hiss and whip of tent flaps, the distant shouts of soldiers.

Marie stared at the wire. She felt as if she had been staring at barbed wire all her life; the camp at Auschwitz, the endless DP camps in Europe, now here. But instead of the black chill sweeping from a flat Silesian plain, the gritty wind that blew her hair came from a grey and sullen Mediterranean.

The stigmata were not as apparent on her, as with many of the others; the hollow-eyed despair that bred like a plague in the DP camps had not infected her. But anyone who had known her before the war would not have recognised her. Because she was thinner, she looked taller, and the lines of her face were more sharply chiselled. Her hair had been shorn a few months before in a camp in Austria to prevent lice and it was still as short as a boy's.

It had taken almost a year to reach Palestine. She had finally found herself a place on board one of the Mossad Aliyah Bet's blockade runners, the *Theodor Herzl*, but it had been intercepted and boarded by a British navy frigate, just off the coast of Haifa. Once again she was behind the wire.

But in her mind she was free.

In her mind, she was engaged to be married to a young German Jew named Netanel Rosenberg. And if she could only find her way out of this place, she was sure she would find him.

443

Tel Aviv

There were seven men and four women standing around Mordechai Yarkoni's desk in the Red House, studying the pencil-drawn map that was spread out on the desktop like a crudely coloured tablecloth. Asher Ben-Zion was among the group, once again field commander of the mission they were planning. The rest were Palmach platoon commanders; they included Rebecca Orenstein, her left hand still heavily bandaged from the wound she had received months before at En Josef; there was also a young and tough-looking camp survivor, leading his first command. His name was Netanel Rosenberg.

Mordechai Yarkoni leaned forward, the light from the single bare bulb making his large brown head gleam like polished oak. ". . . there are sentry towers here and here . . ." he said, stabbing his finger on the map, ". . . and each one has a searchlight. The camp is surrounded by ten-foot wire. Imprisoned inside are six hundred of our comrades from Europe, most of them taken from the *Theodor Herzl* two weeks ago. The British are threatening to send them back to Europe."

He looked around the table, and his eyes were bright and hard with anger. "That will not happen," he said.

"How many soldiers?" someone asked.

"Three hundred," Yarkoni answered.

A low whistle. Three hundred! They would be outnumbered as well as outgunned.

"But there is one vital weakness," Yarkoni added, smiling, and the men and women grouped around the table seemed to relax. "Many of the soldiers in the garrison are unarmed. Their weapons are stored here in the arsenal, under guard. If we can sabotage it, we can effect the escape without having to fight a pitched battle."

"Which units take out the arsenal?" Rebecca asked.

"Yours and Netanel's. You will be in overall command."

"Why don't we just shoot out the searchlights in the towers and cut the wire?" someone asked.

Yarkoni shook his head. "If we do that, we give the British too much warning. We have to get through the wire before we take out the towers." He pointed again to the map. "The main compound is here. We have arranged a diversion, enough to keep the watchtower busy while Rebecca's and Netanel's units enter the camp."

Heads nodded in agreement.

"As you know a dozen of our comrades have infiltrated the camp over the last few weeks. At precisely ten o'clock tomorrow night they will start a fire here on the far side of the tent compound. The intention will be to create a minor disturbance. Throw a few rocks at the sentries, that sort of thing. While this is happening two of our people will shepherd two hundred of the prisoners away from the guards and towards the edge of the compound."

"The sentries on the watchtowers will see them," someone pointed out.

"Of course. But they will think they are trying to escape the fire. They won't shoot providing they don't get too close to the wire." He looked back at the map. "While this is happening, Rebecca's and Netanel's commands will infiltrate the wire here and head for the arsenal. They will take what weapons they can and destroy the rest."

"It's going to break my heart," Asher said.

"Your job is to free prisoners, not to steal arms." He looked at the others. "We will destroy the arsenal with explosives. As soon as they hear the explosion the remaining units will hit the sentry towers, while Asher takes a company of the Carmeli towards the compound. Each man takes two prisoners, and leads them back through the perimeter to the trucks."

"That's all right for the women," Rebecca said, "but everyone knows what men are like. They'll bump into each other in the dark."

Everyone laughed – the women enjoyed the joke more – and then Yarkoni said, "It's a full moon tomorrow night, and the forecast is for clear weather. It will give us enough light. Even the men."

445

"What about the two platoons at the arsenal?" Asher asked.

"As soon as it is destroyed, they fall back and regroup with the units still inside the wire. They will then provide covering fire. There won't be much resistance with the arsenal gone because the British simply won't have the weapons to fight."

"Then why don't we just go in and kill them?" someone asked. Every head in the room turned. Asher looked up to see who had spoken. It was Netanel.

"We are there to defend our people, not to murder unarmed men."

"They are soldiers. They are here to murder us."

"That's not the way we do business." Yarkoni's tone invited no further argument.

Asher stared at Netanel. The harsh light of the bulb accentuated the seams on his face and the coldness in his eyes. The man frightened him a little, and he wondered if he had made a wise choice in this particular recruit. But he had impressed his father-in-law during his training in the desert, and Yaakov Landauer was not the kind of man who was easily impressed. He had chosen Netanel for an additional five weeks' training as a platoon commander.

Asher wondered what drove him. Like all of us, he wants us Jews to have our own country, where we can be safe. But there was something else in those eyes, something more than religious or patriotic fervour. Many of the death camp survivors had a fire in them that had helped them to survive. But with Netanel it was something he did not recognise, something cold and malevolent.

"Any other questions?" Yarkoni was asking them.

No one spoke. Netanel's suggestion had put a chill in the room. Asher could read the faces of the other commanders: All right, some British soldiers are going to die. But it will be battle not murder.

We're not Nazis.

The map was folded away and several of them went outside to fetch the Seder meal. Tonight was the first night of Passover. The matzoh and herbs and roast shank of lamb were brought in, and the ruby red Mount Carmel wine was placed in a goblet by the door for Elijah. They all placed yarmulkas on their heads and Yarkoni picked up the Haggadah and began to read.

"Why is this night different from other nights?" Asher said.

Mordechai Yarkoni spread his hands, palm up, and read from the text before him. "This night is different because we celebrate the most important moment in the history of our people. On this night we celebrate their going forth in triumph from slavery into freedom . . ."

72

Jerusalem

Captain James Talbot of the 6th Airborne Division sipped a glass of chilled chablis. The restaurant was full, but the atmosphere was restrained, and scores of whispered conversations hummed like the summer drone of insects. The porcelain was Bavarian, the glassware was by Mosar, the cutlery heavy Wilna silver. A piano played a soft but unidentifiable tune on the other side of the room.

He noted that most of the clients were senior army officers, or career bureaucrats. He despised the way they dabbed prissily at their lips with their napkins after every mouthful of prawn cocktail, continually sniffed the bouquet of their wine, how they never opened their mouths when they smiled. He hated them all. Except for his brother, of course.

Well, perhaps.

If there was a place to be seen in Jerusalem, Henry

had told him, then it was Hesse's. Hesse himself was a Berliner Jew, a round, garrulous man who had once been chief steward on a boat that ferried Jewish refugees to Palestine, back in the days when it was still a legal occupation. His restaurant was situated in a tiny, cobbled back street behind Jerusalem's most expensive shopping district, Princess Mary Avenue. It had stayed open even through the worst of the rioting of 1936 and 1937, and the piano played constantly except on Friday evenings, the beginning of Shabbat.

"So this is what you were doing while the rest of us were fighting Germans," he said to his brother.

Henry Talbot flushed. "It wasn't my choice, you know, Jimmy."

"Yes, I know. Just joking."

"It wasn't so funny if you were stuck here."

Of course, James thought. Must have been hell. But then everyone wants to be in a war once it's over. "He also serves, and all that."

"You really are a supercilious little shit."

James felt his cheeks flush and he picked up his wine and pretended to concentrate on it. Henry had always been the kind of older brother you had nightmares about. At school he was hopeless at sport, a swot, and a complete wash-out in a fistfight. But at home he was overbearing and fastidious. James had always tolerated it because he didn't want to upset their mother. But there was no damned good reason why he should take it any more.

"Henry, if we weren't in a rather fancy restaurant, I should have to ask you to take that back."

"Don't be an ass."

"It's ten years since you've been home. I'm not your little brother any more."

Talbot sighed. It was true, little James had grown up, although he was rather fonder of the pips on his shoulder than he perhaps had a right to be, in his opinion. By the end of the war the army was desperate for officers. If you could write your own name correctly two times out of three, they made you a brigadier-general.

448

He had last seen James in 1936, on his last visit to England. A long time. He imagined England would be as unfamiliar to him now as his younger brother. Then James had been on the point of leaving grammar school; now, eight years later, he was an army captain with a bristling red moustache, a Military Cross for valour and an uncomfortably working-class view of the world.

He was too big to bully around any more. But damned if he was going to apologise. Especially when he was paying. "Here's the food," he said. A waiter brought two prawn cocktails – Hesse's was famous for them – and they ate for a while in silence.

"I imagine you're rather glad it's all over," he said at last.

"I wish it was."

"Meaning?"

"Meaning Palestine. I feel like a duck in a shooting gallery. At least when we were fighting the Germans there were rules."

"Nonsense, Jimmy. This will blow over. The Jews and the Arabs are always sniping at each other."

James put down his fork and leaned forward. "Blow over? It's getting worse all the time. The bloody Jews are attacking forts and blowing up bridges and warehouses. The Lord alone knows what they'll do next. In another couple of months they say there'll be a hundred thousand British soldiers stationed here!"

Someone dropped a tray in the kitchen. Talbot looked up. Everyone in the restaurant looked suddenly pale. Like Talbot, they had all started at the crash, thinking it was a bomb.

"The government will work something out," Talbot said.

"The government! How many fact-finding committees has Bevin sent over? No matter how many 'facts' they have, those clowns aren't going to understand any more than they do now."

"I suppose you have all the answers, Jimmy."

"Look, a few years ago we were supporting the Jews. Now we're supporting the Arabs. We've twisted and turned this country so many bloody different ways it'll take years to undo the knots! If ever!"

A man Talbot knew from the Commissioner's office glanced over at their table. "Keep your voice down," Talbot hissed.

"It's easy to be objective over here. None of you people saw the Nazis' concentration camps."

"I didn't know *you* had."

"Just one, at a place called Belsen. That was enough."

Talbot buttered his roll. The International Military Tribunal at Nuremberg had begun five months ago, and was still dominating international news. "Is it true? The things one reads about?"

"This isn't something I want to dwell on over lunch, but my one abiding memory is seeing a human skeleton in a striped uniform trying to cut flesh off a three-day-old corpse with the sharpened edge of a spoon. When our interpreter asked him what he was doing he said he was hungry. Form your own impressions."

Talbot watched his brother devour his prawns. Suddenly the seafood was a little too raw and pink. He pushed his entrée away.

"Thank God we won," Talbot said.

"I don't think it's made much difference to the Jews. We don't torture them or use them as slave labour but they still have to live in camps. We don't want them, the Americans don't want them, the Poles don't want them, Russia doesn't want them. The only place that does want them they can't get into."

"This isn't their country," Talbot said. "The Arabs lived here before they did."

"What difference does that make? We've only been here thirty years and we run the bloody place."

"That's beside the point, the thing is – "

"I mean, is there a statute of limitations on ownership? The Romans forcibly repatriated the Jews two thousand years ago. Right?"

450

"What do you say to the Arabs who have lived here ever since?"

"In 1937 the Peel Commission advocated partition. That's always seemed like a good idea to me."

"That's because you're not an Arab and your home isn't inside the proposed Jewish territory. How would you feel if the Americans came along and told you to move to Manchester so the French could take over Guildford?" He realised he had raised his voice and deliberately dropped it back to a whisper. "Look at it this way. Our family's only lived in Guildford for forty years. Some Arabs can trace their roots in a village back to the time of Mohammed!"

James stared at his older brother, surprised by the sudden passion the subject had aroused in him. So unlike Henry. "You've changed colour, Hal," he said.

"I've been in Palestine a long time."

"I hope not too long."

"Don't lecture me, Jimmy. At least my view of things coincides with my duty. A happy coincidence perhaps, but there you are. Don't let your opinions allow you to forget what you're here for."

"I know what I'm here for. To fight another damned war."

Talbot looked away. Jimmy had a point. It was all in the files. In the thirties the kibbutzim had instituted a compulsory premilitary training programme for all boys and girls between fourteen and seventeen. The CID now concluded that the Haganah, although supposedly illegal, had a membership of up to forty thousand, including an elite professional paramilitary unit of fifteen hundred highly trained men and women, called the Palmach.

James was right. If the Jews wanted to make trouble, they were well equipped to do it.

"The one thing I would like to avoid," James was saying, "is surviving the Germans and then coming here and getting shot in some stupid little war I don't want to fight."

"That won't happen, Jimmy," Talbot said.

"Thanks. Just remember to tell that to Bevin. All right?"

Old City

The woman in the black abbayah paused outside the Hass'an Olive Oil Company. She had passed the factory dozens of times this particular evening, in order to familiarise herself with the location, but she was confident no one had noticed her. A tool of enslavement, the veil also gave her the advantage of anonymity.

She stepped into the alley beside the coffee shop, turned another corner into the shadows of a narrow laneway behind the factory. A wooden staircase led to a door on the second floor of the building. She hurried up the steps and tried the handle. It was open. She took a Beretta from the folds of her abbayah and went inside.

Rishou Hass'an shut down the press and locked the doors. It was late, and no sign of his brother. He had learned to expect that. He had hoped Majid might return so he could go home to Rab'allah for a few days but typically his brother had been delayed elsewhere. Probably with a mistress. Never mind. He would go tomorrow.

He reminded himself that Majid was dependable in other ways. Money, for example. It was his money that had made the Hass'an Olive Oil Company possible. Even Rishou was not sure where it all came from. Some of it was profit from Majid's dealings on the black market, some the proceeds from the taxi lease. But Allah alone knew what else Majid was involved in.

It had been Rishou's idea to use the olives from their orchards to start their own press, but it was Majid's money that had made it possible. Now, at least, they would be able to leave something worthwhile for their sons even if the lands around Rab'allah were swallowed up by the Jews.

The old ways were dying. It was apparent that the village could no longer live an existence isolated from the city. Zayyad's influence over them was waning; it was money that mattered now. Money bought cars and suits and rolled cigarettes. Money bought respect.

He looked at his watch. He would go upstairs to the

office and write up the accounts and then he would go to sleep. There was a mattress on the floor of the office for such a purpose.

He lit a hurricane lamp and turned off the electric light. He went upstairs, shivering. Fortunately, Majid had pilfered a kerosene heater from the British stores. He would need it tonight.

He opened the door of his office and a draught of warm air met him. He stared at the glow of the heater, alarmed. Someone was here already! "Majid?" he said.

The door clicked shut behind him.

He swung around. There was a woman, an Arab woman, standing behind the door, holding a gun. He gaped at her.

"Put down the lamp," the woman said.

Something familiar about that voice, he thought, even though it was muffled by her veil.

He put down the lamp. Just then the veil fell away.

"Sarah . . ."

The gun was pointing at his chest. "Just stay where you are."

For a moment he was too shocked to move. Then he grinned and stepped towards her. "Sarah . . ."

"I said stay where you are!"

"I can't believe you're here . . ."

"I just want to talk. Don't come any closer – "

He ignored her, pushing the barrel of the gun aside. He put his arms around her.

"Don't – " she murmured.

The Beretta fell to the floor. It wasn't loaded anyway.

73

Atlit

The ruins of the Crusader fortress brooded on the prom-
ontory above the beach. A full moon hung over the
Mediterranean, a stairway of silver descending from a
star-studded sky of purple-black. The vast city of tents
was silent, but from the skeletal watchtowers fingers of
light probed the darkness for movement.

Asher looked at the luminous dial of his watch. Five
minutes.

"Ready?"

Rebecca and Netanel lay beside him on the dune.
"We're ready," Rebecca said.

"Get as close as you can. The show starts right on
twenty-two hundred. Go for the wire halfway between
the two towers."

Rebecca and Netanel crawled away in the darkness.
Asher saw others follow them, slithering on their bellies,
like black snakes.

The minutes passed slowly. He wanted to urinate badly,
though he knew his bladder must be empty. It was always
like this. The waiting was the worst part.

Shouts went up from inside the camp. A muted orange
glow rose into the sky like a sunrise in miniature. Asher
looked at his watch. Right on time.

The searchlights on the watchtowers swung away from
the wire. Asher started to crawl forward, his Sten cradled
in his arms. A hundred and thirty other shapes followed,

spread along the dunes in a skirmish line, all in black jerseys and black drill trousers, invisible against the night.

Asher heard the crackle of gunfire from inside the compound. Pray God the British are firing in the air! he thought. He peered into the darkness, towards the wire, at the spot where he knew Rebecca's and Netanel's platoons would be at work, but he could see nothing.

The glow of the fire had formed a corona of orange and rose on the night sky. He heard one of the guards on the watchtower shout a warning. By now he would have seen the first refugees start their run towards the wire. The sentry fired one quick burst from the Vickers, the tracers angled very low, urging them back.

Hurry up, Rebecca.

More shots from inside the compound. The searchlights continued to probe the rows of tents but from where Asher lay it was impossible to see what was happening.

Twenty-two o-three. They must be inside the wire by now. Running towards the arsenal. Taking out the guards. They would try to get inside if they could and carry away any automatic weapons and ammunition. Then use their grenades. Perhaps another five minutes to wait, less than three if Netanel and Rebecca ran into trouble.

Asher dared not get closer to the wire.

Wait, wait.

He smelt death on the wind. Whose turn would it be tonight?

The fire was almost out, and the sounds of rioting had died. The searchlight swung restlessly over the compound, then began to work inexorably back to the wire. Asher crawled closer to the perimeter, fifty yards from the base of the tower. He could see the holes in the wire where Netanel and Rebecca and their Palmachniks had gone through. He knew in a few moments the guards would see it too.

Suddenly he heard the harsh staccato of automatic weapons, this time from further away, near the army barracks. The searchlight swung away again. The sentries above him shouted the alarm.

He waited.

They must have located the arsenal. He listened to the sounds of the firefight, winced at every scream, imagined it was one of his fellow Palmachniks. The battle went on too long. Perhaps they can't get inside, Asher thought. Perhaps it's too heavily guarded.

A blinding white light was followed fractions of a second later by a thundercrack. Asher looked up, saw a fireball billowing into the sky, followed by a mushroom of smoke, blacker even than the backdrop of night sky.

"Jesus Fucking Ker-ist!" he heard one of the soldiers shout from the watchtower.

He brought the Sten to his shoulder, aimed carefully at the light, and fired a short burst. A splinter of glass, a scream. More Sten fire from his right and the other light was extinguished.

Men ran past him with wirecutters, and set to work.

Blind panic.

Asher was aware of bodies rushing towards him in the darkness. The instructions the Haganah infiltrators inside the wire had given the prisoners had been instantly forgotten. A shadowy human tide streamed away from the tents towards the perimeter fence.

In the Red House, when Yarkoni was talking, it had all seemed so easy. But suddenly Asher felt himself buffeted by a wave of bodies in the darkness, his own commands lost under the shouts and screams, and he wondered if he and his men might ever be able to extricate themselves and their charges from this chaos . . .

He reached out, grabbed one of the running figures, a woman. "Palmach! Come with me!" he shouted.

One of the guards on the watchtower opened up with his Vickers gun, firing blind into the darkness. His leg went numb beneath him, and he fell. He tried to get up, couldn't. Bullets raked the ground by his head, sand stinging his face. There was a roar as a grenade exploded at the base of the watchtower.

The machine-gun fell silent.

His thigh was sticky wet. His fingers found a jagged hole in his own flesh the size of a small coin. He pressed down hard with the palm of his hand to staunch the pumping blood.

Someone knelt beside him, cradling his shoulders. "You're hurt." It was a woman's voice, a refugee.

"Get to the wire!"

"But you're hurt . . ."

The blood was still squirting between his fingers. Had to keep the pressure on, he remembered from his training.

"Give me your knife!" the woman said. "Quickly!"

He groped in his webbing belt and handed her his knife. He heard her cut through her skirt. She pressed a ball of cloth into his hand. "Hold this on the wound," she said. He plugged the bullet hole with it. He was starting to feel faint from the loss of blood. Had to fight it, had to.

Palmachniks and refugees were stampeding around them. He heard another burst of gunfire. They were in the open, exposed.

"You have to get to the wire!" he shouted at her.

The woman bound the makeshift dressing in place with more strips she had cut from her skirt. "Can you move your leg? Is it broken?"

"I can't feel anything! Get away from here!"

"Not without you."

Asher looked up at her through a red mist of pain. The face of a boy angel, choirboy-cropped hair, huge eyes, dark shadows in her cheeks. She draped an arm around his shoulders, tried to help him to his feet.

Moonlight splashed over the bodies that littered the compound. We'll never make it, Asher thought. The British will cut us down before we reach the wire.

Suddenly three Palmachniks ran towards them from the darkness and he saw the white flash of their Sten guns. Someone grabbed the woman and pushed her away. "Get to the wire! Hurry!" Netanel's voice. He knelt down beside him. "Ash! Where are you hurt?"

"My leg."

"Shit, you're losing a lot of blood. Help me here!"

457

Netanel and a fellow Palmachnik grabbed him under his arms and dragged him away. Asher heard the chatter of a Sten as a third covered their retreat.

He blacked out.

The trucks were waiting, their engines idling, on the road beyond the dunes. The two Palmachniks ran down the sand, their guns slung across their shoulders, Asher supported between them in a chair lift.

The lead trucks started to rumble away, their headlights switched off, heading for the turn-off road that would take them across the plain to a kibbutz twenty miles to the east. They had to be well clear before the British armoured patrols arrived from Haifa.

Asher was hefted into the back of the last lorry. Strong hands pulled him aboard.

The woman pulled away from her escort and leaned inside. "Is he all right?"

"Get away from here!" A Palmachnik grabbed her and pushed her in the back of another lorry, with the rest of the refugees. She saw the man's face briefly in the moonlight. A shaven head almost concealed by a khaki balaclava, the glimpse of a scar under the blacking.

She did not recognise Netanel Rosenberg.

74

Tel Aviv–Jerusalem Road

There were perhaps as many as twenty young men and women in the back of the lorry, dressed in blue denims, ostensibly Jewish labourers on their way to a kibbutz. The lorry rumbled past the barbed wire of the British army base at Sarafand, and headed across the coastal plain to the east. They travelled past vineyards and wheatfields and the towering minarets of Ramle to the maw of the Bab el-Wad, the Gate of the Valley, the twenty-mile-long gorge that guarded the road to Jerusalem.

This was the way that the camel caravans had come in the time of Christ. Titus's Legionnaires had built their forts along this road, and the Crusaders had come this way as they rode against the Saracens.

As they entered the wadi the bell of the red-tiled Monastery of the Seven Agonies reached them on the wind, accompanied by the delicate odour of orange blossom. They could see the Trappists at work in their terraced vineyards, and above them, the grey blockhouse of Latrun Fort where the British sentries would be watching them through binoculars.

Then the walls of the valley closed in on them and they were inside the jaws of the Bab el-Wad, twenty miles of sinuous curves, the white cubes of Arab houses clinging to the steep walls of rock and pine. The Palmach men and women in the lorry fell silent and stared, and were glad of the Sten gun parts the women carried with them inside their brassieres and taped between their legs, grateful for the grenades concealed inside the potato sacks and the spare rifles taped underneath the boards of the lorry. They could feel hostile eyes watching them from every eyrie and they knew they were inside the lion's mouth.

Three hours later they reached the village of Kiryat Anavim and turned a left-hand curve in the road. As they looked down on Jerusalem, Netanel felt the tension drain from his body. He looked up at the glaring white tomb of the prophet Samuel, high on its mountain top. It was from here, legend had it, that Richard the Lionheart looked down at Jerusalem for the first time and wept. Netanel wept also, and he murmured the words of the Passover prayer he had said, a lifetime ago, at a glittering table in Germany.

"Next year in Jerusalem."

The year that had been awaited for two millennia by his ancestors had finally arrived, and he was returned now not with joy but with hatred. The soft young man who had spoken those words in Ravenswald would not have recognised the solemn-faced Palmachnik who rode the lorry down the Jaffa Road towards the rose-coloured walls of the Holy City.

Kfar Herzl Kibbutz

The kibbutz has come a long way in the last ten years, Sarah thought. Now there are lawns and flowers, swings and sandboxes; the school has bunsen burners and microscopes; we have our own hospital; the cottages pile up the slopes in neat rows of red tiles and white walls, the gardens carefully tended; we have electric lights and there are even machines to milk the cows in the barns.

Around the kibbutz, rippling in the heat haze of the afternoon, lay the Judean hills, brown and stark, the colour of dung, a reminder of what the land was before they arrived. They had kept the promise Herzl and the Zionists had made; they had tamed the wilderness. But sometimes Sarah privately longed for the way it was before, when they had first come here. In those days they had been forced to battle the wilderness for every inch of land, and she had not realised how docile and how sad it might seem when it was conquered.

She thought about Rishou. *His heart must break when he comes here. Perhaps it is why he spends so much time in Jerusalem now. When he returns to Rab'allah he must look down at us and what he sees rebukes him twice; it reminds him how his ancestors' land was taken away from him, and it demonstrates how much more advanced our European ways have become. I wonder if he envies or despises us?*

Isaac was playing soccer in the playground with four other boys. *A fine boy,* she thought; *tall and athletic and good-looking.* He was nearly eleven years old. Where had that time gone?

He had been six years old when Asher had joined the Jewish Brigade and gone to fight in Italy. Meanwhile she had started work with the Histadruth in Jerusalem and was spending less and less time at the kibbutz. Yaakov had virtually raised him since then, and now Isaac was almost a stranger to both of them.

Asher limped on to the verandah and eased himself on to a chair beside her. Sarah manoeuvred another chair so he could rest his injured leg on it. "Don't fuss over me," he said.

"You're a wounded hero."

"Your sarcasm is not an attractive side of your personality."

"Talking of personalities, you've behaved like a goat with a thorn in its backside ever since you came back here. What's wrong?"

"I don't like being an invalid."

"It's better than being a corpse."

He shrugged. "I'm not going to apologise."

"Of course not."

"I can't stand sitting round here like a cripple."

"It's not my fault, or my father's."

She watched him wrestle with his pride. He scratched at the dressing on his leg. The bullet had not broken the bone, which was lucky, but it had damaged an artery, which was not.

He grunted, which was as close to an apology as she had ever got from him. Asher and his pride! He nodded towards Isaac. "The boy misses you. You should come back here to the kibbutz."

"You're here with him now. Anyway, my work for the Haganah is just as important as yours."

Asher was silent for a long time. "Are you seeing anyone in Jerusalem?" he said suddenly.

Oh well, you know, just one of my old Arab lovers. "What an extraordinary question."

"I know things aren't good between us."

"I didn't think you noticed these things."

"I pick up little signals. Most men wouldn't notice if they hadn't made love to their wives for a year but I'm very perceptive."

"You've been in Haifa, I've been in Jerusalem. It's hard to be intimate with the Samarian hills between us."

"Why do you think I asked them to post me to Haifa?"

She let the question hang. She wasn't ready for this. Not now.

"When do you go back to Jerusalem?" he said.

"Tomorrow, after Shabbat."

"Why don't you find out if there's something for me to do with the Shai? I'm going crazy round here. The doctor says it will be months before I can rejoin my unit."

Before she could answer, she heard someone calling Asher's name. She looked up and saw Yaakov striding across the lawns towards them. A tall, gaunt figure loped along beside him.

"Ash, you've got a visitor," Yaakov shouted.

Asher struggled to his feet to greet them. "Netya!"

462

"Shalom, Ash!" Netanel grinned. "How's the hero of Atlit!"

Netanel sat on the verandah, smoking endless cigarettes. A vodka bottle was uncorked on the table between them, but only Asher was drinking. "Our unit's been ordered into Jerusalem," Netanel said. "Headquarters thinks that's where the trouble will start."

"We have to keep up the pressure on the British."

"I agree. But there's bound to be a backlash from the Arabs. We can't let them get away with it like they did before the war."

He talks as if he was here then, Asher thought. How quickly he has absorbed our thinking, our ways. He scratched irritably at his leg. "I'm going crazy just sitting round here."

"Does it still hurt?" Netanel asked him.

He shook his head. "It's just the itching. It's getting worse now the weather is warmer."

"You were lucky. You could have bled to death."

"If you hadn't found me so quickly, I would have." He took a swallow of the vodka. "We really shook up the British. I would have given anything to have been in the High Commissioner's office when he got the news."

Netanel nodded, but did not smile. "It's only the beginning."

Yes, only the beginning of the Haganah's war, Asher thought, but nearly the end of mine. He had spent three days after the raid delirious with pain and barely conscious, hidden on a kibbutz a few miles from Atlit. When he was able to be moved they brought him back to Kfar Herzl in the middle of the night in a covered lorry. At first the doctors in the hospital thought he might lose the leg. Asher told Yaakov he would prefer they put a bullet through his head.

He kept the leg.

A few weeks later Yarkoni himself had travelled to the kibbutz to congratulate him in person; the final tally had been one hundred and eighty-six of the refugees freed, just

463

four Palmachniks dead. But Rebecca Orenstein had been one of them.

"She was hit in the first skirmish," Yaakov had told him. "Rosenberg took command. You chose well, Asher. He led them superbly, and his platoon adores him. They say he's not afraid of anything."

Not afraid of anything.

"Have you heard the news?" Netanel said. "The Mufti has reappeared. He's in Cairo, the guest of King Farouk."

"Shit!"

"You can imagine what is going on in Jaffa and Nablus. To listen to the Arabs you'd think Mohammed had been reborn."

"I thought the British had shot the Mufti in Berlin."

"It seems they were saving their bullets for us. You had better get well quickly. We are going to need you."

"We are going to need more Rebeccas too, but where will we find them?" He reached for his walking stick. "Let's not talk about it any more. The vodka's given me a headache. Want some coffee?"

Netanel got up. "I'll get it," he said, and he went inside to the kitchen.

Asher sat and stared at the hills. I wonder who you really are, Netanel Rosenberg, he thought. You talk as if you have been here all your life, as if your own past no longer exists. You never mention Germany, or Auschwitz, any of it. Perhaps if I had been through what you have endured, I would do the same thing.

And yet; he never speaks about women, he never jokes, he never talks about anything except the struggle for the Jewish state. We are all committed, of course. But with Netanel it is more than that. Why do I feel that if we were ever to win, Netanel Rosenberg would suddenly disappear?

Netanel came out carrying a coffeepot and two large enamel mugs on a tray. He poured the steaming black liquid into the cups and sat down.

"Where were you from in Germany?" Asher asked him suddenly.

It was as if a dark cloud had passed across his face. "I don't want to talk about it."

"It's just that I'm German too. Did you know that? I was sixteen when I came out here. My parents were from Bavaria, a little town near München."

"What was the name of the place?"

"Ravenswald."

Netanel said nothing for a long time. "Never heard of it," he said finally.

"Last letter I got from my parents was 1941. I don't know if they're still alive. I've tried to find out. I don't suppose there's much chance."

Netanel stared at the hills, and offered no comment.

"How long were you in Auschwitz?" Asher persisted.

Netanel avoided his eyes. "Too long. Why?"

"It's just that we have a couple of people here in the kibbutz who also spent time there. I thought perhaps while you were here you might like to meet them."

"Like old school chums, Ash? Being at Auschwitz is not quite the same. What do you think we would do? Swap funny stories about the gas chambers?"

Asher shrugged: fair enough. Then he looked into Netanel's eyes and he saw something that Mordechai Yarkoni had said did not exist there. It was there for just a moment and then it was gone.

Fear.

75

Rab'allah

Rishou had built his own house, on the hill just below his father's, overlooking the olive orchards. It was ample evidence, if any were needed, of how successful his business ventures, in partnership with his brother, had been. The house had six bedrooms and two storage rooms, a raised bedstead, an outside toilet and even a primus stove in the kitchen. It should have reinforced his claim as next muktar of Rab'allah, but things were not as they were, and his new home had aroused hostility in the village, not respect. Rishou himself was beyond reproach, but Majid Hass'an, it was well known, had grown rich through his contacts with the British. And the British were now the enemy.

One day I will be forced to choose too, Rishou knew. I will have to disown my brother or become an effendi like him.

Morning. Sparrows squabbled in the olive orchard, swallows swooped among the figs. A white sun chased the mist from the fields.

Rishou watched Khadija on her way down to the well, Wagiha trailing behind her. His wife had grown plump over the years, and his interest in her body had waned. Now that Sarah was back in his life – thanks be to Him – he no longer felt the need to possess her. Khadija did not seem to mind. Either she guessed he had a mistress or she thought he was no longer capable.

He fervently hoped it was the former. She must know

466

there was another woman! Well, perhaps. But Allah alone knew what the women were saying about him at the well. Perhaps he would possess her tonight just to prove to her his manhood was as it had always been.

When he lay with her it was never as it was with Sarah. It was Sarah who, long ago in the apple orchard, had shown him her button of pleasure, and how to caress it. On his wedding night he had tried to locate Khadija's button of pleasure without success. She later told him it had been removed when she was a child.

His relations with Sarah left him both elated and confused. The imam said a woman was intended by God to receive a man as part of her duty, with admiration perhaps for the length of his member and its performance, but to enjoy it as much – or more – than a man was a blasphemy. That wondrous evening of his reunion with Sarah she had reached Paradise on three or four occasions for his one.

He thought about her constantly. At first it had just been for the pleasure of her body. But now he found he longed also for her companionship, her laughter, her wicked tongue. Khadija had never been able to offer him these things. She had been a good and dutiful wife but he did not love her. Sarah occupied his every waking moment.

And he had no idea where his passion for her would lead him.

Sheikh Daoud was to visit his father that morning and Zayyad had requested his presence at the meeting as a courtesy. As he walked the short distance to his father's house, he saw Rahman playing soccer with two other boys. They were using a tennis ball Majid had taken possession of while he had been in the employ of the Talbots.

"Where's Ali?" he shouted.

There were any number of fictions and evasions that Rahman could have employed, but it seemed Allah had made it physically impossible for the boy to tell a lie. Rishou sometimes despaired of him. How did he ever hope to make a living?

467

Rahman shuffled his feet in the dust and did not answer.

Rishou was alerted by this display. He cuffed his son lightly round the ear. "Where's your brother?"

"I don't know."

Rishou hit him again. "Tell me where your brother is."

Rahman looked around. His two friends had disappeared. No help there. "He's gone to al-Naqb."

"Al-Naqb? What's he doing there?"

Rahman did not answer. Rishou grabbed an earlobe and tugged until Rahman was on tiptoe. "What's your brother doing at al-Naqb?"

"He wants to join the Holy Strugglers!" Rahman blurted out.

Rishou released him. Allah help me in my sorrow! He turned around and hurried to the stables, and saddled Al-Tareq.

Sheikh Daoud had aged. The flesh had wasted off him and there were bald patches in his beard and tears in the creases around his eyes. His sons had to help him down from his horse. The old goat will soon stand in the presence of Allah, Zayyad thought. It will take more than a thousand virgins to revive him in Paradise. They say his yard hangs useless between his legs like a water bag hanging off the saddle of a camel. A just reward for living beyond his time and burdening us with his presence longer than is our due.

Zayyad stood at the doorway to greet him, his ceremonial Bedouin sword buckled at his waist for the occasion. They embraced – his body is as light as a child's, Zayyad thought – and he ushered the old man inside. He was sure he could hear the sheikh's bones creaking as his sons helped him sit. Soraya and Ramiza fetched sweet mint tea and a silver platter of halwah.

"May your way to my house always be smooth," Zayyad said.

"A blessing on you also, brother," the sheikh replied. "We give thanks to Allah to find you in such strength and vigour." *It is only your sons who are holding you upright*.

Sheikh Daoud worked his prayer beads between his fingers. "Thanks be to Him. I rejoice in finding you also in such excellent health. It is legend in all Judea how your sons continue to prosper and their houses increase."

"Thanks be to Him," Zayyad said.

The ritual of welcome was, of necessity, long and painstaking, for there were enquiries to be made after the health and fortunes of their many sons and daughters and grandchildren, and praise and thanks duly offered up to God for each.

Finally Sheikh Daoud looked up at the framed photograph of the Mufti that hung on Zayyad's wall, and rasped, "Praise be to Allah for returning our Mufti to us unharmed."

Perhaps He just wishes to purge us through suffering, Zayyad thought. "It is indeed a great miracle."

"He has already spoken on radio in Cairo urging us to crush the Zionists and throw every one of them into the sea."

"*Insh'allah*," Zayyad said, carefully. "As God wills."

"How could His wishes be otherwise? But we must prove ourselves worthy of His help. We must be prepared to sacrifice our blood for an Arab Palestine."

Easy for you to say, Zayyad thought. You already have one foot through the Gates of Paradise. "Tell me, brother, where will all this lead us? Will it bring the young men back to the village, will they again kiss their father's hand when they return to his house? Will it give our fellaheen their own fields or will they still toil for some city effendi who may one day sell the land again, as they sold it to the Jews? Will an Arab Palestine give us back our old ways?"

"Of course," Sheikh Daoud said.

May a leprous camel fart in your face! Zayyad thought. May the testicles of all your grandsons shrivel up like currants in the sun and may your granddaughters all give birth to water melons! You do not even give me the dignity of an honest lie! Whatever happens now, I am the last real

469

muktar of Rab'allah. Our village, our traditions, are dying. The British have taught us rebellion and the damned Jews have brought us Europe and we will never be the same!

"Do you truly believe the British will betray us?" Zayyad said. "They guard the coast against the Jews, and they have stopped all sales of land to the Zionists. What more would you have them do?"

"They will betray us as they betrayed us before. If we are to get rid of the Jews, we must do it ourselves."

Zayyad considered: if he thought it would help Rab'allah, he would gladly fight. But he had seen many olive harvests and although he could not count figures on papers like his sons he could foresee what would happen. But what choice was there?

The distant rumbling of a truck on the road disturbed his thought; as it came closer he heard the screams of women. He stood up and went outside.

They wore the blue denim of kibbutzniks and they were all armed, not with old Mausers and Parabellums like the Strugglers, but with Beretta pistols and Sten guns. They beat their fists on the sides of the truck and waved their guns in the women's faces and shouted insults in Arabic at the fellaheen in their fields and at the crowd gathered outside the coffee house in the square. The lorry rumbled quickly through the village and then was gone, leaving them choking in its dust. It disappeared over the hill, heading towards one of the kibbutzim on the Dead Sea.

Armed and angry Jews. The Mufti was not the only one preparing for war.

Zayyad heard Sheikh Daoud's dry, crackling breath at his shoulder. "Well, brother, what do you say?"

"What I say makes no difference now. Half my young men have already joined your nephew Izzat's band."

"May Allah grant him victory!"

"May Allah grant him just a little wisdom," Zayyad said under his breath.

470

al-Naqb

The meeting place of the Holy Strugglers of Judea was an open secret. Half a mile from al-Naqb was a cave, where the villagers sheltered their goats and cattle during bad weather. Horses grazed on the hill outside and a lone sentry dozed under a nearby fig tree.

Rishou jumped down from Al-Tareq and went inside.

It was dark and cool, the walls were slippery with moss, and the air smelled of mushrooms and goats. There were perhaps as many as two dozen young men, squatting in a circle, cradling a variety of weapons, from ancient damascened swords to First World War Mausers.

Ali crouched against the wall of the grotto, holding Rishou's Lee-Enfield.

Izzat looked up. "Ah, we have a Hass'an in our midst."

Rishou ignored him. Rishou snatched the rifle from his son's arms, and pulled him to his feet. With one push he propelled him through the mouth of the cave.

Izzat stood up. His tone was mocking. "Where are you going, brother? Have you not come to join us?"

"I would rather join a troupe of travelling acrobats."

"Why are you taking Ali? Are you afraid he may become a true Arab?"

"He is already a true Arab. My fear is that if he follows you he will become a true corpse."

"Anyone who dies a martyr for Islam lives for ever in Paradise!" someone shouted.

Rishou turned and faced them. Two dozen pairs of eyes stared back at him, every one of them icy with hate. "He is only just eleven years old!" he shouted at them.

"If he is old enough to fight, he is old enough to join the Strugglers," Izzat said.

"Oh, he is old enough to fight. He is just not old enough yet to recognise the difference between a holy cause and a foolish adventure."

"You don't care about us any more," someone else said.

"You only care about your money."

Rishou turned his back on them and walked away.

Ali stared up at him, his jaw thrust out in a brave but poor attempt at defiance. Rishou held the Lee-Enfield in front of his face. "If you ever take my rifle out of the house again, I shall break off your arm and batter you senseless with the wet end. Is that clear, Ali?"

Ali nodded. "I understand, yaba."

Rishou saw the humiliation in the boy's eyes; also the contempt. "No. You don't understand anything, Ali. When you do, it will probably be too late."

76

Old City

It was hot in the tiny room, and the sweat bathed their bodies and made their limbs glisten like burnished olive. She lay on top of him, delaying the empty moment of their separation. Their sweat had pooled on his body. A droplet of perspiration began its slow march down his cheek and she wiped it away with her finger.

"I must stop coming here," she thought, and realised she had whispered the thought aloud.

"Shhh," he said and held a finger to her lips.

"This is wrong, all wrong. I should never have come back here."

"Put it aside, my Sarah. Just praise God for today."

So easy for you, she thought. You are only betraying Khadija, your wife. When I come here I betray a whole nation, not just Asher. How could I dare risk so much?

A Shai officer, venturing into the Arab Quarter. If I were captured what secrets could the Arabs wring from me? Even if I am never found out my mere presence here is treachery. Is it not enough that I commit adultery against my husband, should I love an Arab, an enemy, as well?

"There is going to be trouble, Rishou. This time it is going to be worse than 1936. Much worse. It is madness for us to continue."

Rishou was silent a long time. Then he said, "When I was a little boy, Zayyad sent me to the school in the village mosque to learn my Koran. In the second sura, Mohammed tells how, you know, it was a Muslim who divided the sea for Moses and saved the Jews from the Pharaoh. It was Muslims who arranged for Moses to meet with Allah on Sinai and receive the Commandments and become People of the Book. In return, he said, the Jews turned everything around, stole our Koran and falsified it, lied about Abraham. I think even back then he was preparing us for the day when we would have to fight you."

"And did you believe him?"

"I did then."

"And now?"

"I was fortunate. My father is a wealthy man, by our village's standards anyway, and he could afford to send me to the Anglican college here in Jerusalem. I formed a different view of the world. But in Rab'allah our imam still describes to us in the mosque every Friday how you Jews kill Arab babies and drink their blood."

"It's a lie. We only do that on festive occasions." She rolled away from him. "We are prisoners of the past. All this hate for things that were supposed to have happened two thousand years ago."

"But don't forget, Sarah, if it weren't for things that happened two thousand years ago, you would not be able to justify being here. Without the past you Jews would be invaders and warmongers. Like this Hitler you hate so much."

She had no answer to that. She stared at him. "Do you hate us?"

"I hate the effendis who sold you the land."

473

"That wasn't my question."

"Every good Arab should hate the Jews. The Mufti ordered it."

"That still is no answer."

He smiled but his smile was sad. He reached out and stroked her hair. "I would like to hate the Jews. It is my duty. But some of you make it very difficult for me. Now let me ask you a question. Aren't you supposed to hate the Arabs?"

"I'm not doing a very good job of it, am I?"

He kissed her gently on the forehead. "If only you had been born an Arab."

"If I had been an Arab I would be in Rab'allah, washing at the well, and you'd be here with a little Jewish girl. Wouldn't you?"

He nodded. He supposed she was perfectly right.

The Al-Rashid was a rundown hotel on the Suq Khan es Zeit. It stood near the seventh station of the Cross, where Christ was supposed to have fallen for the second time.

We all fall, Talbot thought as he hurried inside. But some fall further than others, and with less grace.

In a café on the other side of the bazaar a man in a checkered keffiyeh watched him enter. A few minutes later Levi Bar-Ayal followed, pausing only to pass the proprietor a small bundle of Palestine pounds in return for a key.

Majid was sitting on the bed, smoking a cigarette. He was wearing only a white silk shirt, bright scarlet silk underpants and paisley socks with suspenders. His jacket and trousers hung in the ancient wardrobe. A navy blue and yellow striped tie had been draped neatly over the back of the room's only chair.

Talbot looked around with distaste. The curtains were drawn but in the gloom Talbot could make out a cockroach frozen in trembling apprehension high on a wall in one corner of the room. There were dark and unidentifiable stains above the bed. The inevitable jangle of oriental music filtered in from outside.

He hated himself for coming here. He always promised himself it would never happen again.

"You look nervous, Henry," Majid said. "Like a cigarette?"

"No thanks," Talbot said. He went to the windows and adjusted the curtains, ensuring there were no gaps.

"What's the matter, old boy?"

He was sure Majid was taunting him. If only he wouldn't talk like that, like a public schoolboy during Fag Week.

Talbot took off his jacket and went to the wardrobe. Majid had appropriated the only hanger for himself. He hesitated, then draped his own jacket over a chair and sat down.

"We haven't got long," Majid said. "I have a business meeting at four o'clock."

"Can we just sit for a while?" Talbot said.

"All right." He took a packet of Four Square cigarettes from the bedside table and lit two. He kept one for himself and passed the other to Talbot. "I really think you'd better have that cigarette."

It had begun when Majid had been in his employ at the house in Talbieh. Majid had proved discreet and Talbot had allowed his lapse to develop into what could only be described as an affair. Increasingly tormented by guilt and shame, he was initially relieved when Majid had resigned his post. He had promised himself the liaison was over. Instead they continued to meet in secret, in dingy hotels. One day, he knew, they must be discovered. But he was powerless against the dictates of this dark and unexplored heart of his character.

He was not a passionate man, and it was not the physical act that requited him. It was intimacy. He could discuss with Majid private matters he dared not broach with his colleagues or, least of all, Elizabeth. With Majid he could cast off the ill-fitting role of English gentlemen and diplomat.

Only Majid, and the devil, knew him for what he was.

*   *   *

475

Talbot put his head in his hands. "I think I'm coming apart."

Majid drew on his cigarette. "What is it, Henry?"

"It's everything."

"If you want me to leave I – "

"No, it's not that . . . well, it's part of it, I suppose. It's the whole thing."

"You're not making much sense."

Talbot sat up. His eyes were tired. "Majid, tell me, as an Arab – what do you think of the Jews?" he said.

Majid shrugged his shoulders.

"The Mufti wants them all thrown out of Palestine."

"That dirty little Arab. We should have hanged him when we had the chance."

"Well, what do you think of us, the British? Do you think we have betrayed the Jews? Do you think we should have let them come to Palestine, as we said we would?"

"Of course you betrayed them. You betrayed everyone!"

Talbot noted how easily Majid could switch his allegiance from one moment to another. In one breath he allied himself with the British; in the next he damned them for their perfidy.

Majid shook his head. "Is this the reason you look like shit, Henry? You think too much."

"The colonial service has been my life. I always believed that Britain stood for something good, that we were a civilising force. But now . . . but now I don't know what to think."

"You're getting upset about a few Jews. It's not worth it."

"What is worth getting upset about, Majid? What do you care about?"

"Myself," Majid said, with alarming candour.

Talbot leaned towards him. "There's something I have never told you. When they hanged your brother I was there. I was ordered to attend the execution by the High Commissioner."

"I know."

Talbot stared at him. "You knew?"

"Wagil was always a little simple. What happened was inevitable. I cannot blame you for his stupidity."

Talbot shuddered. "You really are the most frightful little bastard, aren't you, Majid?"

"I suppose I am. Now, why don't you let me help you relax?"

The door was thrown open and a man in a checkered keffiyeh rushed in. He raised the camera and a flashbulb popped. Before Talbot could react the man turned and fled down the stairs.

Talbot sat up, trembling. "Oh my God."

Majid smiled apologetically. "I'm really very sorry, Henry."

Talbot stared at him, stricken. "What?"

"They made me do it. It was a matter of life and death. May Allah burn me on the Day of the Fire if I lie."

Talbot sounded as if he was going to choke. "You . . . you arranged . . . this?"

"I did not want to."

Majid got out of bed and leisurely began to dress. "I'm afraid someone from the Haganah wants to meet you."

"The Haganah?"

"They say if you don't help them, every urchin from Alexandria to Beirut is going to be hawking your picture in the streets as a dirty postcard. They could just be bluffing."

"You utter bastard."

"Look, I'm sorry," Majid said. "But what did you expect?"

When he left Talbot was still sitting bolt upright in the bed, staring at the door, his face the colour of ash.

77

It was Friday evening, the advent of Shabbat, the sabbath
day of the Jews. A cacophony of sound rose over the city,
as the wail of the shofar from the synagogues mingled with
the call of the muezzins and the peal of the carillons in the
church towers. Gaberdine-coated Jews hurried to prayer,
Franciscan monks in brown habits shuffled along, heads
down, in a bobbing sea of black-and-white-checkered
keffiyehs.

The café smelled of grease and coffee and sweat.

She saw him making his way up the hill from Damascus
Gate, a tall figure in a white suit and dark tie, moving with
an awkward, diffident grace. He seemed discomfited by
the jostling of the crowds, as if he expected the mass
should part and move around him. He reached the door
of the coffee house and looked around, uncertain.

Sarah picked up a packet of Four Square cigarettes
and stood them on end on the table in front of her, the
prearranged signal. He blinked in surprise. No doubt he
was not expecting a woman.

He made his way over to the table and sat down.
"Haganah?" he said. He seemed unable to look her in
the eye.

"Yes. You're Henry Talbot."

"I am."

The serving boy put a small cracked cup in front of
Talbot, and filled it with steaming black coffee from a
brass finjan. He moved away again.

"This is without doubt the most despicable behaviour I
have ever heard of," Talbot murmured.

"Is it, Mr Talbot?"

"I am not proud of what I am. But even I place myself above the level of blackmailers."

Sarah controlled herself only with difficulty. She leaned across the table so that their heads were almost touching. "You pompous English bastard. You people sit in your clubs with your Arab flunkeys serving you gin and tonics and when the real world intrudes you start to rail about civilised behaviour! I will tell you what is despicable, Mr Henry Talbot. What is despicable is the world letting Hitler kill millions of Jews in gas ovens and then leaving them to rot in camps all over Europe. *That* is despicable."

"The papers have exaggerated what happened out of all – "

"You think it's just a few little kikes acting up. Is that it? It must be a bore for you. But we're fighting for our lives and our survival and desperate people do desperate things."

"What if I told you to go to hell?"

Sarah leaned back in her chair and sipped her coffee. She smiled. "But you won't, will you?"

"What are you going to do?"

Sarah reached into the breast pocket of her khaki shirt and produced a small envelope. She pushed it across the table to Talbot. He opened it. Inside was a postcard. The black and white photograph was grainy and poorly defined but his own features were clearly recognisable. The caption underneath read: Strange Bedfellows. The British in bed with the Arabs in Palestine.

"Unless you agree to help us, we're going to send a copy to the High Commissioner, and then distribute the rest on the streets of Jerusalem. Your career and your marriage will be finished. If you return to England you will live the rest of your life in disgrace and ridicule. That's what we're going to do."

The card trembled in Talbot's fingers. Flecks of saliva pooled in the corner of his mouth. "*Majid, you little shit!*" he shouted suddenly. All conversation in the coffee house stopped, and the other customers – Arabs, a few Jews – turned and stared at him.

Talbot tore the card into pieces. "Jesus Christ!"

"I'm sorry, Henry," Sarah said, more gently. "Personally, I think what people do in private is their own affair. I don't like doing this. But, be assured, we'll use every weapon at our disposal."

Talbot screwed the torn pieces of cardboard in his fingers into a tiny ball and threw them on to the table in disgust. He put his head in his hands and said nothing. Sarah waited, concerned. She had not expected Talbot to make a scene here in the coffee house. He must surely be aware that just attending such a meeting placed his career in jeopardy. How far could they trust him to keep his nerve?

And yet she also felt sorry for him. What she had said to him was true; she was not proud of herself for this. But what choice did they have? Without Palestine, they had nothing. If they did not save themselves, no one else would. Hitler had demonstrated that.

Talbot raised his head, wiping tears from his face. His voice was hoarse. "What do you want me to do?"

"You're on the High Commissioner's staff?"

"Yes."

"Then I should think our demands are obvious."

He nodded. "Not enough that nature makes me a queer. You want me to be a traitor as well."

"We are all traitors, Henry. Some betray their country, the rest of us betray our principles."

He sneered. "A pretty little speech. Who are you trying to convince? Me . . . or you?"

Sarah was angry with herself for revealing a weakness. She would not make the same mistake again. She fixed him with her eyes. "Just do it, Henry. Meet me here again next Friday. We want to know everything the British are thinking, everything they're planning. If we don't get tangible results we'll destroy you. Is that clear?"

He rose to leave. "You know, you ought to recruit my

wife. She would enjoy your job. In fact, I think she'd be rather good at it."

He went out and was soon lost among the surging Friday evening crowd around the Gate.

Katamon

Katy Antonius was the widow of the most famous Arab historian and writer of his century, while she herself was the most celebrated socialite and hostess of Arab Jerusalem. Guests to her Friday night soirées included the most prominent members of the British and Arab communities. Henry Talbot accepted a gin and water from the white-jacketed Arab waiter and joined a group that included the Anglican Bishop of Jerusalem, a British major and the High Commissioner's Private Secretary. They were discussing a report that the Haganah had blown up a bridge in Galilee.

Talbot found it hard to concentrate on the conversation. His mind kept replaying his conversation earlier that evening with the Shai agent.

We want to know everything the British are thinking, everything they're planning. If we don't get tangible results we'll destroy you. Is that clear?

His attention wandered. Polished parquet floors, evening gowns, the clink of ice, dinner suits, the sparkle of a bracelet, soft ripples of laughter. And over there on the balcony was Elizabeth, sleek and svelte in a black cocktail gown, her father's emeralds glittering at her throat, offering her snow white neck as she laughed to some new predator. Who was it now? Ah, of course, Chisholm, erect and martial in his red-braided khaki uniform and Sam Browne.

"I think it's about time we imposed martial law. What do you think, Henry?"

The Private Secretary was addressing him. Talbot turned

back to the group with practised ease. "I should say it's about time we showed them what we're made of," he said. In his experience, that opinion covered lapses in most conversations. "Now if you'll just excuse me, I must have a quick word with Elizabeth."

It was pleasantly cool on the balcony. A night breeze stirred the trees and carried with it the scent of pine and rosemary. In the Old City a bell tolled dolorously in the carillon of the Armenian convent.

Elizabeth and Chisholm were locked in whispered conversation, the hands that clutched their drinks almost touching. Talbot coughed to signal his presence and Elizabeth looked up in feigned surprise.

"Ah, Henry. Just in time. Major Chisholm and I were just discussing the Jewish problem."

"Have you found a solution?"

"Our feeling is there should be a little more intercourse between the two sides. Don't you agree?"

Chisholm was grinning wolfishly. How wonderful if he fell off the balcony right now, Talbot thought. "The most important thing is that people don't get hurt."

"You're too soft, Henry." She grinned wickedly. "That's always been your trouble."

"I just think negotiation is better than confrontation."

"Well I'm for anything that brings people closer together," Elizabeth said. And she looked at Chisholm.

The little tramp.

"Are we still talking about the same thing, Lizzie?" he said, using the dimunitive he knew she detested.

Chisholm deflected the conversation back to his favourite topic. "I think these kikes have been allowed to go too far. If I was in charge of the army I'd soon have the situation under control. Hitler had the right idea about some things, in my opinion."

Talbot could hardly believe his ears. "Are you serious?"

"Like your wife says, Talbot. You're too soft."

"Almost flaccid, in fact," Elizabeth said.

"Looks like it's time to eat," Chisholm said. "If you'll

excuse me." He walked past Talbot, back to the dining-room.

Talbot looked at his wife. On heat, he thought. I can smell her. "Not quite your type, is he?"

"I don't know. I quite fancy a bit of rough, occasionally."

"Do you have to flaunt it so openly?"

"What's the point of pretending any more?" She put her glass on the balustrade and took his arm. "I shan't embarrass you, old thing. I promise not to fuck him until after dinner. Shall we eat?"

They started with Arab mezze; tiny dishes of hummus, brain salad, eggplant, and stuffed vine leaves. Chisholm dominated the conversation, forcefully expressing the view that the Jews should be brought to order by the use of greater force. Talbot saw the Anglican bishop flush with embarrassment while his own Private Secretary concentrated on his food, disconcerted by such indiscretion.

Talbot was unable to adopt the same diplomatic silence. "But surely," he said to Chisholm, "we must accept part of the blame."

Chisholm's face was a portrait of derision. "The only mistake we've made is letting our bayonets get blunt."

"You sound like Himmler."

"What's your solution? Let them walk all over us?"

"When these troubles first began in 1936, the Jews exercised commendable restraint. At the same time the Mufti of Jerusalem exhorted the Arab population to even greater feats of violence. As a result he got his way. I am afraid both sides learned a very grave lesson from us: that violence would be rewarded."

"Even more reason to show them that's not the case."

"I believe it is incumbent on us to try and find a just and equitable solution. You won't find one on the end of a bayonet."

"But Henry," another voice said, and to Talbot's shock he realised it was his own wife, "surely we cannot be seen to tolerate these Haganah people. I'm only a woman, of course, but it seems to me they are making us look quite ridiculous."

Several of the army officers flushed and found something of great interest on their plates. This unfettered criticism of their best efforts had all but rattled the windows.

Chisholm grinned at Talbot in triumph. "Your wife seems to have hit the nail on the head, Henry. After all, we let them come here in the first place, and now they've turned on us. What's the old saying about biting the hand that feeds you?"

Talbot decided it was pointless to argue further. He had already said too much. Besides, it was not the Jewish problem that weighed in his belly now like lead. It was his personal failure. A traitor and a cuckold, he thought. The absurdity of it all! The focus of my torment is two things I no longer love – my wife and my country. Both have proved to me they are harlots yet still I cling to them. Always I was taught that the essence of a man was to be British, and to be respectable. I have tried to be both these things but I am ruled by fools and married to a tramp.

What am I going to do?

78

The Hill of Evil Counsel

First Secretary Reginald Chandler waved Talbot to a seat.
"Come in, Henry. Sit down, sit down. Take the weight
off your feet." He fussed with the arrangement of papers
on his desk, then sat back, entwining his fingers over his
ample paunch. Sunlight from the window at his back shone
on the grease that had been liberally applied to his thick
grey hair.

Chandler was one of the old school; he had received his
first overseas posting when Queen Victoria was still on the
throne. Talbot sometimes imagined there was dust in the
creases of his face. He was due to retire in just four more
months and some of Talbot's colleagues joked that he was
going to be crated up and shipped back as an exhibit for
the British Museum. Next to the Egyptian mummy.

"Getting warmer, I do believe," Chandler said.

His first remarks were always about the weather. "Yes,
sir. Summer's on its way."

"Indeed. Well, Henry, what can I do for you?"

"I wanted your advice, sir. Something has come to my
attention, and I thought you should know about it."

"Quite right."

"As you know, my wife Elizabeth plays bridge with
some of the women from Katy Antonius's set. It seems
one of the women let slip that her husband had met a
former SS officer, here in Jerusalem."

Chandler's air of bluff good humour evaporated. "I
see."

"I don't know how much credence to give such a rumour, but I thought I should report this immediately so we can check its veracity. It could be a mistake of course, but – "

"Have you told anyone else about this?"

"No, sir. Of course not."

"Good. That's the way we'll leave it then."

"Sir?"

"Look, Henry, I don't like this any more than you, but I'm afraid there's nothing we can do."

"I don't understand."

"Don't be an ass. You understand perfectly well. We can't afford to upset the Arabs."

"You mean it's true? We're harbouring former SS men?"

"Harbouring isn't exactly the word I would have chosen."

"Which word would you choose, sir?"

Chandler's tone became sharper. "As I said, Henry, there's nothing we can do."

"This man could be a mass murderer!"

"We have to look at the big picture. If we want to retain our influence in this region – and if we don't, then we leave it open to the Russians or, God help us all, the Americans – then we have to examine carefully every slice of bread and see which side the butter's on. You know that."

"It's intolerable!"

Chandler fidgeted with his tie. "For your information, there's scores of SS and Gestapo officers in Palestine, maybe hundreds. They're here at the invitation of the Arabs but in the present climate, we cannot do one damned thing about it."

Talbot said nothing. He just stared at him.

"Don't look at me like that, Henry. It's not my fault. Nor yours. We're here to carry out government policy."

"Is this official government policy, sir?"

"Of course it isn't. It's just a fact of life. Now is there anything else?"

"No, sir. Thank you for your advice."

486

Talbot got up and went out. He felt suddenly ill. He heard the sound of children's voices in Guildford Grammar School: *Till we have built Jerusalem, in England's green and pleasant land* . . .

When had it happened? When had his country turned her back on Calvary?

Well, if the High Commissioner and his Private Secretary weren't interested in former SS officers, he knew someone who was.

Rehavia

The block of flats was within easy walking distance of the Jewish Agency where he worked but Asher found that by the time he got there his leg ached so badly it was an effort to stand. He gritted his teeth and limped heavily up the stairwell to the sixth floor.

Anonymous smells of baked bread filtered on to the landing and behind one of the doors he heard a baby crying. Asher found room 613 and knocked.

The door edged open a fraction and a small, dark-haired woman peered out at him. "What do you want?"

"Pray for the peace of Jerusalem," Asher said, giving the current Palmach password.

The woman opened the door and Asher went inside. The curtains inside the flat were drawn and the air was stale. The remains of a meal were still scattered on the kitchen table. There were five other occupants in the flat, four young men, and a girl. A Sten gun lay on the floor on a white sheet, dismantled, and two of the men were carefully cleaning and oiling the mechanism.

One of them recognised him straight away. "Asher!"

"Hello, Moshe. How's things?"

Moshe embraced him. "This is Asher Ben-Zion," Moshe said to the others. "He was in command of my battalion when we were up in Haifa. He led the raid on Atlit." The others seemed to relax. The girl who had answered the door offered him a cigarette.

Moshe gave him a light. "How's the leg, Ash?"

"It's coming along."

"What are you doing these days? I heard you went back to the kibbutz."

"You won't get rid of me so easy. I'm working for the Shai until I can get another combat posting."

"So what brings you here?"

"I'm looking for Rosenberg. Is he here?"

The door to one of the bedrooms opened and Netanel came out. His hair and his clothes were mussed from sleep. He stretched, grinning. "Ash! What are you doing in Jerusalem?"

"I've got some good news for you, Netanel. How would you like to do a little job for the Shai?"

There were only two bedrooms, with a single metal-frame bed in each room, and mattresses thrown on the floor. Personal possessions were contained in the rucksacks that were strewn around the floors. They all had to be ready to leave at ten minutes' notice.

"See how we live in Jerusalem?" Netanel grinned. "Sometimes I think Auschwitz was better."

"If you let your people clean Sten guns in the living-room when there's strangers at the front door, you might soon find yourself behind the wire again."

"You know what sabras are like. You can't tell them anything."

"You forget I *am* a sabra."

Netanel grinned. "No, Ash, I didn't forget."

Asher eased himself on to the edge of the bed, wincing at the pain in his thigh. He massaged the muscle. The climb up the six flights of steps had brought on another cramp.

"How is it?" Netanel asked.

"It aches all the time."

"Some wounds never heal. I know what it's like. I still get headaches from where the Germans beat me once."

He took a packet of cigarettes from the breast pocket of his shirt and flipped it open with his thumbnail. He put one in his mouth and lit it with the glowing tip of Asher's cigarette.

"Been busy?" Asher asked him.

"The Arabs are stepping up their attacks around the Old City. One of my boys was wounded last week in an attack on an Egged bus outside Zion Gate. The week before I lost two more when the British found them with revolvers in their pockets. Enough of my own problems. Tell me about you. What are you doing in Jerusalem?"

"I'm working with the Shai – intelligence. That's why I'm here. Something has come up I thought you might be interested in."

"Not me, Asher. Greatcoats and fedoras don't suit me."

"We don't want you as a spy. We need volunteers for a little job we want done. It's dangerous, of course."

Netanel shrugged. "Tell me what it is first."

"It's Auschwitz, Netya."

Netanel's face lost all expression. "One of them is here in Jerusalem?"

"My wife works for the Shai also. She has a contact inside the British government. He has told her there's a German officer living right here in Jerusalem, in the German colony. He was an SS major at Auschwitz."

"The British are sheltering him?"

"Not exactly. But they're not going to do anything about him, either. So that means we have to. Will you help us?"

"You already know the answer to that." He drew on his cigarette. "What's his name, Ash? Perhaps I know him."

"It's Emmerich. Former SS Reichsmajor Rolf Emmerich."

79

Wilhelmina

There were two Arab policemen guarding the gate. Captain Wilbur Spencer-White, and his driver, Corporal George Taylor, handed their security passes to the Arab sergeant. Taylor joked with him while the officer sat in cold and imperious silence.

"Good day for the race," Taylor said.

The sergeant examined the passes carefully. "What race?"

"The human race."

The sergeant did not laugh. The passes appeared to be in order, but he enjoyed for once being in a position of authority over the God-cursed British. "What is your business here?"

"That is our concern," the officer said. "Our papers are in order. Please let us pass, there's a good chap." He tapped his swagger stick impatiently on the dashboard of the jeep.

The sergeant fumed. Quickly come the dawn when they ran these arrogant sons of whores out of Palestine! He handed the passes back to the British corporal. He gave a lazy salute and turned his back.

"A good day for the race?" Netanel said when they were safely past the guards.

"I actually heard a British corporal say that once," Asher said. "It didn't raise a laugh then either. But it serves its purpose. If someone thinks you're a fool, they become less suspicious of you."

The jeep stopped in the gravel forecourt. Netanel jumped out.

"Good luck," Asher whispered.

"I've prayed for this moment ever since I got out of Auschwitz. I don't need luck. I just don't want it to be over too soon."

"Netya, remember! One bullet is all we have time for!"

"I'll remember." Netanel went to the front door, ramrod straight in his khaki uniform and peaked cap. He adjusted the holster of the Webley Special and rapped on the door with his swagger cane.

The house was classically Arab in style and architecture, built of weathered pink Jerusalem stone with graceful arches and high, vaulted ceilings beyond a central court-yard brilliant with purple flowering bougainvillaea. Arab copper and brass plates decorated the walls and the floors were tiled in bold black and white marble.

"Major Emmerich does not receive many visitors any more," the housekeeper said. Her name was Ilse. She was German also, she informed him, though naturally she had always been totally opposed to the Nazis. "Most good German people did not like Hitler or the things he did. But what could we do? What did you say your name was again?"

"Spencer-White, Captain Spencer-White," Netanel said.

"What do you want to see him about?"

"Official business," Netanel said, putting in his tone the right amount of patronising civility.

"Well, I don't know if he will be able to help you much," Ilse said, and for a moment he detected a curious undertone to her voice and he thought she was laughing at him.

No. He must be mistaken.

Just hurry up and take me to him, he thought. I want to see his face when I hold the gun to his head. I want to remind him about Amos Mandelbaum. I want him to stare into the face of death as Mandelbaum did, and I want him

491

to know who his avenger is. I want the absolution of his terror and his blood.

"Of course Major Emmerich didn't like Hitler either," Ilse prattled on. "He was just a soldier doing his duty." They had reached the sitting-room, a bright room with dusty parquet floors, Persian prints and a Bedouin hunting knife hanging on the wall.

There was a figure in a cane chair facing away from him, towards the garden. Netanel clenched his fists to his sides, trying to keep himself in check. I can't believe it, he thought. I can't believe fate has brought you here!

"You have a visitor, Major," Ilse said.

Netanel looked down at the man in the cane chair.

It wasn't Emmerich.

The body that was there may have once belonged to him. The short blond hair and glacial blue eyes were the same, the set of the features was familiar. But it was like looking at a wax figure that had been left near a hot fire; while one half of his face remained as coldly beautiful as a Teutonic god, the other half appeared to have melted away. The body under the blanket was like a skeleton; the muscles on the left side of his face had wasted away, exposing the pink lower lid of his eye; the eyes were fixed and staring.

This could not be SS Reichsmajor Emmerich.

"You have a visitor!" Ilse shouted in his right ear. "It's a Colonel Spencer-Weiss from the British army. *Verstehen Sie?*"

Emmerich mumbled something incomprehensible in German.

"I don't know if you'll get anywhere today, Captain," Ilse said. "He has his good days and his bad days. Anyway, I'll leave you with him. You give me a call if you want me. I'll be in the kitchen."

"Emmerich?" Netanel said. "Emmerich, do you know who I am?"

There was no response. Saliva leaked from his jaw and formed a dark stain on his dressing-gown. He sat awkwardly in the chair, slumped on to his left side.

492

"Don't you remember me? Netanel Rosenberg!"

He thought he saw a muscle work in Rolf's face. He must understand. He *must*! He took the revolver from his holster and removed the safety. He placed the muzzle between Rolf's eyes.

"Netanel Rosenberg. You remember me, Rolf. At Auschwitz."

The good right eye was utterly vacant.

Dear God, don't do this to me, Netanel thought. He must remember! Let me see one spark of Rolf Emmerich and then I can kill him. Amos will be avenged and I'll be free of this endless torment!

He stared into Rolf's good eye, deep into the black heart of it, but all he saw was a dark reflection of himself.

"Too late," Amos Mandelbaum whispered in his ear.

"Too late," Netanel said aloud.

Rolf mumbled something in German. It sounded like "Ilse". Netanel was aware of a rank odour in his nostrils. Former SS Major Rolf Emmerich had fouled himself.

"Damn you," Netanel whispered. There was no retribution to be had. Not here. Whatever was left of Rolf Emmerich had rotted away inside the skeleton on the chair.

He holstered the revolver and walked out. Ilse came out of the kitchen wiping her hands on her apron. "Going already, Herr Captain?"

Netanel nodded. "How long has he been like that?"

"He was wounded in the head when a Russian Yak fighter strafed the convoy he was travelling in. He got a fever in the hospital afterwards and that's when he got to be like he is. Some days he manages a few words. Did you finish your official business?"

"Yes, thank you," Netanel said.

Ilse proffered her hand and Netanel shook it. Too late he realised what she had done. The sleeve of his uniform rode up his arm and Ilse was staring at the tattooed number on his arm. "You're not a British captain at all," she said, and she laughed at him, her voice thick with loathing. "You're just a dirty Jew!"

493

Netanel snatched his hand away. "Get out of my way," he said.

"Hitler was right about you people. We were doing the world a favour. Perhaps the Arabs will finish the job."

Netanel scrambled for the Webley at his belt. He placed the barrel against her head.

"Go on. Do it," the old woman taunted him.

Netanel lowered the revolver and she laughed at him. He brought it up suddenly, smashing it against the side of her temple, and sent her sprawling across the marble. He stepped over her unconscious body and walked out of the house.

Part Fourteen

PALESTINE, 1946

80

A hot morning, a white sun leaching the pink from the stone walls of the Old City and the blue from the sky. Henry Talbot squinted against the glare while his chauffeur tried to negotiate the traffic below the Jaffa Gate. He looked at his watch. He had an appointment inside the British Security Zone in the western city at four o'clock. At this rate he was going to be late.

"Hurry it up, Moussa," he said, though it was clear there was little Moussa could do except punch the horn even more frequently.

Ahead of them the blunted spear of David's Tower rose into the sky from the citadel, the ancient symbol rising from the choking fumes of traffic and the bustle of the twentieth century. Talbot felt a longing for an ancient, less hurried, time.

Suddenly the Rover came to a complete stop. The braying of horns rose to a crescendo, almost drowning out the faint but unmistakable crack of distant gunfire.

Talbot leaned foreward. "Moussa, what's going on?"

An ancient lorry was stalled in front of them blocking their view of the road.

Moussa shrugged his shoulders. "I don't know, Talbot effendi." He tried to steer around the lorry but it was impossible. Traffic was streaming away from the Gate, completely blocking the road. A donkey cart tried to manoeuvre around a taxi and crashed into a fruit stall, spilling grapes and figs all over the road. An old Arab ran past pushing a bicycle, shouting something about the Jews.

"Wait here," Talbot said to Moussa, though the instruction

was unnecessary. Moussa could not move the car in any direction now.

Talbot ran ahead. A little Jew in a dark suit and a homburg crashed into him and sent him reeling back against the side of a lorry. More people rushed past, Arabs, Jews, women carrying screaming children, all shouting hysterically. An Arab taxi, horn blaring, tried to bulldoze a way through the mob. An Arab woman in a black abbayah fell screaming under its wheels.

What in heaven's name was happening?

A silver Egged bus, the number 2 service from New Jerusalem to the Old City, was stalled in the centre of the square, opposite the tall pillars of Jaffa Gate. A mob of Arabs blocked its path, some of them armed with rifles. All the bus windows had been smashed and blood was seeping under the door on the driver's side to form a widening pool on the road.

"Mother of God," Talbot whispered under his breath.

A British jeep and armoured car were parked on the other side of the square, on Bethlehem Road. Talbot could see the commanding officer leaning on the windshield of the jeep, watching.

Why doesn't he stop this? Talbot thought.

There was a burst of gunfire from the bus. Perhaps some Haganah women had smuggled pistols on board. Whatever weapons they had, it would almost certainly not be enough to keep the Arabs back for long.

He ran across the square towards the British patrol. As he came closer he realised he knew the red-bereted officer in the jeep.

Chisholm.

"I'd get down if I were you, old son," Chisholm shouted at him. "This isn't the place for pen-pushers."

"Chisholm! For Christ's sake, do something!"

Chisholm indicated his driver. "Why don't you squat down on the tailboard on the other side of Corporal Waterson here. We don't want a stray bullet robbing the administration of one of its best clerks."

"Stop this! There's going to be a massacre!"

"Just a few Jews."

"There'll be women and children on that bus!"

"Jewish women and children. No British nationals." Talbot slipped off his leather gloves and eased himself down into the passenger seat. "Get out of the way, you're spoiling my view."

"I'm ordering you to stop this!"

"You can't. You don't have the authority."

Talbot turned round. The Arabs, emboldened by the lack of response from the British patrol, were edging closer to the bus, surrounding it. Two figures, Hassids in black gaberdine coats and brimmed hats, leaped from the bus door and tried to escape. They got just five paces when they were hit by a volley of gunshots and fell.

"Hear the news this morning?" Chisholm said.

"Stop this for God's sake!"

"The Jews attacked one of our patrols in the Old City. Killed two of our boys, wounded three others. One of them isn't ever going to walk again. I knew him, you know. He was in Normandy with me."

"That's got nothing to do with this!"

An Arab, a rifle clutched in his left hand, ran towards the door of the bus. There was the crack of a pistol shot and he fell backwards, arms spreadeagled. For a moment his comrades held back.

"It's time someone taught these Jews a lesson. They can't kill our soldiers and then expect us to protect them from the Arabs."

A blue Fiat, its horn blaring, was nudging its way through the snarl of traffic on Jaffa Road. A Haganah flag trailed from the back window. Chisholm shook his driver's arm, pointing. "Quick!"

The jeep raced across the square to intercept.

A woman, a baby clutched in her arms, ran out of the bus and headed for the Jewish Commercial Centre. Talbot thought she was going to make it. Suddenly there was a single gunshot

499

and she fell. A silence fell over the square. Then the baby started to cry.

The mother did not move.

There were three Haganah in the Fiat, and now they lay face down on the cobbles, their hands behind their heads. Their weapons – a Beretta pistol, a Sten gun and two hand-grenades – lay on the ground behind them. Two soldiers stood over them, their Brens cocked.

"Chisholm, what the hell are you doing?"

"I am doing my duty, old son. These men have been caught in the possession of illegal firearms. They are obviously terrorists."

Talbot turned back to the square. The mob had almost surrounded the bus. There was no shooting now. It was deadly quiet except for the wailing of the baby.

"For the love of God, those people are helpless."

"Unless there's British nationals involved, I'm not obliged to do anything."

Talbot made up his mind. Someone had to do something.

He started to run towards the bus. "Get back!" he shouted at the mob in Arabic. "I am ordering you to get back!"

Their faces were ugly with hatred and bloodlust. He ran through the midst of them and positioned himself across the doorway of the bus, his arms outstretched. "Go home! All of you! I am the King of England and I am ordering you to go home now!"

One of the Arabs raised his rifle, hesitated. Go ahead and shoot me, you bastard, Talbot thought. They'll crucify Chisholm then.

But one of the man's compatriots snatched the gun away. Killing Jews was one thing, killing Britishers was another, even if he was lying about being the King of England.

Suddenly the armoured car rumbled across the square, scattering the mob. Chisholm drove behind in his jeep, his driver hammering on the horn with his fist. Talbot heard someone whisper a prayer of thanks inside the bus. The

Arab gunmen melted away into the snarl of traffic now choking both sides of Jaffa Road.

The jeep rolled to a halt in front of Talbot and Chisholm stood up, leaning on the windshield. "I don't like you, Talbot," he said.

Talbot felt faint. He thought he was going to be sick. "The feeling's reciprocated."

"Whatever that means."

"I shall be making a full report about this."

"Good for you."

Talbot staggered away. Chisholm got out of the jeep and ordered the survivors off the bus. His soldiers escorted them away through the crowds at gunpoint. Talbot saw Chisholm give the Nazi salute to a young girl, then go to the bus driver's door, yank it open, and remove the body from behind the wheel with his boot.

The baby had stopped crying. When Talbot got there it was already dead.

Talbieh

When Henry Talbot arrived home James was sitting in the courtyard with Elizabeth drinking lemon, lime and bitters. Elizabeth looked serene and cool in a long white dress, her hair freshly crimped, and her eyes, Talbot thought, utterly vacant.

James jumped up, apparently relieved to see him. His cheeks were flushed, Talbot noticed. Probably from the effort of talking to her. I wonder what topic of conversation she found to entertain my intense young brother? Contract bridge? Tennis? Male impotence?

"Good Lord, Henry. Are you all right?"

"Sorry I'm late."

"You're as white as a sheet."

"I've just had a rather trying day, that's all."

Elizabeth, he noticed, was regarding him with something less than concern. "Henry, what have you got on the front of your suit?"

"It's blood, darling."

"Anyone I know?"

"I shouldn't think so."

"Jolly good."

Oh, you sarcastic little bitch. "There was some trouble out by Jaffa Gate this afternoon."

"Yes, I heard. Did you get mixed up in it?"

"Yes, I did, actually."

Moussa brought Talbot a Scotch and water. Talbot downed it and handed the glass back. "Bring me another, will you?"

Moussa raised an eyebrow and hurried away.

"Be careful," Elizabeth said, "they say it puts hairs on your chest."

"You should stop drinking it then."

"We're in one of those moods are we?" Elizabeth said. She finished her bitters and stood up. "I'll leave you two to your boy talk, shall I? I'll just go and pluck my chest, Henry."

She went inside, her high heels clattering on the flagstones. There was a long silence. James cleared his throat. "Everything all right between the two of you?"

"Yes, of course."

"I don't want to intrude on anything . . ." He started to get up.

"Oh, for God's sake, we invited you to dinner, you're going to stay and eat it if I have to force-feed you, is that clear?"

James flushed to the roots of his hair. He picked up his drink and lapsed into silence.

"I'm sorry," Talbot said finally. "I'm a bit on edge."

"I can't say I didn't notice." Elizabeth was playing the piano in the drawing-room. The haunting melody of "Für Elise" reached them through the double doors. "This thing at Jaffa Gate?"

"Did you hear what happened?"

"Just that the Arabs attacked an Egged bus and one of our patrols chased them off."

Talbot laughed, but there was no humour in it. "Chased

502

them off! I suppose that's true. They did chase them, eventually. That bastard Chisholm was in command. He wasn't going to do anything at first. He was prepared to let the Arabs murder them."

"Come on, Henry – "

"I saw at least five Jews murdered, Jimmy, including a mother and her baby! He wasn't going to do a damned thing!"

Moussa brought another whisky and Talbot accepted it gratefully. It was almost dusk. The wind rose, keen and fresh, and rustled the leaves of the fig tree over their heads.

"I don't know if it's occurred to you, Jimmy, but our job here is quite simple. We have to hold the Jew's hands behind his back while the other fellow hits him."

James finished his drink. "I can almost understand how the Jerries felt now," he said. "Even if they didn't believe in what they were fighting for, what else could they do? When I was in Europe I was ready to make the sacrifice. Life for king and country, and all that. But if I die in this one I'm going to be awfully pissed off."

81

Row upon row of market stalls, heaped high with the tawny glow of plums and peaches. The square resounded to the shouts of hawkers and the noisy harangue of bartering, but inside the café the sounds of the market were barely audible over the deafening noise of the radio.

Sarah sat in a corner of the room with Talbot. The way they sat, their conversation conducted in whispers, might have seemed to an outsider like a lovers' tryst, except that the man seemed perhaps a little too old and a little too unremarkable for such an exceptionally pretty girl. A casual observer might have guessed also that the woman, in her khaki shirt and blue denim shorts, was not dressed for romance. And there was her manner; as she leaned towards the man her face was strained and angry.

"We know the British are planning something. We are relying on you to tell us what it is."

Talbot raised an eyebrow. "Oh? What is it you know?"

"We know, Henry, that British troops are erecting another camp near Raffa, and that the government printing press has ordered another forty-five thousand blank detention orders."

"Perhaps it's a routine stationery request."

"We also know the administration has nine thousand forms already in stock. What does that tell you, Henry?"

"It tells me you've thoroughly compromised our administration."

"It tells us that Cunningham has plans to make large-scale arrests in the very near future. We need to know who, when and how."

"I don't think I can help you with that."

Sarah smiled, but without warmth. "We have been reviewing the help you have given us so far. It doesn't amount to much."

"I gave you Emmerich."

Sarah shrugged.

"What are you trying to say?" Talbot asked.

"Unless you provide us with hard information in the next seven days Sir Alan Cunningham will receive a postcard through the mail, with views of Jerusalem he has not seen before."

Talbot drummed on the edge of the table with his fingertips. "Do you enjoy your job?"

"No, I don't, Henry. And just for the record, it's not a job. They could never pay me enough to do this sort of thing."

Talbot stared at his hands and said nothing.

"I heard an interesting story about you the other day."

"Oh?"

"One of my colleagues witnessed the attack on the bus at Jaffa Gate. He said you prevented a massacre."

"I'm sure he overstates his case."

"Does he?"

"You think I have some secret sympathy with your cause? Don't be misled, Miss Haganah. It was merely an act of common humanity."

Sarah leaned forward. "What is the difference between saving a busload of Jews, and saving six hundred thousand?"

"About thirty years in prison."

"Look, Henry, if we release this picture, your career's finished anyway. Help us. If Bevin moves against the Haganah, the Jews in Palestine will be defenceless. Like the people on that bus."

"Are you appealing to my humanity or my self-interest?"

"Both."

He looked at his watch. "I have to go."

"Seven days."

"Yes, yes, I understand."

"We can't meet here again. Next time I'll wait for you in Zion Square. I'll go in to a cinema. You follow me in."

"A good picture, I hope. I'll bring the chocolates." He went out into the hot sun, his head hanging, as if the weight of it was too great for his shoulders.

Yemin Moshe

Yemin Moshe was the first Jewish settlement ever built outside the walls of the Old City. It had been financed by the British philanthropist, Sir Moses Montefiore. Marie lived there in a small one-bedroom flat above a grocery store. She had found a job as a clerk at the Histadruth, the Federation of Jewish Labour. They taught her to use a typewriter and with her intelligence and willingness to learn she had quickly been promoted to a position as a stenographer and personal secretary to a member of the central committee.

505

She lived quietly. Each day she left for work at eight in the morning and came home at six o'clock at night, except on Shabbat. In the evenings she made a meal and listened to the radio, then read for a while before going to sleep. She seldom went out. When she first started work at Histadruth she had received countless offers from the men there to go out to dinner, but she had made it clear that she was engaged to be married, and after a while the offers stopped.

She surrendered to the routine of her new life like an exhausted swimmer hauling herself on to a raft. It was safe; she had enough to eat; and she had a warm bed. After Oswiecim and the DP camps of Europe it was the luxury of a queen.

The grocery shop downstairs was owned by a man named Fromberg, and old Berliner Jew who had fled Germany in 1934. Apart from the few casual friendships she had formed at the Histadruth, he was the only other person she spoke to regularly. He had a great bald dome of a head that reminded her of a boiled egg, and a weeping egg-yellow moustache. He was cheerful and kind, and spoke German with her, rather than the Hebrew she was still trying to master.

At first he seemed bemused by the fact that she was not Jewish, but he had quickly adopted her as one of his daughters – he already had six of his own living in the three rooms behind the shop – and she was constantly refusing offers of dinner.

"Fräulein Helder!" he shouted, as she reached the bottom stair of her flat. "Did you have a good day at work today?"

"Yes, thank you, Herr Fromberg." Every day was much like another, of course. But even the worst of days was a day spent in Paradise when she compared it to Oswiecim.

"Hot weather we are having."

"I don't mind it." She went into the shop. It was crowded and dusty and smelled of dried meats and musty cheeses.

"You would like to join us for dinner tonight? My wife

is making schnitzels. I'll tell her to set an extra plate, all right?"

"It is very kind of you. But not tonight, Herr Fromberg."

"Ach, but you never eat! Look at you! If you stand sideways, there is not even a shadow! You need some of my wife's cooking."

"Perhaps another night. I am very tired."

"No wonder it is you are tired. There is nothing of you! When the hamsiin comes, it will blow you away!"

"I will wear heavy shoes."

"My wife is always saying to me: Why don't you get that skinny girl upstairs to come down for dinner? How will she ever get herself a husband looking like a breadstick?"

"I already have a man who wants to marry me, Herr Fromberg."

He frowned, "Ja, ja, well, little Fräulein Breadstick, is there something I can get for you?"

"Perhaps two of your wonderful eggs for my tea." Fromberg's eggs were very popular; he bought them from the Arabs, Arab eggs were free range, but chickens on the kibbutzim were fed special diets and there was hardly any colour or flavour in the yolks.

Fromberg fussed under the counter for the eggs. "Still no luck at the Jewish Agency then?"

"No, not yet. Perhaps soon."

Fromberg became suddenly gloomy, as he always did when discussing Marie's search for her fiancé. The fact of having an unmarried and attractive woman in the flat above him seemed to fret him. It was as if he owned an unmatched shoe.

"The Jewish Agency is inundated with people looking for lost family and friends," Marie said. "They will find him eventually."

Fromberg wrapped her eggs in newspaper and shouted to her as she went up the stairs that his wife would cook an extra schnitzel anyway, in case she changed her mind. Then he sat down to brood. It was not right that such a pretty girl should live alone like that, not going out, not enjoying herself . . . not eating. Sometimes he wondered

507

if this fiancé of hers even existed. He had seen the death camp tattoo on her arm and he wondered if there was not more troubling little Marie Helder than a poor appetite.

Talbieh

There were two empty glasses on the table in the court-yard, and cigarette stubs in the ashtray but only two were smeared with lipstick. Abdollah and Hasna were conspicuous by their absence. Talbot called them in the kitchen and their private quarters but they were nowhere to be found. He felt the cold gnawing of fear as he realised he was about to be confronted with the inevitable.

It was cool inside the house, a fan revolving in syncopatic rhythm, one broken blade breaking the cadence. His footsteps echoed on the parquet flooring. He went up the stairs to the bedroom and threw open the door.

Elizabeth was not quite naked; she still had on most of her jewellery. She was sprawled over the edge of the bed, her feet on the floor, a pillow under her buttocks. Chisholm was not quite naked either; he had not removed his boots. Immaculately polished, Talbot noticed. He was kneeling next to the bed between Elizabeth's legs.

He had a mouthful of ice cubes.

Elizabeth sat up, covering her small breasts with her hands. "Oh, Henry!" She stared at him. "You must think me a terrible flirt!"

Chisholm stood up. Talbot had always believed that it was incumbent on a man caught *in flagrante delicto* with another man's wife to grab his trousers and escape through the nearest exit, but Chisholm made no attempt to leave. He did not even look embarrassed.

Talbot could not take his eyes off his genitals. *Substantial* was the word that sprang immediately to mind. A major and his meat. Perhaps the 6th Airborne were issued with such weapons when they were inducted into parachute school.

Chisholm spat the ice cubes on to the marble. "Can't you knock?"

"This is *my* bedroom. That's my *wife!*"

"Well, I'm using her at the moment, old son. So piss off."

The bastard hadn't even lost his erection. "I'm going to kill you," Talbot said.

Chisholm frowned, genuinely confused. "What with?"

Talbot threw himself at the larger man. Chisholm swung lazily with his fist, caught him on the jaw, and sent him spinning back across the room. Talbot landed on his back, and his head cracked on the marble floor.

"Now stop it!" he heard Elizabeth scream. "That is quite enough! Get your clothes and get out!"

Chisholm dressed slowly, never taking his eyes off Talbot. His boots echoed on the stairs and then the door slammed and he was gone.

Talbot dragged himself to a corner of the room and propped himself against a wall. Elizabeth sat herself on the edge of the bed, holding a cigarette in an ivory holder. She did not bother to dress.

"Do you want me to call a doctor?"

Talbot shook his head.

"It's not very civilised, brawling in one's own home."

"Less civilised than screwing army officers?"

"You're so terribly old-fashioned about these things. What am I supposed to do? If you won't do these little jobs for me, of course I have to call in outside help."

"I just expect some discretion." Talbot put his fingers to his mouth. Two of his teeth were loose. "Chisholm – why Chisholm?"

"Why not?"

"Because . . ." Talbot thought about Jaffa Gate. How could he explain that? ". . . he's not . . . because he's an utter bastard."

"Men who fuck other men's wives usually are." She stubbed out her cigarette in the ashtray next to the bed and stood up. "I'm going to have a shower." She walked out.

509

Talbot hung his head, ashamed. Ashamed of her, ashamed of himself. Ashamed he did not have the physical strength even to punish the man who had taken his wife. Ashamed that God has so misshapen his soul that he did not even want her anyway.

He thought about Chisholm at Jaffa Gate and it seemed to him there was only one way he might recover his pride, and that through treachery. What a strange world.

82

Saturday evening. Crowds milled around Zion Square, harangued by the Arab shoe-shine boys who banged their brushes on boxes to attract the attention of prospective customers. The seductive aroma of roasting coffee lured others into the boulevard cafés on Ben Yehuda and King George V streets, where the European exiles in their shiny double-breasted suits tried to recreate a lost way of life, parading in the latest fashions purchased from shops on Princess Mary Avenue. Stilettos clipped on the pavements, music blared from Arab shops, the harsh cries of the hawkers split the hubbub.

Henry Talbot saw Sarah join the queue outside the Zion Cinema, and purchase a ticket at the booth. He bought a bagel from a Yemenite hawker and ate a few mouthfuls without appetite and gave the rest to one of the shoe-shine boys. He looked up at the hoarding: *Abbot and Costello in Hollywood*.

Had the Haganah woman chosen this particular picture for any particular reason? Was it supposed to put his mind at rest? He bought a ticket and went inside.

He waited a few moments at the back of the cinema for his eyes to grow accustomed to the darkness. There was a sudden shock of laughter at the antics on the screen, the English words subtitled in Hebrew and Arabic. It depressed him how easily the Americans exported their puerile culture.

Sarah was sitting just a few feet away, in an aisle seat at the back. She had probably spotted him the moment he walked in. He ignored the usherette and slipped into the seat beside her.

Another sudden shout of laughter.

"Comedies are ideal for this sort of thing," she said. "When people are laughing they can't eavesdrop and they don't shush you."

"Ah, this is a comedy. I hadn't realised."

"You don't like Abbot and Costello?"

"If I had my choice I would rather dip my head in boiling oil. But we're here now."

"Did you bring the chocolates, Henry?"

"Sorry, I forgot. Will the High Commissioner's files on the Haganah do instead?"

More laughter.

"You have them with you?" Sarah said, her voice suddenly tense.

"A bit bulky, don't you think? But I can get them for you."

"The complete file?"

"Everything."

Sarah took a deep breath. "Well."

"Will that release me from my commitment to you?"

"We'll have to see."

"Have to see? *Have to see?* What more do you want?"

An Arab in a western suit and keffiyeh squeezed into the seat next to them. He sat down and stared in stony silence at the screen. Talbot watched him in the darkness. The man's face was creased with concentration. He could have been watching *King Lear*.

"We start with a famine and move swiftly to a feast. I'm afraid you mystify me completely."

"Do you have a jeep and British uniforms?"

"Of course."

511

"Of course," Talbot echoed. "I can arrange for you to have the file for eight hours. What you do with it is up to you. At the end of that time you must return it to me intact. Is that clear?"

"It's not much time."

"For classified information, it's an eternity. You'll need two men who can impersonate British officers. In other words, a pair of arrogant bastards."

"Where do we make the pick-up?"

"At the Hill of Evil Counsel." Talbot passed her an envelope in the darkness. "Two sets of identity papers. They'll get you inside. And a map of the grounds. You tell me when you're ready and I'll nominate the time. You'll have one shot at this, that's all."

"That's all we'll need."

A whoop of laughter from the audience. A Jew across the aisle was actually rocking in his seat, dabbing at his eyes with a huge white handkerchief. Talbot looked at the Arab beside him. His expression had not changed. Why should he laugh? he thought. How could he understand? For the last thirty years he had been on a collision course with a culture he could not comprehend, a way of life diametrically opposed to the one he had learned as a child. The western suit and the keffiyeh were symbols of the dichotomy the British and the Jews had brought to his land. And here he was, still struggling to understand, still trying to laugh.

And here I am, he thought, selling you out.

Yet someone has to protect the Jews from people like Chisholm.

"Are you staying for the end of the picture?" he said.

"Only if I'm struck with paralysis in the next five minutes."

"There's hope for you people yet then." Talbot got up and went outside. Night had fallen. Judas has met with Caiaphas, he thought. All that remains now is the final kiss.

512

Rehavia

"You can choose whoever you want for this operation, Asher. You know how important this one is."

Asher nodded. "Netanel Rosenberg."

"You don't have to decide straight away."

"He learned English for his father's business in Germany so he speaks it well enough. And he has a flair for acting."

They were in the flat in Rehavia. The windows were open because of the heat but there was no breeze and the room smelled of fried butter from the omelette Sarah had prepared them for supper. There was a bottle of Rishon wine open on the table.

"But are you sure you can trust him?"

"No one is more committed than Netanel – not even Ben-Gurion."

"I'm not questioning his commitment. But the Emmerich job – that could hardly be called a success. He left Emmerich alive and assaulted the hausfrau."

"She saw his tattoo. She was going to raise the alarm."

"We just can't afford any mistakes on this one."

"There won't be any mistakes."

"All right." Sarah fetched an envelope from a drawer in the kitchen. She pushed it across the table and poured herself more of the wine. "New identity papers."

Asher took them out and examined them.

"It won't be as easy as getting into Emmerich's place," she said. "There'll be British soldiers on the gate. If your German friend lets slip with any *dankeschöns* that will be it."

"He won't," Asher grunted. Ever since he had been seconded by the Shai he had found himself taking orders from his wife and he was not enjoying it at all.

She reached into the breast pocket of her shirt and produced a piece of white vellum Basildon Bond, folded into a square. She smoothed it out on the surface of the table. A map had been carefully drawn on the sheet, in black ink.

"My contact drew this for us. Here's the main gate, this is the layout of the driveway and the gardens. The Residency is here. You drive to the side entrance, here. Our contact will be waiting for you at precisely nine fifteen. Don't be early – you'll invite questions – and don't be late, or his nerve may desert him. You will salute, give your name and rank, and accept the briefcase he offers you. You then drive straight out again and head for Kfar Herzl as fast as you can."

"A donkey could do it."

"Yes. Well, that's why I picked you."

He glared at her, then he saw she was smiling and he grinned back. He pushed away the comma of dark hair that hung over his face. "Can this contact of yours really get the file?"

"He says he can."

He shook his head. "For us, it's like having the atom bomb."

She covered his hand with her own. "Just be careful. If you're arrested, they'll treat you as a spy."

His mood changed. He took her hand in his own, toying with the ring on her finger. "Would it matter to you if I didn't come back?"

"I care about you very much."

"It's not the same thing."

"As what?"

"As loving me," he said flatly.

There was hurt glistening in her eyes. She was trying, he thought. She did not mean to be cruel. "Please, Ash."

He pulled her towards him. He kissed her, and she responded, stiffly. Making love from memory, he thought. It did not work, it had never worked from the beginning. But at least she was his, in a fashion, and he could not give her up.

It had been so long. Even now, when they were again under the same roof, her back was turned to him in bed. But tonight he wanted her so badly, and he hoped for miracles.

*   *   *

514

He lay awake for a long time, watching her sleep. In the moonlight she had a face like an angel. An angel and a liar. When he had returned after the war, he had hoped things would be different. Instead, time had only made her comfortable with the gulf between them. Her devotion to him was feigned and her loving mechanical, submission and nothing more. But then, she had never promised that she could ever offer him anything else.

And the tragedy of it was that he considered even that enough.

83

The Hill of Evil Counsel

Locked in a desk drawer in an office adjacent to Sir Alan Cunningham's sitting-room were a number of files, each one stamped MOST SECRET in red stencil. Apart from Sir Alan, only a handful of men had the keys to the desk. Henry Talbot was one of them.

He arrived for work ten minutes earlier than usual, and instead of going straight to his office he went upstairs and along the corridor to the High Commissioner's suite. The corporal on duty at the desk recognised him immediately and unlocked the door to the office. Talbot went inside, unlocked the desk and removed three files. They were marked: HAGANAH, STERN, and IRGUN ZVAI LEUMI. The file marked HAGANAH was several hundred pages thick, and it was only with difficulty that Talbot hefted it under his arm.

He locked the desk and went outside. He signed for the files in the desk corporal's register and returned to his office. He felt surprisingly calm. He squeezed the three files into a black leather briefcase and clicked the lock shut.

There. Nothing to it.

He looked at his watch. Five minutes to nine. Plenty of time. Suddenly his knees started to tremble and he had to sit down. At that moment there was a knock on the door and First Secretary Reginald Chandler walked in.

"Good morning, Talbot. Another warm day by the looks of it."

"Yes, sir."

"Sorry to barge in on you like this. Busy?"

Jesus Christ! "Not at all. Do sit down. Like a cup of tea?"

"Why not?"

Talbot went into the outer office and told his clerk, Mahmud, to fetch two cups of tea. He looked at his watch. Three minutes to nine. How could he get rid of Chandler in less than eighteen minutes?

He went back to his office and sat down.

"You look pale, Talbot. Feeling all right?"

"Fine, thank you, sir."

"Got something to discuss with you. Strictly confidential, of course."

"I see. Nothing untoward, I hope?"

"Good Lord, no. Good news, in fact. As you know, I'll be retiring at the end of August."

Talbot glanced at his watch out of the corner of his eye. What did the old goat want? "You'll be sadly missed."

"Thank you, Henry. Can't say I'm not looking forward to it. Got a little cottage in Esher. Pity the good woman isn't still around. It's going to be pretty lonely without her." Margery Chandler had died six years before.

For God's sake, don't let him get maudlin, Talbot thought. You'll never get rid of him. "At least you'll be able to go and watch some decent cricket. That's something I always miss."

"Suppose so. Anyway, that's not why I wanted to talk to you . . ."

Mahmud entered with two cups of strong tea in rose china teacups. He set them down on the desk and went out again.

Two minutes past nine.

Chandler stared miserably into his cup. "Never met a native yet who knew how to make a decent cup of tea. The Indians were the worst. And they grow the stuff! You know, when I was a junior in Delhi before the Great War . . ."

The sentry wore a khaki uniform and steel hat, and his boots were polished like black glass. He had a rifle over his right shoulder. His companion kept a Thompson pointed at the car as the papers were checked. Neither man attempted to smile.

"Nice day for the race," Asher said.

The sentry ignored him and checked the security passes. "Corporal Davidson and Lieutenant Jenkins."

Netanel tapped on the dashboard with his swagger cane and sighed with impatience.

"Who are you here to see?"

"Is that really any of your business, Sergeant?"

The two men stared at each other.

"We have an appointment with Henry Talbot in the Commissioner's office," Netanel said finally.

The soldier seemed satisfied with that. He handed Asher the papers, albeit reluctantly. "Sorry to delay you," he said. Asher put the jeep into gear and drove through.

"You shouldn't have used Talbot's name," Asher said.

"We had no choice."

Asher grunted. He knew Netanel was right, but Sarah had told them to use the name only as a desperation measure. It was hardly that. As he drove he wiped the sweat from the palm of his right hand on the leg of his khaki shorts. He experienced a familiar tight, liquid sensation in his belly.

He could see Talbot's map in his mind as clearly as if it were spread out across the steering wheel. Instead of following the driveway to the front of the building, he turned off along a gravel drive bordered by rose bushes. He looked at his watch. Nine fourteen.

Perfect.

He stopped the jeep at the side entrance and looked up the steps to the porticoed doorway. It was locked. No sign of Talbot.

He remembered what Sarah had said: If they arrest you, they'll treat you as a spy.

He looked at Netanel. He was lounging in his seat, tapping the toe of his boot with his swagger cane, staring vacantly at the overhanging branches of a conifer.

"Where the hell's Talbot?" Asher whispered.

"He'll come," Netanel said and yawned. "Look at all these roses. The British know how to build a garden, don't they?"

"The point is," Chandler was saying, "Whitehall have still to decide on a replacement for me. So an Acting First Secretary will have to be appointed. It needs to be someone dependable, someone discreet." Someone thoroughly compromised by the Haganah, Talbot thought. "I took the liberty of putting your name forward to the Commissioner."

"My word, that's very kind of you, sir." Good God Almighty, nine sixteen!

"Well, you've worked hard and you've proved yourself thoroughly reliable. You have a great future, young Talbot. A great future."

If only you knew the future I have. In prison or in disgrace. "Thank you very much, sir."

"Of course nothing's been decided yet. If it comes off, the appointment will only be temporary, until someone a little more senior arrives from England. But the experience will stand you in good stead and I'm sure promotion will follow."

"I am really most grateful, sir. I don't know what to say." Look, please just bugger off and let me put my head in the noose without piling on any more pain.

"Well, I just thought I'd let you know. Sir Alan will

518

no doubt inform you officially in due course." He got up to leave.

Then changed his mind.

"One other thing. Now this is strictly in confidence . . ."

"Pine trees," Netanel said. "There were pine trees at Buna." The shadows of the leaves played on the polished visor of his cap.

"Where's Buna?" Asher said. Where was Talbot?

"Buna was the name of the marshalling yards outside Auschwitz," Netanel said. His voice was soft and dreamy. "Strange how you associate one thing with another. When I look at a pine tree I feel cold and hungry. I feel like I want to die."

Asher drummed on the steering wheel. Any moment a British officer would challenge them. Why are you here? What are you doing? Then perhaps Netanel will have his death wish. Asher had already decided he would not let them arrest him. Better to die with a bullet than a rope.

"We give him five more minutes," he said.

"The worst of it is you never leave it behind. I can eat a big dinner and afterwards I still feel hungry. You see, it's not your body that starves, it's your brain. It does something to your mind."

It was the first time Netanel had talked about Auschwitz. He could have chosen a better time.

"It's hard to explain to someone who wasn't there. It was like you died and God sentenced you to hell. It was just like that." Netanel turned and stared at him. "Where did you say you were from?"

"Bavaria. A town called Ravenswald, near München."

"Have you always been Asher Ben-Zion?"

"No, that's the Hebrew name I adopted when I came here. I was a Zionist so – Ben-Zion, son of Zion. And Asher – our Hebrew word for happiness. It's how I felt when I finally came to Palestine. Where the hell is Talbot?"

"What was your name before?"

"Mandelbaum. Why?" Just shut up, Asher thought.

Something is wrong here. I don't want to make conversation. If a soldier comes we're dead, for the love of Almighty God!

Netanel stopped the tapping with the swagger cane. He was suddenly still, his face very pale, staring up at the pine trees.

"If Talbot doesn't come out with that file soon," Asher said, "I am going to go in and get it."

"I was going to keep this to myself," Chandler was saying – Impossible! Talbot thought – "but I shall tell you this in the strictest confidence. It appears my name has been put forward for the New Year's honours list."

"Well, that is wonderful news!" Nine twenty-two. Please, please, please bugger off!

"Isn't it? It looks like a KCMG. Forty years of outstanding service and all that. Margery would have been very proud."

Not Margery, Talbot thought. *Don't let him get on to Margery!*

"We'll all be proud, sir."

"Thank you, Talbot. I can rely on you to keep mum?"

What you mean is, can I rely on you to spread the rumour so I get some kudos before I leave? I can do that for you, old boy. But I rather think I might upstage you shortly, in a rather perverse manner. If you give me the chance. "I shan't tell another soul," Talbot said, and rose from his chair.

Chandler took his cue. As he got up he almost tripped over the briefcase. "Have they been keeping you busy?"

"Just a few files."

"Well, I'd better let you get on then."

When he was gone, Talbot looked at his watch. Nine twenty-six. Great God in heaven! He picked up the briefcase and walked out.

Asher's hand hesitated over the ignition key. "Something must have gone wrong."

When he spoke Netanel's voice sounded curiously

520

detached. "We can't leave, Ash. Either we drive out with the files or they take us out in a pine box. That's it."

"You've got ice water in your veins, Netya."

"Dying the first time is hard. After that it gets easier."

Asher did not have time to ask him what he meant. The side door opened and a tall, pale man in a pinstriped suit appeared. Netanel jumped out of the jeep and met him at the foot of the steps. He saluted. "Lieutenant Brian Jenkins, sir."

"Make sure these arrive safely," Talbot said, and handed Netanel a heavy briefcase. "I shall expect to have these returned to me at five thirty at the very latest."

"Yes, sir," Netanel said, and saluted again. He jumped back into the jeep, the briefcase cradled on his lap.

Talbot watched them disappear along the drive, the tyres crunching on the gravel.

84

Kfar Herzl Kibbutz

On bright warm days the washing lines at the kibbutz would flutter with washing; but today there were no flags of drying clothes flying in the breeze. Instead, the wooden pegs held thousands of sheets of newly printed photographic negatives.

Sarah stood on the verandah of the laundry and stared at the spectacle. The washhouse behind her – as well as the school and the dining hall – had been seconded for the day by the Haganah. Cameras, chemicals and developing tanks had been brought in the previous day by Shai photographic specialists. Fifteen of the kibbutzniks had been placed at their disposal by Yaakov Landauer.

As soon as Asher and Netanel had arrived with their prize, the group had swung into action.

The two men – still in their British uniforms – lounged at a table on the verandah smoking. When Sarah came out, Asher got to his feet. "Got a few snaps for the family album?" he said.

"You would not believe what was in that briefcase," Sarah said.

"Try me."

"It must be everything the British have on us . . . the Haganah, the Palmach, Stern, and the Irgun Zvai Leumi. Thousands of names, in alphabetical order. Age, address, employment, even duties within the organisation. They have far more than we suspected. Far more."

Asher grinned suddenly. "Anything about me?"

"You're listed under 'L' for liabilities." Then she was serious again. "They could destroy us. They have details on our internal structure, how the Palmach is deployed – exactly – weapons estimates, the lot. If they want to destroy us, they can."

"What's the good news?"

"That is the good news." She lowered her voice to a whisper. "We also found a large white envelope, sealed with red wax, bearing the official seal of the British government. It was countersigned by Sir Alan Cunningham and the Chief Secretary of the government. We believe no one else – until today – has seen the contents."

"You're making me curious."

"There are fourteen typewritten pages, an operational order for the military. The code name for the operation is Broadside. The objective of the operation is to destroy the Haganah."

Asher said nothing. He watched the kibbutzniks scuttle back and forwards from the washhouse to the laundry lines.

"There are maps of Jerusalem and Tel Aviv and Haifa, pinpointing the houses of our senior commanders. There

522

are also maps of many of our kibbutzim showing the locations of suspected sliks. There's no doubt now, Attlee wants us destroyed."

"What size operation are they planning?"

"As soon as Cunningham receives the password from Whitehall, he will order an immediate curfew. The operational order then outlines military operations against forty-nine separate towns and settlements using armour and infantry. It authorises the use of RAF and artillery shelling in the event of any resistance."

"God in heaven. When?"

"The operational orders are signed April 16th. That's nearly two months ago. The order to act could come any day."

"All this is making my leg ache. Can we sit down?"

Sarah glanced at Netanel. "This is just between the two of us," she said, and steered him to the other end of the verandah. Asher eased himself into a sitting position on the verandah rail.

"What's going to happen now?" Asher asked.

"We've sent a preliminary report to the Red House in Tel Aviv. Anyone named on the list will have to be moved immediately. We'll need new command centres in all the major towns, and almost every kibbutz will have to make new sliks. We've checked out what the British have on Kfar Herzl for example. They have our weapons cache pinpointed exactly."

"How did they get all this?"

"The CID have been in Palestine for thirty years. Perhaps it's the aggregation of three decades' work, perhaps there's a high-level leak. The important thing is we shift all our pieces before Bevin and the Red Poppies have a chance to checkmate us."

"Thank you, Henry Talbot!"

"Yes. He may not look like Moses but our English gentleman has parted the sea for us. He's shown us the way out."

The Hill of Evil Counsel

Henry Talbot stood at the window of his office and looked down on Jerusalem. It was late afternoon and the city floated on a heat haze like an island rising out of the mist. The sun burned on the golden Dome of the Rock, built, it was said, to commemorate the place where Mohammed rode to heaven on his horse, El-Bureq. The towers of the yeshivoth rose from the ancient Jewish Quarter, where the ones called the Forgotten of God had kept the faith since the time of the Diaspora. The Church of the Holy Sepulchre, built on Golgotha, the site of Christ's crucifixion, was lost in the haze. So many religions jostled for purchase with each other down there; such a history of hate.

Men needed religion, Talbot thought, not to teach them to love, but as a justification to kill. If there had been no Christ, no Mohammed, they would have needed to invent one.

Or perhaps that was what they had done.

If the devil needed a disguise, he thought, then he would call himself God. In that guise he had set Catholics against Huguenots, Saracens against Crusaders, and now Arabs against Jews.

The muezzin high in the minaret of the Al-Aqsa began the call to Asr, the late afternoon prayer. His song echoed around the Kidron valley and the Mount of Olives. Talbot looked at his watch. If the briefcase was not back by five thirty, it was all over for him.

Perhaps it was over anyway.

Judean Hills near Al-Naqb

Netanel cradled the briefcase between his knees as the jeep bounced along between dark stands of pines. The steep sides of the wadi crowded in on them, throwing dark shadows across the road, the echo of the motor reverberating along the rock walls as the jeep laboured up the ridge. The stillness made Asher uneasy.

"What do you want for yourself, Netanel?" Asher said.

Netanel shrugged, and did not answer.

"Come on, what do you dream about? Everybody has a dream."

"Do they? What's yours?"

"I want to start a new kibbutz, in the Negev. I want to build it up from nothing, like Yaakov did with Kfar Herzl. I want to create an oasis in the desert. That's what I want when this is over."

"Do you think it ever will be over?"

"Yes. One day." He stared at Netanel. He had been even more silent and withdrawn since their conversation about Buna. Perhaps, he decided, it had evoked too many painful memories.

Although there were still a few hours of sunlight remaining, the high walls of the wadi had imposed a premature dusk. The pines were black and malevolent, and the air suddenly cool.

"You're a dark horse, Netya, I'll never understand – "

Asher heard a crack like a whip, and he felt the hot draught as a bullet zipped through the air close to his face. He heard a clang-clang as more bullets slammed into the jeep. He stood on the brakes.

"Get out!" he screamed at Netanel.

He grabbed Netanel's shirt and pulled him down the slope beside the road. At the bottom of the wadi they lay on their bellies in the dust and listened.

"Where are they?" Netanel whispered.

"I don't know!" Asher fumbled for his holster. The only weapons they had were standard issue British Webley specials. They were only any use in close combat, not in a sniper duel.

A bullet slammed into the dirt just a few inches away from his face, and he cried out as fragments of stone peppered his cheek.

"The trees!" Netanel shouted. He pulled Asher to his

525

feet and they zigzagged towards a stand of pines. Two more shots whipped at the ground as they ran.

They threw themselves face down in the dirt, breathing hard. Silence, except for the whine of mosquitoes.

"Are you all right?" Netanel whispered.

Asher put a hand to his face. It came away wet with blood. He couldn't see out of one eye. "I don't know."

Netanel wiped the blood away with his sleeve and examined the injury. "You've got a cut over your right eyelid and another one on your forehead. Must have been stone fragments."

"I'm also getting bitten to hell by mosquitoes." Asher twisted around. "Where are the bastards?" He wriggled behind the trunk of one of the pines and stared up at the road. Netanel took up a position five yards away, his own revolver cradled in the crook of his arm.

"Here they come."

A shadow slipped down the hillside towards the jeep. There was more movement on their left, and the tumbling of a small rockfall.

"I'll drill the sons of whores," Netanel whispered.

"Wait until they're closer. We only have ten rounds between us. See how many there are first."

A figure scampered across the road and took cover behind the jeep. Asher squinted into the false dusk. The man appeared to be dressed entirely in black, not like an Arab at all.

But if it wasn't an Arab, then who was it?

"Did you see that?" he whispered.

"Herrgottsacrament!" Netanel said.

They heard whispering somewhere to their left. The words carried to them on the still of the evening with absolute clarity.

Hebrew.

Asher sat up and sang out the words of his religion's most sacred prayer: "*Shma Yisrael, Adonai Eloheinu, Adonai Ehaaa-aaad!*" He drew out the final syllable in the traditional way, in imitation of Ben Joseph Akiba's final dying breath, as he was flayed to death by the Romans.

"Hear O Israel, the Lord Our God, the Lord is One." His voice echoed around the wadi, and was greeted with a long silence.

"Who are you?" a voice shouted, eventually.

"Haganah! Who are you? Irgun, Stern, what?"

He heard someone curse.

Asher stood up, strode across the clearing and scrambled over the dry wadi and up the slope to the road. A man with thinning black hair and tortoiseshell glasses was leaning against the jeep, a Sten gun cradled in his arms. He was wearing a black jersey and black trousers.

"I'm Asher Ben-Zion."

"Moshe Meodovnik."

"Irgun?"

Meodovnik nodded. "We thought you were British soldiers."

Asher ignored him and examined the jeep. There were a dozen bullet holes in the coachwork and the radiator was shattered. Water hissed on to the road, sending up a white plume of steam. Asher roared with frustration and kicked the tyre.

"Shame. Nice vehicle," Meodovnik said.

"Have you any idea what you've done?"

"It was a mistake. These things happen."

Netanel had followed Asher up the slope. "Take it easy, Ash," he said. The rest of the Irgun gang had converged on them now. They were mostly Yemenites, Netanel noticed. Peasants and fanatics.

Asher's right fist took Meodovnik on the point of the chin and sent him sprawling on to the road. He lay there for a few seconds, stunned, then scrambled for the gun that had clattered on to the road beside him. Before he could reach it Netanel was already beside him, holding his revolver to the man's head. "Why don't we all calm down?"

"Sabra prick," Meodovnik hissed.

The other Irgun soldiers had their weapons aimed at Asher. No one moved.

Netanel clicked the safety off his revolver. "Let's just

527

say it's been a bad day all round," he whispered in the Irguni's ear.

Meodovnik put up his hands in a gesture of truce. "Yes. Let's not forget we're on the same side. All right?" He smiled at Asher but his eyes were scored with hate.

Netanel lowered the revolver.

Meodovnik stood up, slowly. "If you informed us of your operations, this sort of thing would not happen," he said to Asher. He turned and marched back up the road. The others followed.

"How are we supposed to get back to Jerusalem?" Asher shouted after him.

"Try walking!"

Asher looked at Netanel, who spread his hands in a gesture of resignation. Asher sat on the running board of the jeep and put his head in his hands. Poor Henry Talbot.

The Hill of Evil Counsel

Talbot looked at his watch. Ten minutes past six. He stared at the driveway leading from the main gates, watching the shadows lengthen. He felt strangely calm; or perhaps tension had exhausted him. The day had lasted a century, a hundred years of fretting and sweating, his attention fixed on the inexorable passage of the hands of the clock.

And, in the end, his reprieve had not come.

The door opened and Chandler looked in. "Still here, Henry? Time to go home, you know."

"Got a few things to catch up on."

Chandler nodded. "Feel like dropping over for a few drinks tomorrow night with Elizabeth? I've asked the Rogersons."

"Love to," Talbot said automatically. "What time?"

"About eight. That all right?"

"I'll mention it to Elizabeth."

The door closed. He turned back to the window. The

Haganah had betrayed him. Oh my God. What am I to do now?

85

New City

Marie's eyes were gritty from exhaustion. She looked at her watch. Almost two in the morning; she had worked over seventeen hours. The little office was cramped and thick with cigarette smoke and the single light bulb did not throw enough light. Someone brought her a cup of coffee but she was too tired to drink it. The typewriter keyboard swam in her vision.

When I am finished here, she promised herself, I am going to go home and sleep for two days.

The Histadruth executive had put their entire staff at the disposal of the Haganah at the start of work that morning. They were typing lists, names and addresses, from photographic negatives. Haganah members, Marie supposed. Each typist had a mirror placed next to her typewriter so she could read the negative in the glass. It was a strain on the eyes and the nerves.

Marie moved on to her last batch of negatives. It was increasingly difficult to concentrate, impossible to type too fast without making a mistake.

RONSKI,	Shlomo
Age:	23
Address:	16 HaHavazelet Street
	Jerusalem
	New City

Haganah Reserve

529

ROSEN,   Michael
Age: 38
Address: Flat 8
                120 Ben Yehuda Street
                Tel Aviv

Known Stern Gang member

ROSENBERG,   Netanel
Age: 29
Address: Apartment 6D
                213 HaNasi Street
                Rehavia

Palmach: *Platoon Commander*

ROSENTHAL,   David . . .

Marie stopped and stared at what she had just typed.
Netanel.
She remembered the last time she had seen him, at the
House in the Woods, when she had given him the silver
Star of David.
Netanel!
At last, she had found him again.

Talbieh

The sun rose over the city, chasing the shadows down the
tombs on the Mount of Olives. The muezzin's voice carried
across the city from the minaret of the Al-Aqsa.
*Allahu Akbar, la illaha Allah, Al-salat khayr min al-
naum!*
God is most great, there is no God but God, prayer is
better than sleep!

For those who can sleep, Talbot thought.

He listened to his household come awake: the clink of cutlery in the dining-room, the sweep of the broom in the courtyard, the smell of coffee roasting in the kitchen. The daily ritual he had always ignored now seemed precious on this last, lonely time.

The hamsiin rushed through the leaves of the fig, fetid from the desert. "Another hot day," he imagined Chandler saying.

Then another, unexpected sound; a vehicle drawing up outside the house, footsteps running on the cobbled court, something thrown against the door. Then the footsteps receded and he heard the squeal of a motor being driven away, very fast.

A few minutes later Moussa entered carrying the briefcase. "Someone left this at the front door, Talbot effendi."

"Thank you, Moussa," Talbot said. He accepted the briefcase and unfastened the straps. A manila envelope lay on top, "TALBOT" written in capitals in red ink on the front. He opened it.

Inside was the postcard, himself and Majid. A photographic negative had been stuck on to it. There was a scrawled, handwritten note: "*We are sorry.*"

"Aren't we all?" Talbot said aloud.

He tore the postcard and the negative into small pieces and went to the double doors that opened on to the patio. He threw the pieces into the air, and let the hamsiin carry them away.

Rehavia

"Moshe Meodovnik," Sarah said. "He's a Russian émigré, came here in 1928 with his family. Maths professor, of all things. He was arrested by the British in 1938 for illegal possession of a firearm and was sentenced to

531

five years in prison. In 1941 he was given the option of finishing his sentence or fighting with the Jewish Brigade. He served with distinction in North Africa and Italy. After the war we invited him to rejoin the Haganah as a regional commander. Instead he joined Irgun Zvai Leumi."

"Couldn't we have told them what we were doing?"

"We never tell the Irgun anything. Officially we have disowned them." The kettle whistled in the kitchen. "More coffee?"

She got up and went into the kitchen. Asher finished his eggs, wiped his mouth with a napkin and threw it on the table in disgust. The Irgun and the Stern gangs were bastard children of the Haganah, radicals and zealots, loose cannons that were a danger to everyone, including the Haganah itself.

"What's going to happen now?"

"By tonight every regional commander will have copies of the file. We even have copies for the Irgun and Stern. They are on our side after all."

"Are they . . . ?"

"Within the week every piece of intelligence the British have about us will be obsolete. As for us, we had better pack up and get out of here today."

"What's going to happen to Talbot?"

Sarah did not answer. Asher rubbed at the sticking plaster over his eye and on his forehead. The heat was making the wounds itch.

Sarah returned with a fresh pot of coffee. "He'll probably spend the rest of his life in prison. And he has me to thank for it."

"It's not your fault. It's not anyone's fault. No, check that. There is someone to blame. Meodovnik!"

"It doesn't help."

"Look, Sarah – "

"It's all right, I'm not going to tear my hair and cover myself in ashes. If I had to do the same thing again, I would do it. I just hope no one ever expects me to feel proud of it."

She poured the coffee.

"It saved the Haganah."

"If we had got the briefcase back in time, we could have saved Henry Talbot as well."

He covered her hand with his. "I'm sorry."

There were tears in her eyes. "It's funny. I'd grown quite fond of him in a way. He seemed kind and he had a sort of dark sense of humour, once you got to know him. I feel responsible."

They drank their coffee in silence. A sense of humour, Asher thought bitterly. Well, the poor bastard is going to need one.

The Hill of Evil Counsel

Henry Talbot arrived at the Residency at eight o'clock. Chandler's car was already there. Moussa pulled up in front of the main steps and Talbot got out, the briefcase clutched in his right hand. He went inside.

Perhaps there was still a chance.

He went up the echoing marble steps to the second floor and walked smartly along the corridor to the desk sergeant. It required an effort of will to stop himself breaking into a run.

"Talbot!"

He turned around. It was Chandler.

"Good morning, sir. Looks like a hot day."

Chandler's face was grey, his skin slick with sweat. There was a voluminous white handkerchief in his right hand. He walked quickly down the corridor, two soldiers wearing the yellow and red insignia of the Royal Suffolks in step behind him.

"Talbot . . ."

Chandler stood there, his Adam's apple bobbing in his throat, stern, disapproving and afraid.

"I had a word with Elizabeth," Talbot said, suddenly

feeling very calm. "I don't think we'll be able to make it tonight."

Chandler did not seem to hear him. "What's in your briefcase, Henry?"

"The missing files, sir."

Chandler snatched the case out of his hand and tore open the straps. He quickly checked the contents and put the case under his arm. He nodded to the two soldiers who were with him.

"These men are going to put you under arrest, I'm afraid."

Talbot nodded. "I see."

Chandler looked as if he might cry. "How could you do this?"

"The same way you ignored men like Rolf Emmerich, I suppose."

"Is that all you have to say?"

Talbot felt curiously light-headed. He wanted to laugh out loud, relieved that it was finally over. What did anything matter any more? In twenty-four hours he had thrown away his whole life but now it was gone the life he had no longer seemed such a terrible loss.

"There is one thing, sir."

"Yes?" Chandler's lips formed a tight, white line.

"Does this mean I shan't be taking over from you as Acting First Secretary?"

86

Rehavia

It had been so long. Would he have changed? What would
she say to him? What if he had found himself another
woman?

She had reached her flat at four that morning, exhausted,
red-eyed and unable to sleep. She had sat at her kitchen
table, drinking endless cups of coffee, watching a lemon
dawn creep over the city; then she had run through the
streets, looking for a taxi.

. . . 213 HaNasi Street, Rehavia . . .

The block of flats was like a dozen others all around it.
She ran up the echoing stone staircase to the sixth floor,
slowed at first by fatigue then by fear. When she reached
the door she no longer had the courage to confront him,
so she hid in the shadows under the stairwell and stared at
the doorway, frozen not in her muscles but in her mind.

She had no idea how long she had been standing there
when she heard noises beyond the door. A man dressed
in white shirt and blue denim shorts and sandals ran out
and leaped down the stairs, two at a time. As he passed
her, she stepped out from the shadows.

He had already reached the first landing when he sensed
the movement, stopped, and looked up.

She could not be sure.

His hair was cropped short, and was peppered with
white. A scar distorted one side of his face, and there
was two days of stubble on his chin. He was gaunt, the
skin stretched tight over the bones.

She tried to remember.

Netanel, her Netanel. Blond hair, neatly parted. Clean-shaven, blue eyed, immaculate in his woollen business suits and polished black shoes. An Adonis face, fresh and well-fed.

They stared at each other.

He started to walk back up the stairs.

"Netanel?" she whispered.

He stopped halfway. "Oh my God." His face turned grey.

She held out her arms. "I'm back from university," she said, but he made no move towards her and finally she dropped her arms and they surveyed each other from a distance, two ghosts in a limbo world, lost of their physical shape.

Acre

The British prison at Acre was a former Ottoman citadel, built on the ruins of a Crusader fortress. Talbot's cell was eight feet by ten feet, and there was no electric light and no toilet. The ceilings and walls dripped with water night and day. The outside wall was sixteen feet thick and the only light filtered in through an archer's slit, a foot high and a few inches wide. Through it he could just make out the tops of the trees on Napoleon Hill.

Although Talbot was allowed neither newspapers nor access to a radio, the cockney warden was a talkative fellow and seemed to be better informed than both the *Jerusalem Post* and the BBC World Service. He had helped keep him sane.

It was almost three weeks since he had been arrested. After his initial interrogation he had seen no one from the administration or the military, and had been allowed no visitors. He had no idea how his betrayal had affected the undeclared war.

536

The government had communicated with him just once. He had received a letter, bearing the official emblem of the Guards, informing him that his brother had been killed while on active service in Samaria.

There were no other details.

Two nights ago, the warden informed him, the British imposed a curfew throughout Palestine and moved in force against the Yishuv.

"One hundred 'fousand men," the warden had said. "One hundred 'fousand! Faaaaark! All over farkin' Palestine! Reckon that's farkin' it, mate! We even 'it the farkin' Jewish Agency itself in J'rusalem!"

I wonder if the Haganah were ready, Talbot thought. I wonder how many they actually caught?

He heard a footfall in the corridor outside, and the less familiar clip-clip of stiletto heels. The key turned in the lock and the warden put his head into the cell. "A'ternoon, Mr Talbot. Got a visitor for ya!"

Talbot stood up.

The scent of perfume preceded her, stunning, exotic. She wore a red silk dress and a black hat with a gauze veil that covered the top half of her face. Tomato-red lipstick, black gloves, an ivory cigarette-holder, and a black leather handbag completed the vision.

She swayed into the middle of the room and looked around, her nose twitching in disgust. "How quaint."

A soldier with a drawn bayonet attached to his rifle followed her into the cell. The door slammed shut behind him. The man stood to attention, his eyes fixed on some point high on the far wall.

Elizabeth examined the tin bucket that stood in the corner. "Have you availed yourself of the facilities today, Henry?"

"Not yet, dear."

"Thank heaven for small mercies." She indicated the archer's slit. "What happened to the window?"

"Builder made a mistake with the plans."

She smiled at him and drew on her cigarette. "Well."

He smiled at her. "Well."

"Have you complained to the management? They could have at least offered you a room with a view."

"This is the presidential suite, I'm afraid."

"Ah. Pity the poor peasants then."

"Quite." He indicated his cot. "Would you like to sit down?"

"I'd rather jump into a pool of vomit." She crossed the room and pinched his cheek. "You look rather pale."

"Haven't been getting out much lately."

"You also smell rather badly."

He shrugged. "Do I? I hadn't noticed."

She turned and glanced at the guard, then at her husband. "Did you hear what happened the other night?"

"I heard there were a few unscheduled night manoeuvres."

"Complete fiasco. The army landed a handful of low-ranking Haganah and a couple of pistols by all accounts. The High Commissioner and the army have all got egg on their faces."

"It must be very embarrassing for them."

"The army say it's the CID's fault, the CID are blaming the police and the police are blaming the army."

"That's good. I was afraid someone might try to blame me."

"Frankly, Henry, I wouldn't care less about any of this, but your behaviour has ruined my social life."

Talbot put his hands in his pockets. "Chisholm been round?"

"Neanderthals have a certain exotic attraction but not for very long. I get so bored listening to him rant about the Jews all the time. It's like going to bed with Heinrich Himmler." She stopped and drew on her cigarette. "You don't mind if I talk about this?"

"It's conversation."

"Just one question. That afternoon you found me with the good major's cock in my hands . . . who were you jealous of? Him or me?"

Talbot looked up at the guard. Still no change in his expression but his cheeks were flushed a cherry red.

"I do have some standards, Lizzie. I just wish you did."

She started to fuss with the collar of his shirt. "Who does your washing?"

"No one."

"I didn't think so." She stared frankly into his face. "I didn't know you had it in you."

"Neither did I."

"I'm leaving Palestine."

"Actually, I am surprised you are still here."

"You'll find this hard to credit, but I've been trying to persuade Sir Alan to help you. Perverse of me, isn't it?"

"A little."

"Didn't have much success until the army's Noël Coward farce the other night. The next morning he seemed undecided."

"Undecided?"

"Whether to have you dismembered or to hush the whole thing up. I think he favours the latter. Otherwise there has to be a trial and no one wants that now. It would make everyone look bad. So it seems they'll just have to let you go. You'll have to resign of course."

"Oh? I was hoping they'd give me my old job back." Talbot sat down heavily on his cot. Freedom. The last thing he expected.

Elizabeth finished her cigarette and flicked the butt into the pail in the corner. Class will out, Talbot thought sourly. She took out her compact mirror and examined her lipstick, then snapped it shut with a gesture of finality. "I'm rather fond of you, you know, in my own way. Not the way a woman is usually fond of a man, I suppose. You're more like a toothless old dog that suddenly proves its worth and chases off a burglar. Yes. More like that, I suppose."

"Aren't you ashamed?"

"Because you're a faggot or because you betrayed your country?"

"Both."

"Yes to the first, no the latter. Politics doesn't really affect me. What you do with other men's bottoms does."

Talbot checked the guard. The man's jaw muscles were clenched and rippling. "So?"

"So, I shall return to England with you and after a decent interval we shall part in a civilised English manner. I do think that's really the only sensible option, don't you?"

"Thank you, Elizabeth."

She sighed and rested her hand gently on his shoulder. "Why on earth did you marry me?"

He shrugged helplessly. Perhaps I just didn't want to face the truth about myself, he thought. Who does?

"Goodbye. Do try and have a wash before they let you out."

She turned to the guard and raised one eyebrow to signal that she was ready to leave. Rather good at wordless commands, Talbot thought. Her talent will be wasted back in England.

After she had gone he sat for a long time, staring at the wall. He had lost his career, and his wife, but apparently he would not also lose his liberty. The rest of his life yawned before him and he wondered with this second chance whether he might make better sense of it this time.

Part Fifteen

PALESTINE, 1946

87

Yemin Moshe

Fromberg looked up when he heard the door of his shop open. He saw Marie heading for the stairs. "Good evening, Fräulein Helder!"

"Good evening, Herr Fromberg!"

"Another hot day! Something from the shop you would like?"

Marie knew she could not escape. She came back down the stairs and took out her purse. "Perhaps some Lebana cheese."

Fromberg wrapped the cheese in some old tearsheets of the *Jerusalem Post* and studied her. She wasn't Fräulein Breadstick any more. Since she had found this fiancé of hers she had been looking fuller, healthier.

Not that he approved of what was happening upstairs.

"You and your friend would like to join us for dinner tonight? Frau Fromberg is making goulash."

"Not tonight, Herr Fromberg. Another evening. But thank you."

He handed her the cheese. "More trouble in the Old City today. The Arabs threw a grenade into a shop in David Street."

"There's always trouble somewhere in the world."

Somewhere in the world! he thought. This is right on our doorstep. How could anyone sleep soundly in their beds? He watched her run upstairs. A lovely girl. When was this young man of hers going to marry her? Not that he could understand why she should choose a man like that. He did not like the look of him. Not at all.

*   *   *

Netanel sat by the window chain-smoking a packet of cigarettes. He was shaking with anger.

Marie threw her handbag and the cheese on the table and kissed him on the cheek. "Did you have a good day?" she said. She went into the kitchen to make coffee.

A good day! Netanel thought.

Some filthy Arab had exploded a grenade in a goldsmith's in David Street. By the time his unit got there it was too late to do anything, and the goldsmith and his son were in bloody pieces all over the alley. Then the British cordoned off the area and arrested two of his men for carrying concealed weapons. *The British!* If they policed the area properly it would never have happened. Instead a harmless old Hassid and his son were dead, and two of his Palmachniks were in prison for trying to do the job the British should be doing themselves. Was that justice?

A good day!

He had tried many times to explain to Marie what he did, but whenever he spoke about his new life with the Palmach, and the struggle for a Jewish Palestine, her eyes assumed a vacant stare and he knew nothing he said would be heard, or remembered. Like the times he had tried to talk to her about Auschwitz.

"Did you hear what happened in the Old City today?" he said.

"Herr Fromberg said something about it."

"The Arabs killed two Jews in cold blood. I saw it."

"Oh, Netanel, there is so much trouble in the world. There is nothing anyone can do about it. Would you like some coffee?"

Netanel shook his head and lit another cigarette, watching the the blue smoke drift through the window. He watched her in the kitchen, grinding the coffee, boiling the water in the kettle, fetching the brass coffeepot. You have hardly changed at all since I knew you in Ravenswald, since that last night in the House in the Woods. Your face is not disfigured like mine, and you murmur happy songs as you work, and there are no shadows in your eyes. No one who did not know you before

544

would ever guess that your insides have been scooped out like a melon.

It is like living with a ghost. I can see you and hear you . . . and yet, you are not real. But if I find a way to bring you back, your memory will certainly destroy me.

What am I going to do?

al-Naqb

The house of Izzat Ib'n Mousa was not as grand as that of his cousins, the eldest of whom had inherited the palatial residence of Sheikh Daoud when he had died a few months ago. There were goatskin rugs on the floor instead of silk cushions; Izzat's wife still ground her own grain with mortar and pestle; and there was no water closet in the back garden, such as the one built by Sheikh Daoud.

Yet Izzat's influence in his village had now grown beyond that of any of the sheikh's sons, for Izzat was undisputed leader of the most powerful Arab militia in the area, the Holy Strugglers of Judea. The Mufti himself corresponded with him through his intermediaries in Jerusalem. When the new Arab Palestine was formed, it was clear that Izzat Ib'n Mousa would be one of its foremost cadres.

Apart from Izzat himself, there were five others in Izzat's majlis, all trusted *fedayeen*, except one. The new recruit was no more than a boy, he had no beard, and his face was grave with determination. He sat cross-legged, conscious that the others were watching him, though their attention was apparently focused on Izzat.

"I have some news from the city," Izzat was saying. "Yesterday in HaShalshelet Street, on the edge of the Jewish Quarter, two young Arab girls were walking home from the market. Even though they were dressed in utmost modesty, they were attacked by a mob of young Jews. They were raped repeatedly and beaten."

"Filthy Jews!"

"We shall have to teach them another lesson . . ."

"Did the British not help them?"

"The British stood back and watched and laughed as they always do," Izzat said. "If we wish to live in peace in Palestine we must rely on our own valour and strength, as the Mufti has commanded."

"May Allah bless him and make him fruitful," Tareq echoed.

"Indeed," Izzat agreed. He clapped his hands and one of his daughters hurried from a corner of the room and handed him a large folded square. She retreated into the shadows once more.

Izzat unfolded the paper and laid it out on the goatskin rug between them. It was a map of the Old City. "The Holy Strugglers of Judea will avenge this crime and teach these dirty Jews a lesson!"

"Thanks be to Him!"

Izzat laid a long finger on the map. "For this mission we will take Tareq's Hillman and drive into the city along Jaffa Road. The British sentries at the checkpoints will have knowledge of you, so you will not be searched."

"Will you not be with us?"

"Not this time," Izzat said. He rarely accompanied them on their missions any longer, but no one sought to question him hard on this point. His authority was unquestioned.

"You will drive past Allenby Square and turn off into Mamillah Road. Your target will be the new Jewish Commercial Centre opposite Jaffa Gate. There you will fire your weapons into the crowds, taking care not to hit any Arabs who might be there. Meanwhile one of you will take the grenade and throw it into the bakery, here. You will exit again along Mamillah Road and head for East Jerusalem."

"Who is going to throw the grenade?"

All eyes turned with Izzat's to the young boy sitting in their midst. "I think perhaps it is time that young Ali Hass'an earns the right to be called a true fedayeen."

Ali did not blink. "I won't let you down," he said.

Old City

The Arab woman hesitated, hurried down the alley beside
the Hass'an Olive Oil Company. What am I doing here?
Sarah thought. I am a whore to my husband and a traitor to
my people. What happens if you are caught? The Haganah
will disown you. Your father will spit in your face.

But she was no longer master of the game she herself
had set in motion and the musk of longing drew her back
time after time. Sometimes they would not see each other
for weeks, for Sarah could never know when it was safe
for her to come. Many times she came to the shop and
Rishou was not there and the disappointment hit her like
a physical blow.

There was a prearranged signal. She would stand at the
window to the shop, and when he looked up and saw
her she would raise her right hand briefly to adjust her
veil and then move on. Rishou would give his labourers
instructions to continue at their work and then go swiftly
up the stairs while they smirked and nudged each other in
silent admiration.

Each time she came she promised herself that this must
be the last time they would see each other. It became her
most devout wish and her greatest terror.

She sat on the mattress, wearing only her khaki cotton
shirt, while he lay naked under the single sheet of the
makeshift bed. A wooden dish containing cold felafel lay
on his chest. Sarah chose one, dipped it in the hummus,
and popped it in his mouth. Then she chose one for
herself.

He grinned at her. "What would a poor apple picker do
without a good lunch to keep up his strength?"

"Then eat plenty. You've more harvesting to do this
afternoon." She ran her finger through the black curls on
his chest, and her playfulness evaporated. "Does your wife
know about us, Rishou?"

"We cannot afford for anyone to know about us."

"Surely she must suspect?"

He shrugged. "Arab women expect their men to have mistresses. As long as they don't spend too much money on them, they don't mind."

"If I thought you loved someone else, I'd want to kill her."

"It's different with us. You know, once my father had an affair with a white woman in Jerusalem. She was a Russian. I was only ten or eleven years old then, but I remember the whole village talked about it. My mother even boasted about it at the well. It gave him an aura of desirability and made her more important. That's how it works."

"It must really irritate you that I'm Jewish then."

He grinned. "Yes, if you really loved me you'd convert. Your parents were Russian. If you would only become a Christian as well, you'd be perfect."

She slapped him, laughing.

His gaze went to the small pile of clothes in the corner of the room. "Why do you always bring a gun?"

"A Jewish girl travelling alone into an Arab quarter? I have to be able to defend myself."

"You wear a veil and abbayah. What danger is there?"

Yes, but Haganah girls always carry guns. "I just feel safer."

He shrugged.

Does he suspect? she wondered. And what difference would it make to him if he knew? She chose another felafel and put it between his lips. "Do you think it will ever be safe for me to come here without the veil?" she murmured.

"Who can say? It is up to the British. They made a bargain in 1939 and the fighting stopped. They will probably make a bargain again. They are good at making bargains."

She wondered if the British would be in the mood to bargain now. A few weeks ago the Irgun had bombed their headquarters in the King David Hotel and blown up an entire wing of the building. Ninety British soldiers and government workers had died.

548

"What if they make a bargain with just us?" Sarah said. "Then you will have to fight them again."

"Not me – the Mufti and the Higher Committee can fight if they want. I am just a humble businessman."

"But what would you do – if there was a war?"

"I would cheer wildly for the Mufti and hide you here in the office until it was all over."

"Perhaps you could hide me in Rab'allah."

"I don't think so." There was a sardonic note to his voice.

"What is Rab'allah like these days?"

"It is changed, Sarah. The people wear western clothes and talk about having radios and cars and wristwatches. The young people shout about an Arab Palestine while they try to turn our little village into America." He sighed. "I worry about my boys."

"Tell me about them."

"Ali is the eldest. He's a good boy, he's tall and strong and he has a quick temper. All he wants is to own his own gun. That's his strength. That's also his trouble. Then there's Rahman. He hardly ever says a word. He's good at his studies, he knows his Koran. He's not a fighter like Ali but he has a good mind."

"Are they good Jew-haters?"

His face was suddenly dark. "If that is what you think of me, why do you come here?"

"But how can you know what your sons think?"

"They're my sons. They think what I tell them to think."

She thought of Isaac. "Perhaps."

"We promised not to talk politics here. You broke the rule."

Sarah did not answer him. She remembered the bombing that day in the Old City, the bodies like raw meat on the cobblestones in David Street. "Just promise me one thing," she said finally.

"What?"

"Promise me whatever happens . . . even if Palestine is in flames, even if we are surrounded by hatred . . . promise me we will always love each other."

The hardness left his face. His eyes were gentle, a liquid black. "I promise," he said. He put the dish aside. "I'm not hungry any more." A small droplet of perspiration had started its long descent between her breasts and he caught it on the tip of his index finger and put it on his tongue. "This food I can live on for ever."

She laughed and took off her shirt. He threw back the sheet and she lay down on top of him.

88

Sarona

The villa was set among pine trees in the old German Templar colony of Sarona. Majid parked his Fiat in the shade of the courtyard and let himself in with his key.

It was cool in the tiled hallway. The whitewashed walls and ceiling were built of thick stone and cold to the touch, despite the heat outside. He stopped at the foot of the stairs. "Ilse!"

"Is that you, Hassim?"

Majid winced. He knew she had other clients but he tried not to think about it. Her candour angered him.

"No, it's Majid," he grumbled.

She appeared at the top of the stairs, and he immediately forgot his irritation. He felt the familiar tightness in his chest and throat at his first sight of her. She had platinum blonde hair, and impossibly white, white skin, like warm marble. So different from the Arab women he had known.

She leaned over the banister in a dressing-gown of violet silk. She put a hand to her long, unbrushed hair. "I wasn't expecting you, darling. I'm not even ready."

Majid's voice was hoarse. "I'll take you just as you are."

She smiled. Her front teeth protruded just a little; it gave her a slightly petulant look that drove him crazy. "Come up then, liebling. I won't be a moment."

He ran up the stairs to the bedroom. He heard water running in the adjoining bathroom. He sat down on the bed and started to remove his clothes. Darling Ilse. Beautiful Ilse.

Expensive Ilse.

But she was worth it. A man like himself deserved a few vices and of all the vices he had ever indulged in, she was by far the most delicious, the most ripe. She had come to Palestine from Berlin just after the war. She had been starving there, she told him. A good day was when you were not raped by the Russians.

Before the Russians came, she said, she had been a good girl. She had been a virgin then. She did what she did now out of necessity. But she was a good girl.

The bed dominated the room, a huge oak construction with carved bedhead and pink chintz bedspread. He threw himself on it, naked, and cupped his hands behind his head. He looked around the room. There were paintings all round the walls, nudes mostly, and wooden statues on the dresser, couples fornicating in various positions. Two baroque mirrors were both angled towards the bed.

But she had been a virgin before the Russians came.

He reached down and massaged himself so that he would be bigger when she came in. He loved the way she gasped and told him how huge he was. He knew she said that to all her lovers – he could not bear to think of himself as a paying customer – but he still suspected that, in his case at least, it was not a total fabrication.

She had chosen a black camisole and French knickers for today's assignation. Her brassiere accentuated soft, ample breasts. A man might lose himself in that valley and never want to find his way out. May the path to Paradise itself be so warm and curving!

"*Mein Gott*," she whispered, "but you are huge!"
"Say it again," he said. "Let all Palestine know!"

She massaged him with warm oil, kneeling over him so that the warm marble breasts quivered inches from his face. Any moment they shall burst out and suffocate me!

He closed his eyes and let her work on him, tried to push away the fretting that crowded in on him, as it had done all day. He tried to forget that tomorrow he must go and see the Britisher major, Chisholm. He tried to forget that with his complicity there would be more raw Jewish meat spread over the Commercial Centre. Some of it would belong to women and children.

"What is the matter?" Ilse whispered and he opened his eyes and found to his horror that he had lost his erection. "Relax! Let Ilse take care of it for you." And she laughed, deep in her throat, and opened her mouth into a perfect vermilion "O".

Majid gasped with pleasure as she encircled him.

Just feel! he told himself. Try not to think what will happen if those dirty Jews start an all-out war in Palestine. Try not to think what that will do to business. He could lose the olive oil company! Or some idiotic bastard – like Izzat – might use his taxi to throw grenades and the Haganah would blow it up and then who would buy a new one?

Allah help me in my sorrow! Try not to think about Izzat! Try not to think what he will do to the man with the biggest sacred member in the whole of Palestine if he finds out that he is also giving information to the Haganah! But how else can I still afford this warm little mouth and breasts of moving, warm white marble?

"What's the matter, liebling? Is he scared of me today?"

Forget about Izzat! Forget about the war and Major Chisholm! Just think how rich you are getting from buying rifles and grenades from the British Quartermaster stores and reselling them in the souks to the fedayeen and the Haganah for five times their cost!

Just think about Ilse and the warm valley that leads to the Gates of Paradise itself.

"That's better," Ilse said approvingly. "What a beautiful minaret. Now I shall return to my prayers."

"Oh yes, yes," he said and at that moment he heard the muezzins summon the faithful while Majid Hass'an gave himself up to his own worship.

Rab'allah

The rattle of donkey hooves. The one sound that Rishou always associated with the village, the sound of peace and order and timelessness. So different from the babel of Jerusalem with its trucks and hawkers and the radios in every souk and café. These days every man with a donkey wanted a motor car.

Like mine.

He got out of the Fiat and went into the coffee house. Zayyad was seated in a corner, with several village sheikhs and elders. He grinned when he saw Rishou. He allowed his son to kneel and kiss his hand in the traditional manner of respect and then they embraced.

"Rishou! It is good to see you! Does business go well?"

"It does, Father."

"And Majid?"

"He prospers also."

A shadow passed across Zayyad's face. "He should come and visit his parents now and then. It is months since I have seen him."

"He works hard." *He works hard at finding women to lie with.*

"Tell him I should welcome having him feast from my plate again anyway. You will take coffee with us?"

"Of course, yaba. And then I must visit my own sons."

They took coffee, and went through the long formalities of greeting that were incumbent even on fathers and sons. Afterwards, when Rishou had taken his leave of the others, Zayyad led him to the door of the coffee house,

553

his arm around his shoulders. When they were outside he whispered, "I wish I did not have to tell you this."

Rishou felt the cold grip of alarm. "What is wrong? Is it my boys?"

"It is Ali . . . I think you must talk to him."

"The Strugglers."

Zayyad nodded. "Talk to him, Rishou. He is so young. It is just the blood in him. He would fight his own shadow just for a chance to prove his worth."

"Izzat! I should have finished with him long ago!"

"Izzat now has bodyguards. He is the eyes and tongue of the Mufti in Judea." He shrugged. "If it was not Izzat, it would be someone else. They won't listen to me now."

"May Allah strike him with a thousand boils and may they all burst at once!"

"*Insh'allah!*"

"Thank you, yaba, I shall attend to my son."

Rahman knelt and kissed his hand at the door of the house, then rose to embrace him. Rishou patted Wagiha on the head and turned to Khadija and instructed her to prepare him his bath.

Bathing was a symbol of his wealth. Because of the shortage of water, only the rich could afford to bathe regularly, while the fellaheen contented themselves with washing only every few months. But Rishou possessed his own well and even had a separate room in his house set aside for bathing. Khadija heated the water in a brass pot and then poured it over her husband while he sat naked on a chair.

Afterwards, he dressed in a new white robe and keffiyeh of red and white check and sat on the rug in his majlis while Khadija and Wagiha served him mint tea. And he waited for Ali to come.

"Yaba . . ."

Rishou stood up and held out his hand. Ali ignored it.

Rishou stepped forward and slapped him hard on the side of the cheek. He heard Khadija gasp.

554

The outline of his hand slowly gelled in crimson on his son's cheek. Rishou sent his wife and children out of the room.

"Have you forgotten the way a son greets his father?"

Ali said nothing.

Rishou hit him again.

"Don't do that again," Ali growled.

"Why? What would you do? Should you kill me, Ali?" He took the knife from his belt and tossed it to his son. It fell on the rug between them. "Take it. See, you are armed now. If you wish to contend my authority over you, pick it up. Go on!"

Ali stared at the knife and at his father and did not move.

Rishou hit him again.

"Is it no longer good enough for you to be an Arab?"

"I am an Arab. A true Arab. It's you who has forgotten."

"So! You are all of eleven years old and you want to preach to me!"

"Izzat says you are a Jew-lover."

Rishou hit him again. Ali took a step back. His eyes were brimming with tears. "If you mention his name under my roof again I shall beat you until your ears bleed. Do you understand me?"

"Then why won't you fight the Jews?"

"Because I do not wish to become a stick puppet pulled this way and that by some fool who calls himself Mufti! Because you cannot tell your enemies by the God of their prayers! Is that clear to you?"

"Izzat says it is because you are afraid!"

Rishou took Ali by the arm and cuffed him again and again and again. Ali screamed and wriggled free. He threw himself on to the carpet and grabbed the knife and slashed at his father's face. Rishou was ready. He grabbed the boy's arm, and twisted it behind his back.

Ali screamed and released the knife.

Rishou spun him around and put an arm around his neck. He forced him to the floor. "You wish me dead,

Ali?" he whispered. "You wish your father dead? But all you have to do to destroy me is get yourself killed! See, it's that simple!"

Ali wriggled like a trapped bird, but Rishou held him fast. "Is it so painful to hear, that I love you so much? When you are dead I shall throw myself in your grave and they can throw the dirt in my open mouth to stop me screaming for I cannot live without my sons!"

"If I die for Allah I go directly to the Gates of Paradise and I shall be welcomed by Mohammed himself and there will be a thousand virgins to wait on me day and night!"

Rishou laughed. "What would you do with a virgin? Play soccer with her? You are just eleven years old!"

He released him. Ali knelt on the rug, his head bowed in defeat. He sniffed and wiped his nose with the back of his sleeve. "Now greet me properly," Rishou said.

Ali turned around on his knees and took his father's hand. He kissed it. Then Rishou pulled him to his feet and embraced him.

My son, he thought. All my love is invested here. Is it ever enough? When was it ever enough?

89

Yemin Moshe

The remains of their dinner were scattered around the table: schnitzel, salad, mangoes and Carmelite wine. Netanel lit a cigarette and leaned back in his chair. Marie had only toyed with her food.

"I don't remember you smoked this much before I went to university," she said.

"I had trouble with my nerves after I got out of Auschwitz."

She blinked rapidly, as if he had said something to her in a foreign language. "Did you enjoy your dinner?"

He nodded. "Yes. It was wonderful."

"Herr Fromberg is always inviting us for dinner. I think he is curious about you."

"Is he?"

"He keeps asking me when we are going to get married."

"Perhaps Herr Fromberg should mind his own business."

"He means well." She stared at him over the rim of her glass. "We can't live like this for ever."

"Live like what?"

Marie put down her glass and stared into the ruby liquid. "Don't you want to marry me?"

"How can I marry you, Marie? For God's sake, how can I?"

"You promised."

"I came to live here because I was worried about you. Because I want you to be well again. But I can't marry you. You have watched me beat another man to death with a club. I am a traitor and a coward."

Her face seemed to crumple, like soft clay melting on a potter's wheel. "Why do you say such things?"

"The man you knew is dead. He died in Auschwitz. I love you, Marie, I will never stop loving you. But I can't marry you."

"You said we could marry as soon as I came home from university."

"That was ten years ago!" He slammed his fist on the table and her glass jumped and the dark wine spilled across the tablecloth.

"But you promised," she said. She rose from the table and went into her bedroom, shutting the door quietly behind her.

*   *   *

557

He had not entered her bedroom in the two months they had lived together. He did not desire her as he once did; that part of him had been left behind, beyond the wire. So every night he slept on the floor or on the sofa.

Tonight he lay in the darkness and listened to her crying on the other side of the door. He looked at the luminous dial of his watch. Almost midnight. She had been crying for two hours. He threw off the single blanket that covered him and groped for his cigarettes. He lit one and went to the window. Marie, please stop.

But it went on and on and on.

She was lying face down on the bed, her head cradled in her arms. He turned on the lamp beside the bed. "Marie, stop it."

He sat her up and cradled her in his arms. Her body trembled, and he felt the wetness on her face through his shirt. She hid her face from him in the crook of his neck. "I love you," she said, gulping in a breath between each word.

He looked down at her, "Just stop, please," he whispered.

"I love you," she repeated. Suddenly he felt her lips on his, and he knew he should push her away. But then her arms were around his neck, pulling him on to the bed. It was as if they were suddenly back in the makeshift bed in the House in the Woods, making love in the candlelight. Those same feelings rushed back to him, unannounced, that same desperate cocktail of need and danger and urgency, the ache of a passion that had almost sustained him through hell.

He kissed her back, desperately, felt the yielding softness of her, and the heat of her body. He had thought this part of him was dead. Perhaps there was a way back after all. Perhaps he could try the maze of his past again and find some different answer . . .

He tore at the buttons of her blouse and ripped it open, and she threw back her head and offered him her breast. He tore off her skirt and fumbled with her underpants.

"Go on, go on," she hissed at him.

"I love you," he said.

"Go on."

"Marie . . ."

"Do it . . . hurt me . . . bite me!" Her voice was not her own.

He tried to pull away but she clung to his neck.

"Go on, rape me, put it in me now, hard, hard!"

"Marie . . ."

He stared at her, and it was like looking at a stranger. Her eyes were glassy with some demonic vision he could not share, her face contorted with hate and fear. It was not Marie at all. And this was not the House in the Woods.

"Go on!" she screamed at him. "Hit me! Hit me!"

"Stop it . . ."

She took his hand and put it in her hair. "Pull my hair!"

"STOP . . ."

"Hurt me, you bastard, you Germans are all bastards!"

He rolled away from her, shocked, as the chasm of Auschwitz yawned between them, and he cursed himself for a fool because he should have known there was no way back. She gave him a look of pure loathing and then the demon of the past vanished as suddenly as it had come and she rolled on her side, like a foetus curling back into its womb. She started to cry, very, very softly.

Netanel heard Fromberg banging on the ceiling below, startled by the shouting. When he left the bedroom Marie was still crying but this time he knew it was pointless to try and stop her.

Damascus Gate

Sarah watched the withered old Arab woman cross the square, her head bowed, the basket of peaches she had brought to the market strapped to her back. She led a donkey on a rope behind her. Her husband sat on the donkey's back, wrapped in his keffiyeh.

559

Perhaps Rishou and I, she thought, save for the grace of two Gods that keep us separate.

She turned back to Majid. "What do you have for me?"

Majid picked up his coffee cup but his hands were shaking and he spilled some of the contents on the tabletop.

"Your nerves are bad," she said to him.

"Is it any wonder?"

"You should try and relax more."

He leered at her. "What do you do to relax?"

"I kill Arabs."

He grimaced, as if he had swallowed something foul. He wiped the sweat on his palms on to his trousers.

"There was an attack in the Old City last week," she said.

"I can't know everything that happens."

"So – what do you know, Majid?"

"I know there is going to be trouble in the Commercial Centre."

"When?"

"Thursday."

"What time?"

"Morning, I think. Some Arabs are going to drive into the centre and throw a grenade into the crowd. That's all I know."

"Have the British been informed?"

Majid wiped the sweat from his upper lip. "Perhaps."

Sarah took an envelope from her shorts and pushed it across the table. Majid picked it up and transferred it to his jacket pocket with practised skill. "I want to stop this now," he mumbled.

"Stop what?"

"Stop these meetings. I can't help you any more."

"You have to help us. You don't have any choice."

"You can't keep squeezing me for ever! One day I'm going to stop. I don't care what you do. Even if they kill me."

"Of course they'll kill you. You know what your Arab brothers do to informers. They'll kill you slowly with their knives and they'll leave you in the street for the dogs and they won't even let your family come and bury you."

Majid's lower lip trembled. "I don't care. One day I'm going to just stop. Do what you like."

"I thought you liked the money," Sarah said, more gently.

"I am still an Arab."

"No, you're not. You stopped being an Arab a long time ago."

"You'll see," Majid hissed.

Sarah watched him leave. Poor little bastard. Her superiors in the Shai had told her to keep the pressure on him but she wondered if he could take much more. She knew they would never carry out their threat to expose him. By the time he reached that trough of desperation there would no longer be any point in punishing him.

She also wondered how many other paymasters Majid had. One day soon, she imagined, he would lose control of his little game and the end would be slow and bloody. If he wasn't such an unprincipled little shit she could almost feel sorry for him.

90

Yemin Moshe

Asher stopped at the top of the badly lit stair and winced at the pain in his leg. Never a day went by that he did not curse the British soldier who had fired that bullet the night of the raid at Atlit. He composed himself and knocked at the door.

After a few moments he heard movement on the other side of the door. "Who is it?"

"Asher."

The door inched open and Asher slipped inside. Netanel looked pale, his face unshaven. "It's late. It must be important."

"It is."

Netanel carefully locked the door.

"Nice place," Asher said, looking around. Compared with the last one. Then he saw her and it was difficult for him to keep the look of astonishment from his face. She was quite beautiful, with chestnut brown hair framing high cheekbones and startling green eyes. Netanel had always shown a zealot's disregard for women and sex. How had he ever found such a girl?

"Marie, this is a good friend of mine from the Palmach," Netanel was saying. "Asher Ben-Zion. Asher, this is Marie Helder."

"Hello, Asher," Marie said. She held out a soft, pale hand and he shook it. Then he remembered. Her hair had grown, the shapeless rag of a dress had been replaced with a soft pink blouse and stylish black skirt. But it was her, he knew it.

"You!" he whispered.

Marie frowned. "I am sorry?"

"You were at Atlit! You were the one who helped me when I was shot! Netanel, this is the girl I told you about!"

"I don't think I understand," Marie said.

"The refugee camp! I was hit in the leg! You helped me. Don't you remember?"

A long, shuffling silence. Netanel and Marie exchanged a look he could not fathom. Asher wondered for a moment if he could be mistaken. But no, it was *her*.

"Where is this Atlit?" Marie said.

Netanel avoided his eyes. "It was dark, Ash. You were in pain. The memory plays tricks."

"Yes, I'm sorry," Asher stammered. "I'm obviously mistaken."

"Netya, why don't you go and sit down with your friend?" Marie said. "I'll make the coffee."

Netanel put an arm round Asher's shoulder and steered him to the table by the window. "Come and tell me the news, Ash. Have you seen Yaakov? How is the old dog?"

Marie made them coffee and then sat down and listened to their conversation, but said little. Asher could not stop staring at her, convincing himself that this really was the girl he remembered. He and Netanel talked about Kfar Herzl for a while and then the conversation returned inevitably to politics and the latest Arab attacks in the city.

Almost at once Marie stood up and said goodnight. "I hope you'll excuse me," she said, "I have to get up early to go to work. Goodnight, Netya. Goodnight, Asher. It was nice to meet you."

"Goodnight, Marie. It was good to meet you also. I hope you'll forgive my behaviour earlier."

"Of course. Goodnight."

As soon as the bedroom door was closed Asher gripped Netanel's wrist. "Is it her? Tell me!"

"I don't know. Is this important, Ash?"

"For God's sake! I thought I was going crazy! Was she at Atlit? Doesn't she remember?"

"I told you, I don't know!"

"She was at Auschwitz, wasn't she?" Asher had noticed the purple tattoo on the soft white underside of her arm.

Netanel looked grey. "You'll make a good spy, Ash."

"What's going on, Netya?"

Netanel tapped his temple with his index finger. "Nobody survives Auschwitz, Ash. Not completely. It does things to your mind."

"But Atlit was just a few months ago!"

Netanel shrugged. "I'm a soldier, not a psychologist."

"Isn't there anything anyone can do?"

"I'm doing everything I can. But it's my problem, all right?"

"Do you love her?"

Netanel threw the heavy silver cigarette lighter on the

table and shook his head. "It's not what you think. She needs someone to look after her. Can we talk about something else? This is really none of your business."

"Have you thought of taking her to a doctor? On the kibbutz we have scores of kids who came from the camps and – "

"I said let's talk about something else."

There were a thousand questions, but Asher felt as if he had already defiled some dark and holy sanctum. After all, Netanel was right, it was none of his business. The girl did not belong to him. "Okay." He tasted his coffee. Cold and bitter.

"You still haven't told me what brings the Shai here at this time of night," Netanel said.

Asher changed the subject with reluctance. He frowned, dragging his concentration away from Marie. "One of our informers has told us there is going to be some action in the Commercial Centre this Thursday."

"What time?"

"Morning. That's all we know. Some fedayeen are driving a car into the centre. They'll have pistols and grenades."

"What do you want me to do?"

"We think the British have been tipped off, so chances are they won't be in the centre. Have all your people there early. Smuggle them in with weapons in twos and threes. You'll need at least a dozen to cover the whole area."

"Do we know what make of car we're looking for?"

Asher shook his head.

Netanel dropped his cigarette into his coffee and jumped to his feet. The cigarette fizzled and went out. Netanel stared out of the window at the night. "Why do we always have to fight running backwards? Why can't we hit the Arabs first for once?"

"You know how it is."

"Yes, I know how it is. And it's shit!"

Asher said nothing.

Netanel let the tension drain out of him in a long sigh. "We'll find them for you, Asher. But I'll tell you one thing.

We're not going to win Palestine unless we start lobbing the hand-grenades back over the wall."

"That's not our job."

"Maybe it should be."

Asher finished his coffee. "Goodnight, Netya." He stood up, hesitating. "Look, about Marie. If there's anything I can do . . ."

"I'm doing everything I can. But it's my problem, all right?"

When Asher closed the door Netanel was still standing at the window, staring into the dark. Asher shuddered. Too many secrets here. Too much he didn't understand.

New City

Major Ian Chisholm swallowed a deep draught of his Goldstar beer and regarded the Arab sitting across the table from him with an expression of transparent distaste. Everyone in the room was staring at the man's tie, for God's sake. Their meetings were supposed to be discreet. Well, if there were any Haganah in the room – and it was not impossible, even though everyone else in Fink's that afternoon was in British uniform – they could not surely suspect that the man with the naked woman on his tie was an Arab informer.

"So what's the whisper, old son?" Chisholm said.

"Thursday morning. The Commercial Centre."

Chisholm sniffed. "I see."

"Ten o'clock."

Chisholm's own Guards company patrolled that particular area. Simple enough to ensure that none of his men was injured; just as easy to keep the Haganah out and help the Arabs do a good job. It would go some way to levelling the scores for the David bombing.

"Remember when the Irgun bombed the King David Hotel?"

"Of course, Chisholm effendi," Majid said.

565

"My best mate had his legs blown off that day. He was with me right through Normandy and the Rhine. Got two awards for bravery. He was wounded in Germany so they shoved him sideways into a desk job. So he comes here and some little kike bastard blows his legs away with a bomb. You reckon that's justice, old son?"

"No, Chisholm effendi."

"Neither do I. So you'd better tell me how I recognise these friends of yours and we'll make sure they don't get themselves into any trouble."

Yemin Moshe

Whirrrrrr. Snap! Click . . .

Netanel started awake, and listened, straining his ears to the blackness. It must be late, there were no lights in the street.

Whirrrrrr. Snap!

He blinked into the darkness. There it was again.

. . . Click . . .

He recognised that sound instantly. He threw himself off the sofa and stumbled towards Marie's bedroom in one movement. The blanket was still tangled around his legs, and he tripped.

Whirrrrrr. Snap!

"*Marie!*"

. . . Click . . .

By the holy name of God, she couldn't be . . .

Whirrrrrr . . .

He threw open the door. Marie sat on the edge of the bed in her nightdress, Netanel's revolver in her right hand. She snapped the chamber shut and held the muzzle against her temple. She stared blankly at the wall.

He watched the knuckle of her index finger tighten around the trigger mechanism.

"*No!*"

. . . Click.

566

Netanel tore the Webley out of her hand. She looked up at him in dull surprise.

"For God's sake! What are you doing?"

"It's all right," Marie said. "I'm just playing a little game with Rebecca."

"Rebecca?" Oily sweat on his face, a weight like cold lead in his gut.

"Don't you know Rebecca?" Marie asked him.

Her gaze returned to the wall, her eyes soft and out of focus, staring at some terrible phantom from her past he could only guess at. He opened the chamber of the revolver. One live bullet.

Herrgottsacrament!

He threw the gun on the bed and sat down beside her. He put his arm around her shoulders. "Oh my God. What has happened to you, Marie?"

"Rebecca says I cheat."

"Who is she? Who is Rebecca?"

"I don't know," Marie said, and her voice was far away and dream-like. "She says she wants to play."

Netanel hugged her to him, but she was as rigid as a statue. God help me, Netanel thought. What can I do? I barely live each day through my own torment. Is that not enough? How can I exorcise her ghosts when I cannot lay my own?

He carried her back to bed. "You have to go to sleep now," he whispered.

Obediently she closed her eyes.

Netanel picked up the revolver and removed the bullet from the chamber. Then he lay down on top of the bed and cradled her in his arms. "Shhh," he whispered. "Go to sleep now. It will be all right. Go to sleep."

After a time her deep even breathing told him she was asleep, but Netanel lay awake long into the night, thinking.

91

Kfar Herzl Kibbutz

The hospital at Kfar Herzl had two wards with ten beds in each, plus a clinic and a basic operating theatre. There was a full-time doctor and three nurses, with a dentist and a psychiatrist shared with three other kibbutzim.

The psychiatrist's name was Levin, and for his visits to Kfar Herzl he shared the doctor's office, a tiny white-washed room that faced the apple orchards. There was a large grey filing cabinet in one corner, with an ophthalmologist's chart hanging on the wall above it. There was no other furniture except for a desk and two chairs.

Levin took his time to fill the bowl of a Meerschaum pipe from a small leather pouch he produced from the pocket of his white jacket. He was a compact, spectacularly handsome man with neatly groomed black hair and intense dark eyes. The single girls on the kibbutz speculated that he looked like Cary Grant, which was a pity for them, because he was happily married with three small children.

He lit his pipe and glanced up at Marie with an expression of almost surprise, as if he had forgotten that she was there. He glanced at the file on the desk. "Miss Helder. May I call you Marie?"

"Of course."

"You live in Jerusalem."

"In Yemin Moshe. With my fiancé."

"Ah, yes, Netanel, Netanel Rosenberg." He sucked on the Meerschaum, and clouds of blue-grey smoke drifted lazily towards the open window. "He brought you here."

"Yes."

"Do you know why?"

"He says I pointed a loaded revolver at my own head."

"Hmm. Do you remember that?"

Marie shook her head.

Levin cleared his throat. "Do you mind being here?"

"I trust Netanel."

"But?"

"I can't believe why I would do such a thing."

"You don't believe it happened?"

Marie traced the contour of the desk with the tip of an index finger, as if she were examining it for dust. "No."

Levin toyed with the pipe, frowning. Difficult. "I wonder why he would imagine something so . . . dramatic?"

Marie said nothing.

"Marie?"

"Perhaps you should talk to him."

"Ah." He picked up the file, flicked through the notes he had taken from his interview with Rosenberg. "You were at Auschwitz?"

Marie stared at him. "I'm sorry?"

"Netanel said you were at Auschwitz."

"My family lived in Ravenswald. It's a small town in Bavaria."

"And what happened to you during the war?"

Marie leaned forward, as if she were straining to hear him. "I am sorry?"

"During the war. What happened then?"

"The war?" She gave a soft, embarrassed laugh. "I was three years old when the war ended."

Levin examined his Meerschaum. It had gone out. He put it between his teeth and relit it. "Marie, this may seem like a stupid question to you . . ." She was smiling at him, not unkindly, he thought. Just enough to indicate that she thought the last question was idiotic enough. He extinguished the match. "What is the date?"

"August 23rd."

"What year?"

"What year . . .?"

"Humour me."

"It's 1938."

A long silence. She stared at him, wide-eyed, as if he were the most stupid and incompetent man she had ever met.

Levin sucked hard on the pipe. Yes, difficult. Very difficult.

Netanel walked with Levin along the dirt path that led from the hospital to the administration building. The path was bordered with rose bushes, and the heavy perfume was thick in the hot, still air. Levin's fists were plunged deep in the pocket of his shorts. His pipe and his pen were tucked into the breast pocket of his jacket.

"Well?" Netanel said.

"I do not pretend to have an easy solution for you, young man."

"I did not come here looking for one."

"No? Then you are a very remarkable person." Levin examined one of the rose blooms. "Beautiful, aren't they? Beautiful to look at, and to smell, and the petals are velvet to the touch. Yet look at these thorns. Razor sharp. Do you know why roses have barbs?"

Netanel shrugged. Was this relevant? "For protection?"

"For protection, yes. Because, despite its beauty, the flower is fragile and can be easily damaged. This is the same as the human psyche. When it is threatened, it tries to protect itself."

"Marie?"

"The ways a person will protect himself from psychic harm are as many and varied as the human personality. Some individuals cope in ways that are acceptable in the society we have created. What we call rational. It takes account of external reality and adjusts to it. Others cope by some measure of withdrawal from reality – as your friend has done."

"Does that mean she's insane?"

"What is insanity? If you look around you at what is

570

happening in Palestine right now, is this rational, is this sane? Everyone is perhaps a little mad. Here in the Yishuv we see so many broken bodies and minds. Most find their way back from their personal nightmares. We can perhaps help them a little but the knowledge we have about the mind is a poor thing beside what we do not know."

"Can you help her?"

"I could try. The kibbutz is a wonderful sanctuary for the spirit. But she does not wish to stay and I cannot force her."

"Then how can I help her forget Auschwitz?"

"Will you ever forget?" Levin put his arm around Netanel's shoulder and guided him along the path. "It is not what we remember that hurts us, it is what we repress. As far as your friend is concerned the year is 1938. She has finished university and returned to Ravenswald to find you gone. She came here to look for you. That is her reality. That is how she intends to live with Auschwitz."

"But the revolver . . .?"

"Yes, that is the problem. There is a part of our hidden mind that is like an umpire at tennis, if you like. It is always keeping score. It knows when we cheat and it accuses us when we sleep."

"She will try and kill herself again. I know it."

"I don't know what to say to you. She doesn't want to stay. You see, in her mind, you are the crazy one."

Netanel stared up at the sky, his hands bunched into fists. "Tell me one thing. What will happen if she does remember?"

"In many cases, if we face our conflict, we can learn to resolve it. But sometimes forcing painful memories to the surface is a very violent process. One has to be careful." Levin studied the gaunt, haunted young man beside him. Perhaps he could do with some help himself.

"I'd like to do what Marie has done," Netanel said. "Forget any of it ever happened. But I can't. Thank you for your help, doctor."

Levin shrugged. A land full of injured minds. There was only so much to be done. The British should not have sent one hundred thousand troops. One hundred thousand psychiatrists might achieve much more.

92

New City

The British had cordoned off the Commercial Centre.

The blue and silver Egged bus was stalled in a long line of traffic behind a roadblock on Princess Mary Avenue. Netanel looked at his watch. A few minutes before ten o'clock. They should have been inside the Commercial Centre long ago. His stomach was knotted with impotent rage. He jumped down from the bus and pushed his way through the crowds towards the roadblock.

Two olive-green Guards armoured cars straddled the road, and the traffic was backed up behind them, choking the boulevard as far as he could see. People were milling around the tanks; bus and lorry drivers shook their fists and pounded their horns in frustration; little Jews in homburgs and carrying briefcases shouted insults at the soldiers; others sat slumped behind the wheels of their automobiles reading their newspapers in weary resignation.

A Guards major watched the mêlée from his jeep. He was surrounded by a phalanx of soldiers, all in steel helmets and battle dress. His beret was perched at a jaunty angle on his head. He leaned on the windshield, staring over the heads of the crowd, as if he were watching a horse race.

Netanel tried to push his way through the mob, but it was impossible. The British were all sons of whores!

He ran back to the bus. A squad of Guardsmen was

already there. Several of them waited impassively to one side, their Sten guns cocked on their hips, while their colleagues routed everyone from the bus and searched them for weapons.

There were seven of his own Palmach platoon among the passengers, four men, three girls. They were safe, Netanel knew. Their pistols and grenades were concealed in intimate places on the women, as was usual practice. The British were meticulous about not compromising the modesty of females during body searches.

Netanel approached the sergeant in charge of the squad. "What's going on? Why can't we get through?"

"Area's been cordoned off, sir." The sergeant's manner was polite but firm. A professional doing his job.

"Why, for God's sake?"

"Security purposes, sir. Who are you?"

"My name's Rosenberg."

"Rosenberg," he repeated. A note of hostility insinuated itself in the soldier's voice.

"That's right."

"Do you mind if I search you, sir?"

"Go ahead." Netanel had been searched many times. He spread his feet wide and raised his hands while the sergeant frisked him. It was then that he heard it. Small arms fire, just a few hundred yards away, from the direction of the Commercial Centre. A stillness fell over the crowd.

Netanel turned to the sergeant. "The Arabs are already in there! Do something!"

The sergeant signalled to his men and they ran back up the avenue, their heavy boots crunching on the road.

A sharp CRACK! Netanel knew that sound. A grenade.

A black plume of smoke spiralled into the blue sky.

"Herrgottsacrament," he whispered.

The Guards major shouted an order and one of the armoured cars detached itself from the roadblock and rumbled slowly back up the avenue towards the Commercial Centre.

A few seconds later a black Hillman screeched out of

the centre, directly in the path of the armoured car. The British officer in the turret of the Dingo ignored it. Moments later the Hillman turned on to Jaffa Road and disappeared.

From the stillness, eerie like the rush of wind, came the sound of screams, the plaintive wounded cries of the innocent.

The sprawling aggregation of warehouses and bazaars, known as the Commercial Centre, was a predominantly Jewish market. The crowds haggled and traded, shoulder to shoulder among the bolts of cloth, bedspreads, shoes and canned food. The shoppers were as diverse as the goods on offer: Hassids from Mea Sherim, Orthodox in white shirts with hand-knitted skull caps, girl kibbutzniks in khaki shorts.

The black Hillman had pulled up in front of a bakery. Ali jumped out. Almost at once the two men in the back produced their weapons, a Colt .45 and an ancient Mauser rifle, and fired indiscriminately into the crowd. The customers in the bakery heard the shots and threw themselves on the floor.

Ali raced inside, stuffed two slices of halwa in his mouth, and pulled the grenade out of his trousers. He removed the locking pin and dropped the grenade on the floor. Tareq had gunned the motor of the Hillman and was already in second gear when Ali ran out of the shop. The boy jumped in as it drove away.

The car door was yawning open as they skidded around the first corner. They were barely out of sight when the explosion blew out the windows of the bakery and hurled pieces of the metal shutters some two hundred yards.

When the British arrived a few minutes later in an armoured car, there were pieces of bloody meat all over the street.

Yemin Moshe

Asher tried the door. Unlocked. A bad sign.

He pushed it open.

Netanel sat by the window with two packets of cigarettes and a bottle of vodka on the table in front of him. The ashtray was overflowing, and the bottle was half empty. "Hello, Ash," he said.

Asher shut the door and sat down. "I heard what happened."

"Twelve dead, twenty-two injured. Can you believe that?"

Asher helped himself to a little of the vodka, straight from the bottle. "It wasn't your fault."

"Do you think that's why I'm like this? That I blame myself?"

"We'll get them next time, Netya."

"Next time! Why does there have to be a next time? There have already been too many 'next times'! Okay, Ash, you're always asking me about Auschwitz, I'll tell you about it. You know what I saw there? I saw men tipping little children out of wheelbarrows into a bonfire! Children, five or six years old, burned alive! Because they were Jews! That was my 'last time', Ash. Every 'next time' after that is an obscenity! It is an indictment against me, against all of us!"

"Please, Netya. It's not my fault, it's not your fault. We did what we could. Let it be."

"Know something? I talked to one of the people who was in the Commercial Centre this morning. He said the Arab who put the grenade in the bakery wasn't more than eleven or twelve years old. Barely off their mother's tit, Ash, and they're throwing bombs at us!"

"There's nothing we can do about this morning."

"Oh yes, there is, Ash. There's a lot we can do."

Asher didn't like this. Was it just the grief and the alcohol talking? Or was Netanel ready to betray the Haganah discipline? "We're not Nazis, Netya, and we're not Arabs. We don't hurt innocents. When you took up

575

arms for the Haganah, you vowed to keep our weapons pure – "

"Pure!"

"Our purpose is defence, not murder."

"You're as bad as my father. You don't see it, do you? All this 'we only shoot in self-defence' stuff is all shit! They're laughing at us! While they know we won't hurt them back they'll keep killing us! An eye for an eye, Ash. Burning for burning!"

"That's not the reason the Haganah was formed – "

"That was fine when you all lived on kibbutzim, when you were playing cowboys and indians. Now we have all European Jewry relying on us, Ash! All the ones the Germans forgot to burn! We have to carve our own land, our own sanctuary! We're not going to do that unless we are prepared to throw the British *and* the Arabs out of Palestine! And let the ends justify the means!"

"Once we start to think that way, we're as bad as the Nazis."

"You were the one who showed me how to fight this war, Ash. But maybe you don't have the stomach to finish it! Don't you know what they did to your father?"

Asher stared at him, confused. "I don't know what they did, Netya," he said softly. "I don't suppose I'll ever know." He tried to fathom the look of tormented rage on the other man's face.

"No, you'll never know, will you?" Netanel spat at him. "You sabras! You think you're tough, you're just sunburned." Netanel lit another cigarette from the stub of his last one. "Get out of here."

Asher left, closing the door softly behind him.

93

Herr Fromberg looked up and saw Marie slowly climbing the stairs to the apartment. "Good evening, Fräulein Helder!"

"Good evening, Herr Fromberg."

"Hot weather we are having."

"Yes. Perhaps it will be cooler tomorrow."

She looks tired, he thought. There are dark smudges under her eyes and the bounce has gone out of her. He wondered if everything was all right between her and this Rosenberg fellow. There had been a lot of shouting and screaming from upstairs lately.

"Nasty business what happened today. Why can't people just let one another alone?"

"I am sorry, Herr Fromberg?"

"Didn't you hear? They threw a bomb in the Commercial Centre."

"There is always trouble somewhere," Marie said and then she was gone. He returned his attention to his newspaper.

There were cigarette butts spilling out of the ashtray and an empty vodka bottle lying on the carpet. Marie shook her head. What a mess he had made! She would have to get him to improve his habits when they were married. "Netya, I'm home!"

No answer. He must have gone out.

She went into her bedroom and threw her handbag on the bed. She sat down at the vanity dresser to remove her make-up –

There were two faces in the mirror. One was her own;

the other was a nightmare from the past. It wore filthy pyjamas, and had a black J stencilled on the left breast. The head was shaved, and the face was encrusted with grease and dirt.

The right fist held a wooden club.

She couldn't breathe. Her whole body shook uncontrollably. She wanted to scream but no sound would come. Her throat closed and she could only shake her head from side to side in silent appeal.

"Remember me?" Netanel said.

She tried to run to the door but her legs buckled underneath her and she fell on to the floor, spilling brushes and a small perfume bottle from the top of the dresser.

Netanel grabbed her by the arm and held his face very close to hers. "Remember now?"

Still she could not answer him.

"What's the matter, little Jew whore? Can't you talk? Perhaps I should take you to see Stürmbahnführer Emmerich?"

"Please . . ."

"So you do remember now?"

She squeezed her eyes shut to block out the apparition. "No!"

"Tell me who I am!"

She shook her head. His strong fingers were squeezing her arm, and the pain was intolerable. "Don't . . ."

"Then tell me who I am!"

She opened her eyes. His face was pressed against hers, distorted and ugly with violence.

"You're Netanel . . ." she whimpered.

"And what am I doing?"

She couldn't say it, couldn't . . .

"*What am I doing?*"

"*You're beating that poor old Jew to death!*"

He let her go and she slipped to the floor. She retched painfully, over and over, until finally she lay panting and exhausted and empty, Netanel took off the cap and threw it on the carpet beside her. He dabbed at the dirt on his cheek. "Boot polish," he said.

He walked out of the room, tearing at the buttons of the pyjamas. She heard him climb into the shower.

She lay on the floor for a long time, not moving. The light faded and the room grew dark. She heard him packing. When he came back he was dressed in a khaki jersey and black drill pants and he had a duffel bag over his arm.

"I am leaving now," he said.

She nodded her understanding.

"If I thought it would help, I would stay. But it won't do any good. I can never forgive myself, so even if you . . . well . . . let's not talk about that. If you think you need to tell people about this, it's all right." He hesitated, as if there was more he wanted to say, but could not find the words. "I am going to call a friend of mine, Asher, Asher Ben-Zion. You remember him? He'll take care of you."

The door closed quietly behind him.

Still she lay there. The wall had been breached and the past trickled in, slowly at first, then faster and faster, like floodwater.

Drowning her.

94

Asher reached the top of the stairs and tried the door. It was open. Netanel said it would be.

He went in. It was night and a faint breeze stirred the curtains. It had blown the pile of cigarette ash from the ashtray and across the table in slight grey drifts. The curtain flicked at the bottle and the glasses.

"Marie?"

He heard a noise in the bedroom. He went in.

She was sitting on the edge of the bed holding a revolver in her lap. She looked up, and her face creased into a frown. "I want to finish my game with Rebecca," she said.

"Netanel called me. He said you needed help."

Her eyes were pink from crying. "I don't think Netanel's coming back," she said.

He gently took the revolver from her fingers. A Parabellum. "Where did you get this?"

"From the souk. They're rather expensive. The war's driving up the price of everything." She seemed dazed.

He sat on the bed beside her and put his arm around her shoulders. "I think you'd better come home with me," he said.

Sanhedriyya

Winter came to Palestine heralded by the hammering of rain against the windows; with the distant hills of Judea springing green from the dry, parched browns of the long summer; and with the shouts of players and spectators at the football matches from the fields behind the YMCA.

A fine mist rolled down the hill from the Sanhedrin Tombs, through the shanty streets of the poor Yemenite Quarter of the city. Netanel Rosenberg stopped outside one of the doorways, and paused to check the window. A blue and white box of Lux soap powder placed in the right-hand corner of the window assured him that the meeting was secure. He wiped the rain off his face with one swift motion of his right hand and went inside.

There were three others in the room: Meodovnik, the owlish mathematics professor from Kiev; Kohn, the Hassid rabbi from Lubin, bald except for the two long ringlets of his religion and tangled beard; and Shoshan, the Yemenite, who sold bagels in Zion Square, his dank strong-smelling sheepskin coat lending the tiny room the heady atmosphere of a barn.

On the face of it, Netanel thought, Rosenberg, the factory owner's son from Bavaria, had little in common with the other three men in the room. In another time and place, Meodovnik, the committed socialist, would have despised me, and I him. Kohn was a fanatical Jew; how would he react if I told him my mother used to make her schnitzels out of pork? And Shoshan! A peasant goat farmer from the deserts of Yemen.

The dream that brought them together was simple. Each had arrived at the same conclusion: that the only way their nation was to be saved was by the establishment of a single Jewish state, along the boundaries of that described in the Bible of their ancestors, from Suez to Acre to the Jordan River.

But first they would have to get rid of the British and the Arabs.

Meodovnik addressed them: "As you are all aware, the British continue with their heinous blockade of our country. Our brothers and sisters from Europe who are arrested on our shores are now being deported to Cyprus, and kept in sub-human conditions in camps little better than those from which they have fled.

"We have demanded that this barbaric practice come to an end immediately. We have had no response. They force us to act.

"The full military court of the Irgun Zvai Leumi has been reviewing recent incidents perpetrated against innocent Jewish civilians by Arab terrorists, and the role played by British soldiers. In particular we have been studying the two worst cases, the atrocities that took place in June and November at Jaffa Gate and the Commercial Centre respectively.

"In both instances, the commander in charge of British forces in the area took no action to protect innocent Jewish blood until far too late. This indicates complicity with the terrorists. The case has been heard and he has been found guilty. The sentence is death. This unit has been selected for the honour of carrying out the execution."

"What is the Britisher's name?" Shoshan asked.

"Chisholm," Meodovnik said. "Major Ian Chisholm."

95

Kfar Herzl Kibbutz

On Fridays, the tables in the communal dining hall were covered with a white cloth, and candles were lit in preparation for Shabbat. The men dressed in their best white shirts and the women in white dresses. After the meal they sang songs and then Yaakov opened the Bible and read them a psalm.

He sat on the edge of one of the long tables, the black-bound volume balanced on his knees. His skin was as brown as leather against the crisp white of his shirt and when he spoke his voice was deep and rich and brown.

"O God, the heathen are come into thine inheritance; thy holy temple have they defiled; they have laid Jerusalem on heaps.

"The dead bodies of thy servants have they given to be meat unto the fowls of heaven, the flesh of thy saints unto the beasts of the earth.

"Their blood have they shed like water round about Jerusalem; and there was none to bury them.

"We are become a reproach to our neighbours, a scorn and derision to them that are round about us.

"How long, Lord? Wilt thou be angry for ever?"

For a few moments no one spoke. Yaakov shut the holy book and the sound of it was like a pistol shot. He looked around at the still, solemn faces. "Who will tell us a story?" It was a tradition after every Friday night meal: the psalm, then the story.

"Asher!"

"You have heard all my stories," he said.

"And none of them are true!" Sarah said. A ripple of laughter.

"Will you tell us a story, Marie?"

All eyes turned to the brown-haired girl at the end of the table between Asher and Sarah. A stillness came over the room. Marie had spoken little since she had come to the kibbutz. She had worked hard in the school teaching the children and had taken her turn in the fields and the dairy, and she had been accepted because she was a friend of Asher and Sarah. But no one knew anything about her. Asher came back to the kibbutz regularly to visit her, and told them simply that she had been in Auschwitz and they should be kind to her.

Now they all craned forward, eager to hear her.

"I don't have any stories," Marie said.

"They don't have to be proper stories," one of the men said. "Just something about yourself. It can be anything."

Marie studied her hands, rubbing at her palms as if there were some stain there that would not come away. "All right," she said. "I will tell you something that happened to me once, a long time ago. It was when I was in Auschwitz." She glanced at Asher. "I know you have all heard stories about the place. I will tell you mine."

She stopped, and took a deep breath. "When the Germans organised the deportations, most people thought they were going to labour camps, another kind of ghetto. So they took whatever they could with them. They were each allowed one suitcase and one knapsack. People crammed in all their gold and their jewellery and their furs and their very best clothes. The Germans knew this. Perhaps that was what they wanted."

She sipped at a glass of water. "You know, when I came to the camp I was lucky. The young girls were sometimes selected for special treatment. I think you understand what I mean.

"I was one of the privileged ones. They did not cut my

583

hair. I wore a red handkerchief around my head. I even had nice clothes. I worked as a courier inside the camp and before that I worked on what the Germans called the Effektenkammer.

"The idea was this: when the people arrived at the camp, the Germans took all their luggage and they sent it to us. Our job was to sort through all the cases and take out anything that was valuable. Then it would be sent back to Germany, to the Finance Ministry.

"One day I picked up a suitcase from our pile and it was very heavy. I wondered what could be inside. Perhaps someone had brought gold bars with them! I forced open the lock and threw back the lid. Inside there was the body of a baby girl. She was maybe eighteen months old."

Marie paused a moment, lost in remembrance.

"Perhaps the mother knew what was going to happen and hoped to save her baby, so she hid her in the case. God knows what happened. Perhaps the child suffocated. Or perhaps the case lay on the station platform overnight and she had frozen. Or perhaps the case had just lain in the pile too long.

"When I showed the child to our guard, he laughed. He picked her up by the leg and threw her outside the hut. He said the Leichenkommando would collect her. Then he sent me back to work."

A long silence. Then Yaakov said, "Does the story have an end?"

"I suppose this is the ending, now. I don't know the little girl's name. But, well – she was a Jew, like you. Perhaps you could all say your Kaddish for her now. Will you do that, please?"

Marie sat on the grass outside the hall, staring into the dark grove of the apple trees. Light from the dining hall threw her profile in silhouette. Inside they were dancing the hora.

Sarah came and sat next to her. For a long time neither of them spoke. "It is so peaceful here," Marie said, at last.

"It's an oasis. For now."

"How are things in Jerusalem?"

"They get worse every day."

"What's going to happen?"

"There's going to be a war, sooner or later. It's inevitable."

"Has Asher heard anything from Netya?"

"Only rumours. He thinks he has joined the Irgun Zvai Leumi."

Marie rested her forehead on her arms. "When I was little my grandmother used to read me fairy stories. The handsome prince always slayed the wicked witch and married the beautiful princess. Good always triumphed over evil. I thought life was like that."

"Not always."

"Do you believe in God, Sarah?"

"I'm Jewish, aren't I?"

"Do you?"

"Well, you know. Sometimes."

"If there was a God, how could there be an Auschwitz?"

"You are asking a good Jew about suffering? It is the basis of our religion. Without suffering we would have nothing to pray about."

Marie's voice wavered. "I never thought suffering was going to be a routine part of my life. So, I try. I battle with my memories but I don't know if I want to come all the way back. What has happened to me has shaken my faith in everything. In God, and in human beings. What is there left to believe in?"

Sarah thought about Rishou. What did she believe in? "Good is like sunshine, Marie," she said. "It goes down somewhere, it shines somewhere else. Now come inside and dance. Tomorrow the sun will come up again. If you can't believe in God, Marie, believe in the sun . . ."

They went back inside, hand in hand.

High above them, from The Place Where The Fig Tree Died, Izzat Ib'n Mousa listened to the singing and spat into the wind.

Jerusalem

Major Ian Chisholm went down the steps of Goldsmith House, ignoring the salutes of the guards. The effects of the whisky hit him as soon as he stepped into the cold night air. A covered jeep pulled up to the kerb and a corporal jumped out and saluted. Chisholm slumped gratefully into the passenger seat.

The jeep travelled slowly along King George Avenue towards the Schneller Compound and Guards head-quarters. Suddenly a black Plymouth pulled out of a side street in front of them.

"Look out!" Chisholm shouted.

The corporal braked and swerved. The jeep stalled in the middle of the intersection. "Idiots!" Chisholm shouted.

Two men jumped out of the car and ran towards the jeep. Chisholm stared at them in dull surprise. The drink had dulled his reactions and it was not until the very last moment that he realised one of the men was holding a Sten gun.

The volley of automatic bullets slammed into Chisholm and his driver chest-high. The corporal died instantly. Chisholm collapsed on to the road, and tried to crawl away on his hands and knees. He vomited blood on to the slick, rain-wet road.

The second man – owlish, dressed in black – ran towards him.

"Help me," Chisholm gasped.

The man held the pistol at the major's temple and fired two rounds. Chisholm collapsed, dead. His assassin took a piece of paper from his trouser pocket and stuffed it inside the jacket of Chisholm's uniform. Then he ran back to the Plymouth and jumped in.

Rain mixed with blood and smeared the typewritten words on the crumpled paper inside the dead man's tunic:

"Let death seize upon them, and let them go down quick into hell: for wickedness is in their dwellings, and among them."

Part Sixteen

PALESTINE, 1946

96

Zion Square

Without his keffiyeh and his robe he could be anyone,
Sarah thought. His thick blue black hair and beard, and
his olive skin, announce his Middle Eastern origins but
the gulf of religion that separates us is suddenly gone
with a simple change of clothing. As he sits with me
here in the café, I in my dress and nylon stockings, he in
a European-style shirt and trousers and expensive leather
shoes, we could be mistaken for rich, modern effendis or
middle-class Arab Christians, or even European Jews. For
one afternoon the barriers of two thousand years do not
divide us.

It had been Sarah's idea, to meet outside the tiny room
in the Muslim Quarter, to go to the cinema, to have coffee
in Zion Square. "I always come here veiled, like an Arab,"
she had told him. "Now I want you to come to me, without
your keffiyeh, like a Jew."

Finally he had agreed.

It was a bright, cool day, a watery sun set in a pale winter
sky. There was snow on the distant mountains of Jordan.

"Did you enjoy the film?" she asked him.

He laughed. "It was ridiculous."

"You sat there the whole time with your mouth open!
Admit it."

He scowled and stirred his coffee.

"You liked Tarzan, didn't you? That is how all you Arab
men see yourselves."

589

"He's an effendi, anyone can see that. He's pale as marble and he has no hair on his chest."

Sarah chased phantoms in her coffee cup with her spoon, and was serious again. "Is it so bad, my darling Rishou?"

"Is what so bad?"

"Coming out with me like this. You take such big strides, trying to walk ahead of me. Sitting here in the café, it is like you are sitting naked on a burning rock."

His face flushed a deeper bronze. No matter what he felt for her, inside he was still an Arab, and his prestige and bearing as a man was everything to him. To walk beside a woman in the street, to converse with her in public, was contrary to all the rules of social behaviour he had ever learned.

But what did you expect, Sarah? You wanted the exotic, the mysterious, the unattainable. Now you want a love affair, as well?

He drank his coffee. "What do we do now?"

"You could walk me home."

"All the way to Rehavia? I shall have to fetch my donkey."

"Yes, but which one of us would ride it?"

He did not answer her. "What do you want from me?" he said finally, his voice bitter.

"More than I have any right to expect, I suppose. I'm sorry."

"Will you come to the factory tomorrow?"

"I'm going to Kfar Herzl. I am going to visit Isaac."

Rishou brooded, moving his coffee cup around its saucer with his spoon. Sarah thought he was sulking because she would not sleep with him, but then he said, "What is he like, your boy? Is he a good son? Does he do what you tell him?"

"I don't tell him how to do anything any more. Perhaps his grandfather does. He works hard, on the kibbutz and at his lessons. That's all I ask."

"Do you see him often?"

"As often as I can. It is better for him on the kibbutz than in Jerusalem. Safer."

"It's something I can never, you know, understand about you Jews. The way you go away and work in the fields and leave your children. And you . . . you come here to Jerusalem for weeks at a time. A mother should be with her children."

"And so we never get to do anything important, or worthwhile. The kibbutz is his family. What do you want? That I should be like Khadija and mind my sons while my husband is off with his mistress?"

She saw she had gone too far. He turned away, white-lipped.

But this was not like him. Something was wrong. "What is it?" she asked him gently. "Tell me."

"You should not leave your son alone so much," he said. "That's what is wrong with Ali. I should spend more time in Rab'allah."

"Ali? What has he done?"

He had never shared a personal problem with her before. She watched him struggling with his pride. "It's nothing."

She reached across the table and touched his fingertips. "Tell me. Sometimes it helps to talk."

It came out of him in a rush. "What do you do with a son who will not obey his father? I beat him and it makes no difference. Well, he should be able to take a good beating now and then. But still he defies me!"

"How does he defy you?"

He seemed on the verge of telling her. But instead he hissed, "You Jews have done this! When you took our land you took our whole way of life! You bring America and Tarzan and motor cars and wristwatches and you have divided us among ourselves! I tried . . . I tried Majid's way. I made business in Jerusalem and tried to build a bridge between this west you have brought and our village. But every time I go back a little more of my Rab'allah has disappeared. Soon our sons will not have respect and our daughters will not have their virtue and there will be nothing left! What have you done?"

591

She spread her hands helplessly, withered by his fury. What was there to say? "You must hate me very much."

The anger left him as swiftly as it had come. "No, I don't hate you. I think of you day and night and I cannot get you out of my mind. If I could hate you my life would not be so complicated, and my dreams would be easier."

They sat for a while in silence.

Finally he said, "Can you come this afternoon?"

Sarah looked at her watch. "But it's getting late."

"Can you do it?" His black, liquid eyes bored into hers.

His eyes! she thought. He makes love to me with those eyes. They look right into my soul. They make it so hard to refuse.

"Please," he whispered. "I'm on fire for you."

Like a moth to a flame, she thought. I know in the end the heat will consume me, but I cannot resist. But rather the fire, than the cold.

"All right," she said.

al-Naqb

How these fellaheen offend me now! Majid thought. Izzat's goathair mats are getting all manner of filth on my suit as I squat here. And look at what he is wearing! His abbayah looks as if it has been fouled by a camel and there is grime enough under his nails to plant vines.

She was right, that Jewess. She said I was not an Arab any more. I have left the village behind. I am a proper effendi, like the man this fellaheen peasant thinks he serves. I wonder if the Mufti himself feels this same degree of contempt for his fellow Arabs?

"I have spoken with the Mufti," Izzat said. "He sends felicitations to all his beloved mujahideen and urges you all to continue your struggle to a great and glorious victory."

There were murmurs of approval from those gathered in the room. Majid looked at them. Munir, Naji, Tareq, from his own village, half a dozen others from al-Naqb he knew only by sight. And Ali of course. Did his father know what a murderous little thug he had become?

"It is clear that the Britishers do not have the belly to do what must be done," Izzat continued. "Killing Jews is man's work."

"Thanks be to Him," Ali murmured.

"I have devised a feat that will make us legend in all Judea. We will take our jihad into Zion Square itself. We will make it clear that no Jew can ever be safe in Palestine, no matter where he goes!"

Majid lit a cigarette. His hands were shaking. Izzat saw it and smiled. "My idea excites you, brother?"

Majid avoided his eyes. "It's suicide."

"What Arab fears death in a holy cause?"

I do, Majid thought. And so do you. That is why you always stay behind and let others take the risks while you take the credit.

Izzat looked around at the sweating, intent faces. "Who will be a martyr for our sacred trust? Which one of you is ready to give his life to Allah?"

"I will go," Ali said.

Izzat grinned. "The boy shames you all." He tousled Ali's hair. "Only eleven years old and he is a lion among lambs!"

Majid suppressed a groan. Ali, you stupid little boy! Do you not see how you have been manipulated? You have not yet lived, and already you want to die!

I will have to tell Rishou.

"I will go!" Tareq shouted.

Others now volunteered their blood, shamed into courage. Izzat chose two more men from his own village. "You are all true fedayeen. Should you not return, know that you will go straight to Paradise!"

Meanwhile Izzat will go straight to bed, Majid thought.

Izzat's eyes shone a little too brightly in the twilight gloom. It put madness in his face. Majid shuddered. He could never come here without imagining that somehow Izzat had discovered that he was giving information to the Haganah. He had started to have nightmares about what they would do to him when they found out. But how could they find out? Besides, the only reason he had agreed to help Izzat was to make him less prone to suspicion.

He just wanted this meeting to be over, to get in his car and return to Jerusalem, to his new villa in Sheikh Jarrah, to his fat wife and his secret whisky cupboard. He wanted badly to shit.

"Majid, you have been a great help to us in our cause," Izzat was saying.

"I live only to serve Allah and the Mufti."

"You still have friends among the Britishers?" Izzat spoke the word "friends" as if it was an obscenity.

"I still have contact with them," Majid said carefully. "That is how I am able to provide you with the weapons you need." It did no harm continually to remind Izzat of this fact. He made a profit, of course. But not as great a profit as he made from the Jews.

"It is necessary that we warn them of what is to happen. We want to kill Jews, not Britishers."

"I understand. I will ensure the Britishers do not interfere."

"Good, good." Izzat shifted his gaze elsewhere.

Majid sighed with relief. Perhaps this time I will not go to the Haganah, not invite this risk. But then I would have to give up Ilse!

And my mistress.

"Before the meeting is ended, there is one final matter," Izzat said. "One of our number has betrayed us."

Sudden, terrible silence.

Allah, help me in my sorrow! Majid thought. I am going to die! He whispered an urgent prayer in the purple panic of his mind, asking God to avert the blow. Izzat could not know! He could not!

"You!"

Izzat pointed his finger.

"You, Khalil Azzem!"

The young man jumped up in alarm and tried to run for the door but Tareq blocked his path. The youth backed against the wall.

Thank you, Allah, Majid thought. I give thanks it is not me!

"Last week during the attack on the souk in the Old City, Munir and Anwar saw you run away! Do you know the punishment for running from battle in jihad?"

Drool spilled out of the boy's mouth. He shook his head desperately. "I did not run from the Jews! The Britisher soldiers were coming!"

"You ran away!" Izzat repeated and he nodded to Tareq. Their former village idiot produced a pistol from the folds of his robe and shot Khalil through the head. He dropped dead on the floor.

Majid looked down at his suit. He had Khalil Azzem's brains in his lap. Ah, Majid, he said to himself. You can cover yourself in fine cloth but in reality you are only two generations from the desert and the desert's laws!

He found it hard to swallow. He could not believe it. Izzat had had the man killed without even hearing out his protest. When had he assumed so much power over them all? He no longer wanted to shit. It was too late.

He rose to his feet and left the house.

He leaned against his car and took deep breaths of the cold afternoon air. He saw Tareq drag Khalil Azzem out of the house by his feet and leave him face down in the dirt. Majid had no illusions what his own fate would be if his own little treacheries were discovered.

Old City

Sarah turned on her side to watch him sleep. She ran her fingers through the tight, black curls on his chest, traced the contours of the muscle to his neck and up to his jaw. He is so beautiful, she thought.

A cane blind had been drawn at the window but she knew by the dusty chevrons of light filtering through the slats that it was getting late. She listened to the jangle of noise outside: the Arab music from the radio in the coffee house next door; the cries of the peanut sellers; the oaths and elaborate compliments of the brass vendor as he bargained with a customer; the shouts of "*Balak! Balak!*" as a trader tried to clear a passage for his loaded donkey. Downstairs Rishou's boys heaved and laughed and shouted as they worked the press.

Madness to come here, she reminded herself, but unthinkable to stay away. It was as if she had been blind and suddenly could see colours again. A grey world had been illuminated with broad, primal brushstrokes. Is it just that I am pretending to be seventeen years old again? she thought. Or perhaps I really love him. God forgive me if it's true! My father won't; Asher won't; nor will the Haganah.

She rolled away from him and reached for her wrist-watch on the floorboards beside the mattress. Almost evening. She got up and started to dress.

Rishou opened one eye and smiled. He loved to watch her dress, loved the strange underclothes she wore, silky, shimmering things unlike anything he had ever seen before.

She looked around suddenly and caught him looking at her. "I thought you were asleep."

"The rustling of the silk woke me."

"All this noise in the street and a little silk wakes you?"

"There are noises a man can ignore and there are some he can't. Is that the sort of thing a tough sabra like you should be wearing?"

"I got it in Princess Mary Avenue. It's my one extravagance."

"My father wears silk underpants. But they are not like those."

"Your father wears silk underpants?"

"Red ones. He got them to demonstrate his power and position."

"Does he show them to everyone?"

Rishou laughed. "Of course not. But the other women see my mother washing them at the well. That is enough."

She picked up her shorts and workshirt. As she dressed he stared at her bottom and sighed. Peaches encased in silk. He caught her wrist and pulled her back down on to the makeshift bed. "Come here," he said.

"It's getting late."

"Stay a little longer. Please."

"Don't beg. You shame your Bedouin ancestors when you do that."

"My Bedouin ancestors seduced camels and robbed their grandmothers. They had no shame."

"I must go!" She tried to wriggle away but he held her tight.

"Why?"

Because my cell of the Shai are meeting tonight in my flat in Rehavia. Because we are blackmailing your brother and we are working out the best way to use him, God help me. "I have a husband."

Suddenly there were footsteps on the wooden stairs that led from the shop. "Someone's coming!" she gasped and scrambled for her clothes. "Is it one of your labourers?"

"They wouldn't dare," Rishou said.

She reached for the abbayah. But it was too late. The door opened and Majid walked in.

Majid's cheeks turned the colour of a ripe tomato. He caught just a glimpse of the girl's face before she threw the abbayah over her head. He reeled back, astonished. Moments later she burst out of the door, a rumpled figure in black, her sandals hooked in the fingers of her right hand. He stood back to let her pass. She ran away down the stairs.

Majid went back into the office to face his brother. Rishou was lying on the mattress, leaning on one elbow,

597

his loins covered by a sheet. "You should always knock first. Isn't that what your Britishers always say?"

Majid could not answer him. His mind was reeling. The Jewish woman, the Haganah spy! How was it possible? The snapshot image of her small brown breasts under her shirt warmed his loins, while the implications of his discovery chilled his heart and numbed his brain. Think before you speak, some instinct warned him.

"You have drool on your chin," Rishou laughed.

"It's not funny!" Majid said. He took a red silk handkerchief from the breast pocket of his suit, and mopped at the perspiration on his forehead. "Who was that?"

"A woman."

"You were screwing her? Here? In the office?"

"I got bored with the book-keeping. There was nothing else I could think of to do."

"Who is she?" Majid said.

Rishou avoided his brother's eyes. "That's my business."

Does he know she's a spy? Majid thought. *Does he know?* If I tell him, I will have to explain my own involvement with the little minx. Or perhaps Rishou is one of her pawns also? He needed time to think. "Your cock's going to get you in a lot of trouble one day," he said.

"*Me!* The fastidiousness with which you treat your sacred member is not exactly legend." Rishou got out of bed and dressed quickly. "Now then," he said, "shall we get to work on these books?"

97

Damascus Gate

Twice a week Khadija and Rahman took the produce from their garden and traded it at the markets in the Old City. In summer, when their baskets were heavy with tomatoes and figs they would ride the donkey cart down the dusty road into the city, but it was a long journey and they would often leave before dawn and arrive back well after sunset. During the winter, when they had just a few eggs and chickens and perhaps some goat's cheese to sell, they walked to the highway and rode in on the silver National Company bus.

Today they had sold just a few eggs and some cheese. People were milling round the buses outside the Gate. Coffee vendors pushed their way through the crowds, the bulbous brass urns that were strapped to their shoulders clanking and jangling, while old Arabs leading ancient donkeys jostled and cursed.

Khadija felt her spirits sag. So many people!

"Can't we visit Father at the factory?" Rahman said. "Perhaps he could take us back to Rab'allah in Uncle Majid's taxi."

"You know he doesn't like us to go there."

"He said I could visit him one day."

"We'll go some other time."

Rahman shrugged, disappointed. Khadija felt sorry for him. He was a good boy. How could she explain to him that they did not visit the factory because she suspected his father entertained his mistresses there?

Rahman grunted under the weight of the heavy basket

on his back. The wooden cage with the chickens was in his right hand. He could barely hold it off the ground. "Let me take it," she said.

"No, it's all right," Rahman said. "I'll carry it."

A good boy, she thought. He always took the weight for her.

The first bus was almost full. There was a goat in the aisle, and women and children spilling out the doors, more people on the roof. "We'll wait," Khadija said.

The oil drum had a capacity of fifty gallons, but the oil had all been drained away. Instead it had been filled with old nails, scrap iron, rusty hinges and glass containers of petrol. Two old rubber tyres held the detonator fuse and a central core of TNT.

The van had been stolen from a garage off Salah ed-Din Road, where some dented front panels were being repaired. There were three men in the back. Two of them were armed with Sten guns, the other man steadied the oil drum as they bumped over the cobbles. The driver wore a keffiyeh and a brown suit.

His name was Netanel Rosenberg.

We need to be feared, Netanel thought. We need to have blood on our hands. We need to be cursed as aggressors and barbarians. Whether German or Arab or British they have to understand that they cannot kill us and not expect retribution.

He was tired of seeing Jewish bodies littering the ground like the carcasses of dogs, tired of his nightmares where children in wheelbarrows fell screaming into the boiling trenches of Birkenau; he had seen enough bodies laid out under seeping blankets in the Commercial Centre and the Old City.

He was crushed by the sin of Amos Mandelbaum. The only atonement possible was the final possession of some sanctuary where such crimes as his could never be repeated.

* * *

Sarah hurried towards Damascus Gate, anonymous once more in her black abbayah. Idiot! she told herself. He beckons, and you follow like some empty-headed houri! There is no future for you with this man. All over Palestine Arabs and Jews are killing each other. What peace can you possibly hope to find with him?

And now you have been discovered! Did his brother see your face, did he recognise you? Fear gripped her heart like a cold fist. You fool, she whispered to herself. You fool!

Consumed by the turmoil in her own mind, she did not notice the van as it rattled by her, black fumes belching from its exhaust. She heard the rear doors fly open and saw a cylindrical drum drop from the back tailboard. It thudded to the ground and began to roll, sparks spitting from the fuse.

She glimpsed a man's face just before the doors closed. He was a Yemenite, his face contorted with hatred. "And I have also heard the groaning of the children of Israel!" he shouted and the doors slammed shut. Someone ran into her and knocked her down and at that moment the drum hammered into the side of a bus and the shock and the heat of the explosion rolled over her.

Sarah looked around. The cobbles were littered with pieces of raw meat. A woman was screaming hysterically, her abbayah in flames.

Sarah staggered to her feet and ran over to her, beating at the flames with her hands. She threw the woman on to the ground. Most of her hair was gone. "My son," the woman whimpered. "Where's my son?"

Then it started. A low moan, followed by another, and another. The entreaties of the injured, like the souls of hell crying for mercy. It rose to an ululation, from all around them. She saw a young boy, his face blackened with burns, holding his own severed leg.

The clamour of alarms and klaxons mingled with the screams. Sarah went to the crippled boy and tried to help him but her hands were numb, and would not respond.

There were strips of skin hanging from her fingers, like loose cotton. She realised she had been burned when she helped the Arab woman. She sat in the gutter, and tried to control the trembling in her limbs, but the shaking would not stop.

The boy slumped on to his back, and she watched his lifeblood leak away on to the cobbles from his shattered limbs. Finally the pumping stopped and he was still.

98

Rehavia

Asher jumped to his feet as the door opened. "Sarah? Where have you been?" He saw the black smudges on her face and clothes. "My God. What happened?"

Sarah could not answer him. He caught her as she started to fall. "What happened to you?" he shouted again, his voice strident with panic.

She was staring at her hands; some charred skin hung in strips. A bundle slipped from under her arm on to the floor. Asher stared at it: a tattered and bloodstained abbayah. It made no sense to him. "What have you been doing?" he repeated but Sarah only shook her head in mute horror.

Rab'allah

He changes each time I see him, Zayyad thought. Which is not often, admittedly. But on each occasion there is another ring on his finger, and on his wrist a more expensive wristwatch to dazzle the eye and invoke the envy of the fellaheen. Now he has a shiny new Plymouth the colour of a tomato and there is even a tooth in his mouth that is made from gold. He conveys the impression that his testicles are made of topaz.

Majid knelt in front of his father and kissed his hand. "Yaba," he murmured. He rose and they embraced.

During the time of Lawrence I went into a brothel in Damascus, Zayyad thought. It did not smell as sweet as you.

"Allah has made you prosperous, I see," Zayyad said.

"Thanks be to Him."

Majid's offspring greeted their grandfather formally. Zayyad saw that Amneh was covered now. How quickly time passed!

Majid waved his children outside, where their mother waited. Zayyad clapped his hands and Rashedah hurried to fetch coffee.

They sat cross-legged on the rug. "I have cried a thousand thousand tears," Majid said. "No Hass'an shall sleep again until young Rahman's death is avenged!"

"*Insh'allah*. I have buried a son and soon I shall bury a grandson. I pray to Allah there are no more graves to be dug."

"The Jews have gone too far this time."

Zayyad did not seem to hear. "Khadija has lost some of her hair and the petrol burned her face and back. However, the scars will not show – provided she never removes her abbayah." Yes, Khadija was a married woman and only her husband would see the signature of the Jewish bombers. But Rahman, poor Rahman. They said his grandson had died badly. His face was so badly burned Rishou had not recognised him. They had identified him by a patch on his trousers.

Rashedah brought the coffee. When she had returned to the kitchen, Zayyad said, "My son, you know the Britishers. Will they help us throw these butchers out of Palestine?"

Majid could not meet his father's eyes. How could he tell him?

"What is it?" Zayyad said. "What is wrong?"

603

"I heard news today. Perhaps it is false."

"What news?"

"It is perhaps just a rumour. But they say the British are to send their families back to England. They intend to leave their soldiers and only the most essential officials here in Palestine."

Zayyad could scarcely believe his ears. May their sacred members turn into snakes and crawl up their arseholes! May their lying tongues turn into jujube thorns and their teeth into hand-grenades! May the Mandoob es Sami's ears turn into bats and eat out his brains! Every golden promise was a shining lie! If the Britishers were sending their wives and their children away, it meant they were getting ready to run from the Mandate and leave them to battle with the Jews, the invaders the British themselves had invited in!

"I have lived too long," Zayyad said.

"The British will not abandon us."

"Yes, they will, Majid. I have seen it coming for a long time now. I just did not want to believe it."

Majid bowed his head. "I don't know what's going to happen."

"I will tell you what will happen. Izzat ib'n Mousa and others like him will have their day. May Allah have mercy on us all."

"It will be bad for business. Rishou and I could lose everything."

Zayyad stared at his son, wondering at his perspective. "Rishou has already lost too much. He has lost one of his sons." He stood up. "Go to Rishou now. Try and comfort him. He has taken this very hard."

When he was alone Zayyad walked through the gnarled and skeletal olive trees to The Place Where The Fig Tree Died, and looked down at the kibbutz in the valley below. He tried to divine the purpose of his god in sending the Jews but he could see no reason to it. They would answer to the dictates of their own religion and their own custom and when it was over they would perhaps see Allah's hand in the curse of the Zionist Jews. *Insh'allah*.

Insh'allah!

Kfar Herzl Kibbutz

It was Sukkot, the Feast of the Tabernacles, the festival that reminded the Jews of the Israelites living in the wilderness after the exodus from Egypt. The kibbutzniks built shelters in the gardens made from palms, myrtle, and willow branches. Isaac had built his shelter on the verandah of the cottage he shared with his grandfather. It creaked in the wind, the top dusted with snow from the previous night's storm.

Sarah sat at the table in the kitchen, her hands heavily bandaged, while Isaac made coffee. He was getting tall, she noticed. Still only eleven years old and soon he would be head to head with her. He was a good-looking boy; he had olive skin and white teeth and exceptionally long black eyelashes that accentuated his dark eyes. He will have no trouble getting girls when he is older, she thought. When he is older? Soon he will be ready for his barmitzvah!

She had taken the Egged bus from Jerusalem that morning. Asher was already here, and she planned to drive back with him tomorrow. It was becoming increasingly difficult to spend much time away from Jerusalem. Every day brought some new outrage.

Isaac brought two mugs to the table and sat down. "How are your hands, Mother?"

"They hurt."

"When will you be able to take off the bandages?"

"Not for another two weeks at least."

"Does that mean you will have to stay here?" There was sudden eagerness in his voice.

"No, I'm sorry, Isaac. I have to go back to Jerusalem tomorrow. I can still do my work even with bandaged hands."

He looked disappointed.

"I'm sorry," she repeated.

"It's all right, I understand." He sipped his coffee. "How are things in Jerusalem? Is there going to be a war with the Arabs?"

"I don't know."

605

"Father says it has to happen one day. So does Grand-father."

"When I was your age the Arabs attacked the Jewish community in Jaffa. Everyone said then that there would be a war 'one day'. Perhaps 'one day' will never come."

"Perhaps we have to make it come. The Arabs have been in Palestine a thousand years and they've done nothing with it. It's time we got them out."

"Who told you that?"

"Maybe I worked it out for myself."

Where did he get such ideas? Not from Yaakov, she knew, or even Asher. What sort of children were they rearing in the hothouse environment of the kibbutzim? There were too many little refugee children now, infecting the others with their parents' venom. Perhaps Rishou was right. She should spend more time with her son. Or perhaps it was already too late.

Sarah stared at the bandages on her hands, remembered the woman in the flaming abbayah, the little Arab boy cradling his own leg in his arms. Would Isaac be standing in the back of a truck one day, pushing barrel bombs into crowds of Arab women and children?

"Perhaps you should just concentrate on your lessons for now."

"School is boring." Then, more eagerly, "Grandfather says I can start military training next month."

"Don't forget, Isaac, in the Haganah we learn to use weapons only to defend ourselves, and our communities. Our watchword has always been *havlagah* – restraint."

"I know, I know. Father has given me the lecture."

"Not every Arab is our enemy."

"The Arabs are dirty and lazy. If they want to fight us, perhaps we should teach them a lesson."

Sarah felt a lump in her throat. When did he become like this? Who was it poured this poison into him? Would he have been any different if she had been here to guide him? She stared into her coffee. "Isaac, you know I love you, don't you?"

606

"Don't start that stuff on me."

"Perhaps I don't start this stuff on you often enough. Well, that's my fault. But some of the things you say, they frighten me. Look at my hands. You know how this happened?"

He stared at her, his face sulky. "Yes, I've heard the story."

"Isaac, I fight the Arabs every day. But I don't hate them. Do you know why? I never learned to hate them. No one ever taught me, and I never stopped to learn. Dirty and lazy? Some of them, maybe. Or perhaps their attitudes to the land, and to life, are different from ours. Are some of them evil? Yes. But so are some Jews." She thought about the Yemenite's face as the van door slammed. "I fight them because I have to. Because we have to survive. But they have a just cause also. Don't hate them."

He squirmed under her scrutiny and looked around for an escape. He found it. "Here's Father," he said. Asher was walking up the dirt path, bundled in a sheepskin coat. He was walking better, she noticed. He would soon be back with his beloved Palmach.

"Shalom, Isaac . . . Sarah." He took off his sheepskin coat, shaking off the snow, and hung it by the door.

"I'll make you coffee," Sarah said.

"Thanks."

"Your leg seems better."

"I go back on active duty next week. How are your hands?"

How polite we are to each other, she thought. He knew, of course, that she was hiding something. The missing hours, her presence in an abbayah at Damascus Gate on the evening of the bombing, she had explained away as an unauthorised assignation with a potential Arab informer. It earned her a tongue-lashing and a reprimand from her superiors at Shai, cold silence from her husband.

"They are getting better," she said. "In fact I was just

talking about Damascus Gate with Isaac. It seems he agrees with what the Irgun are doing."

Isaac stared at the table.

"He thinks we should run the Arabs out of Palestine."

Asher looked at his son. Isaac had been a child when he had joined the Jewish Brigade, a young adult when he had returned from the war. He wondered if there was anything he could say that Isaac would be prepared to listen to. "If that's what the Irgun want, they won't have to worry about the British getting in their way any more."

"You've heard something?" Sarah asked. "It's certain now?"

"It was on the radio just now. The British are evacuating all 'non-essential personnel'. A security precaution, they call it. But everyone knows what it means. They are leaving Palestine."

"This is our chance then!" Isaac shouted.

Sarah's face was stern. "You've much to learn, Isaac. The difference between an opportunity and a final reckoning, for instance."

"Your mother's right," Asher said. "If the British leave Palestine we will have to fight and there's no guarantee we can win."

It was still difficult to accept that the British were finally giving up the Mandate, Sarah thought. It was what they all wanted, and what they all feared. With the British gone their Armageddon would finally arrive, as the Bible had predicted.

In Jerusalem.

The kibbutz was different each time she came, but this time the changes depressed her. Fresh trenches had been dug in the lawns and there were concrete bomb shelters next to the hospital and the crèche. When she looked at the bare branches of the rose bushes, she was overcome with a devastating sadness. So much had been built, now so much was at risk.

"What's wrong, Sarah?" Asher asked her.

"Isaac. He sounds like an eleven-year-old version of Ze'ev Jabotinsky." Jabotinsky was the founder of the Irgun Zvai Leumi and a rabid Arab-hater.

"What do you expect? Every day he hears how the Arabs threw a grenade in this souk, shot that old Jew in the Old City. Face it, Sarah. We all knew a war would happen one day."

"You're looking forward to it."

"I want it to be over, yes."

Sarah stopped beside one of the trenches. The dirt was frozen hard like concrete and there was an inch of snow at the bottom. It looked like a freshly dug grave. "I know Isaac will grow up with a gun in his hand. Why not? I did. I just don't want him to be another Rosenberg, killing innocent people with bombs."

They heard gunfire from the hills above them. They both looked up at the same time, saw a procession wind its way along the ridge from Rab'allah. The ululation of women echoed on the cold air.

"Funeral," Asher whispered, like a portent of what was to come.

The Place Where The Fig Tree Died

Zayyad, Majid and Rishou Hass'an carried Rahman's body to the cemetery. The rest of the village followed behind, taking care not to step in front of the bier, for the angels of death always preceded a funeral. The men fired their rifles into the air, while the women tore at their clothes and their faces and screamed their ululations to a sky the colour of lead.

Rishou did not cry. The Jews had murdered his son and he would not weep for him until he had avenged little Rahman's slow death under the Damascus Gate. He would pay them back for the face that he could not even recognise in death, exact his retribution for his little boy who had watched his life bleed away through his legs.

I will answer you in kind, you lepers, you sons of whores! I will answer you in kind! If it was Ali, perhaps I could have understood. But little Rahman, my scholar, my hopeless liar, my little, quiet wide-eyed son, they have stolen your life and I am not a man if I let them do this and I do not avenge you!

The body had been wrapped in a winding sheet. As they laid the bundle in the grave, his head lain in the direction of *qibla*, Khadija threw herself on top of the bier and screamed her grief at the sky, her own scars still raw and bleeding. The women dragged her away.

Each bystander threw three handfuls of dirt on the grave. Then Rishou bent to his son's ear and recited the confession of faith so he would know the response to the archangel's questions at the Gates of Paradise. Then they buried Rishou's son, while he silently repeated a sulu from the Koran in the echoing despair of his mind:

> We prescribed for them:
> A life for a life, an eye for an eye,
> a nose for a nose, an ear for an ear,
> a tooth for a tooth, and for wounds
> retaliation.

99

Damascus Gate

The markets were under way around Damascus Gate; it was evening and the crenellated walls of the Old City were flushed with pink. The square resounded to the cries of hawkers, the air was redolent with the smells of leather and coffee and sweets and cardamom, the cobbles ablaze with brasswork and cheap jewellery and chick peas and weavings and sheepskin rugs. There was no visible evidence of the carnage that had taken place there a week before. Sarah wondered at the resilience of a people so inured to suffering that they could continue with the everyday routines of their lives after such a violence.

"What happened to your hands?" Majid asked.

Sarah wondered what Majid would think if she told him. She decided it would invite sympathy and perhaps even admiration and neither emotion would be appropriate to their relationship.

"I burned them on a hot kettle," she said.

"You should become more familiar with the workings of a kitchen."

"Cooking is difficult. Outwitting Arabs is much easier."

Majid scowled and drank his mint tea.

Does he know? she thought. Is he playing with me? She could read nothing in his face, nothing. "What do you have for me, Majid. What subterranean rumblings have you heard?"

"Everything is quiet."

"Liar."

"If I knew something, I'd tell you. Have I ever let you down?"

"Who can say? How can we ever know what you have not told us?" She put a brown envelope on the table. "I have a message from my superiors, Majid. They have been very pleased with the little snatches of gossip you throw our way – "

"It is not gossip!"

"– and they say from now on they will pay you double."

Majid started to sweat. "Double?"

Sarah tapped the envelope with her finger. "Perhaps they have heard you are in need of the extra finances. They may have heard that you are behind with your loans on your factory in the Old City. Or they may have heard – but certainly not from your brother, because he does not know – that you gambled away much of last month's profit playing cards with your new effendi friends. Perhaps they know you have a new mistress that you support in an expensive apartment in Katamon and the rest of your money is spent on a German woman in Wilhelmina. Perhaps they want to help you out a little."

Majid reached for the envelope but Sarah snatched it away.

"I cannot do this any more," he said.

"Of course not. I had better get back to my headquarters. I am nervous with so much money in my pocket."

Majid licked his lips. "Perhaps you should be paying me from your own pocket," he whispered.

Sarah felt her heart lurch in her chest. Here it comes. "I don't think I understand you, Majid."

"Your underwear is very pretty," he said, and his eyes were hard and hungry.

She held his eyes. Had he spoken to Rishou? Had Rishou betrayed her? "Have you told anyone?"

He grinned. "Not yet."

"Because if you do, your brother will cut out your liver and make you eat it."

Majid's grin fell away. "Not Rishou . . .?" he said.

Sarah gave him the lie whole. "Betray me and you betray your brother as well!"

She watched the play of emotion on his face and she knew she was safe. "You cannot ask me to keep doing this! It is not a game any more. When the British leave there will be a war."

Sarah raised an eyebrow, and patted the envelope in her pocket.

"Perhaps one last time," Majid said.

"I'm listening."

"Zion Square, Saturday night. They are going to throw a grenade in the cinema."

"What time?"

"I don't know!"

"How many?"

"That's all I know! Don't ask me any more! Isn't that enough?"

"No, it's not. You have to tell me more than that."

Majid licked his lips. "They'll be driving a black Hillman."

Sarah passed him the envelope. Majid tore it open. He counted the money and put the envelope in his jacket pocket.

"This is the last time," he said.

"Of course."

"I mean it! Do whatever you want now. I am a businessman but I am also an Arab! We are finished now."

"I shall be here next week, waiting. With a thick envelope."

Majid stood up. His voice was low and hard. "I don't believe you about my brother."

Sarah did not answer him.

He put his face inches from hers. "This is the last time!"

Sarah watched him disappear among the crowds around the Gate. She wondered. Perhaps this time he really meant it.

Rishou watched Ali make his way back through the olive grove. He was fifty paces off when he saw his father and he checked his stride for only a moment before continuing. Rishou waited, leaning on an olive trunk, his breath crystallising on the evening air.

Ali knelt to kiss his father's hand. "I thought you had gone back to Jerusalem, yaba," he said.

"I know you did. Where have you been?"

Ali shrugged. "I was with some friends."

He has the furtive look about him, Rishou thought. He is not much more of a liar than his brother was. "Where?"

"There is a grotto near The Place Where The Fool Shot His Uncle. In the winter we – "

Rishou slapped him across the face. "Don't lie to me."

Ali blinked in surprise. His voice immediately lost its wheedling tone. "If you knew where I was, why did you ask me?"

"I wanted to see if you would try and shame me again by deceiving me. It seems you have still not learned your lesson."

"My brother is dead! Someone in his family must avenge him!"

"You think I would let his death go unpunished?"

"I don't know. Will you?"

Rishou raised his hand.

"Go ahead and beat me! You won't stop me! I'm fedayeen now!"

Rishou knocked him down.

Ali looked up at his father. The blow had not knocked out any of his truculence. "You can't stop me! I'm going to avenge Rahman."

"No, you're not. I am."

"You?"

"If anyone throws the grenade on Saturday night, it will be me. He was my son. I have the right, no one else."

Ali smiled. This was what he wanted, Rishou realised. This was what he wanted all along.

Rishou pulled him to his feet and embraced him. "I only have one son now. You will not die and break my heart completely. When you're a man you can fight the Jews. But I will not mourn you yet."

A man's fate is written on his forehead, they said. He had tried to chart his own course through the sands, for himself and for his sons. But Allah had prescribed another fate, and he could not turn away from it. He must surrender as the Koran commanded.

Insh'allah. As God wills.

100

Old City

A dull sky enveloped the Judean hills, and icy rain hammered against the windows, weeping grime. The kerosene heater hissed in a corner of the room.

Sarah took off her abbayah, and folded it as best she could on the floor. Her hands had almost healed, but they were still protected with light bandages, and it made her clumsy. She was unclipping the holster with its Beretta pistol when she heard Rishou climb the stairs from the factory downstairs. She was afraid. She had not seen him since the bombing at Damascus Gate.

She had promised herself she would never come back here. I'm like a gambler on a winning streak, she thought. I keep coming back to the table time after time, and I won't be satisfied until all my luck is used up and everything I have is gone.

She waited.

* * *

He closed the door softly behind him. She was about to throw her arms around him but as soon as she saw him she knew. She knew it was over.

"You should not have come," he whispered.

"What's the matter?"

His eyes were like black chips of coal. "You should not have come," he repeated.

"What is it? What has happened?"

"I don't want to see you any more."

Why this cold fury in his eyes? She tried to read some clue in his face, but his features were set like stone. "I don't understand."

He looked at the holster, and the gun. She followed his eyes. "What is it? Tell me," she whispered.

"Are you Haganah?"

She had to lie to him. "Of course not," she said.

"I don't believe you. How many Arabs have you killed, Sarah?"

"Stop it, Rishou. Please! Tell me what's wrong!"

"Rahman is dead."

"Rahman . . . your boy?"

"He was at Damascus Gate."

She was too shocked to say anything.

"You killed him," he said.

She shook her head, bewildered.

"Yes, you did. You murdered him." There were dark pouches under his eyes. He looked like a hunted animal.

"It wasn't us – "

"Do you know what he looked like when I found him? His head was black, like charred meat. And I couldn't find his leg. There were a lot of bodies, perhaps they got them mixed up. I looked everywhere for his leg, but I couldn't find it. So we had to bury him that way. Now, even in Paradise, he will be a cripple. For all of eternity."

"Rishou – "

"I should have paid him more attention. Ali was my firstborn so he got everything. I always thought there would be time to instruct Rahman more when he got older. Now he will never know how to be a man in Paradise."

She wanted to hold him but he pushed her away.

"But why waste tears? There is only one way to make it right for him now."

"I didn't kill him, Rishou!"

"No, but perhaps your father, or an uncle, or a cousin . . ."

"I love you, Rishou! I would never hurt you – "

"Just go away!"

"You promised you would never stop loving me! You don't mean any of this. Tell me you don't mean it."

He shook his head. "You're the enemy now, Sarah."

This cannot be the end, she thought. I cannot bear it if the last expression I ever see on his face is hatred and contempt. I refuse to believe that this is the end.

But she would not let him see her cry. So she turned away from him and reclipped the holster with its pistol. "You fool," she said. "You never knew the worth of any treasure until you tossed it away!"

He seemed to notice the bandages on her hands for the first time. "What happened?" he asked her.

There was no point in telling him now, she decided. She put on the abbayah and brushed past him, out of the door. Anonymous and black, she made her way out of the Arab streets through driving rain.

Rishou watched her from the window. He felt nothing. His thoughts were on Zion Square. After tonight he would weep no more tears for Rahman. After tonight the boy would no longer scream from the heavens for vengeance, for it would be done.

Kfar Herzl Kibbutz

Levin sucked on the Meerschaum. It was no longer alight but he did not seem to notice. "How does she seem to you?" he asked Asher.

"You're the doctor."

"Ah, but you're her friend. There is no definitive scale of measurement when you are dealing with something as fragile as the human mind. What is normal behaviour in one person is abnormal in another. What might be described as depression for you might be positively animated for some of the poor wretches I have seen."

"I really don't know her that well. If Netanel was here . . ." He shrugged. "The last time I was here she was talking about going back to Jerusalem. That seems like a good sign."

Levin toyed with the pipe. "You like her very much, don't you?"

Asher looked suddenly uncomfortable. "Perhaps."

Levin considered. "Something remarkable has happened to her. In my opinion her recovery has been dramatic. The first time I saw her she was in the process of convincing herself that large parts of her life had never occurred. Not unreasonably, perhaps. Now she is learning to cope with the reality of her past. It is much more than I can hope for in some of the people I see. Much more."

"You think she is cured?"

"You mean, is she no longer crazy?" He examined the bowl of his pipe. "Look at what has happened in the world in the last six years. The question is: Are any of us sane?"

Asher found Marie's cottage and knocked on the front door.

"Come in!"

She was in her bedroom, lying on the studio bed, her hands behind her head. She was still wearing the blue denim that was almost uniform for the kibbutzniks, and there was a pale grime of dried sweat on her face and arms. She smiled when she saw him, swung her legs off the bed and came out of the bedroom to greet him.

"Asher!" She kissed him on the cheek. "It's good to see you!"

She was browner and leaner than the last time he had visited, and although she looked physically tired, there was a new lightness about her. "How are you?" he said.

618

"I've been milking cows all day. I'm exhausted." Marie showed him her hands. "Look! Like claws. Have you ever milked a cow?"

He smiled. "Of course. I grew up on this kibbutz."

"I forgot. You're probably one of these sabras who can squeeze the juice out of a watermelon with one hand." She went into the kitchen. "I'll make some tea. Don't ask for milk. I couldn't face it. After the last few weeks in the dairy I think people should drink their tea black and do poor kibbutzniks everywhere a favour."

"You must be doing something right. You look wonderful."

She blushed, pleased with the compliment, and ran her fingers self-consciously through her tousled hair. "I look terrible. I smell like a dairy." She put the kettle on the little primus stove.

"Are they making you work very hard?"

"Harder than I've ever worked in my whole life."

"You'll get used to it."

"Not me. I think I'll try and find something easier. Are they still looking for slaves to haul stone blocks up the pyramids?"

"I think the job's finished now."

"Pity."

He sat down at the kitchen table. "I just saw Levin. We were talking about you. I didn't know you came from my home town."

"Ravenswald? We moved there in 1933! You too?"

"Really, I was only there a couple of years. My family went there from München. I left to come to Palestine when I was sixteen."

"It's where I met Netya. Didn't you know? Didn't he tell you?"

Asher shook his head. He had always thought it strange how Netanel avoided talking about his past.

"There were a lot of things I think he never told me. Perhaps you could help unravel some of the mystery."

Marie's expression was fathomless. "I don't think so, Ash. I have only just worked out my own."

The kettle boiled on the stove and Marie fussed with the tea.

"So. What are you going to do now, Marie?"

"I don't know. I couldn't live on a kibbutz for ever." She smiled. "I suppose it helps if you are Jewish."

"Then what made you come to Palestine?"

"I came for just one reason. To find Netya."

"And now?"

She shrugged her shoulders.

"What about Germany? Are any of your family still alive?"

"I don't know. I don't think I care." She stared across the snow-patched fields. "No, Ash, I couldn't go back. Not now. There would be a ghost on every corner. My house is full of nightmares."

"Well . . . I'm glad."

"Glad?"

"That you're not thinking of going back, I mean."

"Why?"

Asher seemed suddenly shy. "I was hoping you would come back and live in Jerusalem again. I would like to get to know you better. I want the chance to dazzle you with my incomparable charm."

She looked at him frankly. "What about Sarah?"

Asher took his time to answer. "For a long time she was the only woman I ever wanted."

"And now?"

"Now," he said, taking a breath, "now there's you." Marie poured tea into two cups, without looking up. Asher could hear the sound of his own breathing. "Well?" he said, finally.

"You've been very good to me. Not just you, Sarah as well. The two of you have helped me so much these last few weeks . . . I know you aren't happy, Asher. But I don't think I'm the answer."

He shrugged, helplessly.

"Besides, I'm in love with another man."

"Netanel?"

"Don't ask me to explain. There's things I can never

620

tell you about us, things I can never tell anyone. But he's the only man I ever loved. I don't know if I can ever stop loving him. I don't know if I want to." She wiped a smudge of wetness from her cheeks. "Let's talk about something else. Do you have sugar in your tea?"

101

Zion Square

Sarah and Asher sat in the front of a Fiat taxi, watching the square. It was Saturday night, the end of Shabbat; the cafés were full, and the cinema lights were blazing, the posters outside the movie house announcing a new American film: *National Velvet*. Sarah breathed in the rich scent of fresh ground coffee from the cafés and the aroma of roasting peanuts from the braziers of the Arab hawkers.

"A black Hillman," she murmured under her breath.

There were two sergeants from the Jewish Supernumerary Police, both Haganah, patrolling one corner of the square. They had flagged down every black Hillman entering the square that evening, ordered out the occupants – one of them had been packed with angry, gesticulating rabbis – and searched them for weapons. So far nothing.

There were Haganah all over the square. The newspaperman's wife had a Beretta hidden inside the voluminous folds of her dress; the Hassid selling roses from the baby carriage had a Sten gun hidden underneath his flowers; the woman at the cinema ticket booth had a revolver under the counter ready to hand to the usher. Even the couple at the sidewalk café, holding hands and murmuring endearments over the table, were Palmachniks. The girl had two pistols strapped to her legs under her skirt. So did Sarah.

A black Hillman . . .

"How's Marie?" she asked Asher.

"Levin says she's much better."

"Is she still enjoying life at Kfar Herzl?"

"I don't think she will be there much longer. She has been offered her old job back, at the Histadruth."

A fidgeting silence. Then: "Do you like her, Ash?"

Asher stared hard at her. "Are you jealous? Or match-making?"

"I don't suppose anyone would blame you if you – "

"Why do you stay with me, Sarah? What is it? Were you one of those children who liked to pull the wings off flies, is that it? Why are you doing this?"

"I'm sorry, Ash," Sarah whispered, her voice hoarse.

"Look, it's all right. It's not all your fault. I knew when you married me that it wasn't me you loved. It's just that I kept pretending to myself that one day – "

"I do care for you, Asher. I never meant to hurt you."

"I don't understand you at all. You were never a mother, you were never a wife. What is it you want?"

"I wanted something I could never have. It did not stop me wanting it."

"Oh, damn you," Asher said, between his teeth. The Arab boy! All these years and she was still carrying a torch for him!

The two Jewish sergeants were waving down a black Hillman. The driver did not stop; instead, he stamped his foot on the accelerator and drove hard at the first police-man. The car struck his legs and sent him cartwheeling over the bonnet on to the road.

All over the square men and women started to run.

By the time the Hillman reached the front steps of the cinema the usher had a revolver in his hand and had fired two shots into the car's windscreen. The Hillman swerved towards the middle of the square. More gunshots. The usher fell.

622

The newspaper seller fired three rounds into the stalled Hillman. Its tyres smoked as the driver reversed blindly into a line of shoe-shine blocks and then drove away, splintering tables on a sidewalk café. It roared out of the square, heading up Jaffa Road. The rose seller shattered its back window with a burst from the Sten gun.

Sarah had her skirts around her waist, tearing at the sticking plaster she had used to tape two Beretta pistols to her thighs. She checked the clips and threw one in Asher's lap.

"Let's go!" she screamed.

There was water from a smashed radiator and torn tyre rubber on the road. "They won't get far," Asher said.

His prediction was correct. They found the Hillman abandoned at the side of the road no more than five hundred yards from the square, near Hanev'im Road.

Asher stood on the brakes and they jumped out. There was no movement in the Hillman. The windscreen and rear window had been blown in by bullets and the upholstery was showered with bloodied glass. The driver was slumped over the wheel, dark stains spreading over the back of his shirt. Another Arab lay sprawled horribly in the back. The usher's bullet had taken him in the face.

"There were four of them," Sarah said.

Dark, narrow streets led off Jaffa Road into the maze of Mea Shearim, the ghetto quarter where the ultra-Orthodox Hassids lived. "The British will be swarming all over the place in a few minutes," Sarah said.

"To hell with the British! The bastards were going to throw a grenade in the movie house. We've got to find them!"

They ran down the street, following the trail of bloodstains on the paving stones. Their footsteps echoed from the dark, sombre buildings on either side. They heard klaxons in the distance. The army patrols were converging on Zion Square.

An alleyway led off to the right, following the high walls of a synagogue. "I'll go this way," she whispered to Asher. "You check the end of the street."

"Be careful, Sarah."

Asher went on, and she heard the echo of his footfall fade in the darkness. She was on her own.

Sarah was halfway down the alley when she saw the blood. She bent down; there were thick gouts of it on the rain-slick cobbles. They had come this way! A courtyard yawned in front of her, black and malevolent, like the maw of an animal. She took a deep breath, intent on the darkness, searching for movement.

There were houses grouped around the courtyard, their windows in darkness. Whoever lived here had seen, had heard. They are hiding, she decided with contempt. She brushed the thought aside.

On her right was the synagogue wall; on the other shadowy doorways and more laneways, leading off in three directions. She realised she was utterly exposed, framed by splashes of moonlight, a perfect target.

She heard the sirens getting closer. The British patrols would be here soon. Leave it! a voice inside her screamed. The opportunity is lost now. If you don't die in this courtyard, the British will arrest you for the Beretta and you'll spend the next five years in Acre prison.

No. We have to find these killers. We have to show them what happens when they attack us.

She moved to the bottom of the steps, crouched low to make as small a target as possible. She listened and watched and waited.

She heard a small noise, like something being dragged over the cobbles. She saw movement from the corner of her eye, something retreating from the light, into a doorway of a house on the left side of the court.

She ran across the cobbles and braced her back against the bricks, the pistol held in front of her, in a two-handed stance.

She hesitated. It would be easy to fire blind into the shadows, but it might be a cat or a beggar or even a child. She had to be certain of her target.

She edged along the wall.

The shadow moved again.

Now!

"I am unarmed," a voice said in Arabic. "If you want to kill me, go ahead."

Sarah lowered the Beretta and stepped away from the wall.

He was crumpled in the doorway, one leg stretched out in front of him. He was naked from the waist up; his shirt had been torn off to bind the wound in his thigh. He was shivering; shock, Sarah decided.

She tucked the Beretta into the waistband of her skirt. "Rishou," she whispered.

They stared at each other in disbelief.

She supported his weight on her shoulder as she helped him across the courtyard. There were just a dozen steps but by the time they reached the alley the sweat was running off his body in rivulets, and the wound in his thigh had opened again. He was slumped against her now, breathing hard.

"The other son of a whore ran off and left me," he said. "Now a Jewish girl comes back and risks her own life to save me. Are not Allah's ways very strange?"

"At the end of this alley there's a car. If you can reach it I can get you away from here."

"Why are you doing this?" he said.

"Hurry up!" she hissed at him.

He would not move. "Why?"

"Because I love you!"

"But I'm your enemy!"

"You're not my enemy. You're just on the other side, that's all." She looked down the alley. Where was Asher?

They turned the corner and staggered towards the brightly lit street. A few brave souls had ventured out of the shtetl and were standing on Jaffa Road, staring at the shattered remains of the black Hillman, and its grisly cargo. Two Jewish Supernumerary Police had pulled up in a patrol car and were walking towards her.

Sarah saw them and waved them over. "Help me," she hissed in Hebrew. "Haganah!"

They hurried over. "What happened?"

"We were after those filthy Arabs who tried to bomb the square. Moshe here got hit in the leg."

Rishou smiled weakly at them.

They helped her drag Rishou into the back of the Fiat. Sarah slammed the rear door and climbed in behind the wheel. "Good luck," the Jewish sergeant shouted through the window, "and get that damn gun out of sight. There's British everywhere!"

Just as she pulled away from the kerb she turned around and saw Asher appear at the entrance to the alley. He started to run after her. For a moment his face was framed in her rear-view mirror, blank with shock, bewilderment and dismay. He stood helplessly at the kerb, staring after her, long after she had disappeared from sight along Jaffa Road.

"They took me for a Moshe!" Rishou groaned. He lay on the back seat, both hands clutching the blood-soaked dressing on his thigh. His face was chalk-white, and bathed in an oily sweat. Now they were clear Sarah felt her self-control slipping away. Her hands shook on the wheel. "By the hundred holy names of Allah, what were you doing there?" she screamed at him in Arabic.

He fumbled inside the pocket of his trousers, and produced a hand-grenade. "I was to throw this when we reached the square. But I couldn't do it! My little Rahman is dead and I couldn't do it!"

She beat the steering wheel in frustration. "What kind of revenge is it to kill innocent people? You're not like them, Rishou! *Don't try and be like them!*"

"An eye for an eye . . . burning . . . for burning."

Sarah turned off Hanev'im Street and turned left, towards the Nashashibi Quarter. She remembered there was a hospital just north of Nablus Road. She would take him there. "You think killing other women and children will make everything right? You call that vengeance?"

"Don't the Jews?"

"No. *No!* There are some who do, but not us! Not the Haganah!"

"You will, you will."

She slammed the palms of her hands against the wheel. "No!"

"You'd better hurry. I think I've lost a little blood."

"Hold on! It's not much further . . ."

"You knew we were coming . . ."

She kept her foot on the accelerator. If only there were no British roadblocks. She turned on to Nablus Road. So far, so good.

"There's something you have to know, Rishou." She turned round to look at him. He was curled into himself like a wounded animal. He was suffering. "It's about your brother."

"Allah help me in my sorrow . . . that's how you knew?"

She did not answer him. There was no need. "We're there."

The Fiat screeched to a halt outside the hospital. They were in an Arab area now, no place for any woman after dark. Especially a Jewish woman. Especially Haganah.

"Don't get out of the car," Rishou whispered. She reached over to unlatch the door and he kicked it open with his good leg and dragged himself out.

"I'm not your enemy," she said to him.

He did not answer her.

He kicked the door shut and limped up the steps of the hospital, but collapsed before he reached the doors. A man in a white coat rushed out, shouting for help. Two nurses burst out of the doors and helped the doctor drag Rishou inside.

She turned the car around and sped back towards Damascus Gate.

102

Rehavia

Asher was waiting for her when she got back to her flat.
He was sitting in the kitchen, his hands clasped in front of
him on the table, his face grey. She closed the door behind
her and they studied each other, like boxers staring each
other down before a bout.

"What have you got to say, Sarah?"

"What do you want me to say?"

"I want you to tell me the truth. I want to know what
happened tonight."

Sarah did not answer him.

Asher rose from the table and came towards her. "I
don't want to have to report this to Command."

"Oh, don't be such a pain in the ass."

"Tell me what happened! What have you done, Sarah?"

She laboured the words. "The man we were after was
my lover."

"You can't be serious. This is just a big joke, right?"

"You know how I've always loved black humour."

He shook his head. "You couldn't be that stupid."

"Try me."

Suddenly Asher found it hard to breathe. "I don't
believe what I'm hearing! You betrayed us for a stinking
barefoot Arab?"

"I didn't betray us, I didn't betray anyone! I just tried
to save his life! I wouldn't betray the Haganah! If he had
aimed a gun at you I would have killed him. As it was,
he was shot in the leg and bleeding to death. He wasn't
armed. What do you expect me to do?"

"I expect you to do what I would have done!"

"I couldn't! It was Rishou, Ash. It was Rishou!"

There was a long, aching silence. Asher stared at her in blank confusion. "Not that Hass'an boy from Rab'allah?" he said, at last.

"I'm sorry, Ash. I'm really sorry."

No! He couldn't believe it. Rishou! But that was years ago, when she was a stupid kibbutz kid. She was Shai now, and she was his wife! "Please, Sarah, don't tell me you've been seeing him again. Don't tell me this is the affair you've been keeping from me . . ."

She could not meet his eyes.

He uttered a cry like a wounded animal, upturned the kitchen table and kicked the chair across the room. Then he turned on her, his eyes wild and red. "You must be insane! How can you love this . . . this filthy fucking Arab!" He spat the last words like a curse.

"He's not just an Arab, he's a man!"

"Those people are our enemies! We all fight the Arabs every day of your life! How could you do this?"

"I don't fight *them*, I defend *us*. Isn't that what you always say in your great speech about the Haganah? Defence, the purity of arms? I can't help what I feel. I love him. I've been sleeping with the enemy. All right?"

He slapped her. "You whore!"

She hit him with a haymaker, no warning. He fell back into the chair and blinked in surprise. Sarah yelped and collapsed on to the floor, sobbing and clutching her hand.

Asher sat in the chair, for a long time, not moving. The fury at her betrayal, of him, of everyone, settled in his gut like lead and he knew in that moment that he could never love her again. It was finished now. Suddenly he was free of her. "How long have you been seeing him?"

"Nearly a year."

"A year. A *year*. Did you know he would be there tonight?"

"Of course not."

"But you knew he was one of the fedayeen?"

629

"Of course I didn't know! I don't think he's done anything like this before tonight, I swear it! His brother is one of my informants. His *brother*, Asher. His own brother betrayed him."

"What did you do with him?"

"I took him to the Arab hospital on Nablus Road. He'd lost a lot of blood. I don't know if he's going to make it."

If he dies we'll say Kaddish for him at Kfar Herzl, Asher thought, bitterly. Well, that's it. It's over now. What a mess she has got herself in. The thought of her with that arrogant, cock-heavy Arab made him feel physically sick. But at least there would be no more pretending. "Sarah, ever since I first came to Palestine, I was taught the Arabs were our enemies. They stole our food, they burned our crops if we did not guard them day and night. I have spent every day since then with a gun in my hand because always there was the enemy, the Arab, waiting for the moment when our guard was down. I don't understand how you could do this. Not then – not now."

"What are you going to do, Ash?"

"Nothing. After all, it's nothing to do with me any more, is it? I guess the Palmach is my family now." He walked out, closing the door gently behind him. He knew he would never be coming back.

al-Naqb

Izzat looked around the cluster of tight, angry faces. "There is a traitor among us," he said.

The sweat on Majid's forehead caught the light of the kerosene lamp and glistened like metal. Suddenly he was alone in the room. Alone with his western clothes, his bare head, his jewellery, his terror.

"Our brothers Tareq and Naji were martyred two nights ago in Zion Square because someone warned the Haganah of our plan. I now have the name of that traitor."

630

Majid could not raise his eyes. Let him choose another! Allah, help me just this one more time and I shall forsake alcohol, I shall pray five times a day as prescribed in the Koran, I shall make the pilgrimage to Mecca! I am finished with the Haganah now. I gave my word to You in the mosque, did I not? Spare me this one last time!

"You!" Izzat spat and his finger hung trembling in the air a few inches from Majid's face, like a thrown knife shivering in wood.

There was to be no reprieve. He couldn't swallow, couldn't breathe. Every face in the tiny room was turned to him, eyes red-rimmed with hate.

"You were seen at Damascus Gate with a woman, a Jewish woman. A Haganah agent."

He shook his head, tried to find his voice, but he couldn't.

They grabbed him by the arms. He tried to twist free but there were too many of them, he felt their weight on his legs, his chest, his stomach. He cried out in pain.

"Please . . . please . . . please . . . *please!*"

Izzat's knife glinted in the light. Majid tried to imagine the pain. "We could shoot you, but that would be too quick. How long have you been working for the Jews, traitor?"

He couldn't get out any words, so he shook his head from side to side in denial. Someone stuffed a rag in his mouth. "Take off his clothes," Izzat said.

Majid fainted.

Izzat stood over him, scowling with disgust. "Wake him up."

Munir dug his thumbnails into his earlobes. Majid groaned.

"We'll take off his toes first," Izzat said.

There was a soft metallic click! Only Izzat heard it; and when he looked up the barrel of a rifle was pointing straight at his head.

"Let him go," Rishou said.

Izzat blinked in surprise and confusion. Rishou! Zayyad had said he was dying in some hospital in East Jerusalem.

"Let him go," Rishou repeated.

Izzat recovered quickly. Without taking his eyes from Rishou, he nodded towards the others, who were still bent over Majid. "There are a dozen of us, and only one of you, Rishou Hass'an. Do you really think you have a chance?"

"You'll never find out because if you don't release him I'll blow your head off."

Izzat hesitated. Rishou looked pale, he must have lost a lot of blood. He certainly looked unsteady on his feet. Perhaps he could keep him talking. Wait for him to stagger, then grab the rifle.

"Your brother is a traitor," Izzat said.

"Even now I can see your head detaching itself from your shoulders and landing with a hollow thud in the corner of the room," Rishou said. His finger tightened on the trigger.

Izzat realised this was a dangerous game. Rishou might grow weak and collapse, or he might fire before he fell. "He betrayed you, Rishou! That is why the Haganah were waiting for you in Zion Square!"

"No Hass'an betrays his own family."

"He was seen at Damascus Gate with a Haganah woman!"

"Idiot! She's not Haganah, she's a Britisher, she's his mistress! You want traitors?" He nodded at Munir. "Ask that flatulent camel why he left me bleeding in an alley in Mea Shearim! It was Majid who found me and took me to the hospital. Right under the noses of the Haganah! He's a hero! Munir is your traitor!"

"I didn't leave you!" Munir protested. "I went to get help!"

"You ran like a dog!"

Izzat realised the opportunity had passed. Too late to question how Rishou knew the woman at Damascus Gate was not Haganah. All the attention was on Munir now. Well, too bad. A scapegoat was a scapegoat. Someone would have to die for the débâcle in Zion Square.

Majid was still writing and struggling, his eyeballs starting out of his head. It would have been pleasant to kill him, Izzat thought. He particularly wanted that ring on his finger.

Too bad.

"Let him go," he said.

The Holy Strugglers released him, and Majid scrambled to his feet, grabbed his clothes, and ran outside. They heard him vomiting in the alley.

Rishou kept his rifle aimed at Izzat's head. "Harm one of my family and I'll kill you, Ib'n Mousa. It's as simple as that." He pointed to Munir, who was desperately looking around the room for escape. "If that is an example of the kind of men who follow you, then the Jews have nothing to fear."

He lowered the rifle and left.

Rishou staggered and almost fell. He grabbed his brother and dragged him to the car. "Drive," he said.

He collapsed into the passenger seat, fighting the oily waves of nausea. Staying on his feet for so long in that room had required all his willpower. The wound in his leg was like a searing brand.

As they drove away from the house they heard gunshots from inside. By the time they reached the ridge above al-Naqb the wail of Munir's women was already rising into the night, like the wailing of djinn. Izzat had his scapegoat.

Majid dry-retched all the way to Jerusalem.

103

Sheikh Jarrah

Majid turned off Nablus Road into the courtyard of his villa. "You look terrible," he said to his brother, "we should get you back to the hospital."

"Later. I need to talk to you."

"All right. Let's have something to drink first. I need something to fortify my nerves."

Mirham was in the living-room with the children. They looked up wide-eyed at their father and uncle. Majid was pale and shaking and there were evil-smelling stains on the jacket of his suit. His shirt was torn. Rishou's eyes were red-rimmed with pain and exhaustion.

Mirham knew better than to ask her husband questions. She shepherded the children out of the room.

A nice house, Rishou thought. Silk carpets and cushions on the floor, a big Phillips radiogram in polished walnut, beautiful vases, an illuminated antique Koran in a glass cabinet. He had always admired Majid's taste in fine things. Now he knew how he obtained the money to pay for it.

Majid went to a locked cabinet, took a key from his pocket and brought out a bottle of Black Label whisky and two glasses. "Good for the nerves," he said.

Rishou shook his head. "I don't want any."

The bottle rattled against the glass as Majid poured the spirit. "You look terrible," he said to Rishou. He swallowed the liquor in one draught and wiped his mouth with a handkerchief. "When did you get out of the hospital?"

634

"Tonight. I walked out myself."

"Praise Allah you did."

"Yes. Thanks be to Him."

"Did you know?"

"Ali came to the hospital and warned me."

"He's a good boy." Majid poured three more fingers into a glass. "Izzat is crazy. He's jealous of us, Rishou. That's why he wanted to have me killed." He raised the glass to his lips.

Rishou took two steps forward, grabbed the glass and dashed the contents in his face. His other fist took Majid on the side of the head and knocked him down.

Majid landed on his back. "Brother, what are you doing?" His voice came out in a squeal. "What is it? What's wrong?"

"Izzat was right. It was you!"

"You're as mad as he is!"

"You would have let the Haganah murder your own brother!"

"I'm innocent, I swear! May Allah burn me on the Day of the Fire if I lie!"

"I'll roast you myself!" Rishou hauled him from the floor and hit him again. Then he collapsed against the wall. The room spun around him and the pain from his leg made him nauseous.

Majid tried to crawl away. Rishou staggered after him and kicked him over on to his side.

"Please!" Majid screamed.

"Listen to me!" Rishou hissed at him, his fist raised. Majid lay quite still. "You're my brother and I won't let them kill you. But from today don't ever speak to me or show your face near me again. Do you understand?"

"I swear I didn't – "

"Don't! Don't insult me with your lies!"

"The woman! She told you, didn't she?"

Rishou spun around. "What woman?"

"The Jewess! The Haganah spy! She told me you were one of her pawns. She lied to both of us!"

"I don't know what you're talking about," Rishou said.

"It is all right for you now to be so holy, my righteous brother, but how do you think this business started? How do you think we became so wealthy so quickly? Information is like everything else, it's just a commodity, you buy and you sell! Everyone in Jerusalem does it!"

"You bought and sold your own family!"

"I didn't know you would be in that car, I swear I didn't! The others . . . who gives a damn about Tareq and Munir and the rest of them? You think I would have told the Haganah if I had known you were going to be there? Go on, walk away! You want to be a dirty, shoeless Arab the rest of your life, go ahead! It will never be again like it was in Father's day, not ever! The world has changed!" His voice became softer, wheedling. "We have a good business, our own taxi car. We are doing well. I need someone I can trust. I can let you in on a share of a new business I have developed."

"What business?"

"Selling arms."

"To Arabs?"

"Yes, to Arabs."

"Who else? The Haganah?"

Majid did not answer.

Rishou spat on the carpet. "I don't have a brother any more," he said. The door slammed behind him.

When he was gone, Majid fell on his knees, and prayed to Allah, thanking him for his deliverance. Then he fetched the bottle of Black Label whisky, sat down and drank till he passed out.

Part Seventeen

PALESTINE, 1947

104

Rab'allah

Every man in Rab'allah was crowded around the radio in
Zayyad's coffee house. Izzat was there too, with several
of his gang from al-Naqb. The silence was palpable, solid.
Men spoke in whispers. The air was thick with smoke
from the nargilehs, and western-style cigarettes. The
radio crackled and whined, the jangling oriental music
an irritation to their waiting.

How could a man ever imagine that it might come to
this? Zayyad thought. Outrageous that foreigners from
other countries could decide the fate of our holy places.
There had always been Turks or Britishers who were lords
of us, but they had the responsibilities of conquerors, of
great peoples. But to let people they had never heard of
decide what should happen to them was simply a joke and
a violation of human law too overwhelming to be borne.

The United Nations – Zayyad was not quite convinced
of their identity but he inferred they were allies of America
– had sent men to visit Palestine and to impose a solution
on the violence. Before they left they had announced that
immigration should be resumed and land sales to Jews
recommenced. It was clear from this that all the great
peoples had turned against them. What had begun years
ago as a trickle would become a flood and they would all
drown in Jews.

Now these muktars from the United Nations had
announced their sulha. They wanted to divide Palestine
in two, give the Jews the plain of Sharon, Galilee and the
Negev, and put Jerusalem under their own guardianship.

Jerusalem, al-Quds, the Holy! It had been Arab for a hundred hundred years. How could they take it away?

At least Rab'allah would be inside the new Arab state, and if these other countries decided in favour of the sulha, it meant the kibbutz at Kfar Herzl would have to be abandoned. But what kind of effendis would rule them then, Zayyad wondered?

The music stopped and the room fell silent. The United Nations vote on partition got under way. The commentator on Radio Damascus began to shout out his interpretation, and in the background, over the buzz of static, they could hear the drone of strangely accented voices speaking in English . . .

". . . we shall have a roll-call of nations on the partition resolution. A two-thirds majority is needed for passage. Delegates will answer in one of the three ways: for, against or abstain . . ."

The vote began with a country called Afghanistan. Brother Arabs, the commentator shouted.

"Afghanistan votes against."

But then other votes came in, and the commentator began to grow hysterical. Australia, Belgium, Bolivia, Brazil, Belorussia, Canada, Costa Rica, Czechoslovakia, Denmark, Dominican Republic . . . all voted for. Where were these places? Zayyad wondered. He had never heard of many of them. How could they tell them how to live in Rab'allah?

". . . Egypt."

"Egypt votes against and will not be bound by this outrage!" the Egyptian representative screamed.

It was just the third vote against.

Kfar Herzl Kibbutz

In the dining hall the kibbutzniks ringed around the radiogram had the same taut expressions as those in Rab'allah; tension, concentration, and fear was etched into every face. Radio Jerusalem carried the transmission direct from Lake Success in New York.

Isaac looked at his grandfather and wondered what he was thinking. The resolution was a double-edged sword. If the United Nations voted for partition, they would finally have a Jewish state, but they would have to give up the kibbutz it had taken twenty-two years to build. If the vote went against them, they would keep the kibbutz but their future would be plunged again into a melting pot of violence and hatred and uncertainty.

The voting continued. Ecuador, France, Guatemala, Haiti and Iceland all voted for. That made fifteen votes for, six against, more than the two-thirds majority they needed to win.

The Iraqi representative rose to his feet. "Iraq votes against and we will never recognise the Jews! There will be bloodshed over this day! We vote against!"

Liberia, Luxembourg, the Netherlands, New Zealand, Nicaragua, Norway, Panama, Paraguay, Peru. All voted for.

"The Philippines."

"The Philippines votes for partition."

Over the crackle of static they could hear the roar that went up in the hall of the United Nations. Isaac looked at Yaakov. "What has happened?" he asked him.

"I think we're there," he said.

Jerusalem

Asher and Marie sat together at the kitchen table in Marie's apartment on Ben Yehuda Street. The signal from the radiogram was poor and they strained to hear over the static. Poland for, Turkey against. Then the Ukraine, the Union of South Africa, the Union of the Soviet Socialist Republics, all voted for.

"It's going to happen," Asher whispered. "We have the vote! I think we have enough!"

A voice crackled on the radio: "The United Kingdom of Great Britain . . ."

Asher could hear the anger and disdain in the British Ambassador's voice: "His Majesty's Government wishes to abstain."

"The United States of America."

"The United States of America votes for partition."

Thirty-one votes. The Arabs had twelve and needed the last four member countries to vote against to stop the Jews.

". . . The Yemen votes against partition."

". . . Yugoslavia."

". . . We wish to abstain."

That was it. It was over. It had happened. They had a state.

Rab'allah

"This outrage will never be allowed!" the commentator was screaming on Radio Damascus. "Arab weapons will make this so-called partition plan just so much worthless ink on paper . . . !"

The coffee house was silent. Depression had settled over each of them during the vote, like dust on statues.

Izzat was the first to break the spell. "It is a conspiracy of the Americans and the Jews against us!" he shouted, jumping to his feet. "We will fight this to the last drop of blood!"

He stormed out. Pandemonium. The rest of the Strugglers leaped to their feet, fists raised, imitating Izzat's defiance. Shouting curses, they followed him.

The fellaheen also rose to their feet, panicked and murderous in their rage and helplessness. ". . . we must cut out this Zionist cancer from our souls!" someone shouted.

"We will throw the Jews into the sea!"

"Death to the Jews! We will kill every last one of them!"

They poured out into the square.

Only Rishou and Zayyad remained. "*Insh'allah*," Zayyad murmured.

Someone fired a rifle into the air. Soon it was as if a battle was under way in the village. The volleys of gunshots were accompanied by the sound of men's voices, raised in chant: "Death to the Jews! Death to the Jews!"

The commentator on Radio Damascus continued to pour his venom on the partition and the Jews. Rishou got up and switched him off. "If words were bullets all the Jews would have been dead long ago."

Zayyad fingered his prayer beads in steady rhythm. "How did this happen? When did a few Jews become such a problem?"

"It will not end here."

"Of course not. But I fear two things. I fear the Mufti if he makes a war and we lose; then we are at the mercy of the Jews. And I fear the Mufti if he makes a war and he wins; then we are at the mercy of the Mufti. May Allah bless him and grant him increase, of course, but the man has dribble for brains and his farts have more substance than anything that comes out of his mouth. Can you imagine Izzat as his representative?"

"Why does Allah inflict these people on us? We are ruled by hotheads, fools and speechmakers. Look where they have led us!"

"It is indeed hard to divine Allah's purpose in this."

"The Iraqis and the Syrians and the Egyptians have promised to, you know, come to our aid."

"So why does it sound to me like a threat? It is like being attacked by a rabid dog and have a hungry wolf chase him away. I fear what the wolf will do when the dog is gone."

"The effendis sold these Jews the land, now they crow that the world has betrayed them. It is we who were betrayed!"

"Meanwhile the Mufti reclines in Cairo. On the Day of Judgment may Allah have a fat man sit on his balls for eternity!"

The chants and the gunfire went on for hours. Rishou and Zayyad listened, wondering which devil would torment their village the least: defeat or victory.

Kfar Herzl Kibbutz

The sound of laughter and music and singing reached Yaakov from inside the brightly lit hall. Outside the stars were like diamond chips scattered across a sky of black velvet. The air was still and frigid, and the mind quickly sobered. Out here, Yaakov thought, the future seemed less warm, less sure, and less inviting.

He heard movement behind him.

"What are you doing out here on your own, abba?" It was Sarah.

"I will join you all later."

She came to stand beside him. "But what's wrong?"

"Ah, Sarah! All my life I dreamed of this moment. Our own state! Finally a place for Jews to live. But . . ." He shrugged his shoulders, unable to articulate the sadness inside him.

"But you will have to leave the kibbutz?"

"I helped build this. When we came here we created it from swamp and wilderness. When we leave it will go back to the wilderness again."

"You'll build another one. You'll start again."

"Starting again seems much easier when you're young."

"It is worth any sacrifice to have our own homeland."

"I know. And yet . . . yet I am sad for the Arabs too. *Meshuggah*, yes? I've fought them all my life. Yet I cannot stop wondering how they must feel."

Sarah thought about Rishou. He must hate her more than ever now.

"And you, Sarah," Yaakov was saying, "what will the future hold for you after tonight?"

"I never stop to think about it any more."

"I've noticed. Have you seen Asher lately?"

She shook her head.

"Are you going to tell me what happened between you?"

"I don't know, abba. Perhaps I should never have married him."

Yaakov shrugged his massive shoulders. "You had Isaac in your belly. What else could you do?"

Indeed. Yaakov had wanted the marriage, Asher had wanted it. And she had yielded the dictates of her conscience to their urgings and to her own comfort. "Has he said anything to you . . . about us?"

"You're my daughter. He expects it to come from you."

Good, loyal Asher. He deserves better than me, she thought. "I just don't love him any more."

Yaakov's eyes were wounded. He cannot comprehend me, she thought, he never could. "He is a fine young man, Sarah."

"He is the son you never had. The son I should have been, perhaps."

Yaakov reached up and stroked her hair. "No, never say that, I never wished you to be different from what you were."

She put her cheek against his hand. How could she ever tell her father the truth after so many lies? Maybe some other time. After all this was over.

They both heard the gunfire from the direction of Rab'allah and knew it was a portent of what was to come. The harbingers of tomorrow were speeding towards them

645

in the darkness. "Come on. Let's go in," Yaakov said. "They'll wonder where we are."

Jerusalem

On Ben Yehuda Street and King George V Avenue men and women were running along the street banging on doors: "We have a state! We have a state!" An old Chevrolet drove up and down the street, horn blaring. Windows were thrown open, and people poured laughing into the freezing black streets in their pyjamas and bathrobes.

The proprietor of Carmel Mizrachi Wines opened his shop and rolled a vat into the middle of the pavement and began passing out free drinks to the crowd. Someone even climbed on the plating of a British armoured car and offered two glasses to the British soldiers in the turret. The bars and restaurants reopened. Bearded rabbis, sabras with black curling moustaches, bleary-eyed shopkeepers still in pyjamas, yeshiva students in black hats and sidecurls, all sat together to toast "*Lochayim!*"

By two o'clock in the morning the streets were crowded with people and a party was under way. Women in bathrobes, Hassidim in gaberdine coats, Orthodox with jackets thrown over their pyjamas, formed a huge circle and began to dance the hora. Marie and Asher joined them.

Netanel wandered through the same crowds, his hands thrust into the pockets of his greatcoat. How can they be so happy? he thought. Don't they realise they have invited the Arabs to attack them? Don't they know there is going to be a war?

Then he remembered why he had come to Palestine, and, remembering, he understood the reason for their joy. Finally these people had been offered a place to belong, a place where there could be no more Hitlers, no more signs saying "*Juden Verboten*", no more cattle trucks waiting to take them to gas ovens.

If there was to be more fighting, then at least they had a wall to put their backs against.

105

The celebrations ended abruptly. The hangover was painful.

Sarah stared out of the window of the bus at the Commercial Centre, now a smouldering ruin, the streets flooded from the firemen's hoses, the warehouses gutted. Tension stalked the grey streets, and was reflected in the sullen faces of Arab and Jew alike. It was a city in fear, a city on the edge.

For the past year things had been getting worse. The city had gradually been segregated behind huge coils of barbed wire, roadblocks had been set up everywhere, and passers-by were routinely stopped and searched by British soldiers. But since the partition vote the situation had collapsed into terror. Every day came the rattle of small arms fire from the Montefiore Quarter and the occasional roar of a bomb. People rarely ventured out after dark.

Now the bright blue banners hung limp from the lamp-posts along Ben Yehuda Street, like shrivelled party ballons. They were quickly being replaced by black and white mobilisation notices, ordering every Jewish male between seventeen and twenty-five to register for the military.

The day after the vote snipers had ambushed an Egged bus just outside Lydda airport. Five Jews had been killed, and seven wounded. Soon after there were reports of stonings, shootings and stabbings in Haifa, and rioting in Jaffa.

*　　*　　*

The Arab Higher Committee called a three-day general strike. All over Jerusalem, Arab merchants shuttered their shops, painting their shopfronts to distinguish themselves from their neighbours during the inevitable retribution. They painted crescents if they were Muslims, crosses if they were Christian.

Jewish ambulances heading for Hadassah Hospital were fired on, Molotov cocktails were thrown into cafés, synagogues were burned. A mob stormed out of the Old City through Jaffa Gate, wielding clubs and irons bars, and marched down Princess Mary Avenue to the Commercial Centre. As British soldiers stood by, shops were looted and burned, and their owners beaten; several others were hacked to death with knives. Haganah members who tried to come to their rescue were arrested by the British for illegal possession of arms.

What the Arabs had promised had become reality. There would be no Jewish state without bloodshed.

And it had only just begun.

In a high school gymnasium in Rehavia, just a quarter of a mile from Bevingrad and the headquarters of the British CID, was the Haganah headquarters. The Haganah commander for Jerusalem sat in a tiny unheated office, surrounded by maps, his desk piled high with communiqués and intelligence reports.

A bull of a man, a former circus wrestler, film critic, and art dealer, Yitzhak Sadeh, doctor of philosophy, was the founder of the Palmach and a legend in his own right. He wore no uniform and expected no salute. The Haganah had spurned formal army discipline ever since its formation.

He waved Sarah to a chair. "Sit down, sit down." They knew each other well. Sadeh was a friend of her father's, had been almost an uncle to her when she grew up.

He had his adjutant bring coffee, and asked after Yaakov and Asher and Isaac. "Now then," he said at last. "You asked to see me. What is it I can do for you, Sarah?"

"I want a transfer from the Shai. I want to go back on active service with the Palmach."

Sadeh nodded, thoughtfully. "I see. Any particular reason?"

"It's personal," Sarah said.

"As you know, we are preparing for war now, and we need all the able-bodied fighters we can get. We would probably have requisitioned you sooner or later anyway. I suppose you want to join your father's command at Kfar Herzl?"

"I'll go wherever I'm most needed."

Sadeh considered. "I heard you and Asher are having difficulties?"

"It's nothing to do with that."

"I just don't want you to think the Palmach is the answer for your personal problems, Sarah."

How can I explain to you? Sarah thought. About Rishou, about Asher, about Isaac? How can I explain that I lost the only man I ever loved, terribly damaged the man who was my husband, lost my son through guilt and neglect? I have failed and I have come looking for my redemption in this war.

"Look, Sarah," Sadeh went on, "we are outgunned and outnumbered. You were trained as a Palmachnik, so naturally I welcome you, whatever your private reasons may be for coming here today." He went to the map behind him, and slammed the palm of his hand on the Jewish Quarter of the Old City. "This is my immediate problem. Jerusalem. Not on the fringes, but right here – in the very heart. We cannot defend it, but we cannot give it up. On the night of the partition vote, we had just eighteen Haganah in there to defend over two thousand people. We have to get in as many weapons and trained people as we can, as soon as we can."

"I understand. I'll go."

Sadeh looked embarrassed, a difficult feat for such a big man. "Your father won't be happy about this. Once we get our people in, we're not sure we can offer them a way out."

"If I wanted a way out," Sarah said, "I wouldn't have come here. Would I?"

Rab'allah

There were a dozen trucks, their paintwork scoured by desert sandstorms. Uniformed men stood on the back of each one, firing their rifles into the air, beating their fists against the sides as they sang. The people of Rab'allah streamed out to meet them, waving and shouting and laughing, the women running awkwardly in their long black gowns, whooping out long ululating cries.

The Arab Liberation Army had arrived in Judea.

The first truck reached the outskirts of the village. The Iraqi flag had been draped over the bonnet, and a bedsheet flapping on the side, crudely painted, announced: "The Falcons of Baghdad".

"You think we can trust them?" Zayyad said to Rishou.

"You taught me always to trust a stranger but only if I had my foot on his neck. The Iraqis have proclaimed themselves our brothers in arms. Do you think they do this because they are fellow Arabs or because, you know, they would like to send their oil through Jaffa?"

Izzat was running beside the truck, his arms raised in welcome, shouting "Death to the Jews!" When he saw Rishou and Zayyad he broke away from the procession and ran up the slope towards them. He was wearing his new uniform, US army desert combat fatigues, acquired at great expense in one of the souks. He had sewn a patch on the sleeve, an emblem of the Dome of the Rock beneath a red crescent.

"All that is missing are the medals," Rishou muttered.

"The Mufti has declared a holy war," he shouted out to them. "Fifty million Arabs shall fight to the last drop of blood!"

"I imagine if things go that far the last drop will

650

doubtless belong to the Mufti," Zayyad said, "certainly not the first."

"You should be careful," Izzat said. "The Mufti remembers his friends and his enemies."

"I have one foot through the gates of Paradise, ib'n Mousa. You don't frighten me."

"It is not you for whom the warning is intended."

Rishou stared him down.

"Go fuck a donkey," Zayyad said.

"Things will be different in Palestine soon," Izzat said. He turned and ran back down the hill to welcome the rest of the convoy.

"Son of a whore," Rishou said.

"Yes," Zayyad said, "but he's right."

106

The Arab League had financed the formation of the Arab Liberation Army, an irregular force of fanatics, criminals and mercenaries who had been sent to aid the Palestinians while the regular armies massed on the borders and waited for the British to leave the battleground. The Liberation Army had no regular uniforms, no tents, little food and a variable assortment of weapons. The band who had arrived at Rab'allah were mainly Iraqis. They took over the khan next to the coffee house, and camped in barns and abandoned houses. Others simply requisitioned rooms from the fellaheen.

Even Zayyad had been forced into the position of welcoming the Falcons' commander into his own home. He had been persuaded that tents and supplies for the irregular army were just days away.

*　　*　　*

A week after their arrival Zayyad returned one lunchtime from a meeting of the villagers in the coffee house and found the officer sitting in his armchair eating a breakfast of rice with lamb. Zayyad was angry: angry that the Iraqi was sitting in the chair that was reserved for him, and him alone; angry with what he had heard in the coffee house; angry that the officer had ordered Hamdah to fetch for him; angrier still that she had complied.

The man's name was Aziz. He said he was a colonel but Zayyad suspected he was probably only a regular army sergeant who had been made an officer in the Liberation Army in an attempt to impose some discipline on the mercenaries. He was a handsome man with dark, wavy hair, a bristling moustache, and small, dark eyes.

"Sit down," he said expansively, indicating one of the cushions.

Zayyad stood over him, one hand on the knife at his waist. "Do not invite me to sit in my own house."

"I meant no disrespect."

"If you mean no disrespect, get out of my chair."

Aziz considered for a moment. Finally he complied. Zayyad took his place in the armchair – the son of a whore had removed some of the straw through a rent in the cloth! – and surveyed the Iraqi from his throne. This was a better way to begin the conversation.

"Did you sleep well?" he asked Aziz.

"Passably."

"I thought the sun might have bothered you. It has the habit of shining in one's face when one sleeps past noon. It is most irksome."

Aziz stared back at him with an expression of contempt. He clapped his hands for coffee. Hamdah entered. Zayyad growled at her, and sent her back to the kitchen.

"Is something wrong, Zayyad Hass'an?"

"Yes. You are the something wrong. Your company of clowns and thieves and other garbage – I refer to the Falcons of Baghdad, of course. Perhaps not falcons. Perhaps vultures."

Aziz finished his breakfast and wiped the grease from the fingers of his right hand on to his uniform.

"They camp in our olive orchard. They take food and they do not pay for it. They insult our women by leering at them when they go to draw water from the well. Now yesterday two of your men took a donkey and have not returned it to its owner. The poor fellow suspects they may have eaten it after they obtained from it a certain degree of sexual satisfaction. A transport of many delights, no less."

"What do you expect?"

"We expect your men to behave like soldiers – if that is what they purport to be – not like animals. This is our village. You are supposed to be our friends, not our conquerors. These people are poor. They want payment for their food, and they do not want to have the few possessions they have stolen from them."

"So you can go on about your lives here and leave someone else to defend your lands from the Jews?"

"It is not the Jews we are worried about."

"We are here for your protection! We expect that at least you could be grateful for our sacrifice!"

"For myself I don't care about Palestine. I only care about my village. Most of these people are not as well travelled as the Falcons of Baghdad. They have never left this place. This *is* Palestine for them. And it is being raped."

Aziz waved his hand dismissively. "It is regrettable about the donkey. It is probably just a misunderstanding."

"Fucking the donkey or eating it? Which?"

"I will talk to my men about it."

"Thank you, Colonel. It might also be expedient to remind them of the Arab brotherhood. It is a new notion to me, and I am an old man. But my son informs me it is the reason the Jews' blood will flow like a river down the Bab el-Wad. Eventually."

"You cannot expect my men to come here and make these great sacrifices and expect nothing in return."

653

"I never expected that. Some of my poor fellaheen did, but then they are uneducated. Yet it is not a crime to be simple."

"I will talk to my men."

"Thank you," Zayyad said. "One last thing." He leaned forward. "If I ever again find you making my daughter-in-law wait upon you like your personal handmaiden, I shall cut out your heart and stuff it down your throat."

"Perhaps twenty years ago," Aziz said and he leaned over on one cheek and there was a bagpipe squeal as he broke the wind that was troubling him. Then he got up and walked out.

A foul and lingering odour dominated the room. Zayyad's nostrils twitched. Twenty years ago! he thought. *He underestimates me.*

So much for Arab brotherhood.

107

Jerusalem

Across Jerusalem, entire communities had been cordoned off, and the Jewish and Arab quarters were now separated behind rolls of barbed wire. The Jewish Quarter of the Old City was almost completely isolated and the bus was now the only link to the outside world for the ancient community of religious who lived inside.

The number 2 bus took just five minutes to travel from the bus station in the New City through the Jaffa Gate and along the walls of the Armenian Quarter to the southern end of the Street of the Jews. Since the announcement of partition, those five minutes had become an eternity to every Jew now entering the Old City.

The majority of passengers on the bus this morning were Palmachniks; the boys were dressed as yeshiva scholars, false sidecurls glued on to their skull caps, uniforms worn under long gaberdine coats. It was enough to fool the British but as she looked around the bus Sarah knew immediately who was Palmach and who was not; it was in the set of their shoulders and the shadows of their eyes.

Sarah's new identity papers were examined by British soldiers at the checkpoint on Jaffa Road; they identified her as a nurse from the Hadassah Hospital joining the medical staff already inside the beleaguered quarter. She was searched, but not as intimately as the men; this was fortunate for under her skirts she had Sten gun parts strapped to the inside of each thigh.

She peered through the slit that had been cut in the steel plate that now covered the windows. A British army patrol, an armoured car and two jeeps, escorted them through the Arab barricades. The faces in the street were sullen, some openly hostile. When they recognised the faded blue of the Egged bus, several Arabs raised their fists and shouted insults. Some hawked deep in their throats and spat at them. Stones clanged against the metal sides.

Inside the dark and confined space of the bus, there was absolute silence. She imagined she could smell the fear, a rank cocktail of stale sweat and body heat. Sarah felt as if she were passing through the gates of hell. She wondered if she would ever drive out again.

Clang!

Another stone struck the bus. Fists beat on the metal sides.

Sarah tried to control her fear. She looked around at her fellow Palmachniks. Their eyes were concentrated on the slits. Only the genuine yeshivim would look at her, their faces a mixture of bewilderment and resentment.

Suddenly the driver shouted, "The bastards are leaving us!"

Sarah hurried to the front of the bus. Through the slit of the driver's window she saw the British patrol scuttle away along Mamillah Road. The towers of the Jaffa Gate loomed ahead of them. A barricade had been set up in front of it, several dilapidated trucks and ancient cars blocking off the road. There was a welcoming party too, a crowd of forty or fifty Arabs armed with rifles and knives.

Perhaps the British had known about the ambush, Sarah thought, or perhaps they had decided there was nothing to be gained from helping a few Jews. Whatever the reason, they were alone.

There were three other Haganah girls on the bus. One of them ripped open her blouse. Two hand grenades were strapped to her chest with sticking plaster, below her brassiere. One of the yeshiva students jumped up and shouted, "Cover yourself, whore!"

A Palmach boy pushed him back into his seat.

"Where is her modesty?" the young scholar protested.

"There wasn't room for modesty and grenades," the boy told him.

The girl ignored them both. She ran to the ventilating plate at the front of the bus and another Palmachnik lifted her round the waist. She threw open the ventilator, pulled the pin from the grenade and lobbed it towards the barricade.

The effect was like dropping a stone into a pool. The Arabs instantly broke and ran in all directions. Seconds later the grenade detonated with a deafening crack! and a blast of grey smoke drifted across the barricade. As it cleared they saw half a dozen bodies crumpled on the ground.

One of the cars in the blockade had been blown on to its side by the explosion. The bus driver jammed the engine into low gear and smashed through the gap, the side of the bus cannoning off one of the trucks as they went through. Sarah was knocked to the floor.

Then they were bouncing over the cobbled streets inside the citadel. The yeshivim howled in alarm. One of them had fallen forward and smashed his nose. He sagged on to the floor, clutching at his face, blood welling through his cupped fingers.

Sarah clung on. Next year in Jerusalem! she thought. Now she was just minutes away.

The Street of the Jews

They spilled out of the bus and stood around in small groups, amazed at their own good fortune. They put their fingers in the bullet holes that had punctured the metal sides and wondered at how they had escaped.

"I didn't hear them firing at us," Sarah said to the girl who had thrown the grenade.

"Neither did he," the girl said. Two Palmachniks were dragging a body out of the bus.

"One of ours?" Sarah said.

The girl shook her head. "No. A real yeshivim."

Jewish men dressed entirely in black gathered around them. The hostility on their faces, Sarah noticed, was little different from those of the Arabs on the other side of the wall. A rabbi stepped out of the crowd, examined the dead man, and waved his fist at them. "Look what you have done! Why can't you just leave us alone?"

The siege of Jerusalem had begun.

Rab'allah

The blue and white flag of Zion unfurled in the cool wind that grazed the Dome of the Rock, the greatest Muslim shrine in the Holy City. It was a terrifying image, and the young men of the village howled out their rage and their vows of vengeance.

"The Jews have defiled the mosque!" Izzat shouted. "While they still dwell inside al-Quds, our Holy City, no good Muslim may rest!"

". . . Kill the Jews!"

"We will throw them out of the Old City for good!"

There was a roar of fury from the doorway and every head turned in that direction. Rishou limped towards Izzat and tore the postcard out of his hand. "You're a liar!"

"Pictures do not lie!" Izzat shouted, and the fellaheen crowed their agreement. Everyone knew you could not falsify a photograph.

"The flag has been drawn in! A child could do better!"

"Ask your fellaheen if they think it is a lie!" The fellaheen scowled at him, disappointed that he had again sided against them.

"What are you trying to do to these people, Izzat?"

"Are you not an Arab? Does this picture not make the blood boil in your veins?"

"You would drag our whole village into Jerusalem to fight? If we are going to fight Jews, let us do it here, on our own land!"

"The Jews have defiled the mosque!"

The fellaheen again bayed their outrage, and Rishou had to shout to make himself heard. "If they had defiled the mosque we would have heard it screamed aloud on Radio Damascus!" But the fellaheen were no longer listening. Izzat judged his moment to move away and the fellaheen piled out of the coffee house after him.

Rishou watched them go. Allah help me in my sorrow! Izzat is the power in the hills now. Rishou looked at the postcard in his hand, then tore it into small pieces and dropped it on to the carpet.

"He is a lion, that one," a voice said.

Rishou looked around. Aziz, the Iraqi "colonel", was sitting in the corner, drinking coffee and helping himself to a tray of halwa.

"Are the Falcons going to join our young lion in his quest to liberate Jerusalem?" Rishou asked him.

Aziz shrugged and stuffed another halwa into his mouth.

"Did you come here to fight – or eat?"

"We have no orders."

"So you eat our food and sleep in our barns while our young men do the fighting for you?"

"They are just going to throw rocks. When the real fighting starts, we will be there."

"No, if there is real fighting they'll want real soldiers."

Rishou limped outside. Izzat had organised transport. Four other villagers now owned cars, men who had earned good money working for the British before the evacuation. The motor cars were lined up in the square, the drivers gunning the engines and pounding their fists on the horns.

Black-robed women rushed out of the houses holding bowls of goat's milk which they splashed under the wheels as a good luck gesture. Men crammed into the seats, clutching ancient revolvers and rifles. Rishou saw Ali jump into Izzat's ancient black Humber. Seconds later it roared out of the square, bumping over the frost-hard road towards Jerusalem.

108

Old City

The Jewish Quarter of the Old City enshrined the heart and soul of Jewish history. It was built next to the same hill where Solomon had built his temple three thousand years before, when Jerusalem had been capital of Judah. In 600 BC the temple was sacked by the Babylonians, but a second temple was constructed on the same site soon afterwards.

But following Bar Kochba's revolt in AD 70 the entire city was razed to the ground by order of the Emperor

Hadrian. A new Roman city was established there, and all Jews were forbidden to enter. It was the beginning of the Diaspora.

But a part of the western wall of the temple survived, and centuries later, after the Roman Empire had vanished into history, Jews returned to the ancient city, content to live in poverty below the sacred stones while they awaited the coming of the Messiah.

Over the centuries four separate communities grew up inside the Old City: the scholarly and indigent Jews, known to the Arabs as the Forgotten of God; Christian monks who venerated their own holy places around the Church of the Holy Sepulchre, which was reputedly built on the site of the crucifixion; the Muslims, who gathered around the Dome of the Rock, which enshrined the handprint of the Archangel Gabriel; and the Armenians, the very earliest Christians, who had been drawn to Palestine to escape persecution in the fourth century.

In turn, Jerusalem fell under the power of the Byzantines, the Crusaders, the Mamelukes, and the Ottomans. In the sixteenth century it was Süleyman the Magnificent who built a massive wall around the city, effectively sealing it off from the sprawling settlements that were to cluster around it later. On the fall of the Ottoman Empire at the end of the Great War, the British enjoyed their brief nova of thirty years.

But the Old City itself remained immutable, a burning chalice that encapsulated the legends and aspirations of Christians, Muslims and Jews, a mysterious maelstrom world hidden behind the rose pink walls of Süleyman.

The Jewish Quarter itself was an area just four hundred and fifty yards long and three hundred wide extending between the Zion Gate and the Dung Gate. In that teeming ghetto of shadowy bazaars and ancient alleyways, two thousand ultra Orthodox Jews lived in poverty, surrounded by more than fifty thousand Arabs.

It was less than half a mile to the fashion stores of Princess Mary Avenue, but inside the ghetto life was barely different from the time of Christ. The Jews lived as they had lived for centuries, neither seeking nor caring for contact with the outside world. They depended almost entirely on the emissaries who went to America and Britain to elicit *halukas* – "handouts" – for them.

They dressed uniformly in black gaberdines and broad-rimmed black hats, dedicating their lives to the study of the scriptures, their every action prescribed by religious law. A woman who disturbed her husband at his sacred books still risked divorce.

Twenty-seven synagogues and rabbinical study centres – *yeshiva* – towered over the twisted alleys and narrow, steep streets. History stood still here. In the corner of the Elihayu Hanavi Synagogue a crumbling wooden chair still awaited the return of Elijah.

But the world had finally penetrated the walls and now stalked the Street of the Jews. With each passing day the holocaust that had gathered in the ancient land of Canaan became harder to ignore.

The Haganah headquarters in the Old City had been set up in Tipat Chilav, the Drop of Milk, a clinic founded many years before to provide milk for underprivileged children. The garrison was placed under the command of one Aaron Kaplan, an Orthodox Jew from New York, who had served as a captain in the US army after the Normandy invasion. His unit had been first to roll through a camp called Dachau in northern Germany and the experience had left a deep impression on him. At the end of the war he had volunteered his services to the Yishuv in Palestine. He wore thick black tortoiseshell glasses and had the air of a college professor obsessed with his basketball team's recent poor form. He frowned continually, creasing his forehead into deep ridges.

When Sarah walked in he was staring at a large-scale map of the Old City that was pinned to the wall. "Sit down, Sarah," he said, and waved a hand vaguely in the direction of the chair on the other side of the desk.

He and Sarah were both wearing the new Haganah kit:

a work shirt and khaki sweater. Sarah wore shorts, Kaplan olive drab drill pants, both items US army surplus stock obtained from Italy.

"It's like trying to get an octopus into a string bag," he said, frowning at the map. "You put a defence somewhere, the Arabs get through a gap you left somewhere else. Still, nothing a couple of companies of good men couldn't fix. Or good women, of course. Ever been in a siege before, Sarah?"

"No, I haven't, sir." Rank had recently been introduced into the Haganah along with new uniforms.

"Neither have I. In Europe we were always going forward. This is going to be like no other battle I ever fought before."

I wonder if he has the mettle for this? Sarah thought. Any good kibbutz commander knows how to live under siege. They've been doing it all their lives. I wish Yaakov was here.

"What's the situation, sir?"

Kaplan leaned forward. "Sarah, do I look like a happy man?"

She shook her head. "No, sir."

"You're right. One, the Armenians have broken off contact with us. They were our intermediaries for food and water. Now we have to rely on the British. Two, we're short of men and weapons. Yesterday, when you came in, we bribed some British soldiers and we got another bus and three taxis inside the walls. But our total fighting strength is still just one hundred and twenty Palmach and Haganah, men and women combined. Three, our main weapons are revolvers, plus a few Sten guns and hand-grenades. We have one two-inch mortar with a few shells, three Lewis heavy machine-guns, a dozen rifles and some various explosives. The only thing we're not short of is Arabs. Now the Armenians have caved in, they're on all four sides."

Sarah leaned forward. "Yes, but what's the good news?"

Kaplan's expression did not change. "The good news is Ben-Gurion has sent us a cable wishing us luck."

Sarah smiled. "Do we have a plan of defence, sir?"

"The fighting is going to be like it was in Berlin and Stalingrad, window to window, roof to roof, house to house. It's going to be the Day of the Sniper. Imagine you're in a trench in the Great War and you'll have a chance of staying alive.

"Our defence has to be split into two separate areas. The axis line is here." He got up and stabbed a finger at the map. "The Street of the Jews. To the west the quarter runs up a gentle slope to the Armenian Quarter, to the south, below the Zion Gate, it falls away to the Kidron valley. The situation there is not too bad. It's here to the north and the east that we are exposed.

"There's two key positions. Here, the Warsaw Synagogue in the north-east corner. The building is three storeys high, built around a courtyard. There is a yeshivoth attached to the synagogue, but I have evacuated all the students. We have taken it over completely.

"To the east there is a narrow alley called the Street of Stairs. At the far end, here, is the highest building in the whole quarter, the Nissan Bek. It dominates the whole quarter, so it is absolutely critical for our defence."

The door crashed open and an elderly rabbi with a wiry grey beard crashed into the room. A bush of hair exploded from under his broad-rimmed black hat. He seemed to be as wide as he was high and Sarah's first impression was of a grey and weathered bull wearing gold-rimmed glasses.

But any absurdity in the spectacle was quickly banished when the man opened his mouth. His voice had the harsh, hectoring tone of the lifetime cleric. "You are an abomination before God!"

Kaplan blinked rapidly and stood up. "Excuse me?"

The rabbi pointed a gnarled finger in Kaplan's direction. "I have just discovered that your young men and women lie together at night in the yeshivoth of the Warsaw Synagogue! You have turned a place of God into a haven for harlots and fornicators!"

Kaplan removed his glasses and wiped them on a white

663

handkerchief he produced from his pockets. "Why don't you sit down, Rabbi Silverberg?"

The rabbi ignored the offer. "You will stop this immediately! I want your harlots out of my synagogue!"

"They are not harlots, rabbi," Kaplan said softly.

"They fornicate in a holy place!"

"They rarely sleep for more than two or three hours a night, rabbi. I think they might be a little too tired for fornicating."

"Will you or will you not have them removed?"

"I don't think you quite understand the situation. These harlots, as you choose to call them, are as much soldiers as the men. They may sleep in the same temporary barracks – "

"So you admit this!"

"– but they are a fighting unit. If they are going to defend you people, they deserve more consideration of the circumstances."

"Defend us? From whom? We didn't ask you to come here! If you left, everything would be all right. We would live in peace with our Arab neighbours as we have always done!"

"Actually, Rabbi Silverberg – "

"Who is this?" The rabbi noticed Sarah for the first time. His cheeks flushed pink. He stared at her bare brown legs.

"Her name is Sarah Lan – "

"Woman, you offend my sight!" he shouted and walked out.

Kaplan replaced his spectacles on his nose and sat down. "Rabbi Silverberg," he said, after a while.

"Are they all like that?"

Kaplan shruggled. "It seems all those years we prayed for Jerusalem, Jerusalem wasn't exactly praying for us."

Rab'allah

Aziz settled himself in the armchair in Zayyad Hass'an's majlis and clapped his hands for coffee. He was restless. He knew the trouble, of course. It had been months since he had had a woman and every morning his sacred member was as hard as the bone in his shin. When they burned down the kibbutz he would make sure he took one of those bare-legged little Jewesses alive and had some fun with her before he cut her throat.

Meanwhile . . .

As Hamdah bent to pour coffee from the brass finjan, her veil fell away from her face. Not a bad-looking woman, Aziz thought. Not very old, either. He wondered what the rest of her was like, and he felt himself stirring once more. He was bored, sitting around in this disgusting village, eating this putrid food. It was perhaps time he had some fun, some reward for his sacrifice.

Zayyad said this one was a widow, so there would be no trouble about bulling in another man's herd. Probably a long time since she had had some good, stiff Arab cock. She must be desperate for it.

Hamdah quickly replaced her veil. She was about to move away but he caught her wrist. "Come and sit down," he said to her.

She shook her head and tried to wriggle free.

"I said come and sit down. I won't hurt you."

"No . . ."

"I said come here." He started to get angry.

She threw the coffeepot at him and the scalding liquid spilled on his arm. He yelled in pain and leaped to his feet. She ran towards the kitchen.

But Aziz recovered quickly and grabbed her again. She screamed and tried to kick him. By the hundred holy names of Allah she would bring the whole village running in here! He drew back his arm and hit her. She crumpled on the floor at his feet.

She lay on her back, stunned, her long black skirts around her thighs, her thaub ripped at the shoulder. Her veil and hood were torn away and her long black hair fell across her face.

Aziz felt a tight, irresistible ache low in his belly. He knelt between her legs, and pinned her arms over her head.

"Don't pretend you don't want this," he laughed.

She screamed again so he punched her to keep her quiet. He hooked his fingers in the collar of the thaub and ripped down the full length of it. She was plump, with large brown nipples, and a thick bush of hair. He bunched the hem of her skirts in his fist and stuffed them in her mouth. Then he spat on his hand to make himself wet and pushed himself between her legs.

He was almost inside her when the little harlot writhed and twisted away from him. He hit her again, hard, and she yelped like a puppy and lay still, panting and moaning.

He liked it this way.

Soldiering had some compensations.

There were no screams.

When Zayyad reached the doorway he heard only a muffled banging from inside the house and he knew immediately what it was. The primal rhythm and a man's animal moans were unmistakable.

Zayyad took the knife from his belt and went to the back of the house, entering softly through the women's entrance, and crept into the kitchen. He waited for a few moments for his eyes to grow accustomed to the light. Then he went on bare feet to the majlis.

Aziz lay between Hamdah's legs, his arms extended, pinning her wrists with his weight. There was blood on Hamdah's teeth and her eyes were bruised slits. They opened just slightly when she saw Zayyad over Aziz's shoulder; but she did not cry out.

The Iraqi moaned and laughed and murmured something in his own dialect that Zayyad did not understand. His hairy buttocks squirmed and tensed, like bellows. Rise and fall, rise and fall.

The Arab Liberation Army, Zayyad thought. See how they have come to rescue us from the Jews.

Zayyad stepped forward swiftly and cut his throat.

Hamdah's body was covered with dark, slick blood. She rolled into the corner and started to gag and cry at once.

Aziz had not finished dying. It sounded like a pig rutting.

"Cut off his balls and stick them down his throat!" Hamdah sobbed.

"I have killed him. Is that not enough for you? Now go and wash your face and put on some clothes. Then fetch Rashedah. We shall have to bury him somewhere where the dogs won't dig him up."

Aziz finally finished his dying. His legs jerked a final time and he was still. Hamdah crawled out of the room on all fours.

Zayyad cleaned his knife on the Iraqi's shirt. So. What was to be done? Unless they found the body Aziz's soldiers would simply think he had deserted. He would not be the first one. It was better left that way. Zayyad would not risk reprisals against his family.

He frowned in disgust. Aziz had bled all over his prayer rug, staining the image of the Dome of the Rock that had been embroidered into the fine silk. It was a pity. It had been a treasured possession, and had been in his clan for generations.

He would have to burn it now.

109

Old City

They left the Humber near the Damascus Gate and entered the Muslim Quarter on foot. It was late afternoon and the ancient streets were crowded; but the crowds thinned quickly as they drew closer to the Jewish Quarter. By the time they reached the shadow of the great Nissan Bek, they were quite alone.

There were six of them, led by Izzat; Ali scurried to keep pace behind him. The dome of the synagogue loomed ahead of them, dusted with snow. From somewhere inside the Jewish Quarter, psalmody filtered along the alleys on the frigid December air.

Izzat stopped on a corner, twenty paces from the walls of the synagogue. It was achingly quiet. He imagined that the Jews inside the Nissan Bek could hear every whisper.

He addressed the Strugglers, holding a hand-grenade in his right fist: "We will throw the grenade into the Nissan Bek itself! If we see any Jews we will kill them!"

No one spoke. The religious fervour that had captured them in the coffee house at Rab'allah had quite deserted them now.

Izzat handed the grenade to one of the fellaheen from Rab'allah, a man called Ahmad. "I give you this great honour, Ahmad. The women will sing your praises tonight in every village in Judea."

Ahmad stared at it as if it were his own heart, neatly excised from his body and still beating in his cupped palm. He licked his lips and looked at the others. They nodded encouragement.

"What should I do?" he whispered.

"When you get close to one of the windows, just remove the pin and throw it inside."

Ahmad hesitated.

"Do you wish someone else to have this honour?" Izzat said.

Ahmad shook his head. He took a deep breath and started in the direction of the great synagogue. He had gone no more than half a dozen paces, when he screamed and fell spreadeagled on his back. He was dead even before the echo of the sniper's bullet had died away.

The grenade spun from his hand.

Izzat hugged the wall. The others imitated him, sobered by the fate of their comrade. "They must be in the dome of the synagogue," he said. Across the alley a wooden staircase led to the flat roof of a two-storey house. "If we can draw their fire I can take care of the sniper from up there."

No one moved.

"You were all ready to follow me to Paradise half an hour ago!" Izzat hissed. "A Jew fires his rifle once and you are all afraid!"

Ali looked at the cobblestones. A trickle of blood was following the course of the stones in a slow, dark rivulet.

"Is there not one man among you?" Izzat said.

"I will go," Ali said.

From the cupola of the Nissan Bek five latticed windows looked in every direction over the Old City. Below the dome was a gallery supported by three arches, the women's section of the synagogue; by tradition the women prayed separately from the men so they did not provide a distraction. Now the circling tier, with its vantage point over the surrounding streets, made an ideal defensive position.

Two-hundred-year-old Talmudic scrolls had been used to barricade the windows, and an old door had been brought from the cellar and suspended with ropes from the roof of the dome. A sniper lay prone on the door, his rifle aimed down into the street. He had wrapped himself in a blanket against the cold.

His name was Roberto, an Italian Jew from northern Italy. The other Palmachniks in his unit said he had been at Auschwitz but Roberto never talked about it. He talked very little about anything.

Sarah was crouched by the window. "Can you see what's happening?" she whispered. The acoustics of the dome made her whisper echo in the vaulted silence.

Roberto reloaded and stared into the street along the barrel of the British Lee Enfield, his finger still poised over the trigger. "They're thinking it over," he said. His Hebrew was heavily accented.

"Perhaps you frightened them off."

Roberto tried to blow some warmth on to his stiff fingers. His breath crystallised in a brief, wispy cloud. "They'll try again."

If they do, he thought, they won't do any better than their comrade. Roberto took great pride in his marksmanship. He was no higher than his father's knee when he had first gone shooting in the hills above their village near Lake Maggiore. Wild duck mostly. His very first rifle was taller than he was. By the time he reached his bar mitzvah he could hit a running hare at a hundred paces.

In those days he had never considered his talent might one day be required for larger targets.

. . . There!

A figure darted for the grenade that lay on the cobblestones a few paces from the dead man. He fired.

At the same time there was movement on the rooftop of a building opposite and a bullet smashed into the masonry above his head and ricocheted, buzzing around the dome like an angry bee.

Sarah pumped two rounds at the rooftop in reply.

"Did you get him?" Roberto hissed.

Sarah peered over her makeshift barricade, looking for movement. "I don't know!"

Roberto looked down into the street. Another corpse

lay face down beside the first. He had drilled him nice and
clean through the centre of the chest but his momentum
had carried him forward. Even in death one hand reached
for the grenade.

No more than a boy. Pity. Still, it was only an Arab.

Izzat joined the others in the alleyway.

"What happened?" one of the men asked him.

"My gun has jammed," Izzat lied. "But I killed a couple
of them. We've taught them a lesson."

"I think Ali's dead. We can't get across there to the
synagogue. It's impossible."

Izzat shouldered his rifle. "His memory will live long in
our hearts and our songs. Even now Allah is receiving him
into Paradise! I am sure I killed three Jews! Let us go and
celebrate our victory!"

Rab'allah

Rishou parked the Plymouth outside his father's house.
Zayyad met him at the doorway. Rishou knelt and kissed
his hand. "May you live long, Father."

Zayyad's face was grey. "Did you find your son?"

Rishou opened the back door of the motor car and took
the body from the back seat. The boy hung limp in his
arms, his eyes open in death, the face mottled with pooled
blood. There was congealed blood, thick as jelly, over the
hole in his chest.

"I was too late," Rishou said. "Ali has been martyred.
He was killed in the battle for Old Jerusalem."

Zayyad stared at his dead grandson. Soon the whole
future would be rotting in the earth above The Place
Where The Fig Tree Died. "Our heads will always stand
high in his honour. I will tell your mother."

Rishou carried Ali back to his house. He felt as if he had

swallowed stones. May Allah let these Jews live just long enough to bury their own children! he thought. Both his sons were dead now. What else could these Forgotten of God do to him now?

Part Eighteen

PALESTINE, 1948

110

Sanhedriyya

It was the coldest March in memory, as if God had passed judgment on them all. The temperature fell below freezing every night, and the clouds that gathered in slate-grey battalions on the horizons brought sleet and hailstones and rain that made the bones ache with the chill. The days were grey and cold, like death.

There was no kerosene left for heating. Supplies inside the city depended on the daily convoys that battled the ambushes along the Bab el-Wad, and as the weeks went by fewer and fewer trucks got through. The daily rations for an adult inside the city had been reduced to just two ounces of margarine, a quarter of a pound of potatoes and a quarter of a pound of meat.

Meodovnik, Shoshan, Netanel and Kohn shivered in their wet and strong-smelling sheepskin coats as they huddled around the table. Rain had plastered Meodovnik's thin hair across his skull, and fine droplets of moisture glittered on his spectacles in the candlelight.

"I have just received news through my contacts inside the Haganah," he said. "Another convoy has been attacked on the Bab el-Wad. Eleven trucks and three armoured cars were destroyed. The convoy has been forced to return to Tel Aviv."

There was a sharp intake of breath around the table. It was the first time a convoy had failed to get through. The Arabs had cut Jewish Jerusalem's artery. "Bastards," Netanel said.

675

Meodovnik looked around the faces in the room. "The situation in our Holy City is desperate. They are cutting our throats and the British are standing back and watching us bleed. And what do the Haganah do against those responsible? Nothing . . . nothing!"

"They want us to do their dirty work," Shoshan said.

"God's work is never dirty," Kohn corrected him.

"The Haganah are to be respected as pioneers and watchmen," Meodovnik said, "but their leaders are getting old. They think this is still the 1930s. Ben-Gurion still talks about partition, as if it were somehow desirable that Jerusalem should be given up to others. In this city lies our temple, and our heritage. We have prior claim over everyone to Jerusalem and to Canaan. This is our land, promised to us by God and by Moses.

"There is no room for any but God's chosen in God's land. There is no other way, practically or spiritually, than to transfer the Arabs from here to the neighbouring countries. Not one Arab village must be left in Palestine."

"I agree," Netanel said. "The Haganah and their masters in the Jewish Agency have become too fond of talking. My father thought he could talk to the Germans and they killed him in Dachau. If we want to survive we have to use our weapons."

Meodovnik took a map of Palestine from his coat and unfolded it on the table. The road that snaked along the Bab el-Wad was highlighted with red ink, like a vein. "Most of the attacks have been concentrated along this stretch of road," he said. "The Arab forces are drawn from Kader's mercenaries, and the Arab Liberation Army, as well as local gangs of villagers. There are four villages close by: al-Naqb, Deir Jabr, Abu Far'a and Rab'allah. The village that has been chosen for our attack is Rab'allah."

"Why Rab'allah?" Kohn asked.

"Our intelligence indicates that not only do many of the fedayeen come from this village, but there is also a company of the so-called Arab Liberation Army quartered there."

"Let them be on the receiving end for a change," Netanel said.

Kohn frowned. "How many men can we put in the field?"

"For this operation we will be joining our local forces with those of the Stern group. We will form two combat forces of a hundred fighters each. Against us there are perhaps a hundred Iraqis and the same number of untrained villagers.

"The attack will take place at night. One group will sweep from the south-west, the second group will wait along the Jerusalem road to the north. Any Arab that tries to escape will simply be cut down."

Heads nodded in satisfaction. With the advantage of surprise and better weapons, they would deal the Arabs a devastating blow.

"The Arabs must learn there is a price to pay if they want to make war on us," Meodovnik continued. "They must learn we are not only prepared to defend ourselves, we will also strike back."

"And not before time," Netanel said. Ah, Amos, he thought. You would enjoy this moment.

New City

The sunset was a dirty orange stain across the western sky. Ambulances gathered in the bus station as the crowd waited on the slick wet bitumen for the convoy from the coast. Word had spread like flame on dry tinder: today the convoy – forty trucks, two buses, eight armoured cars – had broken through.

The first trucks rumbled into the square. They bore the scars of their battle with the Bab el-Wad; along their flanks were scorch marks made by exploding grenades and petrol bombs, and there were bullet holes punched into the metal and armour. Many of them rode on metal rims, their tyres

677

shredded by bullets. The armoured cars were followed by the buses, all plated in steel, each weighing eight tons. They were bringing in men from the Har-El Brigade, finally back from the battles at Latrun and Kastel.

A hush fell over the square as the doors opened.

The wounded were carried off first, slumped, bloodied, shapeless. Some screamed, some called for their mothers. The onlookers stood and stared, shivering at the cold, stunned with dread and hate and horror.

The first ambulances, bells clanging, hurried away into the dusk.

The crowd pressed forward, crying, hoping, shouting, shoving. Asher pushed his way through the press, his hands plunged into his greatcoat, his eyes luminous in the twilight. There was three days' stubble on his face and his hair was matted and unwashed.

Behind him, they began to lay out the dead on the wet asphalt. The joyous shouts of the reunited were punctuated with the shrill anguish of another who found a friend or father or lover among the shrouded harvest.

Asher walked quickly away. The evening was grey and chill.

There were white handbills pasted everywhere, on walls, on telephone poles, in shop windows:

"We stand to attention before the memory of our comrade . . ." Each name another Jewish boy or girl killed fighting Kaukji's Irregulars in the north, Kader's army along the western corridor, or in Jerusalem itself.

"We stand to attention before the memory of our dead comrade, Menachem . . ."

On Ben Yehuda Street he passed the shell of the apartment block that had been blown apart when British soldiers, suspected Mosleyites, had parked two armoured cars, packed with explosives, in the road early one morning. Fifty people had died in their sleep.

"We stand to attention before the memory of our dead comrade, Michal . . ."

Soon after Asher had left Jerusalem the Arab Liberation

Army under Field-Marshal Kaukji had attacked Kfar Szold, a kibbutz in the far north, but had been beaten back.

"We stand to attention before the memory of our dead comrade, Eli . . ."

Kaukji turned his attention to Tirat Zvi, a kibbutz in Galilee.

"We stand to attention before the memory of our dead comrade, Esther . . ."

In March the Jewish Agency and the *Palestine Post* were bombed.

"We stand to attention before the memory of our dead comrade, Mordechai . . ."

Soon the British would be gone. Then the killing could begin in earnest. Then, Asher thought, they could paper over every crack in the walls of the New City with the names.

"We stand to attention before the memory of our dead comrade, Shimon . . ."

Marie peered out at him from a crack in the door. "Asher!" She threw the door open wide and hugged him. "What are you doing here?"

"Shalom, Marie. Can I come in?"

She pulled him inside. The apartment was cold. There was no kerosene for heating. Her initial excitement at seeing him was replaced with alarm. "Is something wrong?"

"No, my brigade has been pulled back inside Jerusalem. I . . ." he shrugged. "I wanted to make sure you were all right."

His eyes were hollow, red-rimmed with fatigue and horror. He stood in the middle of the room, like a nocturnal creature blinking to adjust to the light. "Sit down," she said, "I'll get you coffee."

He warmed his hands on the coffee mug, staring at the night through his own haggard reflection in the window-pane. Wisps of steam rose from the coffee. He nodded towards the window. "What's that?"

"My window box," she said, and forced herself to laugh.

679

"Every good Jewish housewife in the city has one. There are no fruit or vegetables in the markets. I'm growing tomatoes. Aren't you proud of me? A good kibbutznik, after all!"

"What do you live on?"

She shrugged. "Macaroni. Sardines. But I can get eggs. Herr Fromberg gets them for me. He still has connections with some Arabs and he saves me two fresh Arab eggs every week." When he did not answer her, she said, "I still have this week's eggs. Are you hungry? I can cook them for you if you like."

"Do you remember Leon?" he asked her. "You would have met him at the kibbutz. A tall boy with sandy hair. Always laughing. He was in my brigade. He was wounded when we were fighting at Kastel. We didn't find him till the next morning. We heard him though. They gouged out his eyes and filled the orbits with his testicles." He turned back to the window. "No, I don't want any Arab eggs."

She hugged herself with her arms, not knowing what to say to him. "How's Sarah?" she said, at last.

"I haven't seen her for months. I think she's in the Old City."

"I'm sorry, Asher."

He pulled cigarettes and matches from his overcoat pocket and lit one, with trembling fingers. "Don't be. I'm not."

"That's not true, is it?"

He shrugged.

"Was it another man?"

He nodded. "Yes. Another man."

"What about Isaac?"

His eyes were glassy, unfocused, as if he were looking at something in the far distance. "Isaac. Did you know he wasn't my son? Did Sarah ever tell you?" He drew on the cigarette, composing his thoughts. "She was pregnant with Isaac when I married her. I suppose he was an easy way out for both of us. I was hopelessly in love with her, and she needed a father for her baby. I thought she would grow to love me in time, but of course she never did."

680

"Whose child was it?"

"Some Arab boy from the next village."

"An Arab?"

"Isaac doesn't know. We both thought it better that way." He shut his eyes. "I did my best with him, we both did. But after I joined the Jewish Brigade in 1941 I didn't see him or Sarah for four years. The ties weren't strong enough to keep us together." The candlelight threw shadows across his face and there were dark bruises under his eyes. He looked as if he hadn't slept for days. "Look, I didn't come here to tell you my troubles. I was worried about you. Things are getting bad. I think we should get you out."

"Out of Jerusalem?"

"Out of Palestine. There's British officers with the Arab Legion. They're not bad fellows. They've promised safe passage for anyone who – "

"I won't go."

"Marie, you're not Jewish. This isn't your fight. I'm worried what's going to happen to you if – "

"I'm staying."

"Why?"

"I've got to like it here. I won't go back to Germany and I'm not going back to being a refugee. I stay."

He held up his hands in mock surrender. "All right, all right. I believe you. Thanks for the coffee. I'll look in when I can." He got up to leave. "Be careful."

"Where are you going?"

"There's a barracks for us. In Rehavia."

"You don't want to do that. Stay here. You can have the sofa."

"No. There have been too many sofas in my life." He went to the door, hesitated. "By the way – no, I haven't heard from Netya. I know you wanted to ask."

Suddenly Marie stood up and grabbed his hand. The impulse surprised even herself. She closed the door and pulled him back into the room. She unbuttoned his coat and slipped her fingers inside. "It's cold out there," she said.

681

He shook his head. "Don't do this, Marie. Not if you still want Netya. Don't do this to me again . . ."

"I don't know what I want, Ash. You'll have to help me make up my mind."

"Marie, I loved you from the first moment I saw you . . ."

"Then stay," she murmured. Her mind told her that she loved only Netanel Rosenberg, even though that man perhaps only existed now in her mind. Her mind told her she loved someone else; but instinctively, she followed her heart.

111

Bab el-Wad

Squalls of freezing, slashing rain, the mushroom smell of wet pine needles and damp wool. Rishou huddled around the fire, his eyes red from the smoke. Rain dripped from the branches overhead and droplets trickled under the collar of his sheepskin coat and began their long, slow march down the length of his spine.

The Bab el-Wad was a freezing misery at this time of year but it was the only honourable place for an Arab and a Hass'an to be. What other choice was there? To be like Majid, and hide away in his villa in Sheikh Jarrah and worry over his businesses in the city, like a pig snuffling at a trough after the last scraps are gone?

He had not seen his brother for months, but his fortunes could not be bright. The Hass'an Olive Oil Company was gone, bombed by the Irgun in one of their raids; the taxi had been "borrowed" by Izzat and damaged beyond repair in an attempt to throw a grenade in Ben Yehuda Street.

Majid still worked the black market, no doubt, but how long would he continue to prosper once the British left? That day could not be far away. Villagers who had worked for years at the Allenby Barracks and in the King David Hotel had now had their employments terminated.

Every Arab in Judea was flocking to join Abdul Kader, the Mufti's nephew. Rifles and bullets were for sale in every souk and bazaar; a single rusty bolt-action Mauser was fetching one hundred pounds in the Old City.

Indeed, Abdul Kader was the reason they were camped on this freezing hillside tonight. Finally they had a leader who knew how battles were fought and won, a man of personal heroism and intelligence. Kader had reasoned that the Jews might send their convoy through very early the next day and he wanted to be ready.

And so they waited.

Rishou tried not to think about what would happen when the jihad against the Jews was over. The fight must take place anyway, and he would take his place in the ranks of the men. He would take his vengeance, for Wagil, for Rahman, for Ali, and afterwards he would still have his pride, if nothing else.

He tried not to think about the other fights that would take place after the Jews were gone; the fight with Izzat, for authority in Rab'allah; the fight with the new effendis for possession of their land. Most of all, he tried not to think about Sarah.

If he had to, he decided, he would kill her too.

Rab'allah

Dark clouds scurried across the face of a bright moon. There was just a single guard, an old man with a thick, grey beard. He propped his rifle against an almond tree and lifted his robe to urinate. The splash of his water carried to them clearly on the wind.

When he finished he yawned and stretched and lit a

683

cigarette. Netanel could see his face clearly in the amber glow of the match. The skin was creased and loose, like a well-worn leather pouch.

This was going to be easy.

Too easy! Something was wrong . . .

There was supposed to be a whole company of Iraqis here. Why just one ancient guard? Even for the Arabs, it didn't make sense. "Where are the men?" he whispered to Meodovnik.

"Sleeping."

"Just one guard?"

"They are not expecting to be attacked."

"But just one guard?"

Meodovnik shrugged in the darkness and did not answer.

So cold. Netanel was eager to begin now, needed the heat of action to stop this shivering in his limbs and the creeping paralysis that waiting brings. Let's begin!

He looked at the luminous dial of his watch. Almost four o'clock, almost time.

The earth was cold, and the chill seeped through his greatcoat. The moon disappeared behind another bank of cloud and the shadows of the Irgunis around him in the orchard were no longer discernible. But he could almost feel their anticipation, their excitement . . .

The flare arced over the village like a comet, bathing the flat-roofed houses in a blood-red dawn. The old guard stared up at the sky. Netanel was close enough to see the look of astonishment on his face. Then a sudden burst of automatic weapon fire sent him hurtling backwards and he collapsed like a bunch of empty rags.

Netanel pushed himself to his feet, his limbs numb and stiff. He saw other shadows separate from the ground all around him; the dead rising, screaming vengeance. There was the shock of grenades, the staccato rattle of small arms fire; the pure thrill of hate.

"Yehud Alainou! Yehud Alainou!"

Zayyad woke suddenly from sleep, his heart lurching

684

painfully in his chest. He tried to separate from his dream. He had been talking to Ali. His grandson was riding a white horse to Paradise and he had wanted to buy his rifle.

Screams, gunfire, explosions! Allah help me in my sorrow! What was happening? What time was it? He was bathed in cold sweat.

"*Yehud Alainou!*" The Jews are coming!

He felt Soraya grab his arm, her fingers gripping his flesh like the bite of a horse. "What's happening?" she shrieked at him.

He had to protect the women. Hamdah and Ramiza were in the next bedroom, Khadija and Wagiha were asleep in another. "Get the others!" he hissed at his wife. "Tell them to stay in here and make no noise!"

"What's happening?" Soraya moaned.

"Just do as I say, woman!" He scrambled to his feet, and groped for his rifle, which was propped against the wall in the corner.

"*Yehud Alain –* " Another shot and the screams were cut short.

Zayyad ran to the window and pushed open the shutters. It was like hell had erupted from a hole in the earth. Red light poured from the sky, Rishou's house was a ball of flames. People were everywhere, running and screaming. The whole world was filled with Jews, black spectres with Sten guns, screaming in their sub-human language.

He knelt down, brought the rifle to his shoulder and aimed. The nearest shadow was just ten yards away. He fired and the man collapsed on the ground, clutching at his stomach, and screaming.

Zayyad aimed again.

Suddenly there was a white flash and a deafening concussion. He could not feel the rifle in his hands. The night turned very black; then he felt nothing at all.

Netanel felt the past unravel inside him. He saw Mandelbaum, and the huddled stench of misery on the train from Ravenswald, the children's faces in the wheelbarrows beside the flaming trenches, the piles of rigid corpses outside the barracks at Auschwitz, the dead like bleeding chunks of meat in the Commercial Centre; the raging surf of his fury boiled out of him.

He heard the crack of a rifle from a nearby house, and Shoshan fell, screaming. Netanel took a grenade from the webbing belt at his waist, removed the pin and lobbed it through the doorway, throwing himself on his belly as Yaakov had taught him to do. The shock wave rolled over him and he felt the sting of debris on his shoulders.

Meodovnik ran through the gaping hole the grenade had blown in the wall. An old Arab lay face down under the collapsed masonry.

He heard sounds from the back of the house, like the whimpering of a wounded animal. He took a torch from his belt, and picked his way across the debris. A curtain partitioned the bedrooms. He ripped it down with the muzzle of his Sten gun.

A mass of bodies was huddled into the corner of one of the bedrooms. The beam of the torch picked out staring eyes and a tangle of limbs. Like a litter of whelps, he thought. Here in the darkness was the pulsing, throbbing heart of the hatred; here was the hidden womb that would spawn another generation of hate. No point in just destroying the drones. You must squash the queen and her eggs.

He raised his gun and fired a long burst and in the phosphorus beam of the torch he watched the blood spray up the walls and he kept his finger on the trigger of his weapon until he could no longer hear the screams and the only sound was the laughter of his own release.

The old Arab raised himself to his knees, his face black with blood. At that moment Meodovnik emerged from the smoking ruins of the house. He raised his Sten, about to smash in his skull with the butt.

"No!" Netanel screamed and ran towards Meodovnik, knocked the Sten out of his hands with the breech of his

686

own weapon. He kicked the old Arab back on to the rubble with the heel of his boot.

"What are you doing?" Meodovnik screamed.

"Leave him! He's an old man! Leave him!"

Meodovnik snatched up his weapon, cursing with frustration, and ran off into the darkness.

The old man's body was silhouetted by the flares and the fires. Netanel dragged him back into the shadows. "I'm sorry, Amos," he whispered, and then he was gone too, running back towards the sounds of a battle he no longer had an appetite for.

112

Rehavia

Yitzhak Sadeh looked like he had not slept for a week. He invited Asher into his office and shouted for his adjutant to bring coffee. They talked for a while about the Kastel campaign and then Asher asked him about the situation in Jerusalem.

Sadeh rubbed his face with his hands and groped for his cigarettes. The lids of his eyes were heavy and swollen. "The day before yesterday one of our convoys did not get through. That was the first time. The convoy you came with lost one-third of its trucks and two armoured cars. The fist tightens, Asher. The Arabs intend to starve us to death and the British are going to let them."

"How are things in the Old City?"

"Did you know your wife was there? She asked to go, you know."

"I didn't expect her to hide herself away in a bunker. She's good. Yaakov trained her well."

Sadeh's eyes speculated, but he did not comment further. "In answer to your question – the British try to maintain a semblance of law and order in the Old City but every day there are more attacks. We do not have enough fighters or weapons in there. When the British leave I am afraid our people may not be able to hold out even for twenty-four hours."

The door opened and Sadeh's ciphers clerk walked in. He saluted. It was a new innovation, instigated by Tel Aviv, and one that Sadeh was apparently not comfortable with.

"I think you'd better see this, sir," the man said.

He put the cipher sheet on Sadeh's desk. Sadeh read it quickly and his face darkened. "You'd better come with me," he said to Asher.

Rab'allah

The dawn was pale and grey, a vapid leaking of the darkness from the eastern sky. They were dragging bodies to the clearing and piling them in wind-rows before dousing them with kerosene. Someone tossed a match on to one of the piles and the pyre ignited with a roar and a tail of thick, black smoke spiralled into the sky.

Netanel's nostrils flared at the familiar, sickly sweet smell. He remembered other cold mornings, other red skies, and an odour that clung to the air like a stain.

Birkenau.

The smoke drifted across the clearing, smudging the lemon border of the dawn. In the maelstrom of battle he had seen Jews, his Jews, settle their accounts, and for him there had been no release. He had merely added yet another nightmare to his rich fund. The residue in his mouth was revenge, and it did not taste sweet.

The sun rose in a washed blue sky, hinting at the return of a fleeting spring. The hills were carpeted in verdant green,

688

with patches of scarlet anemones, bright as blood, hidden among the sheltered clefts.

They bounced up the dirt track from the Bab el-Wad Road and as they reached the crest of the hill they caught their first glimpse of the white, flat-roofed village. Asher detected the taint of the smoke on the morning breeze and felt his fists tighten around the wheel.

It was the smell of the dead.

They climbed out of the jeep. The Irgunis stared back at them, their faces white masks of defiance. Like terrible children, Asher thought. Yes, we are responsible, their faces said. We have done this. So? What are you going to do about it?

There were bodies everywhere, like ragged bundles of sheets thrown down. Asher wandered through the narrow streets, dazed, overwhelmed. They had even shot the dogs.

A whole family was crumpled in an alleyway. The wall was drilled with bullet holes, and the women and children and grandparents lay in the twisted aspect of their death. Where were the men? Where was the father to these children, the husband of this woman, the son of this old man?

He turned away, and stumbled over another body. A naked woman lay in the mud, her ankles and wrists tied behind her. She had been eviscerated and the flies rose in a black swarm from the grey-green mass of her belly.

He heard crying from a nearby house. The front of the house was in ruins and an old man lay face down among the rubble. The noise came from the bedroom . . .

. . . The bedroom. Blood sprayed everywhere, the angry murmur of flies. Bodies lay tumbled on each other, as if they had fallen through the ceiling, one woman almost cut in half, her intestines piled beside her like grey sausages. He bent down. All women.

One of the shapes whimpered and twitched.

Just a child. She could not be more than about ten years old, Asher decided. Her body had been protected by one of the other women, but a bullet had taken off her leg halfway up her shin. The stump of her limb was still oozing blood. Asher tore strips from one of the dead women's skirts and tied a compression bandage around the girl's leg.

He carried her outside.

An Irguni was there, his Sten gun propped against his hip. He stared at Asher, then at the child. Behind the spectacles his eyes glittered with hatred. Asher remembered him. Meodovnik.

A Red Cross ambulance rumbled towards them. Asher waved it down. A man in a short-sleeved khaki shirt jumped out. He shouted something to him in German. A Swiss, Asher decided. The man's face was ugly with contempt. He took the child from Asher's arms and hurried with her to the ambulance.

Asher stared at the blood on his tunic, then at Meodovnik. The Irguni had been joined by one of his colleagues.

It was Netanel.

"What have you done?" Asher said.

"They are our enemies, have you forgotten?" Meodovnik said.

"They are women and children!"

"Arab women and children."

Asher took his own weapon from his shoulder and levelled it at the Irguni. "Put down your guns right now."

"Don't be stupid."

Asher removed the safety from the Sten gun. "Do it!"

He was aware there were at least a dozen Irguni around him in the square. He heard them raise their weapons, felt their black muzzles pointed at his back.

"No, Ash." Sadeh strode across the square, and stood between Asher and Meodovnik. "We don't kill other Jews."

"This man isn't a Jew! He's an animal!"

"They have to know Jewish blood isn't cheap any more," Meodovnik said.

"So you slaughter innocent women and children?"

"Nobody's innocent."

690

Asher stared at Netanel. "I don't understand, Netya. What has happened to you?"

Netanel shrugged helplessly. He did not answer.

"Put down the gun," Sadeh repeated.

Asher wanted to be sick. This was not the dream. Ever since he had come to Palestine he had hated and feared the Arabs but he knew he could never do something like this. There was at last something he hated more and he wanted to kill it but Sadeh was standing in the way.

Asher lowered his gun and walked away. In his nostrils the smell of burning corpses, the sweet smell of blood, and corruption.

113

Utter desolation.

Rishou felt as if he were somehow detached from his body, a spectator at his own despair. He felt nothing, except perhaps pity for the tragic central figure, now walking like a ghost among the ruins. He knew pain would come, but it would come later, slowly, a little at a time, so that it would not completely overwhelm him.

A British armoured car was parked outside the coffee house and British soldiers patrolled the alleys or stood around in groups, staring at the corpses. He ignored the soldiers, stepped around the rust-red pools in the mud, and walked slowly up the hill to the burned-out shell of his house.

The barn had not been touched by the flames, but the animals too were all dead. His horse, his donkey, his cows, even the chickens, were all butchered. The flies were at work on the jagged entranceways to the meat.

*   *   *

The door to his father's house had been blown in by an explosion. He stepped over the rubble of stones.

Zayyad sat in his armchair, his face white as alabaster dust. There was a thick bandage wound around his head, but blood had seeped through it, blooming like a rose. His hair straggled from beneath the dressings, lank and grey. It was the first time Rishou had ever seen his father without his keffiyeh.

Zayyad sat slumped to one side in the chair, his left hand clutching at his ribs. "They massacred everyone," he said.

Rishou looked around the room. There were pockmarks in the walls where grenade fragments had embedded themselves. Wagil's photograph lay on the floor, the glass frame smashed.

He went in to the bedroom. Soraya, Ramiza, Khadija and Hamdah were all there. They were beginning to stink. After a cursory inspection he walked out again.

"The Jews did not have time to burn them," Zayyad said, his voice a dull monotone. "The British came."

"Where's Wagiha?"

"I don't know. When I woke up there was a Britisher doctor putting a bandage on my head and my leg. He told me the women were dead. I asked him about Wagiha but he said he didn't know."

"Are you all right, yaba?"

"I want to be dead with the others. That is my only wound."

Rishou walked out. His rage was so cold and so vast he dared not let it from its rein for he had no way to channel it. He walked to The Place Where The Fig Tree Died and looked down at Kfar Herzl and made a silent vow to Allah and to his dead family that he would live to see it utterly destroyed and every Jew in it dead.

"If we lose Old Jerusalem, we might as well lose Palestine," Meodovnik said. "The Old City is our heart. We must not give it up under any circumstances."

"The Haganah do not think they can hold out after the British have gone."

"They must. This is more than a battle for a state. It is a holy struggle. Think about it, Netanel! Why did you survive all those years in Auschwitz if it was not God's design? You are meant for great things, for a great quest. We are the chosen ones. We will restore the temple to the Jews! We will redeem God's chosen tribe!"

Netanel was staring at the table. He was no longer sure whether survival was a destiny or a curse. He had wanted a cause that would serve as his redemption. The massacre of women and children was hardly that. Perhaps the answer lay in Jerusalem itself.

"Begin wants us to get more men inside the Old City," Meodovnik said. "Whoever goes will become the new guardians of the temple."

Netanel leaned across the table towards him. "I'll go. But how do we get inside?"

Meodovnik smiled. He rubbed the thumb and index finger of his right hand together. "It is simply a matter of money."

"We can bribe the British?"

"I have found a British officer who is willing to exchange a moment's myopia for a considerable sum in Palestine pounds."

Netanel remembered a Passover prayer whispered long ago in a candlelit room. "If I forget thee O Jerusalem," he said.

Meodovnik nodded. "If Thy people go out to battle against their enemy, wherever Thou shalt send them, and shall pray unto the Lord toward the city which Thou hast chosen, and toward the Temple that I have built for Thy name: Then hear Thou in heaven their prayer and their supplication, and maintain their cause!"

114

New City

Netanel and Meodovnik crouched in the back of the Solel Boneh truck. Boxes and crates were piled around them, tinned milk, sardines, Cocozine, soap. The truck stopped at the roadblock and they heard the shouts of the British soldiers and the clatter of heavy boots. One of them leaped on the running board to start the search.

The Arabs had cut the number 2 bus route on the last day of 1947 by building a massive roadblock at the Jaffa Gate. Since that time the City of David had been effectively under siege. Twice a week the British allowed a food convoy in through the Zion Gate, provided it was first cleared for arms and ammunition.

It was a slender, vital pipeline.

The man entrusted with that day's search wore the green kilt of the Highland Light Infantry. He had a bristling moustache under a soft beret. His eyes glittered with contempt. "You're supposed to be hiding! I could see you from the back of the fucking truck!"

Meodovnik glared back at him. "You promised us safe passage!"

"Not if you hang out the back and wave to the Arabs as you drive through!" He glanced around to ensure no one was watching and crouched down. "When you get to the gates and the first porter climbs in, you pick up a box and carry it out the back. Don't draw attention to yourselves, all right? It's my arse that's in a sling." He looked over his shoulder once more. "This is the last time. It's getting too bloody dangerous."

"You're being well paid."

"It's still the last time! I could get court-martialled for this!" He stood up, flicking his swagger cane along the boxes. He jumped out. "This one's all right," they heard him shout.

Minutes later the lorry lurched forward. The new guardians of Solomon's temple began the long, slow journey back into the city.

Three armoured cars and a jeep escorted the trucks through serried rows of dark, hostile faces outside Jaffa Gate.

When the convoy reached the Zion Gate a police inspector unlocked the great gates from the inside and sent out half a dozen of his men to dismantle the bars the Arabs had set up on the other side. The first truck backed in and a detail of Jewish porters rushed forward to start the unloading.

The first porter leaped on to the tailboard. He was a boy, no more than seventeen years old, a Hassid with a long, pale face and sidecurls. Netanel and Meodovnik jumped to their feet and he stared at them in astonishment. Netanel remembered the SS guard who had found him in the Leichenauto in Auschwitz; he had looked at him just like that.

Meodovik picked up a carton of tinned milk and carried it out.

Netanel followed him with a cardboard box of tinned sardines. As he brushed past the startled porter the boy recovered enough to whisper after him, "Welcome to hell!"

115

Old City

Sarah realised she had been wrong about Kaplan. He was not the soft metal of her first impression. He was an alloy of discipline and versatility who had succeeded in convincing them all that they would not fold under the weight of the first real attack.

He had forged the defenders into disciplined units. At first they had smoked, or talked, or played chess between skirmishes. Now, when they weren't fighting or patrolling, Kaplan insisted that Haganah commanders give their units intensive weapons training, and even parade them. He held regular commanders' conferences.

Their clothing was still haphazard and privately obtained, so he issued them with armbands and black berets, their first uniform; the officers were distinguished by blue epaulets. Kaplan insisted all the women wear long trousers, so as not to antagonise further the ultra-Orthodox population of the city.

"If we're going to fight like an army," he told them, "we'll have to behave like one."

He employed roofs and long-forgotten cellars as a means of communication between the maze of synagogues and yeshiva and bazaars and alleyways. Gunports were carved from the stone walls, and barricaded with sandbags. He set up a factory to manufacture homemade grenades from cigarette tins and gelignite.

Step by step he turned the Old City into a fortress.

Ration cards were distributed. Blankets and free bread were provided for everyone, and for the first time in the

Old City's history beggars disappeared from the streets. Haganah units policed the streets, to ensure hygiene and to check Arab infiltration.

Maintaining discipline in this honeycomb of vaulted alleyways was the greatest problem. A single sniper's bullet could break the chain of command. So Kaplan split the defence into autonomous military blocks, further dividing each post into battle groups of half a dozen individuals, each with their own combat leader.

A sniper had already taken the life of Sarah's own commander. On his death, Kaplan charged her with the defence of the Nissan Bek.

But water was the greatest problem. Soon after partition the Arabs had blown up the water pipes to the city, and now the ghetto relied on water drawn from ancient cisterns, distributed to the population each day by water carts. Each person received just one gallon a day, for drinking and cooking; the rest was recycled for washing and laundering.

The other great shortage could not be replaced from a cistern; it was people; which was why Sarah had asked for – and received – Kaplan's authority to ask Rabbi Silverberg for help.

The yeshivoth was part of the synagogue, a study centre where students could analyse and discuss the ancient Talmudic texts stored there. Yellow bolts of light angled from the high windows, illuminating an atmosphere thick with dust. The students all wore skullcaps and white shirts buttoned high at the neck, their sidecurls and thin beards framing faces sallow from scholarship and piety.

As Sarah and Roberto entered there was a moment of shocked silence before Rabbi Silverberg rose to meet them. "What are you doing here?"

"We need your help," Sarah said.

Silverberg ignored her and addressed himself to Roberto. "You are not welcome here. Is that clear?"

"We are seriously undermanned," Sarah persisted. "I have authority from my commander to ask for recruits among your scholars. We have lost four men this last week to snipers alone."

The rabbi trembled with rage. Again, he spoke to Roberto. "It is out of the question."

"They do not have to fight, rabbi. They do not have to carry arms. We need men to act as couriers – "

"Tell this woman the taking of human life is an abomination!"

Roberto shrugged and looked at Sarah.

"A pity your Arab neighbours don't feel the same way."

"We had no trouble before you came."

"We just want a little help! We are trying to protect you!"

"Tell this woman we do not want her 'help' – or yours. All the protection we need is God. We shall put our faith in Him, as we have always done." He turned his back on them.

Sarah felt the rage boiling in her. "Rabbi!"

He turned slowly.

"We built Palestine! While you took your handouts and hid your heads in your scriptures, we built Palestine! We redeemed this land!"

"Only God can redeem us! Only God, not you or your killers! Only the Messiah can lead His people Israel home!"

They were interrupted by shouts from outside and the crack of a rifle. "Trouble," Roberto whispered.

Sarah pushed her anger aside. She ran out of the room and into the street, Roberto close behind her.

The attack was disorganised, spontaneous. The Arabs had mobbed the bazaar, dragging two old Jews out of their shops. They had them on the ground, and were beating them with bars and clubs. Sarah took out her Beretta, fell on one knee and fired. At the same time Roberto fired a short burst from his rifle into the crowd.

The mob fled in panic, scuttling into the shadowy alleyways.

Four bodies now lay on the cobblestones. Sarah knelt to examine them. The two shopkeepers were dead, their skulls caved in. She decided they were probably dead long before she and Roberto arrived.

Roberto swore softly in Italian.

"Go that way," she said and pointed to the right. She got up and ran down the alleyway in the other direction.

A bolt of sunlight angled across a courtyard of flagged stones, on walls mildewed with centuries of grime. Shops lined the deserted arcade, honey cakes arrayed in rickety glass cabinets, the shopkeepers' stools spilled in their haste to escape.

Silence.

Then footsteps, softly, like the dripping of water. She wheeled around, aimed the Beretta and squeezed the trigger.

Nothing.

She tried again.

Again.

A face appeared, bearded and grinning. Another and another.

Trapped.

There were four of them, armed with iron bars and knives. Sarah started to back away but the courtyard ended in a high wall and there was nowhere to run. She raised the Beretta again and for a moment they hesitated.

Her finger tightened on the trigger. Please. *Please.*

Jammed!

She let the gun fall to her side.

One of the men whispered something to the others in Arabic and they laughed. She could guess what it was. She knew what they would try and do with her.

She kicked in a glass cabinet and tore out one of the bright, sparkling shards. She held it in front of her, like a knife. "Who wants to be the hero?" she said to them in Arabic. She watched the surprise on their faces. "Which of you will have his name immortalised in song by the women tonight? How the little Jewess cut off his balls and hung them from his ears for decoration?"

They were more wary now, but they kept coming.

One of them raised his arm and pointed, shouting a warning.

Suddenly they turned and ran. The blast of the automatic weapon echoed round the walls like cannonfire, the bullets ricocheting on the cobbles. One of the Arabs fell, the back of his abbayah blossoming with scarlet splashes. He lay prone on his face.

Sarah started to shake. Her mouth was sticky and dry and she could not swallow. She shielded the sunlight from her eyes and looked up to the roof. "Thank God you came back, Roberto."

"Didn't your father teach you anything?" her saviour said. It was not Roberto. "You never ever run down a blind alley."

The blast of whistles. The gunfire had attracted a British patrol. Soon green-kilted Highlanders would be swarming through the alleys.

She looked back up at the roof but the man had gone. She realised she knew that voice. It belonged to Netanel Rosenberg.

She tossed the Beretta on to the roof. She would retrieve it later. She dared not risk being caught by the British in possession of the weapon. Her knees were shaking. She sat down on the step and waited. Death had turned away from her again. He would come eventually, she knew. It was like the siege. You couldn't prevent the inevitable; in the end you were just playing for time.

Part Nineteen

PALESTINE, 1948

116

Kfar Herzl Kibbutz

The first harvest was still on the trees. There were other labours to occupy the young sabras this summer. Trenches zigzagged the cornfields, concrete blockhouses had sprouted among the barley, signs in Hebrew and Arabic had blossomed along the jujube fences:

DANGER: MINES

The spring had been green and short. The wild cyclamen and poppies and cornflowers blazed briefly and then withered under the first scorching breath of the hamsiin, while the kibbutzniks prepared for a terrible summer and bitter harvest.

They sat in grim silence around the upright radiogram in the dining hall, straining to hear over the buzz of the static. There were perhaps as many as a hundred of them, mostly men. Mothers with young children had been ordered back to Jerusalem by Yaakov months before. Those that remained carried their weapons with them night and day, in the fields, in the dairies, in the dormitories, always ready.

Ready for this moment.

". . . the natural and historic right of the Jewish people and the resolution of the General Assembly of the United Nations . . ."

It was Ben-Gurion, addressing the members of the

Jewish Council in the Tel Aviv museum. The British were pulling out early. The waiting was finally over.

". . . we hereby proclaim the establishment of the Jewish state in Palestine, to be called – Israel."

Isaac looked up at his grandfather. Yaakov's face showed no expression, and the others in the room took their cue from him. There were no outward signs of celebration, just grim faces, lovers and husbands and wives squeezing hands.

Yaakov switched off the radio, stood up and went outside.

Isaac followed him. "Grandfather."

Yaakov was staring at the brown hills looming above Kfar Herzl. Just out of sight in the first folding of the valley was Rab'allah.

"All my life I dreamed of this moment," Yaakov said.

"What is wrong?"

"I should have sent you away with the others."

"I would not have gone. You can't treat me as a child."

"You're my grandson and you're only thirteen years old."

"I'm a sabra."

Yaakov shook his head. "When I was thirteen years old I had long sidecurls and the closest I had come to danger was when I dropped a copy of the Talmud on my foot. I was sixteen before I knew anything of politics. I did not ride a horse or pick up a rifle until I was twenty-one, when we first came here to Palestine. Now you haven't even had your bar mitzvah and you tell me you're a sabra."

"I don't understand why you're so unhappy, Grandfather."

Yaakov sat on the whitewashed stone wall outside one of the cottages. "Come here, my boy. Sit down. Look at me. What do you see?"

Isaac shrugged, uncomfortable. His hero seemed suddenly terribly vulnerable.

"I'll tell you what you see." Yaakov pointed to his face.

"Look at these lines. I am getting old. It's not that I mind, it happens to everyone, it is the way God planned. But I am not ready for this any more. I have a daughter in Jerusalem, and I don't know if she's all right, even if she's still alive. And now I look at my grandson and I worry for you also. Do you know what has just happened, my young sabra? We have called down a firestorm on all our heads."

"We will teach these Arabs a lesson for once and for all."

"Will we, young sabra?" He put his arm around Isaac's shoulder. "Perhaps because you are young you just think of all the things you may win. When you get older you fear for all you might lose."

"We can't lose. The Arabs don't know how to fight. You have said so yourself. They have no discipline, no tactics."

"But they have numbers. And now Ben-Gurion has announced the state, the Egyptians and the Syrians and the Iraqis and the Jordanians will all attack us. They have tanks and artillery and aeroplanes. When you have so much, does it matter that your men are not such good fighters?"

"They are lazy and they are cowards. If there is going to be a proper war, I can't wait for it to start."

"Listen, Isaac! These Arabs. They are people, just like us. In many ways we are different, but in many ways we are also the same. We fight them because we have to. But don't let me hear such hate coming out of your mouth. It only makes you ugly."

Isaac bore the reproach, but his face was clouded and sullen. "We will win, won't we?"

"With God's help. Now I must talk to the rabbi. Now is not the time for the hora. Now is the time for prayer." He stood up. "And after the prayers we should double the watch and check our weapons."

705

Sarah Landauer did not hear Ben-Gurion's announcement. She lay on her belly in the gallery of the Nissan Bek, her ears attuned to the deadly, vaulted silence in the streets below. Her eyes scanned the Arab rooftops, outlined in dirty white and grey against the green slopes of the Mount of Olives. The Golden Dome of the Temple burned under a bright sun, taunting them.

Around her, dust hung in the still and sanctified atmosphere, drifting across the faded and extraordinary histories that had passed their quiet centuries on the synagogue walls. The frescoes depicted in lurid agony the destruction of the Temple of Solomon, whose stones lay just a few hundred yards from her sandbagged position in the dome. Above her, the Lion of Judah wept his tears for the downfall of the first tribe of Israel.

Abraham, the Ashkenazi boy who had volunteered as her platoon's courier, flopped down beside her. "Anything?" he whispered.

Sarah shook her head. It was late afternoon and the sun had moved down the sky, fat and lazy and yellow. Its warmth was seductive, and she fought away the drowsiness that threatened her concentration. There had been no firing for hours, but it was dangerous to assume the fighting was done for the day.

"Ben-Gurion has spoken on Kol Yisrael," Abraham said. "He has announced the new state. He has named us Israel!"

"Hear that?" Sarah called to Roberto. "We are Israelis now!"

"Did he mention if this new state would have its own air force and artillery soon?"

"What other news?" Sarah asked the boy.

"The commander says the British are leaving tonight. He says we should expect a big attack soon."

"Thank you, Abraham. Any more grenades?"

Abraham fished in his pocket. A woman called Leah Vultz was making grenades from empty cigarette tins discarded by British soldiers. Children scoured the streets collecting them. Leah then filled them with old nails, explosives and a detonator fuse.

He gave three to Sarah and crawled away.

A brave boy, Sarah thought. The same age as Isaac. Too young to be carrying grenades. As I was too young to be carrying a rifle at thirteen. But then, when I was thirteen it did not occur to me that I had already lost my childhood, and he does not know it either. He will grow up thinking that war is the natural order of life, and perhaps . . . perhaps he is right.

New City

Marie did not hear Ben-Gurion's broadcast either. The Haganah had requisitioned her from the Histadruth as a cipher clerk and she was busy typing coded messages for relay to the Red House HQ in Tel Aviv. A colleague whispered the news to her as she sat at her typewriter. The broadcast meant the British were just hours from marching out of the Mandate. It was no surprise to any of them in the signals office. The British had classified their departure date as Most Secret but the Haganah had known the exact hour for a week.

That evening when she got back to her apartment she went to the kitchen and looked hopefully in the cupboard. Was there anything she could have to celebrate? She found two packets of macaroni but she put them back. There was no kerosene for cooking and it meant leaving the flat and boiling the pasta over an open fire in the courtyard. Instead she opened her last tin of sardines and sat down at the table by the window. She ate slowly straight from the tin, to conjure the illusion of a complete meal.

Ben Yehuda Street was deserted. Snipers and shellfire made it dangerous to loiter in the open. In fact the janitor and the police had warned her it would be best to eat and sleep in the basement of the building with the other tenants, but Marie had ignored their advice. She enjoyed her privacy too much. Besides, Auschwitz had taught her it was fate that decided who would live or die.

Night was falling, and skeins of woodsmoke were smudged across a dirty orange sky like lost souls. In the Arab Quarter electric lights were blinking on, glittering like stars, taunting their dark enemy. The Arabs had long ago cut the power supplies to the Jewish Quarter of the city.

Marie got up and lit a candle.

Since the beginning of May the British had been masters of the Mandate in name only. All over Palestine, the Haganah battled with the militias and the Mufti's mercenary armies for supremacy. The Palmach had wrested away Tiberias, Haifa, Safed, Jaffa and Acre; the roads north to Galilee and south to the Negev were under Haganah control; Kaukji's army had been defeated at Mishmar Haemek; and their greatest asset, Abdul Kader, had been killed at Kastel.

But she knew from the signals flowing between Rehavia and Tel Aviv that Jerusalem itself was all but lost. Yesterday a group of kibbutzim south of the city, known as the Etzion Bloc, had fallen to the Arabs. The inhabitants had been massacred. Atarot, a settlement just to the north, had been hastily evacuated. Now the Transjordanian Arab Legion was converging on the city. British-equipped, British-trained and British-led, they were the trump card in the Arab pack.

After today's announcement by Ben-Gurion, the Egyptians would sweep in from the south, and the Syrians and Iraqis massed on the northern borders would pour down from the Golan Heights. Ben-Gurion had vowed that the Jews would defend every kibbutz, every settlement in their possession, but it was impossible to imagine how they could survive. After mobilising all their reserves they were outnumbered five to one, and they had no tanks, no artillery, and no planes.

She heard the jarring clang of a bell in the street. The

water cart! The distribution took place at night now, because of the shelling and so that less would be lost to evaporation. It was the only time she ever saw queues in the street any more.

She fetched her pail from the kitchen. For a girl from a lakeside village in Bavaria it was still difficult to accept that such a thing as water could become so fragile and so precious.

Like life.

For herself, she did not care if Palestine was Jewish or Arab. So why did she stay, a German Catholic girl, huddled and desperate and besieged, surrounded by foreigners, a family of Yemenites from Aden on one side and Ashkenazi Jews from Kiev on the other?

Why did she stay?

Once the answer was Netanel Rosenberg. Now she was no longer sure.

Sheikh Jarrah

The burst of semi-automatic weapons fire sounded so close, Majid thought for a moment it had been fired in his own hallway. The Jews were practically in the back yard! "Hurry up!" he shouted up the stairs. "We have to leave now! Mirham! Hurry!"

They had been ready to leave for days, and now, at the last moment, she had remembered something that they simply could not leave behind. Suddenly she appeared at the top of the stairs carrying her Singer sewing machine.

"We cannot take that with us! There is no room in the car!"

"I won't leave it behind!" she shouted at him, and then, for emphasis, she stamped her foot. "I won't!"

It was the first time she had ever defied him and after brief feelings of admiration he had an overwhelming urge to slap her face. But that would not do. This was no time

709

for hysterics. He had to get her into the car. His voice became oily.

"But we are not leaving for good," he said. "You think I would leave all this just for a few Jews? Put it back!"

"I shan't!"

"Please, Mirham. It will just be for a few days. When the Jews are thrown out we can return. Two days, three at the most. Just think of it as a small holiday." He wrested the Singer out of her grasp. Even then, she tried to resist. By the hundred holy names of Allah! he thought. It weighs as much as a young camel!

An explosion, very close, rattled the glass in the windowpanes and shook a brass plate from the wall. Any minute the Irgun would be slavering on the front doorstep! He set the sewing machine down at the foot of the stairs and hurried Mirham out of the door. She waddled out, the rich material of her floral thaub rustling as she walked. Like an elephant in a silk bag, he thought sourly.

He took a last look around the room. The upright Phillips radiogram, the ceramics on the walls, the stained walnut cabinet where he kept his Black Label British whisky, the big blue and white vases he had imported especially from Bursa in Turkey, the silk carpets from Damascus and Teheran. What would happen if the Jews found their way in here? If only he had done something before now! But how could anyone have foreseen that the Jews would have had the audacity to try and possess Sheikh Jarrah and Katamon?

He ran down the steps to the courtyard. His house-servant Taha sat behind the wheel of a red Humber, the engine idling. Khemal and Yusuf were in the passenger seat beside him; Amneh and Nafisa, modestly veiled, were in the back seat. Mirham squeezed her bulk next to them.

He closed the door behind her and leaned in. "Taha will take care of you," he said.

Mirham stared at him in shock. "Majid? Where are you going? Aren't you coming with us?"

"I have instructed Taha what to do. You will be all right. I will join you in a few days."

"But, Majid! Where are you going?"

He tapped Taha on the shoulder, his signal to leave. The Humber rolled out of the courtyard, wobbling on its axle, the roof piled high with boxes and suitcases. Mirham leaned out of the window. "But what are you going to do?"

"Goodbye!" Majid shouted and waved. By the morning they should be safe in Amman. It would all be over soon and then they could return and everything would be as it was before.

He still could not believe the British had betrayed them! *Insh'allah*. But the Arab Legion would be in the city in the next twenty-four hours and then they would throw the Jews out for good.

Damned British. You couldn't trust anyone any more.

Old City

The melancholy wail of bagpipes and the rhythmic tramp of boots accompanied the Highland Light Infantry as they marched out of the City of David. The green kilts swung in time with their step. The British, like the Romans and the Crusaders and the Turks, had enjoyed their moment of ascendancy in the ancient city. Even as they left the first gunfire of a new battle erupted behind them.

117

Kfar Herzl Kibbutz

It began just after dawn with a mortar barrage.

The legion had sent nine Dingo armoured cars and a company of infantry up the dirt road from Bethlehem. They had brought with them four three-inch mortars to soften up the kibbutz's defences. None of the kibbutzniks had any illusions why Kfar Herzl had been chosen for this special treatment: it was retribution for what the Irgun had done to their neighbours at Rab'allah.

Isaac leaped out of bed and ran to the window. Clouds of smoke and dust were already drifting through the orchards. He threw on trousers, shirt, boots and the British Second World War helmet Yaakov had given him. He grabbed the Lee Enfield that was propped against the wall and scrambled to the door.

Yaakov was already striding up the pathway to the cottage. He looked calm, his khaki shorts were neatly pressed, the white fringe of hair wet and neatly combed. Crisp, efficient, almost serene.

He must have known, Isaac thought. He has been up all night, waiting and planning.

"Come with me," Yaakov said.

The barrage lasted over an hour. Yaakov and Isaac huddled in a trench beyond the cornfields, feeling the earth hammer under them. It was as if there were freight cars roaring over their heads and pounding into the ground.

When it was over there was a sudden, terrible silence.

Isaac raised his head above the trench and the place he had known from a child was no longer recognisable. The apple orchard was pitted with craters, and half the trees were gone. Most of the timber cottages had been destroyed also, smashed to splinters, their shells crackling with flames. The schoolhouse where he had spent the last eight years had disappeared. The library and the science block had been flattened. Smoke drifted into a pale blue sky.

Filthy fucking Arabs.

"Here they come," Yaakov whispered.

A murmur, like the whispering of bees. He searched the wilderness beyond the fences but he could see nothing. Heat rose from the desert and rippled the brown hills.

But then, what he took to be rocks slowly rose from the wilderness and approached. The armoured cars of the Arab Legion were the colour of the sand of the eastern deserts, the red-and-white-checked keffiyehs of the officers riding in their turrets like flags.

Then the flags disappeared as the hatches closed and their crews prepared for the battle.

The first line of trenches zigzagged behind the jujube fence, reinforced with cement and camouflaged with leaves. A second and third line of trenches were concealed among the cornfields. Yaakov had counted his defenders: eighty-three men and twenty-seven women. The youngest was Isaac at thirteen; the oldest was Yaakov's sister, fifty-eight years old.

"We'll count her as two twenty-nine-year-olds," he had joked.

He had distributed the contents of the sliks the previous night. He kept a precious few hand-grenades in reserve, and deployed the single mortar and a Hotchkiss heavy machine-gun at the rear. To face the armour of the Arab Legion the men and women in the trenches were armed with bolt-action rifles, home-made Sten guns and petrol bombs.

"Can we hold them?" Isaac whispered. The armoured

cars dominated the horizon, nine of them, infantry loping along behind.

"Not for long. Unless we get help from Jerusalem."

It had seemed so easy yesterday. In his Palmach training the enemy was abstract, a dupe for the skills that Yaakov taught them. Now, waiting in this trench, afraid, and afraid of showing his fear, battle did not appear as glorious or as seductive.

He watched an ant at work on the lip of the trench, dragging away the body of a dead beetle three times its size. He focused his attention on its labour, trying to ignore the oncoming roar of the tanks, shutting out his terror.

He prayed for yesterday's bravado to return.

But Yaakov knew what he was feeling. "I was frightened the first time I ever fought in a battle," he said. "I was with the Hashomer near Petah Tiqwa in the early twenties. We were attacked by the Bedouin one night. I remember firing my rifle with my eyes squeezed shut, I was so afraid."

Isaac tried to smile but his mouth was so dry his lips stuck to his teeth. He didn't believe Yaakov anyway. Yaakov didn't look as if he had ever been afraid of anything.

The right flank of the column reached the kibbutz fence. Suddenly the two armoured cars spun around and converged on the five in the centre. The cars on the left flank did the same.

"Shit, the danger signs! We should have taken them down!"

"Why?" Yaakov said, and he was smiling.

"But they were heading straight for the minefield!"

"There is no minefield."

"But you sent out details to lay the mines! I saw them!"

"That was for the benefit of the Arabs who were watching us from the hills. They buried empty tins. Those signs are a means of funnelling their armour towards the centre. Now they are heading for our strongest point – if you can call a few Molotov cocktails and a dozen Sten guns a strong point. We'll see."

* * *

714

Rishou could see nothing except the dust tails of the British Dingo armoured cars. He ran with his head down, his rifle in his right hand, keeping pace with the tanks. He had never fought this way before. In other fights he had always had a clear sight of his enemy. When would the battle start? What would be the first warning?

He remembered the last time he had come this way, running from Rab'allah down to the kibbutz, all those years ago. He had experienced the same feelings then; fear, excitement, anticipation. But then there had been no guns awaiting his arrival, just Sarah.

He only prayed she was not waiting for him this time.

"Wait till they've reached the markers!" Yaakov shouted at the grim, white faces staring back at him from the trenches. Isaac noticed for the first time the painted white stones in front of them, paced out to ten yards. Yaakov had planned everything.

The roaring of the armoured car engines was deafening.

They waited. So close . . .

Racing towards them, twenty yards from the stones, ten . . .

Now. Now. *Now!*

Two petrol bombs hit the leading armoured car and exploded in a hot rush of orange flame. There was the stench of burning rubber and a THUMP-THUMP as the front tyres exploded. Three more petrol bombs hit the armoured car behind. One exploded over the turret and it careened out of control and collided with the Dingo on its left.

A third armoured car veered away along the line of the trenches and was hit two, three, four times by bombs. Its tyres burst into flames, and black smoke billowed from the turret. Isaac heard screams. The hatch slammed open and the crew poured out, like ants from a nest. As they emerged they were immediately scythed down by automatic weapons fire.

Rishou saw the eruption of orange flame on the armoured car ahead of him, felt the rush of heat, heard the hollow concussion of the explosion. There were more explosions to his right and a second armoured car burst into flame.

He kept running.

Suddenly the air around him was alive as the Jews opened fire with their Sten guns. A deadly storm of metal whined past his head, like hordes of angry bees.

The legionnaires had predicted they would roll right over the kibbutz and flatten it under their wheels. But as he watched, bomb after bomb flowered on the turrets and the armour of the cars. Three of the Dingos had lurched to a halt, engulfed in fire and smoke. Another turned directly in front of him and raced for the rear. He had to throw himself clear to avoid being crushed by the wheels.

Perhaps they are going to roll over Rab'allah instead.

Rishou looked around, squinting through the dust. They were gone! The Holy Strugglers who had vowed to fight to the last drop of blood in support of their great allies, the Jordanians, were hopping back across the stones like scared goats.

Allah, help me in my sorrow!

"They're running," Isaac shouted.

Through a break in the curtain of dust and smoke he could see the Arab infantry retreating. Another petrol bomb hit the armour of one of the remaining Dingos, and for a moment it disappeared behind a plume of thick, black smoke. Isaac heard a cheer from the trenches as it backed away, in flames. The remaining armoured car wheeled around and scuttled away.

He suddenly realised he had forgotten to fire his own rifle. He aimed at the retreating Dingo but Yaakov pushed the barrel down. "Save your ammunition. That wasn't the battle, it was just the first skirmish. You'll need every bullet later."

118

Nissan Bek

The man wore a brown jacket and trousers and a black-and-white-chequered keffiyeh. The dynamite was attached to the end of a long rope and he swung it round his head like an Olympic hammer-thrower. Sarah and Roberto saw him at the same time and fired. He arched backwards as if some unseen hand had bent him in half, folding him neatly from the base of his spine. He slumped on to the cobbles.

The dynamite arced through the air and landed out of sight at the base of the building. Sarah waited for the shock . . .

. . . The walls shivered. She saw Roberto's cradle sway giddily on the ropes suspending it from the dome.

When the smoke and dust cleared she saw Arab militia leaping over the body of the dead saboteur. She fired a long blast from her Sten, heard the rattle of small arms fire echo around the Nissan Bek as the other defenders saw the danger.

Less than a minute later, it was over. Bodies littered the cobblestones; one twitched, wounded; another tried to drag himself down the alleyway. Their more fortunate comrades had retreated to the safety of the buildings on the far side of the bazaar.

To her left smoke was rising in black columns from the Warsaw Synagogue. Had the Arabs overrun them? Sarah lay her head on the stone. Her tongue was like leather and her eyes were sore from grit and cordite and the long strain of the day. Bring on the night.

*   *   *

It had started that morning with a mortar attack, and had continued all day. Time and again the Arabs had rushed them, trying to dynamite the walls. First they had used metal cans, packed with explosives and armed with detonators. Then, as their losses grew, they had tried throwing from a greater distance, using rope to launch the mines. So far none of the mines had managed to breach the thick and ancient stone of the synagogue.

She waited for them to come again.

"Perhaps that's it," Roberto whispered. "They probably won't try again until tonight."

"I hope so," Sarah said. She pushed the Sten away and rolled on her back. The Lion of Judah was pockmarked with bullet craters. She could hear the sounds of the continuing battle for the Warsaw.

Avnary, one of her combat group commanders, crawled towards her along the gallery. "The last one did some damage, Sarah. There's a hole in the eastern wall."

"Shit! You take over here," Sarah said. Don't let them attack again now, she prayed. Not until we've fixed that breach.

The local residents had crowded into the basement of the Nissan Bek for shelter when the shelling had begun. Sarah decided there must be more than a hundred squatting in the candlelit gloom. Mothers screamed for children, old women cried, the men kept up the murmurous chanting of their psalms and prayers.

As she came down the steps they leaped to their feet, all shouting at once. Sarah noted that many of them had produced white handkerchiefs, mistaking her in the darkness for an Arab soldier.

"What's happening?"

"Are the Arabs here?"

"Tell them we surrender!"

Her own flagging determination was bolstered by disgust. She put up her hands and screamed for silence. "We beat them back!" she shouted. "We are not going to surrender!"

718

Sullen faces stared back at her. The smell was foul. They had been shut up in the basement all day. Surely it is better to fight, Sarah thought, than hide down here in the darkness and the filth?

"I need your help," she said.

Shuffling, gloomy silence.

"Rabbi Silverberg has made it clear that none of you will fight with us. Well, all right. But you can still help us. The Arabs have blown a hole in the synagogue wall. We need to repair it quickly."

"We cannot help you today," someone said. "It is Shabbat."

"God did not give us the Sabbath so the Arabs could use it to destroy us!" Sarah shouted.

No one moved.

Sarah took her Beretta from her belt. She pointed it at one of the rabbis. "Tell them to help us," she said.

The man stared her down.

Sarah aimed the weapon at his head. "Do not think because I am a Jew you do not need to fear me. Jerusalem is still Jerusalem, with or without you."

Absolute stillness.

"You would dare commit the sin of murder in a synagogue?"

"My people are my religion, rabbi. Let God decide my sins. I will give you until three then I shall have to pull this trigger, if only to maintain my authority over you all."

"You would not."

"One."

He stared at her.

"Two."

She waited.

"Three."

He did not move. Her finger tightened on the trigger.

". . . All right."

Sarah lowered the gun. She could hear her own breathing.

"We will do as you ask. Let it be known that we do this under duress and the sin is on your head."

"Thirty of your best men. If you can call them that," she added and she went back up the basement stairs.

She was shaking from her confrontation with the rabbi, surprised at her own reaction. She had been a moment from gunning him down in cold blood. She had come face to face with her own devil and she was shocked to discover that when forced to choose between the God of her ancestors and the survival of the new tribe of Israel, her tribe, she had felt not a moment's hesitation.

119

Barbed wire had been run across the gap in the eastern wall, and sandbags were stacked high on top of the jagged rubble of brick and stone. Sarah surveyed the results with satisfaction; the rabbi's frightened Jews may not have kept the Sabbath but her Palmachniks might keep the Nissan Bek a little longer.

The Jews filed back to the basement, their faces betraying their loathing. All that still binds us, she thought, is that we are Jews, but we no longer believe in the same things.

Abraham ran along the aisle towards her. "The commander wants you at headquarters," he panted.

Sarah looked up at the gallery. "Avnary! I have to see Kaplan! You have overall command till I get back!"

He waved a hand in acknowledgment and returned his attention to the street.

"Let's go," Sarah said.

*   *   *

Abraham led her back the way he had come, along the new thoroughfares the Haganah had created on the roofs and vaulted alleyways of the ghetto. The towering structures of the Nissan Bek and the Warsaw synagogue gave some protection from the snipers in the Muslim Quarter.

Spirals of smoke rose from the Old City, and the crackle of gunfire increased again as they came closer to the Armenian Quarter.

Abraham led her down some worn stone steps into a courtyard, then ducked through the narrow door of a musty yeshivoth. More steps led down to an echoing underground passage, mildewed and dripping and cold, and they followed it to a flight of crumbling wooden stairs.

They emerged in Kaplan's headquarters in the Tipat Chilav.

The conference was already under way. There were a dozen men and women crowded into Kaplan's office and the air was thick with cigarette smoke. Kaplan cleaned his spectacles, while everyone else shouted and waved their arms and banged their fists on the desktop.

Almost everyone except Rabbi Silverberg and Kaplan seemed to have some kind of injury: a bloodied bandage around a limb, or a dressing obscuring part of their face. Their clothes, like Sarah's, were covered in dust and stained with sweat, and their eyes, almost without exception, were glassy and unfocused. She had seen that look many times before, after terrorist bombings. Horror left an imprint on the face, like a bruise on the skin.

Kaplan looked up as she came in. The shouting stopped briefly as heads turned towards her. "Hello, Sarah," Kaplan said. "What are things like on your side?"

"We're holding, sir."

"Well, that's something." He looked around the room. "I'm afraid these people tell me our western flank is in danger of collapsing. The Armenians have given up all pretence of neutrality. They have allowed the Arabs to occupy the belfry of the Church of Saint Jaques. That put the Zion Gate under crossfire and we had to pull our people back. Now the Arabs are driving towards the Street of the Jews. I estimate we've lost approximately a quarter of our territory already and it isn't sunset yet."

Rabbi Silverberg leaned on the table and stuck his face in front of Kaplan's. "This shelling has been going on for weeks now! How much more are we supposed to take? You have women and children crowded into the basements of the Batei Machse and they are becoming hysterical. What are you going to do?"

"They had their opportunity to leave, rabbi." Sarah looked round. It was the Irguni, Meodovnik. Rosenberg stood at his shoulder.

"This is their home! Our ancestors have lived here for hundreds of years! Why should we leave?"

"That's our point also."

"We must surrender! There is no way that you and your bunch of gangsters can hold out!"

"There will be no surrender, rabbi," Kaplan said, softly.

"We'll see about that!"

Rabbi Silverberg headed for the door but suddenly Kaplan was on his feet. "Rabbi! I warn you now! If anyone – anyone – raises a white flag we will shoot them. Do you understand?"

"You would not dare!"

"If you abhor killing so much I would suggest you not find out what I will or will not dare."

Silverberg shook his head. "You people are monsters."

"Do you understand?"

"May God have pity on you all," the rabbi said and left.

Kaplan sat down again. "Well, I'm glad that was settled amicably."

After the conference ended, Sarah asked Kaplan if she could speak to him alone. Kaplan lit a candle. It trembled as another mortar round landed close by. The sounds of sniper and small arms fire seemed louder in the darkness.

"What is it, Sarah?"

"You invited the Irgun to the conference, sir?"

"We are on the same side. Roughly."

"Do you trust them?"

"Of course not." He shrugged. "But they have finally agreed to fight under my control, if not my authority."

"Have they offered to share their arms as well as their undoubted fighting abilities? My sector is seriously short of weapons, sir."

"All the sectors are seriously short of weapons." He laid his hands on the table as if he was folding gloves. "No, they have not admitted the full extent of their armoury or expressed any willingness to share it. Perhaps when you are fighting the Arabs with your bare hands they may deign to toss you a grenade."

"I doubt it."

"So do I. The point is, the Irgun do not trust us, nor do they like us; and we, in turn, do not trust them. It's a fine start for a new country. Isn't it?"

120

Kfar Herzl Kibbutz

The burned-out skeletons of armoured cars. Charred bodies littered the desert beyond the trampled remains of the jujube and barbed wire. The robes of the dead flapped in the desert wind, and smoke drifted from the shell holes and the shattered, crumbled remains of the trenches.

From somewhere Yaakov heard a man gasping out his life.

Yaakov's face was white from dust and fatigue. He

sipped carefully from a water bottle and handed the flask to Isaac. "Just a little. Don't be greedy. Remember it has to last you a long time."

Isaac drank, just a mouthful, swirled it around his mouth as Yaakov had done, and swallowed. His mouth still felt as chalky dry as it had before.

"I am too old for this," Yaakov murmured. He leaned back against the walls of the trench and closed his eyes.

Yes, he is old, Isaac thought. He'd never seen his grandfather so haggard or so tired. In the passage of just one morning and one afternoon he seemed to have aged ten years. But then I have grown in years too. This morning I was just a boy. Now I am an old man also.

After that first attack the Arabs pounded them again and again with their three-inch mortars. It had gone on all morning until the trenches were a mess of broken earth and leaking sandbags, and nearly twenty of the defenders were dead or lying moaning in the makeshift hospital in the dining hall.

At noon the Arabs attacked again, though with less enthusiasm than before. Again they had driven them back and the wreck of another armoured car lay burning in the desert.

The barrage began again.

Now the guns had stopped. Yaakov looked at his watch. "Five minutes," he murmured. "It will be soon."

Almost as he finished speaking Isaac heard the familiar rumble of the armoured cars. He wanted to cry. The shelling and the momentary elation of the earlier battles had exhausted him. He did not think he could go through it again.

"What plan do we have this time, Grandfather?" he said.

"This time? This time we pray for a miracle."

As he ran behind the armoured cars Rishou thought about Rab'allah. He thought about his wife and his mother and his sister-in-law sprawled in a tangle of limbs in the bedroom of his father's house, his daughter lying in the Red Cross hospital, her mind gone and the stump of her leg swathed in bloody bandages; and as he thought about them, his legs pumped faster.

Izzat was running beside him. The Jews opened fire with their Sten guns from the trenches and Izzat fell.

This time there was no rain of petrol bombs waiting to greet the legion's armour. Yaakov saw two Molotovs fall short of their mark, another explode harmlessly on the leading Dingo's armour plating. It rushed through the sudden blossoming of flame and smoke and roared over the broken trenches, headed towards the kibbutz.

"Fall back!" Yaakov shouted, and he rose to his feet, signalling desperately to the other defenders. "Fall back!"

He grabbed Isaac's shirt and pulled him out of the trench. They scrambled over the broken earth, from shell hole to shell hole. Even as they ran two more armoured cars overtook them, rumbling inexorably towards the cottages and stone dining hall.

He tumbled on his face into a shell hole.

The Arab infantry was right behind them. He raised his rifle and fired wildly. He could not control the trembling in his hands. There was an Arab in an old khaki battle jacket and the black and white keffiyeh of a fellaheen just five paces away. Isaac aimed again. He could not miss.

He fired wide and high.

The man jumped down into the crater, but it was as if he had not seen Isaac. Instead he swung the butt of his rifle at Yaakov's head. Yaakov saw him at the last moment and leaped back. The blow took him high in the chest and he fell.

The old Arab grinned in triumph. Still he ignored Isaac; perhaps he did not consider him worthy of his attention. As he raised the rifle stock to crush Yaakov's skull, Isaac put the barrel of his rifle against the man's temple and fired.

Isaac saw another Arab running towards the hole. He aimed again, and this time his hands did not tremble. He shot the man cleanly through the chest. The man pitched

725

forward and landed face first in the dirt. His hand hung limp over the edge of the crater.

"Quickly," Yaakov groaned and he pulled Isaac out of the hole and they stumbled back through the orchard to the kibbutz.

The Hotchkiss had been mounted inside the concrete blockhouse at the crest of the vineyard. The deep boom of the gun now drowned out every sound on the battlefield. Isaac stumbled and looked back. The heavy machine-gun was cutting a swathe across the orchard, pinning the Arabs down, giving the defenders the chance to retreat.

An armoured car swung out of line and headed towards the vineyards, firing rounds from the three-pounder gun mounted in the turret. Yaakov ran towards it. Rifle fire whipped the ground around him, then one of his legs buckled underneath him and he fell. For a moment Isaac thought he was dead. But then Yaakov rolled on to his back, took a grenade from his battle jacket and armed it. He tossed it into the path of the armoured car.

The blast lifted the armoured car's front wheels from the ground. It roared on, black smoke belching from the turret, stripped tyre rubber flapping useless on the rims. It ploughed into a shell crater and rolled on its side.

Isaac zigzagged through the crossfire. "Grandfather!"

Yaakov lay on his back, clutching at his thigh, little worms of blood spurting between his fingers. "Get to the kibbutz!"

"Not without you!" Isaac pulled him to his feet and helped him in the race for shelter, grateful for the hammer of the Hotchkiss gun on the hill and the unexpected courage he had found in himself.

The dining hall was the only stone building on the whole kibbutz. Yaakov had designated it both as his command post and field hospital. A girl was hunched over a transmitter in the corner shouting an SOS to Haganah HQ in Jerusalem. The wounded littered the floors, bloodied and moaning. Other kibbutzniks were slumped around the walls, paralysed with fear or fatigue, staring blankly into space. People were running in and out, shouting in panic.

When Isaac arrived with Yaakov it was clear that all command had disintegrated and they were about to be overrun.

Two of the Dingos had been stopped by two young kibbutzniks who had blown out their tyres with Sten guns before they themselves were killed by machine-gun fire from the stalled armoured cars. But the remaining Dingo was now traversing the kibbutz, using its cannon, and it had already levelled the remaining dormitories, as well as the clinic and the synagogue. Now it was heading towards the dining hall.

The Hotchkiss suddenly fell silent and the Arab infantry rose from the shell holes in the orchard and started their advance.

Yaakov dragged himself across the floor to the radio operator, smearing blood on the concrete. "What do Jerusalem say!" he gasped.

She took off her earphones and stared at him helplessly, her face a mask of horror. She was too terrified to speak.

Isaac saw a figure run into the path of the oncoming armoured car. He was carrying the mortar in his arms, cradling it like a small child.

It was Levin.

He dropped the mortar to the ground and squatted beside it. He was holding a single shell in his arms. He aimed the mouth of the mortar at the armoured car, fed the round into the barrel and fired.

The armoured car exploded, taking Levin with it.

Rishou saw Levin aim the mortar and he stopped and raised his rifle. But before he could fire, the mortar shell hit the armoured car and the Dingo exploded. A fireball blew out the hatch.

The Jewish defenders had retreated into the stone building at the centre of the kibbutz. He started to run towards it, then suddenly realised he was alone. He looked around. The Strugglers had seen the armoured car destroyed and had lost their courage.

By the hundred holy names of Allah!

Yaakov watched the two remaining armoured cars limp back towards the legion lines, driving on their rims. The Arab irregulars trotted after them. The sun was low in the sky. There would be no more assaults today. Joseph Levin had won them another night.

121

The night was warm and the corpses bloated on the battlefield. The sweet, sickly scent of decay was carried on the night breeze.

Yaakov was pale and shivering. The doctors had stopped the bleeding in his right leg, but the bone was shattered and pain had etched itself into his eyes. But he would not rest.

By sunset he had already reorganised his defenders into new battle groups. Men and women who had been catatonic with fear were roused and given new determination. A detail was sent out to erect a barricade of rocks by the main gate and new trenches were quickly dug around the kibbutz and in a defensive perimeter in the orchards below the blockhouse.

Another patrol set off in the darkness to try and retrieve guns and ammunition from the armoured car Yaakov had disabled with his grenade. But the men returned an hour later with the news that Yaakov had done his work too well. The Dingo's armoury had been damaged beyond repair by the blast.

Meanwhile the kibbutz's weapons expert was busy at the blockhouse repairing the Hotchkiss, which had jammed during the final stages of the battle.

Yaakov gathered the rest of his defenders together and told them that Jerusalem had promised to relieve them the next morning. His belief was infectious. Their flagging morale rallied. If they could just hold on for a few more hours . . .

Later Isaac whispered to his grandfather, "Is it true?"

Yaakov shrugged and smiled. "Is it important?"

Mortar rounds whistled across the night and hammered into the kibbutz. Darkness alternated with the false dawns of flares, as the legion's gunners tracked their trajectories. After each round there were long, aching silences when the only sounds were the chirping of the cicadas and, from very close, the bass rumble of Arab voices.

Men and women lay around the floor in black, empty sleep. The wounded moaned and tossed, others prayed, the mumbling of their words a kaddish for the living dead.

"You were brave today," Yaakov said.

"I wet my pants, Grandfather. I mean it. I really did."

"You did well, none the less."

Isaac took a deep breath. Was this what it was like to be a man? To be so afraid? "I won't make you ashamed of me tomorrow."

"Ashamed? I was not ashamed of you! I was proud. It was I who should be ashamed. I promised Sarah I would look after you. I let her down. I should have sent you away."

"I'm glad I stayed," he lied. "Can we hold on?"

"Tonight we must pray for a miracle," Yaakov said and he took Isaac's hand and made his own silent entreaty to God; for Kfar Herzl, for his grandson, and for his children. But in his heart he knew he would never see any of them again.

Just after dawn the last two armoured cars rumbled

across the orchard, their wheels bouncing over the corpses, deviating only to miss a shell hole or the shattered stump of a tree. Yaakov and Isaac watched from the window of the dining hall, their weapons cradled in their arms. Isaac emptied his pockets and counted his ammunition. He had five bullets left.

The armoured cars stopped at the foot of the vineyard and pumped round after round at the blockhouse. Isaac recognised the father and mother of one of his friends scramble out of the bunker and crawl along the line of the vineyard wall, clutching petrol bombs. Just twenty yards from the legion armoured cars they were spotted and hit by a burst of Bren gun fire. They fell, one of them draped over the wall like a rag doll. Neither of them moved again.

The gunners in the blockhouse hammered round after round at the armoured cars and then the firing ended abruptly. Moments later Isaac saw them making their way back to the kibbutz under cover of the vineyard wall. There was an explosion inside the blockhouse and black smoke poured out of the gun slits.

"They've run out of ammunition," Yaakov said aloud. "They've destroyed the gun."

Now the Dingos rumbled on towards the main gate, bowling aside the barricade of stones as they came. A young girl ran towards them holding a petrol bomb, and was scythed down by machine-gun fire.

"This is it," Yaakov whispered.

They came loping behind the armoured cars, and poured through the gate, heading across the square towards them through the drifting smoke. Isaac fired, again and again, and then heard the terrible click of the hammer in the chamber as the magazine emptied.

"Who has ammunition?" he shouted. "Who has ammunition?"

He turned around and gaped in astonishment. The room was full of bodies. There was just a handful still standing. The rest were dead, or terribly injured. A round

730

from the armoured car had blown in one entire wall. He hadn't even heard it.

Yaakov tore the magazine out of his Sten gun and groped in his field jacket for another. He swore as he realised he had used up his last magazine.

"What do we do, Grandfather?" Isaac screamed.

"There's nothing we can do now, Isaac. Help me stand."

Isaac dragged him to his feet. The bandage on Yaakov's leg was filthy and stained with fresh blood. He lurched towards the open doorway, his arms raised.

My God! He's going to surrender! Isaac realised. He can't! He ran to one of the bodies and snatched the rifle out of the dead man's hand. He aimed at the onrushing Arabs and fired.

Empty.

Yaakov watched him from the doorway. He shook his head.

"It's over," he said. Isaac dropped the gun.

Yaakov went outside. The others followed.

There were a dozen Arabs, fellaheen, their rifles raised to their shoulders. Yaakov came towards them, hands raised in surrender. He was followed by four other men and a woman, Yaakov's sister.

The Arabs were shouting angrily and then one of them screamed, "Rab'allah!" and ran towards Yaakov. There was a bayonet on the end of his rifle and he plunged it into Yaakov's chest. The sound it made reminded Isaac of cutting raw cabbage with a knife. Yaakov made no protest. He fell silently to his knees.

The Arab stabbed again, into Yaakov's stomach.

The other fellaheen began to club their prisoners with their rifle butts. Yaakov's sister had her throat cut swiftly and expertly with a knife. The Arabs left her to crawl around in the dust to die.

Isaac ran.

He ran blindly, swerving around the shadowy figures that loomed ahead of him through the nightmare of smoke and killing. When he reached the olive orchard his breath was roaring in his ears, his legs pumping under him with the desperate speed of terror.

He reached the wall on the other side of the orchard and leaped over it. He was clear. He had got away!

Suddenly there were Arabs all around him.

A group were bent over two bodies, mutilating them. One of the bodies was still wriggling, alive. They looked up, startled. Their leader shouted, and pointed a finger at Isaac.

Isaac tried to run but his legs would not respond.

"Grab his arms and throw him on his belly!"

Three men wrestled him to the ground. He heard his own desperate screams as if they were coming to him from a distance.

"What a pretty little Jew!" the leader said in Arabic. "Let's have some fun with him first!"

The man was laughing. He knelt down behind him and Isaac felt them ripping at his pants and he knew the man intended to rape him.

He screamed again in blind, black panic.

Izzat had never been as excited in his whole life. The metallic smell of blood, the exhilaration of revenge and killing exploded in him like an orgasm, but unlike sex this release went on and on and on and he wanted it never to stop. All the failures and frustrations and humiliations of a lifetime burst over inside him. The screams of the Jews were like a balm. A moment ago he thought the apex of his pleasure was over; then Allah had brought this smooth-cheeked little Jew over the wall and now he could start all over again, and take his leisurely revenge in pain and power.

He tore down the boy's pants and grabbed his hair. He heard harsh male laughter and curses as the men urged him on.

"What a pretty little Jew!" he crowed. "Do you know what I am going to do? First I – "

"Leave him alone," a voice said.

He turned around. A man stood behind him with a gun pointing at his head. It was Rishou.

122

New City

A distant rumble, like thunder. Kaukji's Irregulars were shelling the Old City.

Marie woke and rolled towards Asher. She wrapped her thigh across him, and let her hair fall around his face, a shelter for them both. She kissed his mouth. He came awake slowly.

As she waited for him, images tumbled inside her mind. The House in the Woods, Frau Rosenberg calling out in the darkness, "Is that you, Josef?"; Rolf pushing between her legs: "Say you love me"; Lubanski grinning in the doorway of the Frauenblock, unbuckling his belt. So much to be left behind in the black pit of madness.

Life was, in the end, made up of moments. The past must be released, the future could not be owned. The present was the only certainty, take it, or waste it.

"I love you," he whispered.

"Prove it."

He reached for the drawer by the bed. She stopped him.

"No, I don't want to stop the baby. Make me pregnant, Ash."

"What if . . ." He let the sentence hang.

What if I die? What if this is the last time?

"Then I'll still have part of you."

She took him inside her. Let the night come. What had

733

Sarah said? Believe in the sun. For every end, there was a renewal. The men would destroy and the women would build again. She was not his tribe, but she was his woman. She would carry the seed of the next generation through this next dark time. It had always been the way.

She gave herself to Asher, and said a silent prayer for Netanel, wherever his devils had led him.

Old City

The shooting stopped, abruptly. Netanel heard footfalls on the cobblestones, very close. These sudden silences frayed the nerves worse than the constant shelling. Two Arabs darted across the Street of the Jews. Netanel aimed his Sten gun, and squeezed the trigger. Nothing happened. He smashed his fist against the stock in frustration. Out of ammunition.

Meodovnik ran to the door and hurled a grenade into the street. There was a flash and a jarring concussion. When Netanel looked back the two Arabs lay in a tangled and bloody mess against the far wall.

Meodovnik was crouched beside the doorway, grinning. Suddenly blood welled up between his teeth and spilled out of his mouth. He pitched forward on to his face.

Netanel turned him over. A sniper's bullet had made a jagged entry wound above the right breast pocket of his black jersey. Bright frothy blood bubbled out of it. Lung shot!

Meodovnik's mouth was open and he was trying to gulp in air, like a beached fish. His spectacles were smashed and glass was embedded in his eye and cheek. His fingers clawed at Netanel's arm.

"Get out!" someone was shouting. "We can't hold them any more!"

Netanel picked up Meodovnik's Sten along with his own and shouldered both weapons. He dragged the wounded man to the side door and down an alley.

*   *   *

734

There were two others in the ancient cobbler's shop, both of them Palmachniks, a bearded Ashkenazi and a young sabra woman. The shop smelled of dust and leather and the only light came from a small window that opened on to the alley.

Meodovnik was noisily drowning in his own blood. The Ashkenazi turned to Netanel. "Can't you shut him up?"

Netanel had his hand pressed over the entry wound, trying to help Meodovnik to breathe. The wounded man's lips were blue, and bloody saliva bubbled between his teeth. "He's dying," Netanel said.

"Are either of those guns loaded?" the sabra asked him.

Netanel shook his head.

"For the love of God, we don't have any ammunition either!"

They could hear Arab voices in the synagogue next door.

"Go and get some then. I have a couple of home-made grenades. I'll hold them."

The Ashkenazi looked at Netanel in disbelief. "Two grenades! How long do you think that will hold them off?"

"They're too busy looting the synagogue to worry about us. Hurry, go!"

The man glanced at his companion. He shrugged and jumped to his feet. The woman followed him. They vanished down the alley.

Meodovnik clutched at Netanel's arm. "Don't . . . surr . . . surrender . . ."

A few minutes later he was dead. Netanel slumped against the wall and listened to the Arabs next door squabbling over the spoils.

Kaplan stared at his radio operator. "What do they say?"

"They say reinforcements will arrive soon."

"They promised us help within the hour – guaranteed it – two and a half days ago! How much longer do they think we can hold out?"

The girl stared back at him, helpless and frightened.

Kaplan's red-rimmed eyes and the tremor in his voice betrayed his despair. The sounds of the battle were growing louder. Although the Warsaw and the Nissan Bek were still holding out, the vulnerable western flank of their defence had crumbled away. The Arabs had broken into the Street of the Jews, and were eating away at their defence, advancing into the heart of the quarter, house by house, inexorable, like ants chewing on a carcass.

The sheer weight of numbers was crushing them. Fortunately, none of the Arabs were trained soldiers; most of them were volunteers from the villages or mercenaries raised by the Mufti, and their appetite for looting each new conquest had effectively delayed their own advance. Low on ammunition, Kaplan's defenders were relying more and more on the home-made grenades from Leah Vultz's factory.

"Tell headquarters I want them to shell the area west of the Street of the Jews. Tell him if they don't, there's going to be a massacre."

She relayed the message to Haganah headquaters in the New City less than a mile away and waited for the response. As she did so, she wondered if she would still be alive to see the sunset. In her drawer was one of Leah Vultz's grenades. She knew how the Arabs treated their women prisoners and she was saving the grenade for herself.

Schneller Compound

Yitzhak Sadeh looked crumpled and tired. He leaned on his desk and studied the five young men and one woman assembled in his new headquarters. Just four days ago the office had belonged to the British chief of staff in Palestine, General Sir Gordon MacMillan.

Behind him, on the wall, was a large-scale map of the city. "Ladies and gentlemen," he said, his voice hoarse from days of issuing commands and briefings, "the situation in the Old City is desperate. In the last communiqué, received half an hour ago, the garrison commander said he did not think he could hold out another night. Days ago, I promised them help, knowing I had no such help to offer them. Tonight, however, you have the chance to save Jerusalem from destruction."

He looked at each of their faces in turn. Then he went to the map on the wall. "We think we have found a way in. Here." He pointed to the large square Crusader fortress that stood just inside the Old City wall beyond the Jaffa Gate.

"Aaron, Menachem. Your men will assemble here in the Tannous Building opposite the Jaffa Gate to prepare for the assault. Sophie, what strength do you have at present?" Sophie Zimmels commanded the only armoured brigade the Haganah possessed inside Jerusalem – mostly stolen or illegally purchased British armour.

"Two Dingos and a scout car, sir."

"You will lead them in a frontal assault on the Jaffa Gate. The defenders will assume that is the focus of our attack. Naturally it will be a feint."

There was a barely perceptible sigh of relief in the room. That was the very notion for which they had been bracing themselves.

Sadeh smiled. "Our way in is actually here, at the citadel. There is an iron grille at the base of the wall, perhaps fifty yards from the gate. Yehuda, it will be your team's job to remove the grille with explosives. Once inside, there is a tunnel leading under the main wall to the inner courtyard of the citadel. You will lead your men inside and spearhead the attack. Once you have entry, you will send the codeword 'Maccabee'." Asher smiled at the choice of code. The Maccabees had been the last Jews to breach the city walls, over two thousand years ago.

Sadeh continued. "Aaron and Menachem will then lead their companies inside to continue the thrust through the Armenian Sector to the Old City."

"What about my platoon, sir?" Asher asked.

"I want you to make another assault on the southern side of the city, here at Mount Zion. It will be another feint, to distract attention from our real target, here at the citadel."

Asher nodded, though it was difficult to concentrate. He had got the news that morning. Kfar Herzl had been overrun, no survivors. Isaac was dead, Yaakov too, and most of his friends.

"That is our basic plan," Sadeh was saying. "Now I will go through it with you again, in detail, and I want you all to log your times and positions. Remember, this may be our last chance."

123

Yemin Moshe

Four platoons, Asher thought. Four exhausted, under-strength platoons. It was all that was left of the Har-El Brigade after six weeks of constant combat. They had fought in Operation Nachson, a vain attempt to open up the Bab el-Wad, and had captured Kastel from Abdul Kader. Since their return to Jerusalem there had been constant street fighting in Katamon and Sheikh Jarrah. They had lived for weeks on an average of two to three hours sleep a night. They took Novadrin as part of their daily ration and the tablets now had as much effect on them as aspirin.

The survivors now sat around the walls of the synagogue in the half-sleep Asher knew so well, bright-coloured dreams interspersed with dull minutes of drugged consciousness. The men had a week's stubble, their faces gaunt and shadowed. The women were dirty and lank-haired. Their eyes glittered like psychotics, and most of them carried old wounds. In other armies they would be in the hospital, but the Palmach could offer them no such luxuries.

He wondered how many more of them he would have to sacrifice tonight to deception. Was it just to ask someone to die for an illusion?

"All right," he shouted, "let's move out! We have to be in Jerusalem tonight!" He had not had the heart to tell them theirs was merely a decoy mission. If he had, they might not find the strength to drag themselves up the mountain. Jerusalem was the only incentive he could offer them to make them fight through another night.

Old City

Netanel had become accustomed to the pattern: they would use guns and grenades to hold on to a building until the last possible moment, then abandon it, retreat to the next house, begin again. Exhaustion now held dominion over all fear, the ritual of combat an automatic response, like blinking and breathing. Forget you were running to an ever shrinking heart. Resistance was an end in itself.

Once today he thought it was over, thought he was going to die in the cobbler's shop with Meodovnik. But the Palmachniks had returned with more ammunition just before the Arabs had finished looting the captured synagogue next door. And they fought on.

He fired his Sten gun from the hip, turned, and ran down the alley. Gunfire echoed over the rooftops, a thousand lonely battles being decided inside the honeycomb of steep, twisting streets. Evening sunlight, dirty and yellow, angled through a vaulted ceiling. Ahead of him, deep shadows and a pool of black blood.

He followed the Ashkenazi and his sabra companion

into an anonymous stone building at the end of the alleyway. He flattened himself against a wall, checked the magazine of his weapon, tried to control his ragged breathing.

He looked around. Herrgottsacrament! He was in another synagogue. He understood immediately that it belonged to the Naturei Karta; Rabbi Silverberg himself was wandering along the empty pews studying some obscure text, another old man was bent over a copy of the Torah, his grey beard brushing the ancient pages, yet another stood by the wall, a blue and white tallith shawl across his shoulders, praying and chanting aloud, bowing jerkily from the waist each time he spoke one of the sacred names of God.

"What are you doing?" Netanel screamed.

Rabbi Silverberg looked up. The other two old Jews continued with their private devotions. "You are not welcome in here," the rabbi said.

"The Arabs are next door! Help us!"

The rabbi sighed and closed the text he had been reading. He seemed to make up his mind. "God has decided."

"Decided what?" Netanel screamed. "Why won't you help us?"

The rabbi spoke sharply to the other two men. They looked up from their books and their faces betrayed their dismay. They followed Rabbi Silverberg to the rear door of the synagogue.

Netanel followed them. "Where are you going?"

"We had hoped God might see fit to spare this humble place of worship. That is not His plan, it seems."

"Why don't you stay and fight for it?"

The rabbi looked at his two companions and nodded. They left. He turned back to Netanel. "Young man, you do not understand. The human soul is paramount. What good would it do us to keep our synagogue and lose God?"

The bark of a Sten gun. The two Palmachniks at the door of the synagogue were firing into the street. The Arabs were coming again.

"Have you heard of Auschwitz, rabbi?"

"Of course."

"You know, it's not just the Nazis I blame for Auschwitz. It's people like you. You and other Jews like you have turned us into a nation of weaklings."

"What happens in this world quickly passes. What happens in the next is for eternity."

"You make me sick."

The Ashkenazi screamed and fell, clutching his shoulder. The sabra woman shouted to Netanel for help and kept firing.

"Your opinion of me is of no consequence," Rabbi Silverberg said. "Only God is the judge." He walked away.

Netanel took the light machine-gun from his shoulder and returned to the battle in the street. He wondered what Amos Mandelbaum would say to Rabbi Silverberg.

He wondered what God would one day say to him.

Mount Zion

Asher crouched behind a tombstone in the Armenian cemetery, just yards from the tomb of King David, shouting into the field telephone handed him by his radio operator. He heard a grenade clatter against one of the tombstones. It exploded, and fat chunks of Jerusalem stone scythed through the air.

"What?" Asher screamed into the telephone.

Someone shouted a warning close by – they had found the Arab who had thrown the grenade – and the shout was followed by a blast from a Sten gun as a Palmachnik located the target.

"*What?*"

He could hear Sadeh's radio operator, but her voice was lost to a breaking signal, as if she was shouting into a hurricane.

Then he heard it: ". . . attack . . . been discon . . . heavy fire . . . withdr . . ."

"Do you want us to withdraw?" he shouted.

The answer was garbled, incomprehensible.

"DO – YOU – WANT – US – TO – WITHDRAW?"

"Affirmative . . . code is Ha – . . . repeat . . . is Hadrian."

Hadrian meant the attack on the citadel had failed. Asher slammed the phone back on its cradle on the field pack. Shit! What had it all been for? How many good men and women had he lost again tonight for nothing? *Balagan!* Another hopeless mess!

Suddenly he looked up, astonished. A flare arced across the night sky, and exploded, bathing the Zion Gate and the distant roofs of the Old City in lime green. Asher stared, open-mouthed, then scrambled frantically once more for the field phone. The flare was a signal from his second-in-command. He had captured Mount Zion. The feint had become the body blow and Zion Gate and the streets of Jerusalem were just two hundred yards away at their mercy.

Asher looked at his watch. Two a.m. They would have to be inside the city before dawn for the attack to succeed.

They had three home-made two-inch mortars, known as Davidkas, after David Leibovitch, the young man who had invented them. They were really no more than a piece of six-inch drainpipe and a bomb filled with nails and scrap iron. Their effectiveness was uncertain but the explosion they made when they landed was deafening. The noise often had a greater effect than the bomb itself.

Asher ordered the Davidkas forward to begin a bombardment. He chose two men to lay a one-hundred-and-sixty-pound charge at the base of the gate, then selected twenty of his best fighters – now half the remaining strength of his platoon – and led them towards the gate.

The Davidkas fell silent.

Asher lay on his belly and watched his two sappers crawl

along to the foot of the wall from the Dormition Gardens. Why was it so bright! He prayed for clouds to obscure the moon. He looked at his watch. Almost two fifteen. Hurry. *Hurry!*

The Arabs in the watchtowers must see them.

The minutes dragged by . . .

. . . He waited.

He heard the sappers before he saw them. "Shalom, Asher," one of them whispered.

"It's done?"

"It's done."

He checked his watch again. Surely the mines should have gone off by now? What if the charge failed to explode? How long should they wait before they checked the detonators?

"What time delay did you put on the fuses?" he hissed.

"They're set for two – " He never finished the sentence. There was a brilliant flash, followed a moment later by a massive concussion. The Zion Gate exploded. Dust and stone rained down into the cemetery.

It was long minutes before the smoke cleared. The iron gate stood open, dangling on its hinges. Some of the massive stones around the gate had broken away and lay at the base of the tower. The barricade beyond the gate had been flattened.

"Charge!" Asher shouted and he leaped to his feet and began to run, twisting through the jagged masonry.

He was just a few strides from the shattered remains of the Gate when he realised he was utterly alone.

743

124

Old City

Asher stood under Zion Gate, framed by the moonlight. He knew he was dead. He looked up at the crenellated tower and waited for the fatal shots but they did not come. As if in a dream, he picked his way over the shattered remains of the gate, his Sten held loosely in his right hand. The crunch of his heavy boots echoed around the gatehouse. Keeping his back pressed against the wall, he inched his way up the stairwell to the tower. It was utterly deserted.

The Davidkas and the mine must have convinced the Arabs that they were the focus of a massive attack. They had fled.

He heard a footfall on the cobblestones, saw shadows moving under the walls. He heard Roth, his second-in-command, shouting orders. He ran down to meet him.

"What happened?" he demanded, more astonished than angry.

"We're pretty tired, sir," Roth said. There was a moment's awkward silence. "I think we must have all fallen asleep."

The news that the Palmach had succeeded in breaking the Arab lines crackled through the Old City in minutes. By the time Asher and his men arrived, the Jochanan ben Zakai Synagogue was crammed with people, cheering, crying, laughing. Ultra Orthodox in gaberdines raised their hands to heaven and shouted thanks for their deliverance. Several even ran to embrace his Palmachniks.

And then he saw Sarah. She looks as if she is made of paper, he thought, as if she could step out into the street and be blown away. What has happened to the tough little sabra girl?

She was staggering, jostled this way and that by the crowd. When she saw him her mouth opened in surprise and he thought she was about to faint. Despite every promise he had made to himself, he ran forward and folded her in his arms. But as he embraced her, he felt her stiffen, gasping in pain.

"What's wrong?" he said, alarmed. He felt a thick swathe of bandage under her khaki shirt.

"Grenade fragments. I'm all right. Thank God, it's over."

Asher realised that everyone, even Sarah, thought they had been saved. He wondered if they would still be dancing and hugging each other when they realised he had just nineteen exhausted men and women with him to hold back the Arab tide.

Kaplan closed the door to his office in the Tipat Chilav for the first time in six months. He sat down and hung his head in his hands. "Twenty men? Is that all they could spare Jerusalem? Twenty?"

"We were meant as a diversion."

"A diversion?" Kaplan spoke through his fingers. "For who? The Arabs – or for us?"

"When we informed headquarters we had breached the gate, they promised to assemble reinforcements. They should be here before dawn."

"Where is the rest of your brigade?" Kaplan asked.

"Half of them are here. The other half are holding Mount Zion."

"Forty men? That's all? From a whole battalion?"

"We have spent much of the last two months in the Bab el-Wad."

Kaplan was contrite. "I am sorry, Asher. I meant no

745

disrespect to you or your men. It is just we are very tired and we had been hoping for much more."

"May I suggest we begin evacuating the wounded at once?"

Kaplan nodded, his face blank. A light had been extinguished somewhere behind his eyes. "A few hours ago I thought we would all be massacred. When I heard your men had broken through, you cannot imagine how I felt. Now . . ." He shrugged his shoulders helplessly.

"Our forces are stretched pretty thin, sir. The Arab Legion is converging on the city from the south-east."

Kaplan took a deep breath and with it tried to renew himself. He forced a smile. "It's no use dwelling on shattered hopes. Let's wait until we see what reinforcements Yitzhak sends us."

Sarah lay face down on a mattress on the floor of the Misgav Ledach while a surgeon removed the grenade fragments from the muscles of her back. A nurse held a torch for him, as there was no electric light. There was no anaesthetic either, and Sarah was grey with pain. She held tight to Asher's hand as the surgeon worked and her knuckles were white.

"I'm sorry, Ash . . . I'm . . . I'm sorry . . ."

"It's all right, Sarah. It's all right."

"I'm sorry . . . for every – " She gasped and squirmed as the surgeon probed for another fragment.

"Hold her!"

Asher leaned on her shoulders to hold her still. Oh, Sarah. Some time I should tell you about Isaac, and your father, and Kfar Herzl. I should tell you about Marie. Or perhaps you will never need to know. If you stay here it will be over soon anyway.

"I'm finished here," the doctor said. "The nurse will put on a dressing for you, Sarah."

Sarah searched again for Asher's hand. "Asher?" Her voice was small and wounded.

"It's over now. Relax. Get your strength back."

"Have you any . . . news . . . from Kfar Herzl?"

"They're holding out," Asher lied. "They're all okay."

"I'm glad you're here," she said.

The reinforcements arrived just before dawn.

The men the Haganah sent to save Jerusalem were clerks, teachers, and accountants, previously considered too old for active duty. They had been dragged from their beds and hastily assembled on the makeshift parade ground at Rehavia High School. They had been issued with USN helmets that were originally designed to be worn with earphones, so that they balanced on their heads like huge soup plates. Most were still in their work clothes. But their armoury, at least, was impressive. They each possessed a new Czech assault rifle with eighty rounds of ammunition and four hand-grenades. They had also brought vital supplies of plasma on their backs.

Asher turned to Kaplan. "These people can't hold Zion Gate."

"I was afraid you were going to say that."

"I can't ask my people to do it either. They've fought too long with too little rest and taken too many casualties. I just can't ask any more from them until they're rested."

"So what do you plan to do, Asher?"

"I cannot sacrifice the rest of my brigade to a siege. Anyway, Yitzhak would never allow it. I'm giving Roth orders to pull back to Mount Zion. My people will leave you their weapons and all their ammunition. I'm sorry."

Kaplan shrugged. "What about you?"

"I'm staying."

"Staying? Do you have orders?"

Asher shook his head.

"Then why? I have no choice but to stay. But you . . .?"

"My wife is here, Kaplan. For all that has passed between us, I won't abandon her now."

The Palmach were back on Mount Zion by the time the sun rose above the pink walls of Jerusalem. Later that morning red-and-white-checkered keffiyehs appeared on the battlements of Zion Gate. The Arab Legion had arrived to take over the siege of the Holy City.

125

Old City

The old Arab pastry shop stood on El Wad Road a hundred yards from the Nissan Bek. It was abandoned now, and the wooden shelves had since been ripped out and used for firewood. Broken glass surrounded the charred corona of a cooking fire in the middle of the floor. From the dark corners came the stink of human waste.

The surviving members of the Holy Strugglers of Judea sat around the walls and watched impassively as Izzat placed a fuse inside a sixty-pound charge of explosive, and taped the bundle together. When he had finished he looked around the room: "Which of you wishes for himself the honour of destroying the Nissan Bek?"

Shuffling silence.

Then Rishou spoke: "Izzat ib'n Mousa, your courage is legendary in the Judean hills. Time and again these ill-mannered fellaheen have snatched from you the moment of glory that is yours by right. This time, you lay the charge."

Izzat tried to smile, but the smile froze on his face like a grimace and his eyes were pinpoints. None of the others would have dared speak to him in such a fashion, but Rishou brought with him the authority of his birthright. Ever since the battle at Kfar Herzl, Izzat knew his leadership was under threat.

Now this new challenge. Laying the charge himself was

out of the question. It was for such suicidal tasks that the fellaheen were born. But what could he say? He must agree, and find some excuse later to rescind.

But before he could reply the guard he had posted at the door rushed in. "Ib'n Mousa, there is someone come to see you!"

Every head turned. The newcomer wore a white keffiyeh and spotless abbayah, and carried a new British army Lee Enfield. He was clean-shaven, except for his moustache. He appeared immaculate, compared with the accumulated stains of woodsmoke and cordite and dirt that days of battle had left on the Strugglers.

The man looked around the room. "In the villages the muezzin are calling for volunteers to help in the holy struggle to rid ourselves of these Jews," he said.

Rishou stood up. "Majid, my brother," he said, embracing him.

Since the arrival of the Arab Legion Sarah had recognised a shift in the conflict. Their enemy was now better organised, their tactics more reasoned, their attacks more sharply focused. At the previous evening's conference at Kaplan's headquarters, unit commanders from the western flank had described how every position they lost was now quickly destroyed so it could not be retaken. The extra equipment and supplies that Asher's Palmachniks had brought in had instantly been negated by a superior adversary.

She had noted the increased activity in the Muslim Quarter that morning and she knew another attack was imminent. Her own command was now desperately short of food and ammunition and the only grenades they had were Leah Vultz's home-made explosives that Abraham brought them stuffed in the pockets of his trousers.

Her back was on fire and that night she had been unable to sleep because of the pain. But there was no morphine left in the hospital even for those who had lost limbs or were screaming from stomach wounds, and the seven small metal fragments the doctors had picked from her back muscles seemed trivial in comparison.

And Asher's appearance had given her new courage. At least if she were going to die here in Jerusalem, she would not die alone.

A fellaheen dashed from one of the alleys holding a package of dynamite tied together with string. The hole that had been blown in the base of the wall on the first day had been sandbagged again and again, and barricaded with stones, but it was still the weakest point. The man raced towards it, in an oblique angling run that made him invisible to the defenders at the gunports. Only the snipers in the cupola would be able to see his approach.

For a moment it seemed to his comrades that he might succeed but then there was a sudden volley of sniper fire and he screamed and pitched forward on his face.

"Where's Izzat?" one of the Strugglers whispered.

"He's been summoned to a conference at legion headquarters."

Rishou and Majid exchanged glances. No one had seen Izzat slip away. The sixty-pound charge he himself had prepared and agreed to carry now lay on the cobblestones, a few feet from the dead fellaheen. It was a poisoned chalice. It meant possible glory to whoever had the courage to carry it, more likely it meant certain martyrdom. Who would take it?

A man in a khaki battle jacket leaped to his feet and ran across the street. It was Ahmad, another of the fellaheen from Rab'allah. As he bent to pick up the explosives, a single gunshot from the cupola catapulted him backwards. He jerked and writhed on his back for a few moments and was still.

The Strugglers crouched in the alley and stared at the two new corpses in front of the Nissan Bek. The bodies had been piling up there for five days now and the sun had been fierce. Their stink had created a deadly miasma of death around the synagogue, a psychological barrier as terrible as the sniper fire from the dome.

There was another band of irregulars crouched in a deserted coppersmith's nearby. One of them burst out of the doorway and made his dash for the walls. This time the sniper fire was less accurate and he made almost twenty paces before he fell. He lay on his belly, still alive. His whimpering echoed around the walls.

"I did not expect to see you again," Rishou said to Majid.

Majid said nothing. It was difficult to speak. It required all his concentration to deal with the black panic that had paralysed his limbs. Perhaps if they could just sit here, watch these other men die, and never be required by conscience or by Allah to move, and risk the tearing, violent embrace of the bullets . . .

"I hated you so much. I wanted to kill you."

Majid nodded. That much he knew.

"Why did you do it?" Rishou said. "Why did you betray us?"

Because I needed the money, Majid thought. But also because I did not want to be an Arab. Because I was ashamed of us. I wanted to be a Britisher, and I wanted to be an effendi. Now I have been betrayed also and I am here looking to salvage my pride.

Majid lit a cigarette with trembling fingers. "You never wanted to join these people. Why did it matter so much to you what I did?"

"I thought they were fools, but they were still our brothers."

Another staccato of gunfire and yet another martyr lay sprawled on the cobbles, dark rosettes on the back of his white abbayah.

Rishou turned away from Majid and stared at the bundle of explosives. Majid knew his brother. He could almost hear the train of his thoughts, the twin compunctions of shame and anger driving him to his feet.

"Don't do it," Majid whispered.

"I have to."

751

Majid caught his arm. "It's suicide."

"I came here to fight, not to watch."

Another man sprinted across the alley. Majid thought for a moment he would make it to the synagogue walls but at the last moment a burst of gunfire scythed him down. He tried to crawl the remaining ten yards but a single rifle shot from the dome slammed into him and his body jerked from the impact of the bullets and he lay motionless.

Another fellaheen ran from the coppersmith's shop. Rishou snatched the cigarette from his brother's mouth. "No!" Majid shouted.

Rishou ran for the corner.

He used the early morning shadows on the far side of the alley for cover. Sniper fire chased the other man, caught him still twenty paces from the walls.

They still had not seen Rishou. He picked up the bundle of explosives and ran for the synagogue wall.

Five paces, ten, fifteen.

Majid watched and held his breath.

Sarah finally managed to slam a fresh magazine into her Sten gun and fumbled for a new clip. "There's another one!" she shouted.

Roberto scrambled across the gallery and pushed her aside. He fired, pumping one bullet after another into the street.

"Did you get him?"

"I don't know!"

"Did you see him go down?"

"*I don't know!*"

The architecture of the Nissan Bek made it impossible to see the base of the wall from the dome. Sarah loaded the fresh magazine and stared out of the gunport. Bodies shimmering in the mid-morning heat. There was no movement down there now.

Had the other attacker made it to the walls?

*   *   *

Rishou crouched down, his back pressed against the stone. He was just yards from the protruding barrel of a Jewish rifle at the barricade. He rested a moment to catch his breath. Then he took Majid's cigarette from his mouth and lit the fuse of the dynamite. He tossed it towards the sandbags and threw himself away from the wall. The crackling trails of automatic weapons fire followed him as he sprinted away.

The blast rocked the building on its foundations, and a fine rain of plaster and dust turned the atmosphere inside the Nissan Bek into a choking white fog. Sarah grabbed Roberto's jersey and dragged him with her down the gallery steps to the floor of the synagogue.

The northern wall was open to the courtyard and huge slabs of masonry had crumbled across the ark. Through the floating alabaster dust she could see the Arabs streaming towards them, firing their weapons from the hip.

"Put your weapons on automatic fire!" Sarah shouted.

She ran to the gap in the wall and threw herself on the rubble, firing burst after burst into the onrushing waves of militia and legionnaires. Too soon the magazine was spent, and she had no more.

"Abraham!" she screamed.

He was already beside her, holding out two of Leah Vultz's grenades. She primed them and threw them into the advancing tide. She heard a scream. Roberto was lying on his back beside her, trying to push his own insides back into a gaping hole in his stomach.

There were just three of her Palmachniks still on their feet.

"Out!" she screamed at them. "Out!"

She pushed Abraham ahead of her. Then she half dragged, half carried Roberto from the ruins of the Nissan Bek.

The Strugglers joined with their compatriots from Bethlehem and Shu'fat and Beit Jibrin, and the other countless villages and hamlets of Judea, in looting the Nissan Bek.

Rishou watched a group of men fighting over a velvet curtain they had torn from the synagogue's tabernacle. Finally it ripped in two and they seemed satisfied with this compromise. Others ransacked the remains of the Ark for candlesticks and lamps, or set to work on the bodies of the dead Haganah, rummaging through their clothes for money and valuables before mutilating them.

Rishou found Izzat stuffing pages from a Torah inside his undershirt. "We don't have time for this," he said.

Izzat ignored him.

"We have to press the attack! The Jews are running!"

"You want to leave all this for the legion? It was our blood that was spilled winning it!"

"We didn't come here for this!"

"Tell that to the fellaheen," Izzat sneered.

Rishou turned away in an agony of frustration. "I wonder where he was when the blood was running?" Majid whispered in his ear.

126

Old City

Asher found Netanel on the roof of the Rabbi Moshe Eshkol yeshiva. He flopped down beside him, under the parapet wall. The Arabs were next door.

Netanel's face showed the strain of ten days of nationhood. His thin grey-fair hair was matted on his scalp, and his skull was the shape of a bullet. Fatigue had made his skin more pale and the scars on his face more livid. He grinned when he saw Asher but the grin was cruel and animal. His eyes were flecked with ice blue and empty.

His Thompson sub-machine gun lay across his lap, like a kitten.

"Hello, Ash. Come looking for me?"

He offered Netanel a cigarette. Netanel took one gratefully. They were silent a long time. There were three other Irgunis on the rooftop, and they stared at Asher with undisguised hostility.

"Last time we saw each other you wanted to kill me," Netanel said at last.

"I should never have fished you out of the Mediterranean. You could have died with some honour that way."

"Ah, death with honour. Is that what you think I would like?"

"At Rab'allah they were just women and children. Is that what the Irgun plan to do in the new Israel? Massacre women and children?"

"Don't lecture me, Asher. You weren't in the death camps. It's easy to be civilised when you haven't experienced what barbarity is."

"So that makes everything you do all right? The Nazis are your excuse for everything?"

"I'm tired, Ash. Did you come here to hector me or is there something you wanted?"

"I want to know if your people still have a cache of weapons hidden in the Old City."

"Ah, is that all?"

Asher felt his temper rising. "We're almost out of arms and ammunition. We can't keep fighting without your help. We're supposed to be on the same side. For the love of God, what do you want?"

"I want to be sure you will not surrender. I look at Kaplan and I wonder if he has the stomach for another Massada."

"Just tell me, Netya. Do you have more weapons?"

Netanel stood up and beckoned Asher to follow, down the steps, out of sight and earshot of the other Irgunis. He waited for Asher on the first landing.

He lit another cigarette. "There's a house next to Jochanan Ben Zakai. Go down to the basement. In the

755

corner you'll find two of the stone slabs are loose. The rest of our slik is underneath. Okay?"

"Thanks," Asher said, and turned to go.

"How's Marie?"

Asher turned. He shook his head. "I'll never understand you, Rosenberg. Why did you leave her? Didn't you love her?"

"Of course I loved her."

"Then why?"

"She didn't tell you?"

"She never told me anything. So what is it, Netya? What's the big secret?"

"Do you ever wonder what happened to your father, Ash?"

Asher just stared.

"I'll tell you. He died in the autumn of 1944 in Auschwitz. A kapo beat him to death with a club on the orders of SS Reichsmajor Emmerich. You do know what a kapo was? It was the name the SS gave to inmates in their death camps that they recruited as police. The lowest of the low."

A long silence. "You," Asher said, at last.

"I don't care if you kill me, Ash. A bullet, your knife perhaps. It would be justice."

"Why? You of all people? A kapo?"

"It doesn't matter why. You weren't there, you could never understand. And it wouldn't change anything."

Asher dropped his eyes, stared at the gun in his hands. His Adam's apple worked in his throat as he tried to absorb the barrage of emotion working in him. "Why are you telling me this now?"

"I've lived with this for four years, Ash. Every day and every night it haunts me. I cannot stand the torment . . . any more."

Their eyes met. "The Nazis killed him, Netya," Asher said at last. "You'll never make me believe that it was different."

"For God's sake, I don't want your forgiveness!"

"What do you want? You want me to hate you? I can't.

756

It's like you said, I wasn't there. Anyway . . . how much do you think it killed him when I left? I have my own debts to pay!" A muscle in his jaw rippled. "It's Rab'allah I don't forgive you for."

"I didn't kill any children at Rab'allah!"

"But you were there."

There was a shout of alarm from the Irgunis on the roof. Netanel and Asher scrambled back up the steps. They looked down into the street, staring in utter disbelief.

"Armoured cars," Netanel murmured.

"Impossible," Asher said. But it was true. They were there.

The armoured cars of the Arab Legion followed one of the most familiar routes in Palestine. They came along the Via Dolorosa, the way of Christ's last journey when he carried the Cross to Calvary. In the Christian world it had become known as the stations of the Cross.

For two thousand years the ancient, winding streets of the Old City had known only the click of donkey hooves, and the bleating of sheep. Now the legion brought a new beast clanking into the heart of the ghetto, an armoured car. They used sandbags to coax it up the narrow stone staircases.

Asher and Netanel watched them come, knowing they had no weapons to stop them, except home-made petrol bombs; no obstacle to throw in their path except the rubble already created by the Arab shelling. The Dingos rumbled through the cramped hive of the ghetto, and fired their three-inch cannons from point-blank range into the synagogues and the yeshiva and the final sanctuaries of the Jews.

Rabbi Silverberg leaned across Kaplan's desk. "The sewers don't work. There is no one to collect the garbage. There is no electricity, and nowhere to bury the dead. Our water is almost gone and half the city is destroyed. We have been praying and reciting psalms without interruption for ten days but still there is no end in sight. It seems apparent to me that God wishes us to surrender."

"Battles are not won with psalms, rabbi, they are won with bullets. We still have some left."

"Face the facts, Commander. Your superiors have abandoned you."

Kaplan said nothing. That was what he believed also.

"We should throw ourselves on the mercy of the Arabs!"

"Why not throw ourselves on their bayonets? It's the same thing."

"Have you not heard the broadcasts the Arabs are making from their loudspeakers? They have promised that if we surrender, none of us will come to harm."

"I am sure that is what they would like us to believe."

"Commander, I urge you, in the name of Jehovah, surrender and cease this suffering and end this sin against natural law."

Kaplan stood up and leaned across his desk. "Rabbi, I am telling you, in the name of Israel, I will not."

Asher leaped from the shattered parapet wall. He heard the metallic scream of the Dingo's motor as it inched along the alleyway, just yards away, around the corner of the yeshiva.

It emerged into the shaft of sunlight like some great, dun-coloured beetle, the turret swivelling, searching for targets, the three-pounder gun and Bren feeling for danger, like antennae. Asher faced the monster with a cigarette tin packed with Leah Vultz's dynamite and a few nails.

A burst from the Bren cut him down before it left his hand.

"Asher!" Netanel threw himself from the parapet. The other Irgunis fired long bursts from the rooftop, drawing fire from the tank crew.

Netanel dragged Asher across the rubble into an alley, leaving a trail of dark blood on the stones.

*　　*　　*

All that remained of the Nissan Bek after the legion had detonated a charge of two hundred pounds of TNT inside it was an archway from the north wall. The orange heart of a fire glowed inside the skeletal stones, and the murmur of guttural male voices carried on the night. The moon rode above it, a perfect silver crescent.

The Holy Strugglers of Judea listened as their leader outlined their role for the next day. They were to join the legion's assault on the final bastion of the Jews, the massive Hurva Synagogue.

"Will you be leading this attack?" Majid asked Izzat.

"Of course," Izzat said, but his voice was wary.

"As you led us against the Nissan Bek?" Rishou said.

Eyes glowed like coals in the darkness. The other men sensed the challenge and shuffled their feet, nervous and expectant. Rishou was no longer an interloper among them. They had witnessed his courage and his commitment under the walls of the Nissan Bek.

"It is indeed unfortunate that during the attack I was called away by a legion officer for a vital conference on battle tactics," Izzat said. "After all I am a close relative of the Mufti – "

Rishou spat into the fire in disgust. "What has been happening is Tell or some other legion officer has been asking for fodder to throw at the Jewish guns instead of his own precious soldiers. He wants the Jews to use up all their ammunition on some suitable target – like us. You have been volunteering these poor fellaheen for martyrdom while you gain prestige in the eyes of the legion!"

"You forget. I was there also – "

"No, you forget, Izzat! You were not there! You are never there! I remember at Kfar Herzl, when we ran behind the tanks, I saw you fall, and I thought you had been hit by a bullet. After the battle I could not believe it when I saw you. I looked for a wound. There was nothing. You dropped in the dust of the tanks because you were a coward. Now, that is not so bad, Izzat. My brother Majid here, he will never be a great Arab hero either. But then he does not pretend to be. He does not send other men to their deaths for his own glory. Your Holy Strugglers have run their errands for you for a long time. They have planted your bombs and fired your bullets. And now you want them to die in front of the Hurva for you."

The night was utterly still. Every man stared at Izzat. It was the most deadly of all insults. Izzat would have to answer it with his knife. Now. There was no other choice.

Instead, he got up and walked away.

127

The synagogue was known as the Hurva Rabbi Yehuda Hechasid. The graceful eighteenth-century horizon of the dome towered over the Old City, dominating the heart of the Jewish Quarter. It was the most sacred temple of the Ashkenazi, the immigrant Jews from Europe. Inside, the colours of the Jewish Legion were preserved on the walls, commemorating their campaigns in North Africa and Italy in the Second World War. It was now the last stronghold of the defence of Jerusalem. The Hurva's dome and upper gallery was in ruins, hit repeatedly by mortar and artillery shells. But still the walls stood.

Sarah sat with her back against the wall, staring at the shattered dome above her head. The wounds in her back had become infected and there was no sulphinamide to treat them. Every time she moved they burned like acid. Her eyes felt as if they were full of grit and she was so exhausted each movement required intense mental concentration to force her muscles to do what they should have done as reflex.

The end was close now. They all knew it. It was the eve of La'g Borner, when Jewish children traditionally lit bonfires to celebrate. Last night the bonfires had once again burned all over the Old City, as the Arabs put the quarter to the torch.

Of the two hundred men and women of the original defence, and the eighty replacements brought in when Asher's Palmachniks stormed the Zion Gate, only thirty-five now remained. The rest lay wounded on vermin-infested mattresses in the Batei Machse Hospital or rotted in the sun on its roof. The sweet stench pervaded the whole quarter.

Her Sten gun lay across her lap. It was no more than an icon of her own determination to resist. She had no more ammunition.

She closed her eyes and dreamt. The dream was vivid and bright and confused. She dreamt of apples ripening in the orchard at Kfar Herzl and Rishou whispering in her ear, but she could not make out the words. Suddenly the trees were gone and there was only desert and she was running. There was someone pursuing her, she could feel their hot breath on her back. She pumped her legs faster and faster but the desert sand was soft and slipped away beneath her feet and she could not move. She felt hands reaching out and clutching at her –

She jerked awake and Abraham was crouching next to her, shaking her shoulders.

"I brought you these." He handed her two Player's cigarette tins, the fuses dangling from a hole cut in the tin. Leah Vultz's home-made grenades were all they had left now.

How does he endure this? Sarah thought. He is only a child.

"Thank you, Abraham," she said. "Any news from Kaplan?"

He shook his head. "Are we going to die?"

What could she say to him? What could she say?

"Rabbi Silverberg says we should all surrender," Abraham said.

"Do you think we should, Abraham?"

"Leah doesn't have any more tins for grenades."

761

"Then we'll throw rocks," a man's voice said. Sarah looked up. It was Netanel. His right arm was wrapped in a filthy bandage and hung loose at his side and his face was layered with ten days of grime and sweat. His khaki shirt was ripped and there were jagged holes in his shorts. There was black crusted blood on his chest. A devil in rags.

There were two Finnish Tommy guns slung over his right shoulder. "Here," he said, and he let one of the guns clatter to the floor of the synagogue beside her.

She looked up at him, bewildered.

"It's the last of our sliks," he admitted. "There doesn't seem much point in hiding it any more. Most of my people are dead too."

She picked up the gun and checked the breech.

"There's one magazine left," he said. "After that you swing it over your head, like a club. You can do anything you like with it except tie a white flag to the barrel."

"Why have I been selected for this great honour?"

He seemed not to notice the irony in her voice. "You are still alive and you are still fighting. You have earned it." He was about to turn away. "Asher's hurt," he said softly.

Something squirmed inside her. "Is he dead?"

"He's in the hospital. He took two bullets in the chest, yesterday. It doesn't look good."

Oh, Ash. She felt the wrench of grief in her chest. Yet she knew it was crazy, for they were all damned. There was no reprieve for any of them now. They would all be dead before sunset, and Rosenberg seemed to be the only one eager for the end.

Fifty yards of sloping rubble to the base of the wall. Once it was breached the Hurva would be at their mercy.

Fifty yards of sloping rubble.

The ladder lay behind the shattered remains of a wall, a huge water barrel secured to it with ropes. The inside of the barrel was filled with explosives, and a long fuse extended from the barrel's mouth. Rishou stood beside the barrel, his rifle slung across his shoulder.

"I need three volunteers," he told them. "It is danger-ous, but if you are killed the Mufti says you will go straight to Paradise and Mohammed will honour you himself. More important, if we succeed we will throw these Jews out of our Holy City. They have spat in our faces too long." He paused and studied the exhausted and terrified remnants of Izzat's band. "For myself I have lost my mother, my wife and two children to these Jews. My daughter is a cripple and will never find a husband. My oldest brother I lost to the Britishers. I have had my fill of being persecuted in my own land, the lands of my ancestors. Who will make this final charge with me?"

Suicide, Majid thought.

Two men stepped forward. Majid felt his brother staring at him, but he would not look up. A third shouted, "As Allah is my witness, today we shall kill these Jews or I shall see the Gates of Paradise!"

I would rather see them as an old man, Majid decided. But the thought did not comfort him. He was ashamed.

The four men hefted the ladder, one at each corner, grunting at the weight of the barrel. Rishou shouted a command and they ran from behind the wall and began to scramble over the jagged masonry.

They were halfway across when the first man fell to sniper fire. Ten yards away the second fell and the ladder crashed to the ground. The barrel rocked on its makeshift cradle but held. The third man, beside Rishou, the one who was going to kill the Jews or behold Paradise, ran like a rabbit for the shelter of the synagogue wall.

"Leave it!" Majid screamed at his brother.

Rishou tried to haul the ladder alone over the last ten paces. Then he gasped and staggered, his leg almost buckling under him. Majid saw a scarlet splash of blood on his abbayah.

Majid pushed himself away from the shelter of the wall and ran to him.

* * *

763

The pounding of his heart and his feet, the roaring of the blood in his ears, the crack and whine of bullets, the jarring concussion of a grenade exploding nearby. He heard himself scream his brother's name, was amazed to find himself still running, still upright, still alive.

He grabbed Rishou's arm and dragged him over the rubble to the safety of the wall. In the same movement – he knew if he hesitated for just one moment his courage would be gone – he dashed back to the mine.

It wouldn't budge.

Bullets cracked on to the stones around him.

Yes, yes, the ladder was moving.

He felt the hot flood of his own urine down his leg.

Four yards, three.

He was going to make it . . .

. . . He collapsed over Rishou's body.

Rishou had propped himself against the wall. He tore a strip of cloth from the hem of his abbayah, and bound it around the wound in his thigh. He was grinning. "You did it!" he shouted. "You did it!"

"I did it." Majid smiled weakly and fainted.

128

The synagogue windows had been smashed out and replaced with sandbags. Sarah rested the Thompson on the bags and fired a long burst through the gaping hole in the wall. The magazine was almost empty. Her grenades were gone. Still they kept coming.

Through the narrow gun slit she had seen four Arabs trying to carry a mine across the courtyard. She was sure she had got them all.

Screams echoed around the dome. Someone yelled

something to her. She couldn't make out the words. A warning . . .

. . . A brilliant white flash.

Suddenly she was lying on her back. She couldn't move.

The Scout car had trundled over the rubble of the Bethel section and taken up a position to bombard the synagogue. A three-pound cannon was mounted inside the turret. Its first round had blasted away a section of the wall on the north side. Ignoring the mine, Rishou struggled to his feet and limped towards the breach.

Sarah stared up at the dome. Dust and smoke, drifting. There was a hole in the wall next to her, broken masonry everywhere, a heavy weight resting on her legs. She couldn't move her right arm and it hurt to breathe. She groped with her left hand for the Thompson but it was gone.

The first Arab scrambled over the rubble in the breach and aimed his rifle at her head.

Sarah!

He hesitated, unsure. Your imagination! he told himself. It was just another sabra Jewess. There was blood in her hair, and her face was white with dust. She looked like a scarecrow. It couldn't be.

But under the blood and the caked dirt . . .

He lowered the rifle.

"Sarah?" he said aloud.

He was thinking about the apple trees at Kfar Herzl when something hit him very hard between the shoulders.

Sarah crawled towards him. There was a jagged black hole in his back, at the level of his right shoulder-blade. He was lying prone on his belly, coughing bright blood between his teeth.

"Rishou," she whispered.

His eyes blinked open.

She rolled him over with her good arm. Pink bubbles frothed from the exit wound in his chest, as he tried to gasp in a breath.

"Just hold me, Rishou. It's all right. Just hold me."

Another shell slammed into the synagogue. Sarah cradled Rishou's face to protect him from the shower of plaster and stone. She heard the hammering of a machine-gun very close. An Irguni fired a long burst from his Thompson through the breach in the wall.

"Sarah . . ." Rishou croaked. A trickle of blood leaked from the corner of his mouth. His hand reached for her. "Sarah, I – "

And then she was being dragged away.

"No!"

"We have to get out!" Netanel shouted at her. She tried to resist but then the pain in her shoulder and her leg and her ribs overwhelmed her. The last thing she saw before she passed out was Rishou, choking on his own blood, his hand outstretched towards her.

Majid saw Rishou framed for one moment by the jagged hole in the wall of the Hurva, saw the bullet punch a hole in his back, and even over the deafening confusion of the battle he heard – or thought he heard – the single rifle shot that cut him down. He spun around and saw the sniper hastily withdraw from the shelter of the broken wall below the synagogue.

Majid joined the rush towards the Hurva, saw a black-jerseyed Jew appear at the breach and aim his weapon. Two legionnaires in front of him fell screaming and Majid instinctively threw himself face down. He lay on his belly, exposed and helpless.

He thought he was dead. But when he looked up the Jew was gone.

He crawled over the rubble and found Rishou lying spreadeagled on his belly. He cradled his brother's head in his arms. He was dead.

*   *   *

766

The fedayeen were chanting, firing their rifles into the air in celebration of the victory while others busied themselves with the more serious task of looting. Meanwhile the legionnaires brought in explosives to level the remains of the building.

Majid picked his way back down the slope, ignoring the milling crowds of soldiers. It was difficult to accept that this little pile of broken masonry had seemed so vast just a few minutes ago; the abandoned barrel bomb now appeared so clumsy and stupid.

How could he ever tell Zayyad that Rishou was dead?

Rishou had been the living embodiment of Rab'allah: disowned, ignored, but somehow a point of reference. No matter what he did, he had always been able to gauge his own prodigality by his brother, and he would always know the distance he must return if ever he needed to find himself once more. When he had waved farewell to his family at Sheikh Jarrah he had only to discover that Rishou was with Izzat in the Old City, and he had known his place was there also.

Now Rishou was dead and he felt adrift, rudderless in a world that had changed so dramatically from that of his youth that he no longer recognised his place in it. He tried to identify what he felt and the cold empty fist in his gut was not grief, but aloneness. Rishou had been the one who had known how to meld the old world with the new, tradition with the inevitability of change.

Rishou was his brother and he had been betrayed by his own tribe. In the end, he knew, they all cared more for themselves than they did for each other. It was in their blood, and in their Koran.

He found Izzat still crouched behind the wall. His face was pale and tight. When he saw Majid he jumped to his feet and reached for his rifle. A guilty child found in a neighbour's orchard, Majid thought. That is precisely how he looks.

"I know it was you," Majid said.

767

"What are you talking about?"

"I know it was you."

Izzat's fingers hovered over the guard of his rifle. For a moment neither of them moved. Will he try and gun me down also? Majid wondered. Then Izzat seemed to make his decision.

"Get out of my way," he said and he shoved past Majid and joined the howling victorious mob making their way up the slope. He didn't have the stomach for it, face to face.

He was halfway up the slope when Majid called him back.

"Rishou's dead," Majid said.

Izzat shrugged his shoulders. "He died a martyr in battle. Even at this moment Allah welcomes him at the Gates of Paradise. We shall all mourn him."

Majid shot him through the chest.

129

The hospital had been moved to the basement of the Jochanan Ben Zakai Synagogue. The room was dark, and leached of air, a miasma of stink and sweat and infection. Candlelight threw a shadowplay of defeat and despair on the walls: the hand of a dying man reaching for a nurse; a mother comforting a crying child; a doctor throwing up his hands in frustration. The wounded coughed and moaned in the semi-darkness, among the ancient and mouldering mounds of Talmuds, the diminishing supplies of bandages, the empty serum bottles. There were almost a thousand civilians crammed into the basement also, huddled around flickering candles. The men had tallith shawls around their shoulders and intoned the traditional prayer of the Sabbath Eve.

"Blessed art Thou, O Lord, who spreadest the shelter of peace over us and over all Thy people Israel, and over Jerusalem . . ."

Sarah crawled in the darkness for half an hour before she found Asher. His chest was heavily bandaged and his eyes were closed. His skin looked yellow in the flickering candlelight and there were deep plum-coloured shadows around his eyes.

"Ash . . ."

His eyes flickered open, and his lips moved, but no sound came. His skin felt cold and damp, like wet chamois, and he started to shiver. While the sweat dripped from her forehead on to his face, he began to freeze to death.

"Thirsty," he whispered.

She shrugged helplessly. She had no water.

"Here," a voice said. She looked around. It was Rabbi Silverberg. He held out an ancient leather water-bottle.

Sarah took it, and let a few precious drops fall on Asher's lips. "Why didn't you help us before?" she whispered. "Why did you people never lift a finger to help us?"

The rabbi pointed across the cellar. "Do you see that girl over there? The nurse? That's my daughter. Of course we have helped you."

"But if you had fought with us . . ."

He snatched back the water-bottle. His face was pale.

"Let me tell you something! Before you people came my neighbours were not only Jews. They were Arabs, Christians, Armenians. At Pesach I would invite them in to share the Passover meal with us. We lived in peace here. Our religions did not stand in our way then. Many of your enemies were once my friends." In the flickering light of the candle Sarah noticed the grimy canyons of tears in his white beard. "When you people came you destroyed our lives. Not the Arabs. Not the Mufti. You. You did it!"

A roar, like a freight train crashing through the roof of the basement itself, and a cloud of thick, red dust billowed down the stairs. The legion had demolished the Hurva.

Rabbi Silverberg coughed at the dust, the whites of his eyes luminous in the gloom. "We will bleed with you. We will die here like rats in this cellar with you. But don't ask us to love you!" He offered her the water-bottle. Sarah shook her head. "I am sorry about your friend." He moved away in the darkness.

Asher reached for her hand. His own was cold and greased with sweat. His eyes had closed again.

We will bleed with you. We will die with you. But don't ask us to love you!

So who are my kin and who are my enemies? Sarah thought. Rishou was my lover, and they told me to hate him. Because he was an Arab. Is that all love and hate is, an accident of birth?

And now he's dead. "He's dead," she whispered aloud, trying to make herself believe it. But she was empty of feeling. She was too tired to cry for him now. That would come later.

Except there would be no "later".

Sarah coughed. Her chest hurt where the doctors had strapped her right arm to her ribs. She closed her eyes, rested her head against the wall and waited for the Arabs to come. But all she saw was Rishou lying among the ruins of the Hurva, his outstretched hand reaching for hers.

From the window Netanel could see the smoking ruins of the Hurva Synagogue, and the façade of the Jochanan Ben Zakai. He had expected the Arabs to try to rush the synagogue the previous afternoon, but they had been too busy looting the Hurva and when the legion had finally exploded the charge it was almost evening and the inevitable end had been delayed.

We are not going to die on the ends of bayonets, Netanel reminded himself. We are going to die like a nation, with guns in our hands, not crawling and begging for mercy like dogs.

We will not die with our heads bowed.

Not like Amos Mandelbaum.

He saw movement in the archway of the Jochanan Ben

Zakai. He shifted his position slightly and aimed the Thompson down at the street.

A white flag.

His whole body jerked with the force of sudden rage. Kaplan had promised! Kaplan had given his word he would not surrender! Not after so much!

Two rabbis emerged from the synagogue, carrying a white sheet draped between two poles. He recognised one of them. It was Silverberg.

No! They were not going to surrender! He would not be a prisoner again! He would not grovel for his life!

He aimed the Thompson and fired. The gun pumped four rounds and the clip was exhausted. One of the rabbis lay on the cobbles. Silverberg. The other took up the pole and continued to march across the street.

"*No!*" Netanel tore the magazine out of the gun and scrambled on the floor for a fresh one. His hands were shaking with fury, and he fumbled it.

By the time he had slammed it into the gun it was all over.

People were pouring out of the synagogue into the arms of the Arab Legion soldiers. The street, deserted and sinister a few moments before, had been transformed. People were milling everywhere and the white flag bobbed above the crowd like a cork on an ocean. Arabs in keffiyehs were embracing old bearded rabbis, Hassidic women had their arms around the necks of legion soldiers in khaki battledress.

Netanel felt an almost physical agony as he watched. He aimed the Thompson into the street and considered killing them all. They had all betrayed him. They were weak and they deserved to die.

But finally he let the gun fall on to the floor.

Instead he leaned out of the window and screamed at them, his enemies who were too weak to kill him and his people who were too craven to cower behind him:

"I killed Amos Mandelbaum! *I killed Amos Mandelbaum!*"

*   *   *

Sarah watched the old Jews in their frock coats stream up the basement steps, the women weeping and hugging their children, the old rabbis shouting praise and thanks to Elohim. For a long time afterwards it was quiet, just the moans of the wounded and the purposeful murmur of the handful of doctors and nurses who tended them. It was a stillness as hushed and sanctified as a temple. This was the moment of their sacrifice.

Sarah lay beside Asher, held his hand and waited.

Someone was coming down the basement stairs.

She saw the man's jodhpurs first, then his khaki trousers and a long battle jacket. He had a new British Lee Enfield rifle, held at slope. Then she saw a beard and a hawkish brown face, eyes glittering in the sombre dark, and a red-and-white-checked keffiyeh.

He nodded his head and grinned.

Part Twenty

ISRAEL, 1949

130

Jerusalem

The truck left Netanel Rosenberg in Ben Yehuda Street. He stood on the pavement and watched it rumble away, suddenly an alien in his adopted land. The crowds hurried around the thin, shaven-headed man in the rumpled suit of clothes, ignoring him. He was startled by the flag fluttering from the roof of one of the buildings: a blue Star of David on a white background, the new flag of Israel, a flag he had never seen. And these people, the dark-skinned Yemenites, the Ashkenazi in their fur hats, the black-robed Hassidim, the young women in European fashion, the young moustachioed sabras in their khaki drill shirts, all of them were Israelis.

For months they had told him they had lost; that Palestine was now part of Jordan; that he would be killed. Then one day he and a dozen others were ordered into the back of a truck. He thought they were going to be shot. Instead they were taken to the border and transferred to another olive-drab truck. To their astonishment their new guards spoke to them in Hebrew. They patted them on the back and said they were taking them home.

Suddenly, after months of confinement in the prisoner of war camp outside Amman, after starvation, brutality and even rape, Netanel Rosenberg was free. They bartered for him and brought him home to the promised land. But without enemies, without a cause, freedom was suddenly worse than any prison he had ever known.

*   *   *

He had nowhere to go so he booked a room in a cheap hotel off Ben Yehuda Street. There was a bed with sheets, blankets with no lice, no guard at the door. He was a Jew finally among Jews.

He was also utterly alone. There was nothing for him in this sanctuary he had helped create, for there could never be any peace for the man who had murdered Amos Mandelbaum. Peace was foreign to him, and his soul ached to be back in the Hurva Synagogue. He had expected to redeem his life there, in the new Massada. That would have been perfect.

But Rabbi Silverberg had denied him.

I have kept my promise to the children who died in the fire at Birkenau, to my fellow travellers in the Leichenauto. But I can never receive my absolution from Amos Mandelbaum. Will he always haunt me, in my wakefulness, and in my dreams?

The Place Where The Fig Tree Died

Zayyad Hass'an laid his prayer mat beside the graves of his family and knelt in the direction of Mecca. He prayed to Allah for the wisdom to understand all that had happened, and prayed for His compassion for the plight of his village and for himself.

It was not for him to understand the mind of God, *Insh'allah*.

Rab'allah, such of it that remained, was a part of Transjordan now. Well, that came as no surprise. He had wondered aloud from the very first whether King Abdollah had come to their aid because of his profligate generosity or whether he might want a few border changes as well. The camel does not change his humps at the water hole. One ruler was much the same as another, and he would surely prove less of a tyrant in time than the Mufti.

But was such an insignificant gain worth such terrible

sacrifices? The Jews had more than even the United Nations had wanted to give them, and Arab weapons had been shamed with defeat on every border. The Egyptians were better at sodomising small boys, anyway, everyone knew that; they might just as well have sent a troupe of performing camels as put the Lebanese in battle against the Jews; the Iraqis had enjoyed themselves in Nablus but had not ventured much further; and the Syrians had proved they could shout rhetoric better than most even if they did drive their tanks in reverse.

And the Mufti was still safe in Cairo.

Meanwhile, he, Zayyad Hass'an, had lost his village, two wives, two daughters-in-law, two grandsons, and two fine sons. Here they were, on this hill, asleep beneath these stones, *Insh'allah.*

Insh'allah.

But may the Mufti's sacred member turn into a chicken and peck at his balls until he died! And then may his soul plummet into hell like a stone down a well and roast over a fire until his skin turned black and peeled off like the rind of an overripe fig!

Tears coursed down the lines that time and bitterness had carved into his cheeks. Majid had told him the war was not ended, that every Arab nation had proclaimed the Jewish state as an offence before God, and had vowed never to recognise it. The battle, he had been assured, had only just begun.

The suffering also, he assumed.

Wagil, Rishou, Ali, Rahman. The Jews were gone from the valley. Had it been worth such a price?

Jerusalem

The crowds were back in Ben Yehuda Street. The cafés were open once more and soldiers drank coffee and bought their girls cakes, and rabbis sat at the tables and argued

777

theology. Already people were learning to ignore the concertinas of barbed wire that divided the city. It was life in all its resilience.

Asher sat by the window of the apartment and watched them, his fellow Israelis. Even to be alive was in itself unexpected and he drank in the cold blue morning and the luxury of a future.

The Arab Legion's commander, Abdollah Tell, had proved to be a man of honour. On the morning of the surrender he had allowed the civilians, the women and the wounded to be evacuated. Only the men were taken prisoner. Asher himself remembered very little of those events. For months afterwards he had lain in a Jerusalem hospital bed, fighting for his life.

Beyond the white-painted walls, the larger struggle had continued. Against all expectations, the Yishuv did not collapse with the fall of the Old City. Two weeks after the surrender the United Nations arranged a truce. By then, the Iraqis were penned in the Nablus Triangle, the Syrians and Lebanese had been beaten back by the Palmach in Galilee, and the Egyptian advance had been stopped thirty kilometres south of Tel Aviv at Ashdod.

The two-week truce changed the course of the war. The Haganah used the time well. They were able to smuggle in shipments of arms from Europe: rifles, Sten guns, hand-grenades, mortars, and machine-guns as well as ten Hotchkiss tanks, four anti-aircraft guns and thirty surplus Sherman tanks. They also acquired artillery field pieces and forty-five thousand artillery shells. They even shipped in Messerschmidts and Spitfires from Czechoslovakia. More refugees arrived from Cyprus and Europe every day to swell the ranks of the Haganah and the Palmach.

Meanwhile the Arabs' most potent fighting force, the Arab Legion, was starved of supplies. The United States had forced the British to place an arms embargo on the army they themselves had created. Truman threatened to withhold desperately needed economic aid to the war-battered nation if they refused to comply.

When the truce ended on June 18th, the Arabs faced a

completely new and revitalised enemy. The tide of battle quickly swung the other way.

Asher's doctors were delighted with him. His wounds had healed, although the scars on his chest would be with him for ever, a constant souvenir, death's calling card for some future appointment. He still tired quickly, and was short of breath when he climbed the stairs, but they promised him a full recovery in time.

He was grateful just to be alive.

He heard little Yaakov crying. Marie emerged from the bedroom, holding the infant in her arms. She sat beside him at the window to feed.

When he was better he and Marie had agreed to go to the Negev. They were building new kibbutzim now and he had promised himself he would build another Kfar Herzl there. Little Yaakov would grow up one of the first generation of Jews born in a Jewish state and with luck and God's help he would not grow up with a gun in his hand.

With luck and with God's help.

Perhaps.

The abiding image of the siege that remained with Sarah had been seared into her brain as she was carried on a litter from the basement of the Jochanan Ben Zakai, the evening of the surrender.

Smoke, black as ink, rose from the quarter as the Arab irregulars looted and burned the Bethel district. Meanwhile, some of the shopkeepers had reopened their stores and were serving coffee and cakes to the Arab Legion soldiers, men who had been their enemies that morning.

Our enemies, she thought, can sometimes appear in the guise of friends and our most bitter enemies can sometimes be our sweetest lovers.

She sat beside Isaac's bed as he slept. It had been long months before she received confirmation that he was still alive, many months more before the truce that had led to the exchange of prisoners of war.

He had said little since his return from Amman. He would not speak of his experiences in the POW camp, or what had happened to him at Kfar Herzl. Only three others had survived that massacre.

In time, she was sure, he would speak, and a young spirit could be retrieved. All they needed was a little time.

She stroked his hair as he slept. He was a fine-looking boy, strong and straight and tall. Every day he looked more and more like his father. He would have been proud if he had known him.

A good boy. Good Arab blood in a good Jewish boy.

She wished she had told Rishou, but then, what difference could it ever have made for him, or for her? It might perhaps make a difference for Isaac. She must tell him now, and the truth would be a balm for the hatred and a salve for his scars.

She no longer wept when she thought about Rishou. In the world they lived in, his body had been prohibited to her. But perhaps she could yet fashion another good man from his blood.

The Holy Places are going to pass through long years of war, and peace will not prevail there for generations.

Syria's UN delegate Fares el Khoury, 1948

EPILOGUE

Jerusalem, September 1992

In the late summer of 1992 they were talking about peace, a remarkable thing in a land that has been at war with almost all its neighbours since the state was announced. It was barely a year ago that guests in the Anglican college in East Jerusalem had to leave the dining-room one evening, abandoning their dinners, because of the tear-gas that was drifting in through the windows from Suleiman Road.

Now the tourists and the pilgrims are coming back.

Isaac Ben-Zion tears the top off a Goldstar and leans on the bar in his restaurant off Ben Yehuda Street. His forehead wrinkles into a frown. "I was a major in the Israeli army. I lost a lot of my boys in 1973, fighting the Syrians. And now Rabin is talking of giving it all back to Assad. I don't know . . . he says it will bring peace. But what kind of peace will we have when they are looking down their gun barrels at us from the Golan?"

As afternoon turns to evening I walk back to my hotel along the mall in Ben Yehuda Street. A boy and girl stroll past arm in arm, like young lovers everywhere, except that the boy has an Uzi strapped across his back. Peace seems very far away.

Tonight Mulli Rosenberg will be riding patrol again in the malevolent streets of Bethlehem; on the other side of the Jordan valley Wafa begins another night of exile under the desert high rises of Amman.

As the sun sets the white graves that march up the Mount of Olives fade into grey. This, they say, is the biblical valley of Jehosophat where the trumpets of the

Last Judgment will call the souls of all mankind to the end of the world. Christians, Jews and Muslims are all buried here in expectation of God's final verdict on their actions.

It seems in this land of angry brothers there are so many to be judged. And so few, so very few, to be forgiven.

Do not wait for the Last Judgment
It takes place every day.

Albert Camus